Sisterhood of Suns

Widow's War

by

Martin Schiller

Pantari Press, Seattle Washington, USA

Photo Model: Erika Noble
ISBN-13: 978-0692753637
ISBN-10: 069275363X

Dedication

For "Emily", Lilya, and all the others whose names we will never know. Mere gratitude is not enough, but it is all that we can offer you. Rest well.

PROLOGUE

By 2445 BSE, Humanity had colonized hundreds of worlds. With this great expansion, the very definition of what it was to be 'human' was transformed through the efforts of the Biosyncronism Movement and genetic engineering.

What no one anticipated was the MARS plague. Within a decade, the airborne, gender-specific virus had claimed the life of every human male. Only females managed to survive, saved by advanced genetic manipulation and artificial reproductive techniques.

And in the wake of the greatest plague ever encountered by the children of Gaia, the warlike Hriss invaded, igniting the First Widow's War. Ultimately, Womankind won the conflict and the United Sisterhood of Suns was born. Motherthought became the new philosophy, and 'man' had become a memory.

Now, more than a millennia since these tumultuous times, the Sisterhood enjoys some of the most advanced technology and the highest standard of living in the Far Arm. But change, the only true constant in the galaxy, is in the offing.

Human males, called neomen, have been reintroduced by the radical Marionite Church, and are slowly gaining a foothold in society. The Hriss are poised to wage yet another war, and unknown to the average woman, contact is being established with a human star nation wholly unlike the Sisterhood. A survival of the pre-plague diaspora from Old Gaia, it is a place where men and women still share civilization together.

How these complex factors will affect the Sisterhood or its interstellar neighbors is anyone's guess. What is certain is that the year 1043 ASE is a troubled and dangerous time...

USSNS *Pallas Athena*, Calandra System, Sagana Territory, United Sisterhood of Suns, 1043.03|24|04:16:67

At 04:16:67 hours, Commander Lilith ben Jeni's psiever reminded her of an important event. She put down her cup of tea and opened up a channel to address the entire battle group.

"Attention Battle Group Golden," she announced. "This is the Commander. Today marks the anniversary of the First Widow's War. All personnel not involved in essential tasks will now observe a moment of silence to commemorate the brave women who gave up their lives in that conflict, and in all the wars that followed it. Their sacrifices kept their daughters safe."

An alert chime sounded, and as a group, everyone on the *Athena's* Bridge who wasn't handling something vital, stood at attention. Lilith rose and joined them, while the national anthem, *"United Are We"* played out in all corners of the ship. The same scene was repeated on the *Artemis*, the *Demeter*, and on every ship in the Sisterhood Navy, wherever they where in the Far Arm.

Even though more than a thousand years had passed since the conflict, the experience of the First Widow's War had become graven in the racial memory of humanity, and it's annual observance still exerted a powerful effect. The conflict had led to the deaths of billions, the loss of entire planets including Old Gaia herself, and had engendered the birth of the Sisterhood. It was impossible for Lilith, or anyone else standing there, not to feel a lump in their throat, or to avoid shedding a tear.

Finally, the song concluded, and a collective sigh sounded around the *Athena's* bridge as the assembly turned their attention back to the present, and their duties.

With the raider base destroyed, the *Athena* and her sister ships had resumed their original task of monitoring Hriss communications, along with any other traffic that had the potential of yielding valuable intelligence. This included local conversations between Sisterhood ships, and everyone else in and around the Sagana Elant.

Just before the moment of silence, an odd exchange had begun between the Sagana Territorial Marshals and a T'lakskalan merchant ship. When Navcom saw that Lilith had reseated herself in her command chair, they patched the conversation up to her.

She listened to it carefully as she sipped at her tea. At the moment, the Lead Marshal was speaking.

"*Ssalaksso*, are you in distress?" the woman asked.

"We do not require your asssistansse," the captain of the *Ssalaksso* replied in a rasping lisp that was characteristic of its race whenever it tried to speak Standard. "We have already called for one of our own ss-ships to respond to our ss-situation."

"*Ssalaksso*, we are monitoring your ship and your number one engine is offline. Your number two is also showing signs of immanent failure," the Marshal responded. "At your current power-levels, your orbit will decay completely in six hours."

"We do *not* need your help, *human!*" the T'lakskalan retorted angrily. "One of our ss-ships is ressponding and we are confident that they will arrive in time to render asssistansse."

Lilith called up a holodisplay. According to the data that she saw, the nearest T'lakskalan held planet was at least eight hours away by Null—at best. In the meantime the *Ssalaksso* was in orbit around a J-Type gas giant, and at the present rate of power loss, it was patently obvious that the ship would plunge to its destruction well before any of its fellows could arrive to save it.

Lilith's Third, Mearinn d'Rann, reviewed the data at her own station, and shook her head in dismay. "Their captain has to be completely klaxxy," the Tethyian remarked. "Or hiding something."

"I think that we should drop by and see what we can do to help," Lilith said with a sardonic smile, "in the interests of galactic fellowship of course. Don't you agree?"

D'Rann nodded with a roguish expression of her own, and advised the *Artemis* and the *Demeter* to remain on station. Then she ordered the Helm to take the *Athena* into Null.

An hour later, the warship came back into normal space near the gas giant, and the crippled alien ship. At Lilith's orders, the *Athena* had come out in stealth mode and it would remain that way until the situation dictated otherwise. In the meantime, the dialogue between the Marshals and the *Ssalaksso* was still on going.

"*Ssalaksso*, your number two engine is now at 23%," the Marshal warned. "We have rescue personnel on hand and we can offer you a tow to the nearest safe location."

"Negative, human! We do not want a tow, or your asssistansse. Go away!"

Lilith sighed tiredly and had Navcom contact the Lead Marshal. "Good morning, Marshal," she said when the woman's holo appeared. "We overheard your conversation. Can we be of any help?"

"Good to see you, *Athena*", the officer replied. "We would appreciate anything that you can do for us. The *Ssalaksso* put in at Thenti with trade goods, and after they sold them off, we thought that they'd left our space. But then we picked them up here."

"I see," Lilith said. Although the T'lakskalans had a well-deserved reputation for piracy and trafficking in slaves, there were just as many Tee-Laks that did legitimate business as merchanters. The problem was that even the most honest of them sometimes opted to combine legal and illegal cargos in order to increase their profit margins. Given their dire situation, the odd behavior of the *Ssalaksso's* captain certainly appeared to be pointing in that direction.

The Marshal continued. "We think that they may have had something to do with the disappearance of a four woman Astrosurvey team that was working this system a week ago. But we can't prove anything, and as you know, they're refusing help. I would have insisted on boarding them, but we don't have the numbers or the equipment to force the issue."

"Well", Lilith answered, sitting back and steepling her fingers. "It just so happens that we *do,* Marshal. And I completely agree with you; the situation is highly suspicious and clearly warrants further investigation. Keep them occupied, would you?"

"My pleasure, *Athena*. And thanks again."

Lilith ended the communication and sent a message to Col. Lislsdaater to join her on the bridge. When the Marine commander arrived, she briefed her on the situation.

Shortly after this, two Marine assault shuttles left the *Athena*, headed for the *Ssalaksso* in stealth mode. When they were close enough, they took up positions over the ship's hull, one fore and the other aft. Then they extended their docking tubes, and quietly mated with the alien vessel. That was when Lilith decided to bring the *Athena* out of stealth and had Navcom hail the T'lakskalan ship.

"Merchant ship *Ssalaksso*. This is the United Sisterhood of Suns Naval Ship *Pallas Athena*", the Comswoman announced. "We are responding to a request for assistance from the Sagana Territorial Marshals. You are instructed to comply with an inspection of your ship and its cargo. Respond please."

"This is the *Ssalaksso*. We do not need your help–leave us!"

"I don't think the captain quite understood our message," Lilith remarked. She cut in and spoke directly to the *Ssalaksso's* Captain herself.

"Captain, I am Commander Lilith ben Jeni, and we are not here to offer you our help. You have already refused that from the Marshals, and personally I don't care one nano if you drop to your deaths or not.'

"Before that happens however, we *are* entitled by treaty and by our own sovereign laws—which, by the way, you are subject to by being in our space—to make an inspection of your ship for safety violations, and any contraband. You *will* comply with this, or we will board you by force."

"Do not attempt that *Athena*!" the T'lakskalan Captain hissed. "If you try to come aboard our ss-ship, we will consider you to be pirates-ss, and we will resissst you with armed force!"

His bluster was so outrageous that Lilith laughed aloud. "*And the night dared to call space dark!*" she replied, quoting an old Nyxian expression.

"What does that mean, human?"

Lilith composed herself. "I'll explain it to you shortly, Captain—very shortly."

With that, she ended the conversation and signaled to Col. Lislsdaater. Whether the *Ssalaksso* and its captain wanted to or not, they were going to cooperate.

***

Corporal Kaly n'Deena and Trooper Lena n'Gari had been chosen along with a dozen other Marines to take part in the boarding. The operation, which followed standard protocol for dynamic entries, also involved two Marauder Teams. They would make the initial breach, and then secure vital areas of the ship.

The job of troopers like Kaly and Lena was to follow them in, and not only hold what they had taken, but also render medical aid and assistance to any hostages that the teams managed to locate. They were also responsible for taking prisoners into custody, and towards that end, two additional groups of Navy paramedics and Security Policewomen were part of the boarding party.

Although the troop compartment of the assault shuttle was large, everyone was crowded around the specialized pressure hatch set in the center of its deck. This device employed shaped charges to cut a hole in a ship's hull, and suspended above it was a battlebot, its metal legs folded underneath it like a gigantic arachnid. Once the explosives created the opening, the 'bot would be the first thing to drop down into the vessel. The Marauders would go next, and then everyone else would follow.

As they waited for the 'go-signal', no one spoke, or moved any more than was absolutely necessary. This was for security reasons; now that the shuttle had mated with the T'lakskalan ship, any vibrations that they created could carry through the hull and alert the alien crew. Even radio and psiever traffic had been forbidden. All communications were limited to command and emergencies. Or hand signals.

Unable to do anything more than wait, Kaly remained still and alone with her thoughts. She was scared—she readily admitted this.

Training was one thing, but reality was far different. All of her instructors in Basic had hammered in the fact that unlike an open battlefield, the tight corners of a spaceship could easily hide any number of lethal surprises. And although she had always done well in the simulated assaults, she couldn't help but feel trepidation when she looked down at the pressure hatch.

Her Battle Sister was even more nervous than she was. Lena hadn't been the same since the ground action on CD48 2259, and at that moment, Kaly would have given anything to say something to her, or even think a few words of reassurance, but she couldn't do either.

We'll get through this, Lena, she thought privately, studiously avoiding any activation of her psiever. *We'll be all right.*

As if she had heard this, Lena looked over and smiled. It was a wan expression though, and Kaly found herself hoping that once the action started, that her lover would be able to keep herself together.

Lena wasn't the only one showing signs of stress; a new Trooper, fresh out of Basic, had also been selected for the boarding party. Kaly hadn't memorized her name yet, and had to use the HUD display on her helmet visor to call it up. *'N'Dalla, Gwyn'*.

N'Dalla seemed positively ill, and Kaly reminded herself that she was Troop Leader Da'Saana's responsibility, and not hers. And she didn't envy the NCO one bit. Green Troopers could get everyone killed, including themselves.

Goddess, she thought, suddenly hearing herself, *I'm thinking like I'm an old hand already.* This brought a depreciatory grin to her face. She was still pretty fresh herself, Corporal's arrow or not, and she was in no position to call anyone else a 'greenie'.

Her smile vanished a second later when the order came to breach the T'lakskalan hull. She felt a brief shock under her feet as the charges went off and then the pressure hatch opened and the battlebot dropped.

Its legs extended as it fell through space, and like a kaatze, it landed squarely on the decking below with a metallic 'clank'. It paused there for a moment, ranging its guns around, and when it found nothing to engage, the 'bot stepped out of the way to take up a guarding position.

The Marauder Team descended next, weapons at the ready. Then, after another brief interval, one of them gave Kaly's group the 'all-clear' to descend and join them.

The explosives had sliced out a thick, heavy portion of the ship's outer hull, and this was lying on the decking, still smoking. When Kaly jumped down onto it, she realized that a T'lakskalan had been standing directly underneath the section when it had blown. What parts of its body that hadn't been pulverized into jelly were sticking out of the edges of the heavy plating, including its head and neck. The creature's forked tongue was protruding from its mouth, and it had a look of total astonishment on its reptilian features.

As she took this in, Troop Leader Da'Saana landed next to her, and shook her head at the mess. "Goddess! Talk about the Lady *fekking up* your luck! She must have really *hated* this one!"

"Yeah," one of the Marauders laughed. "I think that just might be a permanent injury."

Horrible as the spectacle was, Kaly found herself laughing right along with them. It really *was* funny she realized—in a gruesome way. Either that, or her combat experiences were starting to alter her sense of humor. She wasn't sure which, but because it broke the tension for an instant, she didn't really care.

The rest of the Marines assembled around the Troop Leader, and as the Marauder Team and the battlebot moved off to secure their objectives, Da'Saana signaled them to begin consolidating the immediate area.

Everyone pulled out hand scanners from their belts and started down the hall, waving them over the bulkheads and the decking.

It was a common practice for smugglers like the T'lakskalans to hide their contraband in secret compartments, but the Marines weren't looking for illicit substances. Instead, the Trooper's were looking for hostages and hidden assailants. The same spaces that could conceal contraband could hide either just as readily. And until every centimeter of the ship had been scanned, searched and cleared, it wouldn't really be considered secure.

A few minutes into the process, Kaly heard the two Marauder Teams announce that they had completed their objectives. The first Team, who had entered the ship just aft of the Bridge, reported that all the T'lakskalans there were in custody, including the captain.

The second one, which had been aboard Kaly's shuttle, had worked their way back to the engine room, and after taking out one hostile, were also in control.

The *Ssalaksso* was going nowhere. But so far, no one had found anything that had justified the captain's recalcitrance. Not even a minor safety violation. Even so, Kaly was as certain as everyone else that there *had* to be something incriminating aboard.

Her squad continued moving and when they reached a junction, Da'Saana had them split off into two groups. Kaly, Lena, and the new Trooper, N'Dalla, went portside while the rest went to starboard. The passage that Kaly's group entered ended after only a few meters and it seemed harmless enough—at first glance.

But something about it raised the hairs on Kaly's neck. She had learned in training not only to look for the obvious when searching a ship, but also to consider a space based on its function and its relationship to the rest of a vessel.

It was the length of the passage that bothered her, she realized. It was too short, and aside from two access panels and a storage compartment, it had no apparent function. And no matter the size of the ship, space was always at a premium. Nothing was ever built that didn't have a clear utility value.

She was just about to mention this to her companions, when N'Dalla's hand-scanner registered a void that shouldn't have been there. Kaly started to turn in her direction when a section of the wall in front of the Trooper popped open.

'What?!" the woman cried. "Wait!"

The T'lakskalan standing on the other side didn't wait. Instead, he shot her. N'Dalla flew backwards, knocking Lena over as she fell.

Kaly fired reflexively, and hit the alien squarely in its chest. It collapsed immediately and she covered the opening with her Mark-7, ready for another enemy. She could hear Lena screaming behind her, and then footsteps as Da'Saana and her group ran up to assist them. But her eyes and her weapon stayed trained on the space in front of her.

"Take care of your Battle Sister," Da'Saana advised her. "We'll check out the space." That was when Kaly finally allowed herself to relax enough to look over her shoulder.

Lena was huddled against the bulkhead, with N'Dalla lying partly on top of her. There was blood all over both of them, and although Kaly wasn't sure if Lena was wounded or not, it was obvious that N'Dalla was beyond saving. The T'lakskalan's shot had caught her just above the neckline of her battle armor, and what was left of her neck was barely keeping her head attached to the rest of her body.

Forcing herself to look away from the hideous wound, she went over to Lena and tried to help her stand, but the young woman batted her hand away

"That's it! That's it!" Lena wailed hysterically. "No more! I can't take it any more!"

The Navy medics had arrived by this point, and they gently pulled Kaly away. "We'll take care of her from here," one of them promised. "The other one's gone."

***

The hidden compartment turned out to be a prison cell for three of the four women from the missing geosurvey team. The fourth member of the team had died resisting the T'lakskalan slavers when they had been kidnapped.

And with the exception of the two aliens who had been killed by the Marines, the entire crew of the *Ssalaksso* was under arrest, and charged with piracy and kidnapping. The ship itself was in tow, destined for Hella's World for training purposes. The Sisterhood Marine Corps always tried to learn from its mistakes, and with one Trooper dead thanks to the ship's deceptive layout, they had the perfect classroom to teach new hatchies with.

None of this was any consolation to the entry teams or to Lena though. Once they had returned to the *Athena*, she was immediately taken to medbay.

Although none of the blood that Kaly had seen had been hers, the young woman had been deeply traumatized by N'Dalla's death. After receiving a heavy dose of sedatives, she was kept for observation and Kaly was forced to attend the trooper's funeral service without her.

When the ritual was finally over, she returned to her rack to change out of her dress uniform. Lena was waiting for her, sitting on the edge of their bed with a dark, haunted expression. "Kaly" she said in a small voice, "I-I just can't take any more of this."

Kaly paused for a moment, and then nodded her head slowly. "I know", she said, surprised at how calm she felt. "What are you going to do?"

Lena drew in a deep, ragged breath, and looked away, not wanting to meet her gaze. "I've asked the Colonel for a transfer. I'm going over to Supply."

Kaly nodded again. In a strange way, she was relieved. Lena would be safe in Supply.

Lena met her eyes. Tears were streaming openly down her cheeks. "Kaly, I'm so sorry. I feel like I'm betraying you, but I just can't do it again. I thought that when I joined up that I could—but--I--just--can't…"

Kaly sat and put a reassuring arm around her Battle Sister's shoulder. "I know, Lena," she said tenderly. "And you're right—Supply is better for you. You'll be safe there. That's what I want for you. I want you to be safe."

"But w-what will you do?" Lena asked, suddenly fearful.

"The Colonel wanted me to consider a transfer after we took out that Hriss base," she told her. "She thinks that I have what it takes for Special Operations. I haven't given her my answer yet."

Lena's eyes widened in horror and she clutched at Kaly desperately. "Oh Kaly!" she cried, "You can't do that! I've heard about them! They go on suicide missions! Don't you see? I want you to be safe too. Please—come with me to Supply—please!"

But Kaly shook her head. "No, Lena. I'd hate Supply, and after a while, I'd start to hate you too. I don't want that for either of us."

The simple truth of this hit home and Lena broke down completely, and wept. Kaly held her for a while, and let her pour out her misery, but they both knew that the Lady had laid out their paths, and they went in different directions.

***

The next morning when Kaly awoke, her psiever sensed the change in her consciousness and transmitted an image of a diamond shaped icon in the right-hand corner of her vision. This meant that she had a message in her virtual inbox. Already half-certain that something was wrong, she sent the command for the message to play. Her heart sank when she heard the first few words of it in her mind, and then she realized that the space in the bed next to her was empty.

My Dearest, the message began, *I know I am a coward, but I didn't want to face you and say goodbye. I went to the Colonel this morning and asked her to expedite my transfer. When you get this, I will already be on my way to Thenti. I know that I disappointed you, and I'll always hate myself for that. I just hope that you'll forgive me.*

I love you, Lena.

Lena was gone.

Kaly felt as if she was being crushed by the weight of a neutron star. She also felt robbed. Robbed of the chance to spend a little more time with her lover before she left, and of the opportunity to say goodbye.

Damn you, Lena, she thought. Suddenly angry, she slammed her fist into the empty pillow next to her. Then, stifling a sob, she rose and put on her fatigues. Whether she was ready to face the galaxy or not, there was still the day's work to be done. She left the pod and headed out into the common area, feeling more like a 'bot than a human being.

Troop Leader Da'Saana met her as she checked in for her work assignment. "She left on the *Artemis*," the NCO said.

Kaly frowned, but said nothing.

"It's like that sometimes," the older woman offerred. "Some women do great in Basic, but when they get a taste of combat, they fold. I had a woman in my platoon just like that when I was a hatchie. She got fantastic scores—-every centimeter the perfect Marine—until she saw her first real action. I think she's working on Rixa in Admin now.'

"Only certain women have what it takes, N'Deena. You're one of them—and you'll have to just shoulder this hurt and march on. That's all soldiers like us can do."

"Yes, ma'am", Kaly replied sadly.

"If you need to take some time for yourself, I can get someone else to handle your duty assignment," the Troop Leader added.

Kaly squared her shoulders and tried to sound stronger than she actually felt. "I think I can manage, ma'am."

Da'Saana saw right through her charade and raised a skeptical eyebrow. "Maybe. Just the same, I want you to take a few minutes and go visit the Ship's Temple. Talk to one of the priestesses and let her do her magic tricks for you. And after she's done, come back and report for duty. Zat klaar?"

"Yes, ma'am."

***

It was another two weeks before Kaly was able to sit down in front of a Com station and compose a message to Lena. Fortifying herself with a deep breath, she began. "Lena" she said, looking into the lens of the holo-cam. "This is Kaly."

She stopped herself right there. It was a stupid way to begin. Lena would certainly know who had sent her the message.

She deleted it and began again. "Lena, I understand why you left, and I forgive you. Please, send me a message so that we can talk. I miss you so much." But this time, she sounded pathetic and whiny, and erased it.

"Lena, I read your note and I understand. Please, send me a message so that we can talk about this. I love you." Initially, this seemed just right, but when she replayed it, she changed her mind. Now she seemed too insistent and demanding. The message joined its predecessors in the virtual waste-basket.

"Lena, I miss you so much. Please send me a message. I need to hear your voice again. I miss you." When she listened to herself a moment later, she didn't sound much better than she had in the previous version. She had never been good at composing personal messages, and this one was proving to be particularly challenging. Letting out a long, frustrated sigh, she threw the clip away, and attempted another.

"Lena, I miss you," she said. "I understand why you left. Please, send me a message and at least let me know that you're all right. I love you." Now, her words felt and sounded just right. Before she could second-guess herself, she saved the clip and sent it off.

She had no doubt that Lena would receive it; the Miliplex, the military component of the omniplex, would route it to wherever she was, using her service number to locate her.

Whether she would reply was another matter altogether. All Kaly could do was wait, and hope.

No answer came though. Finally, after two weeks of waiting, Kaly admitted to herself that she would never receive a reply, and headed straight to Col. Lislsdaater's office.

The Colonel's adjutant didn't make her wait; even on a large ship like the *Athena*, gossip travelled faster than light, and everyone, including the Colonel herself, had heard about Lena's departure. Barely two minutes elapsed before she was standing at attention in front of the woman's desk.

"I heard about your Battle Sister, N'Deena," the officer said, "and for what it's worth, I'm sorry." She paused for politeness' sake and then added, "So, have you come here to speak with me about the matter we discussed?"

"Yes, ma'am," Kaly replied. "I have. I'd like to apply for SpecOps--if that's still an option."

"I thought that you might," Lislsdaater said, calling up a holo. "So I took the liberty of filling out the application for you."

She hit a key on her virtual keyboard. "And now, it's away. I know this is not how you wanted this to happen N'Deena, but I think that once you get through your training, you'll agree that it was all for the best. For both of you."

"Yes, ma'am" Kaly answered. As right as she knew she was, the situation didn't feel 'good' or 'right' at all. At the moment, nothing did.

"I'll let you know when I get an answer," Lislsdaater told her.

Thanks to the Colonel's personal endorsement, Kaly's application was quickly approved and she was given orders to report for training. But because the battle group was still on patrol, she was forced to remain on the *Athena* until they put in at a spaceport. Staying in the rack that she and Lena had shared together, with nothing to do except stare at the ceiling and think, was simply out of the question though, and she immediately requested a new bunk assignment. Corporal n'Darei fully understood, and found her a place on the opposite end of Five-Bar.

From then on, and until the ship made port, Kaly steadfastly avoided going back into her old pod for any reason. The memories waiting for her there were too painful to bear.

Crimson Vale, Larra's Lament, Lalita System, Artemi Elant, United Sisterhood of Suns, 1043.03|22|07:28:39

Ensign Jan bar Daala had sacrificed a week of her shore leave to reach the hidden trail. It was a subtle thing, hidden by bushes and overgrowth, and because only the animals used it, barely visible as anything more than a vague, irregular track. But she recognized it immediately, and knew that further up the slope, there would be points where it would become more obvious, and easier to follow.

Feeling a rush of excitement, she stepped off the main trail and made her way up through the silent forest. The day's light was fading, dying in the arms of the twilight, and Jan made herself hurry. In some places the path was more overgrown than she recalled, and in others, almost completely obstructed by deadfalls.

After half an hour of concerted climbing, she finally reached her destination. It was a small open meadow. Like the trail, its shape had been blurred by the passage of years and new vegetation, but it was still unmistakable. At its far end, bracketed by more overgrowth and small trees, was an opening that led into the hillside. Despite its incredible age, the oval hole was still smooth, and through some agency that Sisterhood archeologists were unable to explain, the forest's vegetation never covered it over.

The passage led deep into the hillside, and into one of the many Drow'voi structures that were scattered throughout the Lament. This one however, was particularly special. It had never been officially catalogued, or explored. Jan bar Daala knew why; except for those that it chose, the site didn't want to be found.

Most of the women of the Lament stayed clear of places like this. While nothing harmful had ever been found inside any of them, they were considered to be haunted, the lonely remains of a civilization that steadfastly defied human understanding.

Jan had even felt this way herself—at one time. But not any longer. Now, this place—and not the town that was officially listed as her residence—was her home. She entered the passageway without so much as a backwards glance at the fading daylight, eager for the shadows.

The darkness didn't last long. As the tunnel began to describe a gentle looping path that wound deep into the very heart of the hillside, its walls began to pulsate and glow. The place knew her, and it was welcoming her back with its light.

At last, she came to what appeared to be a dead end, and for anyone else, it would have been. But as she approached it, another opening appeared in the seamless wall, admitting her into a wide chamber. Like the tunnel, it too was brightly lit, and as soon as she was inside the space, the opening behind her sealed shut.

In the center of the room, two platforms rose seamlessly from the floor. One of them was occupied by a corpse. The body was exactly as Jan had left it, and although it had shriveled down to a point were its dessicated features were nearly unrecognizable, she knew its face well. It was the very same one that greeted her in the mirror every morning.

The other platform was empty of everything except meaning. It was where the marvelous devices of the Masters, still functioning after 20,000 years, had re-created her from nothing more than a few cells harvested from the body lying next to it.

It was also where her new body had not only been gifted with consciousness, but all the memories of her former existence. That, and the special knowledge that the Watchers had known she would need to fulfill her mission.

She reached out to the empty platform, and stroked its smooth surface tenderly. It was a rare gift to be able to revisit the place where one had been born, she reflected. And how the process could have ever frightened her, utterly amazed her now.

If only my old self had only known what had awaited her, Jan thought. *Of the bliss that came from the Sharing, or the joy of serving the Masters. Then she would have embraced her fate instead of running from it.*

But run, she had. Thankfully, the Watchers had prevented her from escaping, and her new life had been able to begin.

Glancing over at her old body, she sighed at the foolishness of her former self, and opened her pack. She had gifts to leave for it, souvenirs of the life she had lived since her rebirth, and she wanted to share them with the Old Jan.

The Old Jan deserved it. After all, they were much more than sisters.

The first items that she brought out were stones from Tetra 5, a place that held many fond memories for her, and she arranged these neatly around the cadaver. Then came the medal that she had earned for her service in the Navy. After this, there was the holo of her and the woman she had had a brief affair with, standing in front of the entrance to the famous Kalia-Vai on Thermadon. All this, and much more, came out of her kit bag, and when she was done placing everything, she stood back, and blew a kiss to the remains.

Then she sang. There were no words to the song that any human would have recognized, and the notes that came out of her throat were purer and cleaner than a normal woman could have ever hoped to produce.

The chamber around her brightened with each note until it reached a near blinding intensity, and then, as she let the melody die, it dimmed down to an almost total blackness. Jan waited in the gloom, knowing that her call had been heard.

Shortly, another light asserted itself. It began as a faint glow, far away and down a nearby passage, and it intensified as the Watchers approached.

They were formless, luminous beings, composed of pure light, and like her, they had been created by the machines of the Masters to stand guard against an ancient foe. Their enemy was only known as the Terrible Ones, who had come from the Deep Beyond to destroy the Masters. And although they had succeeded, they had not destroyed the Great Purpose, or the Watchers, or beings like Jan, who remained loyal to the Master's vision.

Have you seen the Enemy? the Watchers asked as they floated up to her.

Jan shook her head. So far, she had detected no trace of their ancient adversaries.

What of the Singer and the User? Have they awakened yet?

Again, Jan had no information to offer them. "Not yet," she answered. "They remain hidden."

The Watchers accepted this, and drifted closer, as brilliant and beautiful as those who had created them. Enthralled, Jan dropped her pack and opened her arms wide to them in greeting. Their forms merged with hers, and for a time, she and they were one in an ecstatic union that the Old Jan could never have begun to comprehend.

Finally, they withdrew. The parting, and the return to individuality that accompanied it, brought tears to Jan's eyes. But she understood as well as the Watchers did just how necessary this was. She was still needed as an individual. Someday however, she vowed that this would end and she would be allowed to abandon her fragile, human form, and remain with them forever. But not today.

Learn more, they thought to her as they withdrew. *Learn more and keep watch.*

Jan nodded sadly, and watched them leave the chamber. Whether she wanted to or not, it was time for her to depart this special place, and resume her role as a spy, and a human.

CHAPTER 1

Special Military Quarantine Zone, Second Planet, The School, HSL-48 2124A System, Annexed Sisterhood Territory 1043.03|29|03:33:32

At recess, the boys were sent outside to play by themselves, and the girls were kept inside the classroom. They had begun to fidget with impatience when a smiling woman entered the classroom. She wasn't like any of the other women who walked around with guns and shouted all the time. Instead, she was dressed like a normal person, and she sat right down on the floor with them.

"Hello children! My name is Hari n'Kyla," she said. "I am going to be your teacher today. Would everyone like to tell me their names?"

"Where's Miss Mendaza?" one of the girls asked boldly. She was a bright-eyed little blond that N'Kyla immediately identified as a leader.

Such a girl, the Intel officer thought, *if she were properly indoctrinated, could grow up to become an effective clandestine Ops team leader.* Clearly, she would bear watching, and nurturing.

"She's sick," the Intel Officer lied, "but she wanted me to make sure that everyone was keeping up with their lessons." In fact, the woman was being detained and questioned, and she would not be returning. Instead, Intel operatives who had experience educating children would replace her, along with all of the other teachers. Indoctrinating the colony's youngest females in Motherthought, and creating potential covert agents, was one of Captain n'Kyla's pet projects.

Today, she was taking some time to lend her personal assistance to this on-going effort. "Now, let's start with you," she asked the blond girl. "What is your name?"

"Roseya!" the child replied. N'Kyla made a point of noting this on a virtual note pad in her psiever.

"Thank you, Roseya! And what about everyone else? What's your name?" N'Kyla pointed to another girl, who answered her immediately. After she had made a complete round of the room, she smiled at all of them again.

"Now, I'm very new at being a teacher," she told them, "and I don't know what you've been studying, so why don't we try some questions and you give me the answers. And later, everyone will get special treats!" This excited her little audience, and they all leaned forwards eagerly.

"Are you ready?" N'Kyla asked. "Here's my first question: what is the name of your star nation? Does anyone know?"

One of the girls enthusiastically waved her hand. "The *Esteral Terrana Rapabla!"* she shouted.

"Yes, that's right. Now, can anyone tell me the name of the world where the capitol is located?"

"Nuvo Bolivar," another girl volunteered.

"Very, very good! Can you show me on the map where you are—and where it is?"

The child got up and went straight to a simplified star map that was hanging on the classroom wall, and confidently pointed out both locations for her.

"Thank you, Maryaa! That's right! I can see that all of you are very smart young ladies."

Their 'lesson' was just beginning, and she had many more questions for the children. From the scans they had made of their textbooks early on, N'Kyla already knew all of the answers she had gotten so far, but the exchange helped to establish their teacher-student relationship, and more importantly, it lent her the proper degree of authority and trust.

This would be important later, as their relationships developed. And there was always the chance that during these soft-interrogations, the children would let something slip that was entirely new information. Children often possessed far more knowledge than they, or their parents, ever suspected, N'Kyla reflected.

When she realized that they had done enough for one day, she kept her word, and passed out candy that had come directly from Nyx and Nemesis. The little girls had never tasted such exotic delights and she made sure to tell them that the *chocolat* bars and *kelberry* candies had both come from a mysterious and wonderful thing called the Sisterhood; a place that was only for girls. Her audience was very intrigued by this concept.

"Would you like to hear a story? A story about the Sisterhood and how it came to be?" she asked them. The girls leaned forwards, keen to hear the tale.

The one that she told was far from innocent. It had been especially created for this very occasion, courtesy of childhood education experts and psychologists working for the University of Thermadon, and as a favor to the Navy. Every word of it, and every term that it used was couched with an eye towards winning them over, and the Intel officer had made certain to memorize it completely. She also delivered it with the recommended tones in her voice. These too, she knew, would add their subliminal effects to the young minds that were listening.

"Well," she began, "once upon a time, on a planet very far away, there was a girl named Penny. She was just like any other girl. She had a mother and lived in a house with a dog and a cat.'

"But Penny also lived with a brother and a father. These were both men, and they were like any other men. They weren't as smart as girls, nor as pretty, but they were bigger than girls and sometimes they were much, much meaner.'

"One day when Penny asked her mother why they even needed men around, her mother told her that they had to have them to make babies. And Penny thought that this was a very strange thing. But her mother didn't tell her what the men did to make babies, and Penny was a good girl, so she didn't ask her about this again.'

"And every day, and all day long, Penny's mother worked very hard, and when she needed help, Penny helped her. They cooked, they cleaned, and they mended, and when they were done, they did it all over again the next day.'

"The men *never* helped. They just told them what to do, and when they didn't like something, they would become very angry and yell a lot, and sometimes they would even hit the mothers.'

"But Penny and her mother did the best they could, and so did all the other mothers and girls that Penny knew.'

"And every day, the fathers would take the brothers and leave the houses to go have fun. And later, when the brothers were old enough, the fathers would take them to the shining towers in the big city, where the brothers were taught how to run things and what to tell everyone to do.'

"Sometimes, they got angry and fought with each other, and when this happened, they made all the women work even harder so that they could go off and keep fighting.'

"Penny and the other girls never got to go to the towers, and when she asked her mother why, she was told that she couldn't go because she was a girl. Girls had to stay home and work hard with their mothers. That's what the men wanted, and no one argued with them because they didn't want to make them angry.'

"Then one very special day, all the men got very sick; all the fathers and all the brothers. There was nothing anyone could do about it, because there had never been a sickness like this before. Finally, when they became too sick, the Goddess took them all away.'

"Penny's mother and all the older women were very sad at first, because they had never lived without the men and the brothers. And because there was no one up in the big towers telling everyone what to do, or making the city work, things didn't get done, and everyone began to run out of food.'

"Finally, all the women and all the girls went to the city and climbed up into the big towers, where they could see everything down below them, and how it worked. Together, they learned how to get the city to do what it was supposed to do, and then everyone stopped being hungry because there was food again and the lights came back on.'

"Some of the women went to work in the towers and they told others what to do and how to do it, but they weren't like the men had been. They didn't yell, and everyone helped each other, just like they had always done at home.'

"And when Penny was old enough, she got to go up into the tower herself and her mother taught her how the city worked. Every day after that, Penny and her friends, who were now all grown up, went to the city together, where they ran things and made sure that everything got done right. Nobody felt sad about the men or the brothers anymore. They had each other and everything was much, much better."

The girls were utterly amazed, and N'Kyla could almost hear their brains processing, and accepting the new information. Encouraged, she pressed on.

"Now, would you like to hear a little more about the wonderful Sisterhood that Penny and her friends made for themselves after the men were all gone?"

The girls were hooked. They simply had to hear more.

Borrowing from supplimentary material given to her by the University's experts, she began to describe her nation in broad, colorful detail. This too had the proper effect. Her audience was positively enraptured by her account, and by the time she was finished, they were looking forwards to their next meeting with her.

N'Kyla left them, in the care of their regular 'teacher'.

Her students didn't know it yet, but the boys would never be allowed to rejoin the class again. Or that for the rest of their day, and all the days after that, they would be receiving lessons in basic Motherthought, using a primer that had also been created for the class. It was entitled, *'Why Girls Are Better Than Boys.'*

It never hurts to invest in the future, she reflected, crossing the large central gathering area. Her destination was a semi-permanent building that had been erected by Navy Engineers for the Intel Detachment. A military hovertruck was parked near its entrance, and a pair of servicewomen was in the process of unloading boxes of basic household possessions.

These had been confiscated from the townspeople, and they were destined for chemical and metallurgical analysis. Thanks to the School, the ETR had had twenty years to study the Sisterhood, and there was a lot of catching up to do to level the playing field. Nothing, no matter how inconsequential, was being overlooked for its potential information value.

N'Kyla returned the sailor's salutes and went inside the structure, stopping only to have her identity confirmed by the armed guards posted at the entrance.

The interior was divided into cubicles, and in the nearest of these, a pair of women were analyzing some of the currency that they had managed to collect in their sweeps. The ETR didn't use the virtual credit system like the

Sisterhood did. Instead, it still relied largely on archaic paper money called the *Paysoli*.

She leaned over their table and watched the technicians as they went about their work. The designs for the *10 Paysoli* notes they were analyzing seemed rather intricate to her eye, but their supervisor had assured her that they were nothing that couldn't be duplicated flawlessly. If it ever came to it, this had to be a certainty. Any covert agents sent into the ETR would need cash for their missions to succeed, and there was always the possibility that larger amounts might be required to destabilize the ETR's economy.

When they noticed her and looked up, N'Kyla smiled approvingly and then left them alone to do their jobs. Further on, in another cubicle, the results of hundreds of interviews were being crosschecked and indexed. Soon after they had taken charge of the quarantined settlement, everyone living in it had been questioned about literally everything; from the most important details about their civilization, to the tiniest facts about its customs and slang expressions.

The men, and surprisingly a number of the women, had all attempted to plant false information in with the genuine facts, but her staff had anticipated this. By comparing all the data to observed behavior, voice stress analysis and Bioplasmic signatures, they were sifting out the lies, and assembling a factual picture of the life and the mannerisms of the average ETR citizen. Like their currency, this too would be essential material for any deep cover agents.

The only real question that she had was whether or not the Sisterhood would ever use the resources that her unit was collecting. Based on what she had seen so far, this seemed to be the only logical progression for things to take. In her opinion, the two societies could never exist side by side for any great length of time, and the only sensible course of action had to be covert operations, followed by open war.

Even in the Intel community, there were plenty of moderates that were arguing against this of course, but there were also many realists like herself, and goddess-willing, they would eventually carry the day. In the meantime, all that she and her team could do was to continue their intelligence effort, and make ready for the time when they would finally be called into action.

It was tedious, painstaking work, but she was certain that the future would justify their labors.

One of these tasks had been taking far too long for her liking, however. N'Kyla walked out of the central analysis room and down a short hallway to the detention block. Another guard was on duty there, and she absently returned the woman's salute as she went into an observation chamber. At a signal from her psiever, the glass window became transparent—on her side—and she saw that Lieutenant Amandra sa'Tela had already arrived, and had seated herself in a corner of the interview cell, watching their subject quietly.

Dr. Adalpha Martana, the so-called leader of the School was drugged of course, and probably didn't even know that the woman was there, or where he was for that matter. So far, they had been questioning him for eight days straight, and even without sleep and goddess knew how many drugs that had been pumped into him, they were still no further along than when they had begun. Although he was a scholar and not a soldier, he had proven surprisingly resilient.

But now Lieutenant sa'Tela believed that she had a way of breaking past his defenses, and N'Kyla was willing to let the military psychic give it a try. Sa'Tela was widely acknowledged in the Intelligence community as an expert in interrogation, and had the reputation of getting information when everyone else had failed. This certainly seemed to be just such an instance.

Hoping for the best, N'Kyla entered the cell and began the day's session. "Dr. Martana!" she shouted…

…Martana knew her voice, but he couldn't remember whose it was.

"Dr. Martana! *Wake up!*"

He almost had it—he could almost recall who was speaking to him. But he was too tired to seize the memory. *Go away* he thought. *Let me sleep.* That was everything; sleep, blessed rest. To rest forever.

Ice-cold water suddenly splashed over him, jolting him back to semi-awareness. He blinked, but the room was blurry. He couldn't focus his eyes—or his mind—he had--to—sleep.

"Go...away", he croaked. "Let...me...sleep."

"No Doctor. Not yet," the woman said. "Not until you answer my questions."

"Questions...what questions? Go away."

"No, I won't go away, and you won't leave either," she replied. There was a sharp stinging sensation in his arm, but it seemed like it was a thousand kilometers away. Then he felt himself being dragged back from the abyss of unconsciousness.

So close, he thought. He had almost made it to the safety of that nothingness, but *She* had caught him. She always did.

"What...what do you...want?" he begged.

"Answers, Doctor," the woman said. She was cruel like that.

He knew her now. She was the same person who had tormented him for...how long? Days? Years? Forever? He couldn't remember. If only she would just let him go, let him rest.

"What is your mother's name?" she demanded.

The question made no sense. *Why is she asking me this? Why won't she let me sleep?*

"M-Maryya..." he said. "Now...please..."

"And what did she call you as a child?" She was incessant, unrelenting.

"P-popi...my little...p-popi."

"Good, doctor. Now I will let you sleep," she told him. "Then we will talk some more."

Darkness rolled over him like a warm blanket, and he felt himself falling into a blissful oblivion. *At last*, he thought...

...N'Kyla turned to Lieutenant sa'Tela. "Well?"

"I think he is ready now," the officer said with a Kalian accent. "I will take over from here."

Sa'Tela rose and came over to the unconscious man, leaning in close, and then kissing him on the cheek. "*Popi*?" she said, whispering into his ear, "*Popi*? Do you hear me? It is your mother. It is Maryya."

From the depths of his unconsciousness, Martana heard these words as she linked her mind with his. Then a dream began to form. He was a child again, and his mother was there—incredibly, she was alive, and there in his dream with him.

"Mother?" he whispered.

Amandra exerted her talents and reached into his memories until she saw what the woman had looked and sounded like. Then, with infinite care, she brought the dream into focus. "Yes, *Popi*…it's me. It's mama. I need your help. Your mother needs you to help her."

"How?" he asked. She was holding him close now, comforting him, and making him feel safe.

"You need to tell me what you wanted to learn about the bad women," she said.

"Yes—the bad women", he replied, reaching for her. The bad women were here—now. But she would protect him from them.

"Tell me, Popi. Tell your mother."

"W-we wanted to know where they came from," he answered, "and if-if they wanted to hurt us."

"What else, my fine child?"

"We wanted to know if they were--," he answered hesitantly."—if they were different than us."

"Your mother doesn't understand you," Sa' Tela replied. "What do you mean? Please, tell me. I want to know."

There was a brief pause, and Martana took in a deep breath. "About their bodies. We had to find out if their bodies were different than ours."

"Why? Why do you need to know that my darling?"

The man started to weep. "I-I don't know. They wouldn't tell me. Please---I'm sorry. I tried to find out, but they wouldn't tell me."

Sa'Tela caressed his forehead. "Shhh. There now. Don't cry. Your mother isn't angry with you. But I need to ask you something else."

"Yes?"

"Popi, where are the other women? The ones that came in the other ships? Do you know where they were taken? I need to find them. I have to know where they are."

Martana shook his head, and the tears returned. "I-I don't know." Again, he felt her gentle reassuring touch and finally, he quieted.

"Popi," she said at last. "Popi, you have been a very, very good boy, and your mother is proud of you. But now, I need you to be a big strong man and do something. It could be very dangerous, and you will have to be brave for me."

"Yes! Anything," he answered.

"You need to warn everyone," she instructed. "You need to tell them about the soldiers. They have to know that they are here."

Martana smiled. "I already did that, mama!" he said. "I've told them all about it. I've been telling them everything that's been happening here ever since the bad women came."

"Oh, Popi," Sa'Tela responded. "That's wonderful! What a clever boy you are. I'm so proud of you. But how are you doing it? How are you tricking the bad women? They're watching everything."

His voice lowered to a conspiratorial whisper. "The transmitter. We have one that the soldiers don't know about. It's hidden, at a farm just outside of town. The girl knows where it is. She uses it to tell everyone what's going on here."

"What is her name?" Sa'Tela asked. "What is this brave girl called? I want to help her."

"Reesy. Reesy Hernan."

"But Popi, how do they know that it's not one of the bad women just pretending to be her? You know that the bad women lie."

"A code book," Martana answered. "Hidden with the transmitter."

"Oh you are so marvelous, my *Popi*, my beautiful little boy!" she cooed. "And you have helped your mother! Now my sweet one, it is time to sleep."

Drawing from the same memories that had given her his mother's face and form, she retrieved the lullaby that the woman had once sung him to sleep with. The song was very similar to one she had heard as a girl from her own mothers, she reflected.

But it wasn't exactly the same. Nothing about their two civilizations was the same, and never would be.

***

After Dr. Martana had been returned to his holding cell, Hari n'Kyla went straight to her office and summoned Troop Leader Helga Annasdaater. Annasdaater's team had been the same one that had been sent down with the neoman, Jon fa'Teela, to investigate the School when the *Pallas Athena* had first discovered it. Since then, she and her Marauders had been attached to the Intel unit on a semi-permanent basis.

"Lieutenant sa'Tela has uncovered some very interesting information for us today," N'Kyla stated. "Our good friend, Dr. Martana finally disclosed information that will lead us to the transmitter they have been using to communicate with their home worlds.'

"Please arrange to confiscate this device, and its codebook. Apparently, the locals have entrusted one of their young women with the knowledge of its exact location. The Lieutenant can identify her for you. The girl should lead you right to it."

***

Pedaling up to the checkpoint, Reesy Hernan waved to the Marine sentries. Like always, they asked her where she was going, and she told them the same thing that she always did; that she was on her way to visit her grandparents and check on their welfare. And she made certain to maintain her cheerful façade as the troopers inspected the contents of her day bag. She even wished them a good morning as they let her ride on.

It was only when she had left the town behind her that her smile became genuine. Reesy had been born there, and once, she had loved the place. But now her home was a prison—not with bars or fences–but still a place of confinement. Thanks to the Sisterhood, no one was allowed to go anywhere without permission, and everything that they did was watched carefully. Even the sky over her head wasn't free; navy warships prowled the space above her world, making certain that nothing got in, or out.

At 14, Reesy didn't understand all of the reasons behind the occupation, and she didn't care. What mattered to her was that her world was being held captive, and that she was the only one who could maintain their tenuous contact with the rest of her nation. Every adult was under scrutiny, and only young people like herself were able to enjoy anything resembling freedom.

How long that would last was uncertain. For some reason, more checkpoints were going up, more questions were being asked, and there were more surprise searches of everyone's homes and businesses. But Reesy was determined to carry on with her mission for as long as she could. The Republic had to be kept informed about the situation, and with luck, the government would even find a way to shatter the blockade and rescue them from their captivity.

Stepping into her pedals with a will, she rode faster, eager to reach the farm and see her duty done for the week. After that, she promised herself that she would ride on, out into the green, open countryside, and for a while at least, pretend that everything was as it once had been, before the Sisterhood had come.

***

Troop Leader Annasdaater watched the girl through her field glasses. When the Marine was certain that her team could advance without being seen, she signaled the troopers to move.

High above her, flying just on the verge between atmosphere and open vacuum, a Valkyrie aerospace fighter was also keeping an over watch on their quarry. Between the craft in the air, and her team on the ground, there was nowhere that the girl could go that they wouldn't be aware of. Annasdaater was quite confident that in short order, they would complete their mission successfully.

Personally, she was curious to know what capabilities the transmitter possessed. The Navy ships on picket duty above them had maintained a constant surveillance, listening for any signals being sent in the system, and she wondered how they had failed to miss these broadcasts. As she boarded the team's hovertruck, she reasoned that it was probably something that only the techs would understand, but she was still interested nonetheless. SpecOps teams like hers could use something that was that silent.

***

Still unaware that she was being followed, Reesy reached her grandparent's farm an hour later. After checking on them, she made her way to the barn, and walked into one of the last stalls.

There, buried under the hay and muck, was the small hiding place that she had constructed. It wasn't anything elaborate, just an old board covering a hole. The transmitter itself was a tiny device, no bigger than her hand, and it was wired to two metal probes that were sunk deep into the soft earth beneath it.

She checked the battery level, and frowned. Even though it was designed to last for at least a year, it was getting low from all the use that it was being subjected to, and she had no idea how she would recharge it when it finally died. But she shoved this concern aside, fished out the codebook from its plastic bag, and turned the unit on. Then she pecked in the sequence of letters and numbers that the book instructed her to, and sent her message. It wasn't much different than the one she had sent only a week earlier; once again, it warned the Homeworlds that the Sisterhood was still there, and examining everything.

She knew that the signal would take some time to go out. When she had first been given her mission, her father had explained that once she gave the command to 'send', the message went out in little spurts to lower the odds of detection. The same held true for any responses that she received.

Reesy checked her watch, and waited as patiently as she could. There was never any way of knowing if a response *would* come, but she was still required to wait, just in case.

Today, one did. It was the usual inquiry about the troop strength of their captors, and a request for any updated information she had about the Sisterhood's activities.

There wasn't anything new to tell them however. The situation was largely unchanged, and she told them as much. Finally, when the conversation ended, Reesy signed off, vastly relieved that her chore was over. She put the unit, and its codebook, back into the hole and carefully began to cover it over. That was when a shadow fell over her.

***

Reesy, her bicycle, the transmitter, and its codebook, were all brought back to town by hovertruck, and her fellow citizens didn't fail to notice the girl's ignominious return. A few ran off to tell their neighbors, but those who stayed all had an aura of defeat about them, and one or two openly wept. Once again, the hated Sisterhood had out-maneuvered them, and no one knew what the consequences would be.

The moment that the SpecOps team pulled up in front of the Intel Unit's headquarters, Captain n'Kyla stepped outside to meet them. When she saw that their prisoner had been handcuffed, she immediately ordered her released.

"Young lady," she said with an exasperated sigh, "I want to congratulate you for your bravery. You are a credit to the women of your community. But as you can see, your efforts did not succeed.'

"You may go home now—but with one condition: I do not want to hear about you participating in any more covert activities against us. I will not be so forgiving the next time."

Reesy rubbed her wrists and glared at her with pure, undiluted hatred. Seeing the defiance in her eyes, the little girls at the primary school came immediately to the officer's mind. *What magnificent agents these women will make for us one day,* she thought.

"I know that this is hard for you to believe, but the Sisterhood really *is* your friend," N'Kyla told her. "We're the friends of all women, and what we are doing here, although unpleasant, *is* necessary. Think about this when you return to your parents." She gestured to the Marines, who pulled the girl's bicycle out of the truck and returned it to her. Reesy gave them all one last, hard look, and rode away.

N'Kyla watched her leave, and then she walked back into the Intel Center with the transmitter. Once inside, she went straight to one of the techs and laid it on the woman's worktable. "Find out how this thing works and explain why we didn't find it until now."

It took the tech less than ten minutes to find the answer. "It looks like our own technical superiority got the better of us, ma'am."

"Oh? How so?"

"It's nothing more than a primitive radio set," the tech stated, "broadcasting on Ultra Low Frequency just like our psievers. It doesn't even use an antenna—it employs contact with probes in the ground and sends its signal straight through the earth to another set somewhere else, probably no more than a kilometer away at the most. My guess is that at the other end, there is a receiver just as primitive as this one, hooked up to a more sophisticated transmitter, probably an ansible based on what we know of their technology.'

"It's really rather ingenious if you think about it. This kind of tech hasn't been around since the very early 20th century on Old Gaia, during their First World War, and the ansible itself went out of use, for us at least, about a thousand years ago."

N'Kyla frowned in irritation. "So, if it's as primitive as all that, why did we miss it?"

"The signal strength was so low that it probably didn't register to our ships up in space," the tech explained, "As for the ansible, I'd say it probably sends and receives ultra short burst signals, timed for the intervals when we're not directly overhead. Exactly how they know when these intervals are, I can't say, but I'd wager it has something to do with the ansible itself. But I'll know it for certain when we find it."

"Very, very clever," the Intel Officer grudgingly agreed. "There may be more of these damned things scattered about. I'll have the Marauders intensify their searches of the outlying farmsteads and I'll also tell the battle group to change its orbital pattern and listen for any bursts. Good work, by the way."

N'Kyla looked down at the little device and contemplated it. *Yes,* she thought. *Very clever indeed. Having the crew of the Atalanta and their ship to study, they must have realized the parameters of our communications technology. But we were cleverer.*

Once again, she wished a curse on Doctor Martana and his School. With luck, the Lady would hear her prayers, and reserve a special hell just for him.

***

Shortly after this, Captain n'Kyla and her occupation force received a surprise. The *Pentheselea* and its sister ships were making their usual patrols when the listening posts scattered throughout the system registered a ship coming into normal space.

From its warp signature alone, it was immediately apparent that it was not a Sisterhood vessel, and when it openly hailed them in Espangla, any doubts about its true origin were completely dispelled.

"This is the *Resalta* hailing the Sisterhood ships in orbit above the second planet. Please, do not fire on us. We are bearing an important message for your leadership and we come in peace."

The Commander of the *Pentheselea* responded immediately. "And *this* is Commander Shannon bel Suzzyn of the United Sisterhood of Suns Naval Ship *Pentheselea.* You have entered a military quarantine zone. A fighter escort is being sent out to meet you. You will power down and stand by for further instructions—or you *will* be fired upon."

A flight of Valkyrie fighters was already on its way, and the entire battle group had targeted the new arrival.

There was a brief pause, and then the captain of the *Resalta* answered her. "We understand and we will comply. We will follow your instructions without deviation." When they followed this up by powering down their impulse engines, Bel Suzzyn opened a link on her Com to Captain n'Kyla.

"Captain? We have had an interesting development upside. I think you should come up here right away. The ETR is here and they want to talk to us."

N'Kyla didn't press her for any further explanation, and ran to meet the shuttle when it came downside to collect her.

Special Committee for External Relations: Closed Session, 305th floor, The Golden Pyramid, Federal Plaza, Thermadon Val, Thermadon, Myrene System, Thalestris Elant, United Sisterhood of Suns, 1043.04|05|09:12:17

Senatrix Layna n'Calysher sat at the round *baaka* wood table and smiled pleasantly at her fellow politicians, nodding politely to enemy and ally alike. She could afford to be gracious. Her opponents didn't know it yet, but the winner of this meeting would be the Galaxa party, and herself, as its leader. Victory was an absolute certainty.

Although the table itself had been shaped to give the impression of equality, she had had her chair replaced at the very last minute by another that was just slightly larger than its neighbors. And neither her associates, nor her rivals, missed this symbolism. It silently told everyone that she was one of the most powerful Senatrix's in the Supreme Circle.

Another visual reminder was the presence of a Senatorial aide working for her longtime partner in crime, Senatrix Barbra d'Salla. Felecia n'Calysher had been apprenticed to D'Salla earlier that summer, and even though representatives of the Supreme Circle were appointed to their positions based upon the popular vote, N'Calysher had wanted to make it plain that her daughter would someday be her successor. The Calyshers had always been at the center of Sisterhood politics, and simply by being there, the Lady Felecia forwarded their rightful claim upon the future.

Naturally, there had been some objections to the girl's appointment, and also to her presence at the special session. Most of them had come from the Senatrix's enemies in the left-centrist Solidari party and the more radical Unis. Both groups had been quick to point out that the meeting was only open to those with 'Brilliant' level security clearance, and at the time, Felecia had not possessed this.

The issue had been easily resolved however; N'Calysher had simply called in a favor with her friends in the OAE, and her daughter's clearance level had been raised. Not only had this silenced the complainers, but it also created an added dividend. Like her oversized chair, the fact that Felecia had been awarded "Brilliant" level access as quickly as she had been, was another tacit reminder of just how much power N'Calysher herself actually possessed. Very few women enjoyed "Brilliant" status, and receiving it with such alacrity was virtually unheard of.

Smiling at the memory, and at the added fear and respect that it had created, N'Calysher watched her daughter as she brought D'Salla some water. Felecia had dressed herself carefully for the special session, she observed. The young woman was attired in a plain, but well-tailored *comerci*, and as she finished her errand and returned to take her place with the other aides, she presented the very picture of a senatorial assistant.

Felecia is learning to play whatever role is demanded of her, the Senatrix reflected proudly, *and to play it well. She will make a fine politician someday.*

She rewarded her daughter with a slight nod of approval, and then turned her attention to a group of women who had just entered the chamber. Two of them were naval officers and the third was a civilian. The moment that the trio had taken their seats, the Vice Chairwoman formally opened the session with a tap of her gavel.

"Members of the Special Committee," the Vice Chairwoman began. "Thank you for attending this special closed session. As you are aware, over the last several months, we have been engaged in an intelligence gathering operation in the quarantined system of HSL-48 2124A, informally known of as 'the School.' Our mission there has been to determine the nature and technology of our newly rediscovered neighbors, the *Esteral Terrana Rapabla*."

N'Calysher resisted the temptation to laugh derisively. *Newly rediscovered indeed*, she thought. *Hardly.*

Once more, her relationship with the OAE had benefited her. Unlike many of the others sitting in the room, she had known about the ETR for years, and the Sisterhood's clandestine efforts to establish relations with it through the Daughters of the Coast. And it had been her advice to the Chairwoman that had led to the *Pallas Athena* occupying the School.

She was also aware of the consternation that this action was causing the ETR's leadership. More importantly, she knew what the outcome of the special session would be.

Official policy regarding the Republic had already been decided, well in advance of this gathering. It had occurred during a private conversation held between herself, Senatrix D'Salla, the Chairwoman and her Vice Chairwoman. The real purpose of the special session had nothing whatsoever to do with relations with the ETR. But she still had to play her role, and feign surprise.

"Several days ago, an important development occurred at the School," the Vice Chairwoman was saying, "a naval vessel of the ETR's armed forces made contact with our detachment, and requested immediate military assistance.'

"Evidently, the Hriss have shifted their aggression to the ETR, and are currently overwhelming them. Pursuant to this, I have been asked by the Chairwoman to direct this Committee to determine what our policies will be regarding the ETR, and to arrive at recommendations for a response to their plea.'

This was something else that N'Calysher had already been briefed about. According to the OAE, the Hriss had invaded the ETR in large numbers, driven by their perpetual hunger for resources as well as pressure brought to bear against them by their sponsor race. Naturally, the Sisterhood's response to this aggression had also been predetermined at her private meeting. Nonetheless, she made certain to add the right degree of outrage to her expression.

"To help us with our deliberations," the Vice Chairwoman continued, "I have invited the Admiral of the Navy Jora t'Kayna, the Director of the Agency for External Affairs Tara ben Paula, and Captain Hari n'Kyla of the Sisterhood Naval Intelligence Division to join us today. For those of you who don't know her, Captain n'Kyla is in charge of our operations at 'the School' and oversees its day-to-day activities."

The Vice Chairwoman inclined her head to the newcomers. "Ladies, thank you all for the generous gift of your time today." The group acknowledged her, and then the Vice Chairwoman presented the day's itemized agenda.

"Our first task will be to decide whether or not to render military assistance to the ETR. If we elect to do so, then our second item will be to determine whether or not such assistance is feasible, and if so, what form it should take.'

"The third and final matter will be to establish our long-term goals regarding the ETR, and the ultimate fate of 'the School' itself. Now, if no one has any objections, I will begin our session with a general question that I have had on my mind ever since the School was first discovered. After that, we will proceed with opening statements and interviews of our witnesses."

As the Speaker of the Circle, this was her prerogative, and she addressed Captain n'Kyla without any opposition. "Captain? I understand that your recent efforts at the School have yielded some important new background information about the ETR's history. What have you learned?"

"You are correct Madam Vice Chairwoman," N'Kyla answered. "We have made some new discoveries. Thanks to our extensive interviews with the populace, and especially with their children, we've been able to fill in some of the larger gaps and get a much clearer picture of their history."

"Please, enlighten us," the Vice Chairwoman said.

"From what we can tell, the Lost Colonies were originally part of a joint colonization effort. Apparently, it was composed of several countries from the Southern American continent of Old Gaia, and led primarily by the nations of Argentina and Brazil. Like many of the nations that left the Motherworld during the Great Dispersal, they discovered resources in their new territories that changed their economic status overnight. In the ETR's case, this was large quantities of titanium and other valuable metals.'

"Then, during the late period of the Gaian Star Federation, the planets settled by the ETR aligned themselves with the Kaseigian Confederation, and secretly supported their attempt to secede. As you all know, the Kasiegians were defeated by the GSF, and it would appear that the ETR somehow managed to keep themselves out of the conflict and saved themselves from the destruction that was visited on their allies.'

"Afterwards, when the MARS Plague occurred, all contact was lost between the ETR and the Federation. Evidently, they went on to colonize sectors of space that were further and further away from the center of the old government, which only exacerbated their isolation."

Seeing that it was time for her to plant her first seed, N'Calysher signaled that she had a question for the witnesses. At a nod from the Vice Chairwoman, she addressed the officer. "Excuse me Captain, but I think I missed something here. Did you manage to determine how they avoided losing their male population to the Plague? I find that particular detail a bit odd, and I'm sure that this is something that everyone here would like to know."

"Yes, ma'am, "N'Kyla responded. "We found that to be rather anomalous as well. According to their official histories, the Plague mutated into a harmless variant on their worlds. Evidently this spared the majority of their male population from sharing the same fate as the men of the Federation."

"Oh, how *fortunate* for them," N'Calysher remarked dryly, eliciting a smattering of laughter from around the room. "Please Captain, do continue."

N'Kyla went on for a while longer, supplying the assembly with various bits and pieces of the ETR's history and filling in many of the gaps in everyone's knowledge. When she had finished, the Vice Chairwoman called for opening statements. Predictably, N'Calysher's longtime opponent, Senatrix Dana ebed Haria, the leader of the Solidari party, was the first to speak. N'Calysher settled back in her chair, and prepared herself for the inevitable drivel that was bound to come from the woman's lips.

"*Jantildamé*," Ebed Haria said. "I would like to begin by stating that I for one, strongly believe that we should come to the aid of our fellow humans and provide them with the military aid they have asked for. Doing so will not only help to damage the Hriss war machine, but also pave the way for reuniting ourselves with another branch of our Human family."

Typical Solidari rhetoric, N'Calysher thought sourly. *And right in line with their twisted way of thinking.* Despite their pretense of moderation, the Solidaris had always supported the efforts of the lunatics in the Uni party to see neomen integrated into society. This was just a further extension of their misguided policies.

She was far from displeased however; although the Solidaris and Unis had won some great victories for the so-called 'rights' of neomen--and by extension the Marionite cause, today their radicalism would be the very key to their undoing. She would see to that.

Senatrix d'Salla spoke next. They had agreed that she would take the hardline position. This would cast N'Calysher as the moderate, and in the end, help them both to gain the victories that they sought.

"Ladies," D'Salla began, "I must respectfully disagree with Senatrix ebed Haria's assertion. When the ETR learned of our existence, I must point out that they did *not* choose to pursue contact with us. Nor did they return our sailors to us.'

"Instead, what did they do? They held our women captive and *studied* us, clandestinely. And I believe that they would have continued to do so had the Hriss not invaded them. Only now, and after over a *thousand years* of *voluntary* separation, have they come running to us, begging for help. I for one, feel that we owe them absolutely nothing. The Sisterhood would be better served by staying out of this conflict. Instead, we should concentrate on protecting our own space and let them deal with the Hriss."

Appropriate noises of approval and disapproval came from the assembly and the Vice Chairwoman used her gavel to bring the room back to order. When the tumult had died down, N'Calysher took her cue and raised her hand again. She chose what she had to say with great care.

"Ladies, it is true that the ETR could have contacted us before now, and did not. It is also equally true that they did not return our marooned citizens, and I am not excusing them. However, I think that we can all agree that they offer us a 'genetic safety net' should we ever need it, not to mention other benefits that we have yet to discover.'

"And as Senatrix ebed Haria aptly stated, this will also damage the Hriss, which can only benefit the Sisterhood in the long run. Two things concern me however; the first is the disruption to our social order that open contact with such an outdated culture might bring, and secondly, how we could render them aid and still maintain the ability to protect ourselves."

Just as she had predicted, her supportive words caught Ebed Haria and the Solidaris completely by surprise. Up to that moment, the Galaxa party had always opposed *anything* that the Solidaris had ever championed, and none of them had expected such a reasonable response, especially from the likes of her. Seeing their looks of consternation, N'Calysher had to struggle to suppress a malicious smile. The confusion within their ranks was positively delicious.

The Vice Chairwoman waited to see if anyone had anything to add, and when nobody requested permission to speak, she moved on. "Does anyone have another question for our witnesses?"

The leader of the Prosperi party took the initiative, and addressed Admiral t'Kayna. "Admiral, if we do assist them, what is the Navy's position?

Do we have the resources?"

Admiral t'Kayna brought up a holo showing the Sisterhood's naval fleets and their current dispositions. "Madame Senatrix, naturally the Navy is prepared to undertake any mission that the nation demands of it, and we have had plans in place for some time to prepare for just such an eventuality.'

This was an understatement. Although the information had been limited to T'Kayna and her Fleet Admirals, the Navy had been aware of the ETR from the very first day contact had been made by the Daughters of the Coast. They had had decades to plan, and then to refine those plans.

"As it stands," T'Kayna explained, "when the ETR approached us, they supplied data about their own naval strength, and estimates of the size and nature of the Hriss invasion forces. Based on this information, I believe that we could send elements of the Topaz, Emerald and Onyx Fleets as a combined expeditionary force, along with three divisions of Marines, and still have generous defensive reserves here at home."

At this point, Senatrix d'Salla requested to be recognized, and then she asked a question that was crucial to the success of their secret plans for the session. "I have something that either the Admiral or the Director can answer. Ladies, if it ever came to a conflict, what threat could the ETR pose to the Sisterhood?"

The Admiral of the Navy deferred to the OAE Director. "Ma'am," Ben Paula said, "At this point, the ETR is completely mired down in their struggle with the Hriss, and they need our help simply to survive.'

"One reason is that they are hopelessly behind us in technology, and their armed forces are quite small in comparison to our own. Unless we see a radical improvement in their situation, I do not believe that they could be of any danger to us militarily."

Seeing what she believed to be an opening, Ebed Haria waved her hand, and the Vice Chairwoman let her speak. "This question is for Director ben Paula," she said. "Does your Agency know what position the Galactic Collective will take about another war with the Hriss, or if we ever have to pursue it, with the ETR?"

The Galactic Collective was exactly what its name implied, a loose association of interstellar races that had banded together eons before Humanity had even discovered rudimentary flight. Their purpose was to support their mutual and individual interests. Now, after centuries of observation and study, the Collective was finally considering Humanity for probationary membership. There were tremendous advantages to the Sisterhood for such a liaison, not the least of which were increased trade, and new technology.

But membership, even if it was probationary, was not guaranteed by any means. There were many races that hated Humankind and didn't desire to see its inclusion into the Collective. Foremost among these were the Zeta Reticulans, or the Greys.

Before the 22nd century BSE, the Greys had enjoyed almost complete control over Gaia, and had dipped into Humanity's gene pool with impunity. However, the Seevaan Chaotic faction had changed this equation. Seeing its capacity for the very chaos that they embraced, the Seevaans had gifted the human race with interstellar travel and encouraged them to rebel against their secret masters.

The Zeta Reticulans and their allies had never forgiven their former slaves for this, or the Seevaans, and everyone in the chamber understood that the Greys would use any excuse to sway the rest of the Collective against inclusion. And they would certainly challenge whatever policies the Special Committee arrived at concerning another star-nation, even a human on.

Again, N'Calysher enjoyed a tremendous advantage over the other politicians in the chamber. The question had already been answered for her in detail by Ben Paula herself, and she waited patiently as the Director shared what they had jointly agreed to divulge.

"Madame Senatrix," the OAE Director said. "My Agency has made inquiries with the Collective's representatives, and according to them, the entire Collective, including the Zeta Reticulans, are maintaining neutrality on the issue of war--with the usual prohibitions against total genocide, of course. I believe that we can proceed in any manner that does not contravene that stipulation and still be received quite favorably when they take their vote.'

"Evidently, the issue of inclusion does not extend beyond Womankind; the humans living in the ETR are considered separate, and having no sponsor race, lack any standing with the Collective. If anything, we would be the closest thing they have to a sponsor."

While Ebed Haria and the other Solidaris ruminated over this, Senatrix d'Salla pressed the attack.

"Admiral? If we go ahead with this military aid, our armed forces will need to be sustained by more than just mere gratitude. Do you have any kind of cost projection for such an adventure?"

"Yes ma'am," the officer replied. "According to the Government Accounting Department, and our previous experiences in the last two wars, we estimate a total cost of roughly 30 trillion Credits."

"Did I hear you correctly?" D'Salla asked, feigning incredulity. "30 *trillion*?"

"Yes, ma'am", the Admiral responded. "Which I might point out, is roughly half of what we expended to fight the War of the Prophet."

"But that is still not an inconsiderable sum by any standard," the Senatrix challenged, "Is it Admiral?"

"No, ma'am," the Admiral admitted. "Certainly not."

The Solidari leader pounced on this. "But surely," Ebed Haria inquired, "we have such funds available, and if, as Senatrix n'Calysher asserts, there are benefits to having contact between our two civilizations, isn't it worth the cost? As she aptly pointed out, if they survived the MARS plague, then they might be the key that we need to survive another epidemic. That should be motivation enough."

The fool, N'Calysher gloated. She had her exactly where she wanted her now. Ebed Haria had just conceded vital ground to the Galaxa party, and simultaneously weakened herself in the eyes of her supporters. Looking around the room, she could tell that many of the Senatrixs supported what the Solidari leader had just said. But by extension, they had also been forced to concede to Galaxa's position.

Good, she mused, *let them begin to doubt their allegiances. In time, they will abandon Ebed Haria and her pitiful little party completely.*

After that, Ebed Haria would die. Although she could never prove it,

N'Calysher was absolutely certain that Dana ebed Haria had been behind the failed assassination attempt on Nemesis, and the effort to disrupt her negotiations with the Rampart. The woman had failed on both counts, and she would pay for her audacity with her life. But not before she and the Solidaris were completely broken.

Smiling in anticipation of her revenge, N'Calysher made her next move. "Again I must concur with my Solidari colleague, and add my personal note of support for her statement. However, as the Admiral has amply shown, aiding the ETR *will* be expensive. Any war is.'

"Even so, we cannot overlook the possibility that while they are poorer than the Sisterhood, the ETR must possess resources that would be useful to our industries. For example, they would require considerable amounts of titanium simply to field what ships they *do* have. If this is true, then I think that it is only fair that they should be required to give us a fair amount of these materials in compensation."

No one, in any of the factions ranged around her could disagree, and completely unopposed, she pressed on. This time, her question was directed to Captain n'Kyla.

"Captain, I understand that you undertook an analysis of the *Resalta*, compared it to their fleet strength, and arrived at a rough estimate of their natural resource base. Isn't that correct?"

"Yes, Madame Senatrix, we did," N'Kyla answered. "Although a detailed report will be made available for the committee's review, I can summarize it by stating that they are quite well-endowed in terms of raw materials"

I owe a great deal to the Daughters of the Coast, N'Calysher reminded herself. *As does Captain n'Kyla.* Although the officer had conducted the analysis just as she claimed, it had actually been done to cover up the real source, and the amount of time that had been involved in gathering it. The Daughters had been passing it along for decades before the *Resalta* had arrived.

When no one raised their hand to ask for further details about N'Kyla's report, the Vice Chairwoman directed the discussion to the next issue. "Ladies," she said, "I think that we have arrived at our last piece of business:

our long term goals, and the disposition of the quarantined colony." With that, she called for statements from the assembly.

This time, the spokeswoman for the Uni Party, Senatrix t'Tallya, went first. N'Calysher knew T'Tallya well, and had always hated her. In her opinion, the woman was nothing more than an anarchist, thinly disguised as a government representative.

"Ladies," T'Tallya said, "I feel that our long term policy should be nothing less than open contact, and unrestricted trade with the ETR. We can only benefit from our two societies working together, and I believe that the first step in that direction should be the immediate return of the School. It would be perceived as a gesture of good faith, and firmly establish the Sisterhood as a benevolent power, worthy of such a union."

What absolute rubbish, N'Calysher reflected. The Unis had always been a bunch of pro-Marionite revolutionaries with no higher purpose than to wear down the moral fiber of the Sisterhood any way that they could. Even so, their muzzy-headed leader had inadvertently done a favor for Galaxa by mentioning trade.

But it was not the anemic version that the Uni's envisioned. To be even remotely acceptable, N'Calysher appreciated the fact that any agreement with the ETR would have to offer the Sisterhood a decisive economic advantage at every level. And giving the School back as some kind of 'humanitarian gesture' in the process of driving such a bargain was simply imbecilic. She kept her thoughts to herself though, and let her partner react instead.

Senatrix d'Salla didn't disappoint. She signaled to be heard, and then maintained her hardline position as she rebutted T'Tallya's statement. "Ladies," she said, "as you know I do *not* support an alliance with the ETR, and I certainly do not care for the kind of 'open-door' policy the Unis are proposing. We are still dealing with a largely unknown society, and I firmly believe that the wisest course should be one of extreme caution.'

"Towards that end, I think that we should continue with our quarantine of the School, and carry on with our intelligence gathering operation there. I also think that we should consider the placement of agents inside the ETR, not only to gather more information, but also to help us determine what their true intentions are. I, for one, am certain that we will find them to be completely hostile to our way of life, and we can only benefit from the advance warning."

T'Tallya, still caught up in her idealistic zeal, actually seemed as if she were about to stand up and yell out an objection to this, but a reproachful glance from the Vice Chairwoman cowed her into keeping her silence, and her seat. As she settled back down, N'Calysher saw that the time had arrived to close in for the kill.

"Gentleladies," she said in her most agreeable tone, "this seems to be a day when I can clearly see both sides of the issues, and their merits. The Uni Party has sensibly suggested that we should look towards increasing our contact with the ETR, and pointed out the benefits of initiating trade relations. But," she held up her finger for dramatic emphasis, "Senatrix d'Salla has reminded us of the need for caution. As she wisely pointed out, we are dealing with a culture that we know very little about, and must proceed judiciously.'

"In the light of this, I feel that the colony on HSL-48 2124A presents us with an opportunity to accomplish this, and that we should maintain our quarantine. I also believe that the placement of agents in the ETR is equally advisable, if only for the purposes of helping to understand their civilization better than we presently do. And if, Goddess forbid, we should determine that they *are* hostile, such agents could only be an asset to our defense."

There was a long pause, and the Vice Chairwoman looked around the room to see if any of the other Senatrix's wanted to refute this. But N'Calysher had adroitly summed up what many of them were feeling, and had presented them with their own views in a nice, neat package.

No one asked to speak and the Vice-Chairwoman excused the witnesses. "Ladies, thank you again for coming here today." As one, the three women rose, and with a bow from the OAE Director and salutes from the two servicewomen, left the chamber together.

"Gentleladies," the Vice Chairwoman announced, "it is now time to consider everything that we have discussed here today. We will take a two hour break for lunch and then reconvene at 05:41:67 to cast our votes."

N'Calysher met Senatrix d'Salla and Felecia as they headed out into the hall. "Barbra? Felecia? Would you care to join me for lunch?"

"Certainly," her fellow Senatrix replied. "I'd rather avoid the Senatorial Dining Room just now. Too many *raata's* scurrying around down there."

N'Calysher chortled. "No doubt--and all of them fighting over who will get their bits of cheese. My car is waiting on the roof."

The two Senatrix's shared a knowing laugh as they took the hyperlifts to the very top of the Golden Pyramid. N'Calysher's armored hoverlimo was standing by, and as soon as they were aboard, it whisked them across the city to her favorite restaurant, using its special government clearance to take the police flightlanes.

The *Cheyr mis Famme* didn't serve the finest cuisine in Thermadon, but it did excel in two other important areas; its service, and its complete discretion. This made it the perfect place to discuss sensitive, high-level business in comfort.

When they arrived, the *Maitredam* welcomed them warmly, and showed them to N'Calysher's customary table. It was located in a private dining room with no windows, and its own staff of fully screened waitresses. The two Senatrix's had been there many times, and they ordered their usual fare, which were light salads, bread and tea. Although Felecia was quite hungry, she judiciously followed their lead when she selected her own meal.

"So, Feli," N'Calysher said, patting her daughter's hand affectionately. "What did you think of our little session?"

As she asked this, Senatrix d'Salla leaned forwards and paid close attention to the girl as she formed her reply. Like everything else about Felecia's apprenticeship, the question was a test, and a lesson in statecraft.

"Well mother," Felecia finally answered. "I thought that everyone presented what they believed were reasonable points on a very important set of subjects."

"Indeed," N'Calysher returned. "And how do you think the vote will go?"

"I am not sure," her daughter said. "I saw merit in everyone's statements and I'm certain that they will all vote according to their conscience."

Although the Sisterhood's political parties always expected a certain amount of loyalty from their members, Senatrixs were free to vote as they saw fit, even when it went against party lines.

"I do so admire the sense of caution that you've acquired, Feli," N'Calysher remarked. "You dance around the point like an accomplished ballerina. But tell me, my little *dansuar*, exactly which way you see the vote going."

"Why don't you just tell me?" the girl asked her slyly. "You already know, don't you?"

N'Calysher looked to D'Salla and they both grinned. "Yes daughter, we certainly do."

Felecia picked pensively at her salad for a moment, and then looked directly at her mother. "You have some *intima* on them," she said.

This wasn't a question, but a simple statement of fact. During the preceding year, Felecia had learned many things, especially with regard to political power, and its value. She had also come to realize that two important elements helped to create and maintain that power. They were *Intima* and *Terminér,* which translated to '*her underwear*' and '*the hard end*', or compromising secrets and sheer brute force. Together, they formed the core of the Thermadonian art of *Santaj*, or blackmail. Although an old Gaian saying had once made the naïve claim that faith was what moved mountains, the women of Thermadon knew that *Santaj* did a much more effective job. And the two Senatrix's sitting in front of her were its unacknowledged mistresses.

The young woman also appreciated the value of her family's close relationship with the OAE. Their friendship with the Agency guaranteed them both *Intima* and *Terminér* in abundance, and perpetuity.

"It seems," N'Calysher said, identifying a key Solidari Senatrix, "that Senatrix sa'Naari did some favors 'off-the-books' for the NTE Mining Consortium a while back, and thanks to their mismanagement of the mining operations in the Miralindra system, the local economy suffered a recession. You know what that means if it ever came to light, don't you Feli?"

Felecia certainly did. At the very least, it would produce charges of influence peddling, and at the worst, economic treason.

This deadly legal concept was a hold-over from the Star Federation when corporate entities had damaged the nation's economy, either through uncontrolled speculation, or poor administration. Such catastrophic events had given birth to strict laws mandating corporate accountability, with penalties ranging from decades of incarceration in hard labor colonies, to death sentences in the most extreme cases. When it had succeeded them, the Sisterhood had adopted the same laws. Although harsh, economic treason statutes tended to guarantee fiscal responsibility and economic security.

"And T'Tallya and Bel Janet?" the girl inquired, referring to the Uni leader and one of the more prominent members of the Prosperi faction. Although her party was friendly to Galaxa, Bel Janet had always been more sympathetic to the leftists in the Circle. Her vote would be crucial for swaying her compatriots.

N'Calysher shook her head sadly and sighed. "Poor Senatrix t'Tallya has a sexual weakness for neomen, and Bel Janet's daughter has a very serious glass problem."

Felecia took a delicate sip of her water. "I will certainly look forwards to auditing the afternoon session, mother."

Senatrix n'Calysher nodded in approval and then, blotting her lips with her napkin, made a call on her psiever to her own Senatorial aide.

Leesa, she thought. *Please contact the programming director at SNN this afternoon. I would like to see more shows centering on the Lost Colonies.*

I would also like a few rebroadcasts of 'Street of Shadows' to remind women of what life was like before Motherthought. Make sure that you emphasize that this is not an order, merely a favor that her government would appreciate.

Like many media organizations of the past, Sisterhood News Network helped the government by shaping public opinion in advance of any major news development or significant policy changes. The ETR certainly qualified on both counts, and *"Street of Shadows"* was the perfect tool to accomplish what N'Calysher had in mind.

Over two centuries old, the realie centered on the life of a woman living in the 23rd century tenements of New New York. It had become part of the basic Motherthought curriculum that was presented in every secondary school. Along with other strong imagery, it featured a particularly brutal beating and rape scene that was perpetrated by the protagonist's alcoholic husband. This was followed by his murder at the hands of his female victim.

More than anything else, it pointedly emphasized the horrific abuses that women had once suffered at the hands of their male partners. The realie, and others like it, would inspire the proper level of wariness and hostility in the average woman's mind. And later, that same distrust and antagonism could be nurtured and grown. For her part, Layna n'Calysher was not about to let her nation enter into a relationship with the ETR without properly preparing its citizens for the inevitable outcome of such a union.

***

The Special Session went on for the remainder of the day. At the end, when the votes were cast, it was a major victory for the Galaxa party and Layna n'Calysher. The alliance with the ETR was ratified, but with sharply limited contact between their two societies, and the ETR would be expected to provide generous amounts of raw resources to the Sisterhood in return for military assistance.

The quarantine of the School also remained firmly in place, and the use of covert agents inside the ETR had been approved. These measures not only widened the Navy's intelligence gathering operation on HSL-48 2124A exponentially, but they also gave the OAE a vital role in the missions that would eventually be launched from there. And just as she had anticipated, Layna n'Calysher had been unanimously nominated to head the delegation that would meet with the ETR, and present the Sisterhood's terms.

The meeting concluded with her enemies in total disarray and utterly confused about her ultimate aims. The same could be said of her friends as well, including the Chairwoman and the Vice Chairwoman. Although they had been her partners for many years, the time was coming when they would no longer be useful, and even become an impediment to her plans.

N'Calysher regretted the necessity, but to get what she really wanted, they would have to be sacrificed right along with Ebed Haria and the rest.

Once everything fell into place, the Chairwoman's seat would become hers, and when she was ready for it, Felecia would inherit the post. Two Calyshers would go on to serve their nation in its highest office and usher in a golden age for the Sisterhood. Compared to that, everything else was inconsequential.

USSNS *Pallas Athena*, Engineering Section, Calandra System, Sagana Territory, United Sisterhood of Suns, 1043.04|06|02:58:97

"Congratulations, Mariner n'Rachel," Marga bel Lyra said saluting the woman. Sheena n'Rachel beamed with pride and returned the gesture to the Senior Ship's Engineer.

After a year aboard the *Athena*, and endless days of study and drills, she was finally receiving her 'rockets'. The pin on her orange jumpsuit, which depicted an old-fashioned 23rd century cruiser and crossed chemical rockets, told everyone, that at last, she was a full member of the Engineering department, and the ships crew.

Even though a woman could be assigned to a ship, the process wasn't really considered complete until she had fully mastered her specialty skills and also the skills of other key members in her department. In an emergency, every crewmember had to be able to fill in where needed.

This requirement had been a part of the Star Service since its inception, and it went back well before that, to the ancient submarines that had once plied the oceans of Old Gaia. N'Rachel, having accomplished this difficult task, had made the grade.

Corporal n'Darei was standing there among the other well-wishers, and she stepped forwards to add her own congratulations. She wasn't an Engineer, but a personal friend, and she knew how hard N'Rachel had worked to get her rockets. "Good for you, Sheena. You deserve this!"

"Thank you, Tara," she answered, accepting a clap on the back from another Engineer. "I'm just glad it's over. I don't think I could take another snap exam."

"We should celebrate," N'Darei suggested. "I've got a bottle of Kalian Cha'ala in my quarters. Want to drop by and share some?"

N'Rachel smiled, but only the two of them knew that her response was forced. The reference to the Cha'ala was also a covert message that the Corporal needed to speak with her in private. In addition to their friendship, N'Darei was also her control officer, and because she was as new to the OAE as she was to her post in Engineering, N'Rachel had to oblige her.

"Sure thing," N'Rachel agreed. At that, N'Darei left her to celebrate with her peers.

A few minutes later, when she was finally able to break away, N'Rachel went down to Five-Bar and over to the Corporal's quarters. Being the assistant to the Troop Leader and the Colonel herself, N'Darei rated a private space, albeit a small one, and she was waiting for her there.

She wasn't alone. Ship's High Priestess Ophida n'Marsi was also present. Although N'Rachel was aware that N'Marsi was the OAE Station Chief aboard the ship, she had never had any occasion to deal with her, and felt a little intimidated by her presence.

"This is the young woman I was telling you about," N'Darei said to the priestess. "She's willing to work with us on the matter we discussed."

"Yes," Ophida said, giving the Engineer a speculative look, "I suppose she'll do. Tell me, Mariner, are you clear on what we have in mind?"

N'Rachel flushed, still somewhat embarrassed by the whole affair. "Yes, ma'am. You want me to swear out a statement that the neoman made sexual advances towards me—and that he—touched me—in an unwelcome manner."

"Just so," Ophida replied, equally uncomfortable. They had been trying to find something to hang the man with, and after months of frustration, it had finally come down to this tawdry little tactic. Jon fa'Teela simply hadn't cooperated by committing any serious offenses.

"Do you want me to make my statement now?"

"No," the Priestess said. "Not yet. When we are ready, we will ask you for it. In the meantime Mariner, continue to work with the Corporal on the details,"

The young engineer wasn't aware of it, but there were several other women that Ophida needed to enlist in order to make the whole thing seamless. Not all of them were agents, and some, to the Priestess's great surprise, had even been unwilling to cooperate. Despite the healthy dislike that most of the crew had for the neoman, there were still a few among them that were reluctant to bend the truth enough to do what needed to be done. It was inexplicable, but nothing that a bit of *Santaj* wouldn't take care of, she assured herself. They had to get the man, and they would, no matter who they had to go through, or how.

USSNS *Pallas Athena*, On Patrol, Sagana Territory, United Sisterhood of Suns, 1043.04|07|04:16:67

The pilot banked her *Yakolev-1* hard to port and upwards, just to the limits of the planes tolerances. The *Messer* had been turning away from her in a slightly shallower arc and swerved right in front of her guns. Lilya didn't hesitate—it was not in her nature to do so—and she fired a burst of machine gun fire at the other aircraft. The bullets hit, sending pieces of the fighter's skin flying as its pilot tried in vain to avoid her assault. But it was too late for him. In seconds black smoke began to gush from the *Messerschmidt' s* fuselage.

Lilya throttled back, following the other plane like a wolf from the steppes, confident that her prey was dying and patiently biding her time to give him the final *coupe de gras*. The *Messer* broke away, but the maneuver was slow and clumsy.

Her *Yak* followed it easily. Where the German plane had once enjoyed superiority, she was the master of the sky now.

Time for you to die! she thought, triggering her guns.

The burst caused the *Messer* to belch out flame and she saw the pilot trying to open his canopy and escape. Lilya fired a third volley, and her enemy and his plane disintegrated together into a ball of pure flaming hell. As her aircraft flew past the cloud of debris, she felt an exultation beyond anything she had ever experienced anywhere else, even at the hands of the most experienced lover.

"May your bones rot on the soil of the *Rodina* and be scattered by the wolves," she growled. The enemy pilot was one more invader who would not see his precious Fatherland ever again. A savage smile crossed her face.

She was crossing over the front lines now and saw the cities patriotic defenders waving in a wild celebration of the *White Rose's* latest kill. That was what they all called her, even the Nazi bastards; the White Rose of Stalingrad.

As a salute to them for their own sacrifice and bravery, Lilya sent her plane into a victory roll. Then she straightened out and crossed over the shattered cityscape into German held space, seeking out more victims. It was just sunset, but as long as there was light shining over her sacred Motherland, and the great city of Stalingrad, she was determined to kill as many of the Fascist invaders as she could.

The realie ended there.

It took a few seconds for everyone in the classroom to orient themselves, and when Lilith saw that they were ready, she spoke. "That, ladies was what it was like for the women who fought in what they called the Eastern Front during the Second Gaian World War.'

"Unlike the wars of the 21st century and beyond, soldiering up to the 20th century was considered a man's profession, except in the most desperate of times. And only when total annihilation threatened a nation state, would women be offered real equality; the ultimate freedom to live and die for their beliefs just like their male counterparts. Such opportunities were rare, and perhaps the sacrifices that these women ultimately made were all the more precious for that very reason."

'Lilya Litvak was eventually honored as a Hero of the Soviet Union, and female fighter pilots like her helped save their country. But after the war ended, their countrymen, and the world at large, forgot all about them. I'm sure that many of you sitting here today had probably never even heard of Lilya or her fellow female aviators before now.'

"My objective in this class will be to focus on the women who fought in the conflicts occurring before Gaia's Third World War, from the earliest figures that we know of, to the end of the 20th century. I believe that you will find much of it to be both revealing and surprising."

Lilith called up a holo depicting soldiers from the first of the two

American Civil Wars.

"An excellent example is a woman known only as 'Emily'. In 1863, at the age of 19, she ran away from home and joined a regiment in the Union forces, disguising herself as a man. Many women, feeling the call of their nation, did the same, not only for the Union, but also for their opponents, the Confederacy. Unfortunately, in Emily's case, she was mortally wounded at the battle of Chattanooga, and when she was taken before the surgeons, her sex was revealed.'

"The surgeons tried to convince her to divulge her true identity. She refused, but when they persisted, she finally consented. Then she dictated a telegram to her father.

"It read: *Forgive your dying daughter. I have but a few moments to live. My native soil drinks my blood. I expected to deliver my country, but the fates would not have it so. I am content to die. Pray forgive me, Emily.'*

Lilith glanced around the room. "To this day," she continued, "Emily's actual name remains a secret; her doctors took it with them to the grave. But like Lilya Litvak, her sacrifice was not forgotten, and one can only wonder about how many other women like her, died anonymously and will remain lost to history forever."

"Now ladies, if you will bring up your syllabus, you will see the reading list for this class, as well as the dates I have tentatively scheduled for our mid-term and final exams."

Everyone brought up either a holo, or a copy on their psiever, and as they were in the process of reviewing it, Lilith received a message on her own psiever. It was from Navcom.

"URGENT MESSAGE FROM CENTCOM: PROCEED TO THENTI, YOUR SOONEST. MEET WITH SPECIAL SENATORIAL DELEGATION FOR TRANSPORTATION. MISSION DETAILS AND DESTINATION CLASSIFIED 'BRILLIANT'. FURTHER INFORMATION TO BE PROVIDED BY DELEGATION LEADER," it said.

Lilith immediately sent a copy to her senior officers.Then she addressed the class.

"Ladies" she announced with a smile, "This always seems to happen when we are in session, but duty calls. We will have to cut the class short, and reconvene at another time. I will let you know when we can do so. In the meantime, please make sure to read Francine Moore's '*Women in War'*, which will give you more insight into 'Emily' and other women from that time period. Thank you."

Even though the class had been much shorter than she would have liked, her students stood and applauded as she left the room. Mearinn was waiting for her as she exited and Katrinn stood with her.

"Commander," the Tethyian exclaimed breathlessly, "that was everything I had hoped for and more! A wonderful presentation! I can't wait to see the rest!"

Katrinn chimed in, equally enthusiastic. "That realie was amazing Lily! I think my hands are still trembling from that dogfight. I can't wait to tell Ellyn about it when I relieve her."

"Thank you," Lilith replied. "I had a lot of help from the Ship's Computer putting it together. Let's just hope that whatever this delegation needs won't mean that we have too long a delay before the next session. The message was tagged urgent."

The two officers followed accompanied her to the bridge. When they had all taken their stations, she ordered the Helmsmistress to make ready for a transit through Null to Thenti straightaway.

There, they were met by a government shuttle, which docked with them immediately. While Katrinn remained on the bridge, Lilith, Mearinn and Ellyn n' Dira went down to the hangar bay to meet the delegation.

Senatrix n'Calysher led the small party out of the shuttle, and greeted them as they walked up.

"Commander ben Jeni," she said, "Thank you for responding on such short notice. I am Senatrix Layna n'Calysher, and these are my associates Senatrixs d'Salla and Ebed Mariana and this is Captain Hari n'Kyla from your own Intelligence Department, and also Sally bel Mala with the OAE. We represent the Chairwoman's Special Committee for External Relations. I hope that we didn't interrupt anything important."

Lilith shook her head, "Nothing that our relief won't be able to handle, ma'am." She indicated her companions. "This is Captain d'Rann and Captain bel Dira. My First is on the Bridge at the moment and sends her regrets."

"Understandable. Someone has to mind the metaphorical store after all," the politician replied. "Please extend my greetings to her. Now, if we may, might I ask for someplace where we can speak in private?"

"Certainly, ma'am," Lilith responded. "If you'll follow us, we can take our ease in my office." She led the way to the Lifts, and ordered tea and kaafra with her psiever. She was fairly sure that whatever this meeting was going to be about, that it would be a long and thirsty affair.

Once they were in the office, Lilith let the Senatrix take her seat and after the politician had situated herself, she got straight to the point, and told them everything. When the *Athena* had discovered the School, the very existence of the Lost Colonies had been surprising enough, but their sudden request for aid, and the reasons behind it, was even more shocking. Lilith arched an inquiring eyebrow at the woman.

"I was just as taken aback by this recent development as you, Commander," the Senatrix said. "We all were. But they have come to us, asking for our aid in the name of humanity itself. This is a plea that we simply cannot ignore.'

"Because of your prior experience with the School, your ship has been tasked with the job of playing host for the negotiations. Your battle group will not only provide security for this meeting, but also lend a visual reassurance of our naval power."

Lilith had to suppress the urge to smile pejoratively as an old West African proverb that she had once read came to mind; *'Speak softly and carry a big stick.'*

And of all the 'sticks' in the Far Arm, she couldn't think of any that were larger, or more intimidating, than an Isis class warship. The *Athena's* mere presence would lend the Sisterhood a considerable amount of leverage in the negotiations.

"Senatrix, at this juncture," she said, "I must ask that we include our Ships Chief Medical Officer in this conversation. You are proposing to bring these ETR representatives aboard, and I'm sure that there will be certain medical protocols that she will insist we observe."

"Naturally", the politician beamed. "Please include anyone that you believe will help make this historic meeting a success."

Lilith sent a message to Dr. elle Kaari, and a few minutes later, she arrived, accompanied by another physician, Dr. elle'Clayr. Elle Clayr was introduced to them as the Ship's resident specialist in Epidemiology. Both women were quickly brought up to speed, and true to Lilith's words, Dr. elle'Clayr did have an important requirement.

"Madame Senatrix," she said, "the last thing that we want is for this event to turn into a biological disaster, however slight the possibility. Thanks to our stay at the School, we've had the chance to become acquainted with the kinds of viruses that their population has had to contend with, and inoculate ourselves. Conversely, they have also been exposed to our strains and received treatment, all with good effect.'

"However, I should point out that the School *is* an isolated world, and there is still the risk of exposure to something from their inner worlds that we have not yet encountered. The ETR representatives also face the same threat from us in reverse. I must insist that we require them to submit to a short quarantine before coming aboard, and that they allow us to treat anything that has the potential to be harmful to either party."

This was only reasonable; notwithstanding the situation at the School, the doctor was completely correct. Human history was replete with examples of entire societies that had been wiped out by diseases that they had no resistances to, and the MARS plague underscored the dire possibilities that could come from overlooking this. The Senatrix agreed to Elle Clayr's request without hesitation.

"Certainly, Doctor," she replied. "Take as long as you feel you need to. Our meeting can wait until you and your staff is certain that it can be conducted in total safety."

Then she addressed Lilith once more. "Now, if I may, I would like to ask one more thing of you, Commander. We would appreciate the services of one of your Marines during the talks. I'm sure that you are familiar with him. His name is Jon fa'Teela, and we understand that he speaks their language fluently. We have already received some elementary training in Espangla, and we have interpreters to help, but it would be helpful to have Fa'Teela there to catch any nuances that we might otherwise miss, not to mention his public relations value. Can you spare him?"

"I am certain that his commanding officer will be willing to assign him to your delegation," Lilith replied. In fact, she knew that Col. Lislsdaater would be *more* than happy to cooperate. Even though his actions on CD48 2259 had raised him slightly in the Colonel's estimation, there were still many troopers, including the woman herself, who remained hostile to his presence. According to recent reports that Lilith had received, Lislsdaater was still encountering problems placing him in work details without objections being raised.

No one would miss him.

"Excellent!" the Senatrix exclaimed. "Of course we cannot be certain how long our talks might take, but I assure you that we will try to prosecute our business in a timely manner. Although the Admiralty has placed your battle group at our disposal, we would rather free you of this obligation as quickly as possible so that you can return to your normal duties."

"I appreciate your thoughtfulness, Madame Senatrix," Lilith answered with equal politeness. "In the meantime, we'll make accommodations for you on our Officers Deck. You may find the setting to be a bit more Spartan than what you are accustomed to, but my Ship's Activities Officer and Lt. Commander Bertasdaater will do their best to provide what comforts they can."

N'Calysher stood. "I'm sure that everything will be more than satisfactory. Thank you, Commander."

***

Senatrix n'Calysher supplied the *Athena's* Helmsmistress with the coordinates for the meeting. The location proved to be just outside the boundaries of the Sagana Territory in a binary system that boasted a couple of J-Class gas giants and little else. The battle group arrived in the system early, and a few hours after taking up station, their guests finally arrived.

Lilith was on the bridge when the two ETR warships came into sensor range. And although neither of them was scheduled to work, Katrinn and Mearinn had joined her, and Senatrix n'Calysher was also on hand, with her daughter Felecia standing at her side. No one wanted to miss this historic event, or the chance that it gave them to size up their potential allies.

When the *Athena's* screens displayed their information about the ETR ships, Lilith leaned forwards in her command chair and scrutinized the data. Visually, the ships looked surprisingly similar to the kind of heavy cruisers that dated from the War of the Bandits, although they were a bit smaller than the originals and possessed a few features that made them slightly more contemporary.

As a result, she was not surprised in the least when the readouts advised her that they were still using outdated warp engines running at impulse power for their in-system drives. This made them much slower and far less energy efficient than Sisterhood vessels, which employed gravitronic engines for the same task.

"Goddess," Katrinn remarked. "Will you look at those warp trails? Marga would do handstands just knowing that anyone still used it." She was right; their Chief Engineer, Marga bel Lyra, was infamous for her penchant for efficiency. And the ETR drives were anything but.

"Yes," Mearinn agreed with a chuckle. "Those trails could be followed by a blind woman. I suppose that it's a good thing that the Hriss let the Anx'Ma use Null, or they'd have arrived with the Hriss following right behind them."

"I also imagine that any decent stealth capability is out of the question," Lilith opined. "Well, at least our wait should be reasonably short." At best, their drives could only manage half the speed that the *Athena* and her sisters were capable of, which might have added up to hours of waiting had they not come out of warp into normal space where they had. As it was, the battle group still had several minutes to go before the ETR ships could come within shuttle range.

Intent on enjoying their wait, Lilith ordered herself a cup of tea, and as she sipped at it, she centered her holo display on the largest ship, and marveled at its primitive warp drives.

The trip here must have taken them days, she reflected. According to the Senatrix, Nullspace travel was a complete unknown to the ETR, and even more shocking was the fact, that to the best of anyone's knowledge, there wasn't a psi among them, and the psiever, or anything even resembling it, was a totally alien concept. How any modern society could get by without such basic scientific knowledge was completely beyond her. But the Sisterhood had once been in the same position itself, Lilith reminded herself. Centuries earlier.

As a professional soldier, it was their weapons systems that concerned her the most however, and she focused in on this data. Katrinn and Mearinn followed suit, and all three of them reacted with varying levels of disbelief when it appeared.

"Anti-ship missiles," Mearinn observed, "but fairly primitive ones; plasma core drives. I'd venture to say that their guidance systems are probably just as rudimentary. I also see energy gun batteries and kinetic energy weapons, but nothing outstanding."

She was being polite. In reality, they were junk by any modern standard and really belonged in a museum.

"And look at those shields," Katrinn said, pointing at her own display. The ETR ships certainly had them, but they were separate from the engines, fragile, and woefully inadequate.

"And I'm willing to bet that their fusion bombs and planet busters are just as outdated," Lilith added. A moment later, this information came up and proved her correct.

"Well, Lily" Katrinn said. "Now that we've had a chance to get a good look at them, I'd say it's not much of a surprise that they came running to us for help. If this is the best that they have, even the oldest Hriss ships are more than a match for them."

"Which means that if it comes to an alliance, we'll see the largest share of the fighting," Lilith stated.

She glanced over at the Senatrix as she said this. The politician had been listening intently, and while she didn't volunteer anything, she had a gleam in her eye that suggested that she had every intention of using their technological disparity to the Sisterhood's advantage. Lilith certainly hoped so; she and her fellow servicewomen would be asked to put their lives on the line, and she didn't relish the idea of selling them cheaply.

By this point, the ETR ships had come within range and Lilith put aside any thought of politics, and ordered a shuttle launched. Several minutes passed as it made its way to the lead vessel, and after it had docked and picked up the ETR delegation, it turned around and took up station at a mid-point between the two groups. Then, the quarantine process officially began.

Lilith got up from her Command chair. “Well ladies, now we wait for Dr. elle’ Kaari to tell us when we’ll be ready to receive our guests. Senatrix? Can I invite you to breakfast in the Officers Mess in the meantime? We serve a fine meal there, even if I say so myself.”

***

A full ten days passed before Lilith was finally informed that the ETR representatives had received a clean bill of health, and when the shuttle was headed for the *Athena’s* hangar bay, she summoned Senatrix n’Calysher, and her associates. As they rode up in the Main Lift together, the Senatrix spoke with her daughter privately, by psiever.

This will be a momentous occasion, Feli. I am glad that you could be here for it.

Yes mother, the girl replied. *Thank you for bringing me. I am looking forwards to observing the negotiations.*

And well you should, the older woman returned. *It is not often that one gets to observe two star nations reaching an alliance—but not before we make certain that the Sisterhood reaps the greatest benefits from the Pairing.*

Of course, mother, the girl agreed. A hint of cynicism accompanied Felecia’s reply, directly mirroring her own. She reached over, and gave her hand a gentle pat, and then straightened as the Lift doors opened.

Although she had orchestrated the reception with the help of the Ship’s Activities Officer, N’Calysher had to admit she was impressed by the final result. Two triple rows of Marines and Navy women in their dress uniforms stood to either side of a long red carpet that ran all the way from the Lift to the shuttle. The flags of the Sisterhood and the ETR (whose design had been supplied to them courtesy of Captain n’Kyla) were on display to either side of the ladder that led up to the vehicle's doors. There was even colored bunting, in both their nation's colors, draped all around the hangar bay. Captain sa'Vika had done a marvelous job, she observed, and she made a mental note to commend the woman to her Commander. But first, history had to be made.

Now, Feli, watch carefully when the delegation steps out, she advised. *Notice their reactions, however small. This will tell you immediately about their character, and the strength of their resolve.*

The girl nodded, standing alongside her mother and the other delegates as they waited for the shuttle's doors to open. A song (also supplied by N'Kyla) began to play, which the Senatrix supposed was the ETR national anthem.

When the melody had reached its height, an older man roughly the Senatrix's own age stepped out. He was dignified in appearance, and dressed in what she imagined was conservative clothing for his society. But although he seemed to have an air of confidence about him, she noticed that he paused for the briefest of instants before his foot touched the deck plating.

There! she thought urgently. *Did you see that, Feli!? Did you notice how he entered the stage in our little play? I can tell just from that brief hesitation that he is uncertain of himself, and he will be that way during our talks. Now, let us introduce ourselves and begin the dance.*

The Senatrix stepped forwards, and everyone including Felecia, followed her.

"I am Senatrix Layna n'Calysher," she said in Espangla. "On behalf of the United Sisterhood of Suns, we welcome you."

Even if she said so herself, N'Calysher thought that her pronunciation was good and that her delivery seemed natural. It was more than just a diplomatic nicety however; it also sent a message to their guest that the Sisterhood was now studying the ETR, just as the ETR had once used the School to study them. More importantly, it also informed him that the Sisterhood would be on its guard from here on.

The man's eyes widened so slightly that only N'Calysher caught it, and she knew why. He had understood her message perfectly. Then he returned her smile. It came as no surprise to her whatsoever that his reply was in Standard, or that his pronunciation was just as polished as hers.

"I thank you," he said, "I am President Xavyar Magdalana and I represent the Esteral Terrana Rapabla. Thank you for accepting our request for this meeting."

N'Calysher half-bowed politely, and led the man to the Lifts. But not before she sent another message to her daughter. *So it begins*, she thought to her, *the great game of diplomacy, with all of its subterfuge and dissembling. I think that by its end, this day will prove to be a great one for the Sisterhood.*

***

Jon fa'Teela was in Ordstores, and like most of the ship, he had no idea that history was in the process of being made. Instead, he was helping his fellow Marines load boxes onto a hovercart when Troop Leader Da'Saana walked up.

"Fa'Teela?"

Jon put down the case he had been handling and snapped to attention. "Yes, ma'am?"

"You're needed elsewhere," she informed him crisply. "The Colonel loaned you out for a special detail. Get to your rack and change into your dress uniform straightaway. Then meet up with Security at the Five Bar Lifts. They'll escort you from there."

Jon knew better than to even try to ask her what the detail was. At his rank-level, 'need-to-know' generally didn't apply. Instead, he hurried to his pod and changed as quickly as possible. When he had made himself presentable, he went to the Lifts.

The head of Ship's Security, Captain Veera t'Gwen and two of her Security Patrolwomen were waiting for him, and they had a Lift locked open. She gave his bright red dress tunic an appraising look, and then gestured for him to board the elevator with her. "Get in" she said.

The Lift however, did not rise, but stayed where it was.

"From here on out, Trooper," T'Gwen advised, "your assignment is classified "Brilliant" and you have been granted that clearance on a temporary basis for it's duration. You are not to speak to *anyone*, and I mean *anyone*, outside of the mission about any aspect of it. Zat klaar?"

"Ma'am, yes ma'am" he replied.

"Aren't you interested in the details?" the Security Chief asked.

"Ma'am, this Marine is willing to wait until his superior officers see fit to inform him."

"Well, they *do* see fit, Fa'Teela" she replied. "You speak Espangla, don't you?"

"Yes ma'am," Jon answered, trying to look as puzzled as possible, although he already suspected what was going on. The Navy believed that they had scrubbed everyone's memory of the events on HSL-48 2124A, but they hadn't. Thanks to his hidden talents, he still remembered what had happened at the School.

They must have made contact again, he thought. The Sisterhood had to be in touch with whatever nation the School was a part of. He didn't mention his conclusion to the Security Chief, however.

"Good," T'Gwen said. "You'll be working with a special delegation from the Supreme Circle. They are meeting with a group that speaks Espangla. Your main job will be to listen to everything that is said, and to answer any inquiries the Senatrix's might have about these conversations. You will also provide translation services, as they are needed. Any questions?"

"No ma'am."

T'Gwen smiled with satisfaction and signaled the Lift to rise with her psiever. When it stopped and the doors opened, Jon saw that they were outside the Officers Mess Hall. There were more securitywomen on duty there, and the area had been totally sealed off to casual traffic. She gestured towards the entrance, and then stepped back into the Lift. "Have fun," she said, giving him a little wave.

A strikingly beautiful young woman, perhaps not more than 16 standard, and dressed conservatively, met him as he walked into the mess. "Greetings," she bowed. "I am Lady Felecia n'Calysher, and I am an aide to Senatrix d'Salla. I will be your liaison with the Committee. If you will follow me, please."

Jon dropped into step behind her and they walked into a section that had been screened off for privacy with portable partitions. Two more securitywomen were posted at a gap in the screens, and waved them past. Inside, a group of women that he presumed was the special delegation was seated at a table across from another group.

It was a group of men. Not neomen, but men nonetheless. One glance at them told him that with the exception of several wearing unfamiliar military uniforms, they were politicians of some sort.

Felecia did not give him the opportunity to gawk. Instead, she directed him to an open seat next to an imposing looking woman whose resemblance to the girl was immediately apparent. A nameplate positioned in front of her confirmed that she was Senatrix Layna n'Calysher.

The Senatrix inclined her head politely to him as he seated himself and then Felecia leaned in, and whispered into his ear.

"Please listen carefully to what these foreigners say," she instructed, "and be ready to answer any questions that our Committee members might have for you after the talks have concluded. Do you need anything before we begin?"

"Yes, ma'am," he replied. "A glass of water would be greatly appreciated." The girl signaled to someone, and a glass was immediately placed on the table in front of him. As he reached for it and took a quick sip, he caught the eyes of the men across the table. From the looks they gave him, he could tell that they were surprised at his presence, and trying to assess him. Jon rewarded the eldest of them with a slight smile that was not reciprocated, and waited quietly.

Senatrix n'Calysher spoke first and an interpreter relayed what she said. The interpreter's Espangla was halting, but it conveyed the woman's message, and Jon's picture of what was transpiring here was completed, as was his role in it. The 'Lost' Colonies had decided not to remain lost.

"I represent the Special Committee on External Relations for the Supreme Circle of the United Sisterhood of Suns," N'Calysher said, "and I have been empowered by our leader, the Chairwoman, to negotiate with you on behalf of my government. How can our nation be of service to yours, Mr. President?"

The man across from her, identified as President Xavyar Magdalana, replied immediately. "Madame Senatrix, my associates and I have come here in the hope that you will aid us in a desperate time. We are being invaded by Hriss naval forces, and I ask that you assist us in repelling them from our nation's space."

N'Calysher smiled, but it was not a friendly expression by any means. It was sly and calculating. "That is a most precarious situation indeed, Mr. President," she agreed. "And it is unfortunate that our two great nations should endeavor to come together under such unhappy circumstances. Better that we could have become acquainted with one another in a happier setting, and much earlier than now."

Magdalana retained his outward appearance of calm, but her statement had clearly touched a nerve. "As you are aware Madame, our two nations have had their reasons for remaining apart for as long as they have, and I apologize that we did not explore contact with you before the present."

"So, instead you chose to study us through the agency of your little 'School?'" N'Calysher countered. "Tell me Mr. President, did you *ever* intend for the crew of the *Atalanta* to be repatriated to us?"

"Senatrix n'Calysher, I can assure you that the School was not sanctioned by our government. The actions of Dr. Martana and his staff were entirely autonomous. His colony was licensed as a separate, independent community, dedicated to behavioral research, and he had no funding or oversight by us."

"But your intelligence community benefited greatly from his discoveries, did they not?" she retorted.

"I won't say that we didn't benefit from the information that we received from the School," Magdalana admitted. "But again, I assure you that any choices that were made in the handling of the crew of your ship were his alone, and not something that we neither sanctioned, nor controlled. Clearly, his work while well intentioned was misguided."

"Then it would be safe to assume that your government will appreciate why we will continue to keep Dr. Martana and his community in our custody?" the Senatrix countered. "I am certain that since the School is independent of any intelligence effort by your nation, and according to our legal experts, guilty of kidnapping, that such a measure would be considered more than reasonable, would it not?"

President Magdalana's jaw tightened, but he nodded reluctantly. "Naturally. Perhaps in the future we can discuss the return of our colony and its people, but in the meantime, as a law-abiding nation, we fully support your decision."

"I am so glad that such a small issue was so easily resolved." N'Calysher beamed, clearly delighted that she had Magdalana at a gross disadvantage. "I can assure you that the inhabitants of the School are being well treated, and that they will continue to be until the matter can be resolved by our court system. In the meantime, shall we move on to the heart of our business?"

"Yes please," the man said.

With that simple concession, the fate of Reesy and her people was sealed. Politics was an ugly business when all the pleasantries were stripped away from it, Jon reflected.

"You wish for us to commit our naval and ground forces in a joint effort to repel the Hriss aggressors," N'Calysher stated. "You realize of course, that this will require a substantial investment of both material and personnel on our part."

"Yes, Madame Senatrix, we do."

"Then your government is also willing to provide certain valuable resources in return for this sacrifice?" N'Calysher asked, "and generously?"

"Madame Senatrix," Magdalana replied. "While we fully understand that we must contribute something, our nation is not as wealthy, nor as well endowed as your own. We will of course give what we can, but our resources are being taxed as it is."

"Which is a condition that our presence will certainly help alleviate," she responded. "Like your own nation, we are always in need of substantial quantities of metals such as Titanium, not to mention sources of raw fuel and other commodities."

The President's eyes narrowed in understanding. "Yes," he said. "We would be happy to contribute whatever was required to support our joint war effort. Perhaps your government might even consider an exchange of technological advances with us, in the spirit of cooperation."

"Perhaps," N'Calysher replied. "However that would be something that we would have to explore thoroughly before we could agree to it."

It didn't take an expert in negotiations to realize that she had no intention of sharing anything with the ETR—ever. But President Magdalana did not voice any objections. Instead, the man merely whispered to one of his associates, and then nodded. Their situation had to be very bad indeed for this to be their reaction, Jon reflected.

"Then in the name of humanity," the Senatrix announced grandly, "we will be only too glad to come to the aid of our fellow humans. Which leaves us with the delicate matter of how this will be accomplished without upsetting the balance of our respective societies."

"We have some measures in mind regarding that," Magdalana volunteered.

N'Calysher gestured across the table to him. "Please, share your thoughts with us."

"The first would be to completely bar our media from the battlefield, and sharply control the amount of information that they *do* receive."

The Senatrix nodded.

"The other would be to establish our supply bases in sparsely settled systems, located in the border zones. This would allow us to work together without exposing either of us to any unwanted publicity."

"Systems like the one that the School is located in, perhaps?" N'Calysher inquired.

Magdalana winced slightly at this barb, but managed to maintain his composure. "Yes, systems just like that, Madame Senatrix. There are several that we believe would be excellent candidates, and my advisors can identify them for your forces. We would also suggest an exchange of liaison personnel, and ambassadors, in order to streamline communications on all levels."

The Senatrix smiled. "That would only be sensible. Trained diplomats would certainly be the best choice for facilitating relations, and I know that our armed forces will certainly want the best communications possible if they are to work with your military. In fact, we anticipated just such a suggestion, and we have personnel that have been pre-selected for these duties. I assume that you have done the same?"

"Yes, Madame Senatrix," Magdalana replied. "We have, and they can report immediately, if it pleases you."

"It would at that," she agreed. "I am sure that their service will only help to foster the close association that we are both hoping to achieve. Now, perhaps we can return to the issue of your contribution to our war effort and discuss the specifics in greater detail?"

An hour passed, and then the two delegations agreed to take a break. The *Athena's* SAO staff had set up a refreshment table for the participants, and Jon immediately helped himself to a cup of badly needed kaafra. As its warmth rejuvenated him, Magdalana and his party approached the table. Watching the President pour a cup of tea, Jon could tell by the sag in his shoulders, and the look in the man's eyes, that although their alliance would be the salvation of his nation, it would also prove to be an economic defeat. And it made the neoman wonder just how much more N'Calysher intended to gouge the Republic before she was through with them.

The Senatrix herself walked up a moment later, and Jon had to fight the urge to scowl at her in disapproval. Even if she did serve his government, he had come to realize that he didn't like her one nano. From the standpoint of pure, cold logic, her actions might have been necessary, but they still seemed immoral.

Just then, an ETR officer interrupted the unhappy direction that his thoughts were taking him. "Hello," the man said. "I don't believe that we have been formally introduced. I am Admiral Carlaz da Estraddar of the Republican Navy. You are a neoman, I take it?"

"Yes sir." Jon answered, feeling a little uncomfortable at the notion of speaking to a senior flag officer, and one from another nation at that. "I am. I am attached to the Marine unit aboard this ship."

"That is truly fascinating," the officer replied. "I had heard that the Sisterhood only recently allowed men to serve in their military. It must have been very hard going for you when you first came aboard."

Jon answered cautiously. "I did my duty like any Marine would, sir."

"Certainly," the other man said. "One could not expect anything different."

The delegation was returning to the table, and Admiral Estraddar put down his half-finished drink. "Well, back to the battle, eh? It was good to speak with you, Marine. Perhaps we'll have the opportunity to talk some more when these negotiations have been concluded."

"Yes sir," Jon returned, hoping that this would not happen. "Of course."

Several hours passed, and when negotiations had concluded for the day, Jon fa'Teela was dismissed. He was eager to get back to his rack and read some passages from his copy of the *Revelation of Mari* before chow. After the long day he'd had, he craved the relaxation and the comfort that the Scriptures always provided him. He even managed to get as far as the entrance to Five-Bar before Troop Leader Da'Saana intercepted him.

"Not so fast, Neo," she said. "You have another work detail to take care of."

With the ease of long practice, Jon masked his weariness, and simply replied, "Ma'am, yes ma'am."

"You need to get over to the PTS debriefing room," she told him. "The Intel people want you there for some reason. Well? Don't just stand there gawping at me—*burn it!"*

Jon saluted her and returned to the Lifts, resigned to his fate, whatever it was.

An officer from the DNI greeted him at the entrance to the chamber. "Fa'Teela? You men just became obsolete all over again. The brass wants me to take all that Espangla gibberish that you've got stuffed in your head and make a feed with it. That way, women can learn it without having to ask any of you Neos for help. Sounds like a great idea, doesn't it?"

"Ma'am, yes ma'am."

"Yes, I thought so too," the woman said. "Now, take a seat, Trooper."

Jon did as he was instructed, and passively placed the plastic headset over his temples. The reverse feed took only ten standard minutes to complete, and when it was over, the officer had a few more things to say to him.

"Everything's still there, but you can check if you want to. We still need you to be able to speak Espangla, so we left the memories intact. And we'll also want some of your off time to help us prepare a final version of the feed. This is all classified by the way—you know, 'serious-stockade-time-if-you-tell-anyone' stuff?"

Jon nodded. He wasn't surprised in the least.

"Excellent! I'll let your CO know when and for how long we'll need you. And, hey, look at the bright side, Trooper; it'll give you something else to do when you're not sitting in your high chair at the 'big girls table'. Right? Okay, you are dismissed."

The actual process of editing the feed took several days, with Jon auditing the raw PTS signals and making changes, or clarifying grammatical points for the techs. By the time it was done, his entire knowledge of Espangla had been distilled into a single file, and a female instructor-identity had been seamlessly superimposed over his persona.

He knew, without being told (not that anyone *would* have actually bothered to tell him anything) that the Senatrix and her party would be among the first to benefit from it. But they were only the beginning; his audience would broaden to include the entire OAE, anyone in the Navy who was involved in work with the ETR, and every government official who had high enough clearance to know about the situation. Even the Chairwoman herself would take a turn in the PTS chair and receive his knowledge. Without intending it, Jon fa'Teela, who had once made history as the first male to serve in a combat unit after a millennia, had just achieved another landmark. And he would get just as much praise and recognition from the Sisterhood as he always had.

***

Several decks above him, in the privacy of her office, Ophida n'Marsi considered the file floating in front of her eyes, and everything else that had occurred recently. The young Mariner from Engineering had given Corporal n'Darei her statement, and it had been carefully corroborated by other women until it seemed like the truth.

Under any other circumstances, the Priestess would have been highly pleased, and used it against the neoman immediately. With N'Darei's guidance, the Mariner's account was nauseatingly graphic, and best of all, every detail of it matched the times when Fa'Teela would have had the opportunity to do what the woman claimed he did.

In fact, it would have been devastating.

The problem was that current events had rendered it useless. From the moment that she had heard that representatives from the ETR were coming aboard, and what they wanted, she had realized that going after the neoman for sexual misconduct fell far too short of her goals. Although she didn't like the notion of suffering any further delay, the ETR delegation represented a solution to the neoman that was much more satisfactory than what she had originally had in mind.

Accessing her Com, she sent a message out to Thermadon, detailing her thoughts, and waited. Her reply came back only a few minutes later.

"We concur," it read.

Smiling at this, she locked the file and sent a note on to Corporal n'Darei, instructing her to debrief the Mariner and all the other contributors. After all, she told herself, why get the *Fekka konnar* on something that would only result in a dishonorable discharge when she could see him prosecuted for treason. That offense carried a potential death sentence, or at the very least, life in a correctional colony. Either would be more than satisfactory.

USSNS *Artemis*, CD-2212-D System, Unclaimed Space,
1043.04|10|05:03:21

The head cook in the *Artemis'* galley had finally managed to get her favorite dish right, but Erin had no taste for her *squeeka*. They were fat, alive, and swimming about in their bowl of pure spring water, and at any other time in her life, she would have found them to be perfect.

But not today, and not for months. After taking a few desultory bites of the little creatures, the Nemesian finally put down her fork and pushed the tray away from her with a heavy sigh.

She knew the reason for her ennui; she had simply lost her spirit. After a lifetime of accomplishments, somehow, it had slipped away, leaving her nothing but an empty and meaningless shell. It didn't matter that she was Captain of the *Artemis*, or that she had distinguished herself in a hundred different ways. Her inner darkness had overwhelmed all of this like a battle cruiser bombarding a planet.

She also knew what the cure for her condition was. She had known it since the very onset of her depression. She had to find herself again. And the only place where that was possible was on Nemesis.

Returning to the world of her birth meant more than just a long journey though. It also meant attempting a rapprochement with her mothers, Teela and Saly'aa. They had never approved of her leaving the Great Mother Forest to join the Navy in the first place, and although she had earned their grudging respect as a fighter pilot, all of her gains had been reversed when she had gone on to become an officer.

The fact that she now commanded a mighty warship in a distinguished battle group meant nothing to them. The only thing that they understood was that she had walked away from what they considered honorable. Now, she was only a mere 'chair-fighter', at least according to Saly'aa.

Her clan, and most of the other clans on her motherworld shared this narrow attitude. Women who left Nemesis, and failed to pursue worthy professions, faced ostracism. Her sister, Skylaar, had only managed to avoid this fate by accepting work with the Assassin's Guild on Ashkele, but Erin had not. And with Saly'aa also serving the Minna'que'tsa Clan as a *Si'am*, an elder, her situation had only been compounded.

And even if her mothers consented to speak with her, and even if her clan was willing to consider reacceptance, she knew without question that she would still have to pay a heavy price to regain her place among them. Of a certainty, it would take the form of another Tej, but a far more arduous one than the journey she had taken to become a woman. After so many years away from her motherworld, she wasn't entirely certain that she could survive such an ordeal.

But if she failed to take action, if she left things just as they were, her life would continue to lose all of its color, and its substance, until nothing at all was left. That was worse than anything that her mothers, her clan, or even the Great Mother Forest herself could threaten her with. Without her spirit, there was simply no life for her to live. She would be nothing more than a ghost, living in the mists.

Her path was clear, she realized, and all that remained for her was to walk it. Resolute, Erin rose and went over to a display case mounted on the wall of her cabin. It held her Tej knife, preserved from the ravages of time by a stasis field. Like any woman from Nemesis, it was her most treasured possession. The weapon had been created for her by the clan's Bladesinger when she had turned 16, and in preparation for her Tej. Seeing it, some offworlders might have considered it a cruel and primitive thing, but for her, it was an object of great beauty and deep spiritual meaning.

Taking it out from its protective field, she closed her eyes, and gripped it tightly. Then she called on the strength of Fighting Bird, and on all the Mothers and Sisters of the Minna'que'tsa Clan who were, and ever had been.

All of you, hear me, she thought, *I am lost in the forest and you have whispered the way home to me many times, but I have refused to listen. Forgive me, and lend me the strength to lift my feet and take the journey. Bless my steps, and help me reach my goal.*

Uncertain if she would receive this pardon or not, she took the knife with her to her desk and accessed her Com. Lilith answered her call immediately.

"Erin?" the woman asked. "What is it? Is something wrong?"

Lilith is a true friend, Erin thought. *A sister, even if she isn't one of the People.* Somehow, the woman always seemed to know when her heart was troubled.

"I have to go home for a while," she explained. "It's personal business."

Lilith regarded her uncertainly, but she said, "Of course, Erin. You're certainly entitled to shore leave. Once the Treaty with the ETR has been finalized, we'll have to put back into Thenti, and then head on to Rixa. That should give you about a sevenday and a half before I'll need you back. Will that be enough time?"

"It should be," Erin said. "Thank you, Lily."

She cut the connection and stared back down at the Tej knife. There would be pain waiting for her on Nemesis, both emotional and physical, and there was even a chance that she would not survive the experience. But with luck, and the blessings of her ancestors, she would prevail. She had to.

CHAPTER 2

USSNS *Pallas Athena*, Rixa Naval Base, Rixa, Belletrix System, Pantari Elant, United Sisterhood of Suns, 1043.04|13|03:75:75

Despite its significance, the meeting between the ETR and the Sisterhood was relatively brief. As soon as a tentative agreement had been reached, both factions departed for their respective regions of space.

The *Athena* headed immediately for Thenti to return the Senatrix and her party, and then made for Naval Headquarters on Rixa. The Sisterhood Navy had important preparations to make, and Lilith and her staff had been ordered to report to Admiral ebed Cya to learn exactly what their role would be.

As always, they checked in at the section reserved for Incoming Officers, and submitted their log, but this time, there were two messages waiting for them. The first they had fully expected; the *Athena's* command staff, along with the officers from the *Demeter* and *Artemis* were scheduled for a briefing, set for the following day. They all knew without having to be told, that it would center on the first stages of the joint campaign with the ETR.

The second one however, was a complete surprise, and it was addressed to Lilith only. She had been invited to meet with the Fleet Admiral privately, and as soon as possible. Puzzled, she headed for the Admiral's office, and once she arrived, she was shown straight in.

"Commander, I suppose you might be wondering why we are having this private meeting," Ebed Cya said as she took her seat.

"Yes, ma'am. I had wondered." Lilith returned.

"As you know, we are entering into an alliance with the ETR to fight the Hriss. Although the treaty still requires the Chairwoman's signature, we can safely say that it is in place. Once it is officially approved, we will be forming a Special Expeditionary Force."

"Yes, ma'am."

"Which brings me to my business." Ebed Cya reached into her desk and produced a presentation box. It was covered with black fabric, and its lid bore the crest of the Sisterhood Navy, stamped in gold. Lilith swallowed hard, already deducing what it contained, and ardently hoping that she was wrong.

The woman pushed the box across the table. “I want you to have this”, the Admiral said. “And accept what’s inside of it. I’d rather not have to make that an order.”

Lilith opened it, and grimaced, deeply. Her suspicions had been correct. A set of epaulets and matching collar pins, all bearing the two stars of a Vice Admiral, lay inside.

“I know how you feel about promotion to Flag rank,” Ebed Cya said. “The service values everything that you have done with your battle group as a Commander, but current events are calling upon all of us to adapt and to respond to a very unique situation.”

In fact, Lilith had steadfastly refused several offers of promotion from Ebed Cya over the years. In her opinion, her place was on the front lines, not commanding a desk downside as a Flag Officer.

“I’m sorry that it has to be this way,” Ebed Cya explained, “but we need officers with solid battlefield experience to lead our expeditionary forces, and we need them immediately.”

“Ma’am? M-may I speak?” Lilith asked. The room seemed to be spinning around her like a ship without stabilizer controls.

“Do you really need to?” Ebed Cya countered. “I can save you the time and effort, Lilith. You were top of your class at the Academy, and your record since then has only built itself upon that excellence. I was your Strategy and Tactics teacher, so I remember the student that you were quite vividly. And don’t even try to tell me that you would be of more use to me at your present rank. You *have* been useful in that role, but I feel that your talents would be put to much better purpose as a Vice Admiral.”

“But, ma’am I’m not…”

Ebed Cya raised a silencing hand. “Yes, you *are* ready, Lilith. More than ready in fact, and when the Admiral of the Navy gave me this mission, I thought of you immediately, and I not only suggested your inclusion in the Expeditionary Force, but I also mentioned this promotion to her. I told Admiral t’Kayna that in my estimation, you were the perfect candidate. She reviewed your service record, and she agreed."

"Now I realize that it's quite a leap in responsibility, but if it's any comfort, you'll be working under an experienced commander, Admiral Kaysa da'Kayt. I presume that you are familiar with her?"

Lilith certainly was. Kaysa da'Kayt had been one of the principle strategists during the War of the Prophet. She was a native of Trilane, in the Marpesa Elant, where the women were rumored to possess precognitive powers granted to them by a symbiotic silicon-based life form. The Trilanians themselves had never admitted to, nor denied this claim, but Da'Kayt had demonstrated an uncanny knack for knowing exactly what the Prophet's forces had intended at every turn. This, combined with her superlative skills as a tactician, had played a significant role in helping the Sisterhood win the war. Had Lilith been asked for her opinion, she could not have picked a better officer to lead the Special Expeditionary Force.

Ebed Cya saw the recognition in Lilith's eyes, and went on, "I see that you do know her. Good. In addition to Da'Kayt's leadership, you'll also have two other Vice Admirals working with you who have ample Flag-level experience, and they will help you as you step into your new position. Think of it all as a form of 'on-the-job training." The woman chuckled at her wry humor. "In fact," she added, "I wanted you to meet everyone, tonight, at my quarters."

"Yes, ma'am," Lilith agreed, feeling completely overwhelmed.

And like the warrioress she was, Ebed Cya showed her absolutely no mercy, pressing her attack, and giving no room for Lilith to maneuver, nor evade. "As for your specific duties, you will be overseeing the operations of three battle groups from the Topaz Fleet, and their support vessels. You will be working with elements of equal strength from the Emerald and Onyx Fleets under the command of your fellow Vice Admirals, and with Da'Kayt in charge of the entire operation.'

"Believe me. I know how this feels. I was in your position myself once—and if anything, I think I was even more stubborn than you are. They virtually had to drag me in, kicking and screaming to accept my promotion. But-" she held up a finger, "there *are* a few bright points of light to all of this. For one, you will retain the *Athena*—as your flagship."

A wave of relief washed over Lilith. *I still have my ship!* Losing the

Athena would have been too much to bear.

The Admiral smiled, knowing that she had just scored an important hit. "Now although you'll spend most of your time in the field, you'll still be required to come back to Rixa for planning sessions now and again—which will also give you the opportunity to visit Zommerlaand more often. I'm sure that that by itself will compensate you for some of the burdens of command."

Lilith looked down at the carpet and smiled abashedly. She was not surprised that the Admiral knew all the details of her personal life, including her affair with Ingrit. This was a matter of protocol. Because of her rank and responsibilities, she had always been aware of the fact that the *Divis da Naval Intelle*, the Naval Intelligence Division, had kept tabs on her and relayed *everything* to her superiors. Even so, it still felt a little awkward to air such a private matter openly with anyone except her Ship's High Priestess. Despite her discomfiture though, more time with Ingrit *was* a very powerful incentive to be cooperative.

"Yes, ma'am," she finally said. "I suppose that would be another plus."

Her superior nodded. "I thought as much. Now, although she isn't aware of it just yet, your Second, Lt. Commander Bertasdaater is also being promoted. She'll find out tomorrow morning that her rank has been raised to Commander, and that she will be put in charge of the daily activities of your flagship. In the meantime, I suggest that you consider someone to take her place as the *Athena's* Second. Naturally, I will approve whoever you choose; you know your women much better than I."

The obvious choice was Mearinn d'Rann, and Lilith didn't hesitate to say so.

"Consider it done then," Ebed Cya replied. "I'll send the request through right away and she can be informed at the same time as Commander Bertasdaater. That leaves the Ship's Advocate as her Third unless she decides to step aside for someone else--or Bertasdaater has another person in mind for that position."

"Knowing them both, I'd say that N'Dira will stay on," Lilith offerred. "She's a busy woman, but she's always been willing to fill in, and they get along."

"Good," Ebed Cya nodded. "Then it's all set. Now, I have one final item to discuss with you. Pursuant to your new rank, you will be given an office to use when you are here on Rixa, and assigned an adjutant, who will accompany you on this mission."

"An adjutant, ma'am?" Lilith had never needed an assistant before this, and although she knew that Flag Officers *had* them, she had never imagined that she would have one forced upon her. Or that she would be successfully cornered into wearing two stars on her collar for that matter, she thought ruefully. But despite the actions of mortals, the Goddess always tended to see Her Will worked, one way or the other.

"Yes, Vice Admiral," Ebed Cya told her, clearly enjoying the sound of Lilith's new title, "an *adjutant*. In addition to guaranteeing your personal protection, her job will be to act as your administrative assistant, and as a liaison with all the officers under your command. Frankly, given the sheer number of ships involved, you'll *need* an extra body running your errands for you. Her presence, by the way, *is* non-negotiable."

Lilith thought that the idea was patently absurd, but she could only nod her assent, and hope that whoever was assigned to her wouldn't get underfoot when the real work had to be done. "Of course, ma'am."

At this, Ebed Cya stood and Lilith joined her. "Then I think we are done here. Congratulations, Vice Admiral. I'll expect to see that extra star on your uniform at dinner tonight."

"Yes, ma'am."

"Report to my quarters at 07:50 hours. You are dismissed."

Lilith saluted and walked out of Ebed Cya's office. A young, fresh-faced ensign was waiting for her outside. She gave her a crisp salute.

"Ma'am?"

"Yes, Ensign?"

"Ma'am, Ensign Jan bar Daala, reporting for duty, ma'am." From the term 'bar' before her matronymic, and her reddish hair, she identified herself as a native of Larra's Lament in the Artemi Elant. "I'm your new adjutant."

"You're my—adjutant," Lilith replied skeptically. "I see." In her estimation, Bar Daala looked far too young for the role, or even the right to wear a naval uniform for that matter. *Goddess,* Lilith thought. *She's a child.* She even had freckles!

Feeling very old, and very tired, she was sorely tempted to tell Bar Daala to go home to play with her dollies—but kept her tongue.

"Ma'am, permission to speak freely?"

"Yes, Ensign. Granted."

"Ma'am, I know that you are probably thinking that I'm too young to serve with you, but I assure you that I will prove to be more than adequate for this assignment," Bar Daala offered. "I've been on Admiral ebed Cya's staff for 2 years, under Vice Admiral Hana n'Terri."

Lilith had to concede at least one point to Bar Daala for self-confidence. "I am certain that you know your responsibilities, Ensign," she replied charitably. "Just try not to get in my way. And by the way, you don't need to ask my permission to speak from now on. Just talk."

"Ma'am, yes, ma'am," Bar Daala answered, giving her another salute.

"And get rid of the salute." Lilith warned. "While you're at it, just call me 'Admiral' or Lilith when we're in private. Zat klaar?"

"Ma'am, ye-yes, Admiral." The young woman's armed flinched as she began to give her another salute, but she stopped herself just in time.

"So—Ensign," Lilith asked. "I'm somewhat new to my rank, or having an adjutant for that matter. I have a vague idea of what you're supposed to do for me, but I'd like a little more clarity. What exactly *are* your duties?"

"Ma—Admiral, my job is to advise you on your daily schedule, provide you with protective services, and do whatever else it is that you need me to do."

Lilith glowered. Unfortunately, going somewhere very, very far away—and staying there—probably wasn't on the list of the young woman's tasks.

"I had hoped to show you to your new office first thing," the woman added.

Lilith's frown deepened. "Yes, my…new…*office*. Very well, Ensign. Lead the way."

Residence of Fleet Admiral Myrelli ebed Cya, Rixa Naval Base, Rixa, Belletrix System, Pantari Elant, United Sisterhood of Suns, 1043.04|13|07:50:29

What Ebed Cya had blithely referred to as her 'quarters' would have been considered a mansion on any world other than Rixa. Perched on the slopes of Mt. Hypatia, it had been constructed in the Corrissan neo-renaissance style and overlooked the woman's beloved Valley of the Veils, commanding a breathtaking view of the Tritonian Sea.

Bar Daala had driven her there, and Lilith felt a little uncomfortable when the ensign came around to open her door for her. She was perfectly capable of operating her own hovercar, much less managing a simple door, but instead of objecting to this silly formality, she quietly allowed the woman to do her job. She had decided that their relationship was going to be a matter of picking her battles carefully, and this issue simply wasn't worth the fight. It was enough that she had managed to get Bar Daala just to stop saluting her and calling her 'ma'am' all the time.

Another sailor, presumably one of Ebed Cya's own adjutants, met them at the huge entrance door and showed her inside, where another woman took her coat and cap. A third one materialized from nowhere, and escorted her to the Admiral's study.

By the Lady's great name, she thought in exasperation. *Is everything about flag rank nothing but mindless ritual?* Then she reminded herself about Ebed Cya's promise of Zommerlaand, and retaining the *Athena*, and mastered her distaste.

Fortunately, aside from a fourth woman waiting off to one side to serve them refreshments, the only others in the room were Ebed Cya, and three officers. She knew two of them immediately. The first was a personal acquaintance, Vice Admiral Eleen n'Leesa of the Sapphire Fleet.

N'Leesa was only a few years her senior, and they had worked closely together during the War of the Prophet on several operations involving their respective fleets. She had been a Commander back then, and Lilith wasn't surprised in the least that the Durandellan had achieved flag rank. She was a shrewd fighter and an able commander.

The second individual was her new boss, Kaysa da'Kayt, and she was immediately identifiable not only by her confident bearing, but also because of her exotic appearance. Trilanians made their home on a world where silicon-based life forms dominated the environment, including the infamous Szalites that glass crystals were comprised of, and other equally strange symbiotic creatures.

Many of them were microscopic and existed in the very air, making it impossible to avoid contact. Fortunately, most had proven positive in nature, extending the average lifespan of a Trilani woman to well over 250 Standard years, and endowing them with remarkable self-healing abilities.

The cost for this relationship came in radical changes to their bodies that were immediately apparent; their skin was a signature blue in color, with a sheen that came from the microorganisms that had bonded with their dermal cells, and their hair and eyes were a shocking metallic silver, caused by the same symbiotes.

To anyone from outside the Sisterhood, Da'Kayt would have been mistaken for an entirely alien humanoid, and not a member of the greater human family at all. The same could also be said of the Nemesians, and the Nyxians, and many others, Lilith mused. Not that it mattered to her in the least. What affected her instead, was the woman's formidable reputation, and she felt a little intimidated as they met each other's gaze.

The third person standing with Da'Kayt was a complete stranger. But the fact that she was from Lilith's own motherworld was as obvious as Da'Kayt's heritage. The stranger had the classic features of the Old Gaian continent of Asia, and grey eyes that hinted at an ancestry derived from its northernmost peoples.

Ebed Cya came forwards to welcome her. "Vice Admiral ben Jeni," she said. "Let me introduce you to your partners in our little venture. Vice Admiral n'Leesa, whom you already know, Admiral Kaysa da'Kayt, and Vice Admiral Mylee ben Biya, currently serving with the Emerald Fleet."

"It's a pleasure to meet you all," she said, bowing.

The trio smiled politely and returned the bow, but in Ben Biya's case, Lilith detected no warmth, nor anything else in her eyes. And her bow, while proper and precise, seemed more of a formality than any genuine expression of friendliness.

This came as no surprise to Lilith. Like many Sisterhood worlds, a conglomerate of peoples, with different cultures and genetic heritage, had settled Ara. In Ara's case, they had come from widely separated parts of Asia—China, Japan and Greater Eurasia, and they didn't always get along.

Those with strong Chin or Nipaani heritage, tended toward elitism, and were experts at concealing their emotions behind a mask of artificial politeness. Miya ben Biya, whose name translated to "Beautiful Flower, daughter of Precious Jade' in the Chin sub-dialect of Araian, certainly seemed to fit this stereotype. Lilith's own lineage, the Euraasi-Tajikki, were far more demonstrative and open with their feelings, and as far as she was concerned at least, more genuine as people. She almost decided right then not to like Ben Biya on this basis alone, but she fought this back. Despite any cultural differences that might have existed between them, they were still colleagues, and officers, with an important mission to perform and she wasn't about to let any personal prejudice impair that. Even if the woman *was* a Chin.

As for Da'Kayt, her expression was one of true welcome, and her bow to Lilith that of an equal, meeting a friend. "I am just as glad to make your acquaintance, Vice Admiral ben Jeni. I have heard much about you, and all of it has been positive. I think that we shall make a formidable quartet. A little like the Lady and the Three Fates perhaps?"

Lilith chuckled at her use of Selenite religious imagery. "Perhaps not quite *that* formidable Admiral, but we can always aspire."

Da'Kayt conceded this with a smile and a nod that made the crystal beads in her silver hair tinkle softly.

"May I offer any of you a drink to start our evening?" Ebed Cya inquired. "Wine? Or something stronger perhaps?"

Lilith accepted a glass of Tipandian wine, and her companions followed her example, exchanging small talk while their dinner was being prepared, and using it as an opportunity to get a better feeling for one another.

One item in the room helped the conversation along. It was an *Akskakt't*, a Hriss sword of honor, which the Admiral had on display in a stasis case. This was not just any sword though. It was *the* sword, having once belonged to the Prophet himself. The very same Hriss commanders, who had assassinated him and ended the war that he had begun, had presented it to Ebed Cya.

While they were examining the artifact, the announcement came that dinner was ready, and they went together into the formal dining room. And once they had eaten, Ebed Cya directed them out onto an adjacent patio that provided an excellent view of Rixa's three moons. The largest of these, Synope, was just rising over the sea, and the satellite lent its light to the scene, giving the gathering a warm, and intimate feel.

"There is one issue that we must discuss before our evening ends," Ebed Cya announced. She waved to a nearby adjutant and the woman left them alone on the patio.

"It has to do with our relations with the ETR. As you know, since the outset of our alliance, there have been some women who have expressed the concern that the situation might someday change for the worse."

Who wouldn't? Lilith wondered. History was replete with examples of societies that went to war simply because they were too dissimilar to one another. Even so, hearing Ebed Cya voice such concerns aloud was still a bit unsettling.

"Should such an unfortunate event come to pass, you will need to have a plan in place," Ebed Cya said. "I will expect each of you to expend some effort in this direction during your strategy sessions."

"Yes, ma'am", Admiral da'Kayt said, speaking for all of them.

Ebed Cya closed her eyes, and sent a command by psiever. The strains of a classical composition began to play out on speakers hidden in the garden around them. It was a harsh, martial piece that seemed to embody the very essence of conflict and war, and although it seemed familiar, Lilith couldn't immediately place it.

"If you don't recognize it, it is called '*Carmina Burana*'; a very ancient piece from old Gaia, and this particular example is being sung by our own Star Service Naval Chorale," Ebed Cya told them. "I think that you'll agree that it's rather fitting, given its significance." She let them listen a while longer, and then she silenced it.

"Should you ever hear it played in any official message, or receive the word 'Carmina' by itself, then it will mean that war has been declared against the ETR. In that event, you are to prosecute an immediate action against their forces.'

"The counter code for any confirmation inquiry is 'Burana'. With the Goddess's blessings, we will never have to use it, but we must be ready just in case. The ETR are our friends—for now."

Dinner adjourned on this somber note and Da'Kayt, Ben Biya and N'Leesa returned to their own quarters. Possibly as a means of apologizing for forcing the promotion upon her, Ebed Cya offered Lilith overnight accommodations, but after the distressing day she had had, she politely declined the invitation in favor of the familiar. She returned instead to her quarters aboard the *Athena*.

Once there, she shed her uniform, donned her favorite night-robe and settled into her old rocking chair. Skipper of course, wasted no time taking advantage of the situation and quickly ensconced himself in her lap. In the way of all felines, he was fast asleep only a few minutes later. Lilith was careful not to wake him; they had a simple arrangement for times like this. She was perfectly free to do anything she wanted, as long as she didn't move.

Staying where she was, she opened up her latest purchase. It was a rare book that she had bought from her favorite bookseller in the Rixa PX. Just holding it in her hands went a long way towards improving her mood.

The book was a first edition of the classic Martian work, *"Anna 225"*, and the perfect addition to her small library of real books. She handled it with care, gently turning its brittle pages, and finally stopping at one passage to read the words. Some of the archaic terms that they employed completely eluded her, and she had to call up an English-Standard translator program with her psiever. The translation program was one of her favorites, containing not only ancient English, but also many of the dialects of that long-dead language, including the one spoken on Mars at the time.

"What is the true word of God?" she read. *"Is it something that can only be received by a lone man on a mountain, told to him by a disembodied voice that no one else can hear? Or can it come to us by the hand of man, through one of his machines? If God is truly infinite, and all-*

powerful, then why shouldn't His word reach us through a mind that we have created ourselves? Are not our creations simply our children, and as we are made by Him, is their message any less legitimate than what we might hear with our own ears?"

These were the words of the books main protagonist, a follower of the Cubis sect speaking with her inquisitors, who were all members of the rival Sphera group. The story itself was set in a dark period in humanity's past when the developers of two rival operating systems created the first true artificial intelligences.

Possibly as an exercise, or even a prank (historians couldn't agree on which), the writers of the Cubis OS, led by the brilliant but eccentric programmer, Atokada Lynnxa, had given their new AI the monumental task of printing out random strings of letters, hoping to confirm the theory that once it had finished printing out pure gibberish, it would eventually produce all of the written works of mankind. This had been undertaken using networks of super-computers loaded with the Cubis AI. In the process, the theory had been proven correct; the works of Babylon, Greece, Ancient Alexandria, Shakespeare and many others, had rolled out of the printers right alongside previously unknown texts, exciting both scholars and programmers alike. When the AI reached the Christian Bible however, things had gone quite awry.

At first, the copy that Cubis created had been faithful to earlier versions. When the software reached *Revelations* though, something strange had occurred. Instead of merely repeating what had been written there for centuries, new passages had appeared that were later to become known as the *"Revelation of Mari"*—the fundamental text of the Marionite church.

Worse, the new version resisted any effort to erase it, and somehow managed to find its way out of the network and onto the Internet. From there, it had somehow located all existing copies of the previous Bible and replaced them with itself.

Despite vigorous efforts to eradicate what everyone assumed was some form of virus, it soon became impossible to print or present *any* edition that didn't exclude the old version of *Revelations*, and include the new one. From there, it hadn't been long before some people began to firmly believe that the *"Revelation of Mari"* was in fact the true word of their God, sent to them through the AI by His direct Will.

At the same time, the head of the development team for the Sphera OS, who went by the improbable name Demens Segmentatus Proni, had seen an opportunity to discredit his competitors, and set his own AI to create a counterwork. Once again, the Bible that the artificial mind created had seemed very like its predecessors, until it too reached *Revelations*, and then it had promptly come up with a new version. This edition, called *"The Revelation of Marcus"* not only challenged the legitimacy of *'Mari'*, but also resisted deletion or replacement by the Mari copies.

Two separate scriptures, and two religious sects named after the operating systems that had engendered them, came into being. Their presence, and the fanatical zeal of their adherents had eventually led to a religious war that had proven to be just as bloody as the historical struggles between the Catholics and Protestants.

The planet Mars had been the main battleground for this struggle, and Anna, an adherent of the Cubis sect and the *'Mari'* text, one of its millions of victims. She had been executed for heresy, but not before uttering her now famous challenge to her judges. It had only been later, when the MARS plague had done its damage, that the Marionites had emerged as the victors, and Anna herself, had been beatified as one of their saints.

Amazed at the human capacity for intolerance and self-deception, Lilith read on, enjoying the antiquated phrasing and the romantic texture that the authors' language lent to the material. *'Anna 225'* would make for fine reading at the next session of her informal book collectors club, she decided. While there weren't many members aboard the *Athena* who could afford real books, or had the passion for them, there were enough to make the club a viable entity. Saara sa'Vika was part of this group, and Lilith was certain that the Kalian would not only be eager to hear some of the passages from *'Anna 225'*, but would also be green with envy.

Finally, when her eyes started to tire, Lilith set the book aside and called up another cup of tea for herself. She had one last piece of business to get out of the way before turning in for the night. She needed to at least glance at her new adjutant's personnel file before dealing with the woman in the morning.

She didn't expect to read anything interesting, but it was a matter of protocol to learn about a new staff member's background. When the holo appeared, she scanned over the basic details, and then perused Bar Daala's background section, stifling a yawn.

For the most part, what she saw there, she had expected. Born on Larra's Lament, the woman had joined the Navy in 1020.03, had made good marks in her CAFAT and after Basic had attended Officer's Candidate School. Upon graduation, she had been promoted to Ensign and assigned to Rixa as a Command Support Specialist.

It was all rather boring, and routine. According to her record, Bar Daala was, in the colorful lexicon of the Sisterhood armed forces, a 'soft suit'; an officer who had never seen combat of any kind. This would change, Lilith assured herself. Battle Group Golden would see to that with a certainty, especially in the light of their new alliance with the ETR and the Hriss in the equation.

She read on, and then found something that she hadn't anticipated at all. Oddly enough, it had nothing to do with Bar Daala's military career. Instead, it concerned her early years.

Lilith read the notes, and then requested the news clips that were linked to the file. Then, and after watching them, she asked for everything else about the 'Homecomers' and what the media claimed was the Lamentine equivalent of the fabled 'Devil's Triangle' of Old Gaia, or the infamous 'Green Shift' of Tetra 5.

Bar Daala it turned out, was definitely *not* routine, she realized, sitting up a bit straighter. According to the news clips, she had been 16 when she had gone on her Tej. Like many girls, she had followed a route through the Crimson Vale, one of the wilder sections of the great woodlands that Larra's Lament was renowned for.

Then, after two weeks on the trail, Bar Daala had vanished without a trace. Once someone realized that she was missing, an extensive search had been launched. Although the authorities combed the forest, and even scanned it from space, they had failed to find even the faintest trace to confirm that she had ever even been there.

Only a few days after the search had been called off, and she had been declared dead, Jan bar Daala had walked out of the woods into the tiny settlement of Hara's Dell, naked and disoriented. She had had no memory of what had happened to her, and couldn't explain her absence, or her state.

When a doctor examined her, Bar Daala had been in perfect health, but inexplicably, she was missing all of her bio implants. Her psiever, her Inocular--every artificial bio-enhancement that the average woman of the Sisterhood depended upon for daily life--were simply gone.

According to the examiner, they hadn't been surgically removed in any way. Instead, it was as if they had never been there in the first place. No viable explanation for this had ever been determined.

Lilith's eyebrows rose at this fantastic claim, and the fact that disappearances exactly like this had been going on for decades, stretching back to the very first years of the planet's colonization. Although the numbers weren't large in comparison to the Lament's population, the phenomenon of the 'Homecomers' was so common that it had become part of the world's folklore, a paranormal curiosity that defied scientific investigation to such an extent that unlocking its cause was no longer pursued by any serious researcher.

Not quite certain how to take this, she moved on, and learned that like her predecessors, Bar Daala had received replacements; nanorobots had reimplanted her psiever, and she had been given a new inocular implant and Bio-chip. Because of her age, the process of implantation had taken much longer than it did for newborns, and had also required months of follow-up therapy.

Intrigued, but equally baffled, Lilith kept reading. But like the mysterious cause of the Homecomer's disappearances, anything of further interest eluded her. Once her implants had been restored, Bar Daala had been forgotten, and had gone on to become a largely unremarkable figure—-and could have even been considered bland by most standards.

An interesting young woman, she thought, *at one time at least.* She only hoped that Jan bar Daala would be less colorful in her new role as her assistant. Taking a final sip of her tea, Lilith closed the file and made her way to bed.

The next morning found her back on Rixa, seated in a large conference room alongside Ebed Cya, Da'Kayt, N'Leesa, Ben Biya and a group of lesser ranking officers. She felt as out of place among them as a Marionite sister at a Hriss blood-banquet.

She was wearing her new insignia, as Ebed Cya had directed, and it felt strange to be sitting where she was, watching as the *Athena's* command staff filed into the room and took their places across from her. *I should be sitting there,* she thought, *with them. Not here.*

But, 'here' was exactly where she was. And although Katrinn hid it well, Lilith could tell that she didn't seem too terribly comfortable herself. The Zommerlaandar been informed of her promotion to Commander just that morning and although she was wearing the appropriate insignia, Lilith knew from their years together that her former Second was just a bit overwhelmed by the change.

It didn't matter that Katrinn had run the *Athena's* operations on a daily basis for the last three years. Taking a shift as Second was a very different thing than *being* the Commander herself, even if the vessel was going to be Lilith's flagship and they were still going to be serving together on the same bridge. The ultimate responsibility of the *Athena* and Battle Group Golden now rested on Katrinn' s shoulders alone, and Lilith sympathized. Until yesterday, she'd been there herself.

Mearinn d'Rann was at Katrinn's side, and if anything, her demeanor was the complete opposite. She looked quite at home with her new rank as Second. Then again, nothing tended to faze the Tethyian, Lilith reflected, which is what had made her promotion such a natural decision. Mearinn would serve Kat well.

Lilith flashed Katrinn a reassuring smile and then looked around the conference room at the assembly. In addition to the officers from the *Demeter* and the *Artemis*, the Commanders and Captains from Battle Group Silver and Platinum were also in attendance, as were their equal numbers from the Emerald and Onyx Fleets.

Admiral ebed Cya began the briefing. "Ladies, as you are aware, the Sisterhood recently entered into a tentative alliance with the Esteral Terrana Rapabla to provide military aid. I received word early this morning that the treaty was officially approved by the Chairwoman, and only awaits a countersignature by the President of the ETR.'

"With this agreement effectively in place, your task will be to assist ETR forces in repelling the Hriss from their nation's space. Because of the socially sensitive nature of this mission, a strict information blackout will be in effect from start to finish. The official explanation will be that we are lending aid to a neighboring star nation, and no identification will be made concerning their race, or origins. You, your staff, and your crews will all be expected to abide by this, strictly and without deviation. No statements of any kind are to be issued to the media, except by and through this command."

"Operationally, the expeditionary force will fall under the direct control of officers with impeccable qualifications; Admiral Kaysa da'Kayt, Vice Admirals Eleen n'Leesa, Miya ben Biya, Lilith ben Jeni and General Barbra n'Hariet of the Sisterhood Marines. I know that you will all give these women your fullest support, and utmost effort.'

"Admiral da'Kayt will also be your liaison with your respective Fleet Commands, and with ETR Naval command, and she will be responsible for the overall coordination of the efforts of our joint forces.'

"Now, for specifics. Admiral, the briefing is yours."

Da'Kayt rose, and acknowledged Ebed Cya before addressing her audience.

"Thank you, Admiral. Our first task will be to rendezvous with the ETR command staff at a system they call Altamara." Her own adjutant, standing off in a corner with Jan bar Daala, called up a holo of the system, and then zoomed in on the tiny world itself.

"Until recently, Altamara has been a remote trading outpost and servicing facility for ETR merchant ships traveling at the edges of their space. In fact, it was the home base for the supply ships that visited the School before we quarantined that system. Now, in addition to its role as our meeting place, it will also become the central base of operations for our joint action against the Hriss.'

"The Special Expeditionary Force will be the equivalent of two fleets, and composed of some sixty-one ships; nine *Isis* Class Super Battle Cruisers, eighteen *Macha* Class Medium Cruisers, twenty five *Chandi* Class Light Cruisers, some 20 fighter wings, as well as support vessels, minelayers, hospital ships, troop transports and so on. The ETR will also be mustering a force of roughly the same size."

"For ground operations, we will be bringing an additional 87,000 Marines along with us, who in combination with our present contingents, will bring their fighting strength up to a total of ten divisions. So, in short, we can expect Altamara to become a very busy place, both upside and downside.'

"To help with the high ground congestion, a temporary space station is already in the process of being delivered, and it will be used jointly by our two forces."

Another holo popped into view, showing the elements of an MSS unit, the standard modular Navy space station, and then this was replaced by an image of the final product fully assembled in a configuration that favored communications and space traffic control.

"In addition, the 451st and 332nd Combat Engineer Battalions will begin construction of our planet-side facilities. That will begin once we arrive in-system.'

"As you might appreciate from the numbers that I have just mentioned, this will be the largest collection of Sisterhood forces for one operation since the War of the Prophet. I cannot stress how important it will be for everyone involved not only to do their job, but as the space station itself emphasizes, to work together as a team. Ladies, that is all. I thank you for your time."

With this, Ebed Cya rose, and officially dismissed everyone. While they gathered their things, Lilith went over to Katrinn and Mearinn.

"Katrinn", she said, "I'm sorry that I wasn't the one to tell you about your promotion." She had been forced to wake early, and had left the *Athena* for her office on Rixa to prepare for the briefing, missing Katrinn in the process. And she felt terrible about it; after so many years watching Katrinn's skills increase, and hoping that she would one day have a command of her own, she had wanted to be the one to deliver the good news. Instead, Katrinn had received the word by psiever, and then in a brief Com message from Ebed Cya. It was one of those missed moments in life, which once gone, could not be reclaimed. But duty had dictated otherwise, and they both understood this.

"Not a problem, Lily," Katrinn said smiling. "I forgive you. You had things to do and so did I. I'm still getting used to the idea, and it feels damned weird having everyone calling me Commander. I guess you feel the same way yourself."

"Oh I certainly do," Lilith replied with exaggerated sincerity, glancing momentarily at Bar Daala. "And Mearinn, my congratulations and apologies to you as well. Both of you deserve the recognition and I know that you'll do the *Athena* proud."

Nocturne Val, Nyx, Morpheus System, Thalestris Elant, United Sisterhood of Suns, 1043.04|14|09:36:75

Unlike the great sprawl of Thermadon, the capitol of Nyx was a creature of order and symmetry. Nocturne was divided into three distinct Districts that radiated outwards from its center in concentric circles. As their shuttle readied itself for its final approach to Rajani Interworld Spaceport, Sarah explained this unique layout to Maya.

"The Nyxians call themselves the Moonborn," she stated, "and to them, Nocturne is the City of the Moonborn. That center area, which is so brightly lit, is the El'a or the Light District. It is reserved for the spaceport and for the Sunborn, which is what the Moonborn call anyone who is not a native Nyxian."

"Even someone who is only half-Nyxian?" Maya asked.

Sarah responded to the girl's gibe with a patient smile. "To those who don't know me, yes, I suppose I would be considered one of the Sunborn as well. But for those who are acquainted with my mixed heritage, I have the distinction of being called Evenborn; a Daughter of the Evening, someone who is half day and half night by birth."

"In any event, the next District out is the Na'Ela, the Twilight District. You can tell because it is still fairly well lit, but the lighting is subdued compared to the El'a. The Twilight District is the home for businesses that cater to the Sunborn, and engage in off-planet commerce. It is also the location of the famous University of Nyx School of Medicine." She pointed out the window with a gloved finger to a large complex of buildings that took up nearly a quarter of the Twilight District's area. "That is the campus below us."

The shuttle began a slow banking turn, and she directed Maya's attention to the outermost ring. By far the largest, it was separated from the other Districts by a tall wall with egress gates that were situated at various points around it.

"That is the Ehl' Ela, the Night District," Sarah explained. "And the wall you are looking at, is called a light gate. It acts to block out the light from the other two sections and protects the Moonborn from the harmful effects of what we would consider normal illumination."

Maya looked and from what she was able to discern, not a single light of any kind burned in the Night District. *It looks deserted,* she thought to herself.

"The Ehl' Ela is *not* deserted," Sarah insisted. "In fact it is very populated, and well lit, but not by conventional means. The Moonborn use infrared, or Bioplasmic sources instead."

As often as the woman read her thoughts, Sarah's psychic eavesdropping still managed to annoy her. "I wish you'd stop doing that, Sarah!" the girl growled. "It would be nice to at least *pretend* that I have some privacy in my own skull—just for once."

"I will certainly try my best to remember not to rummage around in your mind," Sarah retorted. "Even if your thoughts *are* far too loud to be conveniently ignored."

Maya frowned, but Sarah responded with another enigmatic smile and continued. "We'll be going to the Night District to see a physician I know. She has worked for the Agency for many years, and she will be the one who will initiate your augmentation process."

"So tell me, just *how* will we be able to *see* our way there?" Maya inquired, still bristling from Sarah's mental invasion.

The woman reached into the folds of her traveling cloak and produced what looked like a pair of sunglasses. They were stylish and expensive looking, but otherwise seemed normal enough.

"By using these," she explained. "These are 'nighteyes' and they translate infrared and other light sources into visible bands that Sunborn eyes can perceive. Although as you aptly pointed out, only one of my mothers was Nyxian, I have better night vision than any Sunborn woman. But even I cannot see half as well in the dark as a truly Moonborn woman, and these make up for that deficit. This pair in particular also acts as conventional sunglasses and as a heads-up display for my psiever and other devices.'

"We'll get you a pair of your own when we land at the spaceport. After that, we'll have some free time to explore the city. I really would like to show you Nocturne, Maya; it's an amazing place, quite unlike any other city in the Sisterhood."

"Fine" Maya agreed, somewhat mollified by Sarah's polite invitation. The city *did* look intriguing at that.

Their shuttle touched down, and after they had been granted their exit from the port, Sarah guided her to a shop that specialized in nighteyes. There, the girl quickly learned that prices varied wildly; from cheap temporary pairs, to very expensive ones like Sarah's. When she started to consider one of the more low-priced sets, the woman pulled her away from them.

"This will not be our only visit," Sarah warned, "and you'll want to use your glasses on planets other than Nyx, so you'll need something that will last you and also possesses the right features. The cheaper sets cannot detect some bands of light at all and they rely on batteries rather than your own Bioplasmic energy, which could be a great handicap at the wrong time. And, as Madam n'Fawnelle would undoubtedly say, it is also better to buy a pair that compliments your features."

Maya grimaced, vividly recalling the fussy little dressmaker from their adventure aboard the *Aphrodite*, but she had to agree with the sentiment, and let Sarah guide her over to the sales counter. A real saleswoman helped her to select a pair that was identical to Sarah's—and horrendously expensive. But as she admired them in a mirror after making the purchase, she had to admit that they *did* look good on her, even if she was many credits the lighter for it.

After this, they left the store and made straight for a robotaxi stand.

Although there were many shops in the Light District that seemed interesting enough, Sarah would have none of it.

"Leave off" she said with a dismissive wave. "Except for 'nighteyes', there's nothing in the Light District or even the Twilight District worth looking at. It's all just trash for the tourists. Let's go to the Ehl' Ela and get a taste of the *real* Nocturne."

Maya acquiesced and got into the robocab that Sarah had hailed with her psiever. The vehicle whisked them out of the port area, and through the Twilight District, where it stopped at the foot of the massive Light Wall. There, they got out and walked through the gate into the Ehl' Ela.

It wasn't until she remembered to don her nighteyes that she saw what Sarah had meant about 'unconventional' illumination. With her nighteyes on, she discovered that the Ehl' Ela was just as well lit as the other two Districts, but in bands of light that her Sunborn eyes were incapable of detecting. Where there had been nothing but darkness and shadows, store signs, holo-ads and traffic signals abruptly sprang to life before her. It was as visually 'busy' as any normal street anywhere else in the Far Arm.

And just as her companion had asserted, it was also not uninhabited by any means. While many worlds operated around the clock, 00:01:75 was generally a low point in activity. For Nocturne and its unique inhabitants however, this was the middle of their 'day' and there were many women going about their business all around them. With the exception of themselves, these crowds were almost exclusively Nyxian.

The Moonborn walked along in groups, without the protective Qada's that she was used to seeing them in. Instead, they were dressed in loose flowing shifts or robes, which were embroidered with complex, spidery patterns. Although a few of them wore garments that were silver, or white, the prevailing shade tended to be black. When the girl commented on this monochromatic scheme, Sarah corrected her.

"Its not just 'black' Maya" she said. "Being Sunborn, you can't see it, but there are actually many variations on that color that the Nyxians *can* see and appreciate. I can't discern all of them myself, but I know from my Nyxian mother that there are almost fifty different 'blacks' that are considered by the Moonborn to be as distinctive as red or blue would be for you or I.

And, also, before we proceed any further, I must ask that you lower your voice."

Maya gave her a puzzled expression. She didn't think that she had been talking very loudly at all. Then she realized that everyone around them was speaking in whispers. "Why are they whispering?" she asked quietly.

Sarah replied in an equally hushed tone. "It is part custom, and part physiology. As you know, the Moonborn can see and feel light, and the same holds true for sound waves. For this reason, it is considered extremely rude to speak loudly, or to make a great deal of noise of any kind—except in an emergency. It is also considered to be a violation of another's privacy by forcing them to listen to—and feel—your sounds. On another world, whispering might seem conspiratorial and unfriendly, but here, it is *quite* the opposite."

Maya nodded as a trio of women walked by, moving so silently that she had to look down at the pavement to confirm that their feet were actually touching it. She realized that this was partly due to the soft slippers they wore, but also from the very way that they walked. They seemed more like ghosts than creatures of the flesh.

Once again, Sarah trespassed in her mind. "Yes, Maya, you have it a'right. They have a special skill at passing silently through the world. A Moonborn girl is taught to move that way from her earliest days.'

"Not only is this a part of polite interaction, but it is also one of the reasons why Nyxians make some of the best spies and assassins; they are keenly aware of the impact that their movements make on the environment to a degree that only the Nemesians can match. You should study the Moonborn's way of movement while we are visiting here, and try to emulate them."

Moving on, Maya attempted to follow Sarah's suggestion, but in the end all she managed to do was to come away from the exercise feeling loud and clumsy. For her part, Sarah pretended not to notice her failure, or her frustration. Instead, she stopped and directed the girl's attention to a pole that was mounted in the middle of the sidewalk ahead of them.

It was slightly higher than an average woman and engraved with strange symbols carved at eye-level that were similar to the embroidery on the Nyxian robes. Maya watched as the Moonborn walked up to it, touched the symbols, and then headed off in a new direction. This strange ritual was performed with an almost dance-like precision, and as Sarah led her up to the pole, she finally explained what was taking place.

"This is a 'moon-pole'", she told her. "They are placed at random points all around the Night District, and their location changes every day. The symbols that you see are the Nyxian script, which are partly visual and partly tactile in the manner of the ancient Braille alphabet.'

"Each face of the pole has a symbol that stands for a different direction, and by custom, a passerby must touch the symbol on the pole that is nearest them, and then go where it dictates.'

"This is an expression of a core Nyxian philosophy; although we might have a specific plan in mind for our life, there are times when other forces intervene, and we must adapt. It is a lesson that our entire race learned from the Plague, and the Moonborn have never forgotten this—nor should we. Don't you agree?"

"Um, yes, sure," Maya replied as Sarah touched one of the symbols, and then followed her as she took a sharp left onto a new street. Nocturne was proving to be just as unique as Sarah had promised.

She was so preoccupied with observing everything going on around her that she didn't even realize that she had strayed off the low sidewalk and onto the street. Sarah quickly pulled her back from the path of an oncoming hovercar. As it passed, a flash of soft white light issued from its headlights.

"I should have warned you about that," Sarah apologized. "That is one profound disadvantage that the Sunborn have here. The Moonborn do not use audible warning horns on their vehicles."

"Because the Moonborn can feel the lights instead?" Maya surmised.

"Yes. Please, try to be more aware," her companion admonished. "The doctors here *are* excellent, but I do not want to put their talents to any great test."

Then Sarah's expression brightened. "Well! It seems that Fate has directed us fortuitously indeed! Just up ahead is the Shadow Garden. I had hoped that I would get the chance to share the shadow paintings with you before we left the city. They are a truly Nyxian art form, and something that you won't experience anywhere else. Oh, and even better! The moons are rising."

The woman offered her hand to Maya, and when she took it, pulled her along down the sidewalk. "Come, we must hurry and find a seat for ourselves before they fill up!"

The Shadow Garden proved to be a large plaza, and when they reached it, Maya didn't spot anything that resembled any kind of art that she could identify. Instead of holos or lightweaves, or even archaic canvases in frames, all she saw were what looked like bits of random junk; pieces of oddly shaped metal, twisted strands of wire and irregular sheets of screening, with an occasional piece of colored glass placed here and there with no obvious logic or pattern to any of it.

These haphazard collections of parts were mounted on sets of metal frameworks, which were spaced at intervals from one another. And at various places, there were plain white walls of varying heights. They too seemed to have no discernable purpose.

"*These* are the paintings?" she asked, quite unimpressed.

"No," Sarah told her. "These are the things that help *create* the paintings." She sat down on the nearest bench, and patted the space beside her. "Sit with me and watch."

Maya walked over, and as she took her seat, she saw that it had been situated so that it faced one of the frameworks and the plain wall beyond it. This puzzled her, but when she saw that Sarah appeared to be meditating, she didn't inquire, and kept silent.

The minutes went by, and the light from the three moons increased, bathing the square with their silver light. It washed over the strange bits and pieces in their frameworks, and the shadows created by them began to grow and stretch across the pavement.

The moons rose even higher, and these separate zones of darkness began to come together against the wall. What had begun as haphazard shadows, projected by a jumble of parts, assumed a coherent form, and created a vivid picture of a huge coiling creature that resembled a Durandellan dragon. Hard, distinct zones were created by the pieces nearest the wall, and these worked in concert with the softer edged shadows cast by the items that were further away. All of it worked together to create an image that was endowed with both defined edges and subtle shadings. And the seemingly random pieces of colored glass that Maya had dismissed, magically became the creature's glowing eyes and the jewels encrusting its scales. The end result reminded her of ancient black and white photographs that she had seen in history holos, but with splashes of color here and there to lend the image vibrancy and drama.

But the shadow painting was not yet complete by any means. The moons continued their ascent, and the framework reacted to the shifting light, slowly rearranging itself, so that the image on the wall changed. The dragon grew wings and elongated until it had transformed into a bird of some kind, and then that changed into a fish.

"Did you see the dragon?" Sarah asked. "Or the bird, or the fish?"

"Yes," Maya said in amazement, "I did!" Despite her earlier opinion, she had to admit that she was impressed.

"This is what I meant by shadow-paintings. The Moonborn use shadows and the subtle differences between them to create their artwork. It is something that the first settlers brought with them from Old Terra, and although it was not well known on the Motherworld, and quite experimental there, it became a major form of expression here.

"In addition to her other skills, my teacher, Lady Ananzi is also regarded as one of the great shadow painters, and if we are fortunate, we will be able to see her create one of her masterpieces when we go to visit.'

"She once said to me that shadow painting is more than an art form. It also teaches us a valuable life lesson. As she put it, *'the Sunborn's discards are the Moonborn's art.'* By this, I believe that she meant that we should not overlook something because it seems worthless. It may simply have a value that we have not yet discovered."

Maya nodded pensively. *I guess in a way, most women would see me as nothing worthwhile either,* she thought. *And they're wrong.*

Sarah smiled, but gave no indication that she had violated Maya's mental privacy. "Let us be off," she said instead. "We have our appointment to keep with the doctor."

Dr. Kara elle Taala's practice was only a few blocks away from the

Shadow Garden, in a small complex of medical offices, and they were nearing it when Maya pulled up sharply.

Sarah looked around for the cause and quickly found it. Down the street from them was a Sisterhood Corrections Service work party, being supervised by a single guard. On inner worlds like Thermadon, this would have been a unique sight, but on the more remote 'fringe worlds', like Nyx—the cosmopolitan influence of Nocturne notwithstanding—it was part of the daily scenery of life.

A dozen or so prisoners were hard at work, cleaning the street of what little litter it had. Some of the women were dressed in the simple orange jumpsuits of full-trust inmates, but others were confined in *Cell Suits*.

They resembled EVA space gear in almost every respect, but were bright orange instead of the standard fluorescent green, and they bore the prisoner's number and the logo of the *Sorele Relaga Corectif.* Their purpose was also quite different; they were not intended to protect the wearer, but the general public, and other prisoners, from the women who wore them. They accomplished this by exerting absolute control over the suit's occupant.

If a prisoner did not obey an order, a psiever command to the suit could make it walk the unwilling woman to wherever she had been ordered to go. Given cause, a guard could also completely immobilize the suit, even to the point of cutting off all sensory input.

Worse, all food and elimination needs had to be taken care of through the Cell Suit, giving the Corrections Officers absolute power over even these basic requirements. And in rare cases where an execution was mandated by the court, all it took was a simple command to cease all life support, and the prisoners' existence could be terminated in complete privacy.

The Cell Suit was exactly what its name implied; a prison cell that the offender wore and took with them wherever they went. For that reason, Corrections Colonies had none of the fencing or towers that were the trademarks of more ancient penal institutions. They didn't need them.

"Let's take another street," Maya suggested anxiously. Sarah took note of her grim expression, and knew without having to ask, that the girl was reliving her own experience living in a Cell Suit. According to the Agency,

Maya n'Kaaryn had served one year in the SRC Colony on Alecto for felony theft, and two months of her sentence had been spent in a Cell Suit for fighting with other inmates. She had even undergone the Cell Suit's version of solitary confinement, with only psiever induced behavior modification modules and muscle stimulation to keep her company in the darkness.

"Of course," Sarah replied, taking her by the arm and gently guiding her away. This incident also explained something to her about Maya. When the girl had gone through the first parts of the required training to become a member of the *JUDI's* crew, she had refused to put on an EVA suit, and with such adamance that Bel Lissa had finally been forced to sign off on the module, and move on.

Small wonder, Sarah thought to herself. She wasn't so sure that she wouldn't have reacted in exactly the same way, or even developed chronic claustrophobia. For all its wisdom and concern over the welfare of its citizens, the Sisterhood could be equally as harsh with those who dared to cross it.

They reached the doctor's offices without encountering any other SRC work parties or anything equally as disturbing. It was 00:41:67, an hour past midnight, and the lunch hour. Naturally, the office was open and Sarah showed Maya inside. She had already made an appointment for them in advance, and after the girl had furnished the receptionist with her basic information (which was more or less true, with the exception of her actual identity), they were escorted into an examination room.

Shortly, the doctor joined them. Maya had a strong dislike of physicians and hospitals, having learned to avoid them as a petty criminal, but Dr. elle Taala forced her to revaluate her opinion of 'paints' as they were called on the street, from the very moment that she entered the room.

The Nyxian was a short, middle-aged woman, and she was dressed unpretentiously in utilitarian black scrubs. Her silver-white hair was tied back in a no-nonsense bun, and there was an intelligent gleam in her pale blue eyes, coupled with a wry smile and a straightforward manner.

"Nights blessings" she said, sitting down on a stool near Maya. "So, the Agency wants another operative, do they? Well, that's certainly not a problem, especially since they pay so well.'

"Sarah here has some of the finest components we had when she came to see me, but you'll have the benefit of some of the more recent advances, young lady. The science of Bioaugmentation has come a long ways since I did my work on Sarah. Has she told you what we will be doing exactly?"

"No, doctor," Maya answered. "Not exactly." In fact, aside from a demonstration of her skills and a few chance remarks, Sarah hadn't said very much about the process at all. And now that the mysterious treatment was actually about to begin, Maya was becoming a little apprehensive.

Elle Taala picked up on this immediately, and gently patted the girl's hand. "It's nothing to be afraid of, young lady. In fact, for most of the process, you won't even know that it's going on. No messy surgeries like they used to do hundreds of years ago, or even long rehabilitation periods."

The physician called up a holodisplay. It depicted what looked like a cross between an insect and some kind of flying machine. "The entire procedure is done with nanobots, like our little friend here. We will put them in your bloodstream today, and then they will go about making the changes, following preset programs. It's really a simple outpatient procedure, and once we set it in motion, it takes care of itself. And at the end of it all, when their work is done, the little nanobots will be excreted by your bodies own natural processes."

Maya considered the strange looking machine as the doctor continued. "What our little friends do is precisely what the name 'augmentation' suggests; they enhance your body's abilities. For example, they will install a network of sub microprocessors in your motor centers, and emplace neural amplifiers on specific muscle groups and certain nerve centers.'

"They will also strengthen your joints with bio-friendly metal sheathing, and lay in a web of supportive material to help reinforce your ligaments and tendons. There's even more than that, but I just wanted to give you a basic idea of the kind of work they'll be involved in, which is essentially rebuilding and enhancing—you.'

"The overall process takes several months. You won't have to do anything during that time except take the supplements that I'll give you, and do the exercises that Sarah will lead you through."

"Exercises?" Maya asked.

"Why yes," Elle Taala replied with a wide smile. "As your new capabilities 'come online' as it were, you will have to relearn how to do many simple things, like taking someone's hand without crushing it, or keeping yourself from moving so fast that you injure yourself. The augmentation will heighten your physical abilities by a factor of ten, and trust me, that takes some getting used to. So, Sarah, who has already mastered her added capabilities, will be your guide until you can manage things on your own.'

"Now I realize that all of this sounds rather strange and exotic, but the end result will be a radical improvement on what your body can do and how it will react, which I imagine in your line of work will be a definite gain."

Maya smiled at this, wondering exactly what the doctor believed her 'line of work' was—and then she found herself asking the same question. There was a great deal about Sarah, and the woman's overall motives concerning her future, that was still an unknown.

"I will warn you that there are a few side effects you might have to deal with," the doctor cautioned, "Mainly these will involve episodes of minor discomfort, but they are generally transient in nature."

"Discomfort?"

"Yes. But I can give you something to take if it becomes a problem. Now, do you have any questions for me before we begin?'

Maya was too much a stranger to all of this to venture any inquiries, and merely shook her head. She just hoped that the 'discomfort' Elle Taala was describing wasn't going to be too severe, or embarrassing.

"So, young lady, shall we get to work?" the doctor asked. The woman called up a holo-terminal and punched a quick sequence into its virtual keyboard. A graphic of a woman's head appeared. "Yes, that's you on the screen" she informed her. "I'll be directing the work we'll be doing today from this terminal.'

"Now I'll need to administer a sedative to you so that we can make some alterations to your psiever. These require that you be unconscious, but don't worry. All it will be for you is a short nap and when you wake up, we'll be all done." Elle Taala reached over to the nearest cabinet and brought out a bottle filled with a reddish liquid. She poured this into a cup and handed it to the girl. "Please drink this."

"What is it?" Maya asked.

"The nanobots, suspended in a solution of fruit juice. Once you've consumed it and they've had a chance to enter your bloodstream, we can get going."

Maya considered the cup, and then downed its contents in a single gulp. It tasted just like any conventional glass of juice, and she failed to detect anything that might have been the little 'bots swimming their way down her throat.

A few minutes passed before Elle Taala glanced at the holodisplay and nodded to herself in satisfaction. "Well, our little friends have made themselves right at home, Maya. Time for us to work on your psiever." She produced a small applicator bottle. "Please give me your inocular."

Maya obeyed, and Doctor Elle Taala uncapped the bottle and swabbed the site with the applicator. Then she gestured to the exam table Maya was sitting on. "Please lie back and count from ten to one for me."

The girl lay down and started the count. "Ten, nine, eight…Doctor I don't think it's—"

She lapsed into unconsciousness before she could even finish the sentence.

"They all do that you know," Elle Taala laughed. "I don't think anyone has ever gotten to 'five' in my entire 20 years of practice."

The woman turned on her stool and scrutinized the readout on her holo screen, punching in a coded sequence. "Now to retune her psiever. I'm removing the inhibitor and instructing it to send and receive at a higher bandwidth."

Sarah leaned in to watch the procedure. Although she'd had it done herself, like Maya, she'd been unconscious during the actual process.

"I thought that you'd find this interesting," Elle Taala remarked. "I'm also doing something that we normally do for new mothers, and code-locking it so that you can control when it operates, and at what level. That should give you the freedom to determine when the girl can, and cannot, use its heightened features."

"Thank you doctor. That should prove quite useful," Sarah replied.

"What is the code?"

"A mental command, which I'll need from you now. Please think of a distinctive term that you'll be able to recall easily, and then send it to her with your psiever."

Sarah considered this, and then she chose a word that she knew from the Arai dialect; *'kotama'*. It meant 'magic word,' and she thought it a fitting choice. Once she had formed it clearly in her mind, she 'sent' it to Maya.

The doctor smiled. "There. Good. Her psiever is now keyed to respond to that term. When you need to inhibit her psiever, just think that command word to her, and it will automatically resume a standard performance mode. Send it a second time and it will reset back to the higher level. Now, time for the next step. Did you bring the device?"

Sarah produced a small case from her cloak. The physician took it and opened it. The object within seemed like nothing more than a polished egg-shaped stone, no larger than the end of a woman's thumb. It was dark red in color, with pale green marbling. It was not a stone however.

"Marvelous," Elle Taala said looking at it with a gaze akin to religious reverence. "I do wish that you could tell me what it is, and how it works."

"I could—"Sarah began.

"But then you'd have to kill me—yes, I know the rest, and I also know that it's not just a cliché', not with you at least," the woman replied. "Just the same, I hope that you'll use your not-so-inconsiderable influence someday to change the Agency's policy about this little device."

When Sarah didn't answer, the doctor sighed wistfully. "I had to at least ask. Help me turn her over, will you?" The two of them rolled Maya over, and Elle Taala brushed the girl's hair away from the base of her skull. Then she produced a pair of forceps from the cabinet and carefully removed the object from its case.

"Mustn't touch it now," she said. "I certainly don't need this thing inside of me, as fascinating as that would be." She brushed a little more of Maya's hair aside, and then touched the object to the bare skin. As soon as it made contact, it seemed to melt into the girl's flesh, and in seconds it had disappeared.

"Amazing," Elle Taala declared. "Just its ability to pass through like that would revise and overturn so much of what we know. What a shame it's classified."

"Yes," Sarah agreed. "But it *is* classified."

The doctor frowned, and turned her attention back to the display. The image of Maya's psiever had changed. Instead of the usual sharp outline of the psievers metallic crescent, there was an odd haziness that surrounded it, blurring its edges. To any doctor who didn't know what it was, it appeared to be nothing more than an artifact produced by the medscanner, but the alien device was there, and it had fully integrated itself.

"Well," the doctor observed. "Our wonderful whatever-it-is is in place, and has incorporated with her psiever. You know, even though I have seen this happen before, it's still incredible! It took only seconds for the thing to totally bond with it—and how it knew to do that—-." Elle Taala shook her head in wonder.

"Naturally, you'll make certain to delete the scanner's record of this visit," Sarah interjected.

Elle Taala sighed in resignation. "Naturally."

"And for what it is worth, I am sorry, Doctor."

The physician gave the odd haze one last, longing glance, and then sent the command to delete the recording. "You know," she said. "I once heard it said that any true science was indistinguishable from magic, and in the case of this little thing, I have to admit that whoever coined that phrase was correct. It's not a machine like anything we know. It's more like an organic crystalline growth. It would be a privilege to study it one day."

"Doctor," Sarah replied patiently, "I assure you, that I will mention your interest to my employers, *and* your willingness to cooperate with them in the meantime."

The physician would never get the opportunity that she so desperately desired, however. Sarah wasn't about to mention the woman's fascination with the device to her superiors; her talents were simply too valuable. Instead, Dr. elle Taala would remain ignorant, and alive. And everyone else would continue to believe that the Drow'voi had never left any technology behind.

Only the insectoid Seevaans, who had given the Agency the device, and those humans with high enough clearance, would know otherwise. What the device was, how it worked, and what it was originally intended for was anyone's guess, but it allowed the Seevaans to transmute matter with their thoughts, and gave humans the ability to alter time itself. What Maya now had inside her, interwoven with her psiever, was the very thing that granted Sarah and Skylaar the ability to move faster than the human eye could catch, or respond to.

"Now, it will still be a few minutes before the nanobots complete their alterations. In the meantime, Sarah, I'd like to examine your photo protective skin coating. It's been at least a year since you had the bonding checked, hasn't it? You know it doesn't pay to take chances with skin cancer."

"Yes," Sarah admitted, "a year at least." But Doctor Elle Taala already knew this. She had been the one to administer it to Sarah in the first place, as a little girl.

"Please disrobe." Elle Taala asked, taking up a hand scanner from her cabinet. When Sarah had complied, she ran the device over various spots on her skin, highlighting the coating. Had Maya been conscious, she would have realized that this was the source of the strange rainbow-hued sheen that the woman's skin gave off when the light hit it just right.

The translucent coating was bonded to the cells of her epidermis, and it acted as a barrier against the harmful effects of ultraviolet radiation. Although Sarah was only half Nyxian, without this protective layer, she would have developed melanomas almost as easily as one who was fully Moonborn. And despite the fact that the cure for cancer had been discovered and perfected in the early years of the Sisterhood, it was still not a condition to actively court, nor ignore.

Fortunately, the special coating was very tough, and the bruises that Maya would have seen underneath it, hadn't affected its integrity. They were also something that Sarah never intended for the girl *to* see. Only she and her doctor knew about them, and she wanted things to stay that way. The marks weren't from combat. Instead, they were—personal—and thinking about them, she felt a sudden, deep surge of hatred towards the woman who had put them there.

"Yes," Elle Taala remarked, "Naturally, I won't ask you where and how you got these, but overall your skin seems quite healthy. Just the same", she added in warning, "you'll need to be more conscientious about getting regular check-ups, especially since it's obvious that you're *still* not being too gentle with yourself.'

"Now I realize that the life of an intergalactic super-secret agent tends to fill your calendar with all sorts of universe-saving adventures, but if you neglect your health, you won't be in much shape to battle the forces of evil for very long. Are we perfectly clear on that score, *young lady*?"

"Yes, doctor," Sarah replied sheepishly. Elle Taala was one of the few women in the galaxy that could speak to her like she was a child, and always had.

The physician returned her attention to the display, and Maya. "Ah! All done!" she said. "These new 'bots work so much faster than the older models ever did. Time to rouse our little princess from her magical sleep." The woman administered a stimulant, and when it took effect, she helped Maya sit up with Sarah's assistance.

"Am I…is it…over?"

"Yes," Elle Taala said. "The 'bots are off having a well-deserved lunch. While they're at it, I need you to drink something for me." She handed the girl another cup of what looked like fruit juice. Maya took it from her, and as before, downed it in one gulp. She instantly regretted it.

"Ugh! This tastes awful" Maya exclaimed, "What *is* this stuff?"

"The building material that our little—no, *your* little friends—will need to do their work. It's a mixture of bio-friendly metals and other materials, and you'll need to drink it twice a day so that they can build the components I described to you."

"Oh goddess, this is *shessy,*" Maya grimaced. "Really, must I?"

"Yes, you *really* must," Elle Taala insisted. "You will also want to make sure to eat regularly. The nanobots derive their battery power from your Bioplasmic energy, and they also utilize certain essential minerals in your bloodstream, such as copper. You'll need to replenish yourself so that they can be replenished. So, eat, eat, eat, and don't worry about your figure.

If anything, you'll probably have trouble keeping weight on."

"Is there anything you can do about the taste?" the girl asked, wondering why it was that doctors tended to administer medicines that tasted worse than the maladies they supposedly cured.

"No, young lady, there isn't. Now, up with you! Have Sarah take you to lunch right away, and make sure to drink your supplement twice a day."

Elle Taala reached back into her cabinet and produced three large bottles of the supplement. "That will be one cup-full per dose, by the way. I will also give you something for any muscle spasms you might experience."

"Muscle spasms?" Maya asked unhappily.

"Yes," the doctor replied. "That was the discomfort I was telling you about. While your little friends are at work on your muscles and ligaments, you may have periods where the areas they are altering go into spasm. It shouldn't be too bad, but the medication I'll prescribe for you will help.'

"I'll let Sarah explain the details, but you also have something else going on inside of you that I should tell you about. It's called a symbiote, and I put it in your head." The doctor tapped her own skull to emphasize this. "It's very special and Sarah will make sure that you learn how to use it, and get you acclimatized to what it does."

"What does it do?"

The physician looked to Sarah for the explanation. "It slows down time," her companion finally said.

Maya mouthed a silent "O" of understanding. "So, *that's* how you do your little tricks," she declared.

"*Some* of them," Sarah responded. "Now, please get dressed and we will get lunch for the both of us. I may not have an army of nanobots swimming around in me, but I could certainly use a good meal."

They followed the doctor's advice, and ate their 'lunch' together while the moons were still high in the sky. After that, they found lodgings for themselves. According to Sarah, Maya needed a few days, and even as much as a week for the symbiote to fully acclimatize itself, and she offered to help pass this time by taking her around the city for some more sightseeing. Maya had no reason to disagree, and after a 'good days sleep', they went into the Ehl' Ela for some light shopping.

One of their first stops was a famous local jewelry store, *Onyxxa*, which quite naturally specialized in the Nyxian style. This tended towards the heavy use of platinum, woven in complex, spidery designs that Sarah told her were actually stylized versions of the Nyxian script itself. Like the embroidery Maya had seen on the robes the Nyxians wore when they were not in their Qada's, the items on display were both jewelry and a form of poetry in metal, offset and accented by precious gems. Moonstone and pearl seemed to be the most popular, although there were an equal number that integrated rare black diamonds from Sita and ebony pearls from Tethys into their designs.

One piece in particular drew Maya to it; a graceful necklace that came around to meet together in the center of the wearer's chest where a large black diamond was suspended, ringed by a group of smaller moonstones to compliment its color. According to the tiny holodisplay that hovered nearby, the necklace had even been given a name by its creator; *"The Midnight Song"*, which she guessed had had its genesis in some piece of Nyxian verse of the same title.

While it certainly wasn't the kind of thing that she could ever see herself wearing, it was easy to visualize it on Felecia, and she actually went as far as asking the saleswoman its price. This proved to be truly astronomical, and she politely retreated from the case, looking instead at smaller items that didn't require the credit account of a Corporate President to purchase. Even so, from time to time, her eyes kept wandering back to the necklace. Sarah, who had been watching her covertly, took careful note of this.

Two days passed, and found them at dinner after a particularly enjoyable evening spent touring several of the local art museums. By this time, Maya had become quite familiar with Nyxian cuisine, and she ordered her favorite dishes without having to ask Sarah for suggestions. Nyxian food, she had learned, wasn't just tasty, it was also a pleasure to look at; its chefs worked hard to ensure that it had both the right flavors, and an appealing appearance. It turned out that local flora, from which many of its ingredients were derived, possessed luminous qualities, and these were combined together to create colorful displays.

Maya's personal favorite was *Na'wasi* steaks, seasoned with spices, and dressed with a kelberry sauce that not only gave it a wonderful flavor, but also a lovely magenta glow. A small salad accompanied the main course, laced with more of the kelberries, and these gave off a soft azure light, complimenting the dressing's color and making the salad seem as if it was decorated with luminous gems.

"Are you enjoying your meal, Maya?" Sarah asked, sipping at a glass of water.

"Yes, it's very good."

"I think this might be a good time to try out your symbiote. I am attuning your psiever to a higher frequency and engaging it," she said. She finished her water, put the glass down, and closed her eyes.

Maya noticed the difference immediately. "What—?!!" It felt as if another presence had suddenly joined her consciousness. But it wasn't Sarah. She knew *her* mental signature only too well. It was something else entirely.

"Sarah," she said. "There's something inside me—it's with me—but-"

"But also *not there* at the same time?" Sarah replied, arching an eyebrow.

Maya nodded both in agreement, and wonder.

"I know the sensation intimately. It is more like a 'watcher', an observer inside you, but one who is also somehow—absent?"

"Yes!" Maya said, unconsciously rubbing the site at the back of her neck where the symbiote had been inserted. "That's it exactly! Oh, this feels so *fekking* weird!"

"That's the symbiote. I want you to reach out to it, Maya, and join with it."

"But how do I do that?"

"Relax and focus your entire mind on it. Feel it, and reach out to it. Welcome it into you."

Maya closed her eyes and relaxed, trying to follow Sarah's instructions. As she did so, the feeling of the strange presence increased. She was definitely not alone, but wherever 'it' was, there was a blind spot that her mind couldn't fully categorize.

"It's part of me," she said aloud, "but it's also like it—like it opens up onto something else—*somewhere* else I can't feel, like it's to a place outside—outside of time? I-can't explain it—"

"Don't try, Maya," Sarah told her. "We humans lack the language to accurately describe what you are experiencing, even if we can still perceive it. Now, let yourself go completely. Embrace it."

Maya tried again, surrendering as fully as she was able. Then, quite without warning, she realized that the symbiote's presence and hers had become fused together in some way. She and it were now one and the same being. A sudden shift in her equilibrium accompanied this, as if the chair that she was sitting in was starting to tip over, and her eyes fluttered open in alarm.

A transformed universe greeted her eyes. It was certainly still there, but all the color seemed to have drained away, and everything had a grainy quality to it that reminded her of a badly modulated holo.

There was also a low droning hum in her ears, and as she looked around her in wonder, she saw that all of the women around them had stopped moving, frozen in mid-motion. It took an instant more for her to grasp that they *were* moving, but with incredible slowness, and that the sound she was hearing was actually their conversations playing out at a dramatically reduced rate. The only thing in this strange new reality that appeared to be completely unaltered was Sarah, and the glass that she held up in her hand.

"I have embraced my own symbiote," Sarah explained. Her voice had an odd echo to it. "I did so in order for us to work together in sync for this exercise. Now, catch the glass before it hits the floor, Maya."

Sarah's hand opened, and the glass fell. The moment it left her grasp however, it changed, taking on the same drab, indistinct appearance as everything else, and it slowed, as if it had just encountered some kind of dense liquid medium that was resisting its passage. Maya watched it fall and realized that she could actually see the molecules in the air that it was displacing, moving aside for it as it made its gradual descent.

Minutes seemed to pass as she watched the glass tumble end over end, utterly captivated by its graceful movement. It got nearly a quarter of the way to the floor before she finally remembered her task and reached out to catch it.

That part was easy enough, but the instant that her fingers closed around it, the thing very nearly slipped away. A strong vibration was resonating through it and Maya was forced to tighten her grip. After a few seconds, the pulsations ceased and the edges of the glass became clear again.

"Very good, Maya," she heard Sarah say. "We'll practice this some more, each day. Now you must learn how to release the symbiote."

"How?"

"In the exact reverse manner that you first embraced it. Relax and feel yourself pulling away from its presence. Feel it as being separate from you, apart. Ignore it."

Maya closed her eyes again, and sensed the symbiote sitting there inside of her. She pushed the alien sensation back and away, and another wave of vertigo coursed through her. Simultaneously, the steady drone disappeared from her ears, and when she looked again, the world had resumed its normal pace, color and sound.

"I am going to retune your psiever back to a conventional setting," Sarah told her, briefly closing her eyes. The sensation of the symbiote, which had already become rather faint, vanished completely.

"Once I feel that you are ready, I will allow you to change your psiever frequency for yourself. For now, I will continue to do this for you. In the meantime, would you like to order some dessert?"

"Yes," Maya replied absently, still overcome by what she had just experienced. "Yes, certainly."

She went to bed that night imagining that she could feel the symbiote in her head, watching her silently from the strange non-universe that it resided in, and the more she thought about it, the more the presence seemed to increase. This was impossible though, she knew. It wouldn't react to anything she did unless her psiever was at a high enough frequency, and Sarah had reset it. Even so, the sensation stayed with her until she pointedly forced herself to ignore it.

Eventually, unconsciousness came, and later still, dreams. Naturally, they were strange ones.

She found herself in the Drow'voi Necropolis, back on Ashkele, and just like the dream she had experienced in the tower, she saw it not as it was, but as it had once been. The great stone buildings were unblemished, and Ashkele's primary shone down on the Drow'voi. Once again, she saw their irregular forms, flowing up and down the sides of the cyclopean edifices and working with strange devices. The odd sounds coming from the machines were also back, and she listened to them, trying to piece together what they meant. But just when she thought that she might be able to understand them, the dream faded away and true sleep overcame her.

The memory of these sounds followed her into wakefulness, but no insight accompanied them. Instead, they remained enigmatic, just a whisper beyond the reach of her comprehension. As silly as the whole thing was, the conundrum frustrated her until it was time for 'breakfast' with Sarah in the hotels restaurant, and then she put it out of her mind. There were more important things to focus on.

Sarah had made it a daily ritual for Maya to embrace her symbiote and practice catching the glass. However, the emphasis was being placed on speed now. Maya had to link with the alien device more rapidly, and then unlink from it just as swiftly. The purpose, the woman explained, was simple; to use the symbiote in combat, she would have to master the ability to call upon it at an instants' notice.

When she was satisfied with the day's results, Sarah called an end to their exercise and pushed herself back from the table. "I have some errands that I need to take care of before our departure from Nocturne," she announced. "So you will be on your own. While I'm gone, I want you to practice some of the basic exercises Skylaar has shown you, employing your symbiote while you do them. I will leave your psiever attuned to the higher setting so that you can accomplish this."

"Certainly," Maya agreed, with false nonchalance. Privately though, she was excited at the prospect of having some time alone with her symbiote, and away from Sarah's supervision. She was certainly all for practicing with it, but her plans had nothing to do with any boring martial arts drills. There were more interesting things that she wanted to try out.

The minute Sarah had left her, she changed and left the hotel for the Ehl' Ela district—and the jewelry store that they'd visited.

There, she pretended to window shop until she was certain that no one was paying her any particular attention, and then walked into a nearby alley. Once she was out of sight, she closed her eyes and embraced her symbiote. The familiar wave of vertigo washed over her, and then the world slowed down.

Grinning in anticipation, she stepped back out onto the street and walked into the jewelry store. Inside, she found the saleswomen and their customers frozen in place, completely unaware of her presence, or the fact that they were about to be robbed.

Maya walked behind the counter, past the immobile figures and straight towards her goal. *"Midnight Song"* sat there in its display case, glittering in the light, and just waiting for her to claim it. "Thanks a lot," she said aloud to herself, "I think I will."

And into her carry sack it went.

With the symbiote helping, theft proved to be an entirely new and exciting experience. *I could get to like this,* she decided, moving on to another case filled with some particularly appealing rings. She helped herself to them, and finally to a rather nice little bracelet that simply begged to leave with her.

She left the store feeling quite pleased at how smoothly her caper had gone. She was in such a good mood that she also stopped to pick the pockets of several pedestrians before she reluctantly admitted to herself that it was time to get back to the hotel before Sarah returned.

With that, she broke into a run, moving in and around the still figures of the pedestrians and the hovercars caught in flight, and made it back in what was for her, barely more than ten minutes. The moment that she entered their suite, she stopped and released her bond with the symbiote.

Instantly, time resumed its normal pace, and this was followed by a wave of nausea and vertigo stronger than anything she had ever experienced before in her entire life. The whole world seemed to go into a wild spin, and she felt her legs giving out from underneath her. Only a desperate grab for the doorjamb saved her from falling, and she lowered herself to the floor and crawled to the bathroom. At the toilet, her nausea finally overcame her and she vomited violently.

When nothing was left inside, she kept heaving dryly. Horrible cramps accompanied this, and Maya groaned in pure misery, clutching at the edge of the bowl, and praying for it all to pass. Or for death to claim her. Either outcome seemed perfectly acceptable just then.

"Well? Are you ashamed of yourself?" It was Sarah, the hem of her black cape and the tip of one of her boots was just visible in the corner of Maya's tear streaked vision.

"Yes—"she managed to croak, "—No!—*f-fek you*, Sarah!" She threw up again, but only spittle and a little bile came out.

"I must decline your offer, however heartfelt," Sarah replied, "Did you honestly think that I would let you trot off with your symbiote without keeping watch?"

She dropped a towel on the floor next to her.

"Did you think that I would fail to anticipate *exactly* what you would do once you were alone? Really, Maya, your behavior during our mutual visit to the jewelry store was simply *too* obvious." She laughed heartily at this, infuriating Maya.

"Stop laughing at me, you *bita*!" she coughed. But this only made Sarah laugh even harder.

"Oh Maya," she said, "You mistake my intent! Everyone knows that laughter is the best medicine. I am simply trying to help you."

"Fek...you!" the girl repeated, but weakly. "Ahhh...goddess...*mer de fek!"*

"Now you are becoming repetitious," Sarah observed dryly. Then, "You know, I really should have warned you; the symbiote, while amazing, is still a thing of diminishing returns. And after only a few minutes, the effect of returning back to the conventional time-stream can be rather unpleasant, as I'm sure you would presently agree."

Maya would have answered her with another curse, but a spasm overcame her and she could only moan miserably.

Heedless of her suffering Sarah went on. "That, my little thief, is why it is only used for brief periods, such as in combat. And now that I think of it,

I also suppose that I could have mentioned that the symbiote has to be used responsibly. But then, knowing you as well as I do, I realized that such a lesson would be better learned through the agency of hard experience. You *have* learned something today, haven't you?"

Maya was too exhausted to do anything more than whimper.

Sarah reached down to pick up her carry sack. "Well, shall we see what it was that made all this suffering worth it?" Then after a brief pause, "*Very* nice, Maya! I must commend your taste even if you do lack *any* sense of integrity. Unfortunately however, I'll have to return these items, as part of your lesson.'

"Oh and one other thing," she added reprovingly "when I joined the Agency I never imagined that I would be playing the parental role, but clearly, you leave me with little choice. From now on, you will also consider yourself—'grounded'—yes, I believe that's the term used by most mothers—you are *grounded*, until I decide otherwise. And while I'm off returning your 'loot', please do clean up the bathroom. You've made a terrible mess."

***

Maya wasn't presented with another opportunity to misbehave. The very next evening, Sarah rented them a hovercar, and they drove out of Nocturne to a small settlement named Midnight Corners. Situated at the edge of the Great Nightlands Waste, the town served as the jumping off point for many young Nyxian women setting out on their Tej. Once there, they went to one of the well stocked wilderness supply stores so that Maya could purchase some equipment and personal items for herself, and then, Sarah hired a private ornithopter to fly them out to the Moonspire mountain range. Although Maya was certainly embarking on a Tej of sorts, Sarah had chosen to spare her the added ordeal of having to walk across the desert to their destination, notwithstanding her antics with the symbiote.

"You will have more than enough of a trial as Lady Ananzi's student," she explained. "She is the only woman I have encountered in this life that has ever truly frightened me. She will, I think, test you to your limits over the next year. Enjoy the time you have right now to simply relax and enjoy the desert."

This had been the first time that Sarah had ever mentioned exactly how long the whole training process was expected to take. Looking out at the desert rushing by beneath them, Maya frowned. She didn't relish the idea of being under the woman's thumb for so long, and from her description, Lady Ananzi didn't sound like much of a treat herself.

What little she had seen of augmentation however, offset this. Just the potential of the symbiote alone was enough to make the whole thing worth her while. Even so, she repeated her private vow to herself. When it was all over, *she* was going to be the one to decide when and where to use her new talents. Not Sarah.

The terrain below their ornithopter was largely open desert, with only occasional breaks created by low, rocky hills or weathered arroyos, and in certain places the expanse was illuminated by the soft glow of the local plant life. Sarah regarded the desolate expanse with a positively wistful expression.

"The Nyxian desert is quite unlike any other in the galaxy," she said. "Everything within it is unique. For example, those plants below us are *Jacalya* trees. They give off light to attract creatures who eat their fruit and carry their seeds elsewhere, propagating their species in the process.'

"But there are other plants that use light to fend off predators. There— "She pointed to a bright flash on the desert floor and just off the starboard wing, "that is one of them; the *Nauma* plant. When something threatens it, it gives off a powerful burst of illumination that is created by special chemicals it manufactures internally. The *Jacalya* and the *Nauma* are a good examples of what this desert has to teach us; that everything possesses two sides to its nature, even light."

Maya nodded. Ever since beginning their journey to Nyx, Sarah had become more philosophical than usual and she supposed that it had something to do with the significance that the place held for the woman. Still, she didn't discard what Sarah was saying out of hand. From what she had come to understand, Lady Ananzi was even more inclined towards the mystical, and it had helped her prepare. Besides, as much as she hated to admit it, some of what Sarah had had to say lately actually made a certain amount of sense—and even had some real value—from time to time at least.

Maybe she's getting smarter, the girl decided.

Residence of Lady Ananzi, The Great Nightlands Waste, Nyx, Morpheus System, Thalestris Elant, United Sisterhood of Suns, 1043.04|15|08:33:33

Lady Ananzi's home was a prefabricated set of living modules, situated atop a low hill and sited at the very foot of the Moonspire range. By itself, it would have seemed quite sterile, but the structure had been added to over the years by the artist with bits and pieces of welded metal forms, wind chimes made from bone and wood, and shadow sculptures of varying sizes, all of which combined to give the structure a unique, eclectic feel. A rough wooden awning stretched over the entrance, constructed with dry branches gathered from the surrounding desert, and carefully tended rock gardens, interspersed with live plantings, added to its effect, giving the place a lived in, and even welcoming feel. It was not the foreboding dwelling Maya had imagined for the woman they had come to meet, any more than Captain bel Lissa's home on Ashkele had matched her profession.

They found Lady Ananzi hard at work in a low open space situated at the foot of the hill, melding a piece of metal onto the framework of what had to be a new shadow-sculpture. Her back was turned to them as they walked up, and the melder was giving off a loud buzz as it cold-bonded the molecules of the metal together into a seamless union. Under such noisy circumstances, most women wouldn't have heard the ornithopter's approach, or even realized that they were there, but Lady Ananzi wasn't an average woman. She greeted them without turning around, or even pausing in her work.

"Welcome Sarah," she said. "It has been far too long since your last visit here. Have you brought this girl to be trained?"

"I had hoped that you would consider it, Lady," Sarah said with a half-bow. "And yes, it has been far too long. I have missed this place, and your presence, very deeply."

Lady Ananzi made a few more welds, and then turned off the melder to face them. Just like her home, she did not fit with Maya's expectations.

Physically, she was a short woman, shorter even than Maya, and to her surprise quite heavy. Aggressive health initiatives, and nanobots that removed unnecessary fat, made obesity a rarity in the Sisterhood, and therefore all the more surprising wherever it was encountered. For some reason, Lady Ananzi had clearly not opted for nanobot intervention, or listened very carefully to the Infocasts about the benefits of weight control. Instead, Maya would have placed her at or near 113 kilos.

But despite her unappealing appearance and small stature, her eyes expressed a power that belied her form, and more than hinted at the truth behind her reputation as Sarah's teacher. They were typically Nyxian; blue-almost-colorless, but they had a predatory keenness to them. And when she smiled at Maya, it was a Nemesians's smile, not friendly at all, but challenging and appraising. She seemed very much like her name; a large, fat spider, sizing up something that had had the misfortune of becoming trapped in her web.

"What is your name, girl?" she asked.

"Maya n'Kaaryn," Maya answered, raising her chin slightly.

"I can see the pride in you," Lady Ananzi remarked. "And the guile. The pride I might be able to refashion into self-confidence, and the guile I think I will keep just as it is. Deviousness is a good thing to possess in a universe as dangerous as ours."

She's talking about me like I'm one of her sculptures, Maya thought. She knew better than to resent this though. There were things that she needed to learn, and according to Sarah, Ananzi was the one who could teach them to her.

"What is it you want from me?" the woman asked.

"To learn what you would be willing to show me," Maya replied. Although Sarah had extolled Lady Ananzi's wisdom to her many times, she had never explained the exact shape that it took and this was the only reply that felt safe.

"Caution, as well as guile, eh?" Lady Ananzi observed, stroking her chin thoughtfully. Then she turned, moving with unnatural swiftness, and regarded Sarah. "I will teach her the Path of the Hidden Way–both the

Al'g'aat and the *Daan'g'aat*–the Light and the Dark. If she can learn any of that, then we can see if she can aspire as far as the *Saa'va'a*."

Sarah nodded her gratitude and Lady Ananzi walked up to Maya, extending her hand and raising it so that her shadow fell directly on the girl. "I cast my shadow on it and upon her," she declared, and Maya realized that this was the Nyxian version of a formal oath.

"My thanks for any effort that you would care to expend on her, *Elleshaari*," Sarah said, adding in another, deeper bow.

"Come with me, girl." Lady Ananzi waved for Maya to follow, and led them away from her work area to a large flat spot, fronting a neighboring hill. It was dotted with rocks of varying sizes. The Nyxian considered them, and then pointed to one of the largest stones.

"Watch," she said, assuming what Maya recognized as a fighting stance. Then the Nyxian took a deep breath, and exhaled, thrusting her hand out towards the rock. *"AA-TCHAA!"*

The stone reacted as if it had been hit by some kind of energy weapon. It shattered into a billion tiny pieces, and as they rained down onto the sand, Lady Ananzi looked back over her shoulder at her.

"When you can do *that*, "she said. "Then I might consider your training adequate enough to lend you my name."

***

This is so stupid, Maya thought. *How am I supposed to sit and think about nothing?*

That evening at their Firstmeal, Lady Ananzi had announced that her training would begin by learning the Five Seevaan Disciplines, which she believed were something that every psi had to master.

The first of these, Ananzi had explained, was 'Silence'. The Nyxian had even claimed that any woman who could manage total inner silence for just a standard minute would rule the galaxy. Although Maya had had no idea how just being quiet would grant anyone such great powers, the task itself had sounded childishly simple.

Then she had been sent out to the rock field to attempt it. So far however, things had not been going well, and for the life of her, she could not imagine how the achievement, if she ever managed it, would make her a better fighter, or even help her to move a small pebble, much less smash one to bits.

Taking a breath, she tried again, with the same disappointing results. Finally, frustrated by the entire exercise, she got up and stomped back to Lady Ananzi's home. She found Sarah outside, practicing a martial arts drill.

Seeing her approach, Sarah stopped what she was doing. "How is it going, Maya?"

"How *could* it go?!" the girl responded. "She tells me to think about nothing—and that's exactly what I've gotten done—*nothing!*"

"It's a trick statement," Sarah said, resuming her practice with a move Skylaar called the Fighting Bird. "Lady Ananzi didn't mean for you to actually *think* about nothing."

"I know that!!!" Maya snapped. "But what *am* I supposed to be doing? It makes no fekking sense!"

"Nothing, Maya," Sarah replied. "You are not supposed to be doing anything at all. That's the point. Just sit there and don't let yourself become involved in any mental dialogue. If you can do that, you will achieve your objective."

Maya smacked her forehead. "Yes, *of course*. How *silly* of me. I should have seen that!" Her voice was dripping with sarcasm.

"Maya, it's really very simple; every time you start to think about anything, stop yourself. Don't have the conversation. Try that."

The girl sighed. "Fine, whatever. Back I go."

It actually took several days for Sarah's advice to sink in, but then, during a particularly frustrating bout with herself, Maya got tired of the entire struggle. She decided to stop letting it bother her, and just sat there.

For the briefest of instants, barely an attosecond, her mind stilled completely. The minute that she realized this, the silence was gone, but not the memory of it. She tried again, letting her thoughts drift by, but giving them none of herself. And like the waters on the surface of a pond after its ripples have subsided, the stillness returned.

Ecstatic over her discovery, she sought out Lady Ananzi immediately and informed her of it. The woman was at work on another one of her sculptures, and spared her only the briefest of glances.

"That is a good start. Now, go back and do it again for a longer time."

***

Evening found Maya awake and ready to begin her 'day'. It had taken her a few weeks to adjust to the new schedule of sleeping the day away and working throughout the night, but she understood that changing her routine was just one of the costs that being an agent required. When she was on a mission, she wouldn't have the luxury of setting her own hours. But then, she also wouldn't be under Sarah's control, or Lady Ananzi's, she reminded herself.

After she was finished with them, it would be the sun for her—and as much as she could get of it—until she actually had to go to work. With visions of a warm Tethyian beach dancing in her mind, she walked into the kitchen to make Lady Ananzi her Eventide tea.

Doing this had become her 'duty' as a student, and according to Sarah, it was also some kind of 'honor', although what made it a privilege was completely beyond her.

Some 'honor', the girl thought disdainfully. Skylaar, she could understand. *That* woman had some real knowledge to impart, but so far, aside from her little demonstration on their first night breaking up some rocks, Lady Ananzi had yet to teach her anything of value.

In fact, the entire trip was beginning to seem utterly ridiculous now. Sarah had played the whole thing up like it was going to be some great mystical adventure. But after dragging her across hundreds of light years, and out into the goddess-forsaken Nyxian desert, she'd wound up sitting around contemplating her navel, and playing maidservant.

Frowning in displeasure, she poured the tea into Lady Ananzi's special cup. Sarah had taken pains to emphasize that her teacher liked her tea served at a very specific temperature, and had even sent an impression of this via psiever to make certain that she fully understood.

Which, in Maya's estimation, had been rather silly. It was just tea, and as far as she was concerned, it was 'right' if it was warm enough to drink. And it felt plenty warm enough to her.

Covering the cup with its decorative lid, she took it into the old woman's quarters, eager to be done with her task. Lady Ananzi was waiting for her there, sitting on the edge of her bed. The Nyxian was dressed in a robe, which except for its greater size, was the very twin of the one she had seen Sarah wearing on many occasions. It was a jet black affair with delicate silver designs that combined the graceful Nyxian native script with flowing abstract patterns.

Despite herself, Maya had always admired Sarah's robe, and had even considered getting one for herself. But because that would have also given Sarah the erroneous impression that she was setting Maya's fashions for her, she had never followed through. Still, she mused as she handed Lady Ananzi her cup, it *was* a very nice robe, even if the Nyxian herself was too fat to do it any credit.

Ananzi took an appraising sip of her tea, and then looked up at Maya. "The tea is a trifle cold," she declared. "And apparently, you also don't seem to care for the task of serving it to me. It also seems that you find me to be a bit too fat for your liking."

Even though Sarah still read her thoughts now and again, Maya had come to take her mental privacy more or less for granted, and the woman's remark caught her by surprise. Out of reflex, she began to stammer a hasty denial, but Ananzi was in no mood to listen.

Instead, the Nyxian 'pushed' her with her talents.

A wave of sharp, searing agony boiled up in Maya's skull and the girl clawed at her temples and dropped to the carpet. Then, through the pain filled haze, she heard the woman speak.

"This is your reward for the tea, Maya. It is an important lesson that you are hardly worthy of receiving. No matter what else you learn, you must master the art of hiding your thoughts so that others cannot detect them."

The old woman stood and prodded her with her toe. "You think too loudly girl, and too boldly for your own good. Hate serving me if you wish, dislike my figure—I care not what your opinions are. But learn how to keep them masked, or others just like me will hear you. They will hear you, they will find you, and they will kill you. Now go and speak with Sarah about how to manage this. I wish to wake up alone."

Maya barely managed to crawl her way out of the room. Only when she reached the kitchen did the pain mercifully cease. Even so, it still took her several minutes, lying on the floor, before she could find enough breath or strength to stand. Once she was able, she did exactly as Lady Ananzi had instructed, and sought out Sarah for her advice.

"Lady Ananzi informed me about your little lesson," Sarah remarked, sipping casually at her own Eventide tea. "She also told me that I am to teach you how to serve it properly. I take it that you are interested in learning?"

"Yes," Maya replied sullenly. As painful as the experience had been, she had to admit that whatever Lady Ananzi had just done to her had been impressive. And she wanted to learn how to do it herself. There were more than a few people she knew who deserved to feel that kind of pain, and she was only too happy to oblige them.

Maybe even Sarah or Lady—she started to think, but then she abruptly cut this off. She didn't want a repeat of what she had just experienced.

"Good", Sarah said. "Being careful with one's thoughts, and starving them when they try to become dangerous is part of what Lady Ananzi would have me teach you."

Maya flushed, and glanced nervously towards Ananzi's bedroom. But no retribution came from that quarter, or from Sarah.

"Shall we take the rest of this conversation elsewhere?" Sarah asked instead. "I am sure that Lady Ananzi would like to begin her evening in peace."

Without waiting for Maya's response, the woman picked up her teacup, and its pot, and went outside with them. Maya followed, and they walked down the hill by way of its gravel path, to its base.

"This is where you will learn how to properly serve tea, and to control your thoughts," Sarah said, handing her the cup. She poured some tea into it, stopping only when it was barely a drop away from overflowing the rim.

"I want you to take this cup and walk up to the house with it. Take care to do two things; one, do not spill a single drop, and two, as you go, think only of keeping the tea in the cup and nothing else. If you can make it to the front door without wasting any of its contents, then you will have learned your lesson."

"And if I spill the tea?" Maya asked, looking at the cup doubtfully.

"In that eventuality, you must return here, refill it and repeat the entire process all over again. You will do this until you either succeed, or dawn comes. If you cannot manage the task by the first day, then you will attempt it the next, and the next, and so on until our time here comes to a close."

"*Wonderful*," Maya replied flippantly. The path up the hill seemed fairly smooth, and she imagined that if she just took it very slowly, that she would succeed easily enough.

Sarah was not about to let things proceed so smoothly, however. "You may not use the path up to the house to make your journey," she told her. "Instead, you will take another one. Think of it as a reflection of real life; there are many paths that wind through it, and each one is suited to the person traveling its length. Your path, Maya, is over there."

She was pointing to an area on the hill that had been deeply eroded by recent rains. It was an ugly gouge that scarred the slope of the hill, and filled with rocks and other random detritus. There were plenty of places along its length that offered a climber the chance not only to slip, but even take a good tumble.

"When Lady Ananzi gave me the job of training you today, " shecontinued, "I couldn't think of a route that better emulated the one your own life-path seems to have taken."

The girl glared at her angrily. Her task had just gone from being extremely difficult to absolutely impossible. It was completely fekked. "I'll do my *best*," she snarled.

"No, Maya," Sarah warned. "Don't 'do your best'. Don't '*do*' anything. Just carry the tea to the top without spilling it. I'll leave the pot here so that you can refill your cup if you need to." With that, she set it down on a nearby rock, and departed.

The little wash proved to be just as unforgiving an adversary as Maya had anticipated. On her first attempt, she spilled the cup's contents almost immediately, and returned to the pot muttering under her breath about the unfairness of the whole thing.

Not that her curses aided her in any way. Her second trip proved just as disappointing as the first. The tea spilled again, a little further up the slope this time to be sure, but it still spilled.

Swearing volubly, she went back down and refilled her cup, wondering how she was ever going to manage to finish her assignment, and making ugly statements about Nyx and the shortcomings of its native women in general.

Then an idea occurred to her. *If I take the empty cup and the teapot up to the top, fill it, and then bring the pot back down to the bottom, I could finish this shessy job and they wouldn't know any better.*

At any other time and place, this might have been the perfect solution, and she would have followed through with it. This wasn't the right time or place though. Almost as soon as the deceitful notion had danced its way through her mind, she felt a very convincing facsimile of a physical smack to the back of her head, and immediately after this, received a psiever message from Sarah.

Do it RIGHT, Maya!

To add insult, Maya also heard a second transmission, much fainter than the first. It was from Lady Ananzi, and while she wasn't able to decipher the meat of it, the old woman's derisive chuckle and something about 'guile' did manage to come across. That, and Sarah's own amused agreement with whatever the woman had just thought to her.

They were *both* watching her, she realized. And enjoying themselves mightily at her expense.

Clearly denied what had been a perfectly reasonable answer to her predicament, Maya borrowed liberally from her ample stock of Hriss profanities, and topped off the cup again. Then she gritted her teeth, and started back up the hill.

Sadly, this ascent proved to be just as frustrating as the others, and so did the one after it, and the one after that, and all the rest of the attempts that followed. And even worse, not only did she spill the tea, but she also slipped and fell at least half the time, sustaining some nasty bruises and a matching pair of skinned knees as her only reward.

Like all unpleasant things, the night moved forwards at a crawl, interrupted only when Sarah came down with fresh pots of tea to replace the ones that Maya had emptied. At first, the sight of her doing this, on top of everything else, only added to the girl's foul mood, but eventually her anger surrendered to sheer exhaustion. From there on, her attempts became more of a mechanical process than anything else. The task was clearly impossible, but she also had no choice but to continue with it—at least until Lady Ananzi decided to grant her a reprieve.

By the time dawn had begun to paint the eastern horizon, her exercise had finally assumed truly comic proportions. Looking down at the muddy slope, she saw that for all her efforts, she wasn't any nearer to reaching the top with the contents of her cup than she had been at the very beginning. Instead, all she had managed to do was to give the hillside a good watering—one cup at a time.

Laughing aloud at the absurdity of the entire thing, she half walked, half slid back down to get herself yet another cupful. There were after all, still a few spots that hadn't been wetted down yet, she thought sarcastically, and it certainly wouldn't *do* to leave any job partially undone, even one as ridiculous as this one.

Sarah and Lady Ananzi were waiting for her at the teapot. "It would seem that your cup has been too full to manage the task that Sarah set for you," Ananzi remarked, looking first up at the hillside and then at Maya's dirty and disheveled appearance.

"Personally, I have often observed that anything tends to be impossible when a vessel is too full. This also seems to hold true for those who are too full of themselves. Wouldn't you agree, Maya?"

"Yes," the girl answered quietly, avoiding her eyes.

An acerbic smile painted itself across Lady Ananzi's features. "Having grasped such a fundamental truth, you may resume your duties serving me my Eventide tea. Take care that from now on, *everything* about my tea, including the attitude that it is served with, is done properly."

"Yes. I will, "Maya replied, "Ma'am."

***

When Maya made Lady Ananzi's tea the next evening and delivered it, she was careful to keep her thoughts as neutral as possible, and her opinions about *everything*, rigidly suppressed. As for the tea itself, she had tried to ensure that it was as close to perfect as possible, and when the Nyxian accepted it and took a sip, she held her breath.

"The tea, and even its service are acceptable," Ananzi finally declared. She took the decorative lid and abruptly set it down over a small group of colored stones that had been lying on the table. "Now girl, tell me how many stones were on the table, and what their colors were."

Once again, Maya had been caught unawares, and had no answer. "I'm sorry—ma'am—but I wasn't looking," she admitted.

"No," the other woman replied. "You weren't, and you should have been. It is the mark of a good agent that every detail is observed, no matter what the agent is doing at the time, or how fleeting the opportunity might be."

Maya cringed, anticipating another migraine, or worse. Lady Ananzi only smiled though.

"Have no fear", she said, "—this time. This is an old, old game, designed to train spies for their profession, a game that is as ancient and as noble as the art of espionage itself. It takes time for anyone to master it. For now, you may leave me, and attend to your lessons with Sarah."

Maya was certain that she was prepared for Lady Ananzi after this. The next time that she delivered Ananzi her Eventide tea, she made it a point to get a good look at the little table next to the Nyxian's bed and the color and number of the stones sitting there.

"How many stones did you see, and what color were they?" Ananzi asked her after she had covered them over.

"Two red, one white and three black," the girl replied confidently. Seeing a slight frown starting to appear on Ananzi's features, she carefully added, "Ma'am."

The old woman gave her an approving nod, and removed the lid. "Well done." Then she waved her away. "You may leave me now."

The following evening, Maya repeated her performance, although Lady Ananzi was faster with the lid, and there were more stones on the table. By their third night, she was certain that she was mastering the simple game, and when she brought Ananzi's evening tea, she felt quite ready for the next challenge.

This time though, Lady Ananzi wasn't alone. Sarah was with her, standing near her teacher's bed, and as Maya came in, their eyes met and the woman stepped sideways as if she were merely giving the presentation of the tea a respectful distance. At the instant that she did this, Ananzi also moved, covering the handful of stones on the table with a brightly colored kerchief, so that Maya had only the briefest glimpse of them.

She had been ready for this though, and had been paying complete attention as she entered. When Ananzi asked her, she was able to describe them to her perfectly.

"Very good, Maya!" Ananzi said approvingly. "You take to the game well."

Maya beamed and stood a little straighter. "Thank you, ma'am."

Ananzi took a deep sip of her tea. "But tell me, did you also happen to see the stones on the far table? The ones that Sarah moved in front of when you came in?" Obligingly, Sarah stepped back, revealing another handful of rocks behind her.

"No—I-"the girl stammered. *They tricked me! It isn't fekking fair!*

Her rage was interrupted by a non-corporeal rap on her forehead. It was the very mirror image of a physical set of knuckles, and delivered just as smartly.

"Oww!!" she cried. "*Mer de Fek!*"

"Never let your enemies distract you," Ananzi advised. "The very essence of counterespionage is the use of falsehood and sleight of hand to divert attention. Learn to see everything!"

She didn't have to add that the girl also needed to work some more on keeping her emotions in check. That lesson had already been driven home and Maya had the beginnings of a healthy bruise to carry with her as a reminder.

CHAPTER 3

Residence of Lady Ananzi, The Great Nightlands Waste, Nyx, Morpheus System, Thalestris Elant, United Sisterhood of Suns, 1043.04|21|07:50:01

Twilight was coming over the desert when Sarah sought out Maya in the kitchen. "Lady Ananzi no longer wishes you to serve her tea," she announced, and when she saw the worried expression on Maya's face, added, "She is not displeased with you. Have no worries on that score.'

"In fact, she feels quite the opposite and since you have been progressing so well, she wishes you to take the stone game to a new level. Please put this over your eyes."

She was holding a heavy sash, and Maya obeyed, taking it from her and tying it around her head. After checking to make certain that it was secure, Sarah led her from the kitchen, and outside. Then, like a game she had played in her childhood, the woman made her turn around several times and then stop.

"Now, look up, and lift your blindfold."

Maya complied, seeing the first few stars of evening coming out against the darkening bowl of the sky. She had guessed the bones of what the exercise was when Sarah had shown her the blindfold, and she took careful note of everything above her.

Sarah gave her a little longer to observe, and then directed her to cover her eyes again. Once she had done so, they returned to the kitchen, and there she was allowed to remove the sash. An elzlate pad and a stylus were waiting for her on the table.

"Please draw what you saw. Show every star and its position."

Maya took the stylus and made a sketch of the scene, correcting one or two of the stars when they didn't seem to match her memory exactly. When she was satisfied, she saved the drawing and leaned aside for Sarah to inspect it.

"That seems quite accurate," the woman commented. "Shall we verify your work against the reality?"

"Yes, "Maya agreed, and they went back outside with the pad. There,

Sarah directed her to the quadrant she had been looking at, and invited her to hold it up for comparison. A few of the stars, she saw, were a bit off, and there was one tiny one that she had either missed, or that had not come out when she had been looking. But despite this omission, Maya considered it to be a good copy. Of course, there was no telling if Sarah would give her the pleasure of agreeing with this conclusion or not.

Her companion looked at her rendering carefully, and then the sky overhead. "You did well, Maya," she said at last, and the girl braced for some nasty surprise to follow this. None did.

"We will do this again," Sarah told her. "I would also like you to take the time to study an astrographic program that I learned to work with in my days as a navy helmswoman. It will greatly aid you in your efforts to increase your memory.'

"You will focus on memorizing a particular Elant each week, and then draw its key stars for me, from the perspective of that area's name star." The 'name star' was the central stellar body, after which an entire Elant was named, and it was the nexus for official maps and navigation through the area.

"I think that I should have you start with the one every helmswoman-trainee learns first; Solara, "Sarah suggested. "Yes, Solara it is! Take the time that you need with it, but be certain that you have the stars right when I ask to see your sketch."

"Yes," Maya replied, very nearly adding a respectful 'ma'am', but stopping herself. Lady Ananzi might demand this of her, but she was not about to extend the same courtesy to Sarah. She also didn't care if the woman heard this or not.

Sarah smiled, clearly having done just that, but no retribution was forthcoming. "You will of course add this to your other work," she said instead. "I will still expect you to study all of the training material that the Agency has provided you with."

Maya nodded her assent, and Sarah left her.

As the young woman began her studies for the evening, Sarah observed her from the shadows of the adjoining room. Lady Ananzi joined her a moment later.

I see that you have begun the next great phase of her training, Sharrisaal, the Nyxian observed. They were speaking on a secure psiever channel that was closed to any eavesdropping by the girl.

I have, Elleshaari, Sarah replied, using her teacher's Nyxian honorific. *Through trickery, of course.*

Yes, Ananzi agreed. *That does seem to be the best way to impart knowledge to her. She is obstinacy incarnate.*

Indeed, but I believe that that is also what gives her strength, Elleshaari, Sarah ventured. *I also felt that her memory building exercises had reached the point where she was ready to embark on her real work. I have provided her with the astrographic program.* She inclined her jaw towards the holojector Maya had set up on the kitchen table.

I concur and approve, Ananzi nodded. *And who knows? She might even learn to curb that hot temper of hers in time. Stranger things have been known to happen in this mysterious universe of ours.*

Sarah answered her mistresses' sarcasm with a mental chuckle of her own. *Yes, quite possibly, Honored One. Although like a trip to Andromeda, it is not something likely to occur within a single lifetime.*

Humor aside, they both fully appreciated Maya's potential. Once she had been taught to master her passions, and her formal training was complete, she would not only become an OAE operative in the fullest sense, but one day, assume her intended role as the mistress of the *C-JUDI-GO* herself.

And goddess willing, she would do them both credit in that sensitive position, Sarah reflected.

But like the teacup that she had labored with all night, Maya would first have to be emptied of herself, and then refilled with the knowledge that they would both pour into her. Given the girl's innate stubbornness, this was going to be a laborious process, but well worth it in the end.

***

"The weakness of any society, at any time in history, can be reduced to a few basic factors. These factors are also the same ones that effect humans on an individual basis. Therefore, if you understand how to manipulate these elements to your advantage, then you not only possess the key to controlling entire civilizations, but the individual personalities residing within them."

The speaker in the holo was a grandmotherly type who resembled Maya's first primary teacher, and had more letters after her name than Maya had in all of her aliases combined. The woman was presenting a series of lessons from an official course that every OAE agent was required to take. It was entitled, "*On Subversion: The Covert Disruption of Societal Structures, 25th Edition*" and it was one of a dozen holos that she had been tasked to get through that week.

As dry as the title was, the material it contained was light years more interesting to her than "*Effective Communications Strategies for Interrogation*", which in her opinion, should have actually been entitled "*Effective Strategies for Curing Insomnia.*" And then there were the five stifling episodes that she had to get through of *"Poisonous Plants of the Sisterhood"*. Bor-ing.

According to the virtual 'plexi that accompanied '*On Subversion*', the original edition had been composed for the old Gaian Star Federation almost 1500 years earlier. While it had been edited many times, the wisdom that it had to impart was truly timeless, and borrowed from many ancient sources to make its points.

One of these was someone that Maya had come to admire deeply; Nicholla Machiavelli. The 'plexi had informed her that Ms. Machiavelli had been a Renaissance-era noblewoman, who had authored a short work entitled, *"The Princess."*

Despite the fact that Ms. Machiavelli's thoughts strongly resembled Sarah's mindset, what she had to say about the frailties of human nature, and statecraft, was absolutely priceless. So far, one of her favorite quotes was "*If an injury has to be done to a person it should be so severe that their vengeance need not be feared.*"

Maya had every intention of getting her own copy of *The Princess* as soon as the opportunity presented itself. In the meantime, the holo's speaker concluded with her introduction and began the day's lesson. She took a sip from her kaafra and settled in to listen.

"There are five basic factors which enable the covert manipulation of a single entity, or a group. These are: greed, fear, sex, money and power. Of these, it has often been said that sex, fear and greed are the gravitational centers around which money and power revolve."

This made sense, the girl thought to herself. Everyone wanted to stay alive. And everyone wanted something; whether it was a bigger pile of shiny goodies, or just to feel good, and they wanted as much as they could get of both, and as often as possible. Dangle the hope of survival and the promise of pleasure over them, and their little mouths would water right on command. Then you had them. Simple. Brilliant. *"On Subversion"* was quickly becoming her favorite course.

The speaker went on. "Fear is a universal tool in any society and most of the totalitarian regimes in history employed it as the primary means of controlling their populace. However, wherever it was the sole means of manipulation, it did not produce high levels of productivity, or genuine compliance.'

"As a result, in effective dictatorships, it was often used in tandem with the other four motivational factors, and the combination and degree of their employment depended upon the structure of the society in question.'

"In capitalist societies, greed was the major tool used to control the masses, with money as its lifeblood. In communist societies, it was power and its sister, prestige. And in any form of society, sex was always considered to be a powerful and universal currency for manipulation. This was especially true of any nation that was run predominantly by males, regardless of its ideological structure."

Maya grimaced. Although this was an unimpeachable fact, it was still rather unappealing. Motivating males, such as those who ran the ETR, through sex, while logical, wasn't a method that sounded terribly attractive to her.

That's one tool I'll leave for other agents to use, she resolved. Espionage certainly had its nasty sides, but using sex was one level that she had no intention of sinking to. The idea of exploiting a male's inherent sexual weaknesses to make him do something was just straight-up nasty as far as she was concerned.

Thankfully, the lecturer left this uncomfortable subject behind and focused on something else. "Another important principle," she continued, "is to understand that no society in history, no matter how strong it might appear, is either immortal or impervious to overthrow. No government has ever existed without the consent of those that it governed. Every governmental structure, from feudal kingdoms, to fascist states, to modern republics, has functioned and existed only by the will and permission of those it had power over, regardless of its apparent strength.'

"In order for any society to function, basic services and essential jobs must be performed. On an individual basis, the failure of one person or of small groups to do their part in this process generally has little effect, but when the majority of the population becomes involved in a work stoppage, engages in sabotage or armed insurrection, then the result is the fatal malfunction of the governmental machine.'

"Therefore, the objective of any covert agency tasked with destroying an enemy power is threefold; first, to convince the people to abandon their loyalty and belief in their current system of governance. Second, to willingly support and actively undertake its overthrow, and lastly, once this has been achieved, to accept a new system which is friendly to the aims of the agency that incited the destabilization. To accomplish this, the five major factors that create satisfaction and discontent in humans must be employed, either singly, or in concert, and to greater and lesser degrees."

"Perhaps one of the finest examples of the use of sex and money to undermine a regime can be seen in the history of the ancient Soviet Union on Old Gaia. Its intelligence agency, the *Komitet Bosudarstvennoy Bezopasnosti*, or the KGB, used both to skillfully and successfully subvert intelligence assets from among the ranks of its opposition, the United States of America. The KGB's operations, which utilized large bribes, and male and female 'honey-traps' to compromise key targets, went on for decades, and with stupendous results."

"Ironically, it was the very instability and weakness of their own economy, and the failure of their government to deliver essentials to its own populace that was later used against it by its competing agency, the Central

Intelligence Agency, or the CIA. While the KGB was successful in many regards, the ultimate result was the overthrow of the Communist system, and its replacement by a weaker body which was more readily manipulated to serve the goals of the capitalist United States."

What orbits around, comes back, Maya reflected. Still, as the 'plexi displayed the list of Soviet espionage victories, she had to admit that she admired the KGB's pragmatic grasp of what made people 'tick'. They had been up against a technologically and financially superior enemy, and had still penetrated their defenses using the simplest means possible.

It was a lesson well worth remembering. And the name "KGB" did have a nicely sinister ring to it.

The lecturer was just about to expound on the 23rd century expert, Jen Li-Fang and her interpretation of the use of ego-manipulation to subvert bureaucrats, when Sarah came into the room. Skylaar taur Minna accompanied her.

Maya stood up reflexively. "Sena-Tai!" she exclaimed. "I didn't expect you to come here—"

"Sarah had asked me weeks ago to come and visit you," the Nemesian said. "When she was asked, Lady Ananzi agreed with the idea whole heartedly. We can't have you out here in the desert neglecting your physical skills, now can we Cho-Sena?"

"No Sena-Tai," Maya agreed, giving her a proper bow. "Evening's greetings to you."

"And to you, Maya," Skylaar returned. "I see that your lessons with Lady Ananzi are well under way." Her gaze had fallen directly on the bruise on Maya's forehead, which was still in the process of healing.

"Uh, yes, Sena-tai," the girl replied, self-consciously covering the mark with her hand. "I guess you could say that."

"Lady Ananzi can be a harsh teacher," Skylaar said. "But she is a true Mistress of her Art, and it is an honor to be accepted by her as a student."

"Yes, I guess so, Sena-Tai," Maya agreed, with noticeable hesitation.

"Do not judge her harshly, Cho-Sena," Skylaar advised. "Pain is life's great teacher. It is said that the Goddess created pain in order to warn us whenever we were doing something harmful. It may not be a welcome thing, but without it, we could not know what to avoid, or which path *not* to take. Lady Ananzi understands this, and uses pain as one of her tools to impart her wisdom. I assure you however, that she does not do so out of caprice, but only at need, and only to the proper degree."

"Yes, Sena-Tai." Maya didn't actually concur with what her teacher had just said, but it felt polite to at least feign agreement. As far as she could tell, Lady Ananzi actually enjoyed her little opportunities for torture. But she kept this sentiment as quiet as her mind could manage. She didn't fancy earning herself another bruise.

"Shall we leave the theoretical behind for a bit, and engage in the practical instead?" Skylaar inquired.

Maya was only too happy for the change of pace. "Yes, Sena-tai!"

The Nemesian rewarded her with a friendly shrug and went out the kitchen door with Maya following close behind. Once they were at the bottom of the hill, Skylaar led her through the usual practice drills, and then closed her eyes and sent a command to Maya's psiever, unlocking it and increasing its frequency. Maya wasn't surprised in the least. She was, after all, her teacher, and had every right to know the access code.

"Please engage your symbiote," the woman instructed. "We are going to learn about fighting within the time displacement today." Her own symbiote engaged and for a brief instant, she disappeared, with only a shadowy smear to show where she was standing.

Maya complied, feeling the weird sensation of the 'something else' that represented the alien device, and then as all the color in the world paled, she saw her teacher once more.

"We will begin with a simple punch and block combination," Skylaar said. "Then we will move on to more complex maneuvers."

As eager as she was to train, the announcement that their session would be lengthy worried Maya, and it must have shown, because the Nemesian quickly added, "Do not be concerned about becoming ill. Sarah informed me of your misadventure in Nocturne, and we will space our exertions with proper breaks. This will teach you how to work around the deleterious effects of the implant and garner the greatest amount of time from it."

Maya blushed deeply and dropped her gaze. She had hoped that her escapade would have been kept a secret. But if she had learned anything so far, it was that nothing about her training on Nyx was private. Everyone, including Skylaar, knew what she was doing, and worse, what she had been thinking when she did it. The year that Sarah had promised they would spend on the Nightworld suddenly began to seem more like a century.

USSNS *Pallas Athena*, Altamara System, Frontera Provensa, Esteral Terrana Rapabla, 1043.04|22|06:66:67

Altamara was a mid-sized star system. Its G-2 star had five satellites; Altamara 1, a T-Class world, and its lifeless neighbors, Nanya, Pica, Terresaa and Beya. Despite its remoteness, it was already bustling with activity. Sisterhood naval engineers had laid out a ring of anti-space mines in the outer reaches of the system, and a second one was in progress further in. And over Altamara 1 itself, the space station that would serve as the joint traffic control center was quickly taking shape.

"Welcome to the ETR, ladies," Lilith said. The last ship in their force had just come out of Null and the sitscreens showed another group of vessels already in orbit around Altamara 1, with smaller contingents ranged at various other points. These were identified on the displays as ETR naval ships and the small number of Sisterhood vessels that had arrived in advance of the Special Expeditionary Force.

"It's easy to see why the Hriss have overlooked this place," Katrinn observed. None of its worlds had much in the way of natural resources and Altamara was a long ways away from anything. "It reminds me of something that Grammy's Pairmate used to say all the time; *It ain't nothin, but it sure as heck's the farm right next door to nothin.*"

"Which is good for us," Ellyn n'Dira observed. "We should be able to get ourselves established here without any interference from the Hriss."

Navcom signaled that it had a message waiting. "Admiral, Commander? We've received word that the ETR's Fleet Admiral has arrived, and that he is coming over to the *Boudicca* to meet with Admiral da'Kayt. They sent the message by *ansible*." The tech didn't bother to hide her disbelief.

Katrinn shook her head, mirroring the ComTech's astonishment. "Ansible? Goddess, what's next? Messages sent by telegraph wire? Heliographs?"

Everyone laughed at this, and with good cause.

Ansible transmissions propagated as a wave, using the shortcut of Nullspace to enable instantaneous transmissions anywhere in normal space. But these same waves created vibrations in Null, ringing it like a bell and agitating its unfriendly inhabitants, the Indwellers, to greater violence than they normally displayed. In the presence of such disturbances, the shapeless life forms responded in large, angry numbers and it was believed that many of the early ships exploring Null had been lost due to this unfortunate side effect of the ansible.

The Ansible also had another glaring drawback; it was subject to distortions caused by the nature of Nullspace itself, which could result in garbled, or entirely unintelligible messages. Even worse, it could be easily monitored by anyone with the interest to do so, and jammed just as effortlessly.

For these reasons, the Sisterhood had long since abandoned the Ansible. Instead, modern communications used tight beam signals that were relayed by stationary receivers positioned in Null, or were simply bounced off the fabric of the space itself for periods that were too brief to excite its natives, or be subject to distortion. The fact that the ETR was still employing the Ansible only underscored their image as a backwards civilization.

"Small wonder why the Hriss have been able to anticipate the ETR's forces," Lilith commented acerbically. "They've had their ears pressed to the door the whole time, listening to their Ansible broadcasts. I'd also venture a guess that the ETR's encryption technology is just as antiquated.'

"Com, send a message to the *Boudicca* that I will be on my way to attend the meeting." It was a given that she would be required to attend, in person if at all possible, along with the other Vice Admirals.

"I think an examination of their encryption formats might be one of our first orders of business," Lilith remarked as she rose from her station.

"If they are going to use such an outdated means of communication, we can at least try to make sure that it isn't so easy for the Hriss to decipher it."

She wasn't overly thrilled with the idea of sharing such information with the ETR, but it was better than the alternative of giving away their plans to the Hriss.

***

From the instant she first laid eyes on him, Lilith pegged Alfonza Guzamma as a pompous ass, and a fool. He was dressed in a ridiculous uniform dripping with gold braid and oversized medals, and he carried an archaic gold baton that signified him as the Grand Admiral of the Republican Navy. And as if his basic ensemble wasn't absurd enough, the man had added an equally ornate half-cape to it. The only thing missing was a jewel-encrusted sword, she thought depricatingly, and he had probably intended to bring one along, but had forgotten it.

Apparently ignorant of how preposterous he looked, Guzamma walked into the room with a pronounced swagger that was impossible for anyone to ignore, or respect. Not surprisingly, he was also accompanied by what could only be described as a 'royal retinue' of officers following behind him at a properly subservient distance. As he handed his silly cape back to one of them, Lilith couldn't help but notice that no one in his party was female.

She wondered if this omission had been deliberate, or simply the result of a dearth of female commanders in the ETR military. If it was purposeful, then she knew that she was not alone in her desire to see the man educated about the error of his chauvinistic mode of thinking. If not, then changes in the opportunities the Republic offered to its women were in order. She didn't know one way or the other what the situation actually was, but she imagined that it would make itself plain as their relationship matured.

What was absolutely certain however, were the Grand Admiral's poor skills as a commander. Although intel to and from the ETR was still in its nascent stages, what they had received from their allies had firmly established his record as an incompetent. It had been Guzamma's tactical blunders that had cost the ETR the cream of their forces when the Hriss had initially invaded.

Despite the fact that these reports had been heavily glossed over, there had been no mistaking the pure ineptitude of his disastrous stand against the Hriss in the Cataala Provensa either. There, Guzamma had fully committed his forces without any eye towards an adequate reserve, and the Hriss, who *had* provided for theirs, had overwhelmed and destroyed his fleet with very few losses.

Only his personal friendship with the ETR's President, and that man's own foolishness, seemed to have ensured the Grand Admiral's continued tenure. If history was accurate about the conflicts of the Pre-MARS era, Guzamma was the very epitome of the classic male general in every military force that had ever lost a war; too full of himself to make room for basic tactical sense.

Knowing this, Da'Kayt had carefully prepared herself in advance. She had made certain that their meeting was being held in the *Boudicca's* main conference room, and positioned herself so that she was seated with her back to the statue of the legendary Warrior-Queen.

It was an imposing sculpture, plated with an ancient alloy that the Sisterhood had rediscovered for itself. A mixture of gold and copper, the Orichalcum lent its subject a fiery quality that fully matched Boudicca's own disposition. She had brought the native tribes of England together to resist the legions of Rome, and although her effort had ultimately failed, the Celtic leader had become one of the enduring symbols of womankind's resistance to aggression. In the context of their meeting, Queen Boudicca was also a clear statement to Guzamma that Da'Kayt and her staff were not a group of fainting weaklings that he could overawe.

She had also been careful about how she had dressed herself, and Lilith and the other Flag Officers had followed her lead. None of them was wearing anything grander than what they normally wore, simple day uniforms, and only Jan bar Daala and the other three adjutants looked anything like attendants—and they had been expressly told to keep a low profile, and observe as little ritual as possible. Da'Kayt wanted to disarm Guzamma, by showing him both the Sisterhood's might, and the confidence they had that allowed them such informality. She intended to off-balance and surprise him, just as the Hriss had.

As he strode up to the table, the Trilanian rose politely, and then just as he began to sit, she retook her own seat just a hair ahead of him. This sent another subliminal message; that *he* was the subordinate here, and from the slight tightening at the corners of his eyes, Lilith saw that he had not missed this. *Good,* she thought tartly. *It always pays to set the proper tenor of any relationship from the very start.*

"Good afternoon, Admiral Guzamma," Da'Kayt said, using the Espangla they had all been taught by psionic induction. "I have been looking forwards to this meeting and having the opportunity to discuss our joint campaign with you."

"Yes, yes," he replied with a flippant wave, "My command has drawn up a very workable plan for your forces to follow. It will crush the Hriss in the Argenta Provensa, and open the way to retaking Cataala within the month." Lilith strongly doubted that Guzamma's plan would be anywhere near as effective as he claimed, but she kept this from her expression.

"I look forwards to reviewing it," Da'Kayt returned. "We have also drafted a plan of our own, based on the information that your intelligence forces have provided."

"We will certainly consider anything that our allies suggest," Guzamma responded, clearly employing the word 'we' in its royal sense, "but I must stress that President Magdalana has put me in complete charge, and he has already approved my plan—with the expectation that you would follow it to the letter."

Da'Kayt smiled with pure amusement, and cocked an eyebrow at him. "I am relieved to learn that your President has so much faith in you, Admiral, and I will be happy to evaluate it. But my responsibility lies with the Sisterhood, and any plan will have to be approved by *my* command before we can take part in any of it. We also reserve the right to modify it—as *we* see fit. I am sure that you will be able to make your President understand this."

Guzamma's eyes widened. Clearly, he was not used to being told 'no' however politely, by anyone. "I do not think the President will agree," he countered irritably. "He was quite specific, and he will insist that we follow my plan as it stands."

"Perhaps he will," Da'Kayt agreed, "and perhaps I will have to report back to my superiors that we are unable to work together effectively. Although we certainly value the material assistance that your nation has offered us in exchange for military intervention, I am certain that our forces could be put to good use elsewhere. I for one, had hoped to remain here to fight the Hriss, but," she added a shrug of feigned helplessness, "like yourself, I am only a humble soldier who follows her orders."

"I will speak with the President," Guzamma replied tightly.

"That is very understanding of you," she said. "In the meantime, I will review your plans, and get back with you as soon as possible." Which, given his documented lack of prowess, meant that it would be a very short review indeed, with a *long* list of changes.

"Now," Da'Kayt continued, taking out a czigavar, a habit that she and Lilith shared. "Perhaps we can make the arrangements for the exchange of liaison officers in the event that everything resolves itself favorably? I would like to see that take place as soon as possible."

"Yes," Guzamma answered. "We have candidates selected, and they are ready to report to their posts immediately."

"As do we, Admiral," Da'Kayt returned. "Perhaps we can attend to that detail today?"

"Yes, yes of course."

"Very good," she replied, making sure that her tone conveyed the same royal tone that his had possessed. "We will reconvene in a day or so." With that, she stood, clearly dismissing him.

Guzamma's eyes twitched at the corners again, but he rose, and theatrically clicked his heels together. "Until then, Admiral."

Oh I am going to enjoy our relationship after all, Lilith thought as she watched him leave, his flunkies in tow. From the expression on Da'Kayt's face, she was clearly feeling the same way.

As Guzamma had promised, the *Athena* and many other ships in the Expeditionary Force received liaison officers from the ETR Navy that same day. In the *Athena's* case, the information Lilith had received about their guest was that he held a rank roughly equivalent to a Commander, and captained a ship that fell into a class approaching a Macha-class vessel. After the disappointment of meeting Guzamma, she was curious to see what else the ETR produced when it came to their officers, and eager to learn what she could about their knowledge and tactics. They would be fighting side-by-side soon enough and she hoped that she would encounter something approaching the quality that she expected from her own personnel.

She was waiting in the hangar bay, accompanied by Katrinn, Mearinn and Bar Daala as the shuttle arrived.

"I understand that our guest commands a ship of his own," she remarked as the vessel came in for a landing. "And he's seen action against the Hriss. At least the ETR is sending us someone with some battlefield experience, and not some desk-pilot."

"A male officer", Mearinn said speculatively. The idea was still quite a novelty to all of them. "It should be quite interesting to see what his capabilities are, and aren't."

"I'd think that the Marionites would love the idea, "Katrinn interjected. "A dream come true."

"Well, 'dream' or no," Lilith replied, "he'll be our guest while our forces coordinate their efforts."

As she said this, the shuttle settled down into its landing circle, and its egress doors opened. A tall male in a dark blue military uniform stepped out and looked around. He was easily Lilith's equal in height, and she guessed his age to be about 35 to 40 standard. Dark haired and dark eyed, he also possessed a certain rugged beauty that would have been considered—'handsome'—she thought, recalling the Old Gaian term.

The male made eye contact with her, and then stepped down the egress stairs, extending his hand in what she supposed was some form of greeting. Lilith answered this with a salutation that she had learned to use on Ara, touching her little fingers together and inclining towards him slightly. It was the welcome one gave when the meeting was formal, and for the first time. The man blinked, and withdrawing his hand, carefully copied her bow.

So he is cautious, she decided. But then she reminded herself that the ETR would not have sent someone who was not careful. Although their two nations were allied, there was a great deal of territory that neither had explored, and peace of any kind was always a fragile thing.

"Alla'zi. Enshón di cuna'va," he said in passable Standard, *"dénom ésant Kapitaan Alex Rodraga."*

"*Miya namay Vis-Admiraala Lilith ben Jeni,*" she replied in Espangla. "*Beinvala a la Pallas Athena*"

"Please Admiral," Rodraga entreated, "in Standard only. I want to practice my skills with it as much as possible."

"Certainly, Captain Rodraga," she replied, switching back to Standard with a smile. "My pardon. Welcome aboard the *Pallas Athena.* I have arranged for you to have your quarters in 'Officer's Country'. I hope that you don't mind."

"Not at all Admiral," he said, flashing her a brilliant smile. "I appreciate any—accommodation—is that right? Any accommodation that you'd care to offer me."

"This is Commander Katrinn Bertasdaater and her Second, Mearinn d'Rann," she said, indicating her companions. "They wanted the opportunity to meet you when you arrived."

Rodraga inclined his head to the two women and clicked his heels together as he addressed Katrinn. Unlike the Grand Admiral, it lent him polish and elegance. "*Godag Daar.*"

If Katrinn was surprised that he spoke some Zommerlaandartal, she didn't betray her astonishment. Instead, she simply replied with equal formality. "*Fraal Anref, Kapitaan Rodraga,*" she said.

Just another contribution by Dr. Martana and his little intelligence gathering 'school', Lilith thought sourly. She found herself wondering at just how much the ETR *really* knew about the Sisterhood that it wasn't admitting to.

"My adjutant will show you to your quarters," she offered. "Once you've had the chance to freshen up, I hope that you will join me on the bridge." Bar Daala stepped forwards, and Rodraga handed her his kit bag.

"It would be my great pleasure", he answered, flashing her another dazzling smile. "I've looked forwards to seeing your ship ever since I was informed of my posting."

***

When Captain Rodraga returned and stepped onto the bridge, Lilith was pleased with the reaction she saw. The man hadn't spotted her yet, and frank astonishment was written on his features. He confirmed this when she left her station to greet him.

"Welcome to the bridge, Captain," she said, offering her hand so that he could shake it. In the interim between his departure from the hangar bay, and his arrival on the bridge, she'd taken the opportunity to research the ancient greeting, and its meaning.

"This is incredible," he said, looking at the control stations around them. "What an efficient use of space! My bridge is twice as large as this and I don't think it serves me half as well is this one must."

"Let me take you on a quick tour, Captain," Lilith beamed. "As a fellow naval officer, I'm sure that you'll appreciate its features."

"Yes," he agreed. "That would be delightful."

She led him over to the command chair, floating in its suspensor field. Ellyn n'Dira was doing her turn on duty there, and she smiled and nodded down to them pleasantly.

"This is the Commander's station," Lilith said. "As you can see, her chair can turn in any direction to face whatever station she needs to interact with. The two stations below it, and to the left and right are for the Second and Third Officers. Right now, I'm sharing with Commander Bertasdaater's Second."

Rodraga gazed at the seats, and then up at the gleaming chair with admiration. "I think that I will soon over-use the words 'amazing' and 'incredible', Admiral. Compared to this, my own command chair seems little more than an antique rocker."

"There is much that we have to learn from each other," Lilith answered diplomatically. "Surely the union of our two nations will open the door to vistas that will surprise us both."

"Indeed", Rodraga replied.

Lilith inclined her head towards the Third's station. "This will also be your station while you are staying aboard with us," she said. "You'll have to share it, but when you use it, it will afford you a good view of our operations, and its terminal will call up any display that you require."

"With certain restrictions, of course," Rodraga interjected. Out of politeness, neither of them had mentioned the hard fact that some information—and certain areas of the ship–would be completely off-limits to him. Guest or not, he was still a member of a foreign military force.

"With apologies," Lilith replied.

"Accepted and fully understood, Admiral."

She led him out into the center of the chamber. "To the front and right of us, are the Navcom stations. They handle all of our communications and navigation systems. Up there in the front is the helm itself." Then she inclined her head to her left. "Over there is Fire Control."

"The teeth of your great ship" Rodraga offered.

"The very ones. Like your own ship, those stations handle our defensive and offensive capabilities. And to our left and behind is Environmental and Engineering, and to our right are Science Stations and special terminals that we can assign for specific missions."

Then she took him over to the nearest row of Navcom stations, which at that moment were occupied by busy crewwomen. If the presence of a male in a strange uniform surprised them, Lilith was pleased to note that they didn't show it. For once, Jon fa'Teela's presence aboard her ship had proven to be an asset. The crewwomen kept to their work, and only gave their guest a few fleeting glances. How things were going on other ships in the fleet that had almost no experience with males, was probably a somewhat different matter, she thought dryly.

Rodraga himself seemed completely unaware of his uniqueness and bent over one of the empty stations instead, looking closely at the control surfaces, and then the holodisplays floating in the air above them. The glow from the virtual buttons illuminated and heightened the awe on his features.

"My own ship still uses touch pads and switches," he admitted. "These are holographic are they not? That must cut down on the maintenance of moving parts considerably."

"And what isn't holographic, is psiever-based," Lilith informed him. "There are actually many more controls than what you are seeing, but they are only displayed by the user's psiever in their visual cortex, and manipulated by thought-commands. At a guess, I would venture that you're probably only seeing a quarter of the functions that a technician can really access."

"I won't say that I'm amazed again," he returned with a grin. "I swear."

Lilith shared his smile and pointed at the sitscreens that encircled the cylindrical chamber. "Those are our situation screens, which I'm sure you'll recognize from your own ship. The forward screen is Sitscreen One, and Two and Three are off to our left and right."

"Yes, those at least are familiar to me," he said, "but like everything else that I've encountered so far, they surpass my ship's meager resources. The *Adaventara* has only two, and they are quite a bit smaller."

"We find that three screens serve all of the stations effectively," Lilith said. "And of course, they work in concert with the smaller displays in each area."

"Yes," Rodraga agreed as she directed him back to the command chair, "vital information displayed prominently, where everyone can see it at a glance. A good ergonomic design."

"The arrangement serves us well," Lilith replied with a note of pride in her voice. Then she changed the subject. "I took the liberty of having our lunch brought up to my ready room. Can I offer you some refreshment, Captain? You must be hungry after your long flight here."

"Why thank you, Admiral. I think I would enjoy that."

With her recent promotion and the designation of the *Athena* as her flagship, Lilith had given her old office over to Katrinn and had had a new one constructed for her. Like the original, it was at the rear of the bridge near the Lifts, but on the opposite side. Every so often, she forgot this, and started to go in the direction of her old space, but this time, she was on guard against her own absentmindedness, and guided her guest to the new one without an embarrassing misstep. Saara sa'Vika was waiting for them within, accompanied by an assistant who stood with a covered hovercart. A dining table had also been brought in, and it stood in the open space before Lilith's desk, with two chairs at the ready. The SAO had even added the touch of a linen tablecloth, topped with a decorative flower display, and the fine china that they normally reserved for visiting dignitaries was set at their places. Clearly, the Kalian was pulling out all the stops to make a good first impression on their guest.

"My Ship's Activities Officer, Saara sa'Vika," she said. "Do you have something special for us today, Saara?"

"Yes, Admiral," Sa'Vika replied, her dark eyes twinkling. "I took the liberty of having our chefs create a selection of dishes from around the Sisterhood so that we could welcome the Captain aboard properly."

Lilith and Rodraga took their seats, and Sa'Vika nodded to her assistant who brought the cart close and opened the cover.

"Zommerlaandar baked pork," she announced, "with a Nyxian kelberry glaze, or if you prefer, a very tender Tethyian Netherfish, garnished with Seasprite berries and Sweetweed."

"For your sides, I can offer you wild Jasa Rice from Sita, seasoned with Forxi-spice, and a Nemesian salad medley with either a tart Waxxaberry dressing or a milder Jesha from Corrissa. There is also Kalian black tea, or kaafra from Nemesis. Also, if you are in the mood for dessert, I have some Thermadonian pastries or a fine little Thentian sweetbread that I recently discovered."

Lilith looked over the repast approvingly. "A fitting welcome indeed, Sara. I think I'll have the Zommerlaandar pork and rice. Captain? What can we offer you?"

Rodraga shook his head in bewilderment and laughed. "I am at a complete loss here, Admiral—these foods are all new to me. In this situation, I must defer to my lovely hosts to make my choices for me."

"Try the Tethyian Netherfish," Sa'Vika suggested. "It should prove a very pleasant introduction to our cuisine. And may I add my personal note of welcome to you? This is a historic occasion, and although you will certainly be very busy during your stay, I hope that I can find ways to make it equally as pleasant."

Lilith suppressed the urge to shake her head at this, and instead, sat back as Sa'Vika's assistant served her. True to her nature, the SAO was already currying favor with the man, undoubtedly with an eye towards acquiring whatever little pleasures his nation might have to offer. And she had little doubt that they would soon be seeing exotic items from the ETR making their way aboard ship. For his part, Rodraga seemed completely taken in by her manner and smiled pleasantly as she personally dished out his lunch for him. Sa'Vika was absolutely incorrigible.

As soon as their plates were set before them, Sa'Vika departed from their company with a polite invitation to Rodraga to discuss his nation's cuisine with her—whenever it was convenient for him of course–and left her assistant behind to attend to their needs.

The meal itself proved to be a gastronomical masterpiece. The *Athena's* cooks were always good, but in this case, they had surpassed themselves. Everything was perfect, and to Lilith's satisfaction, she saw that Rodraga was both surprised, and pleased by what he ate.

At the end, as they sipped tea together, Rodraga pushed himself back from the table. "Admiral, that was a truly spectacular meal, "he said.

"I am glad that you enjoyed it", Lilith replied politely. "So, tell me, what do you think of the *Athena* so far?"

"She is an amazing lady," he said, looking directly at her. "She is beautiful, intelligent, and deadly."

Something in his tone told her that he wasn't just describing her flagship, and she felt the color rising in her cheeks. *This man is an unrepentant flatterer,* she realized. It was a wrinkle in the situation that her studies of Human history should have prepared her for. Men, she recalled with some chagrin, had their own methods of manipulation, and could be just as devious as women when they wanted to be.

She suddenly appreciated why the women of the past, lacking the solid foundation of Motherthought, had allowed themselves to be 'swept off their feet' by men like Rodraga. She also understood why he had been assigned to the *Athena*. In addition to serving as a liaison, and presumably a spy, he had also hoped to disarm her with his personality. *I will have to be much more careful with him,* she decided.

"I'm glad that you admire my ship so much," she said, choosing her words, and her own tone, carefully. "The *Athena* is certainly all that you say she is."

"Indeed," he returned, flashing her a bright smile. "So, tell me a little about yourself Vice Admiral. If we are going to be serving together, I feel that we should get to know one another better. What of your people on your motherworld—is that the right term? What are they like?"

"My people?"

"Yes, I am especially curious about the genetic diversity that I've observed since coming aboard. For example, I see what I recognize as Asian heritage in you. We have some people of this descent in the ETR, and it's quite clear. It's in your eyes especially, but their blue color is another matter. It's really quite striking. Where did that come from? Is that a genetic modification of some kind?"

Lilith didn't miss his oblique compliment by any means. "No, it is not, but my nictitating membranes which you also must have noticed, are. My motherworld is a place called Ara, and they were added to help protect us from blowing dust particles. It's quite windy there you see, and they keep down eye injuries. But everything else came from Old Gaia, and nature."

"Where on Gaia, may I ask?" he asked. "My people look to European Spain, and the native peoples of the South American continent."

"My ancestors had their origins in Tajikistan and Uzbekistan," she explained, "in the old Eurasian Union of States, and like yourselves, they emigrated into space when they had the chance.'

"My mothers used to say that Eurasia was the 'crossroads of the world', where everything, the Eastern part of Gaia and the West, came together. They also believed that the best of both were what made us—and everyone else had to make do with what was left over." She laughed at this. "You see, they were very proud of their heritage."

"Yes, evidently," he agreed, joining in her laughter. Pausing, he added, "Admiral, there's something else that I have to ask you. It's been on my mind since we met this morning, and I think it best that I press ahead with it and take my chances. I'm not quite sure how to put it, or even if I *should* ask, and I sincerely hope that I won't offend you."

Lilith cocked an eyebrow at him. "Yes?"

"When I was given my orders to report aboard your flagship, I had expected to meet...how do I say this? Someone more like the Senatrix...someone...much...here I go, so please bear with me...someone older...than yourself. Please don't take offense, but in the Rapabla, our senior leaders tend to be—"

"More mature?"

"Yes. Please, don't take this as a slight. I am sure that you are more than capable, but among my people, such burdens are usually laid on the shoulders of more seasoned officers, and not on a young woman like yourself."

"Tell me, Captain. Just how *old* do you think I am?" Lilith inquired.

It was now Rodraga's turn to blush and Lilith thought that it suited him well. "Vice Admiral—Lilith—in my part of the galaxy, it simply isn't considered polite to discuss the specifics of a lady's age with her."

"We have a very different view on the matter," she countered. "But I do appreciate the sentiment. Again, how old do you think I am? Please, be frank. I promise you that I won't be offended."

The man considered his answer carefully before speaking. "At a conservative guess," he finally said, "I would say that you are 30 years old, perhaps 35 at the most."

"*That* young, Captain? I certainly don't mind the compliment, but you are quite mistaken. I am not 35, nor even close to that, although I must admit that I dearly wish I was."

"Then you are—younger?" Rodraga asked her cautiously.

"Oh Captain, I do so love your flattery!" Lilith laughed. "But no, I am much older. In fact, by twice as much."

Rodraga calculated this for a moment, and then shook his head in disbelief, "You are—seventy!? But—but—you are a young woman! How is this possible?"

"Through advances in medical technology," Lilith explained. "Our science has not only managed to extend the lifespan of the average woman, but effectively combated many of the effects of the aging process. Nowadays, living to 200 to 250 standard years is not uncommon, and for us, 100 is normally considered middle age. So, I suppose by that measure, you were partially correct, and I could be considered by some women to be a *bit* young for my rank."

"Amazing!" Rodraga said. "Ah—There I go! But you see, our best scientists have only managed to extend our lives to half that. It's only a pity that the Hriss had to be the cause of our two nations meeting. I can only imagine what wonderful things our union will bring now that we have been reunited."

Lilith raised her tea-glass and toasted him. "To wonderful things," she said. *Yes,* she thought, *I will have to be much more careful with this man.*

***

Later, after their lunch had concluded, and his shift had ended for the day, Captain Alex Rodraga retired to his quarters. There, he sat on the edge of his bed, and considered all that he had seen.

That he was being observed was a given. Had the roles been reversed, it was something that he would have ordered done, and for the sake of the hidden cameras, he kept his outward appearance calm, and seemingly unruffled. Inwardly, where the surveillance devices couldn't see, it was another matter entirely.

The *Pallas Athena* had been everything that he had been briefed it would be. Compared to his ship, the *Adaventara*, its technology was light years ahead, and he only hoped that the ETR would benefit from their alliance—for as long as that lasted.

But Rodraga harbored no illusions about this. From what he had observed, their two societies were too wildly divergent for the union to be anything but fragile. Only the bond of their common heritage kept it cemented together, and this was tenuous at best.

On the surface, a casual observer might have gotten the mistaken impression that the women who crewed the *Athena*, absent their genetic modifications, were just like their counterparts in the ETR. The Vice Admiral herself would have made a good case for this assertion. Taking away her nictitating membranes, she could have called several of the worlds back in the Rapabla her birthplace, and he even had to admit, that had the situation been different, her beauty and intelligence would have made her the object of his romantic pursuit.

The situation wasn't different though, and she, and her subordinates were not what they appeared to be.

The simple fact was that a yawning gulf of one thousand years separated their civilizations. Not only had genetic manipulation changed their basic definitions of what it was to be human, but their societies had also evolved along entirely different lines and with divergent values.

Nowhere had this been made plainer than when he had been in the Lift on his way down to his quarters. At one of the stops, several passengers had gotten aboard. One of them had been (if his briefings were accurate) a Nyxian. Another was a Kalian, and the third was a Nemesian.

The Nemesian woman had worn the uniform of a fighter pilot, and when she had boarded, he had met her eyes and without thinking about it, given her a polite smile.

Her response however, had not been what he had anticipated. Instead of returning his acknowledgement, her strange slitted pupils had contracted, and she had grimaced back at him, exposing her sharp teeth in a clear display of hostility. Realizing that he had inadvertently committed a grave social error, he had quickly looked away, and this had mollified the woman. But it had been enough to bring everything into sharp, alarming focus.

How someone from his own society would react to a given situation was something that he could anticipate. How a woman like the Nemesian, or even the Vice Admiral, might respond, was another matter. What they believed, what their mores were, or weren't, was still a complete unknown, notwithstanding everything that the Rapabla had learned from the crew of the *Atalanta*. And on a wider scale, what their nation might ultimately pursue as state policy was equally mysterious. The Sisterhood was, at its heart, an enigma. And Rodraga knew, from his years as a combat commander, that enigmas could be lethal when they finally revealed their true nature.

Sobered by this, Rodraga laid himself down on his bed and tried to drift off to sleep. At first, it was a struggle, but eventually he managed to force aside enough of his concerns for unconsciousness to overtake him.

Several decks below him, Ensign Jan bar Daala was also lying in her bed. But she was not asleep, or even attempting to relax in a way that anyone else would have understood. She sent a command by psiever to the room, shutting off its sensors. Normally, these would have remained on, monitoring her and triggering an alarm if any health-related problems occurred, but a privacy option had also been built into the system, and at times like these, Jan exercised her right to use it. It had been a tiring day, on top of an exhausting week, and she was weary of her charade. She was also curious about the *Athena's* strange new guest.

Taking a deep breath, she closed her eyes, and relaxed. Had the room been able to detect her vital signs, the medbay would have been alerted immediately. Her heartbeat suddenly slowed down to almost nothing, and her breathing became nearly imperceptible, but there was nothing wrong with her. If anything, the situation was quite the opposite. For Jan, this was true rest.

She went into a deep trance and felt herself becoming weightless. Finally, when she was ready, Jan willed herself to leave the confines of her body and ascended, reveling in the sensation of absolute freedom that always accompanied this. She had become a being of pure thought, and passed through the door that led to the outer passageway without meeting any resistance. Physical matter no longer held any sway over her.

Floating down the corridor, she felt a familiar longing; to abandon her body once and for all, and remain as she was. But she knew better than to surrender to this desire. It led to nothing more than dissolution and death, and as attractive as oblivion sometimes seemed, the Watchers had forbidden suicide. And she needed their blessing. Without it, the chance to finally free herself of her fleshy prison and join with them forever, would be denied. The only road for her was to complete the mission that the Watchers had given her.

Resigning herself to her situation, Jan made for the end of the corridor, and then took a sharp left turn that sent her through a nearby bulkhead and several neighboring compartments. When she found Alex Rodraga at last, he was fast asleep, and for a time, she simply observed him from a vantage point near the ceiling. Then, she reached out with her mind and tasted his aura.

His energy was fascinating. It was different than the women that she normally interacted with, and yet, oddly similar at the same time. Mindful of the purpose of her visit, and eager to know more about this strange creature, she descended, and entered his slumbering form.

The man tossed fitfully as she joined with him, but his resistance was feeble, and Jan soothed him with thoughts of comfort and safety. Now, if he even remembered her intrusion at all, she would seem nothing more than a fragment of a vague and pleasant dream. She was free to roam his mind unimpeded, and at will.

She searched through it and quickly found his memories. She relived the briefing that he had received before coming to the *Athena*, and felt the concerns that his superiors had expressed about the possibility of a war with the Sisterhood. She also realized that like her, he was an observer for his people, and a spy.

And she perceived that he was deeply frightened by everything that he had seen so far. Replaying all of his experiences since coming aboard, she sympathized. The Sisterhood was intimidating to be sure, but she knew something about them that Alex Rodraga did not. For all their military might, they were not the Enemy, and compared to what the User could do, they were utterly powerless.

When she sifted through his consciousness for any reference to either thing, she found nothing, but she was unsurprised. The Watchers had made it clear that the User and the Singer would come from within the ranks of the Sisterhood's population, and although the Enemy might be anywhere, its taint could only be felt by them, or beings such as her.

Rodraga was exactly what he seemed, just a normal human, ignorant of the workings of the larger universe around him. Satisfied, she moved on, sampling other parts of his past.

She recapitulated his childhood, and the strange world that he had come from, through his own eyes. She saw his parents, and finally understood exactly what a 'father' was. She relived the affairs that he had had with his many lovers, and shared the sweetness and the pain that he had experienced with each and every one of them. She also discovered the deep attraction that he felt for the Vice Admiral, along with the conflicting emotions that accompanied this.

And much, much more.

Finally, she realized that she had learned everything she could. She knew Alex Rodraga now, more intimately than anyone else ever had.

He was not a threat to her ship, and more importantly, he would not be an impediment to her mission. Her work was done. As much as she hated to do so, it was time for her to return to her body. Her parole was over, and her cell awaited.

With infinite reluctance, she withdrew, leaving the man to his dreams, and retreating through the wall, and out of the room. Just then, the Admiral's cat, Skipper, came sauntering by, and unlike the humans around him, he was able to see her perfectly. The creature hissed at her insubstantial form, and Jan backed away from him immediately. Although he certainly couldn't harm her, there was always the chance that one of the *Athena's* psi's would notice the activity, and become suspicious.

They were the real danger. Several of them had already shown some interest in her, and it had taken a constant effort to carefully redirect their thoughts elsewhere. Whether they could detect her when she was out of her body or not, was an unknown and she didn't care to find out. Thoroughly unnerved by the animal's challenge, she left the area and flew through a partition to her quarters.

Stifling a wave of distaste at the sight of her body, she forced herself to descend and rejoined with it. Once again, her heart resumed a normal rate, and her lungs began to breathe. As feeling returned to every extremity, she sighed with her reacquired breath, and then sent a command to reactivate the room's sensors. Then, she let her body take over and gave it the sleep that it demanded, hating it for its weakness.

***

The door to Lilith's quarters opened at Skipper's insistent meow, but not fast enough to suit him. Seeing that she was still asleep, the kaatze jumped onto the bed, making sure to land right on top of her.

Wake up! he demanded.

Lilith swatted at him sleepily. "Skipper, go away!"

I saw something! he told her, walking up the length of her body so that she *had* to pay attention to him.

"Good. I'm glad for you—now let me sleep!" Lilith mumbled, actually having the audacity to turn her back on him.

I saw it, it was-a— Skipper began, broadcasting the image of the strange misty form that he had encountered in the corridor. The problem was, he didn't have any corollary to describe it. *Well—I don't know what it was—but—LOOK at it!*

He sent the image to her, which even he had to admit, was rather confused.

Lilith sighed and rolled over to face him. "Wonderful. You saw something weird and blurry. That's it—no more catnip for you! Now leave me alone or you'll spend the night locked up in the bathroom."

But—

Her expression made it abundantly clear that she would brook no further argument. *Fine!* he agreed. *I'll just sit here and guard you.*

"Thank you. I feel much safer already. Now good night."

Skipper walked indignantly to the edge of the bed and lay down, facing the door in case the 'blurry-whatever-it-was' attempted to come in to *his* cabin. Humans could be so dense, he thought, purring loudly in frustration. It was a good thing that kaatze's were around to save them from their own stupidity.

He didn't broadcast any of this to Lilith however, and let her be. He hated being locked up in the bathroom.

Treetop Station, Nemesis, Rahdwa System, Thalestris Elant, United Sisterhood of Suns, 1043.04|24|02:91:21

Many aspects of travel had changed radically over the centuries. Gravitronic drives and Nullspace transits had replaced chemical propulsion and warp technology, and vessels now hurtled through space at fantastic speeds, and with tremendous efficiency. The distances that humans were able to cover were greater than anything any early spacefarer could have ever envisioned.

One thing remained completely unaltered however. It still took time to get places, and inevitably, there were layovers.

After eight standard hours, Erin taur Minna finally arrived at Treetop Station. It had taken two transits, and an hour-long wait at the Amphitrite Interworld Spaceport in Tethys before she had caught her last connection to Nemesis. Although the realies she had brought with her had managed to stave off most of the boredom of the trip, it had still been a long and grueling experience. She was tired, and hungry.

It was 02:91 hours, and what few restaurants Treetop's common area had to offer were closed, and wouldn't open for another hour. Instead, Erin had to content herself with the meager fare that the vending machine was in the mood to spit out. In her case, this was Kelberry-flavored Nutro and a stale *chocolat* protein bar. The wretched meal was the perfect complement to the homecoming she had received however; no one had been there to greet her.

Although she was certainly disappointed, she also wasn't terribly surprised. She'd sent word, well in advance of her arrival, but her sister Keela was a confirmed 'woodsy' and seldom, if ever, ventured out of the forest for any reason. And she definitely hadn't expected her mothers, or anyone else from the Minna Clan.

She choked down what she could of the Nutro, and stowed what remained of the protein bar in her kit bag. Then, with a weary sigh, she made her way over to the spacedocks to find a ride downside. After a few inquiries, she managed to get a seat on a lumber shuttle headed to the surface. And an hour later, when the vessel had finished loading, she was on her way.

The shuttle landed briefly at the Shadow Lake Lodge before heading deeper into the forest, and Erin chose this as the place to get off. A posh resort for outworlders seeking a taste of the 'Real Nemesis', it was one of the few surface structures that the local government allowed to exist, and it also served as a hub for all of the traffic coming and going from Treetop Station.

The mainstream news had kept silent about the catastrophic failure of its Impeller fencing, and the loss of life that had accompanied this. Erin herself had only learned about it through Keela, and later got the details through some friends in the DNI. Although Keela had downplayed their roles, she and her mate had been the heroines in the crisis, rescuing the daughter of a powerful Senatrix from certain death. It had been real adventure realie stuff, and typical for her sister.

In their mother's eyes, Keela was everything that Erin wasn't, but she didn't resent her sibling for this; she had always been the braver of them, and the strongest. What galled her though, and what had almost made her turn around several times on her trip was the painful admission that Teela and Saly'aa were right to feel as they did about Keela—and equally correct about their attitudes towards her and her life.

She could just picture the expression on Saly'aa's face when she finally made that confession, and hated the mental image more than she hated the Hriss. But like the Tej she hoped they would allow her to undertake as her penance, it was both brutal, and unavoidable.

Frowning at the prospect, she made her way over to the main Lodge building, and looked for any signs of the disaster, but she was hard pressed to find them. The Lodge maintenance staff had done a top-notch job of repairing the resort, and it looked pretty much the same as she had always remembered it.

Because it was spring, it was also the tourist season, and she found the Lodge filled with visitors. She received some surprised looks from many of them, being both a Nemesian *and* a naval officer. But Erin ignored them, and glanced towards the main desk.

The staff on duty there were all *hwa'ni'tem*, women from off-planet, and Erin decided not to approach them. What she sought would only be found among those who had the right to call Nemesis their motherworld, and she searched the Lobby until she spotted another Nemesian passing through. The woman was dressed in a housekeeping uniform, and by her Clan-tattoo, she saw that she was a member of the Haus'ka Clan, making her a neighbor of the Minna, and an ally.

Erin came up and spoke to her in *Kl'all'a*, the Nemesian language. "*Hai'a Sh'tun'aq*, Greetings Sister. I have returned from the *Sh'tchi'Ah*, the Land-Above-The-Sky. Now I journey to my home in Blood River."

"*Hee'ya*," the woman answered. "I can see by your face-mark that you are one of the Minna. But you are also dressed as a *Hwa'ni* sailor—an officer even! How is this possible?"

"It is true that I am garbed as an outlander, s*h'tun'aq*," Erin conceded. "It is because I sought my fortune in battle in the Land-Above-The-Sky. Now I am called to return to the forest to reclaim my spirit. Can you point to where I might find aid and supplies for my Tej?"

"I had heard a tale that one of the Minna did as you say," the woman replied thoughtfully. "You must be that woman."

Then, she stroked her chin and added," There is one who could help you; she is a sister of my Clan. She is employed by the *Hwa'ni* and works in the kitchen here, cooking the life out of their strange foods. She is called Jaala taur Haus'ka. Go to her, and she will help see you on your way."

"*H'sxw'qeh*, sister. Many thanks" Erin replied, making a hand-sign that literally translated to, "May the Great Mother shine the sunrise into your heart." Remembering her manners, she also added, "*Tashi'a'ela'k* "to further emphasize her gratitude.

The woman replied with a pronounced shrug. Erin answered with a shrug of her own, and the two women parted company amicably.

After asking a few directions from the front desk, she found her way around to the back of the Lodge, and the exit from the main kitchen. Luck was with her when she arrived; the woman that she sought was seated on a packing crate, taking her break. When Erin explained the reason for her presence, the woman gestured for her to join her.

"You are in luck, sister," Jaala said. "I have just started my mid-day meal. It is small, but I have a sweetsnake. Perhaps we can share it together?"

Erin's green skin mottled to dark olive with embarrassment at the invitation. It was polite to share food. In fact, custom required it between friendly parties, hearkening back to the desperate early days of the planet's colonization when the first settlers had nearly starved to death, and been forced to pool their rations.

It was also well-mannered to present something in return, and she had little in her kit bag that an omnivorous carnivore would want. Then she recalled the *chocolat* protein bar she had stowed away. Although native Nemesians avoided anything cooked, sweets were, like everywhere else in the Sisterhood and much of the Far Arm, universally accepted. She quickly reached into the bag and offered it.

"It is not much, sister," she said, holding out the bar. But we can share it."

Her companion shrugged gratefully, and took it from her, breaking off a piece for herself before returning it. Then she reached into the small cooler by her side and pulled out the sweetsnake. It was large, fat—and still very much alive.

As she produced her Tej knife, it was Erin's turn to shrug her thanks, and the woman quickly cut it in half. They took their separate pieces and ate the still wriggling sections in companionable silence.

The snake proved to be just as sweet and delicious as her companion had advertized, and Erin consumed it with relish. It tasted just like what it was; home.

When their meal was over, Jaala, in typical Nemesian fashion, got straight to the point. "How can I aid a woman of the Minna Clan?" she asked.

"Although I wear my Tej knife," Erin explained, "I am poorly equipped for a journey to my clan's territory. I also need to store my *Hwa'ni* things with someone that I can trust. Should I return, I will need to recover them."

"It is true," the woman agreed. "You are not equipped as you should be, and you certainly cannot venture into the Great Green in such poor clothing. I will find what I can to help you. Come back here in three hours."

"*H'sxw'qeh,*" Erin said, rising.

Three hours later, she returned and found the woman waiting for her as she had promised. She had a small bundle with her, which included traditional garments, as well as a survival pack, and a chemical rifle.

Erin quickly shed her uniform, which she stowed into her kit bag, and donned the native clothing. It consisted of a simple strap for her breasts, a pair of leather shorts that reached to her calves, and a heavy equipment belt with an assortment of utilitarian pouches. Once she had dressed, she felt much more comfortable.

Next, she checked the rifle. Like the Tej knife, the *Puy'ek'ska*, or Forest Gun, was of Nemesian manufacture. Instead of firing energy bolts, the weapon used shells, fed by a box magazine that was inserted into its rear stock.

As archaic as this system was, the semi-jacketed hollow-tipped projectiles, which were as wide around as her thumb, were more than a match for the forest's largest predators. Their cavities were also filled with the sap of the *Sq'aan'a* tree, a deadly poison, which added considerably to their effectiveness.

It was a familiar weapon, and Erin had learned, as all Nemesian girls did, to use it with great accuracy. She worked the bolt, and chambered one of its massive rounds, pleased with how smoothly it operated. Then she slung it over her shoulder.

"This is more than I could have hoped for, sister," she said, "It is truth when it is said that the women of the Haus'ka Clan are generous. I must repay you somehow."

"The continued friendship of our neighbors is reward enough," Jaala replied. "We of the Haus'ka know that you and your sisters will always do the same for us. Are we not fruit of the same trees after all? Go swiftly along the branches, sister, and may you reach your destination without troubles. I will store your *Hwa'ni* things until your return."

Erin shrugged. "That is good. My thanks again to you. May we live together in prosperity."

"One word of warning," the woman added as she prepared to leave. "Know that women of the Wau'ska Clan have been seen haunting the Roads that twine through our two lands. Although they move through the trees like clumsy *Hwa'ni* and are nothing but *Q'an q'en,* common thieves, be alert for their scent."

Erin's skin darkened at this. Although dueling was officially outlawed by the Sisterhood, on Nemesis and a few other worlds like Sai, and in keeping with the official policy of honoring local culture and customs, the practice was still very much alive. Although harsh by outworld standards, the Returnals who had settled Nemesis had felt that resolving interpersonal conflicts through dueling was part of the 'pure human' aboriginal existence that they had wanted to establish. As a result, Nemesian law, which Sisterhood courts upheld, actually had provisions in it to excuse killings when they could be shown to be 'affairs of honor.'

Blood feuds like the one that existed with the Wau'ska Clan, were not covered by these exceptions, but the *Hwa'ni* planetary officials in their offices up on Treetop Station tended to look the other way when it came to such matters, and unless they became too widespread, let the locals sort things out among themselves. They knew that had they tried to abolish either dueling or feuds, that the native Nemesians would not have stood for it. After more than a millennia of human occupation, such activities were too deeply ingrained in the culture, and Treetop needed the local good will to maintain the system's economy. By far, the most profitable product that the forest produced were life-giving medications, derived from the local flora. And although generous wages were offered to non-Nemesian workers, the task of finding and harvesting these plants was simply too dangerous for anyone but the natives to undertake.

This unique combination of factors made the Wau'ska an item of serious concern for Erin. For reasons that everyone had long since forgotten, they were old enemies of the Minna, and she would be traveling alone for most of her journey. An encounter with a band of them was something that she definitely wanted to avoid.

"Thank you for telling me of this. I shall be careful," she said gravely. "*H'sxw'qeh. Tashi'a'ela'k.*"

***

Movement by outworlders through the forests of Nemesis was generally accomplished by hovercraft, or for brief stretches, by using whatever trails there were on the ground. Of the two, the latter method was by far the more dangerous. Nemesis was home to some of the deadliest predators in the Sisterhood, and the majority of them prowled under the forest canopy. *Hwa'ni* stupid enough to be found there were fair game for them, and once beyond the impeller fencing that surrounded places like the Shadow Lake Lodge, survival for any great length of time was a doubtful prospect.

For natives there was another way, which was not only infinitely safer, but also ideally suited to their body-types and physical capabilities. This was the *Qwal' is' kat'we*, the Green Road. The Green Road was actually a series of pathways across the forest that used the branches of the great trees to avoid the predators below, and provide quick passage from one place to another, free of obstructions. Their growth had been patiently guided by generations of Nemesian women so that key limbs, known as Mother

Branches, met and intertwined with one another. And where gaps existed, additional trees had been deliberately planted, or strangler vines had been trained to span the voids.

This network of aerial pathways was virtually unbroken and crossed the entire length of the Great Mother Forest. Only the Neversaw beast, and the lemur-like Saa'lak which it hunted, shared the Green Road with the Nemesian women. The Road was a horticultural masterpiece that few outside of Nemesis even knew existed.

The Shadow Lake branch of the Green Road began at the edge of the Modrel Cultural Center, and it's first tree was marked by Modrel's *ki'ask'a*, or totem pole, which had been planted there as a signpost for anyone who knew what to look for.

Erin made a gesture of obeisance to the planet's guiding founder as she passed the monument, and searched for the tree. It was easy to locate; not only was it one of the largest in the vicinity, but it also had a pair of wavy lines that had been carved deeply into its trunk. This was the universal symbol for the Road itself.

Seeing this, she tightened the straps of her pack, and with one great leap upward, jumped to the lowest branch and from there to the next one, and then the one beyond that, until she reached the Mother Branch itself.

There was another series of marks on the trunk there, which to any *Hwa'ni* would have seemed to be nothing more than blemishes in the bark. But for Erin, they were as clear as written letters, giving her the distance from the Cultural Center, to the next junction ahead, which was the West Branch Road. The West Branch she knew, led out across the forest until it met with the Great Mother Road and beyond this, the Road that she sought, the Three Sisters Branch, which terminated at her clan's home at Blood River Falls.

According to the marks, her destination was 80 kilometers away, and Erin calculated that it would take her at least two days, and possibly part of a third, to reach it. Squinting up through the canopy, she also saw that it was just after noon, and knew that barring any difficulties, she could expect to reach the Great Mother Road sometime near dusk. Worst case, she would use one of the Nests to spend the night, and complete the first segment of her trip the following morning.

The Nests were places along the Roads where the branches had been woven together to create platforms large enough for women to camp in. To protect its occupants from the Neversaw, the Nests were also regularly painted with a genetically engineered pheromone that signaled 'danger' to the creature. In addition, wherever they were well used, there was the added preventative scent of the Nemesians themselves. The Neversaw had learned to avoid the forest women whenever possible and tended to restrict its attacks to soft outlanders and children who had wandered too far from their mothers. It knew that an encounter with an adult Nemesian woman was a fight with an uncertain outcome.

But absolute safety was never a given on Nemesis. Where the Nests had been neglected, there was always the danger of an attack by a rogue beast, and the prudent traveler kept their Forest Gun and their Tej knife close at hand. Even so, the Nests made travel easier, and Erin reasoned that being so close to both the Lodge and the Great Mother Road, that any that were nearby were probably well maintained.

Her route decided, Erin paused to sense the forest around her. Safe travel along the Green Road was not simply a matter of walking carefully along its branches. It also required the use of all the senses to anticipate the forests conditions, and the activities of its deadly inhabitants. As she smelled the air, and listened to the sounds around her, Erin realized to her chagrin, just how long it had been since she had last done this, and how rusty her wood-skills had become. Years aboard the *Artemis* with its confined, artificial environment had dulled her abilities, and she felt as if she were re-learning to do something that she had once taken for granted.

Damning her outworld softness, she strained herself, trying to read the signs around her. The forest was not a static place by any means; anything that lived in it, or passed through it, left traces of itself for other creatures to detect. After so long, this was an embarrassingly slow process for her, but finally, a clear picture of the world around her, and its occupants, began to emerge.

Her nose detected the musky scent of the Saa'lak, mixed in with the distinctive odor of its fresh dung on the branches above her. Then her eye picked out where a few leaves had been freshly broken off, and places where the bark had been scratched by their talons, exposing the green wood underneath. These signs told her that the herbivores had only recently passed through the area, and when she searched for them, she finally spotted them high above her, grazing on the tender leaves at the tops of the trees.

This was reassuring. Had the Neversaw been near, the herbivores would never have stopped to eat, and would have kept on the move instead. Another encouraging thing was the song of the Kla'laxx, to the north and up in the next great tree ahead of her. The small flying creatures, which were similar to Old Terra's birds, kept silent whenever danger was close.

The Road ahead, for the moment at least, was safe to travel.

Despite this good news however, there was also the scent of moisture in the air itself, and she noticed that the hairs on her forearms had risen slightly. The weather would not hold much longer, she realized. The rains, which nourished the great forest, were coming, perhaps in an hour or less, and they would slow her down considerably.

Not wanting to waste a single minute of the good weather while it still held, she set herself in motion along the Mother Branch. For the *Hwa'ni*, this would have seemed daunting, but for her it was as natural and as fast as walking on the ground. Her prehensile tail gave her perfect balance on the narrow limb, and her foot talons ensured her a sound footing. When she reached it, the end of the Mother Branch joined up with the next tree in the line, and she leapt over the joint, heedless of the dizzying height. Nemesian women had not only been genetically engineered to move naturally among the trees, but they also possessed no fear of heights whatsoever. Like the Aviaa of Tetris, Erin's people were comfortable in such a setting and this, along with their fierceness, was what made them ideal fighter pilots when they chose to leave their motherworld.

Erin kept herself in constant motion, until at last she came to the Great Mother Road itself. This was not only marked out by signs carved into the tree trunks, but by the fact that the branches that composed it were considerably larger than the ones on the West Road—so much so that two women could walk side by side along them, with room to spare. Their wide traveling surfaces were well worn from generations of foot traffic, and she was able to quicken her pace considerably.

By this time however, the weather had begun to arrive. The skies had darkened and the first tentative drops of water were starting to reach her under the canopy. There was a Nest up ahead, she recalled, and she wrestled with the choice to avail herself of its shelter, or press on.

Despite foot talons and retractable claws, travel along the thinner, smaller branches of the lesser Roads could still be dangerous in wet conditions, and while the huge Mother Road presented no such difficulties, she reluctantly had to admit to herself that she was out of shape, and tired. The Nest, she decided, would be a welcome break.

A few standard minutes later, she found it. The platform was off to one side of the great branch. It was smaller than most of its kind, and only seemed able to accommodate one or two women at best, but it was perfect for her needs and she stepped onto it, grateful for the respite that it offered.

With the rain kept at bay by another arrangement of branches and vines overhead, Erin was able to open her pack and inspect its contents without getting anything wet. She found that the the Haus'ka woman had been generous indeed. In addition to an extra set of clothes, a small heat generator and ammunition, she had also packed her some Szz'zllik bugs, wrapped in soft bark to keep them alive and moist. These fat insects weren't Erin's favorite fare, but they far surpassed the stale protein bars that she had brought with her from Treetop, and they were alive and therefore reasonably edible.

Activating the tiny heat generator, Erin dug into her meal with more enthusiasm than she had expected to feel. When she was sated at last, she unpacked a final item, a thing her people called a *Ch'ma'an't'a*. This was a sheet of water-repellent leather that emulated the ancient poncho of Old Terra. It could serve as a personal rain-cover, a small tent, or in her case, a blanket. She adjusted the output of her heater unit, and after making sure that her Forest Gun was near at hand, drew the *Ch'ma'an't'a* over herself.

For a time, she simply lay there, listening to the sounds of the forest around her. The cries of predator and prey mixed together with the soft patter of the rain, the whisper of the wind and the creaking limbs of the great trees themselves. This was the song of the forest itself and her ears recognized its familiar rhythm; it had sung to her as a child, and then a girl, and finally as a woman. As its endless symphony of life, and death, played in her ears, she found it hard to believe that she had not been transported back in time, to a night long before she had ever even dreamed of seeking out adventure in the Land-Above-the-Sky. Somewhere in the act of remembering this, the forest's song lulled her to sleep.

She awoke just before dawn, at that strange hour that was between night and day, and yet neither. It took a few moments for her to get her bearings in the grey gloaming, and then to realize that she was no longer aboard the *Artemis*, but lying in the comforting arms of the Great Mother Forest herself.

The rain had ended, and the fresh clean scent of the jungle greeted her nostrils. It was a heady mixture of green plants, dark rich earth, the scent of a thousand flowers and the odors of the forest's animals, all mixed and distilled into one great essence. Her genetically heightened sense of smell caught every nuance, and she took in deep hungry breaths of it, savoring all its richness like a religious sacrament. It was life, at its most primal level, and in all its glory.

At last, as Rahdwa's light began to gild the world around her in splendor, she broke off from her reverie and began her preparations for the day. Breakfast was what was left of the Szz'zllik bugs and the last of her protein bars, washed down with plain water, and she made brief work of them before packing her possessions and resuming her journey.

When the heavy, damp heat of noon arrived, she stopped to hunt for lunch. This proved to be a large *Lzzk'al* bug—a fatter, tastier cousin of the insects she had dined on the night before, along with a handful of *Gr'vaa'wa* worms. The wood-boring insects were the perfect complement to the *Lzzk'al,* and a handful of sweet *El'as'ka* berries that she found served as dessert and topped off her meal.

With her stomach full and her spirits buoyed, she pressed on, and by the late afternoon, she had reached the Three Sisters junction. Once more, she paused to hunt, and after finding herself another meal, she went along the Road only as long as it took her to find a Nest. She could have continued onwards, but she wanted to be well rested for what she knew she would face when she reached her final destination.

***

It was late in the morning of the next day when she realized that she was no longer alone on the Three Sisters Road. There wasn't anything overt that announced this, just a sense that there were other women in the area. *Who* they were was the question. This was Minna territory, but the warning she had received from Jaala taur Haus'ka about the wandering Waus'ka bands had made her nervous, and she moved along the Mother branches at a slower, more cautious pace. She wasn't happy that this would add time to her journey, but she was still in the process of re-acclimatizing herself to the Great Green, and she didn't want to miss any sign of an enemy's approach by being too hasty.

An hour later, her company arrived. She didn't hear them coming, but she felt the wind as they dropped down from above, and the slight, soft vibration of their feet as they landed on the Mother Branch behind her. She drew her Tej knife, and spun around.

Her readiness to fight instantly turned into embarrassment. It was her sister, Keela. To compound matters, the woman's pairmate, Laaret had descended with her.

Erin's face flushed as she re-sheathed her blade. Had she been able to, she would have gladly crawled into the nearest borehole and hidden herself inside. If the two women had been enemies, they would have had her at a gross disadvantage. It was a mistake that only a *Hwa'ni* and little girls would have made.

"*Hai'a Sh'tun'aq*" she said, trying not to meet her sister's eyes.

Keela ignored her greeting and addressed her companion instead. "Ho, sister!" she said, "Look what we have discovered scuttling among the branches! It is a *Hwa'ni*, dressed up to look like one of us. But see her red hair? That is what gives her away. No one born of our people would have such hair!"

The woman's observation was painfully correct. The natural hair color for Nemesian women was green, like their skin. But Erin had dyed hers shortly after leaving Nemesis for the shock value. And then after a time, she'd simply grown accustomed to the shade and had kept it that way. Keela knew this of course, but couldn't resist the chance to jape her about it.

"And see!" Keela went on, taking all of her in with a grand wave, "She even has a Tej knife, just like a real woman would! There are also victory scars marking her arms!"

"I think that she stole that knife," Laaret remarked accusingly, "And those scars must be from some *Hwa'ni* accident. They certainly cannot be the marks of any great deeds."

Keela's brow knotted and she shook her head. "No, sister, I think that we are both wrong. I think that perhaps this strange creature is no *Hwa'ni* at all, but a Mist-Woman. You know, I had a sister once that looked very much like her. She went off to the Land-Above the-Sky. This must be her ghost coming back to haunt us."

"It is good to see that you are both well", Erin interjected, trying not to fuel their taunting.

But Keela was not done with her yet. "Yes, that has to be it!" she said to Laaret. "I recognize her voice now! The Mist-Woman talks to me in the voice of my long lost sister! And she looks just as my sister did in life, even down to her strange hair. Can this be? Or can this be a person of flesh——and if so—how could she be of our Clan and yet be so careless in the forest?"

"That is a great mystery, indeed," Laaret agreed somberly. "Perhaps she *is* your sister, having lived too long among the *Hwa'ni* to manage herself any better than a little girl would. I think that if that is true, that we should take her to the *Pak'un* before she hurts herself playing at grown women's games."

"Yes," Keela replied thoughtfully. "You are right; that would be best. And if she is a Mist-Woman, she will certainly vanish before we reach our home, and not trouble us any further."

Erin sighed raggedly and tried to redirect the conversation once more. "How are our mothers?" she asked. "Are they also well?"

Keela's expression suddenly softened, and shrugging deeply, she panted. It was a Nemesian's way of laughing. Then she rushed forwards and embraced her. "Greetings my *Hwa'ni* sister! Welcome back from the Land-Above-The Sky! We have missed you here in the Real World!"

***

Like Tetris, Nyx and Tethys, Nemesis was a Bio-World. Its original settlers had believed in the principles of Biosyncronism; a 24th century movement that had espoused two central doctrines concerning the human colonization of other worlds.

The First Bio Principle was that instead of terra-forming a planet to suit humans, that humans needed to genetically adapt themselves to the conditions of the world that they settled on. The result was a radical new idea of what it was to be human, with a wider, stranger variation of racial differences than had ever existed on Old Gaia. The flying women of Tetris, the super-albinos of Nyx, the amphibians of Tethys and the forest women of Nemesis all owed their genetic heritage to this radical policy, and were rightly called by some historians 'the children of the Bio Movement'.

The Second Bio Principle was that the human footprint on the local ecosystem had to be as limited as possible. This shaped a series of laws and practices that severely restricted the construction of artificial structures. It also resulted in some innovative solutions when it came to creating homes and industrial plants. For the Nemesians, the answer was the *Pak'un*.

The Pak'un varied in size, from small versions that housed only a few women, to larger models that could accommodate entire villages. In form, it was a large round platform kept permanently suspended off the ground by a ring of anti-gravity pods. Housing and living spaces sat in a ring atop the platform, arranged around a central common area.

For industrial purposes, such as logging operations, which were allowed under strict reforestation guidelines, special modules could be slung underneath, neatly combining living space for the workers right along with their place of business.

Except for the 'grav units, the Pak'un was constructed entirely out of a combination of local wood and biodegradable plastics. With proper care, a

Pak'un could last for generations, and even hundreds of years. But because of the eco-friendly materials that had been used to make it, when its service life was over, it could be lowered to the forest floor, stripped of its 'grav units, and left to decompose back into the soil, leaving nothing behind.

Floating over the jungle, the Pak'un not only adhered to the Second Bio Principle, but also provided a safe haven for its occupants from the planet's predators. Far from being a drab, strictly utilitarian place however, the Pak'un was first and foremost a home, and the center of Nemesian life. For this reason, the wooden surfaces of the Pak'uns tended to be elaborately painted and carved by the Woodsingers, the master craftswomen of the clan. Many of these vessels were correctly considered to be works of the wood carver's art in their own right.

The Minna Clan counted five Pak'uns as their own; four smaller ones that served strictly as housing, and the fifth and the largest, which also acted as the clan's social and industrial center. It was this fifth Pak'un that greeted Erin's eyes as she climbed up from the Mother Branch to the wooden platform that served it as an aerial dock.

Keela hailed it with her psiever, and as the craft drifted slowly in their direction, Erin drank in the sight of it. Like its smaller companions, it was richly emblazoned with stylized images of Fighting Bird, and in keeping with Minna tradition, the prevailing colors were blue and white. The Pak'un was a familiar sight, and despite her extreme misgivings about meeting with her mothers, a welcome one.

"You never did answer my question, sister," she said as the Pak'un reached them. "How are our mothers?"

"Well enough," Keela replied. "Teela is still the same patient woman she has always been, and Saly'aa is just as stubborn." Then her expression became serious. "You know that they will not look upon your return with any happiness."

Erin nodded resignedly. "I do not expect them to, but I must see them."

"As you will," Keela replied. "But they may not wish to see you."

Her sister's prediction proved painfully correct. When the woman manning the gangplank saw who it was, word was sent that she had arrived, and this was followed by a quick reply; her mothers did not want to come and greet her.

But Erin had traveled too far to meekly accept this. "I will wait then", she replied.

As they started across the gangplank, Keela stopped her for a moment. "I am sorry for this, *sh'tun'aq,*" she said. "But I can at least offer you a bed with us in my *sl'il'tx*. There is an extra *sk'wel'pan* there for you to sleep on."

"H'sxw'qeh," Erin answered.

Because it was midday, most of the women were out in the forest, gathering plants for processing on Treetop, or hunting. The few that remained, mostly the very young who had not yet gone on their Tej, or the very old, worked in the open center of the platform. There, they either sorted what plants had already been gathered, or worked animal skins, talking all the while. It was a familiar sight, and Erin's ears welcomed the sound of their gossip. She had grown up around such scenes, and had learned the subtle nuances of living life among her people that way.

But as she and her companions passed, the women paused and fell silent. They only resumed speaking when they had gone by, and then in conspiratorial whispers. *It is because of me,* she realized unhappily. *To them, I am an outsider.*

Keela didn't miss this, and urged her into her *sl'il'tx,* the living quarters that she shared with her pairmate. "Do not mind them," she said. "They are just foolish old women, and silly children who have no manners. You are welcome with us. Come, sister." Erin frowned back at the group and let herself be led away.

***

That night, she did not fall asleep right away; the sting of her reception, and her worries over her mothers conspired together to rob her of her rest. But the great green moon of Nemesis, Mi'mi'ya, the Whispering Woman, was full and it sat in the sky like a Selenite bride, beautiful and pure. Its gentle, emerald light shone through the wooden slats of the window of her sister's living quarters, bathing the inside of the *sl'il'tx* and touching everything inside with its caress. And her *sk'wel'pan*, the traditional sleeping mat woven from vegetable fibers, was thick and comfortable, smelling of childhood and happier times. In the end, these won the battle, and she managed to drift off.

The next day, she attempted to venture out into the common area again. She received the same cold welcome from her clanswomen as the day before, and after only half an hour of this, went back into her sister's *sl'il'tx,* where she remained. Keela and Laaret made no comment, but carried on with her as if everything was normal.

Erin knew better, though. She also understood that she had no alternative, but to bear it all stoically, and wait.

Another day passed, and then another, before Teela finally came to visit. The old woman had brought her tea set with her in its wooden traveling box. The set was made from dark Chasadan stone, with matching cups, and it was very old, having been passed down from mother to daughter for generations. Bringing a tea set was a traditional gesture that any visitor to another woman's home rigidly observed.

While Keela brewed them all a pot of razor-root tea, Erin followed convention and sat across from her mother, saying nothing. Unlike her pairmate, Saly'aa, or even Erin herself, Teela was short and stocky. But she moved with a greater hesitancy than Erin could ever recall seeing before. Her light green skin also had more dark patches where age had mottled it, and there were wrinkles crisscrossing her face that had never been there before.

She is getting old, Erin realized. It was hard for her not to rise right then and there and go to embrace the woman, but she didn't want to defy custom any more than she already had, and remained seated.

The tea arrived, and for a time, no one drank it. Then Teela took up her cup and sipped at it slowly. Erin followed suit, and waited.

"The tea is good," Teela finally said.

"Yes, *H'ama,*" Erin agreed. "It is."

"It is also good to see you *Ni'na.*"

"And you *H'ama,*" Erin replied.

"But I wonder why you have returned from the Land-Above-The-Sky to the Real World." Teela returned.

"I have returned to find myself again, *H'ama*." Erin said plainly. "I lost my way."

Teela frowned. "Saly'aa knew that would happen when you stopped being a pilot."

"What must I do, *H'ama*?"

"I am not certain", Teela answered somberly. "Saly'aa and the other *Si'am* will have to be the ones to make such a decision. But I will speak with Saly'aa on your behalf."

With that, she drained her cup and signaled to Keela. The younger woman quietly gathered up the pot and the cups, and then went off to clean them. When she returned, they were back in their traveling-box, which Teela took from her. Then, with Keela's assistance, the old woman stood, and left without saying another word.

Another day passed before Erin received any word about a meeting with Saly'aa. When it arrived, it was Keela who was the messenger. Erin was out on the Three Sisters Road, trying to enjoy the morning and her solitude, and this time, her sister was kind enough not to sneak up on her. The two met on a section of the Road that overlooked Blood River Falls, the waterfall that lent the area its name.

"Saly'aa asked me to find you and bring you to her" the woman said plainly.

Erin looked away from the falls and met her sister's eyes. "I am surprised that she agreed to see me," she said. She had fully expected for her mother to spurn her, and had already begun to make plans for her return to the *Artemis*, and whatever life she could salvage for herself there.

"She did not agree," Keela informed her. "She and Teela had a terrible fight."

And Teela won, Erin thought. As irascible as Saly'aa was, Teela always won their arguments in the end. Where Saly'aa was fire, Teela was water, wearing her opponents down through sheer, quiet persistence. It had always been that way between the two of them.

"I will come," she said.

***

Saly'aa was waiting for Erin in the *sl'il'tx* that she and Teela had shared since their daughters had grown to adulthood. As Erin had fully expected, their meeting was to be a formal one. Two other women who acted as elders in the Minna Clan were also present, and Saly'aa was seated cross-legged with them on the pelts of Neversaw beasts, a clear sign of their authority as leaders, and the gravity of the gathering.

Erin entered the room and greeted the assembly before taking her place on the woven mat in front of them. Only Saly'aa did not return the acknowledgement. Her pupil-slits were narrowed with anger and her tail flicked in agitation. The fight with her pairmate must have been truly stellar in magnitude, Erin reflected.

They shared an uncomfortable silence for several minutes before Saly'aa finally broke it. "Who is it that has come to the Pak'un of the Minna?" the woman intoned.

"I, Erin taur Minna," Erin replied.

"There is no one living among us with that name!" Saly'aa snapped. "The one I called *Ni'na*, my daughter, lost the right to bear that name when she abandoned her honor! You are *not* Erin taur Minna, but Erin taur *Ewen'a,* Erin of *No Clan*."

Erin's heart sank, but she bit back the protest that had started to form on her lips. *Erin of No Clan,* she thought. She had lost any right to call herself a Minna. Although she had suspected that this might occur, the reality of it cut into her deeply.

She drew in a ragged breath. "Yes," she finally said. "I am Erin taur Ewen'a"

"And what would this *woman-of-no-people* want with the Minna?" Saly'aa demanded with disdain.

"I would have my name restored, and have a place again among the people I call my family." Erin replied. "I would know what I must do to regain my honor."

Saly'aa panted derisively. "*You* would regain your honor? I am not so sure that it *can* be regained! Look at you! You bear the marks of victories on your arms that I have not seen before. But what of these victories? They are nothing but the deeds of a chair fighter!"

She waved at the scars on Erin's arms, dismissing them completely. "You left your honor behind you—and not only once, but twice! First you left the Mother Forest. If you had stayed like your sister Keela had and served the clan as she does, it would still be intact.'

"But you left against my wishes. Even after this, you could have retained it, like your sister Skylaar. She wins her victories working for the Hwa'ni, but *her* marks are for deeds done by her own hand. *You* left the cockpit of your fighter to let other women do your fighting for you! Now I think that your honor wanders the stars looking for another home and I am not sure that it will ever find you again."

Erin hung her head in shame. "You were right mother," she said quietly. "I admit that. My spirit is sick with the path I have found myself on. I must find my way back." A single tear slid down her face and splashed onto the mat. "Please, I beg you."

An eternity of silence passed before Saly'aa replied. "We will discuss this among ourselves, and see if this thing can be fixed—or if it *should* be fixed," she said sternly. Then at a signal from her, everyone rose and left the room, leaving Erin alone with her despair.

Hours passed, and Erin remained where she was. At points, she thought she heard the sound of voices being raised, and at other times, only silence. Whatever the decision was to be, there was nothing she could do about it though, and she stopped listening. Instead, she prayed to Fighting Bird and the ancestors to look upon her with favor, and give her the chance to redeem herself.

When the *Si'am* finally returned, Saly'aa pronounced their verdict. "Erin taur Ewen'a, we have decided that if you are to regain your name, and your honor, you must pay a price. You must go to the camp of Lay'sa taur Hai'ska, the Woodsinger. You are to ask her to carve a ki'ask'a telling the Real World of your shame—and your redemption—*if* you can find it. You must do whatever she asks, and give her whatever she requires to pay for it."

Erin's heart, already heavy with all that had transpired, now felt as weighty as a neutron star. Woodsingers were not only skilled carvers. They were also shamans, and her childhood had been filled with tales of all the terrible things that they could ask for.

There was no arguing with Saly'aa however, or the demands that tradition placed on her. Her fate, whatever it was to be, was now completely in Lay'sa taur Hai'ska's hands. Hoping that the price would be small never even crossed her mind; that was an utter impossibility.

"Do not return to us until this has been done and the ki'ask'a has been planted on our lands," Saly'aa added. "There is no more I have to say to you. Go away from here today."

Erin looked up from the mat. "It will be done."

***

The Pak'un of Lay'sa taur Hai'ska was located in the Sorrowspring Valley. It was a small craft, floating by itself and housing only the Woodsinger and a few of her apprentices. After a days travel, Erin reached the area, and found Taur Hai'ska and her assistants at work in the clearing below the Pak'un, beginning the carving of a ki'ask'a for the Jee'na clan. Protected by bags of pheromone-soaked scraps of leather and impeller projectors, they were going about their business with no fear of interruption by predators.

Erin descended to the ground and walked up to them. It was impolite to interrupt a carver at their work, so she waited respectfully until the woman had paused for a break before speaking. "Greetings, Woodsinger" she said, "I am Erin taur Ewen'a and I have come to you to have a ki'ask'a made."

The Woodsinger gave her an appraising look. "You bear the markings of the Minna clan, yet you call yourself by no clan's name. What kind of ki'ask'a would such a woman desire?"

"I have come seeking a ki'ask'a of shame, and redemption," Erin answered. Then she related her story.

The carver listened quietly and when Erin had finished, she spoke. "Regaining one's honor is a very serious affair," Taur Hai'ska said solemnly, "and a ki'ask'a that would mark this would be very expensive indeed.

Tell me, what can you pay me for my time?"

Erin reached into her pack and produced the bundled-up pelt of the Neversaw beast. "I have this," she said holding it out for the carver, "the skin of the very beast that I slew on my first Tej. Is that payment enough, Woodsinger?"

The woman took the pelt, and inspected it carefully. "This is a good beginning, but as I said, such a monument would be very costly. I will need more than this to stop what I am doing right now."

"What else would you have of me, mistress carver?"

"To carve this ki'ask'a, I will need an assistant. Your spirit must be part of this work."

"I have only my time to give you," Erin said.

A full minute passed before the Woodsinger replied. "I also need you to help me prepare my workspace," she informed her. Lay'sa pointed towards a pile of rocks at the edge of the clearing. It was about the height of an average woman.

"Those rocks over there disturb the serenity of this place. I need them moved away so that I can concentrate on my work without being bothered by the sight of them."

As nonsensical as the request was, Erin could not object. "Where would you have them moved to, Woodsinger?'

"Take them over to the other side of the clearing where I do not have to see them," the woman instructed. "By the time you have done that, I may have these tools ready for the task that you have asked of me."

Erin rose and went to the pile. Each rock was the size of her head, and looked extremely heavy. She made no complaint though, and started in on her work. By the time the sun was low in the sky, her hands were covered in blisters, and her muscles felt as if they were on fire. But she had finished the job.

The carver, who had been watching her progress, stopped what she had been doing and came over to inspect her work.

"I do not like the new place they are in," she said at last. "Perhaps where they were was better for my work. Please move them back."

Erin stifled the urge to groan and began the process of relocating the stones. She kept at this until the last of the day's light had fled from the sky, and then retreated to a nearby nest, more exhausted than she had ever been before in her life.

When the dawn came, and it was light enough to see, she woke and resumed her labors. Her blisters, which had been a painful nuisance the day before, broke open somewhere in the process, and she was forced to improvise wrappings for her hands from strips of cloth torn from the top she had brought with her. Although it didn't alleviate all of the pain she felt, this measure did allow her to finish moving the last of the stones before the midday meal.

Once again, the carver stopped what she was doing and came over. "This arrangement still does not promote a feeling of harmony," the woman announced. "You must move the stones to another place." She indicated a spot in the center of the clearing. "Move them there and perhaps I will consider carving your ki'ask'a."

Again, Erin made no protest. Binding her hands with additional wrappings, she forced herself to walk over to the stones, and began to move them. The pain in her hands was extreme by this point, and her strength was waning, causing her to drop many of the rocks as she tried to carry them. But even though she wanted to sit down and cry in frustration, she stifled her tears, and carried on.

This is what a hunter does, she told herself, *she ignores her discomfort and fights on, no matter what. I am a hunter of the Minna clan. I will finish my task and nothing will stop me.* It became a mantra for her, lending her strength.

Finally, as she lifted the last stone in place, the Woodsinger came over to consider her work. While she looked the pile over, Erin readied herself for the rejection that she was sure would follow. How she would manage to move the stones a fourth time was utterly beyond her, but she was determined to keep going for as long as her body would allow. It was either that, or throw away any chance of fully regaining her honor, and her name.

"I suppose this arrangement will have to do," the Woodsinger said with grudging approval. "It is a good beginning at least. But I will need you to do something else for me now; I will need better tools. The ones I have here are not adequate to the task. They are too dull. Fetch new ones for me. I think I left a better set in the Pak'un of Tan'yar'a, the Woodsinger of the Ana'gashi clan when I visited her last spring."

Erin knew that the territory of the Ana'gashi clan was several days away using the Green Road, but she had no choice. "I will get them for you, mistress."

"You will use the Nis'ka Road to get yourself there, and none other," the Woodsinger instructed her. "It will shorten the way by several days."

Erin was familiar with the route, if only by its history. The Nis'ka Road was one of the smaller offshoots of the Green Road. Three hundred years earlier, when it had led through the territory of the Nis'ka clan, it had been as important as the Three Sisters Road.

But one of the mysterious diseases that the forest sometimes gave birth to had reduced the Nis'ka's numbers beyond their ability to maintain themselves as a clan. Having no other alternatives, those that had survived the epidemic had left their Pak'uns and intermarried with the Minna and Haus'ka clans. No one lived in the area any longer, nor called the territory theirs, and although it was certainly a shortcut, the Road was indifferently maintained at best. The Woodsinger had given her instructions, however, and her route had been decided.

"I will use the Road as you instruct," she said.

"That is good," Taur Hai'ska replied. Then her gaze became distant, and Erin realized that she was seeing beyond the world around them, into the realm of the spirits. "And when you walk it, take careful note of any strangers you meet along the way."

"I will, Woodsinger." Erin wasn't sure what she had meant by this, but she didn't question her about it. She simply gathered her things and departed.

The Nis'ka Road proved to be just as bad as Erin had expected. For the first kilometer, the Road was easy enough to travel, but as she moved further and further away from the Great Mother Road, its condition deteriorated rapidly. She began to encounter many places where untrained branches had grown across the path, or where strangler vines grew in tangles, blocking the way completely.

In these places, she was either forced to negotiate a way around, or use her Tej knife to cut through. The process proved exhausting, and time consuming. By the end of the first day, she had only progressed a few kilometers, and finally took shelter in the rather dubious safety of a Nest, that from the look of it, had gone unused for months, if not longer. Because of its poor condition, Erin took the additional step of adding some of the Neversaw fear-pheromone to the branches, and then followed through by coating herself with the stuff. It only followed that on a Road as seldom used as this one, that the Neversaw would be much bolder and she didn't want one as a traveling companion, or a surprise visitor in the night.

Thanks to her unease, sleep came with difficulty, and the following morning she awoke to find that a heavy fog had come up around her in the night. Breakfast was a brief affair, and she pressed onwards, hoping that the mists would lift when the sun warmed the forest. But the elements conspired against her just as the foliage had, and the fog stayed thick. Finally, at noon, she stopped to take a short break to apply some more of the Neversaw pheromone and consume a light snack.

As she sat there on her haunches, gnawing on a protein bar, she felt something change in the forest around her. Having already been ambushed by her sister and the woman's pairmate, she knew the feeling for what it was. Someone was coming down the Road. Whoever it was walked very softly though; there were none of the telltale vibrations of a footstep coming to her through the mother branch, and for a moment she doubted her senses.

Then the unmistakable shape of a woman materialized in the greyness, becoming sharper as she drew closer. Erin's hand strayed to her Tej knife, and she tensed as the stranger's features became recognizable.

The woman was about her age, and dressed for the forest just as she was. There was something odd about the cut of her garments that Erin could not place though, and she reasoned that this was because the visitor was from another clan, with different ideas about the design of their clothing.

Not that fashion concerned her just then. The main issue was whether she was an enemy or not, but then Erin saw that although the figure carried a forest rifle and a Tej knife, her hands were empty.

Their eyes met, and the stranger shrugged amicably. "Hello," she said, "Can you tell me the way to the Mother Road?"

The question was complete nonsense. There was only one way to reach the Mother Road and they were standing on it. And there was also something about the way the woman had asked the question—about her entire demeanor in fact—that raised Erin's hackles. Something wasn't right, but its precise shape was as uncertain as the mists around them.

A distant part of her, hearkening back to her childhood, warned her against speaking with supernatural beings, and as silly as this was, Erin instinctively honored it. Instead of answering the visitor, she merely pointed back in the direction of the Mother Road.

"*H'sxw'qeh*, sister," the figure replied, giving her another friendly shrug.

Erin stepped back a pace as the woman walked past and down the branch. As her form disappeared into the gloom, she finally became conscious of what it was that had created so much unease, and she was surprised that it had only half-registered in her mind until just that moment.

It had been the stranger's face mark. Her tattoo had been that of the Nis'ka Clan. Erin was absolutely positive of this. She had come to know the design as a little girl, as part of the education every Nemesian child received to help them recognize clan affiliations. But this was impossible. There were no Nis'ka any more, and no one would wear such a thing capriciously.

Determined to question the woman about this anomaly, she headed after her. Only a few seconds had passed, and she was confident that she would spot her walking along the branch. No one was there to find however. The Mother Branch was empty.

A few more minutes passed before she realized that her pursuit was futile. Somehow, the woman had simply vanished. Erin looked below her, to see if the figure had possibly slipped and fallen to the ground, and then up above her to the higher branches, looking for any sign of an ascent. There was no trace of her anywhere.

A shudder passed down her spine as another piece of childhood knowledge surfaced and she immediately denied it. Mist-Women did not exist, she told herself. Only superstitious clan-women like her sisters, and little children, believed in such nonsense. But the fact that the stranger *was* gone was as undeniable as the mark on her face had been.

Erin left the area before any other strange things occurred.

Thankfully, the remainder of her trip was fairly uneventful and allowed her to put the strange encounter out of her mind. The only exception was a nest of Beth'beks near the Road, and she had taken the simple expedient of treading softly as she had passed them by. Left alone, the bat-like creatures had had little interest in her, their primary prey being the Saa'lak and *Hwa'ni* stupid enough to disturb their rest. And when she finally reached the Pak'un of Tan'yar'a, the Woodsinger was only too glad to give her shelter for the night and the tools she had been sent for.

Unfortunately however, her only route back was the same way she had come, and once more, she found herself on the Nis'ka Road. The fog had also rejoined her, and it not only slowed her progress considerably, but also added to her anxiety.

On the evening of the second day down the Road, she sensed again that she was not alone. This time though, there was nothing subtle about the signs that alerted her. The Mother Branch began to vibrate, faintly at first, and then with increasing intensity and Erin knew, despite all the time she had spent off planet, that it heralded a party of travelers. They were moving fast, and headed her way.

At the moment this occurred, she was between two of the great trees in the middle of the Mother Branch, and there was no place close by to hide. She spared the briefest of glances for the forest floor below her, but the fog made it impossible to gauge her distance from it. The last she had seen, it had been only nine meters below her, but the low visibility left her present elevation, and the safety of jumping, in doubt.

In the middle of her deliberations, she suddenly felt the unmistakable pressure of a hand on her shoulder. She had just enough time to gasp in alarm before an invisible presence pushed her off the limb. Clawing frantically for any handhold, she fell into the mists. A second later, she hit a branch and tumbled off.

Another rushed up at her, and she grabbed for it. It briefly held her weight, but then it snapped and she fell again, crashing through several more limbs before finally hitting the ground. The impact knocked the breath from her, and as she struggled to regain it, she looked up and saw a group of women pointing down at her and shouting.

Even from that distance, Erin recognized them as Waus'ka, and they confirmed this when one of them fired a round from her Forest Gun. The shot missed her by a wide margin, and she knew that had the woman wanted to, she could have hit her easily. Instead, it had been fired as a warning and a challenge, and there was no telling from this how far the group intended to go with things. Clan feuds were complicated affairs and any confrontation could be limited to a simple chase, a good drubbing, or something much more deadly.

Erin had no intention of waiting around to find out which it would be, and scrambled to her feet. A sharp pain lanced through her side, and she realized that she had either broken a rib in the fall, or bruised it badly. But she had no time to minister to it; the band was heading for the nearest tree and climbing down. Cursing all Waus'ka and their ancestors, she gritted her teeth and ran.

Although she knew that she momentarily enjoyed an advantage, it didn't take a Nullspace physicist to understand that her situation was a desperate one. In addition to her injury, the weight of her pack was slowing her down, and her pursuers were comparatively unencumbered.

But the fog, which had impeded her for so much of her return journey, suddenly became her ally. It thickened as she moved along, wrapping itself around her, and concealing her from the Waus'ka women. The fading light added to this effect, and she could hear the Waus'ka calling to each other, trying to find her. By the tone of their voices, she could tell that they were becoming angry, and she smiled grimly to herself.

Then, up ahead, she caught the unmistakable odor of Wasauk beasts. She looked for another direction to run to, not wanting to encounter a pack of the predators, but the footfalls of the Waus'ka behind her decided her course of action for her. She pressed forwards, making as much noise as she was capable of, and desperately hoping that this would frighten the beasts out of her path. Abruptly, the wind shifted in her favor, and she was upwind of the creatures.

Her human scent, intermingled with the Neversaw pheromone she had applied to herself, reached the beasts. They panicked and scattered. But one Wasauk, an old bull who was either too old to join the flight, or too sick, did not run. Instead, he wheeled around on his stubby legs and opened his mouth wide, exposing row after row of arm length fangs. With a roar, he charged at her, and Erin fired into his gullet, shattering the huge teeth and tearing his mouth and tongue to shreds.

The thing died in mid-stride. Ordinarily, this would have given her cause to celebrate, and add a victory mark to her shoulder, but her pursuers were gaining on her and she had no time for ceremony.

Leaping over the still-wiggling corpse, she ran on, her trigger finger ready for anything else that had a notion to offer opposition. But thanks to the wind, and their racket, the forest's children knew that she and the other Nemesians were there, and fled from them. A few minutes later, and without further incident, she arrived at the edge of a sharp drop-off that overlooked a small lake.

Erin knew from her upbringing that such waters, while they looked safe enough, were often home to the Ana'gashi, a species of carnivorous amphibian, and she tried to spot them among the reeds and on the muddy banks. Before she could verify her safety however, or find a way to climb down, there was a loud report and a round flew by her ear. The Waus'ka women had found her again. Hoping that the water was deep enough, and clear of the deadly herpetiles, she dove off the ledge headfirst. Another bullet sought her as she hit the surface and sank, but it missed.

Then a new and unexpected danger presented itself. To her horror, she realized that the additional weight of the Woodsinger's tools was pulling her down to the muddy bottom. With no other choice, Erin wrestled herself out of her pack straps and let the precious thing go. As it sank away into the darkness, she clawed her way upwards, managing to gulp a single, precious breath when she broke the surface.

More shouts came from behind her, and another shot rang out. It too missed, but only by a hairsbreadth, and she dove once more, going deep and swimming for the opposite bank with every ounce of strength she had.

Any doubts she had had about the intentions of the Waus'ka were completely gone now. They meant to kill her if they could.

Rising only to take a few more mouthfuls of air, she spotted a stand of reeds and made for it. It was just the kind of place that the Ana'gashi loved to hide in, and she drew her Tej knife in readiness as she inserted herself into the stand. If they had been there at all however, the amphibians were not in evidence, and she returned her attention to the Waus'ka.

By this point, they were moving down the side of the ledge and making their way towards her. Looking to her right, she saw another stand of reeds only a short distance off, and beyond this, a game trail that led back up into the forest.

Erin submerged again and headed for it, and when the water turned shallow, she half-crawled, half swam until she reached the concealment of the reeds. She hazarded a glance to see how far the Waus'ka women had progressed, and then she rose up and ran for the trail. The Waus'ka saw her do this of course, but once again she had a slight lead on them, and she took full advantage of it, gaining as much distance as possible.

A noise issued out from somewhere up ahead of her, and as she listened, she realized that it was the sound of a human voice. It was faint at first, but as she closed the distance, she even thought that she heard her name being called. She had no way of knowing if the voice was that of a friend, or a clever trick being played upon her by her enemies, but there was no other way to run. Fishing out one of her remaining rifle clips from a hip pouch, she traded it for the empty one, and advanced cautiously.

The voice seemed to grow fainter and further away with every step, and then at last, it stopped entirely, leaving only the sounds of the forest and the cries of the Waus'ka women to fill her ears. Even so, she stayed alert for any sign of an ambush.

Then, a little further on, the trees thinned, and she came out into an open meadow. What she saw there made her gasp.

It was a Pak'un. Half of it had collapsed and the rest was well into the process of rotting away. This in and of itself was not what had startled her; when they reached the end of their service life, Pak'uns were either dismantled for their building materials, or left to biodegrade back into the earth.

What astonished her was that the Pak'uns markings made it out to be a Nis'ka dwelling, which meant that it was at least three centuries old, or even older. Despite the fact that the wood that the Pak'uns were made of was thoroughly treated to resist the depredations of the Nemesian environment, Erin had never heard of one lasting for as long as this one had. The Pak'un was an utter impossibility, sitting right there in front of her.

She didn't have the time to determine the cause of its amazing preservation however. She could hear the Waus'ka women gaining on her, and she weighed her options. Running through the forest was one, but her strength was fading and she knew that it was only a matter of time before they overtook her on the trail. This left the ruined Pak'un, and the desperate hope that the Waus'ka would consider it such an obvious hiding place that they would bypass it. In either case, the odds against her were long.

Erin made her choice, and ran for the Pak'un, hoping that it would offer enough shadows to hide in, or if worse came to worse, furnish her with a place to set an ambush. A huge hole gaped wide on one side of the wreck and as she darted inside, the darkness enveloped her. Navigating more by touch than anything else, she went in as far as the wreckage would allow, and finally found a corner that seemed to offer the best position to hold off an assault.

Covering entrance with her rifle, she braced for an attack. *If this is to be my end,* she vowed, *then so be it. At least I will die knowing I did so with honor.* Her only regret was that her clan would never know that she had finally redeemed herself.

Outside, the Waus'ka had reached the clearing, and as Erin glanced through a gap in the wooden wall, she saw that they were arguing. By their gestures, it was obvious that they were trying to choose whether to investigate the Pak'un, or continue on down the trail. She tensed, expecting that they would end the debate by choosing the Pak'un.

Then she heard someone cry out, and realized that it was the same voice that had lured her into the meadow and the Pak'un. This time, it had come from somewhere down the trail, and well away from the clearing.

As one, the Waus'ka looked up, and ran towards it. Erin waited, and when the band did not return, she knew that whoever it had been had drawn them away. But she wasn't about to count on the ruse working forever, and quickly left her hiding place.

Halfway back to the Green Road, she stopped, slung her rifle over her shoulder and climbed up into a tree. It was becoming dark by this point, and she knew the foolishness of attempting to travel any further. The forest floor was dangerous enough during the day, but travel during nightfall was sheer suicide.

She found a perch in the crotch of two great limbs, and settled herself in for the night. While it certainly wasn't a Nest, it was still a place of relative safety from predators, and it offered potential concealment from the Waus'ka if they returned.

Erin didn't let herself relax right away, but listened for a time, and when nothing occurred, she reached into her belt pouch and took out some *kee'tcha* for herself. The hard, flat bread was a combination of freeze-dried meat and flour made from local plants, and it was an efficient survival ration when it was combined with enough water. She discovered that she had some in another pouch on her belt, and it completed her meal. The chase had exhausted her, and she was famished.

As she ate, she decided that she would retrace her steps in the morning, and if the Huntress was still smiling on her, attempt to recover her pack. She wasn't at all certain of her chances; the pack had most likely buried itself deep in the mud at the bottom of the pond, and there were still the Ana'gashi to worry about. But she held onto what hope she had, and prayed for good fortune. The alternative of abandoning the tools and explaining their loss to the Woodsinger was something that she couldn't bear to contemplate.

***

When first light arrived, Erin climbed down from her tree and sought out the lake. She found that she had been correct about the Ana'gashi inhabiting the place. There were a half dozen of the creatures, who had apparently hidden themselves in the commotion of the day before. Most of them were small things, less than half a meter in length, but one was a big fellow more than a meter long, and it hissed at her as she approached.

Erin didn't waste a round from her rifle, but dispatched the thing with one well-aimed rock instead. It not only killed the beast, but also caused the rest to retreat and keep their distance. As for her pack, this proved much easier to find than she had expected. The mud at the bottom of the lake was shallow and with only a few dives, she was able to wrestle her burden back up to the surface.

By then, it was nearing late morning. As much as she wanted to move on, she forced herself to remain. Her trip was going to be a long one, and she needed the energy that only fresh meat would provide. And despite their looks, Ana'gashi was very good eating.

Great care had to be taken in their preparation though. In addition to razor sharp teeth, the creature's saliva carried a deadly neuro-poison, which was stored in sacs to either side of its great flat tongue. Unless these were properly removed, the meat would be contaminated, and she would be forced to discard it and go hungry.

Prying open its wide, flat jaws, she produced her Tej knife and carefully felt around the teeth with her fingers until she found the bulbous masses. She cut these free, and after inspecting them thoroughly to make certain that she had not ruptured them, and ruined her meal, threw them away. After that, it was a simple matter of butchering the body, and enjoying her reward.

When she had eaten her fill, she hiked away from the lake to the nearest tree in the Road, and started her climb. Her rib pained her as she made the ascent, but the discomfort had dulled considerably from the day before, and she managed to reach the Mother Branch after a few minutes of climbing. Once there, she said a prayer of thanks to the Huntress and her Ancestors for all of her good fortune. After all, she still had all of her survival gear, the precious tools, and her life.

Then she withdrew a piece of the Ana'gashi from her belt pack, and some *kee'tcha*. She still needed to show her appreciation to one other party; whatever it was that had pushed her off the limb and misdirected the Waus'ka with its calls.

"*H'sxw'qeh*," she said, "Thank you, whoever you are." She broke the bread into tiny little pieces and scattered it, along with some of the meat, to the forest floor. The fragments hit the soft earth, and the wind rose up around her, as if something unseen had heard her words, and accepted the gift. Erin listened to it sighing through the trees, and smiled.

Four days later, she reached her destination and handed the Woodsinger her tools.

"These are suited to the task," the woman said, taking them from her. "Now I have one more request to make of you, Erin-of-no-Clan."

"What would you ask of me, Woodsinger?" Erin replied, trying to mask the weariness in her voice.

"You must tell me about your journey on the Nis'ka Road. Did you meet anyone there?"

"Yes, Woodsinger, I did."

"And who did you meet? Tell me everything, and spare nothing."

Erin obeyed; she told her about the woman in the mists, the Waus'ka band, the invisible hand that had pushed her and the strange voice, and finally the Pak'un that she had hidden in.

The Woodsinger listened to her account carefully, closing her eyes at certain points to concentrate on the details. When Erin had finished, the shaman considered all that she had heard.

"I think that you met an ancestor," Lay'sa said at last. "Someone who was a distant relative of yours, after the sickness. After all, the Nis'ka and the Minna did mingle their blood. And perhaps this clanswoman came through the mists to aid you on your Tej, and it was her Pak'un that hid you from your enemies. I do not think that that Pak'un was of this world at all."

"Yes, Woodsinger," Erin replied. From a Nemesian standpoint, all of this made perfect sense, and she forcibly pushed aside her *Hwa'ni* objections when they tried to surface, and simply accepted it.

The Woodsinger had more to say. "If this is so then your labors have been blessed and I cannot ask any more of you without angering the spirits. So, you will have your *kias'ka*. Rest, eat, and when you are ready, we will begin our work."

Erin left the Woodsinger, and did as she had commanded, eating some of the food that the woman's assistant provided her, and although she was tempted to sleep, she returned to the craftswoman as soon as the meal was done. The carving of the kias'ka was too important to be delayed by something as trivial as the need for rest. Rest could wait until her Tej was over.

The Woodsinger handed her a small hide-covered drum, and directed her to sit next to her. A log cut from a S'naw'eya tree had been laid out on the grass and its bark had been stripped away to reveal the cream-white wood that made it so prized by carvers like Taur Hai'ska. A design had also been sketched out on its smooth surface and the Woodsinger's tools were laid out on a vegetable-fiber mat nearby, waiting for Lay'sa to take them in hand and begin.

"Sing for me, Erin taur Ewen'a," Lay'sa said. "Sing about your life, about your honor, and your dishonor. Sing about your battles, and about your Tej. And while you sing, I will carve."

So Erin sang, and as she did, the full weight of everything she had been through overcame her; all the losses, all the gains, the dangers, everything. Some parts she sang with tears in her eyes, and other parts with her voice lifted in joy. She put everything that she still had left of herself into the song and left nothing out.

Through it all, the Woodsinger carved with absolute concentration, as if she was not only creating the kias'ka, but also Erin herself, remaking her into a new shape. By the time the sun had set and the rough outlines of the figures had been fleshed out, Erin knew that the Woodsinger's magic had done its work. She was whole again.

***

It took several more days to finish the carvings and paint the kias'ka. Then, with the Woodsinger's help, a hoverlifter arrived a day later to take the shame pole, and Erin, back to the Minna clan. Although the carving was magnificent, she wasn't certain that it would be enough to convince the Si'am, and especially Saly'aa, to grant her her name, or her honor back. By tradition, these women had the option of refusing the offering and giving her more tasks to complete, or even banishing her forever with no hope of redemption whatsoever.

Her homecoming, and their final judgment, was as much a part of her Tej as the rest of the journey had been however. She had no choice but to face her fate bravely. No matter the outcome, there would be no retreat.

When the hoverlifter reached its destination, she saw that Saly'aa and the other Si'am had gathered in the meadow under the Pak'uns to await her. Their expressions were impassive, and while the crew unloaded the pole, Erin steeled herself for what was to come.

Some of the younger women, including Keela and Laaret, were also there, and with the help of the 'lifter crew, they raised the pole into a hole that had been dug to receive it. This was filled in with earth until the totem could stand upright on its own. When the work was finished, they stepped back, and Saly'aa and the elders came forwards to inspect the pole.

They circled the carvings slowly, taking in every detail, and speaking quietly among themselves. Then they turned as one to face her. Erin's heart leapt in her chest as she waited to hear their verdict.

Saly'aa regarded her for a long time, and then at last, she spoke. "We find it to be a good pole," she said solemnly. "The song it sings is a good song. It will be allowed to remain here so that others might hear its words, and know that Erin taur Minna regained her name, and her honor. May she never lose her way in the forest again."

With that, she and the rest of the elders turned and walked away, leaving Erin alone with her sisters and the other young women. Keela was the first to embrace her, and welcome her back to the Minna, and the Real World.

CHAPTER 4

USSNS *Pallas Athena*, Battle Group Golden, Altamara System, Frontera Provensa, Esteral Terrana Rapabla, 05|08|05:91:34

Somehow, in the process of moving into her new office, her silver czigavar case had gone missing, and Lilith was searching the drawers of her desk for it. She seriously doubted that anyone had stolen it however. It seemed far more likely that it had been stuffed away by some sailor with the intent of returning it to its rightful place in her middle drawer, once she had gotten herself unpacked.

But after an investigation of her desk failed to produce it, she moved on to some boxes that were still sitting in a corner, unopened after all the many weeks since her promotion. With some determined rummaging, she finally found the blasted thing at the bottom of one of them, and felt like cheering.

Instead, she celebrated her victory by igniting a czigavar. A message alert flashed in the corner of her vision as she took her first, triumphant drag. It was from Navcom.

"Ma'am? We have a transmission from Captain taur Minna. Would you like to see it?"

"Yes, please," she replied. She had been wondering how Erin had been getting along on her motherworld, and she hoped that the news she was about to hear was good.

Erin's holo came into view. The display underneath the woman's image informed Lilith that she was still on Nemesis. She was also wearing her Tej knife prominently on her hip, and this detail caught Lilith's eye. Erin had never done this before. Something had changed.

"Erin? How goes your leave?"

"My business here is done, Lily," Erin answered, "and I must ask you to do a thing for me."

"Anything, Erin," Lilith responded.

"I wish to resign my post as Captain of the *Artemis* and take over as Squadron Commander of the *Nighthunters* instead. Can you do this?"

Lilith was speechless. She certainly hadn't expected the outcome of

Erin's trip to be a request for a demotion. "What about Taur Reesha? Isn't she already in that position?"

"Yes, and I have spoken with her," Erin said. "She has already agreed to stand aside and serve under me as a Lieutenant, if you approve of the change." This was a relief to Lilith; the two Nemesians could have just as easily settled the issue by dueling and she couldn't have stopped them short of putting them both in the brig.

"It will of course require that I attend a refresher for the Valkyrie," Erin continued, "and that I re-certify, but I do not anticipate that taking more than another two weeks at the most. In the meantime, Taur Reesha can serve, and my Second, Suzzyn bel Jerra, can continue with her duties on the *Artemis*. She is a capable woman and she deserves the promotion to Captain if you see fit to grant it."

"I see," Lilith said, still overwhelmed by the request. "Well—I certainly don't want to lose you on the *Artemis*, but I could also use you with the *Nighthunters*, and if Taur Reesha is agreeable, then that certainly solves that problem. Bel Jerra's promotion to Captain shouldn't be an issue either. But Erin, I have to ask you—why? I'll approve all of it, but I'd like to know the reason."

"My visit taught me that the squadron is the only right place for me," the Nemesian answered. "I have been wandering for far too long."

Lilith was quite familiar with the Nemesian penchant for honor, and the odd paths that their thoughts sometimes took, so she didn't press her for any further clarification. It was enough that Erin was done with her adventure, whatever it had been, and that the battle group wouldn't be losing her talents. "I'll send the request to Rixa," she said. "As soon as the orders are approved, I'll let you know."

USSNS *Pallas Athena*, In-Orbit, Altamara, Frontera Provensa,
Esteral Terrana Rapabla, 1043.05|08|05:91:34

Erin taur Minna sat back in the cockpit of her F-90A Valkyrie fighter and let the onboard AI take them in for their final approach to the *Athena*. She had successfully completed her refresher course at the Martha McSally

Naval Base on Kevan, and had flown out to the battle group the minute that her re-cert had been issued.

Luckily, a naval convoy had been on its way to Altamara, and they had been only too happy to have her added firepower along as part of the escort force. But aside from a few Indwellers that had gotten too aggressive for their own good, the flight itself had been uneventful, and after a five-hour transit, she was glad to be back in normal space and looking at her old battle group.

When she passed it, she spared only the briefest of glances for the *Artemis*. Despite all the time she'd spent aboard the medium cruiser, the ship was Bel Jerra's now and she was welcome to it as far as Erin was concerned. It was no longer her home, or a part of her life. Her eyes were only for the *Athena*, and the place that was waiting for her there.

The Valkyrie automatically banked to port and then leveled out to line itself up with the supercruiser's hangar bay.

"Ska'neq p'estsha, Erin. Tat'sea'le'pe Athena q'uan-chi." the AI informed her in *Kl'all'a*. "Final approach, Erin. *Athena's* traffic control has cleared us for landing."

"*H'sxw'qeh*," Erin replied. When she'd been issued her fighter, she had insisted that its AI speak her mother tongue in addition to Standard—with Nemesian being the default for internal cockpit communications. Although Erin was embarrassed to admit it, she thought more in Standard now than in anything else, and having everything in Nemesian forced her out of this habit and back into the proper direction.

Another healthy change had been her call sign. Call signs were an ancient tradition hearkening back to the days of air-breathing jets. Normally, they were first given to a new pilot by other pilots, and they tended to highlight something that the rookie wanted to forget. It was only after they had distinguished themselves, and earned the respect of the veterans, that they were allowed to adopt a more dignified name for themselves.

Erin had been through it all, starting off her career like a lot of rookies did by simply being referred to as "*FanF*" which stood for "*Fek! Atre Neu Faam!*" or *"Fuck! Another New Girl!"* but after going through all the usual growing pains, she'd managed to win "*Gungrrl*" for herself. As the Squadron Commander, she had exercised her option and given herself her new name. She was now *"Kis'wa Min"*, or *"Little Bird"*. Naturally, the image of the Minna'que'tsa had been painted on her fighter's fuselage.

Making a sign of blessing towards the graphic and invoking the Ancestors to watch over her and her fighter, she prepared herself for landing. Up ahead of her, the *Athena* was coming up fast, and the Valkyrie had begun firing its braking thrusters. In seconds, the cavernous entrance to the hanger bay engulfed the fighter, and then the landing deck was going past in a blur. As the deck's grav fields locked on to assist it, the AI increased power to the thrusters. The vessel slowed, and then it touched down on the hangar deck and shut down its engines.

By necessity, landing and take-off operations were rapid affairs, and a robot tow came out to her immediately, pulling the vessel out of the flyway and into a spot between several other Valkyries and a Freya Interceptor. The moment that they came to a halt, another 'bot, this time a mobile ladder, drove up and parked itself up against the fighter's body.

While the AI shut down the fighter's systems, Erin removed her helmet, and waited patiently as a metal probe popped out from the instrument panel to her left, connecting with her inocular through a port in her suit arm. When it had been confirmed that her shots were up to date, and she was free of harmful pathogens, the clear canopy swung up and she was allowed to descend the ladder. At the bottom, she paused to drink in the familiar sights and sounds of a busy hangar deck, and then, giving her Valkyrie an affectionate pat, brought out her flight cap.

Like her flight suit, it was Star Service black with silver trim, and in addition to the single pip of her rank, it bore a silver Zommerlaandar owl, its wings spread and its talons outstretched as it dove down towards an unseen prey. The sight of this emblem made Erin shrug with genuine pleasure. It was the ancient symbol of the goddess Athena, and the insignia of her new squadron, the *Nighthunters*.

Giving a crisp salute to the flight crew who had already begun to work under her ship, she stepped away from the flight line and put the cap on, adjusting it carefully until it rode on her head at a jaunty angle. Wearing it on the flight deck of the *Athena*, was something that she had been looking forwards to ever since leaving Nemesis. It signified that at last, she had returned to the right path for her life.

Taur Reesha was standing near the lifts, and Erin noted with satisfaction that her fellow Nemesian had the insignia of a Lieutenant on her own flight cap. The woman was also wearing her Tej knife.

But instead of hanging it at her hip, it was suspended upside down from a strap coming off her shoulder, with a second band securing the huge knife to her chest. This arrangement allowed for a quick, easy draw while sitting in a cockpit, or suspended from a parachute. Erin had done the same thing with her own blade and a glint of approval shined in Taur Reesha's eyes when she saw this. "*Hai'a Sh'tun'aq,*" the woman said, giving her a salute.

Erin returned the gesture and added in a friendly shrug. *"Hai'a Sh'tun'aq."*

"It is good to see that your Tej was a success," Taur Reesha said, also shrugging and nodding pointedly towards Erin's blade. "I had long hoped that you would find your way back to the Forest. It is good that we will now be fighting side by side against our enemies."

"Hee'ya," Erin agreed. "I also bring word to you from your Clan. The Reesha are well, and they sent their greetings with me."

"Many thanks, sister. Welcome back to us." Her double meaning was obvious, and Erin shrugged again.

"Yes, it is well that I am back," she answered.

Taur Reesha handed her an elzlate pad and Erin took it from her. Its screen was loaded with the names of the pilots in her squadron, and as their new commander, she was expected to learn them and memorize their call signs.

She gave the list a quick once-over. It went by seniority and the FanF's were listed at the top, but even if they hadn't been, she would have been able to spot them by their call-signs alone; *'Grhaf'—Gran Horibe Faam, BUG, Giggles, Byewander, and G-Spot.*

The veterans came after them; *Bitch, Blaster, Phantom, Pistollera, Neutron, Princess, Razor, Violet, Chocalat, Freeday, Highline, Meteor, Sady, Spider*, and many more. In total, seventy-five names, and most of them were seasoned pilots, with hundreds of hours of combat time, and just as many kills. It was a good squadron, she decided.

"We've been running regular combat drills to get the FanF's up to speed," Taur Reesha informed her. "I think you will like the shape they are in. Each one has been assigned to a veteran mentor, and none of the vets have complained about their progress."

"Of that I have no doubt, sister," Erin replied. "I'll look forwards to flying with everyone." She tucked the pad under her arm, gave the woman a parting salute and left the hangar bay.

Her first stop was a visit to Lilith to formally report in for duty, and once she had done so, she made her way down to her new quarters in Officer's Country for her last piece of business. Like putting on her flight cap, it was a ritual that would, in its own way, truly end her Tej.

Her possessions had already been shipped over from the *Artemis*, and they were waiting there for her to unpack at her leisure. She ignored most of the containers, and went straight for one of the smaller boxes. This held the display case for her Tej knife. She unpacked it, and set it on the wall in the most prominent spot she could find for it.

It would remain there, and stay empty. Her Tej knife, like her honor, would never be set aside again. Ever.

CHAPTER 5

USSNS *Pallas Athena*, In-Orbit, Altamara, Frontera Provensa, Esteral Terrana Rapabla, 1043.05|09|03:37:73

Despite the pleasure everyone had derived from seeing Da'Kayt put Guzamma in his place, the work that followed that meeting proved to be anything but pleasant. The Grand Admiral had supplied Da'Kayt with a copy of his plan, along with data chronicling the entire war to date. While her superior stood in front of the holo and played an animation of Guzamma's proposal, Lilith realized that his plan was even worse than any of them had ever imagined.

For her part, she certainly didn't object to the Sisterhood bearing the bulk of the fighting. In fact, she and her companions welcomed this. The ETR Navy was simply in no shape for such a task. Even before the Hriss had arrived, its numbers had been small, and the losses that it had suffered since the invasion had reduced it well past the point of effectiveness. This reality, combined with the backwards state of its technology, made the Republican Navy only fit for a supportive role in the campaign.

But what she did object to, and strenuously, was the manner in which Guzamma proposed to employ the Sisterhood's forces. His idea was to deploy the Special Expeditionary Force in a piecemeal fashion, attacking in strength at some points, and assaulting others with insufficient numbers, and all of it without any eye for potential counterattacks. Lilith had very little doubt the Hriss would spot the same weaknesses, and exploit them to their advantage. Although they were ruthless, they weren't stupid—by and large at least.

Lilith took a sip from her tea and observed Da'Kayt as she circled the holo. There was a frown on her superior's face that deepened the longer she examined the display.

Finally, the Admiral stopped and sent a psiever command for an animation of the Hriss invasion to play, showing it from its very onset to the present. As Lilith and the other officers watched, system after system fell to the invaders, and they all took careful note, not only of where the Hriss had finally positioned themselves, but also what they were believed to have put in place there.

The data that the ETR had given them managed to identify most of the ships involved, supplying not only their class, but also their names and unit designations. Lilith recognized quite a few of them from her own encounters, and she requested a match from the *Athena's* computer for the remainder. The results that she received proved quite enlightening—and very encouraging.

"To my eye, the Hriss appear to be taking their sweet time about the invasion," Da'Kayt commented.

Lilith set her cup down and rose to join her with N'Leesa and Ben Biya. Da'Kayt replayed the holo again, pointing out several places on the virtual starmap that supported her observation. "I think that the *Shovelheads* know that they can be leisurely."

"Yes Admiral, I see what you mean," Ben Biya replied.

It was quite obvious that the Hriss had more than enough ships in their invasion force to have completely conquered the entire ETR by this point, but hadn't. Instead, what the hologram clearly revealed was that they were slowly consolidating everything that they took. This meant only two things; that they knew that they could finish off the ETR whenever they felt like it, and that they intended to stay. This was nothing less than an attempt to annex the ETR to Hriss space.

But a relaxed enemy was also an overconfident one, Lilith knew. And overconfidence on the battlefield was a sure recipe for failure.

Then she noticed something about the ships that the computer had identified. Each one had been labeled with its name, and its Clan affiliation. It was what wasn't on the list that really stood out.

"Their forces seem to be mixed," she stated. "They look like a collection of the independent Clans. But unless I missed them, there are no Imperials." To support this, she called up her list for Da'Kayt and the others to look at.

"Yes," Da'Kayt agreed. "I see what you mean. Not a 'regular' in the bunch. I think I know what happened here; I think our *friend* the Emperor sent them here to save his own skin again, or maybe to conduct this war by proxy and hope for the best."

"A clever tactic, even if a damned nuisance," N'Leesa remarked.

"Well, J'akkat'vak'nar is a bit more canny than most of their Emperors," Da'Kayt said. "But I also see a bright side in it for us. They have no real leadership."

Everyone smiled. With the invasion force nothing more than a disparate, squabbling group, this meant that they all had different policies, and objectives. That kind of chaos spelled disaster for any military force, at any time in history, and it was obvious that only the incompetence and inadequacy of the ETR forces had failed to exploit this crucial weakness.

"If we have it right," Ben Biya volunteered, "then as soon as they know we are involved, I think its safe to say that some of the smaller Septs will withdraw."

"I agree," Da'Kayt replied. "As for the larger ones, it will depend on their leaders. Personally, I hope that the Bloody Claw and Star-Rapers stay around for the fight."

She wasn't alone in this sentiment. These two Clans had been involved in the infamous raid a year earlier on the Persephone colony, and the deaths of almost 6,000 women there. Destroying them would redress some of the injury they had done to the Sisterhood. Da'Kayt had the holo zoom in on their stronghold, in the Xapaan system.

"And if we can break them, here in Xapaan," she continued, indicating the system, "we also take the Argenta Provensa. That opens the way to Cataala and everything else beyond it. End of game, and we win."

"What about the T'lakskalans?" N'Leesa asked. They were a third element in the invasion that the ETR had only listed as 'unknown'. The *Athena's* computers hadn't been mystified at all however, and had quickly identified them. Their presence in Republican space, working alongside the Hriss had come as a surprise; the Greys, had never shown any interest in the reptilians, and aside from the Anx'Ma, the Hriss themselves were not in the habit of forming partnerships with other races. They conquered them, or they destroyed them. The T'lakskalan presence was an enigma.

"You have me there," Da'Kayt admitted, highlighting their ships and replaying the invasion. It was obvious from the animation that the

T'lakskalan ships, while accompanying the Hriss forces, hadn't been involved in very much of the actual fighting. Instead, they seemed to have played a role similar to what the Admiral herself intended for the ETR; an occupation and clean-up force.

"Without any intel, my guess, and that's all it would have to be right now, is that they found something that the Hriss want, and they're trading it for the chance to capture themselves some new human slaves."

"That could be a problem," Ben Biya commented. "Rixa will definitely want us to intervene, and maybe even track their shipments down."

"As much as I'd deeply love to, one thing at a time," Da'Kayt answered. "The Hriss are our first order of business, and I think the T'lakskalans will probably run once the missiles really start flying. All I can say for right now, is that we interdict what we can and follow up on *that* war later."

"Aye-yah", N'Leesa agreed. No one was happy with this, but they all understood their priorities. "So, the plan then?"

Da'Kayt expanded the image and centered it on the Argenta Provensa. "I was thinking of following at least one part of the Grand Admiral's plan and hitting the Hriss in the Tiyas system first," the Trilanian said. "We'll need to confirm it of course, but they appear to be garrisoned very thinly there."

She closed her eyes for a moment, and when nothing happened to the display, Lilith wondered if she was employing the prescience the women of her world were rumored to possess.

"Yes," Da'Kayt finally said. "Given its remoteness, I believe that this is still the case. Tiyas first then."

Lilith frowned. The Admiral's carefully framed words hadn't confirmed her suspicions one way or the other. She determined to pay close attention to what they found in Tiyas.

"Once Tiyas is ours," Da'Kayt went on. "I would suggest that we move on to Qyarda, then Santosena, Tensamentra, and save Xapaan for the very end." Attacking in this manner would eat away at the reinforcements that the stronghold would otherwise be able to count on, leaving them alone with only what they had.

"I like it, "Lilith agreed. "May I make one suggestion however?"

"Please."

"As we work our way through Argenta, perhaps we could have our allies and some elements from our own forces initiate some attacks elsewhere, say in the Reganna and Marisal Provensas. They wouldn't be retaking anything—just hitting, running, and hitting again. That might force the Clans to deviate some of their forces away to chase them, and make our going even easier. I say, let the Hriss and their friends worry about holding on to anything."

Although both of the Provensas that she had mentioned were at the opposite end of the ETR, it was plain that the Republic could easily support a raid group. This was especially true in the Catamar Provensa, where the ETR still retained a firm grip.

"It would keep the *shovelheads* running around for a sureness," N'Leesa agreed. "That's provided that our main force keeps up the pressure on them at the same time. They won't know where to send their ships. A merry bit of fun, that."

Da'Kayt stroked her chin as she considered Lilith's proposal. Although it meant splitting her forces, the idea clearly had merit. If she implemented it, it would present the enemy with a combination of classic naval warfare and guerilla-style engagements that would keep them off balance, and on the defensive on two fronts.

"Yes," she finally said, the glass beads in her silver hair tinkling as she nodded. "Yes, I think you are right, Lilith. That is just what we should do. As for the raid group, it could start off small, and then have its strength augmented by ETR forces at need." She paused to take a drag off her czigavar. "So, who wants the job?"

"You have to ask?" N'Leesa responded with a wicked grin. "It 'ill set their drawers on fire, so it's got to be mine."

"Then we have our plan," Da'Kayt announced, finally paying attention to a sandwich her aid had brought for her. "There's one other issue that we have to address before we can implement anything though. It's the matter of keeping this whole operation a secret from the general population.'

"Tensamentra is remote and so are Qyarda and Tiyas, but Santosena has a larger population—although we can't be sure of that now that the Hriss have it. The raider group is going to face the same problem. And the deeper in we go, the more ETR citizens we're going to encounter, and that will only compound the situation."

"I have some thoughts on that as well," Lilith offered.

Da'Kayt looked to her.

"Well, we can certainly operate from space with confidence, just as long as the ETR can control who is up there with us. As for planet side operations, where its sparsely inhabited, I think that we can operate openly and the ETR can 'debunk' any sightings of us as nothing better than the babblings of the lunatic fringe.'

"As for places where there are any significant populations, I'd say we let the ETR do the fighting and have only a few of our women along, dressed in their uniforms of course, to act as advisors. They could call in the air or space strikes and no one would be the wiser. The same goes for any special operations. Of course, some of our more 'colorful' women might need to disguise their appearance a bit."

"Like Trilanians?" N'Leesa jibed.

Da'Kayt grinned. "To name just one group." This was an understatement. Aside from heavily modified women like her, even the most 'normal' woman had (by ETR standards at least) something 'off' about her. Whoever worked downside, however small their genetic modifications, would need to take special pains to avoid civilian attention. It was a small detail compared to the entire campaign, but still something that required attention.

The Admiral turned to her adjutant. "Ensign n'Dayna, take a note and make sure that our ground force commanders are reminded about this, and that they have their women take appropriate precautions." The woman nodded and made an entry on her elzlate pad.

"What about our aerospace fighters?" Ben Biya asked. There were obvious differences between them and their ETR counterparts. Compared to the Valkyrie, just in its lines alone, the ETR *Àgwilya* or 'Eagle' was only slightly more contemporary than an ancient biplane and just about as combat capable.

"Two possible solutions," Da'Kayt supplied. "One, where we can, we limit our fighters to fast, high-altitude runs, and two, where we can't, the Republic simply explains them away as their 'friendly alien allies'.' The fiction of an unknown alien race had been something that the ETR's President had proposed during their initial talks. Now it seemed like the idea might have merit.

"In fact, now that I think of it," she added, looking pointedly at Lilith, "the same thing might work for our more 'colorful' troops. I'll send the suggestion back to Rixa and see if they can persuade the Circle to loosen up the restrictions a bit."

"Good enough, Admiral. But if you ask me, I still think its all *a'dho'pgan*," N'Leesa said.

No one could disagree with her, or her choice of words. *'A'dho'pgan'* was a Gallan phrase that meant "*a two times pain*", and it referred to the unpleasant, but still necessary bi-annual menstrual cycle they all had to endure as an insurance policy against any failure of their artificial methods of procreation.

"Until the Supreme Circle says otherwise, I'm afraid it's a pain that we're stuck with, Eleen, "Da'Kayt responded. "The ETR can't have the news that we exist come out until they feel that their public is ready for it, and we're facing the same issue at home. '

"So, we'll have to remain in the shadows, and the ETR and their fictitious race will get all the glory. As far as I'm concerned they can have it, for how real any of it is. The main thing is that we will be getting the job done, and that's enough."

"Aye-yah," N'Leesa said regretfully. "It's just a shame to think that Guzamma and his cronies will profit, but ah wells. I suppose it could be worse. At least we won't have to dress everyone up to look like a Xee, or something just as ghastly."

She had a point.

Tiyas System, Argenta Provensa, Esteral Terrana Rapabla,
1043.05|11|04:37:37

The two ETR warships came out of warp together, just at the edge of the Tiyas system. The Hriss quickly reacted to their presence, and exactly as Lilith had expected they would.

Confident of their superiority, four medium cruisers headed out to meet the interlopers while the rest of their fleet hung back around Tiyas 5, the one populated world in the system. Normally, the ETR ships would have turned around and warped away from such odds, but this time they didn't. Lilith, Katrinn and Rodraga all listened and smiled at one another as they heard the Hriss captains expressing both their surprise, and delight, at finally having something to kill after months of boring picket duty. The engagement would prove to be much more exciting than they had anticipated, however.

As the Hriss cruisers closed the gap, a dozen more ETR ships came out of warp, and it became obvious to the Hriss captains that a serious battle was suddenly in the offing. Communications traffic increased dramatically, and the remainder of their warships powered up and began to move up to join the units in point.

Then, just as they had agreed, Admiral Guzamma's ships slowed, and then stopped, waiting.

Naturally, the Hriss misinterpreted this as indecisiveness, and the cruisers continued towards them, passing Undsenk, a gas giant with five moons. They had no idea that the battle groups under Lilith's command were hiding in stealth mode on the opposite side of the huge planet.

When the second group of Hriss warships reached the point where they were just inside missile range, Lilith gave the signal that everyone on the bridge had been waiting for. "All ships, this is the Vice Admiral. Power up and come out of stealth," she said.

Simultaniously, every Sisterhood vessel became visible, and the ETR ships acquired target locks on the enemy ships, and opened up their missile doors.

To their credit, the Hriss realized the nature of the trap and did their best to cope with it. Those vessels in the rear hastily accelerated, while the cruisers in the lead continued to close with the weaker ETR force, hoping to engage and destroy at least some of their opponents before it was too late. It was a purely punitive effort though; they knew that they were completely outgunned, out numbered, and doomed.

"All enemy ships targeted, Admiral," the *Athena's* Fire Control announced.

Lilith smiled and looked up to Katrinn. She wanted the pleasure of what was coming next to be hers. "The battle is yours, Commander," she said, gesturing expansively. Over her shoulder, Rodraga rewarded the Zommerlaandar with a smile and a casual, congratulatory salute.

Katrinn grinned back at them, and then addressed her crew. "This is the Commander. Engage all targets. Fire at will." With that, the *Athena* and her sisters launched their missiles in sync.

On both sides of the battle, hundreds of anti-spaceship rockets roared out of their silos, flicked out of normal space, and then returned, discharging multiple warheads as they did so. The number of space borne targets on the *Athena's* displays increased by a factor of ten. Opposing warheads, anti-missile technology and electronic countermeasures defeated many of the warheads, but not all of them by any means.

When these reached their targets, the first of the Hriss ships exploded, followed in rapid succession by their companions. One by one, they were consumed, and a mere three minutes later, the entire occupying force had been completely annihilated.

On the Sisterhood side, there had been no losses, and only a few ships had suffered any damage, and those, minor. But several ETR vessels, including the first brave pair that had served themselves up as bait, had been badly damaged. Despite this, it was still a decisive victory, and a very good start for the campaign.

***

The assault on Tiyas took place at exactly the same moment that Vice Admiral N'Leesa, leading her combined ETR-Sisterhood force in the Reganna Provensa, began the first of her hit and run raids. The overall result among the Hriss occupation forces was exactly what Da'Kayt had anticipated. It was complete pandemonium, especially when the Hriss realized that the Sisterhood had become involved in the conflict.

What had been certain victory suddenly seemed in doubt. And in response, several of the clans left the ETR immediately. But an equally large number remained behind, and offered up a stiff resistance.

The T'lakskalans, also stayed, but rather than lending assistance to the Hriss, they continued to remain on the sidelines and let their allies do all of the fighting. Their absence as an opposing force, while it would have been negligible, made Admiral da'Kayt's job all the easier.

New Lyyrica, Corrissa, Saraswati System, Kalian Elant, United Sisterhood of Suns, 1043.05|19|02:28:41

Just as dawn came to New Lyyrica, Celina entered the main living area of her home, carrying a steaming cup of tea. It was a daily ritual for the musician; she loved to watch the light from Corrissa's sun as it painted the city with its golden brush. The sky outside the huge bay windows was alive with reds and yellows, and the tallest spires of New Lyyrica seemed as if they had been set afire. Out at sea, in the shallow waters of Mandalar Bay, the night still ruled, but its retreat was inevitable. A new day was beginning, fresh with promise.

As the First Daughter of the City of Art watched the spectacle, she tried to recover the fragments of a dream she had had the night before. Designated as a Living National Treasure, everything she did, said or thought, was recorded for posterity by her psiever, but for some reason, there was no record of the dream whatsoever. The musician found herself forced to recapture it the old-fashioned way, through the unreliable agency of her memory.

All that she could recall however, was a woman, who had been strangely familiar, and that the figure had been talking to her. But Celina could not remember her face, nor what she had said, except for the profound sense that the conversation had involved something very important. The only thing that had survived undistorted was a melody.

It wasn't the first time that she had received her inspirations from her dreams by any means. Many of her finest works owed their genesis to this source. This melody was something special though, something apart from anything she had ever encountered before.

It was a haunting, majestic theme, and there was something familiar about it, as if she had heard it somewhere before, and knew on a deep visceral level what it was expressing. But *what* that was and *where* it had been, was a mystery that completely eluded her. All that was left was an enigma, and a deep imperative that she had to bring the song to life.

While she struggled with this conundrum, Celina hummed the tune out loud for the homes' recording devices to capture. Her creative AI patiently waited for her to finish, and then it greeted her.

"Good morning, Celi," it said.

Celina smiled, turned from the window and walked over to her composition chair. "And good morning to you, Clio!"

"That was a lovely melody, Celina. Are we going to use it for the realie?"

The musician pondered this for a moment and then answered. "No, Clio. I don't think it will fit in with what we're trying to create. I think the Goddess sent it to me for another project. It feels—more important."

"Yes, Celi, I understand," Clio agreed, "Listening to it, I got the same impression. There is something about it that demands that it be addressed solely on its own merits. I'll look forwards to working on it with you."

Celina took her seat. "Shall we pick up from where we left off last night?"

"With the forest section?"

"Yes" the artist replied. That particular part of the realie was already 99% perfect, but she wanted to give it one final inspection before getting some breakfast, and starting in on the finale.

Her chair automatically reclined and the built-in realie headset popped up and gently encircled her temples. The room around her vanished and she found herself standing in one of the great forests of Larra's Lament, in the Artemi Elant.

Where Nemesis was infinite shades of green, the woodlands of 'the Lament' as it was known, were all brilliant reds and oranges, and the light from the red giant that the planet orbited heightened these colors dramatically. It was a world of perpetual fall and one of Celina's favorite vacation spots.

The section that they were completing began by taking the audience on a slow journey through the trees, and as they were led to a clearing, the melody, which had been subdued and suggestive, rose. At its highest peak, multiple images of Celina walked out from the woods, singing to her listeners. Clio and she had wrestled with whether or not the images would sing as a chorus from the outset, or if the song would be performed as a solo by one voice. In the end, they had decided to try combining the two arrangements, with the chorus coming in where it was needed most for dramatic emphasis.

As she listened, and watched, she found that she liked that solution. The chorus was just right for punctuating the song without being overpowering. The musician allowed herself to relax and watched the sequence as it went on.

The song peaked, and the multiple images of herself became clouds of leaves that spun upwards in the breeze. These ascended beyond the treetops, taking the viewer with them into the clear sky, where they transformed into glowing orbs of light that spun, and rose even higher.

Then the lights flew into space itself, rushing past the stars in seconds until their final destination became obvious. It was the majestic spiral of the Andromeda galaxy, where eventually, the realie would reach its conclusion.

In the meantime, there were final touches that needed to be made to the forest sequence. It was good, Celina thought, but as she had Clio replay it again, she felt that there was still something missing. It was the air itself, she realized. It felt cool against her face, but not quite enough to achieve the sensation she was trying for. She also thought that the reds of the forest needed more vibrancy. To her eye, they seemed slightly dull.

"Clio, bring the temperature of the woods down a few degrees, would you? And deepen the shade of the reds as well. There's a dear."

The AI complied, stopping at exactly the right levels without being told to. This did not surprise Celina. They had been working together for years and the AI knew her creative process just as well as she did.

Yes, she thought as she watched the modified scene, *perfect*. It was just cold enough to be invigorating, without chilling the viewer, and the reds of the forest were now more inviting to the eye.

"That's it," she declared, rising from her chair. "Lock in those changes, and we'll take a break for breakfast."

"Yes, Celi," the AI answered. "By the way, I was supposed to remind you that you have a lunch date with Madame t'Annya today at the *Annapurna*. It's at 05:41."

Celina had completely forgotten about the lunch date with her producer and she was grateful for the reminder. "Thank you, Clio. I don't know what I'd do without you."

"You'd probably miss all of your appointments," the AI laughed. "What would you like for breakfast?"

"How about *plantaa* cakes with dewberries?" Celina replied, "And some of that wonderful spiced kaafra we had the other day? You know, with the *hinsa* added in?"

"It is on its way, Celi."

Breakfast was ready a few minutes later, and as she ate, the song from her dreams returned. This time, the imagery of the Andromeda Galaxy she had intended for her current project, accompanied it in her mind. The two elements, combined together seemed to call to her. They felt 'right' together.

"Clio, I know that we have to move on and finish the sky to space sequence," she said wiping her lips with a soft *siilka* napkin. "But I wanted to work a bit with that song that you heard this morning."

"I anticipated that you'd say that, Celi," Clio said. "While you were eating, I created a series of variations and an expansion on the melody. Would you like to hear them?"

"Oh Clio," Celina smiled. "You know me too well! Yes darling! Play them for me."

The song began. Rendered in pure musical tones, with a vocal track added in, it had become a thoroughly compelling piece.

Magnificent, Celina thought. It would be a crime *not* to develop it further. But as the melody ended, she wondered what direction to ultimately take it in, and if someone hadn't already created something just like it. It was simply *too* familiar.

"Clio that was lovely!" she said. "Please check and make sure that we're not plagiarizing someone else's work. We *have* to have that music if it's available!"

The AI complied, checking the theme against its library of music. After spending a few seconds comparing it with 1,346,978,432 known songs, and their variations, Clio came back with her results. "It's similar to five previous compositions", she announced, "but it is only a 22% match, and only in certain sections of each work. Based on current Sisterhood Copyright Laws, per the regulations established by the Thermadonian Senatorial Library System, we are free to use it."

"Wonderful!" Celina declared. "Protect it, would you? We'll work on it a bit before lunch. There's something missing, and I'd like to see if we could find it. I think it needs some additional phrasing."

"But, Celi," the AI insisted, "We still have to work on the rest of the current realie. Madame t'Annya told me that it *had* to be done by next week!"

"Alia is a dear," Celina replied using the woman's first name, "but she spends far too much time worrying about her silly deadlines. This is Art, and we have to serve *that* Mistress first. We'll get everything done in time. Come on Clio! Let's play! You *know* you want to!"

"Yes" the AI admitted. "This time *you* know me too well."

Celina clapped her hands together. "Then it's decided! We'll see what it inspires, and then I'll get myself off to that appointment."

They worked with the theme for the next two hours. In that time span, it developed into an even fuller expression, and as the two artists, flesh and virtual, worked together, they both saw that they had something that was better than anything they had ever composed together before. It still needed some work, but it was glorious.

Reluctant to leave it, Celina put on her diaphanous *cxapelo*, a huge brimmed hat that was a distant cousin to the Gaian sombrero, and left for her lunch date. By the time she had walked only a few blocks, she had already conceived the general idea of the realie that would surround her new song. The scope of it was staggering. When it was done, it would be the largest, most complex work that she had ever created.

***

The City of Art was a work of art in and of itself. New Lyyrica had been built 300 years earlier from the income generated by its sister city, Luma, and the orbiting industrial shipyards that Corrissa was famous for. New Lyyrica was the shining center for the creative minds of the Sisterhood; artists, musicians, intellectuals and poets from all corners of the star nation came to it and composed the bulk of its population. And the cities architecture reflected the creative nature of its residents.

Not only did every building have to conform to the usual building and safety codes, but it also had to be pleasing to the eye, and stimulating to the spirit. While there were many heated debates about what exactly managed to achieve this objective, and what didn't, the overall architectural theme of New Lyyrica emulated the Écouter-Nouveau Revival style. A combination of the organic, flowing manner of classic European Art Nouveau and eastern arabesque, nearly every structure was a masterpiece of gentle curves and tasteful colors, complimented by fanciful spires and towers whose only purpose was to accent the streets that they overlooked.

Celina loved the city that she had adopted, and that had adopted her. Even though she was famous throughout the Sisterhood, and instantly recognizable, in New Lyyrica she was just another artist, honored certainly, but free to enjoy her solitude when she wanted it. The city was accustomed to genius, and to being a home for those that the muses chose to bless. Walking down Baez Street, many of the residents recognized her, but aside from smiles, a wave from a flower seller, or a brief greeting by some teenage girls at work on a wall mural, she was left to herself, and her thoughts.

A few minutes later, she reached her destination on the corner of Baez and Joplin. A popular location for poetry readings and art shows, the *Annapurna* was full, but her producer had already gotten them a table outside, and she was shown to it immediately.

Madame t'Annya rose as Celina joined her and greeted her with a hug. "Ah Celina! I see that Clio is doing her job and reminded you about today. How is she?"

"Just as creative as ever," the musician replied. "I sometimes wonder if the galaxy would notice if I just let her do *all* the composing and singing. We're so alike, and she copies my voice so accurately that I think she could create a whole realie by herself and no one would be the wiser."

"Yes, but *you'd* know." T'Annya smiled. "So, how is *'Dreams of Forever'* coming along? Are we on time to meet the production schedule?"

"Yes, Mistress," Celina answered with mock servility. "It will be done as you have commanded. Even better, I already have another project in mind."

Her agent laughed, but Celina could tell that she was also relieved by the news. The woman was a bundle of raw nerve-endings when it came to a deadline. But, just as she was a musical artist, T'Annya was an artist when it came to business. Except for Clio, she was the one who had done the most to propel Celina's career to the heights that it now enjoyed.

"Well," T'Annya said as they sat down. "Tell me about this new project—or should I get something to drink first?"

"As you will," Celina smiled.

"Oh go ahead and tell me! That way I'll know how strong the drink will have to be."

"I already have a working title for it," the musician replied with a chuckle. "It may change, but I doubt it. I am calling it the *Song of Humanity.* I woke up with the opening melody in my head."

"It sounds ambitious," T'Annya said tentatively.

"It is, Alia," Celina said. "I gave it some thought as I was coming here today, and I see it as a portrait of the lives of women throughout the Sisterhood. I want to focus on as many walks of life as I can—the women of Thermadon, the asteroid miners of Agleope, the colonists in the new fringe worlds, and even some members of the armed forces. I want their stories to be told. I want it to be a realie for the audience, about the audience itself."

"Really?" T'Annya was genuinely surprised. Celina's work had always centered on fanciful themes, and up to this point, she had steadfastly avoided anything that addressed social issues.

"Yes." The musician said. "I think that these women have been left behind by the art community, and I want to give them their voice. They deserve it."

"This is quite a departure for you, Celina," her producer observed. "And to get your material, it will involve a lot of travel, some cooperation from the government, and a *lot* of time." She didn't mention the cost, not because she was hesitant to do so, but because expense wasn't an issue. Celina enjoyed a generous endowment from the *Tuluraa Daal Foundation for the Arts*, which not only provided for her living expenses, but also the creation of her realies.

"I just wonder how your fans will react," T'Annya ventured. "This realie may be a little more serious than what they'd normally expect."

"When they see it and hear it," Celina replied. "I think they will react the same way I did, and love it. It's their song, Alia, and it has to be sung."

Waanderstaad Spaceport, Zommerlaand, Sunna 3, Solara Elant, United Sisterhood of Suns, 1043.05|26|05:21:88

When Lilith, Katrinn and Bar Daala entered the civilian terminal together, the kaapers were waiting for them, just as they had expected. And as they had on Lilith's first visit, they tried to prohibit their side arms from entering with them.

This time though, Katrinn was fully prepared, and the minute that the officials began to speak, she produced a flimsy, courtesy of Ellyn n'Dira, which contained an excerpt from the Sisterhood's law, detailing the requirement for military personnel to have their weapons with them at all times when they were downside.

The section also cited several examples of case law supporting this requirement, and also the name of their supervisor, who had been involved in the first dispute. This, and Lilith's flag rank, quickly settled the matter in their favor and they were able to proceed through the terminal without any further interruption. For her part, Katrinn couldn't have looked more satisfied with herself.

Ingrit was waiting for them at the curb, and the instant Lilith laid down her kit bag, the big woman gathered her up and kissed her deeply. "Mehn gaate!" she said when she finally released her. "I missed you two so much!"

"It's good to be back," Lilith answered, a little breathless and blushing. As she picked up her bag, the Zommerlaandar smiled roguishly at her, and then took her by the hand to the hovertruck, with Katrinn and Bar Daala trailing behind.

"Zo *roont*, Grammy's got a big dinner cooking for us back at the farm, and the little one's are about to go nova from all the excitement," Ingrit told them over her shoulder.

"No worries on that score," Katrinn smiled. "I brought them all toys. That should give them something to spend all their energy on."

While they put their luggage aboard, Ingrit leaned in close to whisper to Lilith. "Who's you're friend, Lily?"

In the rush to get to Zommerlaand, Lilith had forgotten to mention Bar Daala, and she flushed again, this time from embarrassment. "My assistant," she explained. "The Admiralty thinks I need one."

"Ah," Ingrit replied, looking at Bar Daala with an odd expression that Lilith couldn't quite decipher. But just as quickly as it had appeared, it was gone, replaced by one of her big smiles.

"Well, let's be off then!" she said. Then she leaned in close to Lilith and whispered in her ear. "I can't wait to get you alone, my darling. I'm going to strip off that pretty little button-oop of yours with my teeth, and then I'll keep you all to myself." Her words sent a delicious tingle down Lilith's spine, and for the third time since arriving, she felt color rising in her cheeks, accompanied by a spreading warmth that had nothing at all to do with shame.

***

For Jan bar Daala, the trip out to the farm was a host of new experiences to tell about on her next visit with the Watchers. Even though she had seen holos of it, she had never been to Zommerlaand in person, and she found its huge fields and open sky a bit overwhelming. But she had expected surprises like that when she had learned what Lilith's destination was going to be, and this tempered her reaction slightly.

What she had not anticipated was the farm itself, and who lived there. The instant the hovertruck pulled up to the front of the farmhouse, and an old woman stepped out to greet them, their eyes locked.

A thrill of alarm went through her as she realized that the woman was some kind of psi, a very powerful one at that, and completely unlike any other she had ever encountered before. And although Grammy smiled at her, her gaze was intent and evaluating. Without intending to, Jan had caught her interest.

The young woman broke off eye contact, and quickly looked away. *The old woman knows,* she thought, damning the circumstances that had brought them together. *Somehow, she knows what I am and if she doesn't, she will soon.*

She began to panic, but the task that the Watchers had set for her was too important to allow for rash reactions, and she forced herself to remain calm. She had evaded psi's before, she reminded herself, and she would do it again with this one, however powerful and strange she seemed. Relying on what had always worked in the past for her, Jan reached out to the woman with her will and projected the feeling that everything was normal, and that she was nothing worth noticing.

Grammy smiled again, but it wasn't the expression of someone who had fallen under her glamour. Instead, she seemed to be—amused.

Jan's feeling of panic spiked. The surprises were far from over though. The next one came when one of the children, Jan thought that she was called Fryya, came out. She was accompanied by several small motes of light that Jan instantly recognized.

She was appalled. *They live here too?* The Watchers knew about these creatures. They had encountered them on many of the worlds that the Drow'voi had colonized. Undisciplined, and unwilling to serve the Masters, the Watchers rightfully considered them to be nothing more than a nuisance, and wherever the machines in the ancient ruins still had the power to do so, the little beings were repelled or even exterminated if possible.

Thankfully, the Lament had been largely free of them, and encountering them there was a rarity. In her naiveté', Jan had always assumed that the same condition held true everywhere else, and in the two years she had been in her new body, nothing she had seen on any of the planets that she had visited had contradicted this. She had even been to worlds where the vermin had never existed at all.

But here they were, on Zommerlaand, and it was patently obvious that they had even managed to form close bonds with humans. Had the Watchers failed here somehow? Or was this a place where the Masters had never established themselves? That seemed an utter impossibility—but the presence of the little pests was equally undeniable.

As this conundrum played havoc with her thoughts, two of the little beings peeled away from the girl and circled around her, briefly inspecting her before rejoining their human companion. It was all Jan could do not to swat at them, and they seemed to know this, circling her a few more times than they really needed to, and actually laughing at her discomfort.

Laughing!!! Jan was outraged and horrified at the same time.

Then, as they retook their places over the child's head, she saw something that frightened her even more. The light of understanding had come into Fryya's eyes.

The evil little bugs just told her what I really am, Jan realized. *She knows!*

The urge to run, as fast as she could, to *anywhere* else, nearly overpowered her, but summoning up all her will, she maintained her facade of calm and went on, playing her role as if none of this was happening. Zommerlaand, with all its wide skies and vast fields, had turned out to be a trap just as surely as any cage, and she had no idea how she would manage to escape it.

Before she could consider her precarious situation any further, Grammy invited everyone into the house and had Fryya show them all in. Taking full advantage of this, the pesky little Alfs came back to encircle Jan again, and one of them even had the temerity to land momentarily on the tip of her nose! But it knew as well as she did that she was powerless to do anything about it, and it flew off laughing at her again.

***

The moment that Jan was out of sight, and earshot, Grammy drew Ingrit aside.

"Who is that woman?" she asked her in Zommerlaandartal. She felt badly about having to keep any secrets from Katrinn and Lilith, but this wasn't a matter that she wanted to involve them in if she didn't have to.

"Katy told me that she's an assistant for Lilith," Ingrit answered.

"I see," Grammy replied. "She is more than that, I think. You felt it too didn't you?"

"Yah, Grammy. I did from the minute I saw her. Her life-fire…"

"Yah I know. She is more like some kind of *gaasten*—a ghost, but with a body she wears around her like an old coat. Watch her as closely as you can," the old woman instructed. "We must learn what she is, and why she has come here with Katy and Lilith."

"You think she might be something bad?"

"I am not certain," Grammy said, "and I am not sure if even she knows. I saw great fear in her when we met, and hatred when the Alfs came to get a look at her. She knew them. So, we watch her. If she is a friend, we will speak with her as a friend. If she is an evil thing, then we will deal with her ourselves."

Ingrit looked in the direction of the farmhouse and added somberly, "Yah, I'll watch her all right. Should I tell Katy about this?"

"Not for now," Grammy answered. "Not unless we need to. She's been too long among the *Vreestaanden*, and she might not understand this thing. But do take Fryya aside and tell her to keep silent; a child's stories are seldom believed, but if they tell them often enough and with enough heart, adult ears might open up."

A raucous caw sounded from the roof and they looked up to see Old Meg gazing down at them. The huge raven had also taken note of Bar Daala's arrival, and they both knew, without Grammy having to translate, what the bird was saying. She would also be keeping watch over their strange visitor.

Grunvaald Haarmaaneplaatz, Vaalkenstaad Township, Zommerlaand, Sunna 3, Solara Elant, United Sisterhood of Suns, 1043.05|27|02:94:67

Katrinn was gone when Lilith got up the next morning, and as she searched for her, she discovered that Ensign bar Daala was still in her room. For some reason, the young officer had been strangely withdrawn during their homecoming dinner, and despite the hour, she seemed determined to stay sequestered.

Lilith was perfectly fine with this. With Bar Daala keeping to herself, there was the possibility that she would be able to enjoy some private moments. Not wanting to jeopardize that, she snuck past the woman's room and went downstairs. Ingrit was in the kitchen, enjoying a cup of kaafra.

"Where did Kat go off to?" she asked as she joined her and got her own cup.

"Katy said something about going over to the *Eddalvaas Haarmaaneplaatz*," Ingrit told her. "Berta is visiting some cousins we have there."

Lilith responded with a silent "ah" of understanding and didn't press for any more information. Ingrit, Katrinn and their sisters Hanna and Marina had all come from the same Pairing, and after Katrinn had been born, their mothers had separated, and left the farm. Neither woman had been back since, because of the painful memories that the place held for both of them. No matter how perfect a relationship was, the years sometimes conspired to make things like this happen, she knew. Even in the best of families.

"And you?" Ingrit asked. "Did you have any plans for today?"

"Not much," she replied, taking an appreciative sip from her cup. "I have some work to do for Rixa, and then I'm free." She wanted to fine-tune the campaign recommendations she would be submitting to Admiral da'Kayt one last time, and ensure that she hadn't missed anything.

"*Gaanskaa gaad*," Ingrit smiled. "I've a bit of work with the 'bots over in the west fields, but the late part of the afternoon is free. Want to go for a ride with me to our lake?"

Lilith had been introduced to the lake on her first visit to the farm, by Ingrit, and the memory of their shared passion there, ushered in a flood of anticipatory warmth. She found herself looking down at her cup, and avoiding Ingrit's eyes like a teenager. The woman had that kind of power over her.

"Yes," she said quietly. "I'd like to see it again."

Ingrit reached over and gave her thigh a gentle, but suggestive squeeze. "*Denn gaaf,*" she declared. "I'll even pack us some supper to take along. The moons will be full tonight. It should be really nice out."

She wasn't exaggerating. It was midsummer in the southern part of Zommerlaand, and later that day, as they rode out together from the farmhouse, the heat had settled down to a temperature that was absolutely perfect; neither too hot, nor too chilly. Sunna was just setting, and as twilight painted everything around them with luminous shades of purple, orange and red, they made their way up through the trees, past the High Place, and out to a broad plain that led to the shore of the lake itself. And just as Ingrit had promised, Zommerlaand's three moons, *Mani, Hjúki* and *Bill* were rising into the sky, full and bright, gilding the lakes waters with a pale golden light.

They rode to a spot that they had discovered together on Lilith's first visit. It was a faultless place just at the edge of the trees, with fine soft grass that offered plenty of space to lay out a blanket and a basket of food. Grammy had come back just in time to pack this for them, complaining all the while that Ingrit 'knew nothing about what to take along for a decent supper', and the old woman had even added in a few special touches. These not only included a fine, sweet salad that she had called '*Kaawl Slaaw*' to go with their fried chikka, but also a bottle of delicious *Aarntwyyn*, harvest wine, to compliment it all. The meal had been put together with a love that they could almost taste as they ate it.

The lake, their supper, and the moment itself, were as far away from the war as anywhere could have been. And the company she was in was just as wonderful, Lilith thought, snuggling into the crook of Ingrit's arm. Sighing in complete contentment, she laid her head on her woman's chest and listened to the sounds of the *chirpii* bugs as their evening symphony kept time with the luminous little *aanzbuggen* flitting playfully around them like Ingrit's mythical Alfs.

Ingrit, ever the considerate lover, let her enjoy all of this in silence, not pressing her about the campaign, or even asking about Sarah. Instead, she simply stroked her hair tenderly, and let out a contented sigh of her own.

Someday, very soon, Lilith vowed, *I'll have all of this, and her, forever.* But then her daughter came to mind. There had never been a day, or even an hour when she hadn't thought of her. And now she knew for a fact that Sarah was alive. Somewhere.

"I wish Sarah was here to see this," she said at last. "I think she would love it."

"Someday, she will be," Ingrit assured her. "Grammy says so."

"Does she?" Lilith asked, looking up at her hopefully. She didn't believe in prophecy, or any of the other superstitions that Ingrit or her family accepted so blithely, but it was still nice to imagine that some of it at least, might actually be true. Especially where her deepest hopes and dreams were concerned.

"Yah. Grammy threw the bones," Ingrit said, "and she told me that you'll be seeing each other again real soon. She even sent a few *Maarkken* out there, just to help move things along. You watch, Lily. It'll all come true."

"I wish it would," Lilith replied, smiling wistfully. "I would love for her to come here, and share this with us." At that, she found herself wondering, if somehow, somewhere, her daughter wasn't looking up at moons of her own, right at that very instant, and thinking the same thing. Of course, that was impossible.

***

Forty-two light years away, on Nyx, it was also early evening. Sarah n'Jan looked up, past the jagged peaks of the Moonspire Mountain range, to that world's moons, *Eris*, *Eros* and *Geras*. Gazing at their light, she inexplicably found herself thinking about her mother, and wondering, for the first time in a very long while, how she was, and where she was.

Perhaps I'll speak to the Agency about contacting her, she thought. Most of the operations that had required her to maintain a deep cover had ended, and there were fewer and fewer reasons to remain separated from Lilith merely for the sake of ensuring her safety. The very idea of having somewhere other than Thermadon, or even her beloved Nyx, to come home to, had a certain appeal. She had been on the move for too many years, she realized. Perhaps it was time to change all that.

But not tonight, she told herself. Tonight she had responsibilities to attend to; Maya was still deep in her training, and Lady Ananzi had tasked her with the job of assisting the girl with her studies. That took precedence over everything else.

Sighing, she turned away from the vista and started up the rocky trail to Lady Ananzi's home to fetch Maya.

Grunvaald Haarmaaneplaatz, Zommerlaand, Sunna 3, Solara Elant, United Sisterhood of Suns, 1043.05|28|06:66:07

Lilith was in Ingrit's bedroom, annotating her campaign files, when the kitchen door crashed open, followed by the sound of running feet. Then she heard one of Katrinn's nieces screaming for Grammy. Leaving the file open, she rushed down the stairs and nearly collided with Berti.

"What's wrong?" she asked the little girl.

"It's Fryya", the child blurted frantically. "She was on Marga, and we told her not to ride her, but she did anyway and then she fell off and got hurt! Please, we've got to get Grammy!"

"Grammy!" Lilith yelled. "It's Fryya. We need some help!"

The old woman had been in the root cellar, and she rushed up and over to Berti. "Where is she, child? Take me to her! Lilith, you go upstairs and get my bag. It's the red one, next to my cedar trunk. I'll see you at the truck."

Lilith pelted up the stairs, and quickly located the bag. When she came back down into the kitchen, she saw Old Betsi hovering outside, with Ingrit at the controls and Grammy already boarding the vehicle. Lilith ran to the hovertruck and handing Grammy the bag, took a seat up next to Ingrit. The instant that she had strapped herself in, they were off, headed out across the fields, leaving a trail of dust and grass blades in their wake.

It didn't take them long to reach Fryya and the other children, and as they parked, Hanna and Marina rode up on horseback. The girl was lying on the ground, with her sisters ringed around her, and when they pushed their way through, she could see that the child's ankle was swollen and deformed. Grammy bent over the sobbing girl and gently examined the injury.

"*Daa armstaad*, it's broken all right," she sighed. "I'm going to have to splint this before we can move her." Grammy reached into her bag, and produced a conventional smart splint that any Navy Medic might have carried in their field kit.

"What? You think I'm all spells and potions?" she said in answer to Lilith's surprised expression. "Katy made sure to get us a few things for this kind of worry. It never hurts to be prepared."

She wrapped the splint around the girl's ankle and as soon as she sealed it, the splint automatically molded itself into the proper shape and size, and inflated. Then Grammy directed them to lift Fryya into the truck.

"We'll want to take her to the hospital in Vaalkenstaad and have them take a look." Her announcement elicited even more tears from Fryya, and a string of apologies for riding the mare in the first place.

"Now, don't you fret about that, *Sötehaart*," Grammy said reassuringly. "You've learned your lesson I think. Now be still while we get you to the doctor."

The ride to Vaalkenstaad took only a few minutes, with Ingrit managing to drive them there at something less than her normal faster-than-light speed. Fryya was quickly admitted to the Emergency Room, and after an hour and a half, returned to them with a cast, an appointment to see an orthopedic surgeon, and a profound new respect for the prohibitions of her elders.

The crisis seemed to have passed.

But two days later, while Lilith was working in the kitchen helping Grammy with supper, Fryya hobbled in. Even to Lilith's untrained eyes, the little girl looked pale and her breathing seemed slightly labored.

"What's wrong, Fryya?" she asked.

"I can't breathe and my chest hurts," the child answered. Grammy made her sit, and quickly brewed her some tea.

"Drink some of this," she instructed. The girl obeyed and sipped at the cup. "It's a mess of herbs to help with chest problems", she said to Lilith, but there was a look of concern in her eyes.

It proved to be well founded. Fryya's breathing problems worsened and then they both realized that her lips were turning blue.

"We have to get her to Vaalkenstaad right away," Grammy declared. "Get Ingrit and tell Hanna and Marina!"

Once again, everyone piled into Old Betsi and this time, Ingrit didn't skimp on the speed. The moment that they arrived, a pair of nurses with a gurney met them. Fryya was whisked into the Emergency Room and everyone was left outside to wait, and worry.

After only a few minutes, one of the doctors came out to speak with them. Lilith clutched Ingrit's hand, bracing herself for the worst. And Hanna and Marina looked like they were ready to faint dead away from pure, undiluted anxiety.

"Your daughter is over in Intensive Care," the woman told them. "But she's all right. We've managed to stabilize her breathing. It's a good thing you got her here when you did, or she might not have made it."

"I told her not to ride *zat fekking* horse," Marina sobbed angrily.

Her pairmate put an arm around her. "It's all right Marina, she's still with us. That's all that matters."

The doctor gave them a moment before going on, "Fryya's breathing problems appear to have been caused by what we call a DVT, a deep vein thrombosis. In Standard, that's a blood clot that lodges in the lungs, and it came from the fracture that she sustained.'

"We've got some nanobots working on the clot right now, but there's a chance that she might experience some issues with her breathing, so I've given her some medication as well.'

"I've also scheduled her for surgery first thing tomorrow. We can't wait for her appointment with the specialist. After she gets through that, she'll need a few days to recover and give us a chance to make sure that everything is under control."

"Can we see her?" Marina asked.

"Only for a few minutes, and only a few of you," the woman told them. "She's under sedation right now and I don't want to excite her with too many visitors."

"You two go in," Grammy urged. "We'll stay out here."

After Hanna and Marina had had their chance to visit with their daughter, Lilith, Grammy and Ingrit returned to the farm. The girl's mothers had refused to leave the hospital, and they had gone back to pick up a few things for them, and to make Fryya's stay a little easier.

Katrinn met them as they pulled up. "I got your message, Lily," she said. While Fryya's mothers had been in the ICU, Lilith had sent her a message via an omni to let her know what had happened. Katrinn had brought a small overnight bag out with her, and she had one of Fryya's favorite stuffed animals tucked under one arm.

"I'll drive those things over," Ingrit offered, taking them from her sister, and starting to head back to the hovertruck.

"Not before eating you won't," Grammy warned. "We all need to get some food into us. After *that* chore's been tended to, you can go."

Lilith didn't feel particularly hungry, but Grammy's tone made it clear that she would brook no disagreements. As a group, they obediently filed into the farmhouse and made themselves eat the quick meal that the old woman served out. It was only when they had consumed enough to satisfy her that they were allowed to depart.

By the time they had dropped off everything at the hospital, and returned to the farm, it was late, and the stress of the day's events had thoroughly exhausted everyone. Lilith followed Ingrit upstairs to their bedroom, and fell asleep in her arms almost immediately.

Someone calling her name, and shaking her, interrupted her dreamless sleep, and at first she didn't know who it was, or even *where* she was for that matter. Then she recognized the voice. It was Ingrit.

"Lily, wake up! Grammy needs us right away! It's Fryya again!"

Lilith sat up and just managed to catch her clothing as Ingrit threw it to her. "What's happening?" she asked, accessing her psiever. It was 08:33:79 in the morning, she realized, and still night outside.

"Fryya's in big trouble!" Ingrit explained. "Old Meg came and told Grammy. *Gaane-an! G*et dressed. We have to hurry! "

Still a little disoriented, Lilith quickly pulled on her clothes and followed her lover down the narrow stairs into the kitchen. Grammy was there, dressed in her special apron covered in Zommerlaandar characters, and Katrinn was with her. Their expressions were grave.

"We have to help Fryya, "Grammy told them. "She is in great danger and she will die if we don't act quickly."

"Then shouldn't we get to the hospital right away?" Lilith asked.

"*Nen*," Grammy said. "There is nothing we can do there. This is something we have to do here and now, or she will be gone before we arrive." There was no doubt in her voice, and one glance at Ingrit and Katrinn told her that they believed everything she was saying unequivocally.

The old woman led everyone out of the farmhouse and up through the dark, damp forest to the High Place. Despite her great age, Grammy moved quickly, and the younger women behind her had to work hard to keep up. Whatever she had in mind was urgent, Lilith realized.

When they reached the familiar tree stump that had been carved into a rough chair, Grammy stopped, and held out her hands. Ingrit took one, and Katrinn the other, and then she signaled Lilith to join them and complete the circle.

"I know that you don't believe as we do," Grammy said, "but everyone has to help with this. Fryya needs us. You must see her in your mind, and see her becoming able to breathe. Picture this as strongly as you can, and send every bit of love and good will you can to her. See it making her well."

Lilith couldn't imagine how this would actually accomplish anything, but she decided that if it made her companions feel any better about the situation, it was worth the effort. She closed her eyes and tried to picture the little girl, lying in her bed with her condition improving.

For some reason however, an image of other people standing over Fryya, kept superimposing itself on her consciousness. They looked like hospital staff, and they were all in a great hurry. She also got the strong impression that they were very concerned about Fryya's welfare.

Lilith willed this unpleasant imagery away, and kept trying to visualize Fryya getting well instead. But a deeper part of her insisted that what she was seeing was real, and that Grammy was right--and as absurd as this seemed, she knew that Fryya *was* in desperate trouble, and that she had to keep imagining a positive outcome, no matter what.

Overcome by a sudden sense of desperation she forced herself to concentrate harder, and the others began to chant. Their words weren't in Standard, or in anything that sounded like Zommerlaandartal. It was something else altogether; pure elemental sounds that seemed older than either language, or any language for that matter.

"Uuuraaa, Uuutaaal, Gaaaraaa, Niiiidaaa, Feh!" they intoned, repeating it over and over.

Listening, Lilith recognized the strange sounds, but at a primal level that defied her conscious understanding, and she also felt their power, resonating at the very core of her being as their chanting rose in volume. At the same time, a warmth began to grow in her hands that she knew wasn't just the body heat of her companions. It was accompanied by an electric tingle, faint at first, and becoming so strong that she could not deny its presence no matter how hard her intellect attempted it.

She opened her eyes slightly, and saw what appeared to be a blue ball of light hovering roughly in the middle of where they were standing. The weird luminous sphere looked as if was pulsing in time with the sounds, and it grew in size and intensity with every repetition. Then abruptly, the chant ended and Grammy uttered one last word. *"Feh!"*

The ball appeared to react to this, and flew up into the air. As Lilith watched in disbelief, it glided away from them over the treetops, and traveled off in the rough direction of Vaalkenstaad before vanishing beyond the trees and her sight.

It was an optical illusion, she told herself. It had to be. A hallucination caused by a lack of sleep and pure suggestion. That, or the coincidental gathering of rare gases from the forest around them, like the will o' the wisps of old Gaia, or the so-called 'ghost lights' of Nemesis. Nothing else made any sense, or fit with what she knew.

Whatever it had actually been, once it was gone, everyone released their neighbor's hands, and relaxed.

"*Saa es vaar*. It is done, "Grammy declared. Her voice sounded ragged and tired. "We can go to the hospital now. Hanna and Marina will want some company after what has just happened. Thank you for helping us, Lilith."

Not quite certain what to make of the whole affair, Lilith joined them as they walked back down the hill to the hovertruck. She didn't ask anyone about what they had just done, nor make any disparaging comments about Zommerlaandar witchcraft. She respected them too much to do that.

She also didn't ask about the strange light either, already anticipating that they would quickly attach some supernatural explanation to it. Instead, she just boarded the ancient vehicle, and tried to catch some sleep as Ingrit drove them back to Vaalkenstaad.

Hanna was waiting for them at the entrance of the hospital. She had been crying.

"Thank you, Grammy. Thank you all," she said as they walked up. "Fryya stopped breathing. They said it was another embolism and they had to resuscitate her. They said...they told me..." Her voice finally broke, "They said that we almost...lost her."

Ingrit and Katrinn surrounded the woman and protectively wrapped their arms around her. "She's all right then?" Katrinn asked.

"Yah", Hanna replied, regaining some of herself. "It was a close thing, but she made it. The doctor said that she didn't know how Fryya did it, but she made it." She looked directly at Grammy, and then hugged her fiercely. "Thank you, Grötdaar."

"There now," the old woman said, patting her shoulder. "That's what family does for each other. It's all over now. Fryya will be just fine from here on out, I know this for sure, so don't you worry. The Gods will watch over her from here on."

She stepped back, her own eyes misted with tears. "Now, come along girl, let's see to Marina. I imagine she could use a little company herself just about now."

They found her in the waiting room, and as everyone embraced and offered comfort to one another, the doors to the Emergency Room opened, and the doctor who had spoken with them earlier, came out.

"I just wanted to tell you that Fryya's stable," she announced. "We're monitoring her of course, but I think she'll be fine. It was a close thing, but she's a strong little girl."

After supplying them with a few more details, she turned to leave, but

Lilith intercepted her. There was something about the whole event that was nagging at her, and she had to put her mind at rest.

"Excuse me, Doctor," she asked, feeling a little foolish for even pursuing the matter, "We met earlier, but I didn't have the chance to introduce myself. I'm Vice Admiral ben Jeni. I'm with the family. May I ask you a question?"

"A pleasure to meet you, Vice Admiral. I'd heard that the Grunvaald Farm had some servicewomen visiting from off planet," the physician replied warmly. "What would you like to know?"

"What time did Fryya have her emergency?"

"What time?" the woman replied, a little puzzled by the question. Then she called up the holochart and consulted it. "Well, she began having respiratory issues at 08:33:10, and we called code on her at 08:35:21, but she started breathing on her own again at 08:36:25. Is that what you wanted to know?"

It was, and the data utterly confounded her. She had been awakened at 08:33:79, and no one had mentioned anything about being contacted by the local Com beforehand. Unless that detail had simply been omitted, there had been no way that Grammy could have known about the event. And they had stood together in the High Place until 08:36, which was the exact same time that Fryya had made her miraculous recovery.

She wasn't about to mention this with the doctor though. She barely believed what it implied herself, and she was certain that the physician wouldn't lend it any credence either. In fact, the woman would probably laugh right in her face. Or suggest mental health counselling.

"Yes, doctor, that's what I wanted to know," Lilith said instead. "Thank you for helping her."

"*Gaanskaa gaad,*" the doctor replied. "Oh, and pass along my thanks to Grammy, would you? It's always nice to have a few extra hands helping out at a time like this."

Before Lilith could press her for an explanation, the woman gave her a cryptic smile, and returned to the Emergency Room.

***

When she had sensed the crisis, Jan had been tempted to follow everyone to the High Place. But the danger of being spotted by the Alfs had been too great to take the risk.

Once everyone had driven off in the hovertruck however, her curiosity got the better of her, and she left her body and trailed behind them to the hospital. None of the Alfs made an appearance anywhere along the highway, and although there had been one uncomfortable moment when Grammy had glanced up in her direction, she was certain that the woman hadn't seen her. Experience had taught her that humans were unable to perceive her in her energy body, and she seriously doubted that Grammy was any exception to the rule.

At the hospital, she went in with the group, and while they were busy consoling one another in the waiting room, she drifted through the walls to where the little girl lay. The child was asleep by this point, and Jan tasted her energy.

Fryya was weak, and although her life essence was low, it still burned within her like a candle fighting to remain lit in a strong wind. With rest, it was clear that it would soon rekindle its strength.

Hovering over the bed, she wondered what it had been like for the little girl, to have come so close to death, and yet survived. She also pondered how it might have been had she lost the battle, and slipped away.

Was there some force, equivalent to the Watchers waiting for her, Jan wondered. Something that would offer her the same bright union, the same sweet joy that they did? If so, then she was certain that Fryya had unwittingly cheated herself of a truly marvelous thing.

Grammy entered the room at this point, and Jan remained where she was, completely confident that she would remain undetected. She was quite mistaken.

Looking directly at her, Grammy's expression became hard. "You were not invited here," she said sternly, "Leave this place now! And be grateful that I do not think you were responsible for this! "

The old woman made a quick, precise gesture and something pushed Jan violently out of the room, right through the walls of the hospital itself and out into a place of pure spinning nothingness. When she became conscious again, she was in her body, back at the farmhouse, and covered in sweat. She rose trembling, not from the chill, but from utter dread. Despite all odds, Grammy *had* seen her, and the old woman possessed even more power than she had ever allowed herself to imagine. The jaws of the trap were closing.

***

After dinner was finished, and everyone had gone to bed, Jan bar Daala lay awake in the darkness, listening to the sounds around her and waiting. When she was certain that the entire household was fast asleep, she rose and made her way outside. She had to get out of the house and into the woods. They weren't the familiar red forests of the Lament, but they were close enough to offer her a little symbolic comfort at least, and a place to think.

All through the meal, she'd felt Grammy and Ingrit observing her. Neither woman had said anything out of the ordinary, but it was obvious that they had been assessing her, and deciding what to do next. Naturally, the Alfs had been there in swarms, feeding like so many flies off the energies of the food that everyone had set aside for them. Although they had left her alone, their simple presence had only added to her disquiet.

Miserable creatures, she thought as she climbed away from the farmhouse. She knew that she had to decide what to do, and before Grammy and the others made the choice for her.

She became so engrossed in her ruminations that she didn't realize that she had walked into the High Place until she was right in the middle of it. After her experience in the hospital with Grammy, the spot made her nervous, and she started to retreat. As she did so, she heard a harsh clicking noise and saw that the raven was there, perched on one of the nearby branches and watching her intently. A pair of Alfs made their appearance next, one of them a bright pinpoint of yellow light, and the other a shade of purple that would have been beautiful if she hadn't hated the creatures so much.

"Go away!" she half-shouted, half-whispered at them. They responded to her command by circling around her impudently, and laughing. As she tried to swat at them, a footfall sounded from behind her and Jan whirled around. Grammy and Ingrit were standing there.

"W-what do you want?" Jan demanded, trying not to stammer in fear, and failing miserably. Ingrit had Lilith's side arm in her hand, and Jan was looking straight down its barrel.

"I think that's a question *you* should be answering," Grammy replied. "We both know what you are not. Now you can tell us what you are, and why you came among us. *Waat sa ja?"*

"What?"

"Waat sa ja?" Grammy repeated in a soft singsong voice. "*Waat sa ja, mina gaasten? Waat sa ja? Waat sa ja?"* Her words began to exert a strange hypnotic effect, making Jan feel drowsy and unfocused.

"I'm Admiral ben Jeni's adjutant," Bar Daala said, shaking off the sensation. "Now, put that weapon *down* and let me *leave!*"

But Ingrit didn't lower the pistol. "*Ehk vaan nej!*" the big woman growled, flicking the safety off. Her meaning was obvious even if her words were completely foreign to Jan's ears.

"I'm a naval officer!" Bar Daala protested. "If either of you do anything to me, you'll both end up in a correctional colony."

"Enough of your lies!" Grammy shouted. She made a sharp gesture with her hand and cried, "*Haala-Tiwah-Feh!*"

Jan panicked. *She knows the Sounds! How is this even possible?* Somehow, Grammy understood the sacred Sounds that the Masters themselves had once used. Her execution wasn't as perfect as theirs, but the power was still there. Before Jan could puzzle this out, an invisible force hit her in the chest and knocked her backwards to the ground. Stunned, and gasping for breath, she lay there, unable to move.

Raw terror took over and she started to leave her body. She had to abandon her form immediately, even if it meant death in this alien place. The Watchers would understand, she told herself.

Grammy had other plans in mind. *"Niida-Ees-Niid!"* she intoned, making another gesture. To her horror, Jan realized that somehow, an unknown power was preventing her from leaving her body. She was trapped inside of herself.

There would be no death for her, and no escape.

The old woman stood over her and looked down into her eyes. Her expression was as hard as an ancient rock, and just as unyielding. "Now, my little *gaasten* we will talk, you and I. And you will tell me what you are, and what you are doing here, *Nake vaar?*"

With no other options, Jan surrendered, and told her everything.

***

Dawn was just beginning to redden the sky when the three women came back down to the farmhouse together. They stopped at the threshold to the kitchen.

"We will not speak of this to anyone else," Grammy told Bar Daala, "It is not a thing that *Da Vreestaanden* need know about."

"Thank you," Bar Daala said gratefully.

"But, you must make me one promise in return, little *gaasten*," Grammy added, her breath misting in the cold morning air.

"And that is?"

"If my Katy, or Lilith are ever in danger, you will use all your powers to help them."

Bar Daala considered this request carefully and then nodded, "My alliegence is to the Watchers, but I will do that for you."

Grammy nodded. "I thank you. And when you meet with the Watchers again, give them my greetings and assure them of our full cooperation. Once the Singer and the User awaken, everyone will have to work together to gaurentee the success of their mission."

"I will tell them that," Jan agreed.

All of them understood that from this point forwards, nothing more would be discussed about this, and the secrets that they had revealed to one another would remain between them.

They entered the building and went their seperate ways; Ingrit to rejoin Lilith, Grammy to her own bed, and Bar Daala to hers. Grammy and Ingrit slept, and Jan rested in her own way.

For once, she was able to leave her body without any fear of discovery, or harassment by the Alfs. Grammy had seen to that. It was what allies did for one another.

CHAPTER 6

Old Gaia National Monument, Sol System, Solara Elant, United Sisterhood of Suns,1043.05|28|02:54:81

Celina gazed out at the asteroid field floating by the view port. As the first stop in her research tour for the new realie, she had traveled to the very birthplace of Humanity, the remains of Old Gaia. The space where the world had once existed was now a National Monument, and a premier stop for tourists traveling through the Solara Elant on their way to the Thalestris Elant and Thermadon.

Her reputation, and the generous assistance of the *Tuluraa Daal Foundation for the Arts*, had gotten her the exclusive use of the tour ship, and while the recorder in her handbag documented the signals coming from her psiever, she gazed out at the Monument's main attraction.

It was a life-size statue of Melina Liang. Her bronze image had been set into a piece of rock that had come from the planet's very heart, and while the vessel made a slow orbit around it, the familiar strains of Pachelbel's *'Canon in D'* filled the observation deck.

"It is quite lovely," Clio commented, knowing that her words would be automatically edited out of the recording. A copy of the AI had been loaded into the recorder before Celina had left Corrissa. She never traveled anywhere without Clio; leaving her behind would have been like leaving a part of herself behind. Which in many respects, was exactly what Clio had become over the years.

"Can you tell me a little of the history about the statue, darling? I might need some background information, and I'm a little hazy on some the details." Celina asked.

"Certainly, Celi. Melina Liang was the daughter of the last President of Earth. The MARS plague had decimated Humanity, and the Hriss, seeing that we had been weakened by it, invaded, starting what would later be called the First Widow's War. Do you wish any dates for these events?"

"No thank you," the musician replied. "Just the general sweep of it."

"Yes, Celi," the AI said. "Despite the advantage the Hriss had in ships, weapons, and personnel, the fledgling Sisterhood Navy fought back, and after many losses, finally managed to destroy two of the main Hriss fleets at the Battle of Formahaut."

"Good," Celina said. "That's exactly the kind of thing I wanted to know! We'll have to make sure to visit the battlefield while we're in this Elant."

There was a pause, and then Clio answered. "I've just made a reservation for us. It's open-ended for whenever we need it."

"Thank you, Clio! You're always so thoughtful," Celina beamed.

"Shall I continue with the history of this monument?"

"Please!"

"Well, the Battle of Formahaut turned the tide of the war, but it also enraged the Hriss, and I'm afraid that this is where the story becomes quite heartbreaking."

"Tell it to me," Celina asked her. "I think I know most of it, but I want to hear it again."

"Yes, Celi. The Hriss immediately dispatched a large force to the Sol system with one objective; the total destruction of the Mother Planet herself. They wanted to punish us for beating them, and to demoralize us. The Sisterhood Navy gathered what forces it still had in the area, and sped to the system to prevent this, but…"

"But it was too late," Celina said, finishing the AI's statement.

"Yes," Clio returned sadly. "It was. The Hriss swept aside the defenses of the Solara system, and reached Gaia before our Navy could stop them.'

"In the last few minutes, the President gave a final address to her people, and then her daughter, a virtuoso cellist, made her own farewell by playing Pachelbel's masterpiece. Legend says that the Hriss began their barrage at the precise moment that she played the final note of the Canon."

"How terrible," Celina said. "And beautiful."

"Yes, indeed," Clio agreed. "But instead of achieving what they thought it would, the destruction of Old Gaia became a rallying cry. The Sisterhood fought harder than ever before, and eventually we succeeded in driving them back to their own space and destroying their armed forces. That ended the war."

“But not the Hriss problem,” Celina observed sourly. “We still had the other wars we would have to fight. I wonder if we’ll ever see an end to them.”

“Perhaps, Celi. Is there any more information you would like me to access for you?”

“No,” she said. “Not unless you can tell me why Liang picked the Canon, in her own words.” This had remained a mystery up to the present day. Many students of Music History had wondered about this, with no consensus.

While the piece played on, Celina listened some more and pondered the question herself. Finally, when she felt that she had heard enough, she stopped the loop with her psiever.

It had not been played as a requiem at all, she decided. As a musician herself, she was certain of this. Instead, she believed that Liang had intended it as a tribute; an acknowledgement of all the beauty that had been Old Gaia herself, and a final expression of human dignity in the face of an unavoidable catastrophe.

Wiping a tear away, she realized that the artist could not have picked a more perfect melody to achieve this. In the final analysis, it was the only one that could have been played for the death of an entire world.

A wave of envy for Liang’s poetic gift surged through Celina and she said a silent prayer for the woman and for all the others who had died with her. When she had finished, she turned away from the view port and headed for her cabin. The monument had done precisely what she had hoped it would. It had inspired her, and she wanted to spend the return trip to Mars working some more on the main theme for the *“Song of Humanity.”* It was still incomplete in certain critical sections.

USSNS *Pallas Athena,* In-Orbit, Altamara 1, Altamara System, Frontera Provensa, Esteral Terrana Rapabla, 1043.05|28|05:98:81

As always, Jon ate his lunch by himself. At first, he had done this because no one had wanted to sit with him, but as his time aboard the *Athena* had lengthened, he had actually come to prefer the solitude. It gave him time away from everyone else, and a chance to relax, alone with his thoughts.

He even had one corner of the mess hall that had become his special place; far in the back and away from anything that anyone might have needed. Although he was no longer concerned that someone would dump out his lunch tray, or add anything unpleasant to it (which had happened on more than one occasion), it was still nice to know that his food was reasonably safe, and given his remote location, easy to keep an eye on.

He was just finishing with his main course as Captain Rodraga entered the mess and got himself some lunch. When the man saw him, he made straight for Jon's table and the neoman felt the slightest twinge of annoyance as he presumed an invitation and sat, but he pushed this feeling aside out of politeness and smiled instead.

"Trooper fa'Teela," the officer said, smiling back. "I had hoped that we would have a chance to talk. I've been rather busy since the conference and I'm sure the same has held true for you."

"Yes sir. It has," Jon agreed. "How are you making out here?"

"Well enough," Rodraga replied, taking a bite from his tray. "Admiral ben Jeni has been a gracious host, although there is a great deal I am still getting used to. I'm sure that you can understand, being a man yourself."

Jon made no comment and kept his attention focused on his tray.

"When I was briefed, among other things I was told that you neomen are the product of a group calling itself the Marionite Order. Is that so?"

"Yes, sir. It is."

"Fascinating," Rodraga commented. "So, a form of Christianity really has survived everything that has happened. I would be very interested to hear some things about your faith. I am not the most religious man, but it would be interesting to learn what the similarities are between what I know, and what you believe."

This got Jon's attention. That, and the fact that Rodraga had placed his right hand on the table. It bore a ring. A ring with a stylized cross. Not the Star of the Faithful certainly, but similar enough to leave him in no doubt as to its meaning.

"I would certainly be willing to tell you what I know, sir," Jon answered, at once eager to do so, and equally uneasy. “But I would have to get permission first.”

“Certainly,” Rodraga said. “I understand fully, and I would not want to put you in an awkward position. If your superiors agree then.” He dropped the matter at that, and shifted his attention to his lunch, and lighter conversation.

Across the room, Ophida n’Marsi took careful note of their meeting, and listened as Jon’s copy of the *Revelation of Mari*, which the neoman carried with him everywhere, relayed what they were saying, in its entirety. The transmission came to her on a closed, encrypted psiever channel, and what she heard made her smile with genuine satisfaction.

Destroying his original copy and replacing it with a bugged one had been the best investment she had made in her entire career as an agent, she thought. She noticed the hesitation in Fa’Teela’s tone of course, but she was certain that it was nothing more than an artifice, created to deceive any casual passersby. If things went in the proper direction, she had no doubt that he would quickly abandon this pretense, and willingly enter into an alliance with the ETR officer.

The only question was how to ensure that this took place, and without alerting either of them, and especially Rodraga, of the trap she intended to lay. The man was clearly speaking with the neoman under orders, and would be especially wary.

Perhaps a friendly nudge of encouragement is in order, she thought, putting down her spork. *‘Friendships are like flowers,’* she quoted to herself, *‘and they should be nurtured, and grown with proper care.’*

She abandoned her meal and walked over to the table wearing her friendliest expression. “Captain Rodraga?” she said, “Ever since you came aboard, I had hoped to introduce myself. I am the Ship’s High Priestess.”

Rodraga stood and greeted her with a slight bow. “A pleasure,” he replied. “I had heard of the Sisterhood’s varied and interesting religions before I was sent here. It would be an honor if you would care to explain them to me some time.”

“Of course,” Ophida said, returning his bow. “The Temple and her Daughters are always ready to serve this ship, and its guests. If you wish it, perhaps I can even arrange to hold services for Trooper fa'Teela and yourself. I have had the chance to study some of Fa'Teela's beliefs, and I am certain that he wouldn't mind the company of a fellow male joining him in his religious observances."

To her satisfaction, Ophida saw that she had caught Jon completely off guard with her invitation. Despite numerous attempts to work her way past his defenses, and gain his trust, he had steadfastly avoided her. Now, he was trapped.

Seemingly unaware of Jon's discomfiture, Rodraga's smile broadened. "I certainly would not wish to presume on Trooper fa'Teela, but I would welcome any comfort that your offices might offer, not to mention the chance to engage you in a comparative discussion of religion."

"Yes," she agreed. "That would be welcome. Anytime you wish it, I am available. Trooper fa'Teela can provide you with the directions to the Temple."

"Soon then," the man replied.

"Soon," she agreed. Although he had made a subtle effort to conceal it, she had also seen the ring on Rodraga's finger, and it had only confirmed her suspicions about his true intentions. The moment that the two men had departed the Temple, she contacted Corporal n'Darei by psiever.

Please see to it that Trooper fa'Teela is ordered, in no uncertain terms, to join Captain Rodraga at the next Sevenday worship service, she thought. *Advise him that this is being done to make our guest feel more comfortable during his time aboard. Also stress that this is an order if he gives you any backtalk. I will see to it that your superiors provide any reinforcement that you need.*

The Corporal was only too happy to comply and sought out the neoman immediately. She told him what was expected of him, and a week later, against his will, he reported to the Ship's Temple as ordered.

The service itself was as close an approximation of the Marionite rituals as Ophida was able to manage, and although it certainly contained some inaccuracies, it seemed to satisfy the men. When it ended, her patience, and her guile, finally paid off.

The pair were in the process of leaving when Rodraga paused at the entrance.

"Jon," he said, "I want to thank you for joining me today. Worship is always better when there are others to share in it." As if to emphasize this, he clasped Jon's hand, and shook it.

That was when Jon felt the small piece of plastic flimsy. As Rodraga withdrew his hand, the neoman instinctively closed his fingers over the message.

From the outset, he had known that associating with the ETR officer was an invitation to trouble, and now he had the confirmation in his hand. For a heartbeat, he considered discarding the flimsy the moment that he had the opportunity.

But he immediately rejected the idea. If the note contained what he believed it did, then his course of action had already been determined for him. He made for his rack, and once there, closed the privacy drape and unfolded the flimsy.

"Your Church is in danger," the message warned,*" and we want to help you before it is too late. If you care at all, suggest Saint Tallia's Prayer for Salvation the next time we meet for worship. If not, then stay silent, and I will understand. Your brother in faith. R"*

Staying silent wasn't even an option. Although the Sisterhood had allied itself with a nation that shared many of the values that the True Faith espoused, the Church itself was under increasing assault. Lately, right wing members of the Supreme Circle had renewed their attacks on the Faithful, and they were fanning the flames of prejudice to life. The New Catholic Church of the Revelation of Mari was facing troubled times, and worse were sure to come if the hard-liners gained enough support. Unless the Church found allies to defend them.

But nothing was ever given by the hand of man out of pure altruism. Jon didn't doubt that the ETR would help the Church, but he was also aware that their aid would come with a price. One that might even involve committing treason.

This didn't bother him as much as it once might have though. He had already betrayed his country once, and that time, the genetic samples that he had risked his freedom for had helped give birth to the Redeemer. If God had moved the ETR to offer their aid to his Church, then treason or no, it was in accord with his will, Jon decided.

When they met in the Ship's temple once again, he would ask for *Saint Tallia's Prayer for Salvation*, just as Rodraga had instructed. And when he recited it, he would not only be praying for himself, but for his Church, and all of the Faithful, everywhere.

Métropol Musé de Arte, Thermadon Val, Thermadon, Myrene System, Thalestris Elant, United Sisterhood of Suns, 1043.06|12|01:25:83

There were many inventions that had profoundly changed the nature of human existence. Perhaps one of the most important of all was incandescent light, which according to official Sisterhood history, had first been conceived of by Ms. Abigail Browning, the secret mistress of Thomas Edison, in 1835 BSE. Seeing its tremendous potential, he promptly stole her idea, and some claimed, 'perfected' it.

Although this invention represented a great step forwards for the species, humanity as a whole had always had the unfortunate tendency to resist radical change, especially when it ran contrary to eons of well-established behavior. It took another 200 pre-standard years for Gaia's children to accept the concept that they were no longer a primitive agrarian society, or yoked to the ancient boundaries of sunrise to sunset to function effectively.

But, by the mid-22nd century, it had finally become commonplace for both commercial and public buildings to remain open, and fully staffed, for the entire 24 hours of Gaia's rotation, and all seven of the days of its week. Profits and productivity soared.

Coming into being after the MARS plague, the Sisterhood had avoided these growing pains, and the influence of the Nyxian culture only helped to support the idea that a truly advanced civilization was able, and willing, to function 'around-the-clock.'

Nowhere was this better implemented than in Thermadon Val. The great metropolis was not only known of as the Capitol, but also rightly held the ancient title of 'the city that never sleeps'. At no point during the day or night, did Thermadon ever slow down, or close its doors to its citizens.

What all this meant for Celina was that the great *Métropol Musé de Arte* was open any time that she wished to visit it, but being a celebrity, she also ran the excellent chance of being recognized, and having her work interrupted by otherwise well meaning fans--even at 01:25 hours. The solution that her agent and the Métropol staff had arrived at was to close the Main Collection and the Gaian Wing for a standard day, citing annual maintenance as the reason.

She arrived just ten minutes after the two sections had been closed, and at the back entrance. A single securitywoman and a senior representative of the Museum staff met her and quickly showed her inside. And even though they didn't openly request autographs, she made certain to express her gratitude for the trouble the Métropol had gone to by giving both of them signed copies of her latest realie, along with additional copies for other staff members. It was the least she could do, and their gratitude, although carefully understated, was still palpable.

When they reached the Gaian Wing, the senior staffer quietly departed, and left her alone with the security officer. This was not out of any concern for theft or vandalism on her part, but simple courtesy. The Métropol wanted to make certain that their special guest was as comfortable as possible, and the officer was there to make sure that anything she needed, she received.

As for the guard herself, she was professional enough to keep a careful distance, and after a few minutes, Celina completely forgot that she was even there. This was easy enough to do; the two wings comprised the greatest works of art of both Gaian and Sisterhood history, spanning from the earliest masterpieces of the Motherworld to the works of the present, and they quickly ensnared her full attention. With Clio recording everything as raw realie footage, she started at the farthest end of the Gaian Wing and took her time moving through it, making her journey a trip through time as well as physical space. She was careful to stop not only at pieces that spoke to her own heart, but also at those that she felt truly summed up the human experience as a whole.

Some of these she already knew quite well, such as the famous *"Head of a Tudor Girl"* by Eleanor Fortescue-Brickdale, or *"Joan of Arc"* created by Annie Louisa Swynnerton, a painting that was so celebrated that it was almost cliché. But there were other works that were less familiar, and they came as pleasant surprises not only for her, but also for her future audience.

One of these had no known artist and had only been given the simple title, *"The Lady of Ajanta."* Celina paused in front of the graceful sculpture and asked Clio to tell her what she could about the piece.

"Unfortunately, Celi, there isn't much to tell," the AI apologized. "It was part of the Great Find of 946.19, and the only thing that scholars know for certain is that it was originally from the subcontinent of India, and created during a period historians call the Harappan era. Shall I define that term for you?"

"No, thank you," Celina answered, a little disappointed. The Great Find that her virtual companion had just referred to had taken place on Mars when construction on the Trans-Amazonia Tunnel had inadvertently uncovered a chamber filled with priceless works of Gaian art. The vault was believed to have been the creation of art thieves operating sometime before the MARS Plague and the destruction of Old Gaia, and because of this, there had been few records accompanying the hoard. Despite the sinister motives behind its creation, the vault had been a gift of incalculable worth to humanity, and there were still many adventurers scouring the surface of the 'Red Planet' hoping to find other caches just like it.

The musician considered the sculpture and then instructed Clio to include it. "I think it will make a nice statement about just how much knowledge has been lost about our origins, and how much beauty," she remarked. Every time that she encountered something as ancient as this, she always wondered what other treasures had become lost in the tumult of history, and completely forgotten. It was something that she wanted her audience to wonder at as well and possibly, to dream a little about what once might have been.

As soon as she was satisfied that she had enough data on the piece, she moved on to the next exhibit; *"A Section of the Villa of the Mysteries: Pompeii, Cubiculum 16"*.

This was actually a section of an entire wall, which had been removed as part of the conservation effort to preserve the treasure found at the ancient Roman city of Pompeii. It was decorated with a mural showing Roman women going about their various domestic duties, and even though they were strangely dressed, and their hair was done quite differently than what a contemporary woman might have considered fashionable, it was their faces that called to her over the centuries.

These were womankind's ancestors, she reflected, her sisters from a vanished age. Although Motherthought tended to view such women with respect, it also saw them as being somewhat less evolved socially and physically, and it held up the Sisterhood, and the women of the present, as the apex of female existence.

While she certainly appreciated her nation for all that it had given women, she privately disagreed with this patronizing attitude. One of her more radical professors in Tertiary had put it best, *"The conceit of those in the present is always to view those of the past as less intelligent, and forget that they were the same as us, but simply enjoyed fewer advantages."*

This wasn't a sentiment that she had any intention of stating openly however. Many women followed the precepts of Motherthought wholly and without question. Instead, she would simply include the footage, and make sure to focus in on the faces. Some of her audience, she knew, would see what she did, and that was enough.

She moved on as soon as Clio had the footage. The next work that caught her eye was entitled *'Mona Lisa'* and its artist was one Leonora Da'Vinci. It wasn't one of the more notable works, and she felt that its use of color was rather crude, but the subject in the painting had a certain enigmatic aura about her, and she made another inquiry with Clio.

"The painting is catalogued by the Museum as the portrait of Lisa Gherardini," the AI replied. "As for the artist, Leonora Da'Vinci is referenced as one of the lesser known renaissance female painters, and she created the work at or around 1503 BSE."

"Thank you dear," Celina said. "We'll include it just for that smile. It's really quite striking."

A few meters beyond, Celina spotted a genuine treasure, *"The Chess Game"* by Sofonisba Anguissola. Unlike Leonora Da'Vinci, Anguissola was well known and highly admired. *"The Chess Game"* depicted the artist herself, at play with her daughters Lucia, Minerva and Europa.

"The Chess Game" was a bright and cheerful piece, and she was certain that her audience would appreciate it. She briefly played with the idea of having Clio delete the Da'Vinci piece. There was only so much time that she had allotted for the museum section of the realie, and it was a *very* obscure work, but then she reconsidered the notion. For the present at least, *Mona Lisa* would stay, and if there were enough room in the presentation to include it, it would make the final cut—as filler.

The years of the paintings advanced as she walked along, leaving the ancient world and the Renaissance behind and carrying her into the 19th century BSE. The works in this section were the creations of such geniuses as Mary Cassatt, Ivana Kobilka and the wonderful Pre-Raphaelite artist, Maria Spartali Stillman. Two of Stillman's compositions vied for Celina's attention and a place in the realie, *"The Rose from Armidias Garden"* and *"Madonna-Peitra"*, and she examined both with care and consideration. Each was an exceptional work, but in the end, it was the beauty of the lighting, and the warm mood that surrounded the *"Madonna"* that won her over.

"Clio," she added as they finished recording the painting. "Could you also send an inquiry to the Museum and see if they have a reproduction of this? It would look simply wonderful in our home, don't you agree?"

"Yes, Celi it would—and we're in luck! They have one for sale, and it's very reasonably priced. Shall I order it, and have it shipped home?"

"Yes, dear. Please do," Celina said with a delighted tone. Then another notion hit her, and she added, "And could you also see about that little Da'Vinci piece? It's probably too obscure to be available, but it doesn't hurt to try, does it? I'm afraid it's grown on me since I laid eyes on it."

"Accessing the catalog, "the AI replied. After a slight pause, it came back with the results. "The *Madonna* has been ordered and is on its way to Corrissa right now, but I'm afraid that we ran out of luck with the other one. The *Mona Lisa* is not part of their normal reproduction inventory, but the Métropol AI did say that it could refer us to one of their vendors who might be able to make us a copy. Would you like me to access the listings?"

The musician sighed. "Yes, I suppose so. I would have to want something no one but an art herstorian has ever heard about. Oh, and while you're at it, can you send for some lunch? I'm absolutely famished."

The guard appeared several minutes later with some sandwiches and kaafra, and then departed. As Celina took her meal on a bench at the entrance to the Main Collection, she considered the melody that had inspired her adventure, and imagined the pieces she'd seen being presented in time with the notes. Even the little Da'Vinci composition seemed to have its place, although she couldn't say precisely why.

But as always, she got the sense that there was something missing in the composition. Ever since she had dreamed about the song, there was an ephemeral element to it that evaded discovery and it frustrated her. The music felt incomplete, as if there was a depth within it that she had yet to plumb.

Clio sensed her mood. "Are you having more problems with the main theme?" she asked solicitously. "I have some additions that I composed that might fill in the gaps." At a nod from her mistress, she sent them via psiever.

Celina listened to them play in her mind, and she had to admit that they *were* good. But as harmonious as the variations sounded, they still felt wrong somehow, as if the music and her personal Muse wanted her to go in another direction entirely.

"They are lovely, "she finally said. "But…"

"It's all right, Celi," Clio replied, with just a hint of disappointment. "Perhaps we can use them for other parts of the realie."

"Yes," Celina smiled. "Yes, we'll certainly do that. You know I can't really put a realie together without your contributions."

This was more than just a salve to her companion's artificial ego. It was a simple fact. What Celina's fans didn't realize was that her AI had actually composed some of her more popular songs, or that her dedication to Clio on *"A Concert for Eversea"* wasn't for a secret lover, but to a computer program. The truth about the two of them was no one's business however, and better left a mystery. A real flesh and blood lover wouldn't have demanded any less.

Celina finished her lunch, and after the guard had taken the remains away, walked into the Main Collection. This portion of the Museum concerned itself with contemporary art, but its definition of 'modern' started with the 20th century BSE, moved on through to the 23rd, through the Plague and finally at the far end of the great expanse, brought the visitor from the early days of the Sisterhood and into what most women would consider the 'present'.

Although she had never personally cared for the works of the 20th through 23rd centuries, the musician made sure to pay homage to some of the established masters from those times, stopping at the most notable pieces before walking on. There was a lot to cover, and she took another break at the end of the 23rd century before going into the area she had been looking forwards to visiting; the Sisterhood era.

There were three paintings and a sculpture that she wanted to make certain to include, but instead of making a beeline to them like some fringe-world schoolgirl visiting the place for the first time, she kept her decorum and paced herself. Even so, when she finally stood before the great impressionist work *"Thermadonian Night"*, it was all she could do to tear herself away from it and move on to lesser creations.

Then she met up with another pair of favorites; *"A Portrait of a Thermadonian Lady"* and *"Martian Sunrise."* Like *"Night"*, these were also impressionist paintings, and she knew that she was lavishing a little too much attention on this style, but she reminded herself that it was *her* realie after all, and neither was as 'hard' as "Night" was, but tended towards realism. At least this argument *sounded* reasonable.

Her final stop for the evening was a paean to the entire Sisterhood and its artists, a patriotic gesture expressed in sculpture. In planning her visit to the Métropol, she had debated which artist would have the final 'say' in this section, but she had wanted it to be a sculpture.

There had been several worthies to choose from. The first had been the statue of Molla n'Dayr, the famous leader of a rebellion against Hriss invaders, with her fist raised in defiance. Another had been *"Portrait in Bronze of Hana Lisa Reese,"* the first woman to fly solo through Nullspace, her space-helmet in her arms, and looking bravely towards an unknown future. But the winner had been a much older subject, which in the musician's mind best expressed the ancient legacy of women and their art. This was a contemporary copy of a 19th BSE century piece, entitled simply; *"Pentheselea"* and it had been sculpted by the renowned Jann Lexxi, a Corrissan.

Celina stopped in front of the twice life-size bronze image of the ancient queen, and lingered there, taking in the details that Lexxi had created; the woman's bow strung and ready, the armor lashed to her body, and finally her face. This was perhaps the most striking part of the bronze. Lexxi had updated the regents' features, doing away with the originals' tendency towards plumpness and a certain vacancy of expression, and replacing it with the face of a more modern woman. A woman who possessed a gaze that was at once determined and fierce, but also filled with wisdom and compassion.

The Métropol must have felt the same way as Celina did about the image, because it had been placed at the very end of the gallery and faced back towards the Gaian wing. Situated like this, the Amazon queen looked back from her place in the present, over the visitor's shoulders, and down through time to the very earliest periods of feminine creativity. She seemed to say to the visitor, *'All of this is ours. Look upon it and marvel. Are we not great?'*

Yes, Celina thought, gazing in the same direction. *We are at that.*

Salta Cia, Altamara 1, Altamara System, Frontera Provensa,
Esteral Terrana Rapabla, 1043.06|16|08:25:52

When the *Oyamay Flaara* arrived over Salta Cia, it was interrogated by traffic control, and after declaring its cargo, received permission to send a launch down to the surface. The fact that one member of the landing crew was a bit old to work aboard a merchanter, and moved with less assurance than his crewmates, didn't raise any eyebrows however. The ETR did things differently, and the man's identity matched the ship's records.

Dressed in a simple crewman's coverall, and carrying a humble kit bag, Bishop da Castraa of the Republican Orthodox Church, was waved through the Customs station and allowed to go anywhere he wanted—as long as he stayed on the ETR side of the town, or in the neutral zone everyone called Dogtown. Hefting his bag, the cleric headed for the *Halflife Club* where his contact, and the first of many guides on his long journey, was awaiting him.

Unlike the Bishop, she really was what she seemed; a member of her ship's crew, the CSS *Fanny Campbell*, out of Corrissa, and although their two faiths shared a common origin, she was a Marionite, and he was not. It was their very commonality and differences that had given birth to the task he was undertaking. The Church had always come to the aid of its own, even if those that they were aiding held to some beliefs that varied wildly from the Truth. The True Gospel would come later, he assured himself, after the dangerous times that they found themselves in had passed.

When his guide was certain that no one was paying them any attention, she led him to a back exit and out into an alley behind the bar. At the far end, there was a ground car waiting for them, and another woman. They got in and the driver took them through the narrow streets to a small, unimposing warehouse.

Inside, were several more members of the *Campbell's* crew, and with them, a shipping box. At their direction, Bishop da Castraa got inside and they sealed him in. The label on the box declared the contents to be '*Live Biological Specimens! Destination: University of Thermadon Entomology Department. Danger! Venomous Insectoids (Species: Hyminoptera Nuvo Bolivaris/Common Name: 'Honey Bees'). Do not Open!'* Because of this, the whirring of an environmental support unit wasn't out of place, and the possibility of anyone opening it up for inspection was highly unlikely.

Grasping the guide handles and activating the hover unit, the crewwomen loaded their freight aboard another ground car, a cargo-model this time, and took it straight to the Sisterhood spaceport facilities.

When they were stopped for inspection, they declared their shipment, and a military policewoman looked at it, and even went as far as scanning it. The fact that it didn't register any biohazards was duly recorded. What was not documented, was that the 'living organisms' within the case actually registered as a single being, and that it came back as humanoid. And a few minutes later, as the *Campbell* headed out from Altamara for the Sagana Territory and the greater Sisterhood beyond, the policewoman said a small prayer to Jesu and Mari, entreating them to ensure the cases' contents a safe journey.

***

Valeri bel Hana of the OAE smiled and sat back in her chair at the workstation the Commander of the *Pele'* had graciously loaned to her. The holo floating before her showed that the *Fanny Campbell* was assuming position in the convoy scheduled to head out for Thenti. The merchanter's captain had listed Tithari in the Telesalla Elant as her final destination, and there was even the remote chance that they might actually visit the place, but the agent knew what their cargo was, and where it was actually headed.

The only question that she really had on her mind was how long they would take to get there, and beyond that, how much time it would take for their undercover agents to document the meeting between Pope Paula VI and Bishop da Castraa.

CHAPTER 7

The galaxy had existed for countless eons, and the passage of a single year was insignificant by comparison—a mere flicker of time that was too brief to be of any genuine consequence.

But for the trillions of intelligent life forms that inhabited its starry reaches, this temporal span seemed much longer, and far more important. Out in the furthest of its arms, the United Sisterhood of Suns marked the New Year as 1044 ASE, and in the Esteral Terrana Rapabla, it had been observed as 3224 AD. For both nations, it was a time of war...

USSMC 93rd Special Operations Training Center, Sniper Training School, Larra's Lament, Lalita System, Artemi Elant, United Sisterhood of Suns, 1044.06|16|02:38:33

Kaly n'Deena had been born in the year 1027.06 at 02:38 in the morning. 17 years later, at the same hour, her birthday occurred in the middle of an open grassy field. She was lying flat, trying to ignore the cold sleet that was raining down on her. Her gillie suit kept out most of it, but some of the frigid drizzle had still managed to find its way past the garments defenses, and the frozen ground underneath her conspired with it to make staying warm nearly impossible.

At least I don't have to pee, she reminded herself. That problem had been alleviated the only way that was available to a sniper in her situation, and she'd learned to just ignore her soiled diaper, and 'soldier on'.

The young woman clenched her jaw tightly to keep her teeth from chattering, and looked through her riflescope at her objective. She had spent the last two days crossing the field, moving only a few centimeters at a time, to evade detection by the Instructors.

Now she was in range of her target, a small white square that represented an enemy asset. She knew that she would have only one chance at hitting it, and the range was extreme. She briefly considered moving closer, and then double-checked her distance, the ambient air-temperature and the speed of the wind around her. The round from her chemical rifle would be affected by these factors, but aside from making the shot only slightly more certain, she realized that moving any closer wouldn't improve the conditions.

After six grueling months of Special Operations Training on Hella's World, which had vastly surpassed all of the hardships she had borne there as a hatchie, and another six at the unforgiving Sniper Training School on Larra's Lament, she was facing her final challenge. It was a pass/fail field exercise that had involved days of land navigation coupled with evasion and detection avoidance.

If one of the Sniper School Instructors spotted her position now, or worse, if she missed the shot, then all of her pain and sacrifice would be in vain. The ancient motto that the school had adopted said it all: *'Un tir, un uspar. Non eçez'*; 'One shot, one kill. No exceptions'. She either succeeded, or any chances that she might have had of becoming a Marine Marauder Sniper were over. There were no options to repeat the course.

Not that I'm under any pressure, she thought. For better or worse, it was time to trust her judgment and her hard-won skills.

Kaly rested her finger lightly on the trigger of her MRS 1400 and looked down her riflescope. With a command from her psiever, she zoomed in until she was comfortable with her sight picture, and then, as a precaution, double-checked her target and the area around it in the infrared and bioplasmic bands. Sometimes, the Instructors hid secondary targets nearby, which represented other important enemy assets, and if they had done so here, Kaly would be required not only to hit her primary target, but also take out the other ones as well. She knew of at least one other candidate who had failed her test by not doing that, and she didn't plan to share her fate.

This time though, the target was by itself—no tricks (unless she'd missed something crucial)—just a straightforward shot. Reasonably sure of her situation, Kaly switched back to conventional light and moved the virtual crosshairs until they met with the weapons actual point of aim. The hairs were centered on the target.

Back in her days in Basic as a hatchie, the weapon she was holding would have surprised her. Then, she had been proud of her Mark 7 energy rifle and absolutely certain that it represented the very peak of the Corps' arsenal. And she had been partially justified; the Mark 7 was everything that Kaly believed it was, and that the Sisterhood had designed it to be. It was tough, reliable, and it had proven itself in combat many times over.

However, it also possessed drawbacks that she hadn't suspected as a raw recruit. Special Operations Teams weren't like conventional units and they had different demands. Premier among them were stealth and silence. As good as they were, conventional weapons like the Mark 7 simply didn't make the grade.

Energy weapons, although powerful, created a very loud and distinctive 'crack' when their bolts superheated the air. Worse, the track of their bolts was visible to any enemy. Magnetic rail systems weren't much better. Like the needlegun and its larger sister, the naval rail gun, their rounds went out at supersonic speeds, making just as much racket.

But by employing the ancient technology of chemically propelled bullets, coupled with sound suppressors, the 'Marine Rifle, Sniper 1400' and other SpecOps weapons were whisper silent, and killed their targets just as efficiently as any modern system would. They were the very expression of the venerable concept, *'La'va Ninor'*, or *"If it works, it needs no replacement',* and the MRS 1400 in particular, was considered to be the premier tool of the Marine Sniper.

Kaly's MRS also had its own name. Just as in Basic, when she had begun Sniper Training School, she had been expected to give her weapon a unique personality. This time however, she had had the chance to prepare, and had made her decision intelligently. In homage to the great female snipers of the past, she had chosen to call her weapon *'Tatiana'* after the great Tatiana Baramzina.

Baramzina had served in the Soviet Armed Forces during the second of Old Gaia's five world wars, and had been credited with 36 kills before being captured and brutally executed by the German Army. Kaly had wanted to memorialize her sacrifice and bravery, and she earnestly hoped that in return, Baramzina's spirit would bless the path that she had chosen for herself—and her shot. The next few seconds would tell, one way or the other.

She let Tatiana's barrel rise and fall with her breathing. On its third descent, she said a little prayer to the Lady and the ancient Soviet sniper, exhaled and fired. The silenced weapon made no sound, and downrange, the round hit its target, dead center.

Kaly didn't stand up to cheer though. Instead, she began the painstaking process of backing away and leaving the area. Unless the Instructors signaled otherwise, she had two more days of backtracking until she reached the concealment of the tree line behind her, and the opportunity to crawl away at something approaching normal speed.

When nothing happened, she resigned herself to her long journey, and moved her body back the first centimeter. But then, to her immense relief, a green flare rose in the air and her psiever flashed with a message: 'EXERCISE COMPLETE'.

No other two words had ever been sweeter. Kaly n'Deena, now the newest Special Operations Sniper, forced a weak smile from her frozen lips, and raised herself slowly.

That night, back at the Training Center barracks, Kaly rediscovered the pleasures of a hot shower and a real bed. Her body, weary from days spent in the cold and damp of the Lamentine forests, begged her for rest. She had two things that she needed to do before she would allow this to happen however.

The first was a quick, but thorough inspection and wipe-down of her rifle, and once she was completely satisfied with its state, her second task awaited. It was to compose a message to Lena.

Lena, my darling, she thought, engaging her psievers record function. *I passed my sniper course today! I am so excited! I am now officially a Marauder, and they told me that they'd be assigning me to a team very soon. I wish you could have been here to share this with me...but...I understand. Maybe when I see you again, we can celebrate. I miss you so much. Love, Kaly.*

She almost even sent it. But then, she did what she had done with all the other letters that she'd composed, and put it in her virtual 'drafts' file instead. There, it would stay.

Kaly had come to accept the fact that Lena just needed time, and space away from her. And while she hated the silence between them, the possibility of driving her lover away forever by pushing things, was simply too great. Instead, it was better to be content with their one sided conversation, she told herself.

Someday, when Lena was ready, she would send her the letters, and if the Goddess was of a mind to bless them, Lena might even agree to share their lives together once again. Until then, all Kaly could do was to keep writing, and waiting. Patience, she had learned, was a valuable quality, not only for snipers, but also for relationships.

The Apex Office, The Golden Pyramid, Thermadon Val, Thermadon, Myrene System, Thalestris Elant, United Sisterhood of Suns, 1044.06|17|03:33:62

Senatrix n'Calysher, D'Salla and Lady Felecia arrived together at the Apex Office ten minutes before the Seevaan ambassador was scheduled to meet with the Chairwoman. All of them, including Felecia, had been to the famous office before, and the Protective Servicewomen on duty showed them in immediately.

Chairwoman Marina bel Rayna and her Secretary of Trade, Hilari n'Teela stood as they entered, and Bel Rayna came from around her desk to greet them. *The* Desk.

It was known throughout the Sisterhood as the 'Defiant Desk'. This iconic piece of furniture was the very same one that the first Chairwoman had sat behind as she had directed their tiny armed forces in their desperate fight against the Hriss invaders of the First Widow's War.

True to its name, it was a solid thing, constructed of dark Nemesian baaka wood and looked as if it were strong enough to withstand the assault of an entire battle fleet all by itself. As many times as Felecia had seen it (and had even played under it as a little girl) it never failed to make an impression on her. The Desk was a symbol unto itself; of strength, wisdom and firm resolve.

"Layna, Barbra?" Bel Rayna said smiling. "Thank you for coming. I always appreciate your feedback after these meetings."

This was Felecia's first official meeting with the Seevaans and the politician made certain to acknowledge this. "Lady Felecia, good to see you here as well. I think that you'll find this educational. The Seevaans are a very unique race."

"Thank you Madame Chairwoman," she replied, adding a small formal bow that conveyed the proper respect for the supreme leader of the Sisterhood. Learning to do business with Humanity's primary benefactor was one of the most important parts of a Senatrix's job. The Seevaans had presented humanity with many marvels, not the least of which was interstellar travel, and their two civilizations enjoyed a lucrative trade relationship. They were also a complex race, and a lot rode on a proper understanding of their nature. Felecia had studied everything she could about them, and she hoped that her first meeting with their representatives would go smoothly.

"So," Bel Rayna said as she returned to her place behind The Desk, "Queen Talaria and her retinue should arrive in about five minutes. Is there anything that the Circle has been up to that I need to know about before she gets here?"

"Not really," Senatrix n'Calysher replied as she took a seat. "The Circle ratified the latest trade agreement with their government last week, and despite a little grumbling from the Uni's, it remains unchanged in its substance. I think Queen Talaria will find it to her liking."

"Good!" Bel Rayna said, clapping her hands together. She closed her eyes for an instant, and then reopened them. "She's here."

Everyone's eyes turned towards the door as it opened and Queen Talaria strode in. She was typical of her species. Standing on six legs, she reached a little over 1.82 meters in height, not counting the small antennae on her long oval head. Her body was a brilliant shade of mantis green, which was not only an appropriate description for the color, but also for her appearance. She resembled the old Gaian insect quite closely, except on a gargantuan scale.

Normally, the noblewoman would have presented herself in all her finery; intricately worked sheaths on her legs, her fore-pincers painted with brilliant lacquer, and her vestigial wings bedecked with jewels. But today, she had a comparatively plain appearance, with only the tiniest bit of clear lacquer visible on her pincers. Female vanity, Felecia thought wryly, was universal, and ignorant of race or origin.

This dearth of decoration was, the girl knew, in deference to the Seevaan celebration of the Great Feast of Purification. Impressed by Humanity's ability to foment chaos wherever it went, and also by its survival of the MARS plague and the prosperity which had followed that event, the Seevaans had taken a hard look at their own society, and found it wanting. They had realized, in the words of the Empress at the time, that their own 'hives were disharmonious and imperfect', primarily due to the presence of males.

Their solution to this problem had been immediate, conclusive, and wholly Seevaan. They had simply eaten them. With the exception of a handful of warriors still serving as ceremonial bodyguards for their dignitaries (at the insistence of another faction, the Traditionalists), their race was now 99% female, and celebrated the cannibalistic genocide of their opposite numbers every year, as a national holiday.

While unique for its scale, the Seevaan custom of cannibalism wasn't anything remarkable. Insectoids had done this for millions of years, from the black widow spider of Old Gaia to the praying mantas that the Seevaans resembled. The only difference was that for them, the practice had been institutionalized, and didn't center exclusively on their males.

From the Empress downward, succession to a higher position in any field was not considered truly complete until one's rival had been slain and completely consumed. There was even a special group of Imperial officials that verified that all body parts had been properly disposed of before a new Empress was permitted to ascend to the great Golden Nest.

Humans however, had nothing to worry about; when asked, the Seevaans were only too happy to assure them that they did not taste good, and were therefore in no danger of joining the menu. How they knew this, and when they had discovered that this was the case, was not a subject for polite conversation however.

Felecia joined the Chairwoman, and everyone else as they rose at the Queen's entrance, and rewarded her with deep bows. Then Bel Rayna addressed the regent, using a form of sign language that had been developed to approximate the intricate pincer movements that the Seevaans used to communicate with. It was something that every accomplished diplomat learned, and even Felecia was familiar with it.

"Greetings, Queen Talaria," the Chairwoman signed, "and my best wishes again on your ascension." Talaria had recently become a Queen herself, after defeating her mother in ritual combat, and then devouring her. Although new to her office, she was, like her predecessor, a shrewd politician and an able diplomat.

"Thank you for mentioning it, Chairwoman," the Seevaan replied with movements that were as elegant as Bel Rayna's were not. Lacking the same body structures, humans would never master the niceties of their language and both sides simply accepted this and worked with it.

"I am sure that you know everyone here, "Bel Rayna said, indicating the other women, "how can we receive the grace of your presence today?"

"I came to compliment you on your decision to defend the human hive you call the ETR," the alien replied. "The Hriss are disharmonious, and defeating them will set things in proper order."

Although flattering, this statement also conveyed that the Seevaans were interested in the conflict, and ultimately, how it would affect relations between their two races. Queen Talaria wanted assurances that any business between them would go on, undisturbed. While she was a Chaotic, the Seevaan notion of this implied that it was focused towards the outside world, and not fomented among friends.

"Thank you, my Lady," the Chairwoman returned. "We saw the necessity to do so when our fellow humans asked us for our aid. In the meantime, I must assure you that our own dealings with your great race will remain unaltered."

"Yes, Chairwoman," Talaria answered. "I had no doubt that with the benefit of your wise leadership, that the status quo would be maintained despite this small disturbance."

"Indeed, my Lady," Bel Rayna agreed. "Since we are on that subject, perhaps we could discuss receiving more assistance from you concerning the Drow'voi material? Our scientists have come quite far thanks to the brilliance of your people, and we would very much like to see the project brought to completion."

Senatrix d'Salla had enlightened Felecia about this before the meeting. An archeological expedition to a Drow'voi ruin on the Sisterhood planet of Storm had uncovered a technology, which if the scientists were correct, would allow for the instantaneous transmission of living matter from one point to anywhere else in the universe. But with limitations; the amount of living material was effectively restricted to individuals or to small groups of women, and over very long distances the process tended to damage, or rewrite their DNA. The Sisterhood already knew how to transmit inanimate matter successfully, but until the discovery on Storm, every effort to send live subjects anywhere, had ended horrifically. However, the Seevaans had deciphered the process, and had been helping Humans to understand it through what had been found at the dig site.

Of course, they hadn't simply given it all away without any expectation of return. Aside from the fact that their aid aggravated the Zeta Reticulans who disliked them only a shade less than Humanity, the Seevaans had been parceling out their help in exchange for increased trade advantages. The Chairwoman and her administration had been playing the game right along with them, exchanging what they had to, for what the nation needed. While it would never replace the transportation of bulk goods through Nullspace, the new Drow'voi technology offered vast new possibilities for exploration, colonization, and naturally, warfare.

"We are certainly willing to have our wise ones expend some more of their time on your great project," Talaria said with a definite 'but' hidden within her signs, "although we will require that the concessions we proposed be implemented in our latest trade agreement. We also insist on retaining the survivor for some time to come. She is still of great interest to us."

The Chairwoman smiled, having already expected this, and signed her acquiescence. "We have incorporated your desires into the latest agreement, and I have been assured by my able companions here, that you will find it to your liking. As for Dr. n'Aida, I am sure that were she able to tell you so herself, she would be more than willing to continue to serve our race in her present capacity."

Once they had learned about what had been discovered on Storm, the

Seevaans had immediately offered their help, but only on the condition that the lone survivor of the ill-fated expedition was turned over to them to examine. Although what use she was to them was a complete mystery to everyone, including Felecia. Thanks to her exposure to the Drow'voi devices secreted in the ruins, Dr. Shandra n'Aida had had her DNA re-written, making her into a strange hybrid of human and what was presumed to be Drow'voi. She had also lapsed into an irreversible coma, presumably as a byproduct of the process.

As for her associates, no one knew what had happened to them, or even if they were still alive. But the girl had no doubt that the Chairwoman was correct about the scientist's position on the matter. Had she been able to. Dr. n'Aida would have surely agreed to the exchange, given the stakes.

"That is pleasing," Talaria responded. "We have much to learn from Dr. n'Aida that may well affect us all. In the meantime, I look forwards to reviewing our trade agreement, and I will send the wise ones to revisit your own learned women. "She paused, undoubtedly for effect and added, "In the meantime, may I ask another favor of you?"

"Certainly, great lady," Bel Rayna said. "How can the Sisterhood be of service?"

"By granting me a mere trifle," the Queen responded. "I am an admirer of your music, and of your great artist, Celina. While our delegation is visiting your wonderful city, perhaps you could arrange for a visit to her studio? I have heard that she was here, working on her latest masterpiece, and I would dearly love the opportunity to watch her at work."

"Consider it done, Queen Talaria," the Chairwoman assured her. "This office is only too happy to showcase the talents of its citizens. I will make the arrangements immediately." Then she bowed.

"My eternal thanks, Chairwoman. May you prosper as Queen of your hive." At that, the Seevaan executed a bow of her own, which despite her many legs and odd proportions, was quite elegant.

USSNS *Pallas Athena*, In-Orbit, Altamara 1, Altamara System,
Frontera Provensa, Esteral Terrana Rapabla, 1044.06|23|02:51:79

The *Athena's* familiar welcome sign greeted Kaly as she stepped aboard the vessel. She had specifically requested the posting and the Goddess had granted her wish, despite the high odds of being attached to another unit. This time, she didn't need anyone to guide her, and after presenting her orders to the sailor on duty, made her own way down to "Five-Bar". Troop Leader da'Saana was in her office, and the normally taciturn woman got up from her desk and greeted her warmly.

"Well, if it isn't Corporal n'Deena!" she said. "I thought we'd finally gotten rid of you!"

Kaly put down her rifle case, and gave her a salute. "It's not as easy as that, Troop Leader. I liked it here so much that I asked to come back. I think it was the food. Is it still any good?"

The Troop Leader laughed. "No worries on that score, N'Deena. The *Hounds* might get all the really *fekked-up* jobs, but we still eat better than any other ground-pounders in the Fleet."

Then she examined the flimsy Kaly offered her. "Marauder Team 5, eh? Those girls are a good group—they've pulled our asses out of the fire a few times. They'll make sure that you get your fair share of the *shess,* and then some."

"That's what I was hoping for, Troop Leader," the young woman grinned.

"Well, I certainly don't need to tell you how to find the pods. You'll want to report in to Lieutenant sa'Kaali when you get there. She runs the Marauder Teams under Major n'Neesa, and 5 has been down since they lost their last sniper. She'll be glad to hear they'll be going operational again. Get with her and she'll introduce you to your team. Her office is just off the ready room for Betsi section."

"Thanks, Troop Leader," Kaly said. "And would you tell Colonel Lislsdaater for me that she was right? SpecOps really was the best decision for me."

"I will, but let's just see how much you like it after you've been on a few real ops with your team," Da'Saana cautioned her. "It's a whole different animal than the kind of action you saw with us."

Kaly simply shrugged. "I'll do my best, Troop Leader."

She found the Lieutenant's office, and the woman herself, waiting for her in Betsi Section. Sa'Kaali seemed to be made from the same stuff as her old DI, Rani sa'Tela, and not just in terms of her ethnicity. The Kalian had the same hard, no nonsense aura, and like the Senior Troop Leader, she seemed every inch the professional trooper. With one notable exception; she was smiling when Kaly saluted her.

"N'Deena?" the officer said, "welcome to Special Operations Detachment 494. I suppose Da'Saana has already told you that Team 5 has been down a woman since they lost one. Damned shame too; Corporal bel Hilari was a good trooper. But," she went on, "now that you're here, Team 5 can get off their lazy cans and start earning their pay again."

"I'm glad to be here, ma'am," Kaly replied.

"Before we go meet your team, I want to give you a leg or two up," the woman said. "Item number first; SpecOps is a lot different than a regular Marine unit. We're more tight-knit, and we're expected to make decisions—good decisions—that most troopers would never have to worry about. What this means is that everyone has to be able to think fast, think without direction, and work well with each other. That's why we call our units 'Teams'.'

"So, you'll meet, try each other out and if it works, you're part of the team. If not, then we'll move you to another team until we can find the right fit, and no blame for anyone. We already know you have the requisite skills just from the fact that you made it through Larra's Lament. It's the personalities involved that concern me now. Do you understand me?"

"Yes, ma'am," Kaly answered. This wasn't a surprise to her. She had heard all about this during her training and she had expected to be on probation with her new team.

"Good. Item number second, and this relates to what I just told you about everyone getting along; Team 5 is a top-notch group. Those girls have seen a lot of action and they know their stuff. Troop Leader n'Elemay runs the team and she's one of the best Team Leaders the Sisterhood has."

Kaly could hear the exception, and waited patiently for the officer to reveal it.

"But, like a lot of our Teams, Five's girls might seem a bit 'strange' to you, at least at first. If you want to start off right with them, just don't say anything about the holos they like to watch. They're a little sensitive about it."

"Yes ma'am," Kaly replied, utterly mystified. *Those must be some holos,* she thought, but she refrained from asking for any clarification.

"Good. Now, item number third, and I'm not quite sure how to put this, but while you're out there in the field with Five...ah *shess*...all right, I'll just say it. Keep an eye out for any 'irregularities'."

"Ma'am?"

"Anything that they, or N'Elemay does that seems like it's out of line," the Lieutenant explained. "I'm not saying that there's anything wrong with Five. Just the opposite. But by their very nature, Marauder Teams have a lot less oversight than conventional units. I am required to tell every new addition that the Sisterhood expects them to report anything that might be a violation of Military Regulations or Sisterhood Law. It's fekked, but that's the way it goes.'

"So, keep your eyes open, and if you witness something that falls into either category, you let me or the Major know immediately." The woman frowned in distaste, but then her expression brightened again. "There, job done. Now, let's go meet your team."

Kaly followed, certain that there had been a lot more that the woman had wanted to say, and she got the impression that some of it even had to do with Team 5 specifically. It had been impossible for her not to miss the slight emphasis in the El-Tee's voice when she'd mentioned the team, and it's Troop Leader.

Whatever, she thought dismissively. *I'll find out for myself soon enough.*

Marauder Team 5 was gathered at the rear of the Marine Quarters in another ready room that also served as a common area for off-duty troopers. Even if she hadn't known who they were, she would have recognized them as SpecOps right away. The rules weren't as tight for the Marauders as they were for the average trooper, and all of them had taken full advantage of this by growing their hair out, or wearing it in non-regulation styles.

The three women were seated on couches, gathered around a holojector. A half-empty bottle of Aqqa sat on a small table in front of them, and all of them were watching the holo intently, their glasses full.

When she and the Lieutenant walked up, Kaly realized that the show that the troopers were playing had been intended for little children. In fact, she recognized it; it was part of a popular series from Zommerlaand, chronicling the adventures of *Laara Lampa, the Clumsy Fairy*. Kaly had watched it as a little girl, and she even recognized the episode.

Weird, she thought, but mindful of the El-Tee's advice, she kept her mouth shut and her features emotionless.

The team leader, Troop Leader n'Elemay looked like a Corrissan but her complexion was pale enough for her to have passed for a Nyxian, and her hair, tied back in a long pony tail, was so blond that it was nearly white, lending itself to such a misidentification. The only thing about her that contrasted with this was her eyes. These were dark brown, and large, lending her a soulful look that might have been more fitting for an artist or a musician.

Her partners were equally striking. One was a Sireeni, with jet-black skin and golden eyes that stood out in stark contrast, and she had added to this effect by incorporating colored glass beads into her long golden hair. This was done in fine thin braids that were long enough to brush against her dark shoulders.

The other woman was a Zommerlaandar, with all the size and muscle of her kind, but she had shaved her hair into a style that Kaly had heard was called a 'mohawk'. Although she had no idea what kind of bird that was, or whether it called Zommerlaand its home, it was apparently bright blue in color.

Compared to them, Kaly, who had let her own hair grow long enough to tie up into two playful braids, felt rather plain and conventional.

"Troop Leader?" Lieutenant sa'Kaali said. "This is Corporal Kaly n'Deena, your replacement sniper. N'Deena—the team. I'll leave you all alone to get to know each other. And everyone—play nice with the new girl or I'll make sure you all go to bed without your supper."

The Troop Leader didn't laugh at the joke, and merely nodded in acknowledgement. No salute, or anything else, and even more surprising to Kaly was that the Lieutenant didn't seem to mind such informality in the least. Instead, she simply turned and walked away.

A whole different animal for sure, Kaly reflected, trying to figure out what to do with herself next. N'Elemay's attention had already returned to the holo and none of the other women seemed interested in providing her with any clues.

Finally, at a pause that was intended on some worlds as an advertising break, N'Elemay looked up again, almost as if to check and see if she was still there, and when she saw that she was, the woman gestured to an empty place next to her on the couch.

"Welcome aboard, "she said. Her accent was soft, with a slight drawl to it that conflicted with Kaly's initial identification of her. It wasn't a Corris-san accent, she realized. It was from somewhere else that she couldn't place. But it also wasn't important, and she took her seat.

As she settled in, the Sireeni pressed a glass into her hands. It was filled to the brim with Aqqa.

"Like the El-Tee said, I'm Troop Leader Ellen n'Elemay. The Sireeni is Corporal Annya t'Jinna. She's our medic, Commo and EWO, and the tiny little woman over there is Corporal Astrid Margasdaater. She's our heavy weapons and explosives expert. She'll also be your security when you work sniper.'

"And before you say anything about it *greenie*, we *like* to watch kid's holos, so if you've got a problem with that, you can go *fek* yourself. Kid's shows have happy endings and we don't get enough happy endings. God-dess knows Corporal bel Hilari sure as fek didn't get one."

Scowling deeply, N'Elemay drained her glass like it was nothing but plain water, and then held it out for the Sireeni to refill. "Try and make sure you live a little longer than she did." She raised her glass in a silent toast to the memory of their fallen teammate and the others joined her.

Kaly waited respectfully, and when the moment seemed right, she took a sip from her own glass. Aqqa was almost pure alcohol, but she drank the evil stuff down without complaint, and made herself watch the holo. She also made a point of ignoring the tears that came to the eyes of her new teammates at some of the more maudlin parts of the show. That, and the fact that they didn't seem to give one nano whether or not she noticed it. Clearly, the holo was a communal experience that brooked no criticism from an outsider.

Which, until she proved herself, was exactly what she was.

USSNS *Pallas Athena*, Madrada System, Cataala Provensa, Esteral Terrana Rapabla, 1044.06|27|05:83:39

Because it offered the opportunity for additional bonding, Kaly was forcing herself to sit through another episode of *Laara Lampa* with the team. The show had just reached a particularly syrupy point, when Lieutenant sa'Kaali walked into the ready room and came to her rescue.

"N'Elemay, your team has an Op," she announced flatly, and instantly everyone was on their feet. "Meet up in conference room 12 in ten for a planning session."

"Well, time to go to work, ladies," N'Elemay said, and then to Kaly,"Get all your gear together. These things move real fast once they're on. We'll probably leave as soon as the briefing is over."

As the other women departed, Kaly felt a strong wave of anxiety wash over her. She wasn't scared—not too scared—but she was concerned about how she would do on her first real 'Op'. She'd been through plenty of simulations during her training on Larra's Lament, but this was going to be her first real mission with her new team. She didn't want to disappoint them by doing something stupid. Or worse, do anything that would get someone hurt, or killed.

Racing to her locker, a thousand different lessons from her training went through her mind in rapid-fire succession, and she finally had to stop in a passage and take a deep breath just to stay calm.

I know what I'm doing, she reminded herself. *They taught me everything that I needed to know on the Lament, and now it all just comes down to doing it, and staying focused. Just...stay...focused...Kaly.* Her nervousness subsided just long enough for her to reach the storage locker.

She reached into the cubby for her rifle and took it out, feeling a sense of comfort from simply holding it. Unlike any other piece of her gear, Tatiana had become a part of her, and hundreds of hours working with it had taught her to put everything else aside; all fear, all doubt, all hesitation, and to focus through it like a light through a lens. Like the light through her riflescope.

Tatiana's plastic and metal felt wonderfully cool in her hands, and as she held the rifle, she whispered the mantra that she had learned in SpecOps School to herself. It had replaced the Star Scout Motto that had sustained her on Persephone, a lifetime before. The maxim was an ancient one, and it had served many soldiers, just like her, and at times just like this. *'There is only the mission,'* it went, *'I am the mission. There is nothing but the mission. I will complete it to the utmost of my abilities, and I will succeed in my mission.'*

This did the trick. Her anxiety retreated.

Slinging Tatiana over her shoulder, she started to check her other gear. The first thing she inspected was her back-up weapon. This was a GSC-19, a compact submachinegun with an integral sound suppressor. It was intended for use in close quarters situations where the larger sniper rifle would have proven unwieldy or impractical, and she was almost as good with it as she was with Tatiana. But it lacked the same deep connection with her that she felt for her rifle. The GSC-19 was just a tool, but Tatiana was part of her soul.

She worked the submachinegun's action, and then inspected its magazines and extra clips. Seeing that it was in perfect, fighting condition, she slipped it around herself and pushed it back and out of the way to inspect the remainder of her equipment.

Like her web gear, her uniform was ETR issue. None of it had the ability to bend light around it and create the perfect camouflage that Sisterhood fatigues could, but it did possess the rudimentary ability to change color based on ambient light levels.

At the moment, her clothing had apparently decided that black and purple were the appropriate hues, and she just hoped that its special fibers would make a better choice once they were downside. She wasn't terribly worried though. If it didn't, then she reasoned that a little good old-fashioned mud wiped over everything would solve the problem neatly.

Thankfully, the equipment that she had strapped onto the webbing, or put into its pouches was another matter. It was all Sisterhood issue, and therefore both familiar and dependable. She made a brief inspection of every item, all the way down to her personal med kit, and when everything had checked out, she added two final items to her load-out; a small needlegun, and a double-edged fighting knife.

As the team's sniper, it wasn't likely that she would ever have any reason to call on either item, but her instructors back on the Lament had all stressed the need to be prepared for any possibility. And Kaly knew, without even having to ask, that her team wouldn't expect anything less.

Finally, she took one last, long look in the mirror at herself, and after applying a few more dabs of face paint to break up her features and reduce her skins reflective qualities, headed for the Lifts.

Four minutes, eighty seconds later, she was standing in the conference room with her team. Most of the other Marauder Teams aboard the *Athena* were also there, and the feeling in the room was positively electric. Everyone had gathered around a large round holojector in the center of the chamber, and Major n'Neesa.

"Ladies," the woman began, "I can now tell you that the Expeditionary Force is on its way to the Madrada system. Your Teams will be landing there in advance, and preparing its single, populated world for a general ground assault. Each team will have its own mission assignments once they're downside.'

"Teams 2, 3, 4, 5, 6, 7, 8, 10 and 11, I'll start with you since you will all be working in the same operational zone. The local resistance forces notified the ETR's Intel people that the T'lakskalans have established a presence on the fourth planet in the system, designated Madrada 4. Evidently, they've teamed up with the Hriss, at least as far as taking advantage of the invasion to grab themselves some human merchandise to sell off elsewhere.'

"While we're unsure if they're also supporting the invasion forces militarily, we do know that they have detained some of the population and have been exporting them back to their home space.'

"The Tee-Laks have established several detention centers for this purpose, but the largest is located in a city called La Maantra, inside some warehouses adjacent to the main spaceport. The spaceport itself has a high strategic value, and in addition to a rescue op, you will also be tasked with taking and securing it until conventional Marine units can arrive to relieve you."

A holo came up displaying the spaceport, and then panned over to a group of three large buildings at its edge. They were overlooked by the ports' main control tower, and flanked by spaceships that Kaly presumed were T'lakskalan. The holo changed again, this time to a close-up, showing the structures in greater detail. A fence of some sort surrounded the entire area.

"We know that the two buildings to the north are being used to house prisoners, with the third one set aside for prisoners of special value, and for processing facilities."

"Processing?" Kaly asked no one in particular.

"Yeah," N'Elemay volunteered, just above a whisper. "The Tee-Laks sometimes chop up some of their prisoners for genetic materials, or just to harvest edible parts. Some races actually do like us, you know—for dinner. I hear tell that we taste just like *chikka*."

The Troop Leader found this funny and laughed quietly, joined by some of the other Marauders. But what exactly was so amusing about something so horrible, if it were true, completely escaped Kaly, and she wondered if N'Elemay was having her on. Then when she saw the serious expression on Lieutenant sa'Kaali's face, she realized that the Troop Leader hadn't been kidding at all.

The Major continued,"The entire facility is surrounded by a conventional 'death wall'. For you greenies," she looked right at Kaly when she said this, "that's an energy field keyed to T'lakskalan DNA. They can go right through it, but if anything else tries, all electrical activity in their body stops. Instant termination. It's very effective for keeping things in, but not out."

"Any idea where the power feed is for the fence?" N'Elemay inquired.

"None," N'Neesa answered. "But if it follows standard T'lakskalan practice, it's most likely inside one of the warehouses, in a secure area. So you'll have to breach it instead."

"Enemy strength?" another Troop Leader asked.

"Only an estimate; the resistance people reported roughly twenty to thirty in the warehouse at the most. Prisoner population is also an estimate, but you can probably count on about 200 or more prisoners at any one time, and if they're really busy, four to five times as many."

"Team 5, your job will be to take the control tower and then cover the other teams as they move into position. Teams 2, 3, 4, 5, 6 and 7 will blow the fence at these spots," she pointed to several places on the map, "and then enter, engage the hostiles and take the facility. As they do this, Teams 8, 10 and 11 will take the ships and neutralize their crews."

"What are the rules of engagement, ma'am?" the Troop Leader for Team 8 asked.

"Weapons hot, engage and take out all non-humans. There are no targets of value among them, so just have fun," N'Neesa said. "As for the captives, secure and render medical aid as needed. I'm sorry but it's going to be a mixed mission, girls. I know how much you all love the 'rush and zap' jobs, but we'll have friendlies to worry about, so watch your fire around them."

"I just fekking hate it ven ve get stuck babyzitting *downziders*," Margasdaater swore under her breath. "Give me za old 'rush n' zap' any time, yah?"

Everyone in Team 5, Kaly included, had to agree. Missions where the only objective was to terminate every living thing within a given radius were a lot easier to accomplish than having innocents to worry about. At least it had seemed that way to Kaly in training.

"That's it then," N'Neesa concluded. "Remember, keep your psiever traffic down to a minimum, and when you speak, speak in Espangla only, even when you cuss, and even if you think you're alone. So keep the Zommerlaandartal, Sitali, or whatever else you normally babble in buttoned-down, Zat klaar? All right, get with your Team Leaders for your specific tasks. Spaceport Teams, dismissed. Teams 12, 14, 16, 22 and 26, you're up next. Front and center."

While the Major began the next briefing, N'Elemay waved for Team 5 to follow her over to a smaller holojector set in another corner of the room. They gathered around it, and the warehouses reappeared, along with the control tower. Then they spent the next five minutes discussing their specific objectives, and examining the layout of the buildings for themselves. When she was satisfied that each of them were crystal clear on the mission details, the Troop Leader led them out towards the hangar bay.

La Maantra Epacia Porta, La Maantra, Madrada 4, Madrada System, Cataala Provensa, Esteral Terrana Rapabla, 1044.06|27|09:16:67

War had always been prosecuted for three basic reasons; to defend against an aggressor or to attack them, to forward political or economic objectives, and lastly, to test new technology on the battlefield. The Nightingale SOI-13 Infiltrator Ship fell neatly into this final category.

These special ships, which delivered the *Athena's* Teams to the surface of Madrada 4, were something very new to the Sisterhood's arsenal. They had been specifically designed to insert small groups of personnel into hostile environments.

The Nightingales were the answer to the latest advances in Hriss scanner technology, which the Zeta-Reticulans had gifted to them as another means to bedevil the human race. As SpecOps missions went, these unique vessels were a vast improvement over the standard Marine Assault shuttle. Even the slight distortion that conventional stealth technology couldn't erase was totally absent. The Nightingales were completely invisible, using a classified process of re-projecting folded light-waves to eliminate any distortion and create the illusion of a seamless, empty space. They were also absolutely silent, leaving behind no engine signatures, or giving off any other emissions that would have otherwise betrayed them. After years of development, the mission that the Special Expeditionary Force had been dispatched to deal with had presented the perfect opportunity to conclusively prove their worth.

Although they were somewhat larger than an Assault Shuttle, they actually possessed a much smaller troop compartment, with barely enough room for two Teams and their gear. This lack of interior space ensured that they would never supplant their venerable cousin, especially when it came to missions requiring large numbers of troopers.

The Nightingales also had no weapons to speak of. With the exception of a pair of energy cannons at the nose, and one pintle-mounted gun at the egress door, everything else had been sacrificed for sophisticated passive sensors and a host of electronic counter measures that would have put a Valkyrie aerospace fighter to shame. The Nightingales had only one function; to sneak in, and if the Goddess favored its intrepid crew and passengers, to sneak back out of places that no Assault Shuttle could ever hope to visit undetected.

But the Nightingale's virtues also presented its greatest challenges. Thinly armored, they were vulnerable to attack, and being totally invisible made the job of flying them into a drop zone, where multiple ships were involved, a very hazardous undertaking. Only the skill of the pilots flying them, and good communications on closed psiever bands, kept any group operation from becoming a tragedy. Such disasters had happened during initial testing, and that was something that every team who rode in them understood.

Descending through the atmosphere to their drop zone, Kaly did what everyone else in the team was doing, and tried not to think about just how fragile their vessel really was. Instead, she stayed focused on the mission, and rehearsed the role she would play in it. And although she wasn't very religious, she added in a tiny prayer to the Lady to watch over them throughout the entire adventure.

The Lady heard her prayers, however half-hearted they might have been, and the Nightingale arrived undetected, and unscathed. It deposited Teams 5 and 7 at one of the two landing zones that were being used as their jump off points. Half the force, including her team, had landed north of the spaceport, close to the control tower, while the other had been dropped off to the south in order to give them quicker access to the T'lakskalan ships, and the warehouses.

Both 'El-Zees' were little more than half a kilometer away from the edges of the spaceport and the Teams at both ends covered that distance quickly. Only a conventional chain link fence stood in their way when they finally arrived at their destination, and this proved no match for the micro-plazer saws that they all carried.

While Team 7 remained at the fence line and covered their advance, Team 5 went through the breach. Kaly followed her teammates, crawling on her stomach, and pausing now and again to break up any noise patterns that her approach might have made. She had been given the job of rear guard, with T'Jinna in front of her, and N'Elemay and Margasdaater taking the point.

Which was just fine as far as Kaly was concerned. As much as she'd drilled for close quarters battle, it was no substitute for real life experience, and her Teammates had that over her by a factor of ten. Her real work was waiting for her, up in the spaceport's control tower.

It was 01:25:87, and the area was quiet. Only a few Tee-Lak sentries at the far end of the field were out making their rounds, or keeping watch over the rows of parked spaceships, and she knew that with the distance, the darkness, and the bulk of the control tower covering them, that the team was practically invisible.

Despite this, Kaly's blood pounded loudly in her ears, and it was hard for the more primitive side of her not to be convinced that the entire planet couldn't hear her heart beating, or every little noise that she was making as she inched along. But no one heard her, or the team, and they stopped when they reached an abandoned service vehicle that had gone to ground halfway to the control tower.

The moment that she was behind cover, she un-slung her rifle and brought the scope up to her eyes. From the scan they'd performed back at the fence line, she already knew that there were two Tee-Laks up in the tower acting as guards, and another who was presumably a traffic control technician. Ranging over the darkened windows, she couldn't spot any of them, until she switched over to infrared, and then she found them easily. They moved around the open room with the casual ease of beings that had no suspicion that they were about to be attacked, and killed.

Kaly kept the rifle trained on her targets and flashed a quick series of hand signs to N'Elemay. *"Both guards confirmed and in the control room, technician also. No sign of alarm,"* she signed in Sireeni. Using hand signs as a means of communication followed Major n'Neesa's admonition to them to keep psiever traffic to a minimum.

And Sireeni in particular, offered another attractive advantage; it was not only extremely versatile and expressive, but coming from an obscure fringe world, largely unknown, even within the Sisterhood. Every SpecOps trainee learned it from day one.

N'Elemay acknowledged Kaly's message with a nod, and then signaled to Margasdaater. It was time for them to move up and get on with the business of taking the tower.

When the Troop Leader left the concealment of the derelict service vehicle, the Zommerlaandar covered her with her GSC-19 until she reached the base of the structure. At a signal from the big woman, T'Jinna took over next, and Margasdaater pelted across the open space to catch up with N'Elemay.

The two women took up positions on opposite sides of the tower's entrance door, at it became T'Jinna's turn to go. Kaly covered her with Tatiana until she reached the others. Once the Sireeni was safely across, Kaly relied on Team 7's sniper to watch her back, and moved across the space herself.

Then, flattening herself against the towers smooth, cold surface, she waited. The next move was up to N'Elemay and Margasdaater to initiate.

The Troop Leader pushed her own GSC-19 to the back and produced another weapon from an oversized shoulder holster; a GSC-4A. To the uninitiated, it seemed just like a common needlegun, but it actually fired chemical-based rounds, and sported a sound suppressor that was almost as long as the gun itself. A smile came over the N'Elemay's face as she readied it for action; an expression of pure delight.

This surprised Kaly. In their short association, she had never seen the Troop Leader smile before, for any reason, and it seemed out of place for this situation.

Looking positively blissful, the woman nodded to Margasdaater, who tried the door. It was unlocked and the Zommerlaandar quietly opened it. Then she reached into her fanny pack and brought out a microbot launcher.

The moment that the diminutive spybot was in the air, it flew through the entrance and into the building.

N'Elemay was the next to enter, with Margasdaater right behind her, followed by T'Jinna, and last of all, Kaly. Still the rear guard, Kaly immediately turned around and covered the entrance they had just come through with her submachinegun and waited as the little bot flew up the winding staircase to the control room itself.

A light tap on her shoulder from T'Jinna told her that they were about to move and she spared a glance over her shoulder. N'Elemay was already on her way up, pistol at the ready, and with the same ethereal smile plastered on her face. Margasdaater was immediately behind her, covering everything ahead of them with her own submachinegun.

The pair moved along with a silent, deadly grace, making less noise than the dust motes that covered everything around them. This didn't astonish Kaly as far as N'Elemay was concerned. The woman had a lithe body that fairly screamed precision and stealth, but Margasdaater *was* a surprise. Despite her bulk, she was every inch as silent as her partner.

T'Jinna followed them, with Kaly straggling behind and feeling every centimeter the clumsy hatchie that she was. When they reached the last length of stairs, just short of the Control Room, everyone paused, and the little 'bot rose up to peer over the edge. The signal it sent back seemed to satisfy N'Elemay, and her smile widened into an expression that would have seemed utterly beatific on any other woman, at any other time. She glanced over to Margasdaater and the Zommerlaandar replied with a smile of her own. Moving as one, they pelted up the stairs and into the control room.

A few brief flashes of light from above her, and a series of muffled clicks were all that signaled that they had entered the space, or told the story of the death they had brought with them. This was followed by the unmistakable sound of bodies soddenly hitting the metal floor.

Kaly looked to T'Jinna, and when the Sireeni started up the stairs, she trailed behind her and took in the scene when they reached the top. The T'lakskalans were all dead. Two of them had neat little holes in the center of their reptilian heads, and the third had a pattern of wounds right up the center of its body, ending at what might have once been its face.

She didn't waste any time ogling the bodies. They were gone, and no longer mattered to anyone, she told herself as she stepped over the corpses. What concerned her more were the windows facing the warehouses. These, she found, opened out, relieving her of the task of cutting a hole with her plazer saw. She picked a good spot for herself, and resting Tatiana in the crook of her arm, surveyed the scene below them.

At the moment, only two sentries were on patrol in front of the buildings. One of the T'lakskalans was hanging back near an entrance door, and the other was walking close to the line of metal poles that made up the components of the death fence. These poles, she knew, were actually transmitters, emitting an invisible beam to a receiver in the next pole that repeated the process. To provide a warning that it was active, and armed, each pole had a light atop it, blinking slowly in the infrared light-band. The entire death fence was essentially a chain, and like any chain, Kaly understood that if one part of it were breached, the entire network would fail.

In the meantime, Margasdaater was settling in near her to provide her with security, and as she did so, Kaly searched around with her riflescope for other enemies, but found none. A follow-up scan on the bioplasmic and thermal bands, revealed the location of the other T'lakskalans and reassured her. They were all inside the warehouses, along with their human prisoners.

She relayed this information to N'Elemay in Sireeni, and as the woman departed with T'Jinna, she resumed her vigil. For the next several minutes, it was simply a matter of waiting and tracking the movements of the sentries while the Teams moved into position to blow the fence. Once that happened, her job would be a simple one; kill the sentries and then cover her side of the warehouses.

One by one, the Teams checked in and advised that they were in position, and that their charges had been set. Kaly focused on the Tee-Laks, working the variables in her head and deciding which of them she would kill first. She chose the one nearest to the death fence and had just sighted in on him when the plan changed, and oddly enough, for the better.

A third Tee-Lak had come into her field of view. He was walking from the direction of the spaceships, and towing a small, wheeled cart behind him. From the disposable water jugs on top of it and boxes that wouldn't fit in the cart's cargo compartment, she realized that he was carrying food and water, most likely intended for the prisoners inside the buildings. The creature was headed straight for the fence, and remembering that it was keyed to T'lakskalan DNA, she contacted N'Elemay by psiever immediately.

Overwatch to Leader. Permission to drop him at the fence? she thought.

N'Elemay had also spotted him, and she was thinking the same thing. If it worked, it would be infinitely more preferable than using explosives and losing any chance of surprising the enemy. But *'If'* was definitely the operative word. Everything would depend on Kaly's shooting skills, her targets position, and a certain amount of luck.

Standby, the Troop Leader replied. There was a brief pause, and then, *Permission granted. All Teams standing by.*

Kaly followed the T'lakskalan's progress, resting her finger lightly on the trigger and keeping her breathing even. As he neared the fence, she knew that the moment was right and went with her instinct.

She fired.

The round spun out of Tatiana, cutting its way through the still night air. An instant later, it met the Tee-Lak's skull and penetrated it.

The creature fell, and Kaly held her breath as she watched the body drop. And when it came to rest, she relaxed. He was lying right across where the invisible energy beams crossed, and the fence, sensing his genetic markers, had deactivated itself. But although the lethal perimeter was down, there were still the two guards outside the warehouse that she needed to deal with.

Quickly, Kaly brought her crosshairs around to the nearer one and fired again. As he joined the first Tee-Lak in death, she began to engage the second guard.

But she didn't need to. Team 7's sniper had already killed him. The fence was down, and all enemies outside of the warehouse were dead, with none of the other Tee-Laks in the warehouse or around the ships, any the wiser.

"Gaanskaa gaad!" she heard Margasdaater say quietly. "That vas zome damn fine shooting!"

Kaly smiled proudly. *More than just 'fine',* she thought. *More like Goddess blessed.* She had only estimated where the first creature was going to fall, and the odds had been long that his body would have landed the wrong way.

No one ever needed to know about this small detail though. Praise, especially for 'greenies', was simply too hard to come by.

With their approach clear, the Teams nearest her shifted from their positions and rushed through the breach, heading for the warehouse buildings. Other Marauders were coming up to join them.

Overwatch, another change of plans. Get ready to leave your position. N'Elemay thought to them. *Team 2 is coming up to take over there. I want you two for the entry.*

A moment later, Kaly heard the sniper from 2 and her securitywoman coming up from below, and when they came in and her relief took up her place at the window, she and Margasdaater left the tower and headed for their Teammates.

Partway there, Team 7 materialized out of the shadows, and joined them. As a group, they went through the fence, moving to the nearest building. There, N'Elemay and Margasdaater repeated their performance at the Control Tower, and made the initial entry. The instant they were inside, everyone else filed in after them, their GSC's held at the ready.

They encountered a long hallway, and as Team 7 peeled off and went left, Kaly followed her companions right. To a woman, no one in either group made any more than the slightest of sounds.

For that reason, the T'lakskalan who came walking around the corner at the far end didn't have the slightest idea they were there. He also wasn't ready for N'Elemay when she shoved the barrel of her pistol into his eye, and fired a 10-millimeter slug into his brain. A second Tee-Lak, who was a few meters behind the first, actually managed to turn around before the Troop Leader cut him down with another shot.

There was a door at the end of the passage, and they knew from the intel they'd received from the ETR, that it led to a large open area where the prisoners were being held. They also knew that above this, was a catwalk and what had been a small office before the invasion. Team 7 was going to handle the upper levels, and their job was to secure the ground floor.

Once again, N'Elemay and Margasdaater took up positions to either side of the door, with Kaly and T'Jinna covering the entrance. They waited there, listening for the signal from Team 7 that they were in position. It came a few seconds later, and both Teams rushed in at the same time.

Kaly had just an instant to take in the entire scene before the shooting started. The prisoners had been chained together in small groups around the warehouses' support pillars. At their feet were discarded plastic water bottles, empty food containers, a few filthy mattresses, and their own bodily waste. And positioned around them at various points in the large space, were their T'lakskalan guards.

"Republican Marines!" N'Elemay shouted in Espangla. "Everyone get down!" The Troop Leader had already picked out her target, a guard who was just starting to turn towards them, and fired, sending him flopping backwards with a slug buried deep in his eye socket.

Kaly had also chosen her own victim and engaged him at the same time. It was another guard standing on the opposite side of the room. Repeating N'Elemay's warning to the prisoners, she let off a burst from her GSC and dropped the Tee-Lak before he could raise his weapon.

Another T'lakskalan, standing nearby, managed to fire wildly in her general direction, but missed her by light years. Margasdaater got him a moment later, along with a third one that was also beginning to react to their intrusion.

Kaly ran for the nearest cover. It was one of the support pillars and when she was behind it, she ranged her weapon around, looking for other hostiles. Upstairs, she heard the brief exchange between Team 7 and the Tee-Laks, and then a muffled 'thump!' as someone threw a grenade.

Then, just as rapidly as it had started, it was over. All the guards on the ground floor were down, and it sounded at least, like things had gone the same way upstairs.

But Kaly and her team members were taking no chances, and kept to their training. To a woman, they'd all found cover behind solid objects, and waited. They knew that even when a target had been mortally wounded, it didn't always die immediately, and could still have enough life left in it to take its killer with it.

After 20 seconds though, it was obvious that none of the aliens were in any shape to counterattack, and Kaly's psiever flashed the 'All Clear' message in the corner of her vision. Leaving the safety of the pillar, she cautiously approached the Tee-Lak she'd shot, firing another short burst into the body, just to make certain. Back behind her, N'Elemay and the others were doing the same thing.

Once she'd kicked the creature's weapon away from it, she finally allowed herself to focus on the prisoners. Most of them were still huddled on the floor in terror, and she started to move among them, telling them in Espangla that they were safe. But some of them weren't; one woman had been hit by the Tee-Laks in the gunfight, and was clearly dead. Another, a man, had been wounded in the chest, and was lying on the ground nearby, coughing up pink foam.

Dropping onto one knee, she pushed her weapon out of the way and opened up her med-kit for a field dressing. T'Jinna came up as she was applying it to the bloody hole, and signed to her, *I'll handle this one. Help me sit him up and then go take care of some of the others.*

Kaly assisted her and then moved on, uttering words of reassurances here and there, and tending to whatever injuries she found among the prisoners that she was trained to handle. They were a mixed group, some men, some women, and to her surprise, quite a few children. All of them sported tattoos on their arms; a sort of bar code that she imagined identified each one of them for their captors. To the smallest of their number, they were all filthy, malnourished and dehydrated.

A few, she saw to her disgust, hadn't died from any weapons fire at all, but had expired in their chains from sheer neglect. Despite the food containers and water bottles scattered around the place, it was obvious that the T'lakskalans had been indifferent about the state of their captive's health.

She didn't know it, but she was about to find out just how unconcerned they had really been, and why. As she was giving one of the children the last of the water from her canteen, N'Elemay walked up and holstered her pistol.

"N'Deena, get over to the processing center at Building Three and relieve the team there. They're needed somewhere else."

Kaly couldn't help but notice that the Troop Leader had finally addressed her by name—not her first name certainly—but still, by name. She'd passed the team's test, she realized, or at least part of it. Now, she was officially a person, not just a 'replacement'.

"Yes, ma'am," she answered, careful not to salute the woman. SpecOps training stressed that superiors were never saluted in the field. All that accomplished was to mark them as targets-of-value for an enemy sniper. Instead, she just turned on her heel and headed out of the warehouse the way they'd come.

Outside, the spaceport had become transformed. Instead of darkness, firelight illuminated the entire area, creating sharp zones of brilliant flickering light and deep shadows. The source was the T'lakskalan ships. Somewhere in the middle of the firefight, the other Teams had assaulted and destroyed them.

When she reached Building Three, another Marauder met her there. "You my relief? Good," the other trooper said. "There's a fight starting up at the entrance to the port. Looks like the Hriss have decided to pay us a visit. Stay here until we can spare someone to relieve you."

With this, a group of Marauders ran by and the woman followed after them, leaving Kaly by herself to play the stupid hatchie and pull guard duty on an empty building. It was more fun than a girl had a right to have, she mused acerbically, settling in for the wait.

A short time later, she heard gunfire off in the distance, and then flashes of light accompanied by short, sharp explosions that she knew were grenades going off. Things got quiet after that, and they stayed that way.

Eventually a group of Marauders materialized out of the night, and Kaly recognized one of them as the woman she had relieved.

"Thanks," the trooper said. "We're all done up there. Your team is on the way down to get you. They should be along in a few minutes. While you're waiting, take a look around inside. We've gotten all the intel we need and we're going to blow it. It's quite a sight; you don't want to miss it."

Kaly wasn't sure that she really wanted to see the processing facility, but it was better than standing around in the cold, doing nothing. So in she went.

Even though she had been told about what it contained, this still hadn't prepared her to experience the reality. The moment that she stepped inside the building, she regretted her decision. The processing facility was one of the horrors that all veterans saw in wartime, which once seen, was never forgotten.

Portable cells that had been built for single occupants, lined the far wall of the main room, and like the other accommodations she had seen in Building One, the cages were filthy and reeked of human waste, sweat, and most of all, raw despair. This wasn't the worst thing about the place, however. There was much more.

Containers for storing liquid, and others for solids, were stacked against another wall, and the team that had seized the place had opened several of them. Knowing that she was doing exactly the wrong thing, Kaly went over to them. She *had* to see what was inside.

The liquids container nearest her was filled to the brim with a reddish soup and what looked like chunks of meat floating in it.

No, she realized in revulsion. Not just meat. It was human flesh. The solids container sitting next to it was even worse. Body parts were stacked neatly inside of it like products awaiting sale in a butcher shop; arms, legs, and other indefinable parts that she knew, if she really tried, she would recognize. And from the tattooed bar codes on one of the severed arms, there was no doubt about their origins.

Kaly stepped back, utterly appalled. But she still hadn't seen everything. Her retreat had taken her to the doorway of an adjacent room and as she bumped into the doorframe, she looked over her shoulder.

A conventional plazer saw, the kind that workshops used for cutting up large objects, was situated in the center of the room. It was a table-mounted model, and its latest 'job' was waiting on its work surface for completion. This was a headless, footless human torso.

There was also a freezer unit nearby. Whoever had searched it had left the door open, and inside were more bodies, set on hooks like slaughtered animals. All of them had been neatly gutted and hung there, ready for 'processing' that would never come. They too, had bar codes on their arms.

This was all that her stomach could handle, and she bent over and threw up until nothing else could come out. When she finally stood, N'Elemay was there, waiting patiently. Kaly wiped the vomit from her lips and the Troop Leader handed her a pair of incendiary grenades.

"Burn it," the woman growled. "Burn this whole fekking goddess-damned place to the ground!" Then she left her alone to do what needed to be done.

***

That night, with the battle over, and the Madrada system firmly under Sisterhood control, Kaly tried to sleep, but the pictures going through her mind defeated her. No matter how hard she tried, images of the severed limbs and the hanging bodies kept coming at her. Other memories quickly joined them. Of her first time in combat, and the bodies in the Gathering Square on Persephone, commingling into an unholy union of horror that refused to show her any mercy at all.

Finally after an hour, she gave up the struggle, got dressed and walked down to the exercise facility that had been set-aside for the Marines. There, she worked out until she was utterly exhausted. Then she showered and returned to bed.

The tactic didn't work. The images came back, and renewed their assault on her overtired mind. Knowing that more drastic measures were required, she left her rack a second time and headed for the only place that offered any possibility of peace; the ready room.

Just as she had expected, N'Elemay was there, sitting by herself with a bottle of Aqqa, and watching an episode of *Laara Lampa* on the holoplayer. The woman looked up at her as she walked in.

"I can't get them out of my mind," Kaly explained. "I keep seeing them."

"Welcome to my world," N'Elemay replied grimly. She held out the bottle of Aqqa to her. "Try this. It helps me—sometimes."

Kaly took it and gulped down a mouthful of the stuff, feeling the warmth of it hit her middle and then spread out through the rest of her. As wrong as she knew it was to resort to it, the Aqqa made her feel good, and she took another drink from the bottle and joined N'Elemay on the couch.

That was when she really noticed the nanotattoo on N'Elemay's upper left arm. The woman had taken off her fatigue blouse, and with nothing on but a sleeveless top, it was impossible not to see it. The little 'bots moved in unison to a pre-programmed pattern just under her skin, creating a delicate scrollwork that shimmered and shifted as if a physical breeze was blowing against it. On these scrolls were women's names, written in ornamental Standard. There were a lot of them.

N'Elemay caught her eyeing the *nanotat* and answered her unspoken question with a single word. "Friends."

Kaly knew from the darkness in her eyes, that every name was someone who had died. Someone that N'Elemay had cared for.

They didn't speak after that, and watched the holo together, sharing the bottle between them. N'Elemay proved to be completely correct about the Aqqa. It did help, and by the time the show ended and Kaly had staggered off to her rack, she finally understood why the team watched what they did. Happy endings *were* important—and they really were *damned* rare.

Zenithia Productions, Agamede District, Thermadon Val, Thermadon, Myrene System, Thalestris Elant, United Sisterhood of Suns, 1044.06|27|06:25:99

Zenithia Productions had gladly loaned out the use of their studio to Celina while she was in Thermadon, and being the finest facility of its kind in the Capitol, she had been just as pleased to accept their offer. The realicording equipment they had was a true dream to work with, allowing her the widest range of possibilities available outside of her own studio in Corrissa, and a nearly infinite selection of samples to weave into her raw tracks.

There was the same high level of quality when it came to the musicomp systems. The programs were easy to use, and when she inputted her basic ideas for the soundtrack, Clio was able to integrate them with the resident

AI to create some truly marvelous compositions. There would be a great deal more to splice in of course, but her project was definitely coming together very quickly.

The Zenithia staff was as magnificent as their facilities. She hadn't had to bother Clio with anything as mundane as water, or the occasional mug of kaafra. They had anticipated her needs with all the insight they had as professional musicians themselves, delivering it at just the right times without interfering with her work flow in the least.

This had left her dear artificial partner, and herself, free to work virtually uninterrupted. That, as many artists had learned painfully over the centuries, was extremely important. Everyone had heard of the poor poet, Samantha Taylor Coleridge who had lost the final lines to her great work "*Kubla Khan*", thanks to a knock on the door at an inopportune moment.

This was why, when a call came for her through the front offices, she was more than a little surprised, and annoyed. There had already been several calls, mostly from fans, but these had been artfully fielded away from her by Reception. This call had managed to get past them however, and she took it, albeit reluctantly. She had been in the very middle of an important bridge between a street scene in downtown Thermadon and an upswell in her main theme, and she was in no mood for whatever trivialities the outside universe had in mind. Nothing, not even the immanent nova of Thermadon's primary, or the very end of the universe itself, was as important to her as finishing the section properly.

She was wrong, but she wasn't aware of it, yet.

"Yes?" she asked absently. Her attention was focused on the timing of a key set of notes to a wonderful burst of traffic she had caught with her 'cam. It looked just like a school of Aerfin flyerflish on Tetra, with all the life and power of those strange creatures. The music that she was trying to add to it would communicate this sensation to her audience—assuming that she got it just right, and was allowed to complete it.

"I am *soo* sorry to bother you Celina, but this *is* quite important." It was Hanna n'Jerri, her host on Thermadon, and the Director of the *Tuluraa Daal Foundation.* N'Jerri had access to her, any time she wanted it, although Celina was glad that she was still being deferential about making use of the privilege.

"It's no problem, Hanna," Celina dissembled, desperately hoping that it wouldn't be a request for another dreary interview with some music critic. "What can I do for you today?"

"I don't imagine that you've heard, but the Seevaans are visiting the capitol," the woman informed her. N'Jerri was completely correct, Celina hadn't. Galactic politics simply didn't interest her.

"Apparently they're fascinated by human music, and the leader of the Chaotic delegation, Queen Talaria, has asked for the chance to meet you."

"Oh, Hanna, I'm just too busy for that...I simply can't..."

"Celina, I completely understand," the woman replied soothingly, "but this *is* important. The Seevaans are one of the Sisterhood's closest allies in the Far Arm, and its greatest supporters with the Collective.'

"And Queen Talaria is in line to become their next Empress. We simply *can't* turn her down. Besides, she's something of a fan of yours; her Head Handmaiden told me that she's played just about every realie you've ever made."

Celina's brows knitted unhappily. She could just imagine how Queen Talaria had become familiar with her work. Xee merchants, forever on the lookout for a chance to make more money, had pirated many of her realies, and repackaged them under the horrid label *"Maggot-Hymn Productions."*

Not only had these illegal copies netted the Maggot-Hymn Consortium tidy sums, but the Xee had also added to their profits by soliciting advertisers and splicing in subliminal messages that hawked their wares. Celina's attorneys had been litigating the matter for years in the Xee court system, but so far, had enjoyed little success. In the meantime, illicit copies of her work had made their way to just about every corner of the Far Arm without netting her even a single demi-credit.

"Yes," Celina answered, trying her best to conceal her irritation. "I certainly wouldn't want to snub such an important fan."

"Good!" N'Jerri exclaimed "I'll tell her Seneschal that they can come by the studio today then. Say about 05.83?"

"No. That won't do," Celina retorted. "Clio and I need to be able to do our work without any distractions. I can't have them in the studio getting in the way."

"Celina, I'm sorry," N'Jerri apologized, "but they specifically insisted on seeing you work. Please, this is a big favor for the government. They're in the process of negotiating for some new tech from the Seevaans, and some of it hinges on a chance to watch you while you're in the middle of your creative process. Please, do it for your country!"

Celina would have preferred to end the call right then and there with an emphatic 'no!' but the hard reality of funding, and its source, gave her pause. She hated the idea of having an audience with her in the studio, even one as august as the Queen and her retinue, but reality was what it was. Besides, she told herself, she could always make up for anything that she failed to accomplish the following day, or even later that same evening if she forswore sleeping.

"All right," she finally said. "They can come here, but only for an hour or so. After that, I want them *out*. I need to work!"

***

Queen Talaria and her entourage arrived only a few minutes late, and just enough to be in fashion, but without giving insult. She had three Handmaidens with her, and also two male warriors. Celina had seen Seevaans before, both in holos and when she had attended state functions, but the warriors were something new to her.

These rare creatures were slightly larger than the females of their species, and in addition to armored sheaths covering their bodies, they carried large pole arms with their secondary set of fore pincers that were set with huge blades, which for all their gilding and jewels looked as if they could cleave a Hovertank in half.

Watching them assume their places at the door, she found it hard to believe that such formidable looking beings had been all but completely annihilated. As she came forwards to be formally introduced by Hanna n'Jerri to Queen Talaria, she thought that perhaps Motherthought had been correct about creatures like them. Despite their brawn, their history certainly seemed to support the idea that males of any kind were actually the weaker sex.

"Celina," N'Jerri said. "Allow me to introduce you to Queen Talaria ne Hadrada ne Jannisha ne Maallata ne Keevesha of the House of the Chaotics, first royal daughter to Her Celestial Empress Quellatesha."

Celina brought her hands together, the back of her thumbs meeting one another, folded her fingers slightly, and bowed. This was the best approximation of the greeting a respectful Seevaan vassal would give, with allowances for human anatomy. Talaria, in keeping with her station, but with respect for Celina as an artist, replied by inclining her thorax, and brought her fore pincers closer, but didn't touch them together.

"Tell her that the honor is all mine," Celina said, looking up into the Queen's multifaceted eyes. N'Jerri nodded and made a quick series of hand gestures, which the Seevaan regarded before answering with her own rapid pincer movements.

"Queen Talaria says that it is she who is the one being honored," N'Jerri told her. "She says that ever since she first heard your music she looked forwards to being in the presence of such a great artist."

Celina knew enough Seevaan pincer-speak to sign out her own thanks for this gracious compliment. Even though the Seevaans *were* a distraction, and although she doubted that she would get anything meaningful done while they were around, compliments from any source were always nice. Especially when they came from a being as important as Talaria was.

"Well," she said through N'Jerri. "Everyone--please, make yourselves comfortable. Clio and I were just working on an important bridge for our latest realie production."

The furniture in the room, aside from her seat at the mixing controls, consisted of a couch and some chairs. None of these were suited for the Seevaan anatomy, but her guests didn't seem to mind at all. Instead, Queen Talaria and her attendants appeared to be content to settle themselves down on their rear legs in a half crouch. Then all of them became as still as jade statues.

Doing her best to ignore her exotic audience, Celina returned to her chair and reopened the raw file she had been working with. She was just about to ask Clio to replay the musical track when loud clicking noises sounded behind her, nearly startling her straight out of her seat. She spun around to see that the Seevaans, led by Queen Talaria, were all rapidly clicking their pincers together in nothing that resembled any intelligible pincer-speak.

"Hanna? What are they doing?" she asked N'Jerri.

"Umm-sorry Celina," the woman replied. "I should have prepared you. They're…practicing their enthusiasm."

"What?"

"Polite Seevaans prefer to rehearse their applause so that they can express just the right level of appreciation when it's appropriate. I'm afraid that with everything else going on, Queen Talaria and her staff just haven't had the opportunity until now to get it just right."

"I *see*," Celina answered. "So, are they satisfied? Do they need a few more minutes? I can go and take a break if they need time to work on their routine."

"No, no," N'Jerri said, waving her back into her chair. "I'm quite certain that they've properly prepared themselves. Please, Celina, go on."

Celina gave her audience a long, doubtful expression, but returned to her work. This time, she managed to get as far as the first few bars of the music before the Seevaans responded with more clicking, which if anything, was even more passionate than their practice efforts.

"Hanna?"

"Yes, yes, Celina…sorry about that," N'Jerri replied. "They really do admire your work. They're just a little excited is all." She was making rapid, frantic gestures to the insectoids at the same time, trying, as politely as possible, to convince them to curb their enthusiasm. To her relief, Queen Talaria and her group ceased applauding, and went absolutely still once again.

Just the same, Celina took the precaution of putting on a set of headphones. She knew that this might be perceived as rudeness, but if she were to get *anything* accomplished, blocking out her guests spontaneous bursts of excitement was going to be the only way.

She started in again, re-playing the *Song of Humanity* and carefully matching up the holofootage with its timing. It wasn't long before she became utterly entranced by the melody, and equally certain that her guests would be just as enthralled by it. Their reaction was not what she, nor N'Jerri had expected however.

As she hit the final note, Queen Talaria gave out a shrill whistling sound. Instantly, her guards, who had been as still as statues up to this point, came to life. They immediately wheeled to face the door, leveling their pole arms at it. The Handmaiden's meanwhile, had produced long, wicked-looking daggers and raced to take up positions around Celina and the keyboard. There, they faced outwards, trembling with agitation. Talaria had also reacted, leaping out of her repose and skittering up to the musician.

Celina was still processing this abrupt change when the Queen grasped her, gently enough, but quite firmly, and raised her up out of her seat. The musician squealed in both surprise and terror as the alien held her level with her multifaceted eyes and proceeded to speak to her with her secondary pincers in gestures that were too rapid to decipher.

"Hanna! What in the Lady's name is she *doing*?!" she yelled. The Seevaan had pinned her arms to her side, and she was beginning to loose circulation.

"I-I don't know," N'Jerri answered, starting to move towards her. That was a mistake. The Handmaiden nearest her reacted, swatting at her with her secondary fore pincer. The blow sent the woman flying with a grunt. Only her impact with the couch saved her from hitting the wall and sustaining a serious injury.

Perceiving the threat to her mistress, Clio intervened. "Celi! I've called the police! They are on their way! I've also alerted building security!" Neither measure did anything to grant Celina's release from the creature's powerful grip, however.

N'Jerri struggled to her feet, and kept a wary distance from the Handmaidens. She circled around the assembly instead, with the nearest Handmaiden wheeling in time to track her movements, dagger at the ready. The woman stopped when she was within the Queen's line of sight and signed to her.

Queen Talaria turned her head and regarded N'Jerri carefully. Then she answered, and the woman translated her words. "She wants to know where you heard the song you were playing, and she wants to know now. It's quite important."

"What!?" Celina responded, wondering if her guests had gone insane. "Tell her that I didn't hear it anywhere. It's my song. I wrote it."

N'Jerri relayed this, and it provoked a series of gestures from the Seevaan that were even more emphatic. Her grip on Celina also tightened.

"Oww!" Celina cried, "Tell her to let me go! I think she's breaking my arms!"

"I will! I will!" N'Jerri said, signing frantically to the insectoid. Thankfully, her communication finally had some effect; the Queen's hold slackened slightly. She didn't release Celina though, and repeated her question.

"Tell the Queen that I wrote it! I swear—no one gave it to me!" She had never imagined that one day she would be in fear of losing life or limb to a giant bug obsessed with plagiarism.

N'Jerri was beginning to reiterate her statement to the Queen when the door to the studio opened. One of the Zenithia staffers, who apparently hadn't been alerted about the emergency, began to enter, carrying refreshments. The guards reacted to this intrusion by swinging at her with their weapons. Fortunately, they missed decapitating the woman, but one of the blades scored a hit on the tray that she had been carrying. It went flying, tumbling through the air in perfect accompaniment to her shriek of surprise and terror. As it crashed to the floor she backpedaled and ran for her life.

"Hanna!" Celina hollered. "Do something!! Tell her it came to me in a dream, that's all! I heard it in a dream and recorded it when I woke up!"

The nanosecond that N'Jerri signed this out, the Queen set Celina down. But she didn't back away, and neither did her attendants relax or change their positions in the room. Outside, the musician could hear the Police arriving and coming down the hall. Talaria seemed oblivious to the commotion however, and signed out something else.

"What is she asking now?" Celina asked.

"She wants to know what else the dream told you."

Now she was absolutely certain that Talaria and her companions were unhinged, but she answered nonetheless. "All I know is that there was some woman in it, and after she gave me the song, she told me that it was important. I can't remember anything else."

Queen Talaria finally stepped back, and at some unheard signal, the guards retreated from the door and her Handmaidens re-sheathed their daggers.

The Queen signed again. Her gestures were much slower now, and clearly intended to be fully understood by the two humans. N'Jerri shared what she had to say.

"Queen Talaria graciously begs your forgiveness, and says that the song that you were given is indeed very important. She says that you must finish it, that it is not complete."

"How did she know—?" Celina started to ask.

Her question was cut off as a squad of heavily armed Thermadonian Police officers entered the room, weapons drawn. They didn't fire however, and they were followed in train by a senior policewoman and another woman who was dressed in a plain comerci.

The woman in the suit moved up to the front of the group, and bowed deeply to the Seevaan Queen. They signed to one another at length, and then the woman turned and addressed Celina and N'Jerri.

"Lady Celina, I am Leesa bel Farra with the State Department," she said. "I will be providing an escort for the Queen and her retinue. On their behalf, and the Sisterhood's, I deeply apologize for the terrible misunderstanding that occurred here today."

"Misunderstanding? Yes, well, of course—"

"Please be advised that we will be in touch with you shortly. There are certain matters that we will need to discuss at a more opportune time. I'm sure that you'll want to rest after all this excitement."

"I would, but—"

"Good day jantildamé," the woman said with another bow. She left them, with the Seevaan party and the police following behind her.

"Hanna," Celina said as she watched them leave. "That is positively the *last* time I will *ever* give anyone permission to visit me in the studio! I don't care if it's the Lady herself!"

The State Department representative kept her word. A full day went by before Reception notified her that she had a call from Bel Farra. Her agent, Madame t'Annya had also joined the conversation.

"Lady Celina, "Bel Farra began. "I hope that you have recovered from the events of the other day."

"I have," Celina replied, more than a little irritated at the reminder of the fiasco, and the interruption that the call was causing. After the Seevaans had left, she had been too upset to work, and had lost a full day just recuperating. To stay on her self-imposed schedule, there was a lot that she had to catch up on. "How can I help you?" she asked. Then offhandedly, she greeted her agent. "By the way, Alia, hello."

"Celi," T'Annya said in a careful tone that instantly warned the musician that she was about to ask her to do something she wouldn't like, "Ms. bel Farra, and the Sisterhood need a favor."

"What is it?" Celina asked, looking suspiciously at Bel Farra's image.

"Lady Celina, once again, let me extend our sincere regret for the way the Seevaans conducted themselves. But it seems that your work provoked their response. They didn't quite explain it to us, but evidently your song has some kind of deep symbolic significance, and they were quite unprepared to hear you play it. Had we known this, we would have tried to prevent them from visiting, but as it was, we were caught just as unaware of the situation as you were."

"Yes? And?"

"As you recall, Queen Talaria requested that you complete your piece, and we would like you to oblige." This sounded reasonable enough to her. Which only meant that whatever was to follow, wouldn't be.

"Fine. Go on."

"After speaking with the Chaotic delegation at length," Bel Farra continued, "the Chairwoman has requested, as a personal favor to her, that you agree to one other thing. She asks that you promise not to publish it in any form. Ever."

Celina was positively floored. "W-what?! Are you all insane?! That's the most outrageous thing I've ever—"

"Celi, Please" T'Annya interjected. "They've explained it all to me. It's a matter of national security. You have to cooperate. Please, just listen to me!"

Celina didn't listen. She severed the connection.

It took several more calls to the studio before she felt calm enough to speak with her agent again. By the time the woman was done speaking, she was still furious, but reluctantly willing to cooperate. She hated herself for doing this, but she still agreed.

When the call finally ended, she did two things; she ordered a strong drink for herself, and then had Clio bring up the files containing some of the other pieces she had been working on. Compared to the *Song*, they were, in her opinion, quite second rate, but she had to salvage her project somehow. She had learned early in her career that when *shess* talked, money walked, and she needed her funding, and the government's good will too badly.

Bel Sharra Memorial Spaceport, Cyrene District, Thermadon Val, Thermadon, Myrene System, Thalestris Elant, United Sisterhood of Suns, 1044.06|28|00:30:14

Kaly n'Deena was not the only woman to finish training that year. Maya n'Kaaryn had also just completed a full year on Nyx. She had finally managed to learn how to meditate and she was even able to keep her mind still for a few seconds.

More importantly, she had gained a great deal of control over her thoughts and by extension, her passions. And in addition to a host of new knowledge and skills, courtesy of the Agency's prescribed training course for new agents, Lady Ananzi had gone on to train her in the use of some of her talents. She had even learned to break up rocks with her psiever-aided will. Small ones to be sure, but rocks nonetheless.

Now she was on a hiatus of sorts, a break between what Ananzi had called her 'basic training' and learning 'real knowledge'. That, whatever it was, was slated for later, when she returned to Nyx. In the meantime, she had come back to Thermadon for what Sarah had called her official 'graduation to the next level'. Maya wasn't certain what shape this would take, or why they needed to visit the capitol for it, but she had learned, thanks to many pratfalls and bruises, to just accept the process and see where it would lead.

When they exited the Spaceport terminal together, Sarah's aircar was waiting for them at the rain-wet curb.

"Greetings Mistress," it said as it opened its doors for them.

"Hello again, Aria," Sarah answered. "Aria, this is Maya. She will be a frequent passenger from now on. Please remember her and do as she says unless I countermand it."

"Certainly, Mistress", Aria responded cheerfully. "Welcome aboard Maya!"

Maya nodded politely in the general direction of the dashboard, acknowledging the greeting.

"Mistress, I'm so *glad* that you came home!" Aria said. "I was getting lonely in that stuffy old garage. Is there a chance that we will have an adventure tonight?"

"It is quite likely, Aria", Sarah replied. "Did the special weapons package that I ordered for you get installed?"

"Yes! And it really is quite wonderful! I simply *can't* wait to use it!" A display of the car's systems appeared on the windshield HUD, and a section of the vehicle, showing its internal components, flashed on and off enthusiastically.

Sarah scrutinized the data, and then waved her hand, banishing the image. "You may have your chance tonight, Aria. Right now, I am sending you some coordinates in the Industrial district. Please take us there."

"Certainly, Mistress!" the AI chirped. "Oh this is going to be fun! I just know it!" The cars engines started, and they rose smoothly up and away from the terminal and into the lines of traffic flying above the spaceport. As the hovercar found a position for itself among the other vehicles and assumed level flight, Sarah looked over to Maya.

"I want to tell you about a creature that once lived on Old Gaia," she said. "A magnificent beast called a 'lion'. Have you ever heard of it?"

Maya shook her head. Old Gaian history had never really interested her very much.

"A pity," her companion frowned. "You should look this creature up when you have the chance. The females of this species, the 'lionesses', were formidable hunters. The Goddess designed them to be the perfect killing machines, and they performed that role with a flawless efficiency. Nothing could challenge their primacy '

"They killed to eat, they killed to feed their young, and they killed to defend the cubs from other predators. And when their young were ready, they taught them how to kill for themselves, wounding their prey so that the cubs could practice on them, and learn."

Sarah paused, letting Maya absorb this. Then she continued.

"Now there was also another creature that lived alongside the lioness. It was called the 'jackal'. The jackal was much smaller than the lion, and by itself, it was unable to bring down the kind of large prey that the lioness could.'

"Instead, it followed behind them, and when they killed, it lived on whatever scraps the lioness and her children saw fit to leave behind.'

"When you and I first spoke on the *JUDI*, you might recall that I told you that you and I were of a different cut than most women, and that you needed to become greater than you were. It was either that, or risk becoming someone else's prey. Do you remember that conversation?"

"Yes," Maya replied. She did, vividly.

"You have grown since that time, Maya. But tonight, you must make an important choice; whether you will go on being a jackal, slinking at the edges of life, and surviving upon whatever you can scavenge, or become a lioness. Lady Ananzi, Skylaar, and I, have all shown you your teeth and claws, but now you must decide whether you will use them or not."

So, Maya thought. *This is it. I'm here to kill someone, maybe even several someones.* She looked away from Sarah, and out the window at the city lights rushing by, and considered this. The issue of whether she could ever take a life was something that had come up in her mind many times during her training, and she had always arrived at the same conclusions.

Most women were expected to wrestle with their 'consciences' and their 'morals' when it came to this subject. At least that was how it always went in the adventure realies. But except for Skylaar and Felecia, she had never really cared about most people. They had always just been 'marks' to her; people that you hustled, or temporary accomplices that provided something useful before you threw them away, or before they did the same thing to you. That's how it worked.

She had also never believed in the so-called value of human life. Growing up on the pitiless streets of Ashkele, she had witnessed enough death and injury to understand that the Goddess was fickle when it came to the fates of her children. They lived, they died and they suffered—and nothing *ever* intervened to save them. Not even her. As far as Maya was concerned, Humanity was alone, and anyone who said differently was just filled with *shess*.

But what *had* always bothered her, and was bothering her right then, was whether she was truly ready for the challenge. She didn't care if Sarah would be satisfied with her performance or not, but Skylaar's opinion of her *did* matter, and despite the fact that she had come a long ways in her training, the prospect of actually *applying* any of it to a real life situation was quite daunting. The very last thing that she wanted to do was *fek* up and disgrace herself in her teachers' eyes.

There was also something else that troubled her, though not as profoundly. Before coming to know Sarah, Ananzi and Skylaar, she had always thought of herself as a thief—a damned good one in fact—but never an assassin. If she had to kill someone this night, she knew that she would be crossing a threshold; from what was familiar and even comfortable in its own strange way, and over into a dark, yawning uncertainty of a life.

Sarah had crossed that boundary already, many years earlier, and seemed almost smug about it. But so had Skylaar, she reminded herself, and in order for her to complete her own journey, she knew that she would have to join them and cross that line.

In the end, it really wasn't a choice between the jackal, or the lioness, Maya decided. The jackal had stopped being an option since her first day of training with Skylaar. Now it was only a matter of completing the process.

"Who are we going after?" she finally asked.

Sarah rewarded her with a pleased smile. "I am sure that you recall the terrorists who tampered with the impeller fields at the Shadow Lake Lodge."

Maya grimaced, and crossed her arms in front of her breasts. It was impossible for her *not* to remember them. The failure of the force fields on Nemesis had nearly cost her and her lover their lives. "So, this has something to do with them?"

"Everything," Sarah responded. "The Agency had a hard time of it, but they managed to track down the Bio Action Army cell that was responsible for the attack. They are meeting at the warehouse we are headed for. And the terrorists don't know it, but tonight we're going to see our business with them settled, permanently. You are here to help us finalize the matter."

Good, Maya thought. Killing them didn't bother her one nano. They had tried to murder her and Felecia, and they would try it again if they ever got the chance. So, it was a simple equation; for her and Felecia to live, they had to die. Now. Tonight. Log off, end of line.

"Fine," she said with a leaden finality. "I'm ready. Let's get this over with."

***

At 00.61.70, the streets of eastern Thermadon were relatively quiet, and not all of the factories and facilities in the area were operating at full capacity. This was especially true of the sector Sarah had taken them to. Most of the warehouses there were closed, and no one was around to notice the dark hovervan, or Sarah's *Falcaan 490* as they parked together at street level. Another van arrived at the same time and positioned itself at the opposite end of the street.

Sarah pointed to a warehouse in the center of the block. "That building is where the terrorists are meeting. Our teams will make the initial entry and take the building. Did you check your needlegun?"

Maya nodded. "Yes." It was loaded with a full clip of poisoned 'smart' rounds.

As she said this, a group of women dressed in masks and black fatigues got out of the hovervan next to them. They were all carrying military grade energy weapons and from the way they held them, Maya could tell that they were seasoned professionals.

At a hand-signal from their leader, they moved soundlessly towards the warehouse. The same thing happened down the street at the other hovervan.

Reaching the entrance together, the two teams took up positions to either side. One of the women did something at the door, and abruptly stepped away. There was a bright flash of light, and the door blew off its hinges. Before it had even finished hitting the ground, the two teams rushed inside.

Only a few seconds elapsed before Aria made an announcement, "Mistress? The Team Leader reports that they have neutralized five targets, and that two are in the back of the building headed towards a rear exit."

"Good," Sarah said. "Maintain a watch on the area and let me know the progress of the remaining targets." The *Falcaan* was tied into the city satellite network and was monitoring all life forms in the vicinity.

"Yes, Mistress," the car replied. "Do you really think there's a chance we will see some action tonight? I've been in the garage sooo long…"

"Perhaps," Sarah told it. "Continue monitoring, please." The woman closed her eyes, and then reopened them. Maya knew that she had been communicating with someone by psiever, but the conversation had been on a closed channel. Whatever had transpired brought another smile to Sarah's lips however.

"Mistress!" the car said excitedly. "The two targets have exited the rear of the building. They are entering a hovercar and its engines are powering up."

"Good," Sarah answered. "When it leaves, follow it."

The *Falcaan's* own engines came to life and the vehicle started to rise immediately. "It's a red *Aerhawk 760*, Mistress," the car announced with clear disgust. "Oh, I *hate* those models! They think they are *so* special. It will be a pleasure to run it down!"

"I always love it when someone has the opportunity to enjoy their work," Sarah remarked dryly.

A split-second later, the *Aerhawk* burst out from behind the warehouse and ascended rapidly. But the *Falcaan* was already climbing to give it chase. The steep angle pressed Maya back into her seat as the vehicle clawed its way into the air after its prey.

The *Aerhawk* spotted them, and banked hard, but *Aria* stayed with them as they flew over the rooftops. "Mistress?" the car inquired. "May I use the weapons package now? I would certainly like to see how well it works."

Sarah glanced briefly out the window before responding. "Not yet, Aria. I want them brought to ground at a better location. Maintain pursuit. Also, have we had any police units dispatched to this event?"

"No Mistress. They seem to be re-routing their units away from us."

"Well, that is a change for the better," Sarah returned astringently. "I suppose they learned their lesson from the last time that they interfered with Agency business. Continue monitoring their Com-bands however. It only takes one ambitious officer to spoil things."

Up ahead of them, The *Aerhawk* had finally realized that it was not going to throw the *Falcaan* off of it by mere speed, and a second later, something discharged from its belly. An alarm registered immediately on the *Falcaan's* HUD display: "WEAPONS DEPLOYED!"

"Evading! Engaging Countermeasures!" Aria declared. Whatever it was that the *Aerhawk* had dropped, burst open, and the Falcaan responded by rising and banking sharply. Maya's stomach lurched and she held onto the armrests for dear life.

Below them, in what had been their flight path, a series of small explosions went off as the bomb-lets the *Aerhawk* had discharged, detonated.

"Ooo! That was a dirty trick! And just like an *Aerhawk* to try it!" Aria complained. "But I'm faster and my countermeasures are much smarter!"

The *Aerhawk* cut in its thrusters and headed for a line of traffic in the sky ahead of them. Even at this early hour, it was busy, and Maya wondered if the driver, or the car's AI, was crazy enough to try and fly through it.

They were. The *Aerhawk* flew straight into the oncoming air traffic, sending other drivers careening away in all directions to avoid a mid-air collision. As it was, at two aircars *did* collide. One spun down towards the ground until its emergency chutes deployed, and the other, still intact enough to manage it, limped towards the nearest rooftop in a controlled descent.

Up ahead of them, the Interworld Trade Center dominated the skyline. Next to the Golden Pyramid and the Bel Sharra control tower, it was one of the largest buildings in Thermadon. The gigantic complex hosted some of the most important businesses in the Sisterhood, and housed upwards of 720,000 employees even at its quietest times. In seconds they were on top of it, flying in and around its massive tubeways.

"Aria, this is becoming rather tedious," Sarah said as they caromed under a tubeway close enough to see the women inside scurrying for safety. "We are near a good location to bring them down. You may go ahead and use your weapons package. But do *not* destroy the *Aerhawk*! I want them reasonably undamaged."

"Oh thank you Mistress!" the car answered happily. "I know you'll like the new additions. Engaging missile."

Maya felt a gentle 'thump' as the missile launched, and then her eyes followed its trail as it sought out the other aircar. Then, at the last second, instead of hitting the *Aerhawk* squarely, it swerved to the right and detonated itself to the side and rear of the vehicles' engines. The shrapnel and the energy from the blast had an immediate effect; the hovercar's right engine fragmented and a thick ribbon of dark smoke poured out. The *Aerhawk* wobbled, and rapidly lost altitude.

"I also have a railgun that I can use," Aria offered.

"That's very sweet of you," Sarah replied. "Please wait for them to clear the buildings, and then you can destroy their left engine with it. I'd like them brought down in the Park."

The *Aerhawk* was barely managing to avoid the rooftops by this point, and still dropping. In front of them, was a large area filled with trees that Maya recognized immediately; N'Dayr Memorial Park. As the *Aerhawk* cleared the last structure between it and the park, Aria fired her railgun.

The *Aerhawk's* left engine turned into a cloud of metallic fragments. This was all the punishment that the machine could take. It smashed through a row of trees and came down at a steep angle into an open playing field, skipping along the ground like a rock thrown across a pond. Halfway across, it finally came to an abrupt halt, nearly flipping over before burying its nose in the soft soil.

"There!" the *Falcaan* declared with a pronounced note of triumph. "That's where you belong! In the dirt! Not flying in *my* sky!" Then, with a hopeful tone, it added, “Can I strafe them now, Mistress?”

“No, you may *not*,” Sarah retorted. “Descend to ground level and let us out. Then assume a parking orbit overhead and monitor for any traffic.”

“Oh, very well, Mistress,” the car responded sulkily. Then it added, “And thank you. That was quite satisfying—even if you didn’t let me finish them off.”

Sarah laughed as the *Falcaan* landed smoothly on the grass. When it came to a complete stop, the vehicles gull-wing doors opened and she stepped out, needlegun in hand. Maya drew her own weapon and joined her.

The wreckage was just ahead of them. The *Aerhawk’s* right engine was on fire, and the flames illuminated the field around them with a flickering orange light. On the passenger side, the door was partly jammed in the dirt and Maya heard someone inside, trying to kick it loose. Then it popped open and a figure emerged.

Sarah calmly brought up her needlegun and fired a short burst. The figure collapsed back into the shadows with a grunt.

The driver’s side door swung open next. Thanks to the light from the fire, Maya could see the driver clearly. She was an older woman, rather plain in appearance, and could have been any worker at the spacedocks—but the weapon in her hand was something that a dock rat would never have carried.

This is it, Maya told herself. This was the moment of truth. Her entire universe seemed to slow down and compress around that single instant. Intellectually, she knew that this wasn’t an effect from the alien device in her skull, but a natural reaction. Everything in the galaxy had narrowed down to only one thing; the energy gun in the terrorist’s hand--and the fact that it was being raised towards her.

Then, as if her own hand possessed a will of its own, Maya pointed her weapon and pressed the trigger. The rounds sizzled and hissed as they left the barrel and her target cried out and convulsed as they stitched a bloody pattern across her chest. Then she fell back into the *Aerhawk’s* cabin, and went limp.

Lowering her needlegun, Maya realized that her hands were shaking. It wasn't from fear though. It was from pure adrenaline. As time resumed its normal pace around her, it was accompanied by a feeling of pure euphoria, as if she had been drinking and the rush had just hit her. A strange as it was, she felt—good.

"Well done, my young lioness", she heard Sarah say. "Well done."

***

A dark hovervan arrived several minutes later. While its occupants got out to clean up the wreckage scene, Sarah led Maya back to the *Falcaan*.

As soon as they were airborne, she contacted the Ops Leader, and what the agent told her put her in an expansive mood. In all, seven members of the terrorist cell had been eliminated, including one who had been positively identified as their leader.

Sarah took them straightaway to the *Orfeo Café* to celebrate. At the restaurant, there was a surprise awaiting Maya; Skylaar was sitting at Sarah's customary table.

"Greetings Cho-Sena," she said. "I understand that tonight was your graduation, and I wanted to be here to congratulate you. This is a profound moment. I believe that the ancient Gaians once referred to it as 'making your bones'"

"T-thank you, Sena-tai," Maya replied, not quite grasping the reference. It seemed to be a night for obscure imagery.

"Your first kill can be quite a powerful experience," the Nemesian remarked as the young woman took her seat, "I know that mine certainly was."

"Who was your first, Sena-tai?" Maya asked, taking a deep drink from a glass of wine Sarah had just handed her.

"An alien sentry," Skylaar stated. "I was about your age when my teacher took me out on my first real mission. I had just jumped over a wall and landed right next to the creature. I broke its neck using one of the techniques I showed you before I even realized that I had done it. My hands couldn't stop shaking afterwards."

"Yes! That's exactly what happened to me!" Maya exclaimed. In fact, her hands were still a bit unsteady.

Skylaar saluted her with her glass. "Trust me in this Cho-Sena, they will get much steadier, given time and practice."

After this, they shared a companionable meal together. When it was done, and Maya had drunk all the wine that she could handle, and still more or less stand, Sarah bid goodbye to the Nemesian for the both of them and helped the young woman stagger to their aircar. Maya fell asleep as they lifted off, and she was only half-conscious when they landed again at Sarah's apartment.

The woman brought her inside, and after tucking her into the large bed, placed a gentle kiss on her forehead. She was proud of Maya, and pleased that all her plans for her were finally coming to fruition.

The future could only get brighter.

Apartment of Sarah n'Jan, 409th Floor, The Otrera, Agamede District, Thermadon Val, Thermadon, Myrene System, Thalestris Elant, United Sisterhood of Suns, 1044.06|29|03:76:02

Thanks to all the wine she'd consumed, it took Maya a minute to remember anything at all about the night before, but then she recalled the chase, the kill, and the restaurant afterwards. She also had a dim memory of Sarah bringing her into the apartment and then, after tucking her into bed, leaving on some errand. She listened to the sounds around her, and then realized that for the moment at least, she was alone. Sarah was still wherever she had gone off to.

The girl cracked her eyes open just enough to look out the window and saw that it was late morning, or possibly even early afternoon. She briefly debated staying right where she was and enjoying the delicious warmth of the covers, and the chance to snooze a little longer, but she also felt hungry. Finally her hunger won her over, and she got up and wandered out into the central living area. There was a kitchen just off of it, and she set the autochef to work right away, making her some kaafra, with breakfast to follow.

Once she had her beverage in hand, she went out onto the spacious patio and took in the view. Sarah didn't go cheap, she observed. The apartment was somewhere well above the 400th floor, and like its neighbors all around it, in an expensive building.

The view was quite naturally, breathtaking. Thermadon stretched out and away from her, glittering in the bright sunlight like a field of gems left out by some giantess, and she could see down through the corridors of the colossal buildings all the way out to Bel Sharra spaceport and beyond. Despite the fact that she was downtown, all the traffic was far below her, weaving through the perpetual shadows of the great metallic structures with hardly a sound reaching her ears. Only the occasional bird, or the wind greeted her ears.

Very expensive, Maya thought, and like Sarah herself, quite isolated and solitary.

She spent a few more minutes taking in the view, and then went back inside. Breakfast was ready, but she told the autochef to keep it warm, and went exploring instead. Even though she knew that Sarah didn't spend all of her time there, she was curious to see what the apartment could tell her about the woman.

There wasn't much however. Although everything was stylish, new and well kept, none of it stood out as unique, or gave away any clues about Sarah's personality. It was as if everything in the place had been put there to give the appearance that the space was lived in, but without saying very much about the owner.

I should have known, she told herself.

Disappointed, she returned to the kitchen and ate. Generic or not, the autochef, like everything else, was top of the line, and her scrambled chikka eggs and soyaham were cooked to perfection. When the last speck was gone, she addressed the apartment's AI.

"So," she said to the air around her. "What's your name?"

"Greetings mistress!" a familiar voice answered. "I'm sorry for not wishing you a good morning, but I didn't want to disturb your peace."

"Good morning, Aria," Maya replied. Another non-surprise; Sarah wouldn't have trusted anything but her favorite AI to oversee her living space.

"Good morning Maya."

"Where is Sarah…no, never mind…when is she coming back?"

"She didn't say. My transportation component is still parked where she left me, and she hasn't given me any updates."

"Okay," Maya said. "Did she leave any messages?"

"No, Maya, she did not."

Maya put down her napkin and stood. "Well then, it seems that I have the day to myself. And I don't want to spend it here watching holos. The only solution is to go shopping, don't you think?"

Then, just to be on the safe side, she used her psiever to access her credit account. Thanks to her share of the *JUDI's* earnings, the sum waiting for her was impressive, even by Thermadonian standards. "Yes, shopping it is! Aria, please call a cab for me."

"Yes, Mistress Maya."

By the time Maya had dressed, the cab was waiting for her outside, hovering against the patio. While she had been getting herself ready, she'd also browsed the city omni, and had found just the place she wanted to go. "I won't need a round trip," she told the cab's AI as she stepped aboard. "One way only."

***

Avé Aerocar produced some of the finest, fastest and according to some critics, most dangerous hovercycles in the Sisterhood. Of these, the *Raptor 110 SE* was the very apex of the Avé product line, boasting enough thrust to easily outmatch and outperform any of the other high-end sport aircars and 'cycles in the skies. One of them was now Maya's.

The dealership didn't sell very many Raptors, thanks to their hefty price tag, and they had been only too happy to rush the custom modifications that Maya had wanted the moment she'd unlocked her credit account for them to debit.

The hoverbike was a dream made of alloy and plastic; jet black with a blue 'ion trail' design that she'd picked out to accent its curves, and a custom motto painted on its fuselage; "SCJM", short for "*Seul Culpa Je'va M'arrete*," or *'Only Guilty If You Catch Me.'* The saleswoman had even been kind enough to place a call back to Sarah's apartment to download a copy of Aria into the machine for her. She had also thrown in a free set of matching flying leathers as her way of saying, 'we want to thank you *VERY* much for the outrageous amount of money that you have just irresponsibly thrown away.'

People could be *so* nice when there were lots of credits involved, Maya thought as she sat on the dealership rooftop. The day around her was still quite beautiful, the air was fresh, and she had her hands resting on the controls of a machine that no sane woman would ever dare fly. Never having considered herself sane however, this presented no serious obstacle.

"Well, Aria," she said to the Raptor. "First things first. I think you need a new name if you're going to be riding with me. And a separate account. I like my privacy."

"Of course, Mistress Maya," the AI answered. "I have just cut my connection with my home database. We are now quite alone. What name do you wish to call me?"

Maya considered this, and then said, "Rebá. Yes that's it, that's what I'll call you." This was Standard slang for 'rebel'. "Please, just call me Maya."

"Yes, Maya," Rebá replied.

"Good. Now that that's settled, let's go for a ride. Show me what you've got." The Raptor's engine came to life underneath her, and it lifted smoothly into the air.

"Any particular destination, Maya?" it asked.

Maya locked herself onto the bike, read the gauges one last time, and flipped down the visor of her helmet. She was tempted to fly the machine straight through the normal flightlanes, but after a year under Lady Ananzi and Sarah, she knew better. As much fun as it might have been to terrorize her fellow motorists and flaunt the traffic laws, the last thing that she needed was to earn their ire. Neither woman might have been present, but if she had learned anything, it was that there were consequences to her actions. Not always immediate ones, but still inevitable. She had plenty of recent, and painful memories, of what their displeasure could bring.

Frowning at the maturity that she was being forced to adopt, she replied, "Back to Sarah's apartment...the long way. But take the Freeflight lanes, Rebá, and when we get there, don't spare the thrust."

The hoverbike obliged. Thrusters igniting, it roared off the roof into space, leaving the dealership behind in seconds and banking sharply to avoid a collision with another pair of towers by flying neatly between them. In seconds it was through the narrow passage, and rising just like the bird of prey that was its namesake.

Maya took over manual control and sent the hovercycle into a climb that took it above the normal flightlanes and into the Freeflight zone. A distant relative of the ancient German Autobahn, the Freeflight lanes had no speed restrictions, and few rules governing the vehicles that dared to use it. In a city where surveillance, rigid customs and bureaucratic restrictions were part of the daily landscape, Freeflight allowed the women of Thermadon the one place where near absolute freedom existed. It was also something that neither Sarah nor Lady Ananzi could object to. What went on there, however uncontrolled, was perfectly legal.

As her mistress had requested, Rebá engaged the 'bike's thrust to full, and the machine roared past the other vehicles nearby as if they were only hovering in place.

"Oh goddess--Yes!" Maya cried. "I *like* this!" Rebá was magnificent, and when she saw that they were nearing Sarah's building, she was so pleased, that she had the AI continue onwards, riding out to the very edge of the city and then back again, just for the pure joy of it.

When she finally arrived at the apartment, it was late in the day, and Sarah had returned. Maya wasn't worried however; she had taken the expedient of calling Aria at one point, and leaving word.

Not that this completely mollified Sarah, who met her at the door.

"If you are going to ride one of those—things," the woman said with palpable disapproval, "I will insist that you agree to a connection to Aria and a priority override by her. I don't want you to be tempted to test out your machines capabilities anywhere that might get you into trouble."

Maya started to open her mouth to protest, but Sarah waved her to silence. "That is non-negotiable. I will not jeopardize the investment that we have made in you to some spurt of teenage exuberance. When you are not in Freeflight, you *will* obey every traffic law. I know how hoverbike riders are, and as a motorist myself, to think that you have joined their ranks is not only not surprising, but in equal parts, quite terrifying."

The girl knew better than to argue this, and maintained her silence. As it turned out, she had little time to enjoy Rebá over the next ten days. Sarah set her hard to work practicing her drills, memorizing astrographic images and studying more Agency approved material. When she had finally reached the point that she was absolutely positive that her skull would burst from all the knowledge that was being poured into it, Sarah announced that they were going on a trip together into the city.

Their destination was Aria's garage, and what Sarah called a 'fitting.' She hadn't explained what this was, but Maya could tell that something about it profoundly bothered the woman, so she didn't press the matter. She was simply glad to be out, riding her hoverbike behind Sarah's vehicle, and she didn't want to spoil the experience by angering her in any way.

The garage itself had no signage indicating what it was, and it occupied a rather plain looking block of light industrial businesses, just one of the many anonymous tenants. Maya knew, without asking, that it was an Agency place, and that its owner wasn't looking for any customers. As they drew close, the automated doors recognized them, and opened.

A young woman was waiting in the landing area. She was dressed in a plain grey jumpsuit, and Maya guessed her to be in her mid 20's. Like Sarah, she was pale and her hair was jet black, but it was tied up into two thick, glossy ponytails. She smiled at them, but there was something in her eyes that reminded Maya of Lady Ananzi. Something cold, calculating, and possibly even cruel.

"I'm Trina," she said as they parked. "But my friends all call me 'T'. You must be Maya." She held out her hand, and Maya saw that her nails were surprisingly long and sharp. Her canines were equally as long, which could have either been the legacy of a Nemesian ancestor, or a cosmetic addition. Whichever the case, they were oddly appropriate.

Maya took her hand, and Trina glanced over at Sarah. "You forgot to mention that she was so *cute*."

Sarah grimaced, and changed the subject. "I brought her here to see what you could do with her hovercycle, and to get her fitted for her suit." Her tone also implied, *'and nothing else.'*

Trina smiled suggestively, and then her gaze flicked back to Maya. "Let's take care of business then. First, your bike." She looked over Maya's shoulder to the Raptor, and with another sassy grin, walked past her. "A Raptor 110," she said appreciatively, "you're not only cute, but you also have *very* good taste in 'bikes."

She turned and addressed Sarah again. "I can certainly do something with this. The standard pursuit package then?"

Sarah nodded, and again Maya sensed her disquiet.

What is it with these two? she wondered. There was definitely something going on between them, and she knew without having to ask, that Sarah was unlikely to explain a thing about it.

"Do you want a defensive package as well?" Trina was saying.

"Yes," Sarah responded stiffly. "With an override, keyed to myself."

Maya had only the vaguest idea what they were talking about, but she reasoned that it was similar to the modifications that Aria-as-an-aircar possessed. Sarah, she knew would explain it all, later and when and if she was in the mood to do so. In the meantime, Maya was more interested in the interplay between the pair, and what was lurking behind it.

"I can do that," Trina answered. "It will take about a week, maybe less to put everything together. Can you spare the bike for that long?"

"She may need it over the next day or two, but I can have it delivered to you by Threeday," Sarah replied. "I'll have the usual courier come by with it."

"Oh, now why go to all *that* trouble?" Trina asked. "Little Maya can just fly it by. I'm sure that she wouldn't mind the trip." By her tone, it was obvious that she had much more in mind than simply sparing the services of a courier.

Sarah shook her head, just a shade too vehemently. "*No.* The courier will *do.*"

Trina frowned coquettishly, and then a wicked expression came over her features. "Very well. You'll *pay* for that of course."

This exchange was enough to make Maya absolutely certain that the woman was Sarah's lover. In all their time together, Sarah had never mentioned having anyone in her life, and it was only logical that she would have picked someone from inside the Agency. But there was something much more to them than that, she decided.

"So," Trina declared, "shall we take care of your fitting then?" She crooked her finger at Maya and smiled, exposing her fangs. "This way, pretty Maya."

They went out of the garage and into another room that housed a number of storage lockers, a workbench and a variety of dull grey crates, some of which were clearly labeled, *'Property of the Sisterhood Navy'* or *'Property of the Sisterhood Marine Corps'*.

Trina ignored the crates and went up to one of the lockers and opened it. There was a black bodysuit hanging inside. It was the very sister of the one that Sarah was wearing, made of the same pleather-like material, and behind it, on another hangar, was the twin of Sarah's black cloak. Even the ornate broach that was pinned to it was a perfect duplicate.

Trina let her examine the items, and then she picked up a hand scanner from her workbench. "Well, time to strip, Maya! For me." Another iniquitous smile came to her lips, and Sarah's frown deepened considerably.

Maya had undressed for someone before; on the *Star of Aphrodite* for the dressmaker, but there had been none of the suggestiveness that was oozing from Trina, and as she complied, she began to feel a deeper sense of anxiety about the woman, and the entire situation. The very last thing that she needed was to become the object of Sarah's jealousy, if things between them were as she thought them to be.

Trina grinned and passed the scanner over Maya. Clearly, she was enjoying herself immensely, and at Sarah's expense.

"Very good!" she announced. "Now all we need to do is send the data to the suit." She pressed a button, and the bodysuit responded. Its molecules shifted and rearranged themselves, and in seconds, the proportions of the suit changed, shortening and reshaping. With another signal, the cloak behind it did the same thing. Whatever they were made of, Maya realized, it was not pleather or cloth, or any conventional material for that matter. It only looked that way.

"*Vala!*" Trina declared, gesturing expansively towards the garments. "All done! You see? All very quick and simple. Now, be a good girl and try them on for me." She gave Maya another exaggerated moue. "Please?"

Maya glanced at Sarah. Her expression was bland, but the look in her eyes told Maya that she was seething at Trina's performance. For her part, Maya certainly appreciated the sentiment. The woman was a total *bita*, she decided, and just as cruel as she had suspected.

Despite her increasing dislike, and her dismay that Sarah had picked such a partner for herself, Maya put the garments on, and found that they fit her perfectly. The cape felt slightly ridiculous and as she settled it over her shoulders, she had to remind herself that it did have a practical purpose; it rained on Thermadon frequently, and it also lent its wearer a certain level of psychological privacy in an otherwise crowded environment. Even so, it would take some getting used to, and she had no idea how, or if, she would ever be able to bring it with her when she rode her hoverbike.

As for the bodysuit, she had always assumed that it had some functionality. But *what* exactly, had never been explained to her by either Sarah or Skylaar. Now it seemed as if she might get an answer—unless Sarah did what she always did, and wrapped it up in another frustrating layer of mystery.

At least it compliments the cape, she thought.

"Well, look at you!" Trina said. "Every inch the proper Thermadonian out for an evening's pleasure. And that black really does wonders for all the gorgeous blond in your hair." Then she pointed into the locker. "There are matching boots and gloves in there as well. It certainly wouldn't do not to have everything carefully covered over, *would it* Sarah?"

Sarah grimaced again, and Maya saw that she was actually clenching her fists, and pointedly looked away. Yes, Trina was a bitch. Definitely.

Trina reached in for the boots and gloves herself, and handed them to Maya. As they came close to one another, Maya flinched involuntarily, and Trina laughed and stepped back, her expression saying, *'don't worry. I won't bite you—right now.'*

The moment that Maya had finished putting everything on, Trina went to another locker and brought out one final item. It was a knife. It was in its own sheath, which seemed to be made from the same material as the body-suit. She gave it to Maya, and let her draw it.

Its blade was double-edged, a good 20 centimeters long, and *very* sharp. Its surface also gleamed with a beautiful semi-gloss black finish that caught the reflections of the room around it like a sorceresses' mirror. Maya had never seen its like, and behind her, Sarah leaned in for a closer look.

"A little gift for you, pretty Maya," Trina purred. "It's a *Carrissa.* " The word meant 'lover', or more accurately 'sweet one'. "In my opinion the *Carrissa's* are the best around, especially if you *reaaaly* care about someone. Wouldn't you agree? Sarah certainly thinks so; that's what she carries."

"I-I suppose," Maya answered. She had changed her mind about Trina. She wasn't just a weird bitch. She was downright *klaxxy.*

"What is that finish?" Sarah inquired, taking the knife from Maya and examining it closely. "It feels a trifle heavier than I'd expect. Is this a coating of some kind?"

Trina clapped. "Ooo! Clever Sarah gets the prize!" Then she planted her hands on her hips and spoke as if she were giving a lecture to students who weren't terribly bright. "It certainly is a coating. The Agency calls it *Malandrium,* and the Seevaans gave it to us. According to our big green bug-buddies, it's created when iron is compressed by gravitational forces equal to a black hole."

"When it gets squashed down that far," she continued, pinching the air with her thumb and index finger for emphasis, "it becomes liquid, and the bugs have managed to find a way to keep it like that just long enough to apply it as a coating.'

"So, you see, this process not only gives us a wonderful new weapons coating, but also definitively proves the mechanical principle that the right amount of pressure, applied in just the right place, can make wonderful things happen. Why…come to think of it, that's just like *sex!!*"

Sarah's eyes narrowed down to unhappy slits. "Yes. And *Maland-* stands for?"

Trina pouted, and pretended to examine her nails. "Oh, it's from 'Malinda', and 'Sandra', which means 'mal', 'black' and 'defender of humankind' in old Gaian. Or so I was told. What I just gave pretty little Maya is only half a micron thick, and it's still able to penetrate anything that we have. If it passes our trials, the Agency is considering it for use on armor plating, and even juicy new rounds to shoot our enemies with. Isn't that just positively delicious?!"

Despite her irritation, Sarah's eyebrows rose. "So, what did our benefactresses ask of *us* in return for this gift?"

"Oh, just some silly little thing having to do with music," Trina replied, waving the subject away into irrelevancy. "They like our music, and they're willing to give the coating away…I'm sorry, but I'm just in rare form tonight, and its all thanks to Maya…the Seevaans are willing to give it away…*for a song!*" She laughed at her own humor, but neither Sarah nor Maya joined her.

"It is nice to know that the Arts are getting an opportunity to support the defense effort," Sarah replied astringently. "We'll certainly evaluate it, and let the Agency know what we think." She handed the blade back to Maya who put it into its sheath.

"Oh, just go ahead and put it on, Maya," Trina insisted, and examining it, the girl was unable to see exactly how to accomplish this. The sheath had no obvious loops for a belt to fit through. Nor did she happen to have a belt.

Trina grinned again, her canines gleaming. "Just put it against your leg, sweetness. It will do the rest. Or…if you want…I can do it for you."

"No," Maya answered,"I can manage." She bent down and pressed the sheath to her calf, and she had to admit that she was impressed by the result. The sheath and the material of the bodysuit seemed to find each other, and bonded together into a seamless union. Whatever she was wearing was definitely *not* leather, or cloth, or any other fabric she had ever heard of.

Trina's grin widened. "Perfect! The knife suits you. So, I'll expect you back here with your hovercycle in a day or so."

Sarah glared and immediately corrected her. "I *said* that the courier would bring it."

"I had to at least try," Trina replied with counterfeit shame. "But do feel free to drop by again, any time little Maya. In fact, Sarah, you should think of bringing her by when you come this way again. I'm sure the three of us can find *something* to talk about other than business."

Sarah didn't rise to her bait. "Maya, lets go. We have another appointment."

Trina laughed, a rich evil sound, and watched them leave.

Maya followed Sarah's lead as they flew away from the garage, and then when she saw her signal, landed with her on a nearby rooftop. She got off her bike, intent on complaining about her stupid cape flapping everywhere, and about just how weird she thought Trina was. But as Sarah exited her aircar, Maya took an involuntary step backwards. Sarah's expression was absolutely crazed.

Abruptly, the woman grabbed her by the forearm, and shook her roughly. "You will *promise*," she snarled, "that you will *never*, *ever* go to that garage by yourself. *Ever!*"

"But, what—?!"

"Ever!"

"Fine! Ever," Maya answered. Then, "So, what is it about her? What's going on between you two?"

Sarah's features twisted with barely restrained fury. "*That* is a question that you will never ask me again." Her voice had a deadly undertone that made it quite plain that there would be terrible consequences if Maya violated this. And wisely, the young woman decided not to press the matter. Instead, she simply nodded passively.

Sarah released her grip, and then stamped back to the *Falcaan*. "We have an appointment," she said over her shoulder. "To meet with Senatrix n'Calysher for lunch. Don't get lost, or get yourself into any trouble."

Themiscrya Tower, 900th Floor, Penthouse Level, Agamede District, Thermadon Val, Thermadon, Myrene System, Thalestris Elant, United Sisterhood of Suns, 1044.07|09|04:36:67

It began to rain shortly after they left the garage, and the foul weather only added to Sarah's dark mood. She was absolutely livid with Trina, but even angrier with herself for her outburst.

Maya should have never seen her acting the way she had, she told herself, out of control, emotional, and worst of all, weak. It undermined the very foundation of everything that she was trying to accomplish. And she knew that this was also precisely what Trina had intended; to goad her to the breaking point just for the pure sadistic pleasure of making her lose her self-control in front of her apprentice.

That's what the woman always did. She used her own emotions against her. Overcome with anger, Sarah slammed her fist on the hovercar's dash and cursed. "*Bita!*"

This made her feel better, but only slightly. They still had their lunch with the Senatrix ahead of them and she wasn't about to let "T's" little victory poison it. Ordering Aria to assume control, she performed one of the breathing exercises that she'd learned during her travels. It was from Zommerlaand, and it had always helped to give her her strength back, and her focus when she needed it the most.

Making the *Maarken* of 'Isa, the Icicle' with her forefinger, she held it up in front of her face, and closed her eyes. Then, with a deep breath, she relaxed; letting the force of primal ice cool her passions, and slow her thoughts. "Iiiissss," she chanted. "Iiissss, Iiissssss. Ice instead of fire, calm and focus over unbridled passion."

She repeated the mantra over and over. At last, when serenity had returned, she lowered her hand and reopened her eyes. According to the HUD, they were nearing their destination, Themiscrya Tower, the home of Senatrix n'Calysher.

"Aria," she said calmly, "take us up to the private flightlanes and on a course to land at the Senatrix's residence."

"Yes, mistress," the AI replied, making the aircar ascend even as it acknowledged her command. Behind them, Maya's hoverbike copied the maneuver and followed them upwards through the storm. The sight that greeted Sarah's eyes as they came through the cloud tops finally brought a smile to her face.

The N'Calysher residence occupied the penthouse of the 900-story skyscraper, and as such, it was the most exclusive dwelling in a building that housed the very cream of Thermadonian society. The Themiscrya Tower was a gigantic cylinder, made up of individual 'apartments', all of which easily outsized what would have otherwise been considered palatial mansions on the ground, and the Senatrix's residence capped all of it off like the crown of a queen. It was a huge half-dome, encircled by a generous balcony dotted with elegant gardens.

The architect who had designed the residence, had decreed that like a piece of royal jewelry, the structure should catch the sunlight and reflect it back in a glorious display that everyone in the city would be able to see, and admire. Her grandiose plan had been to have it plated in pure gold to achieve this effect.

But this had not been implemented, not only due to the prohibitive cost involved, but also because a more weather-friendly alloy coating had offered itself up as an alternative. Despite this substitution, the woman's original vision still managed to dazzle and captivate the eye. And after their journey through the darkness below, the bright sunlight flashing off the penthouse dome was nothing short of utterly spectacular.

Sarah hadn't really expected anything less however. For a woman whose family had dominated Sisterhood politics for centuries, such opulence was only to be expected.

It was also a given that the residence had an array of hidden defensive weapons that were the equal of its elegance. The Senatrix had many enemies, and Sarah was certain that no expense had been spared to ensure a proper welcome for anyone coming to do her, or her family, harm. She didn't see any of these lethal devices of course, but she wasn't surprised either. An obvious display of firepower would not only have made it easier for a potential attacker to plan around it, but in her mind at least, would have come off as rather gauche.

Naturally, the N'Calysher residence had its own hovercar dock, and an auto-guidance function that allowed her the luxury of relaxing as it guided the two vehicles inside. Settling back in her seat, Sarah smirked when she saw that Aria had altered her own skin to a golden color which came suspiciously close to matching the penthouse's glory. For an AI, Aria often tended to vanity, she thought wryly.

Her good mood had definitely returned.

Sharra, the Senatrix's Chief of Security was there, accompanied by several of her underlings, and greeted them warmly. "Sarah! Maya! It's so good to see you again," She gestured for one of the other women to take Maya's riding helmet and both of their capes. "The Senatrix has been looking forwards to seeing you. She has arranged for your lunch to be in the Solarium."

Even without her talents, it was obvious that Maya was fairly bursting at her hull plates to ask if the Lady Felecia would also be joining them, but Sarah also noted with immense satisfaction that she was refraining from doing so. Although it had been over a year since the two lovers had even seen one another, Maya had clearly gained a large measure of self-control. Lady Ananzi's efforts, in that area at least, appeared to have paid off handsomely.

Naturally, Sharra had anticipated Maya's question, and simply volunteered the information. "The Lady Felecia will also be joining us. She had a pressing engagement, but when she heard that you were coming, she changed her plans and decided to take her lunch at home."

Maya's eyes lit up with excitement, but then she regained her stoic manner, and merely inclined her head in acknowledgement. "Thank you Sharra".

No one, least of all Sharra, was fooled. But the woman only returned the nod, and then waved for them to follow. "Ladies? If you will come with me."

Sarah had never visited the N'Calysher residence before, and it proved to be just as refined on the inside as it was on the outside. The hangar area opened onto a large domed foyer decorated in the Neo-Renaissance style, and the overall scheme was a subdued gold that emulated the great dome that covered it.

Niches, containing priceless works of old Gaian art, occurred at intervals around the chamber, and the ceiling itself had been painted with a superb reproduction of Hillaari bel Teresaa's immortal *"Goddess Rising,"* which played surprisingly well in the round. Overall, it was a space that had been designed to impress the visitor, and remind them of the powerful patrician that Layna n'Calysher was.

Beyond it, Sarah found that the rest of the home was no less spectacular, and equally clear in transmitting its messages of influence and wealth; exquisite Corrissan furniture was everywhere, offset by fine carpets from Sita that were clearly expensive, but without being overstated or vulgar. And again, Gaian artwork predominated, including several works that Sarah had heard were occasionally loaned out for exhibit at the Métropol.

Seeing all this, she was filled with admiration for the Senatrix's good taste, and promptly made a mental note to acquire copies of some of the pieces for her own residence. Although she kept her apartment carefully neutral, there were some things that she encountered that were simply too fine not to include. Of late, her residence had begun to seem sterile to her, and it felt like it was time to liven it up a bit—without giving away anything too sensitive, of course.

Unfortunately, Maya had no eyes for their palatial surroundings; all she sought was the sight of her lover, and Sarah couldn't help but smile to herself at the terrible and compelling force of teenage infatuation. Thanks to its grip on her, when they reached the Solarium, Maya barely noticed that aside from the Senatrix and Felecia, that another guest was also joining them.

Not that she would have recognized the woman, Sarah reminded herself. To date, Maya's entire experience with the Agency had centered on the *JUDI's* crew, and DNA encoded flowers. Sally bel Mala could have been anyone as far as the besotted girl was concerned.

Sarah knew full well who she was though, and while she allowed Maya to enjoy her reunion with Felecia, she acknowledged the OAE agent. "Ms. Bel Mala," she said. "It has been awhile."

Sally bel Mala was not just 'any agent' though, any more than a black hole was merely a 'slight gravitational anomaly'. She was the Department Director of the OICD, the Operations Integration and Coordination Department, which oversaw and synchronized all of the Agency's operations throughout the Sisterhood, as well as in all neighboring regions of space. Bel Mala's hand was in every significant action that the Agency involved itself in, and she answered to no less than the Director herself. Sarah had become acquainted with her during some of her own clandestine missions, but they had only met a few times in the flesh, at planning sessions for some of the most sensitive tasks. Seeing her here, meant that something very important was afoot.

"I'm glad you could come and join us today, Sarah," the Spymistress answered. "I know that your protégé's training has kept you rather busy."

Then Bel Mala turned to Maya, who had finally managed to realize that there was something else in the universe other than Felecia. "It is a genuine pleasure to meet you Ms. n'Kaaryn. Sarah and Lady Ananzi have both reported good things to us about your progress."

Maya responded to the compliment with a careful half bow, the kind that one made when the status of the other person was uncertain, and when she stole a glance at Sarah, all she received was the slightest headshake.

Now is not the time to ask any questions, Sarah thought to her. *Listen and learn.* Wisely, Maya accepted this, and remained impassive.

"Now that we are all here, shall we lunch?" Senatrix n'Calysher interjected. "My chef has prepared a light meal that I think will be conducive to our meeting." She gestured to the elegant table behind her. It was set with fine Corrissan silver, atop elegant Sitalan lace and offset by a colorful spray of flowers that were so delicate that Sarah guessed that they had been imported from the world of Flora in the Sagana Territory, which was known for its exotic blooms. The window behind all this, and framing the blooms, was constructed of double-paned pressurized material that had been made to look like decorative leaded glass, and it commanded a truly heart stopping view of the city below.

Everyone took their places, and lunch was served. The food was as impeccable as the setting and while they ate, the conversation stayed carefully focused on nothing in particular. Finally, at its conclusion, Felecia, much to Maya's palpable regret, excused herself, citing another pressing engagement.

Sarah understood the reason immediately. Despite her relationship to the Senatrix and to Maya, the young woman was not intended to be privy to anything that was about to be discussed.

"Sarah," N'Calysher began, once her daughter had departed, "I invited you here today because there have been some important new developments that affect the Sisterhood."

Sarah arched an eyebrow, and waited patiently for the woman to reveal the substance of her business.

"Several decades ago, we became aware of a pre-plague human society located in a region of space adjacent to the Sagana Territory," the Senatrix began. "This star nation has no knowledge of Motherthought whatsoever. Instead, they live like Humanity used to, before the MARS plague."

She gave Sarah a moment to digest this, and then went on. "Unfortunately, all of our sisterly attempts to make contact and negociate an alliance with them were met with silence. However last year, our Navy came across one of their colonies and finally managed to convince their government that it was in their best interests to open up a meaningful dialogue with us."

"Since then, the Esteral Terrana Rapabla as it calls itself, requested and received, an alliance with us for military aid in order to repel Hriss aggression in their space. This was subsequently furnished to them, in exchange for certain material concessions."

Although this news definitely qualified as 'incredible', Sarah didn't display any surprise. She simply took a sip from her kaafra and smiled back at the woman with an expression of mild interest.

"A special expeditionary force was dispatched to handle the Hriss issue, and the joint campaign that it has been engaged in since then has been quite successful," the Senatrix continued. "In fact, we are anticipating victory over the invaders quite shortly."

Now the Neversaw becomes seen, Sarah thought, quoting a well-known Nemesian expression to herself. An intact pre-plague society would certainly be a problem. Without any question they would be archaic, anarchistic, heterosexual—and thanks to this unhealthy combination of factors, potentially divisive to the Sisterhood's very way of life. They would have to be destroyed, she decided.

"After a year of participation in this joint venture," N'Calysher said, "The Supreme Circle and the Chairwoman have decided that it is finally time to introduce the ETR's existence into the public discourse."

Sarah nodded in understanding, and enjoyed some more of her kaafra.

"A full disclosure will be made to the Sisterhood about them, and about the heroic assistance that we have been providing to them in the name of

Humanity. We believe that if this news is introduced to the average woman in the correct manner, and with the proper education to support it, that it will not have any significant effect on our society.'

"Naturally, we will also make certain that the citizens of the ETR are made aware of the situation, and our existence. We feel that they have as much a right to know the truth as our citizens do."

The news would also cause quite a bit of embarrassment and upheaval for the ETR's government, Sarah mused. Their credibility, and their support, would suffer badly when the populace realized that they had been aware of the Sisterhood for decades, and had concealed it.

With luck, it could even be the beginning of a concerted effort to destabilize and destroy the ETR. Sarah certainly hoped so; the Sisterhood would surely win the war with the Hriss, and there was the future to look to, after all. A future that mandated a friendly neighbor. Her smile widened, and N'Calysher, seeing that she fully appreciated the subtleties behind her words, gave her one of her own.

This was Bel Mala's cue to speak. "To help with this process, and aid other initiatives that we plan to undertake, we would like to enlist your able services." She glanced at the Senatrix and the politician immediately rose from her chair.

"Ladies, I'm afraid that I must apologize," N'Calysher said. "But I just recalled that I have an urgent holo-conference to take in my study. Please enjoy the use of the Solarium in my absence."

She left the room. Sharra, and the other servants also departed with her.

Plausible deniability, Sarah thought. The Senatrix obviously wanted to be able to state, under oath, and in any examination by a psi, that she had not heard, nor had any knowledge of what was about to be said next.

Bel Mala continued. "I realize that in the past, you received your missions by genetic courier, but we decided that the tasks we have in mind for you should be delivered in person. We also felt that a face-to-face was appropriate, given your latest promotion."

"My promotion?" Sarah asked with just the right amount of nonchalance. She absolutely loved how the OAE did business. Everything, even promotions, were kept a secret until just the right moment.

"Yes," Bel Mala replied. "The Director deeply appreciates the results that you have achieved for us, and she wanted to reward you with the post of Sector Chief for the Sagana Territory, with a commensurate raise in your pay grade.'

"This will put you in complete charge of our operations in the area, and you will be answerable only to the Director and myself. Ms. n'Kaaryn will also be officially added to your staff with a G-10 pay rating to start off with. Which," she added looking over at Maya, "means a paycheck from the Sisterhood, as well as the chance for advancement as you prove yourself."

It also meant that Sarah was no longer just a senior field agent. If she wanted to, she could leave the fieldwork to others and sit behind a desk, and even have the freedom of living something that approached a normal life.

If she wanted to, she reminded herself. The notion of making contact with her mother came to mind again, and she wondered if this was the time to broach the subject. But she decided to wait, and see how the conversation progressed.

"Please extend my deepest thanks to the Director," she said. "How would you like me to begin my term as Sector Chief?"

"With some field work, I'm afraid. Normally, we would have been happy to have you delegate it to a subordinate, but the operation requires that the most experienced operative we have be engaged to handle it. I apologize, but the Director specifically asked for you. She has a great deal of faith in you, Sarah, and she simply wouldn't consider anyone else."

"No apologies are needed, ma'am. It would be my pleasure to serve her," Sarah replied. "What would you have of me?"

"We would like you to make a personal visit to the ETR, and contact several influential women there. This will be in direct support of our efforts to publicize the historic union of our two nations, and help lay the groundwork for its future. We've had a small group working inside the ETR for the last ten months, and they provided us with the identities of the women you are to meet with."

"Oh?"

"Yes, a Captain Hari n'Kyla of the DNI assembled the team from volunteers, and its being run by another officer of hers, Lieutenant Amandra sa'Tela. Sa'Tela's supposed to be one of the best psi's that they have. Of course, since their operation will be under your control, you can change out anyone you don't want, but in all fairness, they've been doing a great job so far."

Sarah nodded. She would certainly consider the Lieutenant and her women, especially given such a recommendation.

"Because of the sensitive nature of this affair," Bel Mala continued, "we would like you to keep your dealings with your contacts absolutely confidential, and that you convince them to accompany you back to Thermadon to meet with Senatrix n'Calysher and her Special Committee."

"Of course," Sarah replied. "I also suppose that my entry into the ETR is to be just as—discreet?"

"Naturally," Bel Mala answered. "We want complete discretion maintained in every aspect of this matter. To help you accomplish this, you will be provided with transportation assistance by the Navy."

"My thanks," Sarah said. "But I would prefer to use my own ship for such a venture. Captain bel Lissa has a great deal of experience in such things, and her skills would prove invaluable here."

"I have no problems with that--for the infiltration," Bel Mala said, "but the Agency would prefer that you employ a naval warship for the return trip to Thermadon. I'm sure you can appreciate the reason why."

Sarah certainly could; a warship would both impress and intimidate their passengers. It also meant that the Goddess had just played her hand in the situation. The ETR was located in the operational zone for the Topaz Fleet. And it only stood to reason that the *Pallas Athena* was involved in the campaign there, if not leading it. Her opportunity, she realized, had just arrived. "May I specify the ship?" she asked.

Bel Mala nodded. "If they don't have vital duties to perform elsewhere, yes you certainly may."

"I wish to bring them here on the *Pallas Athena*," Sarah said. "Is she available?"

Bel Mala's eyes widened, ever so slightly, and there was a short pause as the Spymistress considered her request, and all of its implications.

"Yes," the woman said at last. "That vessel can be made available. I'll contact the Navy and make the arrangements." The look she gave her as she spoke these words communicated the rest. *'Best of luck to you when you see your mother again,'* her features said *'you'll need it.'*

Sarah understood. Of a surety, it would be a difficult meeting at best, but she expected as much. Even so, as the Selenites often said, there was 'no other road' for her to take.

"Who am I being sent to retrieve?" she asked, steering their conversation back to the main subject.

Bel Mala reached into a pleather valise waiting at her feet, and handed over a pair of flimsies. "Ms. Rozza Ramara with the Republican Associated Press, and Ms. Sanda Ernan. Ernan's a leading feminist radical."

Sarah glanced at the flimsies, and then back to Bel Mala. "A *feminist?* How...quaint."

The whole concept of female 'equality' was completely irrelevant to a civilization created by, and run by, women. The fact that the ETR was still struggling with such an archaic concept not only emphasized the mixed nature of their society, but also amply demonstrated just how backwards they truly were.

"Yes," Bel Mala said with a wry smile of her own. "She's one of the few that they have. Some of her thoughts tend towards the fundamentals of Motherthought, but even she hasn't quite reached that level...yet."

With our guidance, however, she will, Sarah assured herself. And in the process, Ernan would undoubtedly provide the Sisterhood with a pool of sympathetic women who could be employed in any future 'efforts' that the Agency had in mind for the ETR. "And the journalist?"

"One of their leading female reporters," Bel Mala answered, "with a penchant for challenging the current regime, and a reputation for being very aggressive about how she does it. She's no 'feminist' certainly, but she's willing to speak the truth."

"Yes, the 'truth,'" Sarah remarked mordantly. The Spymistress joined in her laughter.

"There are two other pieces of business that the Agency wishes you to undertake. They are somewhat more sensitive in nature, and involve our long term plans for the future," Bel Mala said. "To be successful, the Director believes that they utterly depend upon your experience, and no one else's. I concur with this opinion."

Sarah invited her to continue.

"We understand that you know a certain businesswoman in Ashkele, one 'Lady d'Ershala,' do you not?"

Sarah did, and only too well. 'Lady' d'Ershala, aka Hana t'Lari, aka Vera bel Myssi, aka Shella bel Terri, ad-infinitum, was the largest dealer of glass in the Far Arm, and quite possibly, anywhere in the known Universe. The woman had been trying for years to convince her to enter into a partnership, and to use the *JUDI* to fly her filthy stuff into places she had had difficulty delivering to. Sarah had always refused her, and in a few cases, she had emphasized her denials with force.

"We would like you to make her an offer," Bel Mala explained, "which we are sure she will accept. She can have complete access to the ETR, with our blessings and support."

"Provided that...?"

"Provided that she agrees to terminate her operations in the Sisterhood within a reasonable period of time, and limit them to this new, untapped, and might I add, competitor-free environment.'

"To seal the bargain, she must also agree to help us locate and eradicate any other individuals involved in the trade who currently operate within our borders. Glass must move into, and remain confined to the ETR. We are particularly interested in seeing her target members of their military as her customers. I like to think of this as a form of cross-cultural exchange."

Unable to contain herself, Maya sent Sarah a message by psiever. *Glass? Sarah we can't get inv—*

Sarah cut her off, abruptly. *BE* SILENT! *I will NOT warn you again!* To reinforce her resolve, she 'pushed' the girl, sending a brief, but intense wave of pain coursing through her skull.

Maya grimaced and her signal abruptly terminated.

Sarah waved for Bel Mala to go on. "Please, do forgive that interruption, and continue with what you were saying."

"Do you believe that Lady d'Ershala will be receptive to such an offer?" the woman asked.

"Undoubtedly," Sarah replied. As much as she herself hated glass, she understood the devastating effect that it would have on the ETR. If they were as backwards as they had been described, they would be completely unprepared for it. More importantly, their government would be faced with an entirely new set of problems to deal with. "What else would you like me to do?" she asked.

"Once Lady d'Ershala begins her enterprise, she will certainly become acquainted with influential figures in the ETR's underworld," Bel Mala said. "When this occurs, we would like her to furnish you with introductions, especially to anyone who provides sexual favors to the regimes' more powerful and wealthy males."

"Of course."

Sex had always been one of the deadliest and most effective tools in espionage. History had shown time and time again that men were fools, and that the more powerful they were, the more foolish they tended to behave in the bedroom. Engaging high-paid prostitutes and mistresses, or 'boyfriends' would give the Agency access to the ETR's deepest state secrets, and invaluable leverage for *Santaj* whenever they wanted it.

Seeing that she fully understood, Bel Mala presented her with her final task. "The last item I wanted to discuss with you was the Marionite problem."

Sarah's pulse, which was already racing, fairly leapt. She had infiltrated the dissident group many years before, and she had always wanted to see them eliminated.

"Since the onset of our alliance, there has been mounting evidence to suggest that the ETR intelligence services intend to enlist the Marionite Order to help them in the event that hostilities break out between our two nations. And recently, a representative of their largest religious organization, the Republican Orthodox Church, was smuggled into the Sisterhood by Marionite sympathizers. We believe that this man was in fact an intelligence agent, working on behalf of his government to secure an alliance between them."

Again, Sarah merely nodded, and maintained the appearance of indifference.

"The Agency would like you to use your contacts among the Marionites and to do whatever you can to ensure that they not only *do* join forces, but that ample proof is gathered about their dealings with one another. Your effort will be in support of other agents who are already working undercover and investigating this matter."

"It will be my very great pleasure, ma'am," Sarah responded sincerely, recalling a visit to one of their clandestine genetics laboratories.

It had been just after Maya had gotten herself trapped aboard the *JUDI*, and they had come there to deliver genetic materials as part of the Agency's efforts to track their secret project. While they had waited for their payment, a neoman had served her and her crew kaafra, and at the time, she had wondered how 'he' would have fared against her in hand-to-hand combat. Now, it actually seemed that she might get the chance to find out after all.

Despite all of the unpleasantness with Trina, it was proving to be an utterly glorious day after all.

***

On the way back to her apartment, Sarah's mind was moving at warp-speed as she considered the implications of everything she had been made privy to. That, and what a reunion with her mother might bring. Her thoughts were a heady mix of excitement, desire—and trepidation, all warring for dominance.

Despite this, she still couldn't help but notice Maya, sitting across from her, and staring pensively out the aircar's windshield.

"Maya," she finally said. "I will need your full attention tonight. This is an invaluable learning opportunity for you. You have been given the rare chance to observe the subversion of an entire nation, from the outset to its completion. That is a precious thing indeed."

The girl spun in her seat to face her. "But *glass*, Sarah? *Fekking* glass?!" she spat. "I thought that the *JUDI* didn't peddle that *shess*. *Deas dam va!*"

Sarah sighed tiredly. "Maya, take one lesson from today away with you. As members of the Agency, we will do whatever we have to for the Sisterhood. No exceptions, no arguments, no 'picking and choosing' what suits us, and what doesn't. We do it."

She gave the girl a long, hard stare, punctuating her statement. Although it was obvious that Maya wanted to argue the matter further, she exhibited more of the restraint that she had shown in the Senatrix's residence. She simply folded her arms over her chest, and went back to gazing sullenly out the windshield.

With the subject effectively closed to any further discussion, Sarah returned to her private ruminations. Maya didn't know it, and probably would not have believed it had she been granted the knowledge, but she had no intention of letting Lady d'Ershala enjoy the fruits of her profits for very long, or the privilege of continuing to draw breath either. The Agency hadn't asked her to terminate the woman, but she was certain that they wouldn't mind, once she had performed her service to her country, of course.

A courier from the Agency was waiting for them when they arrived at her apartment a few minutes later. She had brought data spheres containing digests of everything that Captain n'Kyla's team had gleaned so far from the School and the ETR. There were also detailed files on Ramara and Ernan, and a PTS realie that contained a concentrated course in Espangla.

As soon as she had taken possession of the data spheres, and seen the messenger on her way, she grabbed herself another cup of kaafra, and made Maya sit next to her as she played the first holo. The hours passed, and finally when the young woman couldn't keep her eyes open any longer, Sarah banished her to her bed with an absent wave of her hand. She was back to studying the material even before the girl had begun to stagger out of the room.

Shortly after this, however, she received a private message, and after reading it, reluctantly put down her work. It was from Trina and it said, *"I told you that you'd pay for what you did today. Come see me right now.'T"*

Had it been anyone else in the Far Arm, Sarah would have either ignored it, or sent back a rude reply. But she couldn't do either. Not when it came to Trina. Taking care not to wake Maya, she dressed and went to her aircar.

"Destination, mistress?" Aria asked.

"You know where," Sarah replied darkly. Aria had automatic access to all her messages, including this one. She knew whom they were going to go see.

The trip took only twenty standard minutes, and when they landed at Trina's garage, the machine pulled into its servicing slot and powered down without voicing any protest, or asking its mistress questions.

Trina was waiting, and as soon as Sarah had exited the vehicle, she led her out of the service bay into her private apartment. When the door had slid closed, the woman turned to face her.

She had met Sarah wearing nothing except a pair of black elbow-length leather gloves, and a *strapaadi* belted about her waist. This item wasn't something that women spoke about in polite society, but anyone, at any level, would have recognized the thing instantly. It was a common sex-toy that had been a part of the human arsenal of pleasure for centuries, even before the Star Federation had existed, and the Sisterhood had seamlessly adopted it. While its basic shape no longer bore a close resemblance to the male sex organ that had inspired it, it still possessed the same size and general outlines.

What made it uniquely a part of the Sisterhood were its internal workings. The modern strapaadi took full advantage of psionic technology. In addition to its gross ability to cause physical stimulation, a user could also send signals through it directly to the brain of the person on the receiving end, creating the illusion of additional sensations. Alternately, they could program the device to 'play' a specific set of feelings, and tailor this to the needs of their partner.

Trina's particular strapaadi differed from the common variety. It had been custom made for her, and with much darker purposes in mind. Like all other models, hers also sent signals, but in addition to pleasure, it could also create pain, and at any level that she desired. Of the two, Trina preferred pain.

Seeing her wearing it, Sarah groaned softly, in both longing and dread. She knew what was coming next and she was powerless, and equally unwilling, to resist.

They said nothing to one another for a long time, and then, quite without warning, Trina stepped forwards and slapped her in the face. Instead of reacting with violence, Sarah simply stood there with a vacant expression on her face. The persona of the self-assured, elegant predator had fled from her, replaced by absolute passivity.

Trina smiled cruelly and slapped her again, this time with the back of her hand. The impact sent Sarah's head rocketing sideways and as she staggered, the woman grabbed a handful of hair that had escaped her bun and pulled her in close. A few tears ran down from Sarah's eyes, but still, she did nothing.

"You've been gone for far, far too long this time," Trina hissed. "And then you toyed with me by bringing little Maya here. That wasn't nice." She kissed her, but it was a forceful savage thing, utterly devoid of affection.

"Now you'll have to make it up to me," she growled, biting the woman's lower lip and drawing a tiny bit of blood. "Say that you'll make it up to me."

When Sarah didn't answer, Trina reached out and grasped her nipple from under her blouse, twisting it painfully with her fingertips. "Say it!"

Sarah winced. "Yes-I will…"

With that, Trina spun her around and pushed her against the wall, pulling down her pants with one expert tug. "Oh yes. You certainly will."

As Trina made the first thrust into her with the strapaadi, Sarah cried out in pain. This only increased Trina's excitement though, and she spared her nothing.

***

Hours later, Sarah lay listlessly on the bed. Her body was covered in bruises, but nowhere that her clothing couldn't conceal them.

Trina traced one of the marks that she'd put there with her long artificial fingernails. Her touch was almost loving, but her eyes were cold as ice as she surveyed the woman's body. Sarah stayed where she was, letting her do this, just like she had let her do everything else, and then watched as Trina rose and dressed herself.

"I hate you," she finally said, but with only a ghost of the violence that she was truly capable of.

Trina smiled as she pulled on a blouse. "Yes, I suppose that you do."

"I should kill you," Sarah added, staring up at the ceiling, but there was no conviction in her words. "I should stick a knife in your guts just to see the surprise on your face as I push it through you."

Trina laughed over her shoulder as she walked to the bathroom. "Yes, you really should. But you won't. You need me too much—I complete you."

Someday, I will do it, Sarah vowed. It was a hollow promise though.

***

The idea of partnering with glass dealers had made it hard enough to fall sleep, but then another dream about the Drow'voi intruded on Maya's slumbers. She was in the Necropolis again, and like her previous visions, everything around her had been restored to its former glory.

Once more, she listened as the Drow'voi manipulated their incomprehensible machines and created strange, enigmatic sounds. This time however, a glimmer of understanding came to her. Somehow, she knew that these sounds were not just an accidental collection of noises. Although they had no melody that her ear could trace, there was a pattern to them, and as she listened some more, it dawned on her that it wasn't music after all, but a mathematical formula of some sort, expressed in sound. It was as if the Drow'voi had communicated their numerical values with tones, rather than symbols. The dream receded away from her at this point, and she returned to consciousness recalling an odd fact that she'd picked up in Primary; that on a certain level, mathematics and music were actually one in the same.

Her eyes opened, and she wondered why the dream had ever come to her in the first place, and why it seemed to be recurring. It wasn't as if she was interested in the Drow'voi. Her childhood in the Free City notwithstanding, the ancient builders of the Necropolis had nothing to do with her life. They were something that only crackpots and 'fringie' xenoarcheologists really cared about, and she certainly didn't consider herself to be a lunatic like them. Dreaming about the creatures made absolutely no sense. When no answer presented itself, she finally dismissed the whole thing as some kind of weird mental hiccup, and got out of bed.

Shambling out into the living area, she found that Sarah was still hard at work. Somewhere in the night, the woman had shed her clothing for a nightgown, and then abandoned this to wear nothing at all. She had also unbound her long black hair. And her silver hair spike, which sometimes saw service as a weapon, had been taken out and lay on the carpet beside her.

Even with her long tresses concealing most of her pale back, it was impossible for Maya not to notice the bruises on it and on her shoulders. Or the cuts. Some of the injuries were new and fresh, while others seemed to be in the process of healing, or had healed. Whatever had happened to her had been going on for a long time, the young woman realized.

Suddenly sensing that she was there, watching her, Sarah gasped in alarm and hastily covered herself with her nightgown. Maya pointedly looked away, knowing that she had just witnessed something very private, and deeply painful. She went into the kitchen immediately.

"You know you really should get some sleep," she said, keeping her tone as light and as casual as possible.

Sarah joined her, her robe now belted tightly around her. Her eyes were filled with emotion, and for a heartbeat, it seemed as if she were about to say something, but then she changed her mind and went back out into the living area.

"I'll sleep soon enough," she said from there, and if Maya had had any doubts at all about the nature of the marks, the husky tone of the woman's voice and the slight hesitation, banished them completely.

Trina made those, she realized. Two surprising emotions accompanied this; a deep pang of pity for Sarah, and an even deeper loathing of Trina.

She finished making her kaafra and went out into the living area. There,

Sarah gave her another long, haunted look. Then she transformed, suddenly sitting up straight, and once again becoming strong and confident. A careful fiction now existed between the two of them, an impossibly fragile thing that survived only by their mutual consent, and silence. Without having to ask, Maya knew that there would never be any discussion about the marks.

"So?" she inquired, desperate to redirect things in *any* other direction, "What do we know about the ETR?"

"That they are everything that I expected them to be," Sarah answered. "They are primitive, unstable, alienated, and internally divided. This Captain n'Kyla and her little group have done an amazing job, especially considering the short time period that they have had to work with. The material that they have provided is quite in-depth, and thanks to it, we should be able to depart soon, and begin our work in earnest. I think that a trip to the School, and a meeting with this Captain n'Kyla, and then on to Ashkele, would be a good itinerary."

"Yes," Maya agreed. Despite herself, a frown escaped her. Not only was the purpose behind their journey to Ashkele highly distasteful, but it also meant that they would be leaving Thermadon without giving her a chance to see Felecia again.

She didn't object though. The last thing she wanted just then was to agitate Sarah any further. Instead, she asked, "When do we leave? "

"Soon," the woman answered. "But before we can do so, I want to study some more of this material and see what else the Agency can provide. We also have some additional business that will need attending to before our departure, which will include the PTS training material on this language they speak. Apparently some neoman working for the Navy compiled it. Evidently, the Marionites also speak it, and he learned it from them."

She shook her head in wonderment, and added, "In the meantime, you can busy yourself with your studies. Skylaar will be coming by in an hour. You are to dress in your bodysuit, and she has also requested that you bring your cape with you."

Reasoning that the class would most likely center on learning to use the garments for defense, Maya asked, "Won't you be coming with us?"

"No," Sarah replied tersely. She was already bringing up another holo on her player and turning away to watch it.

***

Skylaar made her appearance precisely at the top of the hour. As she and Maya left together, Sarah spared them only the briefest of glances before losing herself in her studies again.

"Sarah seems quite busy," her teacher remarked as they stepped into the lift that would take them to the apartment's private garage.

"Yes," Maya returned. "A new assignment."

"Does something about it trouble you? I can feel your unease, Cho-Sena," Skylaar inquired.

"No, Sena-Tai," Maya replied. "Not the assignment."

"Sarah then," the Nemesian guessed. "Visits to Thermadon can be quite complicated for her. You will find this out the longer that you know her."

The woman had a true gift for understatement, Maya thought. "Yes, Sena-Tai."

"I have known about her friend, and their relationship, for some time," Skylaar informed her. Amazement registered on Maya's face, and she went on. "Sometimes, in the great struggle of life, even the bravest and purest of spirits can become warped and scarred by what they have been forced to endure.'

"For them, oftentimes the only peace they can have is in the arms of the very darkness that they have fought against for so long. Do not judge her for this, Maya. That is not your place. You have not walked through the same fires that she has. Instead, be what a fellow warrioress should be; a friend and an ally. Lend her your sword in battle, understand her if you can, and where you must, grant her soul the privacy it has earned."

"Yes, Sena-Tai," Maya said. She only hoped that the struggle her teacher was describing wouldn't change her the way it had Sarah. She couldn't see herself pairing with someone like Trina, or doing the things that she imagined they did to one another. An involuntary shudder went up her spine at the very notion of it.

"Now, on to today's lesson," Skylaar said as they reached the aircar. "I imagine that you have been wondering why I asked that you dress yourself as you did."

Maya nodded, and got inside the vehicle with her.

"Your bodysuit is much more than a piece of clothing," she explained. "It also offers you protection against edged weapons and even most needlegun rounds. When cut, or shot, it will not only protect you, but heal itself."

Maya held up an arm, and gazed at the leather-like material with a newfound respect. "What about the cape? Please tell me that it does more than just make me look silly and get caught in 'car doors."

Skylaar shrugged, which Maya knew for her version of a grin. "Yes, Maya. It is much more than that." She reached over and twisted the large gem on the clasp that held the cape on Maya's shoulders. Immediately the special micro sensors in the fabric activated, mimicking the colors of the cars interior to such perfection that wherever it covered her, her body seemed to vanish into thin air.

"What?! Hey!" Maya exclaimed. Now she knew exactly how Sarah had pulled off her little vanishing act the first time she'd spotted her outside her hostel. She had always wondered about it, but for one reason or another, had never gotten around to asking her.

Skylaar turned the gem again, and the cape became opaque. "You agree then? That it has a better use than getting all tangled up?"

Maya shook her head, vigorously.

"You will also find that it has several useful compartments," the woman added, "which I am certain Sarah will help you fill up with all sorts of nasty little toys."

She shrugged again, this time at her own humor, and sent a command to the hovercar to lift off. "Today's lesson is to acquaint you with these items, and then explore how they can be used in combat. However, I would also like to take the time to learn about another weapon. One that is the closest to my spirit—the sword."

Because the day was sunny, Skylaar took them to N'Dayr Memorial Park. Although there were many other women there who were also taking advantage of the fair weather, she found them a spot that was reasonably private, and then had Maya perform her usual drills. For this, she was allowed to remove her cape and work out in her bodysuit, which to her surprise, did not cause her to overheat as she had feared it would. In addition to its antiballistic properties, something in its material also had the ability to bleed off excess body heat. It was actually quite comfortable.

After she was satisfied that Maya had enjoyed enough of a warm-up, Skylaar had her put her cape back on, and demonstrated not only how it could deflect various attacks, but also the ways it could be used against her by a skilled opponent.

Then, she moved on to the lesson she had promised her. The K'aut'sha Fighting School had originally adopted the sword from the Saian culture, where it played an important symbolic role. Unlike the dramatically curved blades the Saians favored however, the Nemesian *Ka'na'quehs,* or *Ka'na* was closer in design to the ancient Japanese *katana* of Old Gaia, and was handled in much the same manner. Maya had already seen a *Ka'na'quehs* before, during some of the first lessons she had ever had with Skylaar, and at the time she had privately considered it to be a rather primitive, and anachronistic weapon.

When Skylaar handed her one and led her through the basic draws and cuts, and then let her work out with it, free form, her feelings about it changed. While the Nemesian worked with her own sword alongside her, Maya's sense of time fled, and before she knew it, she had fallen in love with the *Ka'na'quehs*.

It wasn't that she had been wrong in her initial impressions. The sword had proved to be everything that she had originally supposed it to be. It was hopelessly antiquated, completely outclassed by more modern weapons, and more than a little impractical in many situations—-but it also possessed grace, and beauty. Moving with it felt more like a dance than a drill, and there was an elegance to her movements as she made her cuts that she had never tasted before.

At last, sunset arrived, and to her regret, Skylaar called an end to their session. "I can see that the song the *Ka'na* sings is as sweet to your ears as it is to mine," she observed. "I had hoped that you would find it so. We will practice with it some more in our future lessons together."

Maya bowed deeply to her teacher. "Thank you, Sena-Tai. For everything."

CHAPTER 8

Apartment of Sarah n'Jan, 409th Floor, The Otrera, Agamede District, Thermadon Val, Thermadon, Myrene System, Thalestris Elant, United Sisterhood of Suns, 1044.07|13|03:01:96

While they breakfasted, Sarah announced what Maya's plans for the day were to be. "The Lady Felecia was unhappy that she had to leave us at lunch the other day, and she has requested your presence," she told her. "You may go and see her. I will however, expect you back here in the morning. We have some business in the city and then we will be journeying offplanet for an extended period. You will need to pack for that."

Maya was overjoyed, and she didn't waste her freedom. The instant that her breakfast had been consumed, she rushed to the bedroom, dressed, and made her way straight for the roof, and her hovercycle. Rebá's powerful engines and the Freeflight lanes made certain that she reached the Themiscrya Towers in less than half an hour.

Felecia was at the entrance of the penthouse, dressed in her own flight leathers. They were designer-wear of course; Felecia would never have gone riding in anything less, and her helmet was just as stylish and expensive. She looked utterly gorgeous.

"Oh Maya," she cried, running past the securitywomen and straight into her arms. Completely oblivious to their audience, they kissed deeply. And when they parted, there were tears in Felecia's eyes, but they were from pure happiness, and she brushed them away with a smile.

"I've missed you terribly."

"Let's get out of here," Maya said.

Felecia glanced at the securitywomen, and then back to her. "Yes, please!"

"Any place in particular?"

"Anywhere but here!" Felecia declared. "But first I need to drop by the office for something. Can we do that? Senatrix d'Salla has been working me to the very bone and I have to take care of something for her before Oneday. Really Maya, she's such a slavemistress. She's worse than a

T'lakskalan!"

Maya laughed, glad to be going anywhere with her lover. Then Felecia gave her the location and they were off, soaring over the city together like two birds that had just been freed from their cages.

***

The *Eirene Museum of Fine Art* had been raised during the first century of the Sisterhood, and like everything else in Thermadon, it had been constructed on a massive scale and in the Neo-Renaissance style. Decorative pillars offset huge gilded domes and ornate cornices, but unlike later structures that would emulate this architectural style, the bulk of the building was made from dark grey stone. Instead of making it seem depressing however, this choice actually worked in concert with the gilding and lent the building an air of dignity and stateliness.

The museum had once housed artwork from all over the Sisterhood and even Old Gaia, and for centuries, its uppermost story had followed the dictum of a now-defunct Thermadonian tradition; the topmost floors of the public building had once housed government officials and their families. The idea had been to make them more accessible to their constituents, at least symbolically, and also to save on the cost of creating special, separate residences that tended to cloister their occupants from those that they served.

But as times had changed, the art had been relocated to the *Métropol*, and replaced by science exhibits. In more recent years, the residence floors had been vacated, and converted into government offices and storerooms.

The Eirene still managed to attract a handful of visitors, but it had been largely forgotten by most of the city's population. As Maya circled over it, she was struck by its fading grandeur. And if a building could have been said to have emotions, she would have called this one sad, but still proud despite its obvious neglect.

Thanks to the dearth of visitors, it was easy to find a spot to land, and once they were down, Felecia led them up the broad stairs at the front, and past a sign that advised that this was not only the museum, but also the local offices of her patroness, Senatrix d'Salla.

A single watchwoman was on duty in the lobby, and she waved to Felecia with an absent familiarity as they walked by. "Come along, Maya," Felecia said, returning the woman's friendly gesture, "I know a way that will get us upstairs faster than going all the way to the Lifts."

With a conspiratorial wink, she beckoned Maya over to a non-descript spot along the wall. When she pushed against it, a hidden door revealed itself. "This place is filled with service passages," she explained.

"And you found them all on your lunch breaks?" Maya asked.

"No, of course not," the girl replied, taking her by the hand and leading her into the narrow passage beyond. "Before they moved Senatrix d'Salla's offices in here, the upstairs was still a residence. This is where I grew up, until my mothers moved us over to the Themiscrya towers. We were actually the last government family to live here."

"It must have been a wonderful place to play," Maya observed.

"Oh, it was," Felecia said. "I used to pretend that I was a princess, and that this was my castle."

Maya smiled at the imagery as they made their way down the corridor to a small elevator. The Lift took them up a few levels, and then opened up onto another corridor, which was just as deserted as the first one had been.

Further on, there was another hidden door, but this time, when they walked out of it, it was immediately apparent that the floor had been unused for some time. Thanks to the attentions of maintenance 'bots, there wasn't any dust to indicate this. Instead, the place had the distinct aura of loneliness and the hollow echo of a place that humans seldom visited.

"Another short cut," Felecia said to her over her shoulder, "and it's also a very special place that I like to visit now and again. I wanted the chance to share it with you."

They entered one of the smaller rooms just off the corridor and Maya saw what she meant. A child's tea-set sat atop an old plastic cargo crate in the middle of the chamber, surrounded by other bric-a-brac that had been left there, and long since been forgotten.

"We used to have our tea parties here," Felecia explained as she picked up one of the tiny cups. "We would pretend that this was our royal court and that all sorts of important and interesting women were coming to visit us."

Maya grinned suggestively "Mmm, I like tea. *Very* much."

Felecia blushed, recalling their first tea together on the *Aphrodite*, and the passionate lovemaking that had accompanied it. "It wasn't *that* kind of tea, Maya," she said. "We were *very* little."

"So, that's all you did here as a child?" Maya asked her. "Have tea parties?"

"No," Felecia answered with a trace of hesitation. "We also did…other things."

"Such as?"

"Well, we did play a few tricks…" Felecia admitted.

Maya's interest was piqued. "Oh?"

"Well," Felecia went on, "nothing *nasty*. Really, we were *very* good girls."

"But…?"

"There was this *one* time…well, you see the museum is supposed to be haunted…"

"Haunted?"

"Yes, by a young girl that used to come here to sketch the artwork. They say that when she died, she came back to haunt the museum forever because she loved it so much."

"...Annndd?"

"Well," Felecia said, her face reddening, "It was the Selenite Feast of the Dead and we dressed up in sheets and painted our faces white…just to celebrate…"

"We?" Maya prodded, "you really mean 'you,' don't you? I can tell just by the tone of your voice."

"Yes, it was me," she admitted, "but the other girls helped! We used the service corridors and snuck up on one of the securitywomen."

Then Felecia burst into giggles that made her seem very like the little girl she had been at the time. "Really! I didn't mean to scare her so much! She actually screamed and dropped her flashlight and…and…I…didn't…know…someone's…hair…could…really stand…on end…like that…"

The rest was lost in laughter, but Maya was able to guess the rest. "So, did she ever come back?"

"Yes," Felecia said, finally managing to bring her mirth under control, "but she refused to work at night ever again."

"Felecia!!" Maya exclaimed with mock severity, "*shame* on you!" Then she gathered her in close. "You'll simply *have* to be punished for being such an evil little girl!"

"I might just enjoy that," Felecia answered. "Come with me. There's something else I want you to see."

She took Maya's hand again and led her out of the room, down the hall, and through a series of passages, until they came back out into the part of the museum that still enjoyed regular use. She stopped when they came into a large round chamber that served as both a planetarium and a holotheater.

"The watchwomen are off somewhere else doing their rounds," Felecia informed her.

"After your prank with the ghost, I'm not surprised," Maya chided. That earned her a playful slap on the shoulder.

"No!" Felecia declared. "Not because of any *'ghost'*, silly. They're just doing a little favor for the Senatrix's Office."

"Speaking about the office," Maya said, putting her arms around her again. "We didn't really come here to get anything at all, did we?"

Felecia lowered her eyes for a moment and then looked up coyly. "No, we didn't. I just wanted to share this place with you. It's special for me, and…"

Maya gave her an inquiring expression.

"…and I was hoping that we might…make love, here," she finally said, her voice nearly a whisper. Then she closed her eyes and the lights dimmed. They were replaced by a perfect holo of the Milky Way that spun slowly overhead like a dancer made of pure light. Maya looked at the image with a delighted smile before revisiting Felecia's gaze.

"I also brought something for us," the girl added.

"Oh?"

"Do you remember our picnic—on Nemesis?"

Maya certainly did. They had traveled to the jungle world so that her mother could attend a secret conference. Even though the Imaging Safari itself had nearly cost them their lives, the picnic they had enjoyed before the disaster had been exceedingly pleasant.

"I brought…oh, you'll probably think that it's utterly shameful of me, but…"

"You brought—*what?*" Maya asked, enjoying the game.

Felecia paused, and then said, "Do you remember the *Converger* that I told you about? I brought it here, and I wanted to try it with you—if you don't mind."

Maya recalled her mentioning this during the picnic. Supposedly, it allowed a pair of users to exchange their psiever signals, and let them perceive physical sensations from the perspective of their partner. The device had sounded very exotic at the time, and she had to admit, also quite intriguing. "No," she said, "I don't think it's shameful at all, and I don't mind a bit."

Felecia's blush disappeared, and she reached for a small bag that had been sitting nearby. Opening it, she brought out what appeared to be a very conventional realie player with two wireless headsets. She put one of these on, and handed the other to Maya. And then, as they kissed, she activated the device with a thought.

The effect that it had was shocking. Maya felt a sharp wave of vertigo, and then she realized that she wasn't standing where she had been. She felt—different—and when she opened her eyes to look, she saw her own face, looking right back at her. Then, with a gasp, she realized that she was actually inside of Felecia's body.

Felecia-as-Maya smiled at her with an expression of wicked, sensual delight. "What do you think?" she asked. The sound of her own voice surprised and disoriented Maya almost as much as hearing it with Felecia's ears did. *Do I really sound like that?* she wondered.

"I'm not sure," she replied in Felecia's voice. "But I—I think we need to spend some time with this thing."

Her partner smiled, and they kissed again, deeply, and sank down to the floor together. The sex that followed was unlike anything that Maya had ever experienced before; she learned things about her lover's body that would have been impossible to know any other way. She also understood, without having to ask, that Felecia was making her own amazing discoveries about her, and her most intimate needs. This alone, made the entire experiment with the *Converger* priceless beyond any measure.

The greatest surprise however, was waiting for her at the very end. Maya had readied herself to feel it in Felecia's body, but right before the instant of completion, her lover sent another command to the device. The data stream to their two psievers immediately merged, becoming one common signal that they both received simultaneously. Orgasm came for Maya, but in both bodies, at once, and with such intensity that afterwards she was amazed that she had actually survived such absolute bliss.

Finally, Felecia switched the device off, and once again, Maya felt herself firmly seated in her own body. She was completely exhausted, and totally overwhelmed by the experience.

"Well?" Felecia said, rolling over to look at her. "Did you like that?" Neither of them had the strength to stand just then.

Maya reached out, and stroked her cheek tenderly. "Yes," she answered. "I did. Very much."

They lay quietly together for a while, enjoying the simple pleasure of being together. Then, after a time, Felecia broke the silence.

"What was it like on Nyx?" she asked. "With Lady Ananzi?"

"It was hard," Maya answered. "And there were some parts that I really hated. But I'm glad that I did it. I learned some things there."

Felecia didn't press for the details. Nor did she need to. Thanks to her mother's connections with the OAE, and a confidential source very close to Sarah and Maya, she already knew about everything that had transpired on the Nightworld, and all about Maya's 'graduation' in N'Dayr Park. "You've changed," she said instead.

"Well, I certainly hope that you like the new me," Maya returned half-jokingly.

Felecia didn't respond, but drew Maya's arm in closer and snuggled against her. Without willing it, the memory of their farewell to one another at Bel Sharra Spaceport came back to her. They had just completed a harrowing trip to Thermadon from Nemesis, and they had both believed that it would be the last time that they would ever see one another again. And with this, her mother's words to her as they had left Maya and the *JUDI* behind, returned as well.

"Care for her as you will, Feli," the Senatrix had said, *"In fact, I encourage your friendship. The day may come when Maya will be the captain of that valuable little ship, and you will need all the assistance that she can offer you. Her affection will guarantee her aid.'X*

"But never let her be anything more than a friend. When you do marry, it will be to someone who will help you consolidate your power base, not to a common smuggler. She is, and must always be, a useful tool, and nothing more."

At the time, she had hated Layna n'Calysher for saying this. But now, she understood her mother's true motives. As hard as it had been to accept, the Senatrix had presented the universe to her daughter exactly as it was, stripped of all its lies and fantasies.

Like the OAE, Maya promised her the power the she would need to become the Senatrix she was destined to be, and also the ability to survive and destroy the enemies that she would inevitably make. She still loved Maya—deeply in fact—but a part of her now understood and appreciated her for what she really was.

Maya was more than a lover. She was also, as her mother had described her, a valuable asset.

"Yes, Maya," she finally said, rolling over to face her. "I do like the new you. Very much." They kissed.

Office of the President, Presidential Palace, Nuvo Bolivar,
Magdala Provensa, Esteral Terrana Rapabla, 1044.07|13|05:85:15

President Xavyar Magdalana cut the ansible connection, and leaned back in his chair to rub at his temples. Grand Admiral Guzamma had been complaining to him again about the *putaya* the Sisterhood had set over him, and he had threatened to resign his commission unless this 'affront to the national honor' was properly addressed.

Magdalena knew that Guzamma wouldn't actually resign. The man cherished his title too much, but that didn't alleviate the stress that he placed upon his leader every time he carried on like this. The simple fact was, *putaya* or not, Admiral Kaysa da'Kayt was accomplishing what Guzamma had failed to do. The Hriss were slowly losing their grip on the ETR, and retreating.

Magdalana also had no illusions about the situation; the Sisterhood was their ally for the moment—but only that. The most pressing issue facing the Republic was what would happen to his nation when the Hriss were finally defeated, and they found themselves alone together on the battlefield.

Thanks to the Sisterhoods intervention, the Republic's Navy had survived and was rebuilding its strength. But there was no question about its being able to match the United Sisterhood of Suns in terms of military technology. That simply wouldn't happen. The Sisterhood guarded its secrets too well, and his own scientists were too far behind for any sane man to imagine them winning an arms race. The race had already been run, and the Sisterhood was the clear winner.

The Sisterhood did possess one potential weakness, though. And exploiting it was the only real defense the Republic would have, *when* and not *if*, a conflict broke out between them.

His ancestors had faced the same problem more than a thousand years earlier. Then, as now, the Republican Navy had been small, and ill equipped to resist the larger Gaian Star Federation. Out of necessity, they had joined forces with the Kaseigian Confederacy. Even though it hadn't saved them, the MARS plague that the Kaseigians had developed, and its cure, had spared the Republic, and decimated the Star Federation.

This, and the peace that it had brought with it as its legacy, had shown the way for the future. Almost from the very moment that the Daughters of the Coast had made contact with the Republic, his predecessors' advisors had urged the sponsorship of a black project. And the *Atalanta* and her sister ships had only underscored its urgency.

Its objective had been to create a bio-weapon that could save the Republic again, this time from the Sisterhood, and the President had agreed. But unlike the homogenous Star Federation, the genetic diversity of the

Sisterhood had proven too vast, and the project had been stalled for years.

The fact that two decades had gone by after that without any threat coming from the Sisterhood had only added to the lack of inertia behind *Lida Medica SA's* efforts. There had even been calls to scrap the project entirely, several times. Then the Sisterhood had arrived at the School, and the Hriss had invaded, and these two events had forced everyone to revaluate *Lida's* work—and renew their efforts with even greater vigor.

Now, Magdalana could only hope that they would finish in time. The stakes were far higher than they had been for the early Republic; although the Gaian Star Federation had been powerful, they were nothing compared to the Sisterhood in terms of pure military might. If the scientists at the *Lida* facility failed, or worse, were somehow discovered, the price would be more terrible than he even wanted to contemplate. Politics was always a gamble however, and he understood that true leadership sometimes required having the courage to throw the dice.

Reaching into his desk, he brought out the latest classified report from the work-site, and re-read the request that the Lead Researcher had sent. In bland, scientific language, Dr. Adolpha Sanchar had asked for something that had truly horrified him the first time he had seen it, but now that he had had the chance to think the matter over, he appreciated the cold logic behind it.

In the end, it really was the only course of action that they could take, he decided. Without giving Sanchar what he was asking for, the project would never be completed, and the ETR would remain defenseless. It was as brutally simple as that.

Magdalana had always done his duty, first as a military officer, and then as President of the Republic. This could not be the exception to a lifetime of service. He simply had to agree.

Carefully uncapping his pen, he signed the authorization. Dr. Sanchar would get what he wanted.

And may God have mercy on us all, he thought.

Special Military Quarantine Zone, Second Planet, The School, HSL-48 2124A System, Annexed Sisterhood Territory, United Sisterhood of Suns,

1044.07|16|03:75:55

Captain n'Kyla greeted Sarah and Maya with a formal bow as they walked up to her in the School's central gathering square. This was partly out of politeness, and partly at the genuine pleasure of receiving them. DNI Command at Rixa had advised her that important agents from the OAE would be coming to visit, and that all her hard work at the School was about to be fully recognized. After more than a year of intensive analysis and study, the government finally appeared to be ready to take things to the next level with the ETR—the right level—and she couldn't have been more pleased.

"Ms. n'Jan, Ms. n'Kaaryn? Welcome to the School," she said.

"Ever since I first learned of your efforts here," Sarah replied, "I've been looking forwards to seeing it firsthand, and the opportunity to meet you. I think that we will accomplish great things together."

"May I offer you any refreshments before we take the tour?" the Intel Officer asked.

"No thank you," Sarah answered. "We took our ease on the *Penthe-selea* before coming downside. Perhaps we can adjourn to your office instead? I have so many things to ask you about."

N'Kyla smiled. "Would you let me show you around the town itself first? Then we can visit the Intel Center. The lifestyle of the natives is rather interesting to observe. One might even call it quaint."

"I should think that 'backwards' might be a more fitting description," Sarah ventured.

"As you say, Ms. n'Jan, "N'Kyla conceded. "Although they do offer a fascinating snapshot of their nation."

"Indeed," Sarah replied, arching her eyebrow as she surveyed the town. In her estimation, it wasn't much to look at. Nearly all of the buildings were one-story affairs, constructed from a combination of manufactured and local materials, with only the main meeting hall, aspiring to another half-story. *Mere hovels compared to what we build for ourselves in the Sisterhood,* she thought with disdain.

The central street wasn't paved either. Rather, it seemed to be made of compacted earth, although she did note narrow sidewalks for the natives to move about on.

There were also very few vehicles in evidence; mostly small electric affairs, or slightly larger versions used for hauling bulk goods. Primitive machines, with archaic chemical batteries as their power sources, she decided. The initial finding that the ETR was behind them in technology by at least two hundred years was apparently quite accurate.

And aside from the Marine troopers on patrol, and the crew manning an armored personnel carrier at the end of the street, there were only a few people of any kind in evidence, and they all appeared to be women. Either the rest of the women, and their pet males, were out working in the surrounding fields, or everyone else was indoors watching their arrival.

Just like superstitious aborigines, Sarah reflected. Too terrified of something more sophisticated than themselves to risk leaving their hiding places.

The women that she did see made a good accounting of themselves at least. Although they tried to hide it behind masks of false docility, she didn't miss the pure hatred that radiated from their eyes as she and her companions passed.

This at least, said something positive for the ETR. Their women weren't the cowed creatures that one would have expected from such a hopelessly deluded society. Perhaps Captain n'Kyla's notion of recruiting their young women as agents had merit, she concluded. There was definitely promise there.

Then they encountered another woman, and her child. This woman didn't bother to conceal the venom in her expression, and glaring at them, hurriedly ushered her offspring indoors.

It was a boy.

Sarah didn't let this affect her, and smiled pleasantly to the woman as she fled from their presence. It also served as a forceful reminder of just how far the ETR would have to go before it was properly evolved. Any right-thinking woman would never have allowed a little man-creature like that to appear in public, much less let herself *conceive* one in the first place. But then, she reminded herself, they *were* savages.

The incident did bring to mind something useful however. It was a question that many women, including herself, had been asking for some time. If war with the ETR did occur, a Sisterhood victory was a given, but the peace that would follow was the problem. What *would* they do with all the ETR's men in such an eventuality?

Separate communities, perhaps? Special camps as some had suggested? Or even something more—drastic? At the moment, the 'male question' was only an intellectual exercise, but she knew that the situation could easily change.

Sarah didn't have a ready answer for this conundrum, but it was something that she would certainly ponder as they continued with their mission. If she arrived at an acceptable answer, she would certainly pass her recommendations along to the Agency. And who knew? There was always the chance that someone in power might even be inspired by her suggestions to alter the course of State policy.

Spacedocks, Ashkele Free Port, Ashkele, Hallasa System, Frontier Zone, Xee Protectorate, 1044.07|18|07:08:39

For the first time ever, stepping out into the spaceport on Ashkele actually felt good. More than a year had passed since Maya had last been there, but it might have been a lifetime for all the changes that she had gone through. Instead of repelling her, the stinking air, and the chaotic bustle of the alien inhabitants now welcomed her like old friends. As she took it all in, she realized that for all its glaring flaws, the lawless metropolis suited her like nowhere else in the galaxy ever would. It always had, and she had simply never acknowledged it. She was home.

Bel Lissa and Zara greeted them at the Port exit with an armored hover-taxi, and as soon as they had been granted their exit, Zara walked straight up and gave Maya a hug. The old engineer had never been one to allow formalities to stand in her way.

"Goddess, Maya! Welcome back," she said, stepping back to look at her. "Look how you've grown! Only a year gone and you've become a woman!"

Maya blushed, but said, “It’s good to see you too, Zara. Have you been keeping busy?”

Bel Lissa joined them, and embraced her with a little more decorum. “Not busy enough. A few runs here and there, but nothing as challenging as the kind Sarah sends us off on. The *JUDI’s* missed you both. So, are you back on business, or just taking a break between jobs?”

“We have some business here in the city,” Sarah stated, coming up to the group with Skylaar just a step behind her. “Once it has been completed, we will require the *JUDI* and your services.”

“Oh?” Bel Lissa asked, nodding an acknowledgement to Skylaar. “Are we going anywhere special?”

“Very.” The fact that Sarah had answered with only one word communicated the rest. Their destination was classified, and potentially dangerous.

Bel Lissa grinned wolfishly. “Good. The *JUDI’s* always up for a challenge.”

“Ay-yah,” Zara agreed. “Been damned boring ‘till now. So, got the time for a stop over at the *Nulltrekker* first, or are you three going about your work straightaway?”

Sarah smiled. “I think that we can spare an evening.” It had been a long trip from Thermadon after all.

Residence of Lady d’Ershala, Ashkele Free Port, Ashkele,
Hallasa System, Frontier Zone, Xee Protectorate, 1044.07|18|08:75:19

Skylaar parked her hovercar in the shadows. It was a non-descript vehicle, neither too plain, nor too flashy, and it blended in perfectly with the other vehicles there. They had landed in a street in the residential section of the Free City, and the large walled compounds that lined the avenue gave the area a deceptively claustrophobic feeling.

After she had set the lethal anti-theft devices on the machine, the three of them walked to their destination. Their cloaks, activated for stealth, made certain that what little traffic there was, didn’t notice them, and Sarah’s talents ensured that anyone that might have been too observant for their own good, promptly forgot what little they might have seen.

The compound that they were headed for was like any other in Ashkele and surrounded by a wall that followed the local architectural norm. The barrier was a massive thing, constructed of gigantic blocks taken from the Necropolis itself, and therefore impervious to breaching by even the heaviest of vehicles. It was also as high as two tall women, and topped by a nearly invisible, but deadly energy field, that was only evident from the telltale shimmering in the air above it, and the small antennae that served as the transmitters. Maya knew from experience that on the other side, there were most likely plantings of blisterweed, razorfang flowers, and a whole host of sensors.

Skylaar regarded the wall for a moment, and then produced a small metallic sphere from her belt pack. She thumbed something on its side and the little ball floated upwards until it was level with the top.

The air around it suddenly shuddered, and then the energy field above the wall went still. In its place, was a perfect circle of clear, unmoving space. Whatever the sphere was, it had opened up a neat hole in the field, Maya realized.

Skylaar gave her companions a glance, and then jumped. Her leap took her to the top in a single bound. Sarah went next, only a shade less powerfully, and then gestured for Maya to join them.

The young woman moved up doubtfully, but as she came nearer to the wall, she was amazed to find that her body felt as light as a feather. The miraculous little ball had not only created a gap in the energy field, but somehow, it had also lessened the force of gravity all around it. Grinning at her discovery, she jumped upwards, pleased and amazed at how easy it was to reach the top. Another feature of Skylaar's device revealed itself as she did so; she made no noise whatsoever. Sound waves, it turned out, had also been suppressed.

Thanks to the cyclopean blocks, the summit of the wall proved wide enough for the three of them to lie flat on, and look down into the garden without being seen. As Maya silently took her place next to her companions, she vowed to ask Skylaar what her miraculous device was, where it had come from, and how she could get one for herself. The Nemesian always seemed to have the really neat toys, and as far as she was concerned, it was high time that she acquired some playthings of her own.

Resolved to handle this important matter at the earliest possibility, she peered carefully over the lip of the wall and saw that there were indeed blisterweed and razorfang bushes, and just a little further on, two human sentries. Her nighteyes, which Sarah had insisted on, proved their worth, revealing a third sentry as well. There were also others, she saw, some T'lakskalans, and other alien races, scattered throughout the large gardens, but the group below them seemed to be the largest, and she wondered how they were going to manage their attack.

'They' actually turned out to be Skylaar. Sarah gestured for Maya to wait and the Nemesian raised herself up slightly and then pushed off into space. Her maneuver took her well past the deadly vegetation. Halfway to the ground she executed a perfect mid-air roll that brought her to land right between the two guards. Even as her feet touched the earth, her arms shot out, and a pair of razor-sharp spikes flew out from her hands. The sentries crumpled.

Still moving, she rolled forwards, coming up again on her feet and fluidly plucking a third spike from a sheath on her back in the same motion. It went spinning across the lawn and toppled the third guard before the woman even had the chance to turn around. With all the sentries now down, Skylaar came to a halt, and nodded back up to her companions.

The area was clear, and Maya was utterly enthralled. As terrible as Skylaar's deed had been, she had moved with all the grace of a dancer, transforming the assault into a thing of sheer, fluid beauty. Killing, Maya had learned during the previous year, was an art form just like any other, and Skylaar was without question, a virtuoso performer. When the operation was over, she promised herself that she would train even harder than ever.

In the meantime, Sarah was descending. She dropped, tumbled and landed only a hair less perfectly than Skylaar. Then it was Maya's turn. She did a passable enough job, but she also felt every small error that her body committed. To add to this, her nighteyes flew off her face as she came to a stop, and she had to scramble to grab them up.

Thankfully, they had been made of idiot-proof plastic, preventing any damage, and neither of her companions seemed to have noticed her fumble, or were simply pretending ignorance. Embarrassed, she put her glasses back on and followed them as they moved into the garden.

Yes, she thought. She would definitely have to train much harder.

They encountered another sentry a few minutes later, and Maya expected them to attack the woman. But this time, something else occurred. As the woman realized that they were there, and began to bring her weapon to bear, Sarah simply raised her hand and whispered, *"Sleep!"* The guard promptly collapsed, unconscious.

The same thing happened to another pair of guards, one human and the other an alien from a race that Maya couldn't categorize. The next group however, were all slain without any hesitation by Skylaar, and Sarah assisted her.

They went on like this, eliminating some and sparing others, and Maya was unable to discern either rhyme or reason behind their choices. She didn't press for any explanation though. Whatever their motives were, it had something to do with their respective assignments, and she had not been included in the information loop. Besides which, she reminded herself, she had her own targets to worry about when they finally reached their objective.

This was in the main house itself, and the trio moved along its length until they arrived at a large set of glass-paned doors. There was an office inside, and Maya instantly recognized the figure of Lady d'Ershala, seated at her desk. A wave of loathing for the woman, and regret, warred within her as she observed the glass dealer. As much as she might have wanted it to be otherwise, D'Ershala was not to be hers.

Sensing her turmoil, Sarah glanced at her. *Maya,* she thought, *Forget her. Concentrate on your targets, and engage your symbiote.*

***

Lady Eniya d'Ershala had earned herself the title of 'the Queen of Glass' through a combination of a keen business sense, innate organizational skills, and absolute ruthlessness. Of course, there were many beings in the Far Arm that wanted to supplant her, and while the majority of them posed only minor inconveniences, there were some cases where they actually managed to become real nuisances. She was in the middle of discussing a particularly difficult individual, and her lethal solution to the problem, when she realized that the large picture window behind her had somehow just come open.

A trio of shadows passed through the room an instant later.

Before her bodyguards could react to the threat, they were falling to the floor, and then three women materialized out of thin air. Instead of panicking, Lady d'Ershala maintained her calm, and remained motionless. She knew that had she been their target, she would have been dead already. Even so, she was also savvy enough to understand that it didn't pay to exacerbate a delicate situation.

Her lieutenant, Nina bel Trudi, was not quite so fortunate. D'Ershala caught the glint of something spinning out from Sarah's hand, and then Bel Trudi gave out a strangled gurgle and dropped to the carpet. Only when her body had come to a complete standstill did D'Ershala spot the knife impaling her chest.

The glass dealer knew Sarah and Skylaar from her dealings with them, and she recognized Maya because she kept regular tabs on the *JUDI's* crew. Seeing her playing the part of an assassin was just a bit unexpected however. The last she had heard from her spies, Maya had been an engineer's mate, and a *very* junior member of the *JUDI's* compliment. Something quite interesting and dramatic must have happened in the interim, D'Ershala decided.

It was also equally clear, just from the way that the girl held herself, and the look in her eyes, that Maya dearly wanted to add her corpse to the pile of bodies on the carpet. But somehow, Sarah, Skylaar, or the pair of them together, were keeping her in check.

Again, this was an interesting development. Clearly, Maya n'Kaaryn would bear much closer scrutiny.

"Greetings Sarah, Skylaar…and Maya," she said. "May I ask you what this is all about? And can you tell me why you just killed my best bodyguards *and* my closest advisor?" She suspected that she already knew the answer, but she had learned the wisdom of always asking for clarification when it came to business matters.

"Think of it as a gesture of good faith," Sarah replied, kneeling down and retrieving her *Carrissa* from Bel Trudi's body. It came out of the cadaver with a wet scraping sound and she wiped it clean on the corner of the dead woman's blouse before she straightened.

"As you may have already surmised, Bel Trudi was in the employ of one of your competitors, and these guards, and quite a number of others on your staff, were also traitors. Together, they represented a possible complication to what will otherwise prove to be a very lucrative transaction for you."

"And you, I take it, are here to broker that?" D'Ershala asked, arching a speculative eyebrow. "Considering your long-standing position on glass, I must admit that your presence surprises me somewhat. Have you experienced a change of heart perhaps?"

"In a manner of speaking," Sarah began, but a noise from the hallway interrupted her. "More of your security is on the way. Unless you wish to see them destroyed as well, please have them stand down so that we can talk with one another like civilized women. I assure you that they are loyal to you, and it would be a terrible waste."

In the meantime, Skylaar and Maya had already turned towards the door, with their weapons, both seen and unseen, at the ready.

"Frankly, I'm not entirely certain that I *don't* wish that," D'Ershala confessed. "After all, they *did* fail to intercept you before you reached my office. Perhaps they should be removed, and replaced." She took a pensive sip of her wine, and then changed her mind, "Then again, perhaps there has been enough killing for one night."

She closed her eyes, and sent a psiever signal to the forces massing out in the hall. The commotion beyond the door ceased immediately. "So, to business then?"

"Yes," Sarah replied. She went on to explain Bel Mala's proposal in detail. Naturally, she didn't mention the Agency by name; it was quite likely that there were listening devices in the room, recording the entire conversation. And if it came to it, the only party that anyone would be able to identify would be her, and she had no concerns about adding another stain like that to her soul.

"I see," the woman said when Sarah had finished, "And what if I refuse the offer, or simply pretend to accept it, and then go on to do as I wish?"

"Please, Lady d'Ershala, I don't think that we need to sully this otherwise pleasant conversation with any vulgarity," Sarah replied smoothly. "I am sure that a seasoned businesswoman like yourself understands the consequences, especially once you realize exactly *who* my friends are."

"I think I already do," D'Ershala said. "I have my own sources, and I think I've known for quite a while who you are involved with. You can have my answer right away. It is, unequivocally, yes."

Sarah smiled. "I knew that once we had a chance to really talk with one another, that I would find you agreeable. Now to specifics."

She went on, telling D'Ershala about the existence of the ETR, its archaic societal structure, and most importantly, its known weaknesses. By the time she was done, the glass dealer was genuinely glad that she had decided to cooperate with the Agency, and she had no regrets at all about severing her present ties and relocating. Compared to the potential that the ETR represented, the profits that she had enjoyed in the Sisterhood were nothing. It was even possible, she later mused, given the sheer amount of wealth that the shift in markets would create, that she might even manage to earn herself a measure of respectability. Many statesmen—and stateswomen, throughout history, had started out just like her, and had gone on to become revered as great leaders. Like prostitution and drugs, crime had always been the partner of politics, and contrary to what some hopeless idealists claimed, it *always* paid, and paid well.

***

If nothing else, Maya had learned to bide her time. Lady Ananzi had taught her this, and even Sarah had contributed.

She had also discovered the maxim, '*La vendet es un plata qua es la buan a servit fredda,*' 'Revenge is a dish best served cold.' It was an ancient saying from Old Gaia that had been coined by an unknown author, and been adopted by the women of Thermadon. It had become her motto as well.

And in Lady d'Ershalla's case, it definitely applied. Sarah had made it quite clear that the Glass dealer was off limits—at least until the Sisterhood had no further need of her. Then she would be fair game.

Thanks to D'Ershala, and the filthy stuff that she peddled, Maya had been forced to witness the slow destruction of one of her only loves—someone who had been just as precious to her as Felecia was now. Shyla was the secret of her early teens; another street urchin like herself who had succumbed to glass' seduction, and had been consumed by it.

Glass defiled everything that it touched, and those who lived on the streets of Ashkele were easy prey. Misery was their bread, leavened with desperation, and for them, the drug promised the illusion of peace, and pleasure. Shyla had fallen for these lies, and glass in turn, had taken her life. No one remembered her now, except for Maya, and thanks to her mental prying, Sarah.

When the time came, she would hunt the Queen of Glass down, and kill her as slowly, and as painfully as possible. Another lesson that she had learned during her time with Lady Anazi and Sarah was that the longing to commit murder was a hunger in its own right, and just as valid as the need for sex or food. She was eager to satisfy it.

Offices of the Republican Associated Press, Bolivar Cia, Nuvo Bolivar, Magdala Provensa, Esteral Terrana Rapabla, 1044.07|25|05:20:01

It was lunchtime, and the lobby of the Republican Associated Press was empty, but even at its busiest, the pretty young woman on duty at the reception desk rarely missed anyone who came in off the street. As a result, when she glanced down at her magazine, and then back up again, she was startled to see a pair of women standing directly in front of her.

"Pardon me," Sarah said. "But I have some important footage that I would like to give to Rozza Ramara. It concerns the war."

"If you'll give it to me, I can have it delivered to her," the receptionist replied, flashing a professional smile to emphasize her authority.

"I am afraid that the material is quite sensitive in nature, "Sarah returned, giving her a smile of her own. "I must insist that I deliver it to Ms. Ramara personally."

"I'm sorry, but Ms. Ramara is quite busy, and that would be impossible," the woman countered. "But I can get her secretary for you and see if she can come down to set up an appointment."

"That won't be necessary," Sarah said. "You will tell me where Ms. Ramara's office is and I'll go there myself. You will do this for me now."

The receptionist began to object, but then she felt an odd pressure in her forehead, and quite suddenly, the request seemed very reasonable. In fact, she realized that it really was the *only* way to solve the problem.

"Yes, you're absolutely right," she agreed. "That won't be necessary. I'll tell you where her offices are, and you can go there yourself. You'll find them on the 22nd floor in the News Department. She is in the first office on the right. Would you like me to call her and let her know that you are on your way?"

"That won't be necessary," Sarah answered. "Thank you for handling this matter so adroitly."

"My pleasure," the woman replied, this time rewarding Sarah with a smile of genuine gratitude. It really *had* been a pleasure, she realized. In fact, for the first time since taking the job, she felt as if she had finally had the chance to do something truly useful. Filled with a deep sense of satisfaction, she watched Sarah and Maya leave the lobby and board an elevator.

***

"Don't you think making her feel so happy about helping us wasn't laying it on a bit thick?" Maya asked her companion.

"Call it artistic license," Sarah replied. "I could have *'pushed'* her to help us without adding that little touch, but she'll come away from our encounter feeling, for a day at least, that her life had some purpose to it. Most people in her position never achieve that, and because our interaction was so pleasant for her, she will be far less likely to question anything else about the event."

"A good point," Maya agreed, filing this lesson away for future reference.

When they stepped out onto the 22nd floor, they encountered another receptionist. She too tried to run interference, but like the one in the lobby, she quickly decided that it was *far* more rewarding to let them pass. In short order, Sarah and Maya were standing at the door to Rozza Ramara's offices.

Inside, Ramara was trying her best to ignore the migraine that had been stalking her the entire morning, and failing. With the war on, intense pressure was being brought to bear on the News Department, and on her. Not only did her Department have to keep up with rapidly changing events, but they also had to discover the real stories concealed behind the sanitized version that the Military Public Affairs people were serving up to the press.

It had been hard enough in the last war with the T'lakskalans to get uncensored stories from the front lines, but now it was virtually impossible. The Republican Navy had actually gone so far as *banning* reporters from roaming the war zones without a military handler to escort them. One of her best journalists, Felix Gonzaala was still being detained by the government for violating this stricture.

The RAP's lawyer was on the case, and it was quite likely that Gonzaala would eventually be released, but the situation was still maddening. The Republic had been founded on the principle of a free and unobstructed press, and despite their naked censorship, the present government actually had the gall to wrap itself in the flag and claim that it still adhered to this noble legacy. It was total crap!

Even worse, most of her fellow journalists seemed to be content with this. Instead of reporting the facts, the majority of them spent their time well behind the lines, lapping up whatever pap was dribbled out to them at the official press conferences, and then regurgitating it to the public, almost verbatim.

The press release in front of her was a fine example of such garbage, she thought sourly. It concerned a battle in the Nevanas system and consisted of nothing but dry statistics and grand pronouncements about 'inevitable victory' and other tripe.

It mentioned nothing whatsoever about the cost in lives, or anything substantial about the Republic's new allies, whoever or whatever they were. The government still hadn't described them as anything more than a 'friendly member race' from the Galactic Collective. And it was still persisting in its ridiculous claim that this unknown alien group had demanded anonymity in the interests of *'maintaining intercultural balance by avoiding premature contact.'*

Pure unadulterated drivel! The ETR had made contact with other races before; the Xee, the Hriss, the T'lakskalans and many others, and it had always weathered the shock of each meeting without any great social upheaval whatsoever. The idea that after all that, that the identity of their benefactors would somehow prove to be too much for the minds of the average citizen to handle was patently absurd.

What could be so strange and terrible about a friendly race that the powers-that-be don't think we can handle? she wondered. The real story was out there, waiting to be told, and it had everything to do with their mysterious allies. She was positive of it.

Getting that story was another matter though. As Felix Gonzaala had amply demonstrated, going out to the war zone was an exercise in futility. In addition, all of her usual sources in the Republican Department of Defense had steadfastly refused to leak even the smallest details to her about what was really going on.

Hence, her headache.

With a deep sigh of resignation and frustration, the reporter finally surrendered to her migraine, and reached into her desk for a painkiller. For the moment at least, the press release was going to be the only thing she would have to work with for the nightly newscast.

Ramara dry-swallowed the pills and called up her holographic keyboard to begin the unhappy task of making the announcement sound something remotely like real news. A woman's voice startled her.

"Ms. Ramara? I was told that you were a reporter with a thirst for the truth. I have some information about the war that might interest you greatly."

"Who are you?" Ramara demanded. Her secretary hadn't scheduled any appointments for her that day, and she didn't recognize the two women.

She also hadn't heard either of them enter her office.

"My name is Sarah n'Jan, "the taller of the pair answered. "My companion is Maya n'Kaaryn. We apologize for surprising you like this, but I have some footage that we think you will want to see. It concerns the Republic's allies." The strange, pale woman stepped forwards and held out a rather plain looking data-cube.

Like any veteran reporter, Ramara understood that identifying a source was just as important as the information they provided. While Ms. n'Kaaryn seemed normal enough, and Sarah's Espangla had been nearly flawless, she hadn't missed the slight, unidentifiable accent she had, or the foreign sound of their names. Taking the 'cube from her, the reporter tried to read both of them for any subtle clues that would betray their true origins.

Their clothing was new, she observed, but slightly out of date. This was nothing terribly revealing in and of itself; many women tended to dress in 'retro' styles, and fashions changed so rapidly that what was out of style one week, might be its very height the next.

It was Sarah's complexion that kept capturing her attention. It was much paler than the reporter was accustomed to seeing and she noted the odd rainbow-colored sheen to it. Cosmetics were the most likely explanation, but she couldn't recall any ETR planet where such a look was currently in vogue.

Their body language was also noteworthy. Something in the way the pair stood there was 'off'—as if the contents of the room were not entirely familiar to them. It was a subtle thing, which most people would have missed, but Ramara was a keen observer and she noticed little details like that.

Taken singly, each of these things meant very little, but combined together, they argued that whoever her guests really were, they were *not* from any major world. *One of the outlying systems*? she wondered. *A frontier colony perhaps?*

She inserted the data-cube into her desktop player, hoping that in addition to whatever it contained, it would also yield more information about its messengers.

The scene that appeared in the holo field above her desk an instant later was a shot of a group of ETR warships in orbit over an unknown planet. It wasn't anything that she hadn't seen before and could have just as easily been stock footage from her own Network's archives.

But then the scene changed. The holocam panned past the Navy ships to another group of vessels off to their port side, and zoomed in. As their details became clearer, her pulse quickened.

These ships were *not* Republican vessels. They were similar in some respects, but only barely. In fact, she realized, that in comparison, the Republic starships seemed almost primitive, as if the unfamiliar vessels in the holo owed their lineage to the same designers, but had evolved beyond them into something far more sophisticated.

The holocam gave her an excellent view of their markings, and where there was any lettering, the characters were strangely familiar to her eye, but also just different enough to make them hard to translate with any certainty.

The camera pulled back, revealing where it was positioned. It was viewing the scene from another group of ships just off the starboard side of the Republic squadron.

Ramara had had years of experience covering stories that would have overwhelmed most reporters, and she had always managed to keep her journalistic distance and professional calm. But what she saw as the holocam presented its widest view, made her jaw drop like a cub reporter covering her first real story.

The shot plainly established that the footage was not being taken from a Republican starship, but from one of their alien companions. The holo was *not* official government footage.

"Where did you get this?" she finally asked.

"From some friends of mine," Sarah told her. "They wanted to make sure that someone with real journalistic integrity had the chance to view it."

"This isn't from the Navy, is it?"

"Not from your Navy, no", Sarah replied.

"I'm sorry—*what?*"

"My friends want the truth to be told," Sarah answered enigmatically.

"There's much more that you need to know and your government does not want this to occur."

"*My* government? *My* navy?" Ramara repeated, her eyes narrowing. A story she had seen several years earlier suddenly came to mind. It had been one of those offbeat, speculative shows that centered on outré topics like reincarnation and ghosts, and for that reason she hadn't really paid much attention to it.

The episode in question had focused on an old myth that another branch of humanity had somehow survived the MARS plague, and had gone on to pursue its own destiny somewhere beyond the furthest reaches of known space. At the time, she had considered it to be complete nonsense, fit only for consumption by fringe lunatics and eccentrics.

Now however, she was starting to wonder just how crazy the idea really was—and by extention, how crazy *she* was.

"I know you're not from Nuvo Bolivar," she finally said. "Where are you *really* from? Who are you?" She already half-suspected what the woman's answer would be, and the very notion was completely improbable, even insane. But the question *had* to be asked.

Sarah merely smiled. And with that simple expression, she answered Ramara's inquiry better than any words could have ever managed.

"You're not from anywhere in the ETR, are you?"

Sarah didn't answer this. Instead she said, "My friends would like to give you the opportunity to be the first journalist to uncover the real story. The truth behind the help your government is getting in its war against the Hriss. Are you interested?"

Despite her incredulity, Ramara was too seasoned a reporter to hesitate for even an instant. "Yes," she replied. "I am. When can I meet with these friends of yours?"

"In two days" Sarah said. "Meet me in front of your offices here at 12:00. A car will be waiting for you. You may also bring a camera operator, but we must insist that that person also be a female. You should both make sure to pack yourselves overnight bags and to plan on being gone for at least several days."

A female camera operator? Why in heaven's name would that be im-

portant? she wondered.

Ramara left this unvoiced however. The story was simply too valuable to quibble over such a small detail. *I'll use Yúna*, she decided. Yúna Ageelar was one of the few camerawomen working for the RAP.

"In the meantime," Sarah continued, "we will leave some more footage for you to examine at your leisure. I trust that you and your associates will find it to be of equal interest." She produced a second data cube, and placed it on the desk.

"Thank you," Ramara said.

Sarah and Maya turned, and began to walk out of the room.

"Wait!" the reporter said, rising from her desk. "How do I get in touch with you if I need to?"

Neither of them responded, and they walked out into the reception area, closing the door behind them. Ramara went after them, but when she stepped outside, they were gone.

An intern was just coming out of the elevator, and she stopped the young man. "Two women just walked out of my office," she said. "Did you see where they went? Did they get on the elevator?"

The intern gave her a puzzled look and shrugged. "I didn't see anyone Ms. Ramara. I'm sorry—should I call Security?"

"Never mind," Ramara replied. "It's nothing."

She went back into her office and played the second data-cube. When it was over, she had her secretary cancel all of her appointments for the next four days, and left a message for the News Director to come down to her office right away. Her headache had not only vanished, but she felt better than she had in months.

***

When they were back out on the street, Sarah hailed them a cab.

"That was a pretty spooky act you put on back there," Maya remarked.

Sarah shrugged. "Every great actress understands that the right amount of shadows help to create interest and suspense. Besides which, she wouldn't have expected anything less from a pair of 'strange alien visitors'.

I know that I certainly wouldn't have."

"Well, next time tell me," Maya insisted, "and I'll make sure to polish up my antennae. So, where to now, my mysterious extraterrestrial leader?"

"I am in the mood for a really good cup of kaafra," Sarah informed her as a yellow and black vehicle pulled up to the curb. "Capt. n'Kyla was kind enough to tell me about a little place that not only serves the best that these primitive people have to offer, but also plays host to many interesting speakers."

"Sounds like a nice break," Maya agreed. Not that she believed for one nano that they were going there for anything but business.

She knew Sarah better than that.

***

Sanda Ernan stepped down from the stage and found herself a seat in the corner of the coffee house. The next speaker was an inspired woman, and she generally enjoyed listening to her impassioned addresses, but tonight she had to admit that she felt tired. She ordered herself a strong cup of coffee, hoping that it would reenergize her. She wanted to show her full support, but she needed the energy.

The woman began her speech, and Sanda listened, considering the content, and the state of the Movement itself.

When will women finally realize that the only path to true freedom is to throw off their male oppressors? she asked herself.

She'd tried for years to get her sisters to see the light, and except for small victories, it seemed as if the struggle between the sexes would never end. It was hard sometimes, to keep up the fight when so little seemed to really change, she thought unhappily.

Absently, she rubbed at the angry red bruises on her wrists. They were souvenirs of her latest arrest; this time for chaining herself to the doors of the city government center during a protest. At her arraignment, the judge had warned her that another arrest would lead to a longer stay in jail. *Much* longer.

Sanda didn't care about imprisonment though. It was simply the price that had to be paid for the revolution. *If only more women were willing to take such risks. Then we would be even closer to realizing our victory.*

But so many weren't willing. Comfort, even if it was really only disguised slavery, was what mattered to most of them, and it sickened her.

"I enjoyed your speech," Sarah n'Jan said, taking her by surprise. "It was truly inspirational. It is only a shame that more women haven't taken your message to heart, or are ready to make the sacrifices that are needed to make it a reality."

What the woman in front of her had just said was so close to what she had been thinking that Sanda found herself blinking in astonishment.

"May my partner and I join you?" Sarah asked, indicating herself and Maya.

"Please," Sanda replied, gesturing to the empty seats at the table. The two women sat down.

There was something different about them, she realized. Sanda wasn't sure exactly what 'it' was, but they were not typical members of her usual audience.

"Your ideas concerning the leadership role of women are very important," Sarah told her. "It was refreshing to hear the truth put so clearly."

Sanda smiled at these encouraging words, feeling her energy and her fire returning. "I have struggled for years to get the women of our nation to understand one single thing," she replied. "Women can run the Far Arm better than the sexist patriarchy ever could."

"We already do," Sarah said with an inscrutable smile.

"I'm sorry—*what?*"

Her guest didn't repeat herself. "I represent a group of powerful women who believe as you do, and want to contribute what they can to see your movement grow and succeed."

"Who are these women?" Ernan asked.

"Friends," Sarah answered, "Powerful women who understand that the male domination of your society has stunted the potential of women in order to serve its own selfish ends. They wanted to show their support for your work by making a small donation to the cause, and to ask that you honor them with your presence at a meeting of like-minded visionaries."

She produced an envelope and pushed it across the coffee-stained table. "This is a small token of their appreciation, given with the hope that you will consider accepting their invitation."

Sanda Ernan looked at the envelope, and seriously considered refusing it, but the women across from her seemed sincere, and thanks to the money-centered power structure that men had established to keep women in perpetual servitude, even the Movement had to rely on cold, hard cash. It was the only way to ensure that its message was printed and distributed.

She took the envelope reluctantly, and opened it. There was a *lot* of money inside.

"It is only a small gift," Sarah said, "to show that the women I represent are serious revolutionaries. Can you spare a few days of your time to speak with them?"

"I-I think I can," Sanda responded. 'Where do they want to meet?"

"Because they might face persecution for daring to challenge the patriarchy, they have asked that the location remain secret. If you accept their invitation, I will contact you in two days, and escort you there."

"Tell them that I will come," Ernan responded.

"Very good," Sarah replied. "I will meet you two days from now at this place. Please make sure to pack for several days. And tell no one about this. The male hegemony has a vested interest in preventing any meeting where women of power might reach an accord that would threaten their authority, and sadly there are too many enslaved women who might be tempted to betray us."

***

Sanda Ernan had not been quite as taken in as she had led Sarah to believe. She had lived the life of a revolutionary for too long to allow herself to fall for easy promises. But in the end, the money, as detestable as it was, had proven quite real, and the promise of more, and the support of powerful backers, had simply been too much to refuse.

At least until she discovered the real motives behind the offer. If it was some clumsy attempt by law enforcement to entrap her, she intended to expose it and make the women of the Republic aware of the desperate lengths that their society would go to keep them subjugated. If it were real, then it was worth the secrecy and the risk.

Two days after their meeting, she sat at the same table, with her day bag packed and a tiny micro recorder hidden in her pocket. She knew that if they were working for the police, that her hosts would find it, but she had also taken the precaution of contacting several friends, and a female lawyer friendly to the Movement, and had told them enough about the meeting to guarantee that there would be an inquiry made if she found herself in a holding cell. None of this was comprehensive protection by any means, but it was better than blindly walking into a trap, and being a revolutionary sometimes involved taking calculated risks.

Sarah and Maya arrived right on time, and escorted her to an electric car waiting at the curb. The *'lectri* was plain, but one of the more expensive varieties, and when she got in, she discovered that the women had not come alone.

Instead, she was sharing it with two other women, one of whom she recognized with immediate distaste, and relief. It was Rozza Ramara, and another woman that she assumed was her assistant. This allayed her concern that the entire affair was some form of 'sting' operation. The reporter and her helper would never have been asked to come along had that been the case. Not that this made their presence any more appealing.

"What's this self-serving media-whore doing with us?" she demanded. Ramara was nothing more than a tool of the male-run information network, and hardly worthy of the company of any true feminist. All the woman really cared about was advancing her own selfish objectives over the needs of her fellow women.

"The women that I work for understand the need to retake control of the media in order to guarantee that women hear the truth about their oppressors." Sarah explained patiently. "To do that, we need the help of women like Ms. Ramara and her camerawoman.'

"I certainly understand your reservations, but she *is* committed to the truth, just as you are, even if she is not a dedicated revolutionary. Please, I ask that you welcome her and her assistant, if not as sisters, then at least as allies in our struggle."

There was something compelling about Sarah's petition, and Ernan found herself agreeing, albeit reluctantly. "Very well," she said. "Any woman who lends a hand in our struggle is a sister--in spirit at least."

This was all that anyone could have hoped for, and the ride out of the city into the desert that surrounded it was a quiet one. Not a companionable silence, but the stillness of a grudging truce.

When the 'lectri finally reached a remote location in the Mid-Desert, it turned off the main highway and onto a dirt road. They drove on for many more kilometers after this, until they were far out in the desert, where even the distant lights from the highway had vanished in the darkness. Then, inexplicably, the car stopped in what seemed to be the middle of nowhere.

"*This* is our meeting place?" Ernan demanded. Of all the spots she could have picked, it seemed the least likely of anywhere on the planet, and once again she was starting to have her doubts about Sarah and her promises.

"Please sister" Sarah entreated. "Be patient."

They waited together for several minutes and then, just when Sanda was about to demand that they end the farce and head back to the city, a bright set of lights appeared on the horizon.

"Our transportation has arrived," Sarah announced. The lights increased in magnitude until Ernan realized that they belonged to a ship. A spaceship.

The *C-JUDI-GO* came in for a landing, kicking up dust and debris as it settled down several meters from the 'lectri. Sarah and Maya got out first, urging the other women to follow as its cargo bay swung open.

Captain Bel Lissa met them as they walked up the ramp. "Nice to see you two again," she said in Standard. "I had a hell of a time keeping off the local sensor net. It may be primitive, but it's still a pain in the *arsh* to evade. I take it these are our guests?"

"Yes," Sarah answered. "We'll need to get them situated in the crew's quarters. Those should do until we can rendezvous with the *Athena*."

Rozza Ramara and her camerawoman came up to them at this point and interrupted. "That language you just spoke," she said. "It's not Espangla.

What is it?" The young camerawoman had also turned on a small holocorder and was starting to point it in their direction.

Sarah reached over, and gently pushed the lens down towards the decking. "Now is not the time for questions, Ms. Ramara, or for recording anything. You will have your story, and much more, very shortly, but I must ask that your associate erase that footage right away."

Ramara looked to her assistant and nodded, and Yúna immediately complied.

Satisfied, Sarah smiled. "Now, if you will all follow me, we will show you to your quarters for the flight."

***

The *JUDI* came out of Null and paralleled the orbital track of the system's only planet. It was a burned out cinder that had met its end when its primary had gone nova a million years before. For that reason, it was the perfect place for a clandestine meeting, having no value whatsoever to anyone except scientists who specialized in studying such phenomena.

The *Athena* was on station, using its stealth capabilities and the background interference created by the remnants of this primordial cataclysm to its fullest advantage. Although Bel Lissa and her crew knew that the warship was there, it was not until the *Athena* resumed a normal running mode that they were able to see it on the sitscreens.

The distance between the little merchanter and the giant warship closed, and when they were near enough, the naval vessel took over the helm and auto-guided them into its hangar bay. At Sarah's request, Maya had brought Rozza Ramara and Sanda Ernan up to the bridge to witness the event.

"My sweet God!" Ramara said as the *Athena* grew in size. "Is *that* where we are going to meet these 'friends' of yours?"

"Some of them," Sarah replied. "But the real meeting is scheduled to occur somewhere else, and that ship will take us there. As you can see, you were correct in your supposition that Maya and I were not from the ETR."

"But who—? Where—?" It was one thing to suspect the incredible, but quite another to encounter it in the flesh. The reporter's head was spinning.

"All in good time, Ms. Ramara. In the meantime, your assistant may now begin filming," Sarah advised her, "with one proviso; she is not to film myself, nor any of my associates. As I am sure that Ms. Ernan here can appreciate, our effectiveness is only possible through anonymity."

Ramara nodded dumbly, and then remembered herself and waved to her camerawoman to begin filming the incredible spectacle unfolding on the *JUDI's* sitscreens.

When the *JUDI* landed in the hangar, everyone filed down the ladder and into the cargo bay. Sarah stopped the party when it arrived at the egress hatch.

"I must apologize for all the mystery," she said, "and for all of the questions that I have left unanswered, but I felt that the best explanation would be better furnished by my countrywomen."

With that, she opened the hatchway.

As they stepped out of the merchanter and into the hangar bay, Sanda Ernan and Rozza Ramara looked around them in wide-eyed amazement.

Sally bel Mala walked up to them, accompanied by a naval officer. "Welcome aboard," the officer said in Espangla. "If you will come with us, we will show you to your quarters for the duration of our trip."

"I-I don't understand," Sanda stammered. "Who *are* you people? What *is* all this?"

"This is the United Sisterhood of Suns Naval Ship *Pallas Athena*," the officer informed her. "And my name is Lieutenant Lissa t'Neena. I'm with the Sisterhood Naval Public Affairs Office."

Then she indicated Bel Mala. "My associate here is with the Agency for External Affairs. They're a small liaison group that handles diplomatic relations with nations like your own. We will do our best to be your guides while you are staying with us."

Sanda didn't quite believe what she had just heard, or anything that she was seeing for that matter. "The *Sisterhood*? Was that what you just said?" Just then, it dawned on her that she had not seen a single male, anywhere.

"Yes," Sarah replied. "She did. There is a great deal that your government has not seen fit to tell you. But it is a very long story. Perhaps you would like to hear it over dinner? It has been quite a while since we all ate and I think that it is something that you will want to be seated for."

While Lieutenant t'Neena and Bel Mala led the little group towards the Lifts, Sarah held Maya back.

"I believe that we have just witnessed history in the making," Sarah remarked solemnly. "A small event and only a handful of women certainly, but the beginning of something truly momentous. What will it give birth to, I wonder?"

"I don't know," Bel Lissa interjected as she joined them. "But here's hoping that whatever it is, the Goddess will watch over her daughters. In both nations."

The three of them made the Lady's sign and then Sarah left them. She was headed towards the Command Center to speak with the Vice Admiral, and to reunite with her mother.

***

A Marine trooper showed Sarah into Lilith's office, and she took a seat and waited. When the door behind her slid open, she drew in a deep breath and tried to compose herself.

Lilith stepped inside, and seeing her there, did a double take. Then the older woman went around her desk and sat down. There was a long silence as the two of them regarded one another, and then Lilith produced a czigavar and began to smoke it.

Her hand, Sarah noted, was trembling. "Mother," she finally said.

Lilith's nictitating membranes flicked across her eyes and she blinked. It was something that Sarah remembered that she did unconsciously whenever she was very emotional, very upset, or both.

Lilith extinguished her czigavar and put it down on her desk. It was a quick, angry motion. "Damn you, Sarah," she hissed. Her eyes were bright with pain.

"Mother, I had no choice."

Lilith stood, the very epitome of hurt and anger. "Ten years, Sarah! Ten years of not knowing if you were alive or dead!" The tears came next, streaking down her face. *"Damn you!!"*

"Mother, I'm sorry."

"Sorry?!" Lilith cried. "You're *sorry*?!! You could have sent word! You could have at least *told* me that you were *alive!"*

It was Sarah's turn to rise, and she started to walk over to her. "I couldn't," she said. "I can't explain all the reasons, but I couldn't."

"Couldn't? *Couldn't?!* Aren't you some kind of—of *spy*—or something?" Lilith spat. "You could have sent me some kind of 'secret message'. Isn't that what spies do?!" She turned away from her, angrily crossing her arms over her chest.

Sarah reached out and touched her shoulder. "Mother, I'm sorry."

Lilith whirled around and slapped her. "Ten *years*, Sarah! Ten years of worry—ten years of—*nothing!*"

Then she collapsed into her daughter's arms. "Oh goddess! All that time wondering, worrying…" The rest was lost in deep, heart wrenching sobs.

Sarah gathered her in close, and stroked her hair as if she were a child. "I've missed you too, Mother," she said quietly.

When the two of them finally emerged from Lilith's office several minutes later, their eyes were both red and sore from weeping, and Katrinn hesitated to approach them.

"Kat," Lilith said, her voice husky with emotion, "This is my daughter, Sarah."

***

After they had parted company, Lilith made arrangements for Sarah to have her quarters in one of the guest cabins on the *Athena*. On an Isis Class vessel, these were located in 'Officer's Country' and were always kept available for officers-in-transit, or the occasional visiting dignitary. Sarah accepted the offer, and when she mentioned them, Lilith extended the same honor to Bel Lissa, Zara and Maya as well. She also asked that all of them join her for dinner together later that evening in the Officer's Lounge.

Privately, Sarah was relieved that Lilith had included her friends in the invitation. After their painful reunion, she wasn't ready for any more time alone with the woman. Enough old wounds had been opened for one day, and the presence of the *JUDI's* crew would provide a much-needed buffer for the both of them. They would have years to talk and mend their breaches, and rushing things would only foul the process.

Sarah found her cabin with the help of Lilith's adjutant, Ensign bar Daala. The young woman struck her as a bit odd, but she wasn't able to put her finger on why she felt this way.

When she focused on her a bit more to get to the bottom of it, she abruptly decided that it was nothing worth concerning herself with after all. Bar Daala, she reasoned, was obviously capable, or she wouldn't have been given such a critical posting in the first place. Besides which, she had more important things to concern herself with than the peculiarities of some junior—*very junior*—officer.

One of the most pressing issues that she faced was how to dress herself for the evening. The rule for visiting officers when dining aboard a naval ship was to attend in uniform, whether one was an active or retired servicewoman.

Sarah had separated from the Star Service with the rank of Captain, and she was reluctant to thrust this, and the memory of her disappearance, into her mother's face. Protocol required it though, and Lilith was a stickler for such things. With great misgivings, she sent her measurements to the Ships Stores and ordered them to fabricate her uniform.

It arrived only a few minutes later, and she verified that her service ribbons included one that declared her to be a retired servicewoman. Her mother would be expecting to see this.

She also made sure to add another item to the blouse, just below her ribbon awards. It was the small black rose insignia of the OAE. Although she knew that Lilith would find it offensive, she felt that she had to make a statement to her that that part of her past *had* be acknowledged, if not in the present, then as a matter for a future conversation between them. Notwithstanding her mother's feelings, she was proud of her Agency association, and she wanted the woman to know that.

Shedding her civilian clothes, she dressed herself, mildly surprised that after all the years since she had worn the uniform, how natural it still felt.

Then, arranging her long hair into a neat and reasonably military bun, she inspected herself in the mirror. After patting a few hairs into place, and giving a tug on her tunic to straighten it, she went out into the common passageway to collect her crewmates.

Just as she had, Bel Lissa and Zara had donned uniforms appropriate to their former ranks, and included their own OAE pins. Sarah smiled with relief and gratitude when she saw this. She hadn't asked them to put the pins on, and they could have just as easily left them behind and still satisfied regulations. But they hadn't, and she was glad for their support. Now her mother would have to deal with not only one Agency representative, but three.

Nodding her thanks, she led them down the corridor to collect Maya. They caught up with the girl as she was coming out of her quarters, busily fussing with her cravess. Unlike her crewmates, Sarah had given her very specific instructions on how to dress herself. And although Maya and social polish where certainly not on intimate terms, Sarah had to admit that she was pleased with the final result, and uttered a little prayer to the Goddess, asking her to bless Madame n'Fawnelle of the *Star of Aphrodite* for her influence. The comerci that Maya had chosen for herself complimented her complexion nicely, her hair was perfect, and her make-up was properly understated.

But even though she had the dressmaker to thank for much of this, Sarah had to award the girl some credit of her own. Given her chequered past, it was highly likely that the only time that she had ever worn a comerci before had been in court, as a criminal defendant, and despite this lack of experience, she had managed to do a tolerable job.

Sarah only had to make a single small adjustment to Maya's cravess to bring it to perfection, and added a stern warning to her not to fidget with it, or with her stiff collar for the remainder of the evening. With that said, they sought out the Officer's Lounge.

Lilith and Admiral da'Kayt were already there, the latter having been aboard on other business, and invited at the last minute. Although Da'Kayt was completely unaffected by her appearance, it had precisely the effect on her mother that Sarah had expected. The uniform summoned up a tiny frown, and when Lilith recognized it, the OAE insignia only deepened her scowl. But the woman kept any sharp remarks to herself, and greeted her companions cordially enough, although she did give them the same unhappy look, mixed with a certain measure of wary appraisal.

Saara Sa'Vika catered the meal itself, and while it was quite without parallel, the conversation was another matter entirely. Neither she nor her mother could figure out what to say to one another without treading into forbidden areas, and they were forced to keep their remarks carefully neutral.

Thankfully, Bel Lissa, Zara and Da'Kayt came to everyone's rescue, borrowing on their common experiences during the War of the Prophet to keep things lively, interesting, and most importantly, safely clear of any possible controversy. By dessert, not only had they all become reasonably comfortable with one another, but Lilith finally seemed to approve of her friends, having accepted the fact that they were veteran naval officers like herself, and that if nothing else, Sarah had at least been in good company during her adventures.

This didn't exonerate Sarah of course, but it did mitigate things between the two of them to a large degree. And for that little victory, Sarah was in her friend's eternal debt. She was even able to relax enough to loosen the death grip she had been keeping on her napkin all through the main course.

In the end, the dinner, for all its initial awkwardness, proved to be a success. No one pressed their luck by lingering over dessert, however, and by a wordless, mutual consent, the group broke up shortly after it was finished.

Sarah also had other business to attend to while she was aboard, and while she could have gone straightaway to see to it, she chose not to. Dinner had left her emotionally exhausted, and she gave herself the luxury of spending the remainder of the night alone in her cabin instead. The only allowance that she made to duty was to send a short message to Maya, advising her of their appointment the next morning with the Ship's High Priestess.

Like the meal, the occasion was to be a formal one, and she added the caveat (with some private amusement that she carefully edited out) that Maya was to attire herself in her comerci again.

Not only was this suited to the occasion, but it also served as a form of punishment. Despite her admonitions to the contrary, Sarah had caught her, when she had thought that no one had been looking, tugging at the edges of her collar during their meal. Whether the girl liked it or not, Sarah was determined that Maya would eventually become reasonably civilized. If she was going to be a representative of the OAE, she had to learn to at least *act* the part.

***

Sanda Ernan and Rosa Ramara had also had a gathering of their own to attend. Once they had been assigned their quarters, Lieutenant t'Neena and Bel Mala escorted them to the Officers Mess and saw to their meal. As they ate, Lt. Commander Mearinn d'Rann joined them. She had come not only to formally welcome them aboard as Katrinn's Second, but also in her capacity as a Professor of History, and used the opportunity to tell them the story of the Sisterhood, from its very inception, to the present.

Rozza Ramara was positively electrified by the tale, and it's potential. It was nothing less than the story of the century, if not the millennium. When her Network broke it to the public, she knew that it would shake the very foundations of her society. Even better, she would be the one to tell that story, and do most of the shaking.

With T'Neena's permission, she had her camerawoman record the entire lecture, and then, once the meal had been concluded, she convinced the officer to take her on a tour of the ship itself, after agreeing that certain areas would be off limits to filming. Ramara had been aboard military vessels before, and she was more than willing to consent. Even with this prohibition in place, she knew that she would have enough material to last for a lifetime.

The impact of Mearinn's impromptu class was no less profound for Sanda Ernan, but she reacted quite differently than the journalist. All through Mearinn's discourse, she had remained silent, asking only a few short questions here and there, and when Ramara and T'Neena had departed together to begin their tour, she had requested to be shown to her quarters. As soon as she arrived there, she had only one additional favor to ask of her hosts; for a holoplayer and any additional material that related to the Sisterhood's history. Mearinn saw to it that this was provided, and Ernan remained sequestered in her cabin for the rest of their journey.

USSNS *Pallas Athena*, Altilyar System, Magdala Provensa,
Esteral Terrana Rapabla, 1044.07|28|03:75:61

Reverend Ophida n'Marsi had been well prepared for her meeting with Sarah. She had been told in advance by her control officer that a senior OAE official would be coming aboard, en-route to Thermadon on high-level business. And exactly who she was.

The fact that *'Galenthis'*, as Sarah had once been code-named, was now the Sagana Sector Chief had been somewhat of a surprise, but the Priestess had been a senior agent for too many years not to simply accept the fact, and deal with N'Jan's new status accordingly. Tara ben Paula didn't appoint women to such high posts haphazardly.

If Sarah n'Jan had been given the job, then Ophida was quite confident that she had earned it, although how she had done so would most likely never be disclosed. Not that this mattered overmuch; secrets were simply part of the job.

What did concern her though, was that the woman was now her superior, and that her Intel files needed to be ready for review. Thanks to the notice she'd gotten, she had had plenty of time to see to this however, although there hadn't been very much for her to tidy up. Her station was well run and her agents scattered throughout the Expeditionary Force were not only observant, but also timely and exact in their reporting. When Sarah arrived, Ophida was confident that she would be quite satisfied with what she found.

She made a final entry in the holofile in front of her, and then settled in to wait for the woman. Sarah didn't keep her long, and when she arrived, Ophida noted that her assistant was accompanying her.

The Priestess didn't know Maya n'Kaaryn personally, but she had heard of her, and if the rumors were true, she was Sarah's personal protégé—an extremely rare honor that was only conferred on equally unique individuals.

From what she had been told, Ms. n'Kaaryn had come to the OAE from outside normal Agency channels, and whatever her particular talents were, they had been valuable enough to allow her to circumvent the usual selection processes. Ophida made a mental note to find out more about her, if she could. Someone that unique bore watching; either for signs that she was a potential ally, or an adversary.

As an Assistant Priestess showed the pair in, Ophida bowed politely, and automatically vacated her chair. Then they were alone.

"Ms. n'Jan and Ms. n'Kaaryn, welcome. May I offer either of you any refreshments?"

Sarah waved off the invitation, and took the chair, while Maya positioned herself off to one side and remained standing. Just from the way that the young woman held herself gave Ophida a little more insight into her.

Sarah, or someone else, had been training Maya for 'wet work'. It was obvious. And if she survived the process, she was going to become as dangerous as Sarah was one day, the priestess mused. It was an interesting piece of information, and also a reassuring one. For an old woman like herself, the knowledge that the next generation would be just as capable as the one that had preceded it was very comforting.

"I am not here to inspect your files," Sarah began. "I know all about your work, and I am quite certain that everything is in order, and of the highest quality. My assistant and I are, as you are aware, engaged in a very sensitive mission and we have little time to waste."

Ophida waited respectfully.

"I would however like to take the opportunity to congratulate you on the initiative that you showed with Jon fa'Teela and the ETR Liaison Officer. It was not something we could have afforded to miss.'

"The Agency completely believes as you do; that the Republic will use Rodraga to make contact with the Marionites, through the neoman, and as part of an ongoing counterintelligence effort against us.'

"The Director feels that if the Marionites can be convinced to align themselves with the ETR that they would represent a substantial and well organized fifth-column that could be called upon by the Republic in the event of hostilities. Like yourself, we *want* that alliance to occur—and for ample documentation to be gathered for later follow-up actions."

May the Goddess be praised, Ophida thought. Not only would Fa'Teela be brought to justice, but the Marionite abomination would be destroyed along with him. She kept her expression bland though, forcefully suppressing the tears of joy that wanted to flow down her wrinkled features.

"I also understand that you may have other individuals serving with the Expeditionary Force that have been identified as Marionites," Sarah continued, "or subversives that might pose a threat. Is that not so?"

"Yes, ma'am," Ophida answered. "It is. I know that you are in a hurry, but may I show you their files?"

Sarah indicated her assent, and a signal from the Priestesses' psiever opened the holofiles. One of them concerned Troop Leader Ellen n'Elemay, and Sarah paused and read it in detail. A moment later, she closed her eyes, and accessed her psiever. When she reopened them, she dragged the Marine's file off to the side and briefly reviewed the others.

"Continue to maintain your watch," she said at last. "And if you can encourage any complicity in treasonous acts, so much the better. When the time is right, the Agency wants to be able to clean house thoroughly."

"Yes, ma'am," Ophida replied, her spirits rising even higher. Everything that she had just shown Sarah had also been presented to the previous Sector Chief, but the woman had simply ignored it, despite her best efforts to convince her of its gravity. Sarah n'Jan on the other hand, clearly possessed a much wider vision. Tara ben Paula had picked wisely, the Priestess decided.

"One more thing, Reverend," Sarah added. "I just spoke with my superior. She wants you to remove N'Elemay from your watch list, and delete her file. I have forwarded a copy of it to Thermadon."

Ophida was taken aback. "Ma'am?"

"See to this immediately," Sarah instructed. "Her case will be handled at a higher level."

***

Sarah and Maya left the Temple only two minutes later, and while Maya headed to her quarters to pack, Sarah sought out her mother on the bridge. When she entered, Lilith saw her and stood up from her station. The *Athena* was about to transit into Null, and once the ship completed the process, they would be arriving over Thermadon. Then they would be forced to part and both of them would be too busy to say any farewells.

"Mother," Sarah said, approaching her. "It is almost time."

Lilith glanced briefly at the sitscreens and then with a regretful expression, at her daughter. "Yes. I know."

Sarah reached out to take Lilith's hands in her own. "Mother, I will miss you," she said. "And I *am* sorry—again."

Lilith gathered her in and hugged her. "I will miss you too, Sarah. Goddess, if only Jan could have been here, with us, right now to see this…."

When she stepped back, she brushed a few tears from her eyes. "Stay safe, and send a message when you can."

"I will mother," Sarah promised.

"You'd better," Lilith warned, wagging a finger at her. "I know where you work now and I know how to find you!"

They shared a smile and a moment of teary laughter. Then Sarah stepped back a pace. "Goodbye, mother."

After another, final embrace, Sarah left the bridge to collect Maya and their special guests. On her way down to Officer's Country, she made a vow to herself. This time, her departure wouldn't be like it had been a decade earlier. She wouldn't just vanish and leave Lilith alone again, wondering about her fate. She was home now, and she intended to stay there.

***

Thermadon Val, Thermadon, Myrene System, Thalestris Elant,
United Sisterhood of Suns, 1044.07|29|07:50:83

A military shuttle met the *Athena* in orbit and immediately transported

Ernan, Ramara, and their escort, downside to Bel Sharra Memorial Spaceport. From there they were whisked off by hoverlimo to the *Euxine Plaza Hotel*, one of the cities finest establishments. Once they had been checked in, they were informed of a meeting scheduled for them at the Golden Pyramid, to meet with a group of Senatrixs led by none other than Layna n'Calysher herself, the following morning.

Neither woman felt like spending the evening waiting in their rooms however. Excited by the great city, both of them wanted to get out and see the Capitol for themselves. Rozza Ramara, true to her calling, immediately asked for, and received, an escort through Thermadon to film some of its marvels, courtesy of the Sisterhood News Network. And Sanda Ernan quickly followed suit, requesting her own private tour as well.

In Ernan's case, Sarah and Maya acted as her guides, along with an aide from Senatrix n'Calysher's office. Their first stop was the Government Center, in the very heart of the city.

It had been late in the day when they had arrived on Thermadon and a rainstorm had just ended. This had left the air fresh and clean, and the light from the planet's primary bathed the scene below their hoverlimo in a magical golden radiance. As the vehicle slowly circled the Government Center, the sunlight flashed brilliantly off the sides of the great Golden Pyramid and caressed the shape of Concordance Hall, which sat by itself in the middle of the vast plaza.

Even at that advanced hour, tourists from all around the Sisterhood still dotted the great expanse, or filed into the buildings in groups to visit the historic attractions. Of all of them, it was Concordance Hall that held Sanda's attention the most.

"That building" she asked, pointing down at it. "That's Concordance Hall, is it not?"

"Si'dà, jantildam," the aide responded. "Yes, gentlelady, it is."

"And that is where the Sisterhood's founding document is kept?"

"*Si'dà, jantildam*. Would you like to visit it?"

"Yes," she said, "I would. Very much so."

The aide briefly closed her eyes, and the hoverlimo made a smooth banking turn and descended. Although she had learned about psievers aboard the *Athena*, and had seen them being used, Ernan still found them a little startling. Controlling things by thought and speaking mind-to-mind, as the aide had just done with the limo's driver, was just one of the many things that she had been trying to wrap her mind around since encountering the Sisterhood.

The vehicle landed smoothly in the very center of the vast plaza. Normally this was a 'no-landing' zone, but the status of the 'limo's special passengers and the fact that the aircar had government transponder codes, meant that they were free to land just about anywhere they wanted. Thermadon was at Sanda Ernan's feet and Concordance Plaza was definitely no exception.

Ernan was the first one out of the vehicle, and as everyone followed her, she walked resolutely to the foot of the marble steps that led up into the Hall itself. There, on a low, broad pedestal, a fire was burning in a brazier. She stopped in front of it, and then looked over her shoulder at the aide.

"This is the Flame of Unity, am I correct?"

"Yes, gentlelady," the young woman replied.

"Tell me about it, please."

"It burns perpetually, gentlelady, and it is never allowed to go out," the aide told her. "It represents the united worlds of the Sisterhood and our resistance against the forces of chaos. It is the undying symbol of civilization and community."

Ernan nodded. "And fire is also the weapon that banishes the enemies of that community. Isn't that also correct?" There was a gleam in her eyes, partly from the light of the flame itself, and also from something else, much deeper within her soul.

"Yes, gentlelady."

Ernan considered the flame for a long moment, and then walked resolutely up the steps. At the summit, were two Marines in their scarlet dress uniforms, holding polished Mark-7 blasters. They were part of an honor guard that maintained a continuous watch over the Hall, and stood at attention to either side of the entrance like statues. The woman regarded their impassive young faces carefully, and then with a slight nod of acknowledgement to them, she walked into the Hall itself.

Maya flashed a questioning look at Sarah.

Watch, Sarah told her by psiever, *and learn. You are about to witness something truly marvelous.*

Maya followed her, not quite certain what was going to happen next.

They found Ernan standing in front of the Concordance itself, which was protected by a stasis field in an airtight display case. The case was set on a massive marble pedestal and framed by the flags of the Sisterhood, and its armed forces.

Maya had seen copies of the document before, and like everyone else, she had read it in primary. It was a noble text certainly, but also something that one tended to take for granted, as part of daily life. By Ernan's posture alone however, she could tell, that for her, standing before it was more akin to a deep religious experience.

The girl started to move forwards to join the woman, but Sarah stayed her. *Let her be*, she advised. *Let the Sisterhood speak to her alone.*

Several minutes went by before Sanda turned and walked past them, deep in thought. She went outside and looked out across the colossal city. The metropolis was just beginning to come alive with the lights from its massive buildings and the endless ribbons of traffic that coursed between them. With the last rays of light shining through it all, the city looked like a place out of fable, powerful, and yet almost unreal in its magnificence.

Sarah waited until she sensed that the moment was right to approach her. When she did, the woman regarded her with a fierce, haunted expression.

"You can't imagine what it was like," Ernan said, her voice breaking. "All these years, all the sacrifices that we made for the Movement...and now...all this. You were out there all along, and none of us even knew about you."

"Yes" Sarah agreed, "We were."

Ernan pondered her answer, and then asked, "What do you want me to do?"

"We want you to do what is right, Sanda," Sarah replied. "Our sisters demand nothing less of any of us."

USSNS *Pallas Athena*, Altamara System, Frontera Provensa, Esteral Terrana Rapabla 1044.08|13|04:58:17

Lilith learned about the government's disclosure in an official communiqué from Rixa, and she sighed in relief when she didn't hear the strains of *Carmina-Burana* being played along with it. The secret was out, and they weren't at war with the ETR.

After confirming that Da'Kayt had also seen the message, and didn't require her presence, she ordered up some tea, and invited Katrinn, Mearinn and Col. Lislsdaater up to her office to watch the civilian news clips with her. The first holo began with a special news bulletin from Thermadon.

"Sisterhood News Network was advised this morning by the Chairwoman's Office of Public Information of a historic development. One year ago, contact was made by one of our Long Range exploration ships with a previously unknown star civilization," the announcer began.

"This nation, calling itself the Esteral Terrana Rapabla, is reported to be a survivor of the Pre-MARS era Gaian Star Federation. In addition, the OPI informed SNN that shortly after making contact, the ETR approached the Sisterhood for military assistance to combat Hriss aggression in their space. This aid was provided and there is currently a successful operation being conducted by our naval and Marine forces to repel the aggressors.'

"When asked why there had been such a long delay in making this announcement, the OPI stated that it had been necessary to guarantee the operational security of our armed forces. Their spokeswoman added that while there is still a need to maintain a high level of security to ensure the success of the Navy's mission, it had been decided that a general announcement could finally be made to the public.'

"The OPI did not furnish any details to SNN regarding the nature of ETR society, or the name of the ship that made the initial discovery, but promised that additional information would be released shortly. They also advised SNN that the Chairwoman will be making an official statement to the nation this evening at 07:50.'

"To comment on all of this, SNN reporter Hilari n'Mara has invited Dr. Layrri t'Sharalese of the University of Thermadon at Thenti to join her for a special edition of *'SNN Top Story'*."

Hearing these names, Lilith recalled N'Mara from her own interview about Jon fa'Teela, and remembered seeing T'Sharalese being featured on a sensationalist show about the Lost Colonies.

The scene cut to a studio set with the reporter and Dr. t'Sharalese sitting together, and N'Mara began her interview, "As some viewers might remember, Dr. t'Sharalese staked her reputation on the claim that fragments of the Star Federation did manage to survive the Plague, a contention that earned her the ridicule of many of her colleagues.'

"Bravely refusing to abandon her theory, Dr. t'Sharalese went on to explore ruins found on Phantasma 9-A, a world located at the very borders of Sisterhood space in the Sagana Territory. Dr. t'Sharalese, you must be very excited by this announcement."

The doctor was. "Yes, Hilari. This is a total vindication of years of research and hard work. I know that my team on the Phantasma Project is just as happy as I am to hear the news. I was sorry to learn that the news also involves problems with the Hriss, and my prayers are with our servicewomen, and the people of the ETR."

"As are ours, Doctor," N'Mara agreed soberly. "Now, with regard to the ETR itself, the government's release didn't include very much information, and our viewers would like to know anything more that you can tell us about them. Can you give us any idea what they might be like, based upon your research?"

"Well, Hilari," T'Sharalese replied carefully, "We can really only speculate at this point, but based on what my team uncovered on Phantasma 9-A, we are certainly looking at a society with the capability of interstellar flight, and technology that at least approaches a level similar to our own."

The interviewer nodded. "Based on your findings, do we know if they have values similar to our own? Do they embrace Motherthought for example?"

"That's impossible to say at this stage," the academic replied, "The dig uncovered artifacts that date before the MARS epidemic, and those indicated that the residents, on Phantasma at least, were a mixed-sex population. Whether they became completely female like ourselves at a later point, or not, is something that we will have to just wait and see. Whatever the case turns out to be however, the discovery is certainly a milestone in xenoarcheology."

The journalist knotted her brow in concern. "Doctor, I must ask you a difficult question. Is there any possibility, as some have already begun to suggest, that the ETR might ultimately prove to be hostile?" Everyone, including Lilith knew that she was also asking, '*...and come here?*'

"We didn't find any evidence of that at our dig site." Dr. t'Sharalese answered. "Of course, it's always possible."

The interview went on like this for a while longer before it concluded and SNN returned to their normal programming.

"That reminded me of a bedtime story my mothers once told me about two blind women, who had never seen a *Haaraxx*, and tried to describe it just by touch," Katrinn remarked tartly.

Lilith had to agree. She'd heard an Arai version of the same fable, and N'Mara had shed just about as much light on the nature of the ETR as the blind women had with their *Haaraxx*, and had probably created more concern than she'd managed to allay in the process.

If she only knew, she thought to herself. She sent a command for the next news item to play.

It was the Chairwoman's address to the nation. Marina bel Rayna was the 105th woman to serve the Sisterhood as Chairwoman. At 175 standard years, she still carried herself like a much younger woman, and Lilith hoped that she would look half as good when she reached Bel Rayna's age.

A veteran politician, Bel Rayna was composed and relaxed as she stepped up to the podium, and she made a point to smile and wave at several of the journalists that she knew personally. Behind her, Lilith caught sight of Fleet Admiral ebed Cya, the Commandant of the Marine Corps, General Hanna Tannasdaater, and their superiors, Admiral of the Navy Jora t'Kayna and Secretary of State, Sussyn ebed Sandra. Like the Chairwoman, they were all playing their proper parts, and offsetting her calm demeanor with stiff, businesslike expressions that assured the public that they were on the job, and ready for anything.

"Gentleladies of the Press," Bel Rayna began, "as you know from an earlier announcement, some time ago, the Sisterhood made contact with a heretofore undiscovered branch of the Human family, the Esteral Terrana Rapabla. You are also aware that the ETR subsequently approached us, requesting humanitarian aid in the form of military assistance, and that this help has been provided.'

"This is clearly a momentous event in history. For centuries, we women believed ourselves to be alone, the sole survivors of the MARS plague. Now we know that we were not the only ones to weather that terrible calamity.'

"I am here tonight to share this news, and assure you that we will not only help our new friends to combat Hriss aggression, but work to foster closer ties, once the emergency has passed.'

"I have been advised, by the Secretary of State, and the Command Staff of the Navy and Marines, that we are well into the process of defeating the Hriss forces. I have also been in contact with the Hriss Imperial Ambassador. He has declared that the forces which we are engaging are criminal elements who are in no way associated with their government, and he has also pledged that they will receive no aid whatsoever from the Throne of Bones."

Lilith had to chuckle at this. While they were certainly independent of the Imperium, the Hriss clans bought all of their ships, weapons and spare parts from the Imperial Navy, and even received technical assistance from regular navy personnel—all in the name of 'self-protection' of course. But she could understand why the lie was being told; after so many defeats, the Throne of Bones didn't want to risk another open conflict, and for the moment at least, it was also in the Sisterhood's interests to confine the situation to the ETR.

The Chairwoman went on. "For reasons of operational security, we must keep all information about the ETR to a minimum, however, as the OPI release stated, we will disclose what we can, and in the proper time and measure. For now, I can only tell you that the ETR is a friendly nation, and that we have formally recognized them. And as soon as circumstances permit, an exchange of ambassadors will take place, and embassies will be formally established in our respective capitols. That said, I will now open the floor to questions."

With the floodgate opened, the journalists nearly trampled each other to death as they vied for the Chairwoman's attention. Many of the questions that they asked her were patent attempts to manipulate Bel Rayna into divulging more than she intended to, and old hand as she was, she not only deflected them, but managed to make the questioners feel good about it. The press conference ended without anything additional being revealed. This left the newswomen with only one other time-honored option; pure, useless speculation.

In SNN's case, it took the form of a series of interviews with 'average women' in various parts of the Sisterhood. The reaction that they received was mixed. Some women welcomed further contact with the ETR, some didn't, and underlying everything was a deep concern about the true nature of this newly discovered society, and it's ultimate intentions.

When they had seen enough, Lilith paused the holoplayer.

"So, what does all this mean for us, in Standard?" Mearinn asked.

"That our job just became easier," Lilith said. "Rixa made it clear that our forces are now free to operate openly in the ETR. We don't have to pretend anymore. So, Colonel, your girls can throw away their ETR rags and start dressing like proper Sisterhood Marines again."

Lislsdaater brightened at this, and sat up a little straighter. Of all her officers, the Zommerlaandar had been the least pleased with the masquerade. Lilith supposed that it was a Marine thing.

"However," Lilith went on, "our operations still remain classified "Brilliant" until further notice. No details regarding it, or about the ETR, are to be shared outside of military channels. The same applies to the existence of the School, and anything to do with the *Atalanta*. I imagine that the government will get around to dealing with all that, just as soon as they decide what kind of 'spin' they want to put on it."

Privately, they were all wondering the same thing; what form such announcements might take, and what had actually happened to the two crewwomen who had accepted their offer of repatriation when they had first discovered the School. Given the secrecy involved at the time, it seemed likely to Lilith at least, that they had had their memories scrubbed the moment they had come aboard the USSNS *Pentheselea*, and replaced with something fairly innocuous. In all probability, they were living out rather bland lives somewhere in the Sisterhood, without any notion whatsoever about their former existences. But like Dr. t'Sharalese, she could only speculate.

"Well, now for the ETR reaction," Lilith said, calling up the file.

"Oh, this should be a *hüüt*," Katrinn remarked dryly.

The first scene they saw was a shot of Rozza Ramara, standing in front of what appeared to be police ground cars. They were facing a road that ran towards a small town, surrounded by empty farmland.

"In reaction to the disclosure made by Republican News Network of the true identity of our allies," she said, "President Magdalana declined to make any comment, but his Press secretary advised this reporter that a statement would be forthcoming. The citizens of the Republic are not waiting for a speech, however. Instead, some of them have already responded in a dramatic fashion.'

"Right now, I'm standing in front of the town of Alquibar, on Picala 15 in the Magdala Provensa, where a group of women have seized control. According to Colonel Jyuan de Jehesa, the local Garda Nacia commander, the radicals took over the town at noon today, and are holding the entire male population prisoner. Their leader, Yúna Santavaar, who is a member of the radical feminist group *La Ermanyaa*, made this statement to us:'

"We are the women of the Republic, your sisters, your wives and your mothers, and we will not allow ourselves to be second class citizens any longer. The Sisterhood of Suns has been the inspiration for us to declare our independence from the male-dominated government, and we call on all freedom-loving women to join us.'

The newscaster continued. "So far, the women have refused to surrender the town or their weapons, and local authorities are continuing in their efforts to negotiate a peaceful end to the tense situation. When asked for his reaction, the local governor, Sencha da Reyavaal refused to speak, and the President's office was equally silent. We will continue to cover this story as events develop.'

"In the meantime, there have been equally strong positions taken by what could be called the 'opposition' to the Sisterhood. Chief among these was made by Bishop Manel da Florze of the Republican Orthodox Church, who is known for his outspoken views against the rights of women."

The scene cut to a quiet study, all dark wood and lined with real books. A man in ritual garb, and identified as the Bishop, was seated, facing the holocam. He appeared to be quite upset.

"This *'Sisterhood'*," the cleric sneered, "if it is *really* what it is claimed to be, goes against the beliefs that every decent, hardworking citizen of the Republic holds dear. Our nation has always embraced family values, and the union of men and women as God ordained it to be. Allying ourselves with such a state is a betrayal of everything that we believe in, and President Magdalana should excuse himself from office for entering into this shameful pact."

"What about the military aid they have been giving us?" the off-camera interviewer asked. "Don't you think that we owe them our thanks for helping us fight the Hriss?"

"We owe them nothing!" he replied, waving his hand in angry dismissal. "God delivered us from the Hriss, not some group of misguided perverts. They are an abomination and we should shun any association with them!"

The broadcast returned to Ramara. "The reaction on the street has been mixed. Here are some of the opinions that we heard from the average citizen, gathered during a series of on-the-spot interviews with the men and women of Nuvo Bolivar."

The first interviewee was a woman.

"Well, I think the Sisterhood is a great thing", she said. "The idea that there's a nation of women out there running things is something the Republic should pay attention to! We could use more women in power here." As she said this, a man pushed his way into camera view.

"Bullshit!" he said. "Women can't even drive a 'lectri! How in the hell can they run a whole star nation? I say back to the kitchens with all of you!"

The 'cast immediately cut away to another man. "This Sisterhood—surely it has some place for men in it? I mean, how can such a society exist without us? I'd like to know…and if there's room for me, I'll go. I've always thought of myself as a woman trapped in a man's body."

The next shot was of a pair of teenage girls, decked out in the latest *Xenyo-punka* makeup and jewelry. "Yeah!!" they chimed enthusiastically, "Jet-on Sisterhood!"

After this, a fairly sedate, and reasonably normal looking woman was asked for her views. "I don't know," she said doubtfully. "It all sounds so…well, I don't know about women being with women. I mean, thank you for helping us…I guess. Anyhow, I have to get going."

The final interview was with a woman who looked like a businessperson. She was well groomed, calm, and faced the camera with confidence. "The Sisterhood?" she said. "Of course. It's only the next logical step in our evolution. I think we'll see it happening here, very, very soon." Before the reporter could ask her to explain what she meant, she smiled enigmatically, turned and walked away.

The file reached its end, and Lilith decided it was time to take a deep drag from her czigavar. "Well," she said expansively, "wasn't *that* fun? I'm *sooo* glad that we've already been through such teething pains."

"Yah," Katrinn agreed. "That was a bit hard to watch. What *kraanksingaan*!"

"Yes, you are right, Katrinn. Utter chaos," Mearinn said. "And it will only get worse. I just hope that those poor women in Alquibar get some help. Theirs is a brave effort certainly, but it is ultimately doomed to failure."

"That's not our problem," Katrinn countered. "We have the Hriss to deal with and that's more than enough for us to worry over."

What none of them could know was that Senatrix n'Calysher had also seen the same clips, and unlike them, she had the power to do something about the situation in Alquibar. Light years away, on Thermadon, she waved for her assistant to come forwards.

"Please contact the Admiral of the Navy," she instructed. "I think that those women in Alquibar could benefit from some of our assistance. In complete confidence, of course.'

"I'd also like the OAE to try and find out who that businesswoman at the very end of the interviews was. She seemed like a very sensible sort to me, and she might prove useful to us in the future."

"Yes, ma'am."

By the end of the day, orders had been cut for the OAE to locate the enigmatic professional and to see if she was amenable for recruiting. The Office of the Commandant of the Marines also received instructions, and it immediately sent a message to Major n'Neesa aboard the *Athena*.

Her mission was to dispatch a Marauder Team to the beleaguered town as soon as possible. She chose Team 5.

Maristown, New Covenant, Bethlehem System, Telesalla Elant, United Sisterhood of Suns, 1044.08|14|07:91:67

Sister Erynn n'Avenal read the latest communication from Jon fa'Teela. He'd written it to her using the Book of Numbers Cipher, concealing his real message in lines of innocuous scripture. Jon was worried.

'The Sisterhood seems to be moving closer and closer to war with the ETR.' he had written, *'They have let the news out that they have been helping them, but from the 'casts they've allowed us to see, it only disrupted the ETR. This can only lead to further troubles and I fear that the Church will be singled out. I am praying for all of us.'*

Even though he wasn't aware of it, Jon was an astute politician, she thought, and might actually serve the Faithful in that very capacity one day. Of course, she had already known about the so-called 'secret war' from its very outset, not only thanks to Jon and his dispatches, but also from others who served even more silently than he did.

She had also seen the news clips he had referred to, and had deduced the same potential outcome. The only fruit that disclosure could ever produce would be to discredit the ETR's current government and foment disharmony among its people. That, in turn was a prelude to war.

And when it was over, people like Sanda Ernan would be placed in power. More importantly, the very existence of the Church would be imperiled. N'Avenal had no doubt whatsoever that the right-wing elements of the Supreme Circle would find a way to use the conflict as an excuse to persecute the Faithful. If one considered the situation from their perspective, it all made a certain satanic sense, she reflected.

But the Church would not be caught unawares. For decades, it had created a secret network of believers spread throughout the Sisterhood; women who not only risked their freedom on a daily basis to spread the Gospel of Mari, but also stood ready to help the Church in it's darkest hours.

Accessing her Com terminal, she composed a letter to the Holy Office of Her Supreme Pontiff, Pope Paula IV and when she was satisfied with the contents, she sent it. Most Sisters would never have presumed such a thing, but N'Avenal was no average cleric.

Aside from her duties as Jon's spiritual mentor, her other sphere of responsibility was serving as the *Praepositus Generalis* of the *Societas Mariaa,* the Provost General of the Society of Mari, making her the leader of the Church's equivalent of the OAE.

Her job was nothing less than guaranteeing the security and survival of the Church itself. Her message to Her Holiness had been simple, sent in a cipher that even the OAE did not know of—yet. It had read; "Your Holiness, I believe that the time has come to initiate preparations for the worst."

The Pope would know exactly what this meant, and with her blessings, secret arrangements would be made. Sympathetic ship captains would be paid retainers, officials bribed handsomely, and key members of the Faithful would begin preparing safe houses. More importantly, the Daughters of Eve would begin to make their own plans. They were something that even Pope Paula didn't know about, and with Jesu's blessing, never would.

If the terrible day of persecution *did* arrive, the *Societas Mariaa* would be ready, and the Sisterhood would pay dearly for its sins. The Daughters of Eve would make certain of this, and their recompense would be in blood.

Alquibar Pobla, Nuvo Bolivar, Magdala Provensa, Esteral Terrana
Rapabla, 1044.08|17|06:94:88

The 'siege' of Alquibar, as the media was now calling it, had gone on for several days, with no real change beyond who was negotiating with the women holding the town, or what they were offering. All services had been cut off, and police and local detachments of the Garda Nacia blocked every road. Their commander expressed his confidence that the lack of food, water and electricity would force the rebels to capitulate, and see the male hostages released without bloodshed. He might have even been right—if the affair had been kept between the militants and his forces.

The arrival of a Nightingale infiltrator over the restricted airspace changed the equation however. It evaded detection with very little effort, and settled itself down in the town square. Once it was concealed from view, it went out of stealth mode for just a minute, and its passengers disembarked. Most of the women holding the town were at its perimeters, stationed behind makeshift barricades, but a few had been tasked with guarding the town center, and the bank, which had become the unofficial command center for the radical group.

Seeing the Nightingale, and the strangely dressed women walking out of it, they did what they were supposed to do. They gave the alarm and leveled their weapons at the strangers.

"Stop where you are!" one of the guards demanded.

Troop Leader n'Elemay raised her hands, and behind her, the rest of Marauder Team 5 did the same. "We are friends, sister," she said. "We have come from the Sisterhood to help you."

"We'll see," the woman replied doubtfully. By this time, other women were joining her, and at her signal, they disarmed the team. Although Kaly didn't much care for the idea of having her precious Tatiana taken away from her, N'Elemay had made it clear on the ride downside that turning over their weapons would be mandatory. They needed to establish trust from the very start.

The young woman frowned, but gave the rifle over to the nearest woman. To her relief, the guard handled it with the respect that it deserved, and slung it carefully over her shoulder before patting her, and her companions down.

"You will come with me," the first woman told them. At her direction, they were marched into the bank. Kaly couldn't help but notice that although they had been forced to turn over their arms, they had not been bound, nor had they been ordered to keep their hands up. This was a good sign.

A table, clearly appropriated from the bank's break room, had been set up in the middle of the lobby, and a portable lamp that was similar to the kind Kaly had seen brought out on summer nights back on her mother-world, illuminated a trio of women. They were older than the guards, and from their look, two of them had been asleep when the team's presence had been announced.

The third, and the youngest of the group, regarded them suspiciously. She had a thin face, and a hawk-like nose, and her expression was one of deep distrust. Like her companions, she was wearing surplus ETR fatigues, and a dark pink beret decorated by a Venus' Mirror with a fist rising from its center.

From the information that had been provided to them in their briefing, Kaly knew her as Yúna Santavaar, the leader of the group, and she recognized the insignia on her headgear as the symbol for their movement. As for the pink beret itself, she recalled hearing that in the old Star Federation and in the ETR, the color was traditionally considered to be a 'woman's color' and represented passivity (although she couldn't imagine why). She had also been told that *La Ermanyaa* was attempting to 'reframe it as the color of female power'. Personally, she hated pink, but the sentiment at least, was noble.

"Who are you?" Santavaar demanded. "Why have you come here?"

"We are from the Sisterhood," N'Elemay replied. "We have been sent to help you."

The woman's eyes narrowed in distrust. "Easy enough for you to say. How do I know you're not just lying to us?"

"You want proof then."

"I do. You could just as easily be *putayas* working for the men, sent out here to fool a bunch of stupid women."

"Agreed," N'Elemay returned. "We could be what you say—but if we were, then what about the vehicle that brought us here—or our equipment?"

"Some kind of new military hardware," Santavaar challenged. "Men are always dreaming up new ways to kill each other."

N'Elemay sighed. "True enough, and certainly possible. But we can do other things that your military can't. Getting in here was just one of them. I need you to believe us and listen to me."

"I'm sure that you do," the woman retorted. "But I'm not sure that I need to *do* either thing."

N'Elemay frowned, and then closed her eyes. Kaly tensed, knowing that she was sending a psiever signal—and what was coming next.

More Marauders seemed to appear out of thin air all around them, dressed in full fighting armor. They trained their weapons on the guards, and the women at the table. Anticipating trouble, Team 5 hadn't come alone. Teams 12 and 7 had also made their way into the town by Nightingale, and they had simply been waiting for the signal from N'Elemay to act.

"*Now* will you listen to me?" she asked.

Having no alternative, Yúna Santavaar and her associates did listen, and the negotiations began. It took the better part of an hour to convince the rebel leadership that their effort was hopeless. In the end, what made them agree to do what the Troop Leader was asking of them was what she offered in exchange.

***

The next morning, just before dawn, the first units of the Garda Nacia cautiously made their way into the town. Even though their observation posts had confirmed that the rebel sentries had all left their positions, and that there was no sign of life in the rest of the town, they were wary of ambushes. When none came, their concerns changed, and to a man, they began to dread the possibility that they would find the rebels, and their male prisoners, all lying dead somewhere from an act of murder-suicide.

This fear proved groundless. After twenty minutes, every one of the hostages had been located. All of them were alive, and aside from some cuts and bruises, unharmed.

But the women who had held them captive were absent. To the immense shock and disbelief of the Garda's commanding officer, every single one of the rebels had somehow managed to vanish without a trace. The only sign of them was a large piece of graffiti, spray-painted on the bank's wall. It was the Venus' Mirror again, but this time, instead of a clenched fist, its hand was giving them the middle finger. And underneath this was a cryptic message: *"We'll be back!"*

Naturally, a priority planet-wide alert was sent out on all military and police channels, and the media engaged in the wildest speculation possible about the whereabouts of the militants. Some journalists placed them in Nuvo Bolivar, and others postulated that they had scattered into the countryside. A few even came close to the truth when they suggested that the women had somehow gotten themselves off-planet and traveled to another system in the ETR.

In reality, the tiny band was safely ensconced aboard the USSNS *Cathay Williams*, headed with its Macha class escort, for Larra's Lament and the Marine Special Operations Training Facility. Women such as Yúna Santavaar and groups like *La Ermanyaa* were simply far too precious to abandon, and they would have their uses in the months and years ahead.

As for Kaly and her team, as soon as they had completed the exfiltration, they were ordered out on another mission. It wouldn't be nearly as easy, or as short as Alquibar had been by any means.

CHAPTER 9

Nancaan District, Angelaz Cia, Treya Angelaz, Santosena System, Argenta Provensa, Esteral Terrana Rapabla, 1044.08|20|01:86:70

The fundamental strategy of conquering a star-system was a fairly straightforward process. First, the enemy was engaged in space, and once they were defeated, assault forces were sent to deal with whatever the opposition had in place 'downside'. Of the two phases, the battle in space could be comparatively brief, while operations on a planet's surface might be protracted in nature, even with the benefit of fire support from friendly assets in orbit.

The Special Expeditionary Force had multiple systems to contend with, and a large enemy naval presence spread throughout them. Admiral da'Kayt's solution had been to focus on speed, superior technology, and surprise, to defeat the Hriss clans in space, and then to have the SEF move on after every successful engagement to the next star system. This tactic effectively stranded the Hriss ground forces, and kept the SEF from becoming bogged-down in any one location.

The dirty job of actually consolidating control of the planets themselves, and eliminating stranded Hriss assets, fell to the ETR regular army, which followed behind the SEF naval forces, and Sisterhood Marine units.

SpecOps played a vital role in this. The basic mission of the Marauder Teams was to insert themselves well in advance of any conventional forces and conduct reconnaissance and sabotage operations. They were also expected to train and assist local resistance forces where they existed, so that these indigenous units could serve as advisors and scouts once the regular infantry and armor arrived.

One star-system where this was slated to occur was Santosena in the Argenta Provensa. The SEF was still busy back in Qyarda, and ETR ground forces were finalizing their control over Tiyas, with Tensamentra scheduled as their next stop. For the moment at least, Santosena was firmly under Hriss control, both in space, and downside.

The USSNS *Nancy Hart* had been sent out ahead of the Expeditionary

Force to deliver Marauder Teams to Treya Angelaz, which was the most populated world in the system. The *Hart* was a veteran of many SpecOps missions, and when it entered Santosena, the light cruiser deftly slipped past the Hriss picket-ships without raising the slightest alarm. Once on-station over Treya Angelaz, it discharged its cargo of Nightingales and then assumed a hidden, standby position on the dark side of the world's only moon.

The Nightingales didn't loiter. When they were clear of the *Hart*, they snuck down to the surface of the planet and dropped their Teams, and all of their supplies, at pre-designated landing-zones.

For Team 5, this was a rubble strewn vacant lot at the very edge of the Nancaan District in Angelaz Cia, the largest and most strategically important city on Treya Angelaz.

Team 5 was just one of ten teams that had been assigned to help the indigenous population carry on their fight against the Hriss in Angelaz Cia. They had been exhaustively briefed in advance about the terrain, local customs and the language. The PTS feeds in Espangla in particular, had been augmented by live tutoring courtesy of Captain Rodraga and Trooper Jon fa'Teela, and Rodraga had been responsible for giving them additional details about the people that they would be working with.

The team's mission entailed what SpecOps did best; blowing things up, and teaching other people how to blow things up better. Thanks to the disclosure made to the ETR populace about the Sisterhood's existence, this task had been made even easier. The team would be able to operate openly, and use their own equipment instead of second-rate ETR hand-me-downs.

They were also on Treya Angelaz for the long haul. The best estimate that they had been given was a couple of weeks, and up to a full month downside before they could expect conventional ETR and Marine units, or any space-based fire-support. And for Kaly, as the newest team member, this was to be her first extended mission.

Even though the rendezvous had been prearranged through the ETR liaisons with the local guerilla forces, the team wasn't taking any chances with their security. The instant that they were out of the Nightingale, they took up positions, activated their camouflage and made ready with their weapons, waiting for either an attack, or the arrival of their hosts.

A good 10 minutes passed before Kaly spotted a humanoid figure rising up from behind a pile of rubble and making its way towards them. She automatically centered her rifle on the figure's head, and dialed up the Bio and Thermal scans as she zoomed in. It was a human, she saw, a human male dressed in a combination of ETR camo fatigues and civilian clothing. Not that this was any relief, or gave her any cause to cease tracking him with Tatiana. According to Captain Rodraga, some members of the human population of Angelaz Cia had turned traitor and were trying to save their skins by actively aiding the Hriss.

The male walked into the open, put down his weapon, raised his hands and waited. From the shadows off to the left and behind him, Kaly heard N'Elemay issue the prearranged challenge. "Dog", she said.

"Town", the man answered, giving her the correct countersign. He was a friendly.

N'Elemay and T'Jinna stood, but Kaly and Margasdaater stayed where they were, continuing to scan the area for hostiles. N'Elemay and the man spoke for a minute, and then the Troop Leader sent a psiever message out to the pair. They could abandon their positions. The team was moving out.

More resistance fighters appeared out of the shadows. They were as ragtag as the first man, and Kaly realized that several of them were actually children and teenagers, the oldest being no more than 12 to 14 Standard years at the most.

Like the adults in their party, they were well armed, and all of them had the same hardened, battle weary expressions. War had never spared the young its horrors, and when there weren't enough adults left alive to fight, it often drafted the young to carry on with the struggle.

At a command from the adult male, the little band helped the team carry their heavy cases, and they started off together. Their guides led them through a tangled maze of broken buildings and wrecked vehicles. Kaly had been made aware that the city of Treya Angelaz, or simply 'Angelaz' was divided up into three districts; Pica, Nancaan, and Fortema. The Hriss occupied Pica, where the city spaceport was located. The rest of the ruined metropolis was only theirs during the daytime however. At night, Nancaan and Fortema belonged to the resistance forces, but not without continuing challenge from the Hriss.

Once, the party was forced to stop and wait while armored hover vehicles flew overhead. Their guides, whose clothing lacked the optical invisibility, IR, Bio and Thermal protection that SpecOps uniforms possessed, used the rubble and the derelict vehicles around them for concealment instead. Knowing what she did about ETR equipment, Kaly knew that this maneuver really amounted to a desperate hope that the Hriss scanners wouldn't turn their way. Which, the Lady mercifully decided, they didn't.

Then, from somewhere off to the north, there was the hollow 'whump' of a huge explosion, followed by weapons fire, and the vehicles near them departed, heading off towards the disturbance at top speed.

Hand signs in Sireeni from N'Elemay told Kaly and the rest the story. The resistance, knowing that they were headed in, had arranged for a little 'distraction' to make the going a bit easier. They had blown up a local supply depot. Keeping low and moving along behind the remains of a brick wall, Kaly had to admit that even though they were poorly equipped and badly outnumbered, the city's human fighters did have some serious *gyna.*

Five minutes later, they were joined by another small group of men and one woman. They were also armed, and from the direction they had come, she guessed that they had been the cause behind the explosions. The woman made eye contact with her as they met up, and they gave each other brief nods of acknowledgement. Although they were from two entirely different societies, separated by centuries and radically different belief systems, the silent exchange between them expressed what they *did* have in common. They were fighting the same war, against the same enemy.

The guerillas guided them through the devastation and into a building that looked like it was ready to collapse at any moment, from the outside at least. But as they moved into the shadowy interior, Kaly saw that it had been carefully shored up to prevent the walls from actually falling. Further in, they came to a staircase, and went down into a basement. At the rear of the chamber, the wall concealed a hidden door, and beyond that, a long passage that was barely high enough to stand in.

A ladder had been positioned at the end of this, which led down to another passage, and another, until they came out into what had been a sewer tunnel when the city had still been a place for people to live their lives in. From here, they transferred through a break in the tunnel wall and into a much larger tunnel that was instantly identified by it's rusted single rail as an abandoned mag-way. There, a wall with a heavy door had been built, blocking the passage. It had slits cut in it that Kaly guessed were weapons ports and looking around her, she was also reasonably certain that the tunnels they had been moving through had been planted with explosive charges, and other nasty traps, all along their length.

When they reached the armored door, it opened, and her surmise about the slits proved correct. On the other side, a resistance fighter, another man, was manning a heavy energy gun similar to the kind that her own forces used, and there was a homemade control box nearby, with wires running back out to the mag-way tunnel. The man smiled at them as they passed, and Kaly made sure to return his friendly expression.

Another armored door lay beyond, and an armed fighter also manned it, and behind him, was a final door, set off to the side. This opened up into a tunnel that had once been used for service access to the main mag-way lines.

Here, the fighters had taken the space and partitioned it off using scavenged materials to create niches for living quarters, weapons storage, communications, and in one chamber that had once housed machinery, even a makeshift hospital. The place was crowded, and ripe with the odor of human bodies, and when she came nearer to the hospital, she could smell blood and underneath this, the fetid odor of sepsis. She very nearly gagged, but when she saw that her Teammates and the Resistance fighters were unaffected by it, she fought the reaction down.

The cramped space was also lit, using what had once been work lights, strung along its 'ceiling'. This was also lined with sheets that had been made from ETR uniform blouses. Knowing from her own experience that the cloth had a limited ability to mask IR signatures, she understood their purpose immediately. They were a primitive form of shielding from Hriss ground scans.

And in gaps between the sheets, she spotted an additional layer of metal plating. Metal, she recalled from her training, was the one thing that T'lakskalan seeker beams couldn't penetrate. This makeshift arrangement wasn't the most secure, but it was better than nothing at all, and with the shelter being deep underground, and in a remote area, only added to its overall effectiveness. The insurgent's hideout was as secure as such limited resources would allow, and for the time being at least, it would be their home and base of operations.

Their original guide and his companions led them past the other residents of the place, who greeted them with either cautious smiles, or expressions of careful reserve. On the whole, the fighters were clearly glad to have assistance in any form, but by the uniforms and the gear the team wore, and word sent out in advance about them by the ETR, they knew Kaly and her sisters for foreigners, and therefore an unknown quantity.

At a wider spot in the tunnel, which had been created by digging into the walls to either side, they met the local resistance commander. He was dressed in the same assortment of scavenged clothing as his fellows, and he was bearded like most of the males were, but his facial hair had been carefully trimmed, and he possessed an unmistakable aura of leadership. N'Elemay stepped forwards and immediately introduced herself.

"Troop Leader Ellen n'Elemay," she said, extending her hand as they had been taught,"United Sisterhood of Suns Marine Corps, Marauder Team 5."

The man gave her an appraising glance, and then he smiled and shook her hand. "Captain Carloz Morana," he returned. "1st Garda Nacia, Angelaz Cia."

At the pre-mission briefing, the team had been told that the local resistance was made up from remnants of the local civil militia and civilian volunteers. They were divided into three groups; the guerilla fighters, irregular scouts, and an underground element that was composed of slaves in Hriss captivity. This group funneled vital information on enemy troop strengths and movements through the irregulars to the guerilla bands.

Morana had also been mentioned in the team's briefing. Before the Hriss take-over, he had been a Corporal, but had become an officer both by default, and personal merit. He was reputed, by the ETR at least, to be a very competent resistance leader and had been put in charge of their area of operations.

"We were told about our new allies," he said. "Welcome to Treya Angelaz. You'll find plenty of Hriss to kill here I think."

"We were hoping so, Captain," N'Elemay replied.

"Private Estabanya will show you were you can stow your gear, and get you some food, " Morana said. "I am sure that after your long trip, you are all hungry."

His eyes fell on the large cases that they had brought with them, and N'Elemay obliged his curiosity by opening up the first two.

One of these held rations, sent from the ETR, and intended for the fighters. According to their briefing, the resistance survived only by what the irregulars could scavenge from the ruins, what they managed to catch, or what the slaves smuggled out for them. Rat, Kaly recalled, was often the main course.

The second case was even more welcome. "Medical supplies," N'Elemay explained.

She opened the third case last, and Morana's eyes sparkled with pure delight. Inside of it were Harpy-10 ATAA Anti-tank/Anti-armor rockets, and shoulder fired launchers. These state of the art weapons had been sent straight from the Sisterhood Armament factories on Nightshade, in the Artemi Elant, and some wag had even taken the time to use lipstick to add the imprint of her lips to the case, and written in grease pencil the phrase, '*Ton ave la baiz*', 'Given with a kiss'.

"Some gifts for the Hriss Hovertanks, courtesy of the Sisterhood," she explained.

Morana grinned. "How thoughtful. I will look forwards to helping you to make a proper presentation of them."

"I can show you to where you'll be staying," a woman's voice said from behind Kaly. She turned around to see the woman who had helped guide them in. "I am Private Marisol Estabanya." She was also rather attractive, and Kaly didn't miss the hungry gleam in Margasdaater's eyes.

"Fraal anref, shöna dar, "the Zommerlaandar said, stepping forwards and extending her large hand. "I am Corporal Margasdaater, and zis is my

friend Corporal n'Deena. I am very pleased to meet zuch a beautiful voman in a place like zis."

The Private blushed deeply, caught off guard by the compliment—and the fact that it had just come from another woman, but she did smile back. Kaly was scandalized. Margasdaater was utterly brazen.

N'Elemay caught the exchange, and signed to them both in Sireeni, *You two! Stop chasing 'split' and pay attention!*

Kaly was beginning to protest her innocence when the lights overhead went off and then on again in rapid succession. Captain Morana, who had been in the process of showing the Troop Leader the overall disposition of the Hriss forces in Pica, held up his hand.

"There is a flyover coming," he told them. "The Hriss regularly scan this district from space to try and locate us. Please forgive the interruption and the darkness."

With that, he glanced over to one of his guerillas, who was standing next to a large switch. The man activated it and all of the lights, and everything else, including communications equipment, went dead. For the next few minutes, everyone stayed where they were and kept silent. Then, at his command, the lights came back on, and all activities resumed.

Morana continued with what he had been saying as if there hadn't been any interruption at all. "The local Hriss forces are composed of elements from the Skullsplitter and Blood Reaver Clans. Their leader is a junior chief called M'Kwa'tan'tka.'

"So far, his policy has been to keep his units, and especially his artillery, clustered around the spaceport, and he has only sent out a few patrols to try and engage us. Either he is satisfied that we are not a threat worth dealing with, or he doesn't want to get his nose bloodied.'

"Whatever the truth is, Hriss activity in Nancaan has been limited largely to automated scavenging operations. We have a raid party going out shortly to disrupt one of these. I would like to invite you to join us."

Knowing that this would be an excellent opportunity for each faction to see something of the other's mettle, N'Elemay immediately accepted, and volunteered Margasdaater's expertise. When he heard what the Zommerlaandar had in mind for the mission, Morana was very pleased.

***

Kaly recognized the machines working below them with instant distaste. The automated scavengers were exactly the same models that had been used by the Hriss on her motherworld to strip it of its vital resources, and they were committing the same atrocities here.

The robots traveled together in a group like the ancient trains of Old Gaia. The machines in the lead performed the initial processing. They were huge squat things that moved along on broad, flat tracks. Enormous open maws set with gigantic teeth, dug into the ground and fed the material onto belts, and from there, back to row upon row of whirling metal blades, and hammers the size of hovercars.

It didn't matter whether they encountered a building, a vehicle, or a part of the landscape; everything that the mechanical mouths consumed was shredded, pulverized and sent out the rear to a second group of robots behind them.

These were smaller units, with finer teeth and metal vacuum hoses that collected the tailings and chopped everything down into more manageable pieces. This was then conveyed to the final group where everything was automatically sorted by material into long rolling bucket cars for storage, and eventual collection.

The scavenger train moved in perfect unison, letting nothing slow it down or alter its formation. And where it had passed, only a swath of flat, dead earth remained, stretching away until it disappeared on the horizon. Like their makers, the scavenger machines were ruthless, inflexible and destructive.

Kaly looked over at her companion and sympathized with the churning emotions behind her grim expression. It was hard to watch your world being completely raped of everything and then have the added agony of watching it happen slowly. But like her, Marisol Estabanya was a soldier, and knew that here at least, a stiff price would be exacted from the Hriss.

The woman pressed a button on her binoculars and readjusted their focus. "No tanks," she whispered. Like Kaly, Marisol was a sniper, and she was providing security while Margasdaater worked with the guerilla fighters below them.

This wasn't the first time that either she or the Garda had dealt with scavenger trains, and according to Captain Morana, whenever the trains were attacked, the hovertanks came. To date, the guerillas had been unable to prevail against them and the team was hoping to reverse this negative trend.

A moment later, the Hriss machines reached the spot that Margasdaater had chosen for their ambush, and when they did, she sent her signal. The bombs buried under the ground were primitive things, constructed from rockets and artillery shells that the resistance had either stolen from Hriss depots, or what had been left behind after the regular army's defeat. Their triggers used only plain wire and a simple electrical charge to initiate everything. As primitive as this was however, the arrangement still served quite handily.

When the IED's went off, they punched up through the bellies of the lead machines, gutting their innards. Black smoke and flame belched out of the collector mouths and the cruel metal teeth scattered in all directions. The rest of the train, now leaderless, ground to a halt, impotent and useless. It was a wonderful sight.

Barely two minutes passed before a pair of hovertanks made their appearance. The scavenger train had been moving through the middle of the ruined city, creating its own avenue of destruction, and the hovertanks followed their trail, their turret guns ranging angrily around them for something to shoot at. From the concealment of a ruined building there was a sharp report and a rocket flew out at the nearest one. Because of the tank's shielding, the blast did little beyond angering its crew, and the monster turned and fired towards what the gunner thought were the humans serving the launcher.

Its partner joined in the fusillade, turning the building into rubble and clouds of dust. As a result, neither of them were prepared for the two additional rockets that came at them from the rear. These were Harpies, and when they hit the tanks, they punched right past their shielding and destroyed them easily.

Even as the last bits of shattered armor were hitting the earth, a message came over Kaly's psiever; *All team members! Extract and move to rally point 'Freda'.*

Kaly was already in motion. One lesson she had learned early on in her Sniper Training was the basic concept of 'shoot and scoot.' Snipers *never* stayed in one place very long. Marisol, lacking a psiever, hadn't received N'Elemay's message, but she was experienced enough to have anticipated it, and followed Kaly without being told.

In the meantime, the Hriss had a few things to say about the loss of their tanks, and they made their reply with artillery. Kaly heard the hollow reports of their long range field guns down at the spaceport opening up, followed by the shrill whistles of rounds coming down overhead. A nanosecond later, the area immediately above the scavenger train erupted as thousands of bomblets unleashed their destructive power.

Typical Shovelheads, she thought as she took cover. They were so intent on killing their enemies that they didn't worry about the thin possibility that their comrades might still be alive, or the fact that they were doing the team's job for them, and destroying all the robots that the IED's had missed. She blew a grateful kiss up the Goddess for having made them as stupid as they were, and then sprinted to join her companions.

***

The next couple of weeks went badly for the Hriss and their leader M'Kwa'tan'tka. More of their automated scavengers were sabotaged, and they lost so many tanks that they finally ceased sending them out on punitive missions. They also stopped inadvertently destroying their own equipment with artillery.

Instead, their tactics changed over to the use of air power, seeking out the guerillas by sensor. But when this failed, thanks to the team's instruction on better concealment techniques, and an emphasis on remotely initiated weapons, the invaders resorted to a more old-fashioned technique. They sent out ground troops on reconnaissance-by-fire missions, and in company sized units. It was a good response, in theory, and it failed precisely because it was a theory. It was also the perfect opportunity for Kaly and Marisol.

When the Hriss sent out a particularly tempting group, the two snipers and their security were waiting for them, along with a combined party of guerillas and team members. The Hriss patrol was moving down the center of one of the few streets that was clear enough of rubble to make a column formation possible, and Kaly had to admit as she watched them in her riflescope, that their spacing was good. None of the warriors below her position was too close to the next one in line, and they all seemed well armed, and alert. The presence of a hovertank flying overwatch above them lent the unit a great deal of firepower, and they had made good progress, moving deep into the Nancaan District.

As the warriors reached a pre-designated spot in the road, Kaly sent one short burst on the radio-headset the Garda had lent her to talk with Marisol. Then, sighting in on a warrior walking point at the head of the column, she counted down from five to one.

At 'one', she fired and so did Marisol, who had targeted a warrior in the middle of the formation. Both Hriss went down at the same instant. Caught in a sudden crossfire coming from two directions, the Hriss scattered to either side of the road, finding what they believed was excellent cover to reply from.

Kaly and Marisol were already moving to other positions however, and Margasdaater had a surprise of her own for the Hriss; charges had been buried right under where some of the warriors had positioned themselves. Their 'excellent cover' turned into a death trap when the Zommerlaandar set them off.

Some of the surviving warriors ran from their positions in a panic, and improvised claymores that had also been set in place, either ended their flight, or drove what was left of the group right back into the killing zone.

The hovertank responded to this carnage with fire from its main and secondary guns, trying to land a lucky shot on their unseen enemies. It missed hitting anything by a light year, but any shame that its crew might have suffered was ended when a Harpy rocket destroyed it.

Now completely alone, the remaining Hriss infantry was in total disarray. Kaly and Marisol took advantage of this, picking off the survivors with the help of their teammates. By the time they had finished shooting, the entire column had been wiped out to the last warrior.

N'Elemay paused only long enough to compose a final message to the pursuers that were sure to come. It was delivered in two parts.

The first was conveyed with a can of spray paint, and she gave Captain Morana the honors. The man painted a quick "1st Garda" on the shattered remnants of a wall near the largest pile of Hriss corpses.

Kaly didn't understand what this was intended to accomplish and T'Jinna enlightened her by psiever. It was, she learned, an ancient gang custom that had migrated from Gaia to the cities on Delgen, Thermadon and the darker parts of Corrissa. It warned intruders that they were trespassing into forbidden territory. Territory that the 1st Garda owned. Although the team had played a significant part in the operation, it was SpecOps protocol to give the credit wherever possible to native forces. Marauder Teams weren't interested in publicity, and they didn't need their egos stroked. It was sufficient that they had helped to create the success.

N'Elemay inspected the graffiti with a critical eye, and then she said, "I think it's still missing something," and turned to Margasdaater. "Astrid, what's your opinion?"

"Yah, za *Shovelheads* may not underztand zomething zo complicated. I have an idea." The big woman went over to the bodies and knelt down, taking out her combat knife.

While Kaly watched with nauseated fascination, Margasdaater sawed off the head of one of the Hriss warriors with the big blade. The Zommerlaandar went about her task quite cheerfully, and once it was loose, she took her gory prize over to N'Elemay. Together, they impaled the hideous thing on a piece of pipe that Morana had found for them in the rubble. As sickening as it was, Kaly had to admit that it conveyed a message that any language, or level of intelligence, would understand clearly, and without any need for translation.

The words of an Instructor from SpecOps School came back to her as they left the gruesome tableau behind them. *'War is hard,'* the woman had said *'and sometimes we must commit acts that the average woman would never understand, or could ever bring herself to do. Get used to it.'* This was just another level of that learning process.

***

That night, Kaly found it hard to sleep. Not because she was unaccustomed to sleeping in the field, but due to the closeness of the bunker-tunnels, and the lack of privacy this created. It made it completely impossible for her not to notice the activities of everyone else around her. Especially the male-female couples.

A few spaces down, Marisol and Captain Morana (who, much to Margasdaater's profound disappointment, had turned out to be the young woman's bed partner) were together. And the sounds of pleasure that Marisol was making made it quite clear what they were doing behind the privacy drape.

Get on with it already! Kaly thought, gritting her teeth. Personally, she couldn't imagine what it would be like to make love to a male, and she really didn't want to, nor did she need such an incomprehensible act going on right next-door. Even so, as she listened, she realized that Marisol didn't seem terribly unhappy about what was taking place at all.

Shock and horror followed right on the heels of this. *Goddess! It would be just like doing it with an animal!*

Unable to stand it any longer, she pulled out a field dressing from her belt kit and stuffed pieces of it into her ears. It didn't block out everything, but it helped her ignore enough of the racket to drift off.

Several more days passed, and after a particularly successful raid against a Hriss supply area, the fighters returned to their hideout, and celebrated all of their recent victories with the team. A lot of Aqqa and some local stuff the fighters called *Mezacal* got passed around, and Kaly managed to get herself truly and thoroughly drunk, right along with her sisters.

So drunk in fact, that she barely noticed N'Elemay and Morana talking intently, and then leaving the impromptu party together. Or the bottle in N'Elemay's hand.

Kaly put it out of her mind right away. The taciturn Troop Leader often went off on odd errands, and speaking in private with the resistance leader was certainly her prerogative.

Later that night, and in the face of more important events, she forgot all about it. She was fast asleep when she felt someone shaking her awake. It was Margasdaater.

"Kaly! Get oop!" the woman said. "Za Hriss are zearching za tunnels—ve have to bug out!"

Despite the effects of the alcohol in her system, Kaly was up and dressed in less than a minute. Grabbing her gear, she followed Margasdaater into the larger common area. Everyone there was moving fast, carrying out whatever they could, and heading out of the shelter for the tunnel beyond.

N'Elemay was waiting there with T'Jinna. "We're to assist a rear guard to cover the escape and delay the Hriss," she said just as a pair of guerillas rushed by with a stretcher loaded up with one of their wounded.
"Once the main party is clear, we'll rendezvous with them at another hideout."

Corporal Estabanya ran up to them. "I am to make sure you stay clear of the traps we have set for *diya Putadaza*." This was a slang term the Garda often used when referring to the Hriss. It meant 'Sons of Whores'. Kaly grinned right along with everyone else, even though the meaning of the slight eluded her somewhat, and followed the team out of the shelter.

Once outside, Marisol played out the wires from a makeshift control box, and they moved together to a junction of the service corridor and the main tunnel. Then they waited.

The Hriss weren't long in coming. Their arrival was heralded by the distinctive sound of a battlebot tromping down to the armored doors, and then the screech of the barrier being torn from its hinges.

The warriors came next. These were not regular infantry; they were the special Honor Killers, the rough equivalent of a Marauder Team, and they followed behind the 'bot with great care, letting it go through the entire shelter before risking entry themselves.

When the Hriss were all inside, Marisol tripped the arming switch for her box. But when she pressed the button to set off the explosives concealed in the dwelling, nothing happened.

No one was terribly surprised. Either the 'bot, or the warriors, had found the wires and disarmed the devices. The intent had not been to catch them with the improvised weapons however—that had merely been a gamble that had not paid off. The real plan had been to delay their pursuers long enough for the guerillas to escape, and the give the team further opportunities to misdirect them.

N'Elemay had her companions remain where they were until she heard the door at their end opening up, and then she hurled a simple flash-bang grenade in its direction. The loud report had its intended effect. The Hriss and the 'bot fired in their direction, and as they retreated down the tunnel, the Honor Killers ran after them.

A little ways in, the team came to a junction in the tunnel. There were more explosives packed in there, in a hollow that had been carved out of the cement walls, and a simple trip wire served as the trigger. Margasdaater reached into her hip pack and produced a spool of wire, and tied a long length of it onto the arrangement, turning it into a pull-cord. Playing this out as she went, she backed away from the device while the women behind her made for another intersection further on.

Once everyone was there, N'Elemay halted them and produced a microbot launcher, discharging the tiny 'bot back down the passage they had just vacated. Right away, it began transmitting images of the Hriss battlebot peering into the tunnel like some trepidacious prehistoric insect.

The Hriss Honor Killers hung back and let the machine probe ahead for them. As soon as the 'bot found the booby trap, it paused to examine it, and seeing the wire leading off into the darkness, began to bring its manipulator arm into play to sever the line and disarm the device.

Margasdaater smiled, and let a GSG-20 grenade fly. The 'bot spotted the munition as it came around the corner, and its AI decided to engage it first, giving the Zommerlaandar the second that she needed to pull the wire. To its credit, the 'bot managed to shoot the GSG down on the wing before the explosives went off and blew it to bits. Down the tunnel, the Hriss could be heard yelling in anger and then the passage was filled with blaster fire and grenades of their own.

But the team was already on the run again, and leading them well away from the main body of the Garda fighters. Shortly, they came to another trap. This was a simple box, suspended inside of what had been an overhead air vent, and like the first device, a trip wire activated it.

Instead of explosives, it contained a species of poisonous insect that Marisol later told Kaly was called the *masqyara*, or 'death mask' beetle. Its venom was fatal to either humans, or as the guerillas had learned, the Hriss, possessing an enzyme that broke down flesh at a horrific rate. And there were hundreds, if not thousands of the venomous things inside the box. The moment that the group was well clear of it, Marisol let the beetles loose and then everyone gave the spot the distance, and respect, that it deserved.

This proved to be something that not even a battlebot could have handled, and although the Hriss finally resorted to a few grenades to clear the creatures out, it slowed them down even further, and enraged them more than ever. The game went on and on like this for several more minutes, and the frustration of the Honor Killers reached almost comedic proportions.

But like all things good or evil, the time came for it to end. Realizing that they would not catch up to their quarry, the Hriss warriors ceased their pursuit and let another agency take over for them. Kaly became aware of the change when the sounds behind them grew distant, and then ceased altogether. Then, from overhead, something rebounded down through the air vents. A slight 'pop' followed, and the tunnel behind them became filled with a thick white gas. No one needed any explanation of what this was, and with Marisol in the lead, they quickly found a ladder up to the surface and evacuated the passage.

There was another Hriss patrol waiting for them on the surface, but the Goddess was with the team. The warriors hadn't been prepared to cover every possible exit and had been keeping watch on another manhole. As the women came out from behind them, the warriors turned around in surprise.

The one nearest Kaly was an officer. She knew this because he carried a medium sized *Akskakt't*, a Sword of Honor that she recognized from a class in Hriss weaponry back in Basic. Instead of going for his pistol, the creature roared and drew his blade, slashing out at her with it even as it left its sheath.

Kaly stepped backwards to avoid the strike, tripped on something and fell backwards, which is what saved her life. Thanks to her clumsiness, the blade missed making a cut that would have otherwise slit her wide open from hip to sternum.

Hitting the ground, she fired her submachinegun at the creature. The 10 mm rounds ripped their way straight up through the center of his body, tearing into his armor and spattering her with greenish yellow blood. The officer fell, and another warrior, who had just been making ready to fire at N'Elemay, saw the blade leave his leader's hand and broke off his attack to leap for it. The Hriss never abandoned their Honor swords, even to the point of dying for them if they had to.

He never recovered the weapon however. N'Elemay shot him with her own submachinegun, and then as he fell, fired over his descending body at another warrior who had been standing right behind him. The firefight, as such, was over in seconds, and all the Hriss were either dead, or mortally wounded.

While Kaly wiped the gore out of her eyes, Margasdaater reached down and picked up the sword. "Nice vork, Kaly! Zis is your's", she declaired, handing her the weapon. "You hold onto zat—it's vorth plenty of credits if you ever vant to zell it."

Still a little stunned by the speed and violence of their encounter, Kaly stood and absently took it from her, sticking it into the rear straps of her web gear so that it rode out of the way across her shoulders. It made her look like some Nemesian martial artist, and she definitely didn't feel like one at the moment; just a clumsy 'greenie' who had managed to get lucky.

Next to her, N'Elemay administered the coup de gras to two warriors who weren't quite dead, and then, putting her silenced pistol away in its oversized holster, signaled for everyone to move out. Her smile, as it always was at a time like this, was blissful. And from the look in her eyes when she glanced at Kaly, the young woman could tell that her Troop Leader was proud of her.

The moment passed, and N'Elemay urged everyone to follow Marisol deeper into the ruins. A dozen minutes later they found another underground entrance and a tunnel that eventually led to their new hiding place.

By the time the team stumbled into their cots, it was dawn.

To express their unhappiness about the raid on their tunnels, the team went out with the Garda the following day. Their mission was another ambush on a Hriss infantry company.

The intel that they'd received had come from slaves working for the Hriss, relayed through the irregular couriers. According to the breathless boy, junior chief M'Kwa'tan'tka had been replaced for his incompetence, Hriss style. After he had been publicly beheaded, a new leader was put in charge, calling himself T'Kan'at'kvet.

T'Kan'at'kvet was supposed to be a cannier opponent than his predecessor, and had immediately decreed that incursions into Nancaan be increased in both frequency, and aggressiveness. Not that this bothered the team or Captain Morana overmuch. The hapless M'Kwa'tan'tka had promised the same great things, with dismal results. They intended to see to it that T'Kan'at'kvet shared the same fate.

Following his edict, a punitive force of two companies of infantry had set out from the Spaceport that same morning and were reported to be marching straight down the middle of the district, clearly intent on another reconnaissance-by-fire mission. The success of any ambush on a force of this kind utterly depended on the accuracy of the intelligence that the attackers received, and when he was asked, Morana assured them that his source in the underground had always been reliable.

Initially, his claim seemed sound. The irregular scouts located the Hriss detachment easily, and once it was clear which direction they were taking, the team and a select group of guerilla fighters used the tunnel network to move to a spot ahead of them where Margasdaater would set up her explosives.

It was the perfect location. That portion of the city was made up of multistory buildings, and the road that the Hriss were using was lined on both sides not only by these tall structures, but sizable piles of rubble, making any deviation difficult and slow. To make it even more ideal, the road turned sharply at the far end and was partially blocked with debris, creating a narrow choke point that would force the warriors to pick their way through it to the other side. The team had no intentions of letting them manage to get that far though.

Once they had arrived, Kaly found a 'hide' for herself on the third floor of one of the office buildings lining the road that gave her the best view of the kill zone. She had commandeered a badly dented desk to set up a rest for Tatiana, and although the gaping hole in front of her, which had once been a window, was large, she was well hidden by the shadows and a piece of plastic screen that she had scavenged for herself. To add to her stealthiness, she had darkened her skin, and wore a special poncho that was made of the same material as her fatigues. Activated, it mimicked the colors and tones of the room around her to perfection.

Marisol was crouched next to her, acting as a spotter and watching through her riflescope for the first sign of the enemy. The young woman had borrowed another poncho for herself and had taken the additional step of taping over the lenses of her scope so that only a thin slit was exposed to any reflected light. She was almost as well hidden as Kaly.

With all of this in place, Kaly was fairly confident that they would be invisible to anyone, or anything passing by below them. Just the same, the two of them took care to move as little as possible and said nothing as they did what snipers did best. They waited.

Just as she had been trained, Kaly made sure to alternate between looking down Tatiana's scope and away again, in order to rest her eyes and stay aware of the environment around her. For the moment, nothing was moving on the rubble-strewn street outside. And except for the wind whistling now and again through the blasted window, and the occasional sounds of what resembled birds, the only noise that came to her were from little falls of broken masonry, and small animals skittering nearby.

The silence was broken a few minutes later by a low rumble that Kaly immediately identified as the fans of a hovertank. Then she heard the unmistakable sound of footfalls mingled with the miscellaneous noises made by web gear, packs and moving bodies.

A short transmission sounded in her earpiece. It was Captain Morana. "Enemy closing; counting two infantry companies, one tank."

She leaned into her rifle and looked down her scope. Then she saw the tank, flying over the narrow street, and in its shadow, the first of the Hriss warriors. Her finger moved to rest lightly on the edge of the trigger and she brought her breathing under control. The lead warrior was still too far away for any kind of decent shot, and she wouldn't have fired without an order in any event, but when the trap was sprung, Kaly had decided that he would be the first one to die.

Her concentration was interrupted by another signal from Morana. "Be advised: the column is stopping. They are *not* in the box. Repeat—they are not in the box! Wait one."

That's strange, she thought, and a feeling of foreboding began to creep up on her. But then she told herself that it was just as possible that the company's commander was simply playing it safe. The choke point was an obvious hazard, and any soldier, human or Hriss, would have wanted to approach it with caution. If her assumption was correct, she expected to see a few warriors sent out as scouts next, running point for the rest of the column. No one came forwards however, and they were all still too far away for Margasdaater's explosives to have any effect.

Another message sounded in her earpiece, and it thoroughly chilled her blood. "All team; heavy lifters reported moving inbound from the east and northwest." These were the Hriss equivalent of heavy-duty assault shuttles, and they were not only capable of carrying troops, but also armor.

A second passed, and then Morana came on the Com again. His voice had the unmistakable edge of stress to it. "Lifters confirmed! Unloading near our position—we've got tanks! Scouts report ten coming from south, five from northwest. They must have dropped the Lifters down on us from space!"

Kaly swore, and N'Elemay sent her a message of her own, straight to her psiever, but she already knew what it would say.

Kaly—it's a trap! Bug out! Meet up in the tunnels and head to the junction at grid Dana 2. We'll regroup there.

She snatched up Tatiana and started for the stairs, with Marisol right behind her. From somewhere outside, she could hear the tanks. They were coming in fast, the rumble of their fans shaking the dust from the broken walls around her.

The pair took the stairs two and three at a time and then leapt down the final flight to the ground level. Slinging Tatiana around her shoulder, Kaly hefted her submachinegun and exited the building first. For what might lay ahead, she knew that her rifle would be useless.

She ran with Marisol out into the street and the sunlight blinded her momentarily, but then she caught sight of their escape route; an open manhole that led to the sewers below. Her teammates were running for their own boltholes, and she didn't allow herself to worry about them. They would all reach safety, Kaly told herself. Everything would be all right.

All of a sudden, one of the Irregular scouts ran out in front of her, one of the young boys. He paused when he reached the manhole and waved for her to come to him. The sound of the tank fans were much louder now, and Kaly yelled to him over their roar.

"Don't stop! Get down there!" In her raw panic, this had come out in Standard, and she quickly repeated the instruction in Espangla.

The boy hesitated, obviously waiting for her to accompany him to safety, and he yelled something back to her. Whatever it had been, was lost forever a second later when the entire side of the building next to her abruptly swelled, and then burst open like an overripe fruit.

A Hriss hovertank emerged out of the dust cloud and came into the street, nearly on top of her. Kaly dove and rolled, more out of instinct than from any acrobatic skill, and just missed being squashed flat by the falling bricks that were showering down all around her. Then she was on all fours, scrambling out of the way as the tank turned on one fan to face the small figure at the manhole.

"Jump!" she screamed. But the boy had waited too long and the tank opened up on him with its secondary guns, spitting out a stream of depleted uranium rounds. One of these hit him, and his leg disintegrated at the knee, sending what was left of the severed limb flying one way while the rest of him went the other.

Kaly would have given the Goddess anything to have been able to help him, but she was powerless against the armored monster. Instead, she did the only thing she could and dove for the nearest pile of rubble.

Another hovertank came through the hole created by its brother and shot at the manhole and the wounded scout with its main gun. This was a heavy energy cannon. The street around the hole erupted into a mass of flame and flying debris, and Kaly brought up her arm to shield her as pieces of the pavement, human flesh and metal flew everywhere. Something hit her forearm, followed by a sharp, white-hot lance of agony.

When she looked down at the limb, she realized that a sliver of metal roughly the length of her forefinger had impaled it, going right through the meat and exiting out the other side. Blood spurted up around the shrapnel immediately, and she stared at the wound, dumbfounded by horror.

Then Marisol was there, grabbing her up by her web gear and half pulling, half dragging her to the feeble safety of a low wall. Someone in the tanks saw this, and the lead machine turned towards their position and began to rake along the barrier with its secondary guns. Marisol had been in the process of opening up a field dressing, and she dropped the bandage, screaming for Kaly to move again. From somewhere, Kaly's legs obeyed, and as she ran, the wall behind them shattered into powder.

The tank crew grew tired of their cruel game, and brought the main gun to bear. There was a red flash, accompanied by a loud roar and everything in front of Kaly vanished in a cloud of dust, flame and flying debris. She felt herself being lifted up, off the ground into the very heart of the maelstrom. The sensation was almost peaceful; time seemed to hang in midair with her, completely suspended. And with the exception of a loud and persistent ringing in her ears, the scene was utterly silent.

An impact with something hard broke the spell and simultaneously drove all the air from her lungs. Kaly grunted in pain, and stared up at the open sky, dazed. *So this is it,* she thought. *This is where I die.*

Anger surged up through her. If this *was* really it, if it was her last few nanoseconds of existence, then she wasn't about to meet her end without fighting back. She wouldn't give the Hriss the satisfaction of meekly surrendering to her fate. If she had to die, she wanted her epitaph to read, *'She died fighting!'*

With a cry of agony and pure determination, she levered herself up from the ground and brought her weapon to bear with her one good arm. The tank was directly in front of her now, looming over her like a malevolent alien predator waiting to devour her whole. And Death, ever the patient one, was only a breath away, waiting on the sidelines to snatch her up when the end came.

"F-Fek you!" she snarled, letting off a burst of automatic fire. She knew that it was a useless gesture—but it was all the defiance that she still had left to offer.

Predictably, the slugs did very little beyond scratching off some of the machine's paint. Its main gun began to swing down at her, moving with an almost leisurely slowness, and Kaly prepared to meet her Goddess.

Suddenly, the machine exploded, transforming from her executioner into harmless fragments of flaming trash. Kaly blinked in incomprehension.

Before it could avenge its fallen partner, the second tank met with the same fate an instant later. As the shattered hulk embedded itself into the ground, N'Elemay and T'Jinna came out from behind a nearby wall, toting a pair of Harpy rocket launchers, their barrels still smoking from the anti-tank missiles they'd launched.

Death retreated, to await another chance, on another day. It had all the time in the universe to claim Kaly n'Deena.

Her Teammates carried her into the tunnels, and then handed her off to the Garda. She was hustled from there to the makeshift hospital the guerillas had established, and treated immediately. Somewhere in all of this, she passed out.

Hours went by, and when she finally came to, she was staring up at a patchwork collection of uniform cloth and steel plating. Her head hurt, her side hurt, her arm hurt and she couldn't move her right leg without that hurting as well. Fearing what she might behold, she looked down at her body, and to her relief, saw that she still had all of her limbs. The ringing in her ears was also still with her, but it wasn't as loud.

She looked down and saw that Margasdaater and N'Elemay had come in.

"Zo," Margasdaater said. "You're oop? Gaanz gaf! You vant a drink maybe?" She helped Kaly to sit up, and brought a canteen to her lips. The young woman only managed to take in half a sip before she coughed it out, instantly nauseated. It was Aqqa, not water.

"W-water", she managed to croak.

"Don't give her alcohol, you stupid Zommie yokel!" N'Elemay growled, pushing Margasdaater out of the way. "Stand aside!!"

She offered her her canteen and Kaly drank from it gratefully.

When she had had enough, the Troop Leader let her back down gently. Then Kaly asked the question that she had to ask. "How bad?"

"Not zo bad, Kaly," Margasdaater volunteered cheerfully. "Za doc says you have a couple of broken ribs, a broken ankle and zat your arm vill heal up now zat they pulled zat big piece of metal out of it. Za rest is all just cuts and bruises and za little knock on za head zat you got—and oh ya, n' maybe a little shock. Oh, and zey also zaid zat your inner ear got a little messed up too. But you'll be okay."

"Marisol—did she make it?"

N'Elemay shook her head gravely. "No. She didn't. Internal injuries. The 'paint' told me that it was something called 'blast lung.' It doesn't always hit right away. She died on the way back."

Kaly closed her eyes and felt a lump in her throat. Marisol had been a good fighter, and a good woman, for all the short time that they had known one other. She had also saved her life, at the cost of her own.

It wasn't fair. But life wasn't fair. Most times, it was just a big steaming pile of *shess*.

"I'd like to sleep," she said, suddenly feeling incredibly weary. N'Elemay reached out and lightly traced a design on her forehead. It was a cross, the girl realized, and a thousand questions raced through her mind. But the woman's touch was soothing, and she left them unasked.

N'Elemay whispered something, and as Kaly drifted off, she thought that it had been, "May Jesu and Mari stand watch over your dreams and speed you back to health." But the Troop Leader had pitched her voice so low that she wasn't completely sure—and she was too tired to really give a *fek* one way or the other.

***

It turned out that the operation's security had been betrayed by one of the human slaves in exchange for the promise of slightly better living conditions. The perfidious bargain was never kept however. Before the Hriss could either execute the traitor themselves, or reward him, the other slaves working for the underground exacted their revenge and killed the man with homemade knives.

This was only a thin comfort to the Garda and the team. Marisol, and the young Irregular scout had not been the only ones to die; the guerillas had lost three others and almost twice as many had been wounded, some of them severely.

With Kaly and the other survivors on the mend, operations against the Hriss had to be severely curtailed, limited only to reconnaissance missions, small-scale raids or occasional joint efforts with other forces and their Teams. Until the regulars arrived and attacked the Hriss in earnest, the 1st Garda and Marauder Team 5 were effectively out of action.

There was also one final insult, and it was dealt out solely to Kaly; her beloved Tatiana had also been a casualty of the failed ambush, bent into a misshapen mess by the same explosion that had injured her. The ruined weapon had been brought in a few days after the event, and it sat against the wall across from her cot, a mute testament to the extent of the disaster. Despite several offers to remove it though, Kaly insisted on keeping it right where it was. She knew that she would heal, and she was determined to see to it that Tatiana was fully repaired. And when she was well enough again to wield it, she would bring its crosshairs to bear on the first Hriss that she came across, and kill the *fek*—for Marisol, and for herself.

***

ETR regular infantry landed at the end of that same week, aided by Naval ships lending them massive fire support. Thanks to the team's efforts, the warships were able to destroy all of the major Hriss assets, including their artillery and armor, which made the infantry's job more of a mop-up operation than the heavy assault that everyone had anticipated. Kaly and the team were relieved and in short order, transported back to the *Athena* for some badly needed, and well earned down-time.

Although she was feeling much better by this point, Kaly was ordered to report to Medbay as soon as she was on board, and after a thorough examination of her injuries, she was prescribed an aggressive course of nanobot re-growth therapy. The biggest area of concern hadn't been her ankle though, but the damage done to her inner ears from the explosion. The 'bots responded to this right away, and with their care, it didn't appear that it would prove to be a permanent disability.

Her healing was by no means an instant process however, and she was given a prescription for painkillers and forced to accept the use of a plastic composite cane to get herself around, with *very* limited duties. Walking out of the Medbay, or more correctly hobbling, she felt like an old woman, and truly hated the stares that she received.

She tried to walk under her own power all the way to her first destination, but finally accepted a lift from a passing tram. When she reached the Armory Bay, she sought out the Head Armsmistress. Tatiana's remains had been sent upside with the team, and the woman was well aware of what she wanted.

"I can craft you a new rifle using some of the parts from this one," the Armsmistress told her. When Kaly started to object, she explained herself. "Trooper, the receiver is too badly bent for me to repair, and the barrel is a complete wipe."

She didn't add any commentary about the scope. It had been squashed flat, and looked like a very dead kzizka bug.

Kaly grimly accepted the verdict, and after receiving an estimate for how long the work would take, headed for her next appointment: Lieutenant sa'Kaali's office. They'd gone through the usual debriefing of course, so Kaly already knew that it had nothing to do with the mission, and she suspected what it was actually about. She was right.

The Lieutenant had a small presentation case in hand, and a plasti citation accompanying it, and she handed it to her as she tottered in.

"Corporal, this is for you. The Sisterhood wants you to know that it is grateful for your sacrifice." Then Sa'Kaali saluted her.

Kaly responded with the best salute she could manage, and opened the case. There was a small red service ribbon inside, along with a full-sized medal for her dress uniform. Most troopers nicknamed the award the 'Blood Ribbon', and it was given for injuries suffered in combat.

But as much as she wanted to, Kaly didn't refuse it, or share her thoughts. She simply thanked the woman and made her way back to Five-Bar and her teammates.

When Margasdaater spotted the award case, she teased her mercilessly. "Za great Blood Ribbon!" she declared. "Now you need to go out and get yourzelf zome *real* injuries—maybe a hangnail next time, yah?"

Kaly scowled at her. "I think it's stupid to give out an award just for getting hurt," she said. "Marisol got herself killed. What did she get? Fek-king nothing."

The Zommerlaandar frowned, and then her features brightened again. "Ach, Kaly," the woman said, playfully clouting her on the shoulder. "*Gaane an!* You've got to laugh or you'll just go fekking klaxxy—ve get zo many of zose dumb zings. I zhink zat maybe I have enough now to build a little house out of zem. Hmm…and maybe, zomeday I vill! You'll see! And vat a house it vill be—all red and shiny!"

Her imagery was so patently absurd that Kaly was forced to laugh. It also banished some of her gloom, and she sat down with everyone, glad to be off her feet, and free of her hated cane.

As a bottle of Aqqa was passed around, the very last thing on her mind was the party that they had held with the Garda, or N'Elemay's strange dis-appearance at the end of the affair. It was only a few minutes later, after they had finished watching another episode of *Laara Lampa* that this came to have any meaning.

The show had just concluded, and instead of returning to their racks, everyone was staying around the couch and taking their ease, sipping their drinks out of plastic cups. For some reason, Kaly had always found that Aqqa actually tasted better when it was served in cheap plastic cups, and she imagined that this was probably due to some sinister chemical reaction between it and the polymers, but she really didn't care one way or the other. Anything that made the stuff halfway palatable was just fine with her.

"I vonder vhat zose vomen zee in zem," Margasdaater was asking. She had been referring to the female Garda members and their attraction to their male counterparts. Like Kaly, everyone on the team had been exposed to the two sexes coupling with one another during their stay in Treya Angelaz, and the Zommerlaandar's question was a natural one—if left unvoiced by anyone until just then.

"I've wondered too. I've wondered what it's like," Kaly added in a small voice. "I mean—you know, to 'do it' with—one of—*them*." Despite her best efforts, her morbid curiosity had haunted her since the night of the party with the Garda. She was half certain that her question would earn her some well-deserved ridicule, and she prepared herself for the scorn of her companions. But she had had to ask it, just the same.

Kaly didn't get the censure that she had feared, however. Instead, she received the shock of her young life.

"It's not bad."

It took a second for her to register who had just said this. It had been none other than Troop Leader n'Elemay, and suddenly her departure on the night of the party became shockingly obvious. She and Morana had gone off, bottle in hand, and done—the unthinkable.

Kaly's mouthful of Aqqa sprayed out in all directions as this hit home. "Y-you?!" she coughed. She couldn't believe her ears. This was Troop Leader n'Elemay, one of the toughest women she had ever met! A Trooper's Trooper! A Sisterhood Marine, through and through.

N'Elemay's expression was deadpan, and she didn't blush, or show any other sign of emotion. "I was in the mood, so I took care of business," she drawled. "I'll never give up women for men, but they're not bad. Just in case you're wondering, I got a friend of mine in medbay to give me a little something before we went downside. I wouldn't want any little 'souvenirs' following me around in my kit bag for the rest of my life."

Kaly took a long hard pull directly from the bottle. The woman hadn't only 'done it' with a male, she'd actually *planned* for the possibility! In fact, it sounded like she'd 'done it' before—several times at least.

Not only was this a stunning personal admission, but she knew that if it got out, it could also earn the Troop Leader a court martial for *'committing an unnatural act unbecoming a Marine'*. Kaly was also now half-certain that this was precisely what Lieutenant sa'Kaali had meant when she had used the term 'irregularities'.

Everyone else sitting there also understood the gravity of the woman's confession, and the fact that N'Elemay had shared it with them, spoke volumes for the trust that she placed in all of them, including Kaly herself. Deeply honored, the young woman made a choice, and it was for her teammates. There would be no report about this, to the El-Tee, or to anyone else. *What happens in the team, stays in the team,* Kaly vowed. *In my team.*

As she came to this decision, she felt a more profound respect for N'Elemay; the woman didn't give a damn for anything. She had done what she had wanted to, and had told the rules to go *fek* themselves. Kaly certainly didn't agree with the act itself, but as she sat there, thinking it over, she admired the woman for her independence.

Later, when the group finally retired for the night, Margasdaater pulled her aside, just before they reached their racks. "N'Elemay vouldn't say it," the woman told her, "but she likes you. Ve're all glad to have you vith za team, Kaly. You did good down zere on Angelaz. I vanted you to know zat."

"Thanks, Astrid," Kaly replied. "It's good to have a home."

"Zere's zomething else," the Zommerlaandar added. "Zomething you should know about N'Elemay. Ve're zisters now, and it's important zat we know all about each other, yah? Even za zecret parts."

"Like what?" Kaly couldn't imagine anything more intimate than N'Elemay's earlier admission, and she braced herself for the next astonishing surprise that the Goddess had in store for her. It had been that kind of night.

"She's not from Corrissa—zat's vat most women zink."

Kaly had already figured out that much on her own and she waited for her companion to enlighten her.

Margasdaater looked around to see if anyone else was near enough to overhear her, and when she was certain that they were alone, she spoke. "She's really from Faith. You know zat place?"

Kaly certainly did; Faith was one of the three Marionite systems. It not only explained the Troop Leaders ease, but also her familiarity with men. And it confirmed what she had heard the woman say over her in the field hospital, and also the cross she had drawn on her forehead.

Troop Leader n'Elemay was a Marionite.

If anything, this was even harder for her to believe than the fact that the woman had actually coupled with a man. N'Elemay just didn't seem to her like what she had always pictured as a 'typical' Marionite. Not that she was entirely sure *what* was typical for them. But she didn't let this overwhelm her. She was still a little numb from the first revelation about the Troop Leader, and the Aqqa was only helping her desensitization along. She just accepted it instead.

"Okay," she said. "What about you? T'Jinna? Are you Marionites too?"

"Ach, nen!" Margasdaater returned with a chuckle. "I'll ztay vith the vays of the za Alte Volk, and T'Jinna keeps to her Lady of Zilence."

"So, next question; why is she here?" Kaly asked. "Why the Marines?" The Marionites were a despised minority, and it surprised her that after all the poor treatment they had suffered at the hands of the Sisterhood, that any of them would want to risk their lives for it.

"It's her nation too," Margasdaater said simply. "Even if it zpits on her and her volk."

Kaly had to agree. It really *was* N'Elemay's nation too, right or wrong. The location of her motherworld didn't change that basic fact one nano. And the Hriss would kill a Marionite just as quickly as they would any other woman. But she did find herself wondering if this was going to be another secret she would have to worry about keeping. "Does anyone else know about this?" she asked.

"Yah," Margasdaater replied with a casual shrug. "Za Corps knows, and of course za El-Tee and za Major too, but zey just let it all go by-za-by. Zat's za way za Corps vants it; za Sisterhood needs all za good troopers zat zey can get, and she keeps a low profile besides. Zo, alle gaaf."

This made Kaly doubly glad she had resolved not to be the 'good little trooper'. It might have been her official duty to report the incident on Treya Angelaz between N'Elemay and Morana to the El-Tee, but it would also have given the Corps a planet-sized black eye, and cost them a good Team Leader in the process. The Corps didn't exactly shower rewards on troopers who fekked up *that* much. She also didn't harbor any resentment for the El-Tee for asking this of her; the woman had her job to do too, and in her own way, she had tried to warn Kaly away from making a terrible mistake.

"No problems," Kaly said. "And no worries. Good night, Astrid."

***

Another shock was waiting for Kaly, and everyone else, the following day. The team was in the armory, using its workshop to inspect and adjust their weapons when Lieutenant sa'Kaali walked in. Her expression was subdued, and she marched straight up to T'Jinna and signed something to her that Kaly didn't quite catch.

The dark woman blinked, and then Kaly saw her sign a reply. *No,* the Sireeni insisted. *It's not true! This isn't really happening. This is some kind of dream!*

The El-Tee shook her head and signed back, *I'm sorry. This is real. Truly, I'm very, very sorry.*

T'Jinna dropped the assembly she had been working with and collapsed into the officers' arms. Everyone stopped what they were doing and rushed over to join them. Something awful had just happened.

Lieutenant sa'Kaali gathered the Sireeni in close, and handed N'Elemay the flimsy she had brought with her. The Troop Leader read it.

"*Mer de fekking fek*!" N'Elemay growled, and then she wrapped her own arms around T'Jinna. Confused and worried, Kaly looked to Margasdaater for an explanation, but the Zommerlaandar was just as mystified as she was and took the flimsy from N'Elemay's outstretched hand.

"It's her zister," Margasdaater said quietly. "She vas on the *Cleopatra* in za Colombyen Provensa. A Hriss missile got zem. Za ship vas lost. All hands."

"Oh goddess no," Kaly exclaimed, tears welling up as she went to T'Jinna. The Sireeni was sobbing in grief, and if anything, the lack of vocal cords made her despair all the more heart wrenching for its absolute silence. Kaly felt utterly helpless and could only join with the others in holding her tight.

Everyone stayed together like this until Margasdaater gently pulled the woman away and led her off to her rack. Later, when Kaly stopped by to see how she was doing, she found T'Jinna sitting on the edge of her bed, staring at a holo.

The scene in it was at night, and there were literally hundreds, if not thousands of lights glowing softly. Coming closer, she saw that these were actually lanterns of some sort. Some of them were earthbound, and others were floating up into the evening sky. From somewhere, she recalled that the Sireeni women observed a celebration they called the Festival of Lights. It was held in the deepest part of their summer, for them the eighth month, and it was done to invoke a blessing on the home, and to memorialize relatives who had passed away the year before.

T'Jinna noticed her and looked up sadly. *It was our favorite holiday,* she signed. *Maneeya loved to sit with me and watch the lights rise.* Fresh tears came to her eyes, and Kaly sat down on the bed to lend what comfort she could.

N'Elemay came along right then, and glanced at them and then at the image. "We'll have to go downside," she said flatly, and promptly left.

An hour later, the team had assembled at the hangar bay, and with the assistance of a sympathetic Marine shuttle crew, got themselves a trip downside to the surface of Chacital, one of the planets that the SEF had retaken when they had won control of the Agwalar system. The shuttle landed at the only spaceport that was still halfway functional, and disembarked.

Somehow, N'Elemay had, with Saara sa'Vika's assistance, gotten her hands on a lantern very similar to the ones in T'Jinna's holo. It was constructed of some kind of light papery material and had a tiny flame producer inside.

The team took it to the very edge of the spaceport. By this time, it was just after sunset, and as the darkness gathered around them, T'Jinna signed a little prayer to her sibling's memory and triggered the igniter inside the lantern.

It rose slowly, and then the warm currents of air caught it and it ascended, higher and higher into the darkening sky. Kaly said her own prayer to the Goddess as it rose, and caught the furtive little cross that N'Elemay had sketched out with her right thumb.

Like everything else that they did, they marked this occasion together as well, each of them in their own ways. Kaly looked away from the Troop Leader to the lamp and watched it with her companions until it joined with the stars overhead, and vanished from sight.

That evening, a Marine from Willa Company, a regular trooper that Kaly had seen visiting the SpecOps section from time to time, joined them in the ready room. She had brought a little hard case with her, and T'Jinna looked up at her expectantly.

"What name do you want?" the trooper asked as she opened the container.

T'Jinna signed out her sister's name, Maneeya t'Jinna, and the woman took out what Kaly recognized as an injection gun for nanotattoos. The device was similar to a normal medical injector, but it had a palm-sized screen attached to it for viewing tattoo designs, and a stylus to edit them with.

While the trooper turned the device on, and accessed the tattoo pattern from the injectors' memory, T'Jinna pulled up the sleeve of her blouse, exposing a beautiful animated tattoo that was a duplicate of the one on N'Elemay's arm. The only exception was that her scrollwork had been created by a group of gold-colored nanobots so that the design stood out sharply against her black skin, fluttering there like some strange midnight apparition.

With the pattern called up, the trooper traced in the name with her stylus, and after selecting the font that she preferred, turned it around and showed it to the Sireeni. Once T'Jinna had approved it, the woman placed the tip of the injector against her existing tattoo and fired. The moment that they were under her skin, the new nanobots went to work quickly, joining those that were already present and assuming their place in the animated pattern. It only took a few minutes before the name was properly displayed, and it looked as if it had always been a part of the design.

"Anyone else need any work done while I'm here?" the Marine inquired.

N'Elemay raised her sleeve next. This time, Kaly saw something there that she hadn't seen the first time. Her scrollwork had an added detail that was so subtle that it had gone unnoticed. Intertwined with everything else were three tiny four-pointed stars that winked in and out of sight; the Marionite symbols for Jesu, Mari and the Holy Spirit.

The Troop Leader gave Kaly a long meaningful look and then said, "I'd like the name of 'Marisol Estabanya' put on mine. She deserves that."

The artist made no comment, and got straight to work. When she had finished, Margasdaater went next, making the same request, and the Marine quietly obliged her. After that, the woman started to pack up her things, but Kaly stopped her.

"Can you make one for me?" she asked. "I have a few names that I'd like put on it. Marisol's is one of them."

"Not a problem, trooper. Roll up your sleeve."

***

There were very few 'perks' for being on a Marauder Team, but one of them was being freed from the work details most Marines had to perform aboard ship during downtime. With her injuries, this was particularly so for Kaly.

Finding herself with a full day of nothing to do, she decided to connect to the ship's omni network with her psiever. The SAO's department posted daily listings there of activities that were available for off-duty personnel, and Kaly wanted to see if there was anything scheduled that she could participate in.

"Military History 102, 21st-23rd centuries BSE," one entry went, *"Prior enrollment in the University of Thermadon Extension Program and completion of MilHst 101 required. Contact Lt. Commander d'Rann."*

While Kaly had certainly completed her primary education, she had never gone beyond it into Secondary or Tertiary, and even the prerequisite course sounded just a bit too advanced to tackle. She paged on to the next listing.

"Beginner's Knitting," another announced. Definitely not. She hated knitting.

"Introduction to Portrait Drawing," came next, and this mildly interested her. She wasn't much of an artist, but she had always wondered about developing the talent for drawing. But not enough to take the next step and

register for the course however.

She paged on. *"Cooking Kalian Cuisine,"* followed. *No,* she thought. *I burn water.* Putting her in a kitchen was certainly a recipe. For a disaster.

"Folk Guitar," offered itself up next. She'd often heard that Commander Bertasdaater was quite an accomplished musician, and she had even tried to learn to play herself when she was much younger. It was a distinct possibility, and she saved the listing to her personal file.

Finally, she saw one entry that truly grabbed her interest. *"Book Club Meeting: readings and appreciation. Open to new members. Book contributions also welcome, but not required. All ranks eligible. Location: Officers Recreation Lounge, 07:91:67 hours."*

Kaly had never shared it with anyone, but old books had always fascinated her. She had never actually owned one, but one of the women serving on the Mother's Committee on Persephone had, and she had always wanted to hold it in her hands, and feel the texture of its pages as she read it. Feeling a brief pang of sorrow at the memory, and then sent her acceptance. The event date and time were automatically added to her psievers' personal calendar, but she didn't really need this; the meeting was only an hour away.

She spent the next 100 minutes showering, tending to her rack and inspecting her gear and then she headed over to 'Officer's Country'. The sailor standing watch there confirmed her enrollment, and then pointed the way to the Recreation Lounge. Kaly had never been in the section reserved for officers before, and she felt a little out of place as she walked along, trading salutes with everyone she encountered.

No one challenged her however, and when she walked into the lounge, Saara sa'Vika was waiting at the entrance. The Kalian was a welcome sight. Although she was an officer, she was also the woman everyone came to for every little pleasure the Ship had to offer, making her a friendly face in an otherwise strange and new situation.

Kaly still saluted her however. "*Alla'zi*, Is this where the Book Club is meeting today, ma'am?"

"It is, and welcome," Sa'Vika said, gesturing for her to cross the threshold and then directing her over to a linen-covered table.

"Did you bring your own book? No? Well, no problem at all. You'll want to grab a pair of gloves, and make sure to get yourself some tea and sandwiches too. These readings can be very thirsty work."

Kaly took a pair of white gloves for herself, and glanced over her shoulder to see who else was attending the meeting. To her alarm, she realized that one of them was none other than Vice Admiral ben Jeni herself. Next to her was the male officer from the ETR, Captain Rodraga, and the Admiral's aide (whose name Kaly couldn't remember for the life of her) and finally Lieutenant Commander d'Rann. They were all seated around a low table, and chatting quietly.

The presence of so much brass made her feel nervous and awkward; she wasn't at all sure what the protocol was, and she deliberately hesitated over a plate of cucumber sandwiches as she tried to decide how to handle the situation.

Sa'Vika picked up on her unease and came up next to her. "There's no need to be nervous," she said in a half-whisper, "In the Book Club, everyone is the same; a lover of reading, and old books. You can relax, Trooper."

"Yes, ma'am," Kaly responded. She took up a plate and helped herself to a few of the other items that appealed to her, and hesitantly joined the group. After Sa'Vika had taken her own place, the only open seat was between the Vice Admiral and Captain Rodraga, and Kaly took it tentatively.

Once she was seated, and despite Sa'Vika's reassurances to the contrary, she still sat as straight as possible, and kept her feet flat, and her mouth shut. When the Vice Admiral looked over at her, she also made certain to give the woman a courteous nod of acknowledgement. It wasn't the salute that wanted to spring out of her, but it was better than nothing, and the Vice Admiral only smiled back, and returned the gesture. Kaly relaxed, by small degrees.

"Well," Sa'Vika began. "I think this is everyone that could make it tonight. Chief Engineer bel Lyra is standing watch, and sends her regrets. Now, I understand that we have a few treats this evening. First, we have a new member, Corporal n'Deena. I also understand that Captain Rodraga has brought a book with him from the ETR. Captain?"

"Thank you, Captain," he replied. He put down his tea and reached into a briefcase he had brought with him. Everyone, Kaly noted, had something similar to it sitting next to them. When he opened it, he took out a smaller metallic case, and inside of this was a book. She could tell as he lifted it out, that it was old, but she knew that most books were, and in a day and age when nothing had been printed on real paper for centuries, probably quite rare and fantastically expensive. Being from the ETR made the object even more exotic.

"This is the third edition of *"Selected Tales from A Thousand and One Nights by Sir Richard Burton*," in Espangla," he began. "And edited by Jyuan Escarra. As you can see, it's in a little less than mint condition, but the paper is still in good shape, and although worn, the faux leather covers are intact. Thankfully, it was sewn in signatures, or the glue that most publishers used at the time would have lost all its effect centuries ago."

He handed it over to the Vice Admiral, who examined it, and then opened it up with great care. She ran her fingers lovingly over the page before her and looked back up at him.

"A beautiful copy," Lilith said. "Absent a bit of aging at the borders, the paper is certainly in wonderful condition and the signatures seem quite sound. You know, I don't think I recognize this particular version, Captain. Can you tell us a bit about it, and perhaps share a passage or two?" She handed the book over to her adjutant, who relayed it over to Lt. Commander d'Rann to look at.

"A pleasure," he replied. "The publisher was Santosaa iya Marva, a firm that was in Diolores, on Estraddar and it was printed in 2441 BSE. The story I would like to share from it is the classic comedy about the Hunchback, the sultan's court jester. I think everyone will enjoy it, even if they have heard it before."

As Rodraga was saying this, the Tethyian completed her inspection, and to Kaly's immense surprise, gave the tome to her. She took it, holding it as if it were made of spun silicon, barely daring to breath, and afraid that she would somehow damage it if she actually opened it. She quickly returned it to its owner, and he smiled at her, and opened it himself without any hesitation.

Then, he began to read to them. Thanks to Kaly's knowledge of Espangla, she was able to follow along with the man's recitation, although some of the words he shared were antiquated, and hadn't been included in her PTS trainer. Those, she was able to more or less guess from their context and they really didn't detract from her overall experience. Unlike everyone else, the story of the Hunchback was completely new to her, and by the end of it, she was laughing right along with the rest of them. The ancient farce had lost none of its humor after being translated into a foreign tongue, or the passage of millennia.

"That was quite wonderful. You were right by the way, I have heard the story before, but it is still a good tale," Lilith said. "Your book would certainly make a fine addition to my small collection. Perhaps you would consider a trade?"

"What did you have in mind, Admiral?" Rodraga asked.

"State secrets, perhaps?" she replied with a sly smile. "Absent those, perhaps my copy of *'Anna 225'*? It's in about the same condition. It was printed on Mars—an English translation."

The man put down the book and rubbed his chin thoughtfully. "That would depend on the secrets of course. I'm certain that my superiors would agree that some things are more important than a nation's security, but then again, the book you are offering me is just as tempting, and would probably be less problematic for our two governments."

Lilith laughed. "The book for the book then?"

"Let me think on it," he returned. "I still might be willing to turn traitor, but if my courage fails me, may I at least have the chance to examine your copy first?"

"At your pleasure," she agreed.

Seeing an opening, Sa'Vika spoke. "Thank you for sharing with us, Captain. Now, I also have something special that I would like to present." She reached into her own case and produced another small volume. It seemed to be just as old as the one Rodraga had shown them.

"This is something I have been holding onto until just the right occasion came along," she told them. "Tonight seems to be that time. It is another English book of collected poems, entitled *'Great Love Poems of the Ages'*, and it features one particularly rare piece, penned by none other than Edgar Allen Poe."

Her companions seemed to know who this was, but Kaly remained lost until she accessed the Ship's Omni and made an inquiry. After that, she was simply mystified. A writer of horror and the supernatural didn't seem to be a likely candidate for a love poem, much less one that was considered great, but she was willing to let the piece prove itself, or establish that the editor who had chosen it was as mad as Poe had been.

Sa'Vika opened the book. "The poem is entitled *'Annabelle Lee'* and it was first published after the author's death in 1849 BSE. It is believed to be about his pairmate, his *wife*, Virginia, but some scholars dispute that. Whatever the woman's true identity, he managed to create what was, I think at least, one of the finest love poems ever written. But let yourselves be the judge."

Everyone, Kaly included, set down their tea, and waited intently as the Kalian took a sip from her own cup, and then began to read.

"It was many and many a year ago," she began, *"In a kingdom by the sea,*

That a maiden there lived whom you may know by the name of Annabel Lee;

And this maiden she lived with no other thought than to love and be loved by me.'

"I was a child and she was a child, in this kingdom by the sea: But we loved with a love that was more than love—I and my Annabel Lee; With a love that the winged seraphs of heaven, coveted her and me.'

"And this was the reason that, long ago, in this kingdom by the sea, a wind blew out of a cloud, chilling my beautiful Annabel Lee; So that her highborn kinsmen came, and bore her away from me, to shut her up in a sepulcher in this kingdom by the sea.'

"The angels, not half so happy in heaven, went envying her and me—Yes!—that was the reason (as all men know, in this kingdom by the sea). That the wind came out of the cloud by night, chilling and killing my Annabel Lee."

"But our love it was stronger by far than the love of those who were older than we--of many far wiser than we—And neither the angels in heaven above, Nor the demons down under the sea, can ever dissever my soul

from the soul of the beautiful Annabel Lee'

"For the moon never beams, without bringing me dreams of the beautiful Annabel Lee; And the stars never rise, but I feel the bright eyes of the beautiful Annabel Lee,'

"And so, all the night-tide, I lie down by the side of my darling—my darling—my life and my bride, in her sepulcher there by the sea, in her tomb by the sounding sea."

Kaly was so moved by the passage that she finally found the courage to speak aloud. "That—was so beautiful," she said, wiping at a tear that had formed in her eye. The editor had not been *klaxxy* after all, she decided. And for some odd reason, the poem also made her think of Lena, wherever she was, and how desperately she missed her.

"I am glad that you enjoyed it so much," Sa'Vika said. "There are many other fine works in this little book. Perhaps, since you have no book of your own, you would enjoy borrowing it, and reading them? As a way of welcoming you to our circle?"

"Oh!" Kaly exclaimed in shock. "Oh no! Ma'am, I couldn't—it's much too fine!"

"I know that you'll take good care of it," the officer said. "Borrow it for a week or two and then get it back to me. If not," she added with a sly gleam, "then I know right where to find you."

She held it out to her, and unable (and truth be told, unwilling) to refuse, Kaly took it from her.

The meeting ended a half an hour later, with the Vice Admiral and Rodraga still negotiating their trade, and with an invitation to Kaly to return for their next session. Still unsated, Kaly left, and went back to her rack. She read '*Great Love Poems*' until her psiever informed her that the Third Watch was beginning.

USSNS *Pallas Athena* and Downside, Salta Cia, Altamara 1,
Altamara System, Frontera Provensa, Esteral Terrana Rapabla
1044.09|23|03:76:02

It was the 23rd day of the 9th month of the Standard Year. This date was a special one for many of the women serving in the Special Expeditionary Force. On Old Gaia it had once been the Autumn Equinox, or the Wine Harvest, and one of the great festivals of the year. Even though on many planets, including Kaly's motherworld, this occurred on a completely different day, the date itself was still observed as a sacred occasion. And in deference to this, small decorations could be found in every corner of the ship where they didn't impede operations, and the Enlisted Mess was festooned with brown, yellow and orange plastic crepe ribbons. Saara sa'Vika had even added little place settings of simulated leaves, with tiny holocandles set in their centers.

Seeing all this brought a mixture of happiness, and melancholy to Kaly as she remembered the celebrations she had once enjoyed with her family on Persephone. Pushing back the memories that reminded her that none of them were still alive, she sought out Margasdaater and T'Jinna, and sat with them at their table. N'Elemay, she noted, was absent.

"Where's Ellen?" she asked, pointing to the empty chair she normally occupied. She also hadn't seen the woman at morning mess.

"Zis is one of her great holy days," Margasdaater told her, her voice kept carefully low. "She's fasting, and praying in her rack. We von't see her tonight eizer. She'll stay in zere until tomorrow. She always does zat ven zere are holy days."

"She must be lonely," Kaly observed, unconsciously echoing the words that her departed lover, Lena had spoken about Jon, "All by herself in her rack with no one to share it with."

"*Vemiskliet*, she is," Margasdaater agreed. "But she always zpends it by herzelf, and ve all leave her alone until za day has passed, yah?"

Kaly heard the friendly warning in her friend's words. "Yah, Astrid, sure thing." Then she started in on her meal. Once she was done, she took leave of her Teammates and instead of heading to the gym, or back to her rack to read some more of her poetry book, she went directly to the Ship's Library.

She wanted to know more about the Marionites, and by extension, her Troop Leader. Until coming to the team, she had never really cared one way or the other about the Marionite belief system, but now that she counted one of them as family, she felt that she had to at least try to learn more, and if possible, to understand,.

The references that the library offered her were vague however, and they presented the Marionites, in an odd, and somewhat incomprehensible fashion. As near as she could puzzle out, they celebrated the first birth of their Redeemer figure, but they felt that his death was also very significant, and claimed that he had somehow been transformed into an immortal figure that would not only be reborn, but also save Humanity in the process. And their holy days, as Margasdaater had stated, involved a great deal of fasting and prayer.

Being raised a Demetrian, she certainly understood the concept of personal sacrifice as an essential element of worship. Back on Persephone, every religious holiday had been marked by an offering to the Great Mother, given by the participants as a way of expressing thanks to her for her gifts. The Marionite custom of fasting and privations seemed to be similar to this, but how the death of Jesu was involved, or why all of this made him the 'Savior of Humanity' completely confounded her.

One small nugget of information did manage to surface clearly; for the Marionites, the 23rd of the 9th was considered to be one of their Festivals of Light, a fire festival just like its Demetrian equivalent, and it was also observed with candles, either real or holographic. She then learned that it was the custom among the Marionites at such times to wish one another well for the coming months, and marking the occasion by presenting a candle to their friends and loved ones.

An idea struck her as she read this, and finding little else of value, she signed off the terminal and made her way down to the PX. There were still plenty of holocandles for sale there, and she purchased two of them. With these in hand, she went down to Five Bar.

Her first stop was N'Elemay's rack. The privacy curtain was closed, but Kaly could see the light of another holocandle flickering through it, and as she paused, she spied the woman's silhouette outlined by the soft light.

Keeping Margasdaater's prohibition in mind, Kaly didn't disturb her, but walked past as quietly as she could and left one of her candles on the common table at the end of the pod, a place that she was sure N'Elemay would find it. After this, she moved on to her next destination.

Jon fa'Teela wasn't in his rack, as his shift was only halfway done, and Kaly was grateful for this small mercy. She still felt guilty about keeping silent when he had been passed over for promotion and decorations, and a face-to-face meeting between them would have been too awkward to bear. Making sure that she was unobserved, she took the second holocandle and placed it in his rack, right on his pillow.

Her gift would be anonymous, and she only hoped that its discovery would bring him the same joy she hoped her first candle would give N'Elemay. It certainly wouldn't atone for her inaction, nothing really could, but it was a kindness nonetheless, and the least she could do. She didn't know if Jesu and Mari were actually real and watching her, or if the Great Mother herself was witnessing her act. She only hoped that someone out there, somewhere, would note the gift, and allow it to offset a portion of her sin against Fa'Teela.

***

N'Elemay heard someone coming by her rack, and instinctively closed her little copy of *'The Revelation of Mari'*, tucking it out of sight under her pillow. She also stuffed her tiny Star of the Faithful under her tank top and pulled down her left pant leg, concealing the *circula* that she wore around her ankle. Any one of these items, had they been seen by a hostile unbeliever, might have landed her in trouble. Especially the *circula*.

Constructed of simple wire, the ankle bracelet sported sharp barbs that bit into her flesh deeply enough to draw blood when it was fastened tight. Other women, not of the True Faith, would have considered it cruel, and because its use also involved 'damage to Sisterhood property', she was committing a punishable offense simply by wearing it.

But she didn't care what those who lived their lives in darkness believed; their very bread was ignorance. Her only concern was that by discovering it, they might interfere. She could not let that happen.

For her, and for many of the Faithful, wearing the *circula* and devices like it, was an act of deep devotion and sacrifice. Mortification of the flesh was the only sure way to purge oneself of sins, and on this day, an especially fitting measure.

May I suffer as Jesu suffered for me, she thought, tightening her hand on the anklet and driving its barbs in even deeper. As she did this to herself, the footfalls outside paused, and she realized that whoever it was, was depositing something on the common table jutting out from the wall between the racks.

When she heard the woman retreating, she peered out carefully to see who her visitor had been. She just managed to catch sight of Kaly before the young woman turned the corner and disappeared. Then she saw the holocandle that her teammate had left, flickering cheerfully on the table.

Astrid or Anniya must have told her about me, she thought, leaving her rack and going over to cradle the present in her hands. It was, without question, one of the finest gifts that she had ever received from anyone in a very long, long time, and far more than she deserved. Taking it back with her to her rack, she re-closed the drape and carefully set it alongside the one that she had purchased for herself.

"Merciful Mother Mari," she said, her voice barely more than a whisper, "I thank You for this wonderful Light—and for moving the heart of an unbeliever in the midst of this terrible and lonely place."

"Mother of God, You have always shown me mercy and I can only try," she continued, her voice beginning to break, "to repay your infinite kindnesses—your infinite patience with me—with my love." She blew a kiss upwards, saluting Mari herself. "Thank you, Gracious Mother."

Then she addressed her son, the Redeemer, whom she knew was also listening, "Jesu, Son of God, Son of Man, Light of the Universe, I am even less worthy of you. You walked among us—-and then you gave us the greatest gift that anyone ever could; your life—that we might all be saved. Even…even…me…" She hesitated there, choked with emotion, and half blind from the tears that welled up in her eyes. Finally, when she felt ready, she continued.

"Lord, I am a flawed and imperfect thing, my soul is small and shriveled with sin and weakness, but despite all of my wickedness, you still sacrificed yourself for me.'

"How can I ever repay you? I can only pledge you what little I have, what I always have pledged; my love and my service, and if you demand it, my life. Praise be to the heavens for your name, Jesu, Son of Light!"

This was as much as she could bear to say aloud.

Will I know heaven when my time comes? she wondered desperately. *Will my sacrifice and devotion be enough? Can I remain unwavering in my faith until that great day arrives?*

She was no missionary like Jon fa'Teela, with a mighty purpose to sustain herself with. She was only a simple soldier, with a soldier's faith, and she was ashamed to admit, a soldier's doubts. It was hard for her, surrounded as she was at all times, and on all sides by ignorance and persecution, to remain strong.

But her struggle was nothing compared to what Jesu's had been, she reminded herself. She had only her own soul to worry over, not all of humanity's. Compared to that, her struggles were insignificant, and no price could ever be asked of her that was too high to pay.

Thanks to the True Word of Mari, she also understood the actual nature of the battles that she was destined to fight, and what the universe really was. For someone of real faith, like herself, it was more than just a random collection of stars spinning mindlessly through the void.

In actuality, it was a place of testing; a bleak, and desolate purgatory where the forces of Light and Good battled with the Darkness and Chaos for the possession of her immortal spirit, and those of her sisters and brothers.

And even though they called themselves the Hriss, or the T'lakskalans, or half a dozen other names, she wasn't fooled in the least. These were nothing more than poorly crafted disguises. They were, and always would be, the children of the Evil One, the howling demons of the dark that could never hide themselves from the revealing Light of Truth.

On the day that she had decided to join the Marines, she had sworn two oaths. One had been worldly, given to the Sisterhood to defend it from its enemies. The second had been a spiritual promise. It had been made to Jesu and Mari, vowing to repay them for their infinite Light and Love with the only coin that she had to offer. Her willing sword arm.

Every enemy that she had slain since, she had slain in their names, banishing the darkness so that the light of God could shine into every corner of the Galaxy—one bloody meter at a time. This was why she only smiled in battle; not out of any love of killing like some believed, but because it was only when she was battling evil face-to-face, that she felt the full bliss of God's light. At such times, it filled her completely, banishing all her doubt, all the weakness from her soul, and shielding her with its power like the glittering, golden armor of an archangel. But this was something that no unbeliever, not even her teammates, would have ever understood, or could have hoped to experience.

N'Elemay completed her devotions, and after putting the *Revelation* back into its hiding place, briefly considered going to the ready room to watch another *Laara Lampa* holo to help her relax. Normally, her prayers would have been enough, but she had been under so much stress, that she knew that she had to find something more to help settle her soul. The holo, as appealing as it was, wasn't what she needed, and she discarded the idea for something else. Something that was much more satisfying, and easier to find, down in Salta Cia. She also knew exactly how to go about getting it once she got there.

Her mind made up, she changed out of her fatigues and into her service uniform. It was a few steps below the red, white and black dress uniform, and grey in color, but of a much finer cut than the clothing she had been wearing, and generally reserved for semi-formal occasions. It would be just perfect for what she had in mind.

She added each layer on with care, making sure to maintain its neatly pressed look, and even included a blue Marine-issue cravat to her ensemble. As a finishing touch, she caught up her hair in a tight, neat bun that would have made her Drill Instructors proud, and donned her blue beret.

The Blue Beret was an ancient holdover from the Gaian Star Federation, and had once been worn by their elite troopers. Originally, the color of the headgear had symbolized the scheme of the GSF Flag, which itself was an evolution of the even older United Nations flag. The advent of the Sisterhood hadn't changed the beret's color scheme at all, or the link that it shared with the national flag. Like its predecessors, the banner of the United Sisterhood of Suns was also sky-blue and white.

Instead of displaying the UN globe or the GSF Star however, it was emblazoned with the sun, sword and starship of the Marine Corps. This insignia rode on the beret as a gold embossed pin, and as she faced herself in the mirror on her rack, N'Elemay made certain that the headgear was properly creased and folded, and that the symbol was prominently displayed. She spent a few more seconds after that making a final inspection of her appearance, and then left Five Bar for the Lifts.

On the way, she met another Marauder, from one of the other teams. She didn't know the woman by name, but they had seen one another often enough to have a passing congeniality. The trooper also knew her, and her reputation.

"Going somewhere special?" the trooper asked, more out of friendliness than from any real interest.

"Yes," N'Elemay answered with her usual deadpan tone. "Downside. I need to have a little fun."

The Lift arrived just as she said this, and she stepped inside without waiting for the other woman's reaction. The doors stayed open just long enough for her to see it though. It was a sudden look of comprehension, followed by a profanity, and then the trooper starting to turn, and run.

N'Elemay knew exactly where she was headed; to go and find Lieutenant sa'Kaali. Everyone in *Hekate's Hounds* understood that N'Elemay had some very strange ideas about what constituted 'a fun night out', and the trooper had obviously, and correctly, assumed that the El-Tee would want to be prepared for the aftermath.

***

Salta Cia, or 'Jump City', was a typical boomtown. Before the alliance between the Sisterhood and the ETR, it had been nothing more than an automated refueling depot for merchant ships working at the edges of ETR space, a general store catering to their crews, and a combination restaurant and hotel.

Once the military forces from both factions had established themselves there, it had transformed itself overnight, and like all such places throughout history, its population had swelled in size to match the changes. What had been a hamlet of barely 1,000 souls had grown to almost 10,000 civilians, most of them imported from the ETR, and a single dusty street had turned into multiple blocks, filled with new buildings.

The town was officially partitioned into three sectors. In the west, it was Sisterhood territory. In the east, it was controlled by the ETR, and in the middle there was a neutral space commonly referred to as 'Dogtown' for reasons that had been lost shortly after the title had been bestowed upon it.

Technically, Dogtown was off limits to both sides, except those with special passes, and naturally, this immediately attracted both factions to it, with or without said passes. To keep some semblance of order, a joint force of Sisterhood Navy Shore Patrolwomen and their ETR counterparts, patrolled the place and controlled access to the other parts of town.

Not that this delayed N'Elemay greatly. She was able to wrangle a ride downside on a shuttle ferrying supplies, and then a lift from a Navy hovertruck that took her past the checkpoints and right into the center of town.

From there, she made her way on foot to a bar. Although she had never been there before, she knew all about *"The Halflife Club"*.

The *Halflife* was one of the few bars in Salta Cia that catered to a mixed clientele, and as she entered it, she saw ETR soldiers—male soldiers—on one side of the room, and Sisterhood women on the other.

The men were loud and boisterous, and the male civilian working security at the door looked nervous. N'Elemay wasn't concerned in the least, and took a seat at a table that sat in the very middle of the bar in what was an informal 'no-man/no-woman's zone.' This earned her a few glances from the males, which she pretended to ignore. In reality, they were just what she had been hoping for.

Raised on Faith, N'Elemay understood men better than any of the other women in the bar--and these men in particular. She had been raised among the neomen, and had not only worked alongside them, but had even called several of them her lovers.

The men here though, were not cut from the same righteous cloth. Instead of being prayers-in-the-flesh to God for the Redeemer's return, these males were very much like those who had existed before the Plague. Some of them, like Captain Morana, were noble, intelligent, and caring beings, and like the neomen that she had known on Faith, fully worthy of her body.

Others though, such as the ones openly leering at her from their side of the room, were not. Instead, they were everything that Motherthought accused them of being; base, cruel creatures, and in her eyes, an affront to God and his great design for men and woman. And when it came to such filth, she fully agreed with the Sisterhood's position, even if the underpinnings of their philosophies differed radically. Men like them were only worthy of her contempt.

They did have one saving grace however, at least as far as her designs for the evening went. They were stupid, and therefore, easily manipulated.

N'Elemay ordered herself a glass of water from a serving woman, and as she received it, she subtly altered her posture, arching her back just enough to accentuate her breasts, and making sure to be rather dainty about taking a sip from her drink. She also made certain to exchange glances with the ugliest and loudest of the males, batting her lashes and regarding him coyly.

The man was obviously drunk, and one of his fellows, who was only a shade less unattractive than he, nudged him encouragingly. Sauntering over on unsteady legs, the ungainly pair came over to her together.

"What's a fine looking lady like you doing here tonight?" one of them asked in truly horrible Standard. He reeked from a combination of cheap liquor, and a sour musky odor that had to be his natural scent.

"You want a date with me? Maybe find out what its like?" The creature leaned in close and gave her a toothy smile. His breath proved to be just as sour as the rest of him. "You know honey, that's sure a sexy little beret you have on. Does it mean anything, or are you just wearing it to turn me on? 'Cause if you are, its working."

N'Elemay put down her glass, and smiled up at him, feeling the beginnings of the bliss that she had sought coming over her. "I'm just finishing my water," she answered sweetly. "Now, why don't you go away or you'll find out what this beret *really* means."

"Water!?" the man guffawed. "Here—let me buy you a real drink!" He reached out and tried to take her glass away from her.

That was a serious mistake. Before his fingers even got half way around it, she had him in a wristlock and had slammed him down onto the table. Her other hand was around his windpipe, squeezing it shut. All the while, a truly dazzling smile was spreading across her face.

"As I told you, *little man*. I was just finishing my water." With that, she released his wrist and took the glass from his limp hand, drinking the contents down as he writhed on the tabletop. He was starting to turn purple.

Seeing his distress, the man's partner decided to intervene, and came at her. One of the first principles that she had learned during the hand-to-hand-combat phase of her SpecOps Training was that fights were not intended to be drawn-out affairs. The objective was to down an opponent quickly, and with the greatest economy of effort. N'Elemay had been one of the top students in that particular module, and she applied its principles to the letter.

Keeping her grip tight on her captive's throat, she simply turned and threw the glass straight at the oncoming male. It shattered squarely in the middle of his forehead, slashing it open and sending gouts of blood streaming into his eyes. The man reeled back, moaning and holding his bleeding face in his hands. Blinded, he was effectively out of the fight.

But a third man clearly didn't take any of this to heart, and not only decided to join in, but to attack her from behind, yelling something in Espangla that sounded very much to her ears like, "You fucking dyke bitch!"

She wasn't overly concerned with the exact content of his words though. Instead, as his hairy arm came around her neck, she reacted, releasing her first opponent, who was now quite unconscious, and sunk her fingers deep into the muscle of her new attacker's wrist and forearm. The man cried out in pain, and she rose slightly, bent forwards at the waist, and sent him flying into space. He hit the floor with a loud impact, but quickly regained his footing, yelling something else, that this time, was completely unintelligible.

N'Elemay waited calmly as he charged at her. The instant he was close enough, she responded to the attack with a jumping kick to his solar plexus, followed immediately by a hammer blow to the back of his neck as he folded over. He promptly collapsed into an insensible heap.

For a nanosecond, the bar around her was utterly still. Then the women reacted, cheering at her performance, while the males responded with cries of anger. But none of them attempted to rescue their companions, or to engage her. Instead, it was the nervous looking man working security that came up.

"You need to leave," he warned her. "Or I'll call the Shore Patrol."

Still smiling, N'Elemay primly patted down the few stray hairs that had escaped her otherwise perfect bun. "No troubles" she said quietly. "I was finished anyway."

She had been right to come here, she decided. She really did feel much better.

***

The moment that N'Elemay was back aboard the *Athena*, a Corporal was waiting for her, and escorted her immediately to Lieutenant sa'Kaali's office. News of the fight had traveled faster than an anti-ship torpedo flicking through Null.

"I understand that you were involved in a brawl, Troop Leader. At a mixed bar in the Neutral Sector," the officer stated.

"Ma'am, yes ma'am, I was," N'Elemay admitted.

"While it is vitally important that we educate our allies about the composition of our forces, and that we familiarize them with the fighting abilities of the Marauders in particular, what you did tonight is *not* how the Sisterhood wishes to accomplish that goal. Am I making myself clear?"

"Ma'am, yes, ma'am!"

"Good. Consider yourself officially reprimanded. Dismissed."

N'Elemay saluted her and started to leave.

But the El-Tee had one more thing to say. "By the way Ellen, next time you go, take me along. I hear the water is good down there and I wouldn't mind sharing a glass with you."

"Of course, Lieutenant."

Word of the incident at *The Halflife Club* spread to more than just the

Lieutenant, or even the crew of the *Athena*. From that point onwards, ETR troopers pointedly avoided *any* woman wearing a blue beret. They were also more polite in their interactions with regular Marines and navy women. There were only a few exceptions to this, and one of these would prove dangerous.

***

Trooper Manel Alvara was drunk. He'd been working on this since early that evening, and now he felt good and loose.

Just the thing to wash away the taste of the stockade, he thought. He had just finished doing a week in lock-up, for theft of supplies.

A week was nothing though, and so was the theft charge. He'd done more time than that back on Nuvo Bolivar, and he would have done a lot more if they'd ever caught him for any of the really serious capers that he'd pulled. But cops were idiots.

As it was, he was working off a sentence for felony assault through military service, and sometimes it seemed worse than doing straight time in a regular prison. Being sent to this godforsaken place certainly was, he thought. He took a long pull off his drink and looked across the bar at the women drinking there.

No, not women, he decided. *Not real women. Saapa Putayas*. That's what they were, lesbian whores. They all thought that they were so damned superior with their fancy ships and weapons, but it was all just plain luck as far as he was concerned.

If we had any of their stuff, he told himself, *they'd be nothing*. Nothing but the putayas that they really were.

He'd heard all about the lone blue beret that had rocked the place while he'd been in the 'stocks of course, and he still couldn't believe it. In his estimation, she'd probably just found a few of the worst troopers to pick on.

Hell, the troopers that she beat up were probably queers themselves.

Reassured by this conclusion, he took another swig from his drink, and then one of the women caught his eye as she walked up to the bar. She was a little thing, and putaya or not, he had to admit that she was pretty fine looking.

She was also all by herself, and he put his drink aside, and walked up to her. A few of the other women glared at him, but he ignored them.

"You look lonely," he said. "Did you come here to see what a real man feels like?"

The woman looked up at him. "Go away," she said. "I'm with someone. She'll be back soon."

"You mean your *putaya* girlfriend, don't you?" he grinned. "That works. I can do both of you. I'd enjoy that!"

"Fekka je Konnar!" she hissed, taking her drink and leaving the bar.

Manel laughed at her back. "Go back to your girlfriend, bitch," he said. "Prolly couldn't handle me anyhow!"

The security man walked up. He was hefting a piece of pipe, and from prior experience, Manel knew that he meant business. "Time for you to leave."

"Sure. It's a shitty bar anyhow," Alvara sneered. "Nothing but *putaya* here."

"Out!!"

When he came out into the street, he almost walked over to another bar, but then he realized that he had to take a leak, and pissing on the wall of the place that had just thrown him out sounded like a damned good idea. A narrow alley separated the building from its neighbor and he squeezed in and worked his way back to where the passage opened up onto a tiny yard. There were a few trashcans there, a chair, and someone sitting in it.

It wasn't an employee however. It was the little *putaya* from inside, he realized with a smile. "Well, lookie who's here!" he slurred, forgetting all about his need to urinate. "Did you come out here looking for me after all?"

"I told you to go away! *Gan se Ca!*" she growled, starting to rise. Until that moment, he had actually been in a good mood, but her stuck-up attitude suddenly made him angry, and he grabbed her by the shoulder. When she cried out and tried to pull away, this made him even angrier. And a kick to his shin took him right over the top.

"Saapa putaya!" he snarled, cocking his fist. When he brought it down into her face, he felt the soft flesh squash under its assault, and then the

bones in her face crunching wetly as they yielded to him.

The rest of her was going to submit to him as well—when he was damned good and ready. For the moment though, hitting her felt so good that he did it again, and again.

Finally, he tired of this, and that was when the real fun began.

***

Shore Patrolwoman Marla ebed Rena thought that she had finally gotten used to Salta Cia. Or at least to the putaya's. The fact that women would actually sell their bodies to men had horrified her at first. Then, this had resolved into anger, and finally simple disgust. In her opinion, Salta Cia, or at least the Neutral Sector, was as close to an open sewer as a town could be and still be livable.

The prostitute that they were dealing with had wandered over to the Sisterhood side to complain that she'd been robbed by one of her so-called 'customers', in the ETR sector of course, and way out of their jurisdiction. The woman probably knew that the ETR MP's wouldn't do a thing about it, and had just assumed the Sisterhood could and would. To top it all off, by the scars on her arms, Ebed Rena could tell the putaya was also a glass addict. *That* little treat had made its way to Altamara and over into the ETR faster than the Expeditionary Force had.

Her partner was in the process of trying to convince the woman to give up her 'job' for something worthy of herself, and failing miserably. But Lissa was new to Security, and still learning about police work. Her advice was going right in one of the putaya's ears and out the other side like a ship transiting Null.

"I don't care about all that! I just want my money back," the woman retorted. "That *fiho da marca* robbed me. You've got to get it back!"

Her partner was about to explain to her about the limits of their powers in the ETR sector—again—when the Com flashed a message. They had a call in Dogtown, the one place were they didn't have any limitations on their police powers.

"Ma'am," Ebed Rena interrupted tiredly, "we have to go. You can make a report about this incident at the checkpoint. It's right up the street."

"But—"

"But—make a report and we'll contact the ETR about it. Come on, Lissa." She was already moving towards their hovercar.

Her partner joined her and they took off from the curb. Behind them the putaya was stamping up to the checkpoint, already forgotten.

"What do we have?" Lissa asked.

"Some kind of assault at the *Halflife Club*. One of ours was involved."

"Shess, I just hope it's not some of those damned Marauders again," the woman frowned. The last time, it had been, and the three ETR troopers had been pretty banged up. On top of that, they'd had a whole galaxy worth of angry ETR Shore Patrolmen to deal with when they got there. It had been an ugly scene, and they'd had to call for back up just to settle things down.

This time though, it had nothing to do with the Blue Berets. A couple of Sisterhood sailors met them outside and frantically waved them into the bar. Ebed Rena didn't see any males hanging around, and the women that were there looked like they were ready to go nova. When they reached the small yard in the back, the reason became horribly clear.

"Her pairmate was just here," someone said. "I think she's gone out looking for him."

"*Dees dam va!*" Ebed Rena barked. As she broke out a small med kit from her duty belt and opened up a field dressing, she shouted over her shoulder to her partner. "Get a med team down here now and get a description out on that pairmate and the suspect. Burn it!"

***

Manel watched the Sisterhood cruiser pass, and ducked into the shadows. *Well, I screwed up again,* he thought ruefully. But all he had to do was go a little bit further and he'd be back in his own sector. Then it would all go away. He had a couple of buddies there who would vouch for him. Then it would be his word against the putaya's. That would teach her—right on top of the little lesson he'd taught her in the alley.

Another cruiser flew by and he backed further into the shadows, but despite the situation, he had to grin. *Yeah,* he thought, *I taught her real good.* He felt himself getting aroused all over again just thinking about it.

Just then, a noise sounded behind him, and he turned around, expecting to see a Shore Patrolman and hear a challenge. But it wasn't a Shore Patrolman. It wasn't even a man. It was one of the really weird looking Sisterhood women, with green skin and a tail. She also had a knife in her hand as long as his arm.

He started to say something to her. But before he could finish, her slitted eyes narrowed and she growled like the animal that she resembled, becoming something right out of one of the worst nightmares he'd ever had about Hell. With a hiss, she leapt at him.

From very far away, he heard himself scream.

***

When the military policewoman shone her flash-beam down the alleyway, it illuminated a horrific scene. A Nemesian Marine was standing over something on the ground and she was covered in blood. As the light played on the mass at the woman's feet, the policewoman realized that it was a body, or what was left of one.

The ETR trooper lay face up in a pool of gore with an expression of terror frozen on his face. There was a huge bloody stain between his legs, and something small and wet lay nearby. Her mind matched it with what she knew of male anatomy, and processed what it was, or rather, had been.

As the realization hit home, she drew her sidearm. "Military Police! Drop the knife!"

The Nemesian spun on her heels to face her, Tej knife at the ready and hissed, exposing her canines.

"Drop the knife *now* or I *will* shoot you!" the policewoman warned. Her finger began to tighten on the firing stud.

The Nemesian blinked, and then she seemed to come out of her spell, and shrugged. "I offer you no resistance, sister," she said, gently putting her knife down on the blood soaked ground and exposing her hands. "My honor has been satisfied."

***

By the time Col. Lislsdaater arrived at the crime scene, it had been cordoned off and a combination of Sisterhood MP's and ETR Shore Patrolmen were keeping the curious away. A crowd of Sisterhood sailors and Marines ringed one end of the area, yelling obscenities, and an equally large group of ETR soldiers and sailors were on the other, doing the same. The mood was ugly, and Lislsdaater knew that the situation was just a spark away from turning into a full-scale riot.

"What happened?" she asked the senior-most patrolwoman.

"The Nemesian's pairmate was assaulted by an ETR trooper back behind the *Halflife Club*," the Troop Leader said. "His name was Manel Alvara. He had just been released from the stockade after doing time for theft. He also had a long record of other crimes, and he was out here serving a stint with their army instead of going to prison. After the assault, our Marine tracked him down and cut him up with her Tej knife. We have her in custody, and the Ship's Med Team is treating her pairmate. From what I heard, she's in pretty bad shape."

"How bad?"

"Well, I'll leave anything official to the 'paints', but they say the ETR trooper sexually violated her, ma'am, after beating her severely. She has a broken jaw, a busted cheekbone and a couple of shattered ribs. They also told me there's the good possibility of some internal injuries."

"Is that the ETR trooper over there on the ground?" Lislsdaater asked.

"What's left of him," the officer replied. "Like I said, the Nemesian sliced him up pretty good. The MP who took her into custody said that when she arrested her, the Nemesian had just finished cutting his genitals off."

"Nemesians do tend to react a bit harshly when the honor of a loved one has been sullied," Lislsdaater remarked casually. "But at least she saved us the trouble of hanging the man."

Although it had never been invoked against a male due to the intercession of the MARS Plague, the penalty in the Sisterhood for rape—by anyone, male or female—was death. Lislsdaater was glad that the matter had been handled without the drama of a lengthy court trial, albeit in a rather gruesome fashion.

And good riddance, you fek, she thought. *I just hope that it was slow, and painful.*

Then, just when she was beginning to think that her evening couldn't get any more unpleasant, her counterpart with the ETR arrived. His face was scarlet with rage.

"Colonel," he said. "We want the *woman* responsible for this atrocity up on charges. In fact, we want her placed in *our* custody right now!"

"Straight to business and no kiss to sweeten it up, I see," Lislsdaater returned flippantly. "Then I will be equally businesslike with you. The answer is no, Major, in fact, let me rephrase that; *fek* no. You can take the matter up with an Advocate if you want, but the *woman* you are referring to is a Sisterhood Marine, and she falls under *our* jurisdiction, not yours. We'll keep her."

"We'll just see about that!" he snarled. "In the meantime, I can't be held responsible for the actions of my men. The news has gotten around about what that woman did to one of their own, and there's going to be trouble! You can count on it!"

"Let's hope that you are mistaken," she replied coolly. "I'd hate to be forced to order my troopers to open fire on a mob, especially since we're all supposed to be such good, close friends."

The Major's face went from red to purple. "We're going to get her Colonel! And she's going to face *our* courts, not *yours*. I know how you Sisterhood *women* are, and you won't get away with just a slap on the wrist for this."

"Best of luck with that," Lislsdaater said sardonically. "Now if you don't mind, Major, I have other things to attend to." She gave him a salute and turned smartly on her heels without bothering to see if he returned it or not.

USSNS *Pallas Athena*, In-Orbit, Altamara 1, Altamara System, Frontera Provensa, Esteral Terrana Rapabla, 1044.09|30|08:97:25

At a kilometer in length, getting to some places aboard the *Athena* on foot could be exhausting. While an interior shuttle system and the Lifts did their part to facilitate travel, a simpler and healthier alternative that most large naval vessels employed was the venerable bicycle.

Although it performed the same job, it wasn't the bike of Old Gaia however. Instead it was composed of plastics derived from carbon nanotubes, Kevlar, nylon, and host of other materials that gave it an overall weight of less than 0.9 kilograms, and a structural strength that far surpassed its predecessors.

The bicycles reserved for officers were housed in racks just outside of the entrance to Officer's Country. Lilith selected one for herself, unfolded its wheels and its handlebars, and set off down the main corridor that ran the length of the deck. She actually enjoyed riding when the opportunity presented itself. Not only was it good exercise, but it also gave her a chance to be alone with her thoughts.

She had a lot to think about.

Tensions between her forces and their ETR counterparts had been rising steadily since the onset of the campaign. Guzamma had become increasingly discontent with his reduced role in the conflict, and several of his commanders had deliberately deviated from their operational plans with his tacit approval. She had also received reports of altercations taking place between personnel on the ground, at Salta Cia and elsewhere. All of this had been anticipated however, and none of it had been serious enough to merit any real concern—until now.

The violation of Sailor Suzzyn t'Neena, and the bloody retribution exacted by her lover, had not only caught her command at something of a loss in terms of an appropriate response, but had also exacerbated the situation between the ETR and the Sisterhood to the boiling point. Almost as soon as Trooper Vala taur Tanna had been taken into custody, the local commander of the ETR naval forces had been on the Com with Admiral da'Kayt, demanding that the Marine be turned over to him.

She'd refused him of course, but according to what she had reported to Lilith when *she* had called *her* looking for explanations, the normally unruffable Admiral had nearly resorted to profanities before the man had backed off. Da'Kayt had also requested—actually ordered—that Lilith get as much detail as soon as possible about the event and get back with her. Hence, her impromptu bike ride.

Even Captain Rodraga had been affected by this turn of events, she reflected. Just after her call from the Admiral, she'd met him on the way to her bicycle, and while he was as polite as always, their brief conversation had been noticeably stilted, and his smile had seemed forced. She didn't blame him for being upset about the incident, but she also didn't welcome this disruption to their working relationship.

The whole thing was a goddess-damned mess, Lilith thought, as she pulled up outside of Conference Room 12, and walked in. She couldn't wait to find some resolution that would set things back on an even keel.

N'Dira had already seated herself, and Katrinn, Col. Lislsdaater and the Ship's Security Chief, Captain Veera t'Gwen were also present.

"You know," she said as she joined them, "I love having a good, set routine, getting through my day, knowing exactly what I'm going to do, and when to do it. It's just too bad that I never get to actually do that. It would be *really* nice once in a while."

"Hello, Lily," Ellyn n'Dira said. "Sorry to spoil your day."

"It happens to everyone, and especially Vice Admirals." Then she told them about Da'Kayt's call. "So, what do we have?"

"As you know Taur Tanna is in the Brig," the Advocate told her. "She was brought upside just as soon as Shore Patrol had her in custody."

"What is the situation in Salta Cia?" Lilith asked. This was directed to Lislsdaater and T'Gwen.

"'Strained' would be the most polite way to describe it," Captain t'Gwen answered. "Marya and I agreed to close down Dogtown, and we have our girls staying at the ready for riot duty if it comes down to that."

"Good," Lilith said. "Does Taur Tanna have council yet?" It went without saying that there would be a court martial.

"Yes, I assigned Lieutenant Manda n'Nyle to her case," N'Dira said. "I've also recommended that N'Nyle have Taur Tanna's case heard on Rixa. She agreed to the change of venue, and it was approved by the Advocate General's Office."

"That's a good idea," Lilith agreed. "Admiral da'Kayt also feels that way. When we spoke, she even suggested the idea. Getting Taur Tanna away from here will certainly help ease things a bit."

"A bit," N'Dira replied. "But only that. The ETR's JAG office contacted me right before you arrived, and they demanded that we remand Taur Tanna to them. I told them where they could file their request."

Lilith grinned sardonically. "That was very helpful of you, Ellyn. So, what do you think Taur Tanna's chances are in court?"

"Fairly good, actually," the woman answered. "The Sisterhood Code of Naval Justice allows for 'crimes of passion' in cases where a life has been taken outside of a wartime setting, and temporary insanity can be demonstrated. N'Nyle will certainly try to make a case for that, and given the eyewitness testimony, and especially the statements Taur Tanna made to bystanders, and to the Patrolwoman who arrested her, I think she'll succeed.'

"The prosecution will probably try to counter by challenging their testimony and citing the element of premeditation. After all, she did go out looking for the man, and theoretically had the time to cool off.'

"But I don't think those objections will go very far. Crimes of passion have been allowed in the past, even where premeditation existed, provided that the time period from the incitement to murder and the commission of the act wasn't too great, and this affair didn't take more than a few minutes at the outside.'

"If N'Nyla can't make this argument, then she could cite the Nemesian Planetary Code, which would also argue that Taur Tanna as one of their citizens, was one hundred percent justified. As for the Thalestris Elant's codes, they don't take a position one way or the other, but there have been similar cases heard before their courts that establish the precedent of exonerating women who have taken a life in 'affairs of honor'.

"The court will also have to take into account the fact that no man-on-woman rape has occurred since the MARS Plague, clearly contributing to Taur Tanna's overall state of mind. N'Nyla will certainly use the appalling nature of the rape to its fullest advantage, and she won't have to try very hard to be convincing on that score."

Lilith inclined her head in understanding. Although woman-on-woman rapes did occur, they were fairly rare, and they had none of the shock value that the rape of Sailor t'Neena had. Her physical violation pushed every button that Motherthought had instilled in the average woman, and Lilith was no exception. She was too professional to say it out loud, but she was glad that the man who had done it was dead, and that he'd died the way he had.

"So, what do you think the judgment will be?" she asked. "Any guesses?"

"If I had to gamble," N'Dira responded, "I'd wager on 'Not Guilty, with Prejudice', and most likely a less-than-honorable discharge for 'gross conduct unbecoming a Sisterhood Marine,' with time served. But you never know anything for certain until you're in the court room."

Lilith sighed. "I suppose that's better than a correctional colony. I also don't imagine that her people back on Nemesis will hold her actions, or a 'less-than-honorable' against her."

"No, they won't," N'Dira said. "If I know anything about the Nemesians, she'll probably be considered a role model for their little girls."

"Goddess save us from other 'examples' like her, or victims like her mate," Lilith replied, and they all made the Sign of the Lady. Then she looked over at Katrinn. "Kat, I want her on the first transport heading out to Rixa."

"Already being taken care of, Lily."

"Good. Colonel, Captain, Dogtown is to remain off-limits to all personnel until further notice, and keep your people on their toes until the air clears a bit."

Everyone rose to leave and carry out their orders, and Lilith lit a czigavar for herself. Then, after taking a deep drag from it, she got on the Com and called Da'Kayt back.

***

Erin taur Minna also had an interest in Taur Tanna's situation, not only as a woman, but also as a fellow Nemesian. When she had the opportunity, she went down to the Brig, and asked to see her. A Security policewoman escorted her to a visiting room, and the Marine was brought in.

Her fatigues were gone, and she was dressed in the plain white jumpsuit that all naval prisoners wore, with only her name and service number stenciled on the chest and the back of the garment. But some blood from a wound on her upper arm had managed to seep past the dressing medbay had applied to it, lending a grotesque splash of color that drew Erin's eyes right to it.

She knew what the source of the injury was without having to ask. Taur Tanna had done it to herself with her Tej knife just after killing the ETR soldier, as a mark of honor for victory in battle. Erin regarded the woman with understanding, and respect. Taur Tanna had satisfied her honor, and that of her mate.

"*Hai'a Sh'tun'aq*," she said to her in *Kl'all'a*. "Tell me sister, are you well?"

"As well as one might expect," Taur Tanna replied with a shrug. "They say I will be facing a court martial on Rixa."

"I will send word to your Clan," Erin assured the woman. "I know that they will want to hear of your deed and know that you are well."

"It is often said that the Minna are very kind," Taur Tanna said. The Tanna Clan called the forests on the opposite side of Nemesis their home and the two groups had little, if any contact. "It would seem that this is true. *H'sxw'qeh, sh'tun'aq*."

"And what of your *Tej'q'ues*, your Tej knife, sister? What became of it?"

"It was taken from me when I was arrested," Taur Tanna answered. "They said that it is evidence of my crime."

"I can see no need for that," Erin said. "Didn't you admit your act of honor to them?"

"*Hee'ya*, I did. I told them I had killed the *Shu'man hwa'ni'tem* to avenge my pairmate."

"Then I shall get the knife from them," Erin told her. "They will have no need of it. I will also see to it that it is properly cared for by your Clan until you are set free."

"Again, you are too kind to me. I will not forget it, and someday, I will repay you for the favor."

"*Tashi'a'ela'k*," Erin answered. Then she took her leave of her, and made straight for Captain t'Gwen's office, where she requested to see the *Athena's* Security Chief.

T'Gwen still had the knife, locked away in her evidence vault, and she had been waiting to send it, along with her prisoner, to Rixa for trial. But when Erin explained her purpose, she proved quite understanding. After clearing it with Lt. Commander n'Dira, who agreed that it wasn't really required, T'Gwen gave it over to Erin's custody.

It was some time before the opportunity arose to do so, but when it did, Erin had the weapon shipped back to Nemesis, and to Jaala taur Haus'ka at the Shadow Lake Lodge. She only worried over the matter until confirmation came back that Taur Haus'ka had received it. After that, all of her concern disappeared.

Jaala taur Haus'ka and her Clan understood the meaning of honor and obligation. It was not even a question of whether they would deliver the knife to Taur Tanna's relatives or not. No matter the trouble involved, Erin knew they would see the task to completion, and when it arrived, the Tanna would hang it in a place of honor, and sing of Taur Tanna's great deed. For them, for Erin, and for any true Nemesian, honor was all that really mattered. The Great Mother Forest taught that essential truth to all her children, and deeds like Taur Tanna's, only served to reinforce it.

Highway 70, Bujara, Jujoya System, Marisal Provensa,
Esteral Terrana Rapabla, 1044.10|07|00:001:71

Like any military force, the vast majority of personnel serving in the Sisterhood armed forces worked in functions that supported their front-line troops. As a result, when Lena had applied for the Quartermistress' Corps, her application was accepted immediately. Her service record had guaranteed her a posting on Rixa itself, but with the forging of the alliance between the Sisterhood and the ETR, her situation had rapidly changed. She found herself reporting for duty on Bujara instead, in a forward supply depot that supported ETR elements left behind by Admiral n'Deesa's fast moving raider force. Their job on Bujara was to mop up the planets' remaining Hriss defenders.

The young woman wasn't overly pleased with her new assignment, but it was still a far cry from serving in a front line combat unit. Her duties consisted of transporting supplies from the depot at the spaceport and hauling them by hovertruck out to secondary storage areas, and back again. At the moment, she was on just such a mission, and had gone out with a partner, carrying a load of spare parts in a hovertruck that they had requisitioned from the depot's motor pool.

The 'trucks left-hand anti-grav pod had been acting up lately, and when she'd been issued the vehicle, the mechanics in the motor-pool had promised Lena, on the Goddesses honor, that it had been properly serviced. But right in the middle of the desert, and exactly halfway to their destination, the suspensor pod let out a low whine, and expired.

Her co-driver who was riding shotgun, tried to contact the supply depot immediately. But with all the action going on nearby, the frequency was jammed with chatter. The truck was effectively grounded until it was quiet enough for someone to hear them, and either come to tow it out, or replace the pod itself.

The two of them were in the process of deciding whether a 32-kilometer march back to base was a better alternative than spending the night in the cab, when they spotted the headlights of another hovertruck. They could tell immediately that it wasn't a Sisterhood vehicle, and Lena recognized it as an ETR machine. As it drew closer, they got out, and Lena waved, feeling a little embarrassed at being broken down. After all, the Sisterhood was supposed to have better equipment than the Republic. But a ride was a ride, she told herself, and things happened to everyone.

The ETR 'truck stopped short and several men got out. Like everyone else serving in the battle zone, she'd been given a PTS course in Espangla, but she hadn't had the chance to actually practice their allies' language very much. Now it seemed that her opportunity had arrived.

"Hoyaa" she said, *"Graciar pey aya altomar. Siyas mechanica a*

destaril. Mayas a la tormovila ate la depara attendensmo?" Thank you for stopping. We've broken down. Can you give us a ride to the next depot?"

Instead of greeting her, or agreeing to give them a lift, the soldiers surrounded them and inexplicably, raised their weapons. Lena's eyes went wide in shock and surprise.

"Estay asto da Ermanda Unita da Saalas!" she cried, amazed that they had somehow failed to recognize that she and her partner were Sisterhood Marines. The weapons stayed trained on them.

"Mannas Arrebar! Nolo sey Mavar!" one of the men barked.

She couldn't believe it. He was ordering her to raise her hands! It had to be some kind of mistake. She automatically started to obey, but her partner had no such intentions.

"Listen here," the woman said angrily in Standard, "We're with the Sisterhood, you idiots. Put down those weapons now!"

To Lena's horror, the ETR soldier fired his weapon. A hole the size of Lena's fist opened up in her partners' chest, accompanied by a puff of bloody steam. The woman staggered backwards gasping for breath with a look of total astonishment painted on her features.

As she flopped backwards onto the sand and died, Lena screamed. That was when the soldier nearest her raised the butt of his blaster and brought it down on the back of her head.

***

When Lena returned to consciousness she was no longer in the desert. In fact, she wasn't on Bujara. Instead, she found herself shackled to a low metal bench in a small cell. Her fatigues were gone, and in their place, she was wearing a simple gown like the ones she had seen in hospitals.

From the vibrations alone, she knew that she was aboard a ship of some kind. She heard the sounds of someone walking by after this, and called out to them, wincing as her head forcefully reminded her of the injury it had suffered.

"Hello? There's been some kind of mistake," she yelled. "Take me to your Commanding Officer so I can speak with him." But whoever it had been passed her by, heedless of her entreaty.

An hour, or more passed. Then a slot opened in the wall and a tray of food popped out. It wasn't anything that she was used to eating, and a wave of nausea destroyed any appetite that she might have otherwise possessed. Sickened, she pushed the tray away and gathered her feet up underneath her, trying to figure out what was going on, and what to do next.

Maybe we're at war with the ETR now, she thought with a chill. There had been speculation on and off between her fellow Marines that this might happen, and it was the only plausible explanation for what was taking place.

Which meant only one thing: she was now a prisoner of war. The lecture she'd heard in Basic on that subject came back to her, and Lena began to panic. But the horrors of captivity that had been described there had been at the hands of the Hriss, she reminded herself. The ETR were humans, and would certainly observe some of the same conventions that the Sisterhood would.

At least she hoped that this was the case.

Time went by without any resolution, and she slept. Finally, her cell door opened, and a tall, dangerous-looking ETR soldier waved at her to step out. When she obeyed, the man clapped a pair of manacles on her wrists and led her down a long passageway, lined with cells just like her own.

In the process, she discovered that she was not alone. Another woman, dressed in Navy black, was also being escorted just ahead of her, and Lena resisted the urge to call out to her. It was better to wait, she decided, and to speak with whoever was in charge instead.

At the end of her journey however, all that awaited her was a long docking tube, and a hard steel bench, which she was immediately shackled to. There were other women there, including the Navy woman, and as soon as the guards left them alone, Lena leaned over and whispered to her.

"Are we at war?" she asked.

The sailor shook her head doubtfully. "I don't think so," she told her. "Just before these apes took me, everything seemed fine. We were even talking with them, telling each other jokes. Then they turned on us. I think this is something else, but I don't know what."

Lena was about to ask her what she meant by this when one of the guards returned.

"Shut up!" he yelled in thickly accented Standard. Then, just to show that he meant business, he produced a stun baton and flicked it on. Lena shrank away from the crackling energy field and kept her mouth shut for the rest of the trip.

Some time later, more guards appeared and they went down the line, unshackling everyone, and making them run out of the ship into waiting ground transports. Lena tried to get her bearings and determine where they were, or anything else that would have proven useful, but aside from establishing that they were inside some sort of military base, she was completely disoriented.

When the transports stopped, they were herded into a building that looked and smelled like a hospital. There, she was taken and put into another cell.

It was rectangular in shape, with just enough room for a cot and a combination toilet and sink. The chamber also had a pair of heavy doors; the one that she had been brought in through, and another at what she reasoned was the head of the room. Both portals had tiny observation windows, and looking through one, she saw a hallway, and another cell across from her.

Above it was an electronic sign displaying a name and a number. It was a Sisterhood name, and the number was definitely a military service identification number. The place was some kind of prison for Sisterhood women, Lena realized. She backed away from the window, and sat on the edge of her cot, weeping in despair.

Eventually, a meal was served to her through a slot in the wall, and despite her misery, she consumed it. When rescue came, or an opportunity to escape revealed itself, she knew that she would need every bit of her strength to take advantage of the situation.

More time went by, and then, abruptly, the lights went out. With no other options, Lena lay down in the darkness and forced herself into a fitful sleep.

Some time later, they came back on again, and a pair of guards dressed incongruously in something resembling spacesuits came into her cell. Once she had been re-shackled, they took her into an exam room. In the middle of the space was a metal table, and when Lena spotted the restraints that it was equipped with, she panicked.

"No!" she cried, trying to back away from the table. But the guards grabbed her by her arms and lifted her small squirming form up and onto it. She tried to kick them away, to bite them, to do anything to resist, but their hard plastic suits prevented her from dealing them any injury. In short order, they had her strapped down securely.

Then they left her there, and her fear grew exponentially. When she was finally certain that she wouldn't be able to stand another second of waiting, she heard the door hiss open. An elderly man dressed in the same kind of white plastic spacesuit that the guards had worn, entered the room. From behind the transparent visor, his face seemed kindly, and he even smiled at her.

Despite her terror, she realized that he actually wore glasses, and the sight of them reminded the part of her that was still vaguely coherent just how archaic the ETR really was. No one wore those anymore.

"Good evening young lady," the man said in Standard. "I am Doctor Adolpha Sanchar. What is your name please?"

"N'Gari, Lena, Trooper 412345679!" she answered, feigning bravery.

"What is the world of your birth?"

"N'Gari, Lena, Trooper 412345679!" she repeated.

The man looked at her thoughtfully. "Yes, of course," he finally said. "Name rank and serial number, just as required." He sighed tiredly and went over to a small table filled with instruments, selecting a syringe.

"You and I are going to become very well acquainted, Miss n'Gari, Lena, Trooper 412345679," he said. He walked over to her and without warning, jabbed the needle into her arm.

Lena cried out, but the man was completely unaffected.

"You know," he said, expertly drawing out a sample of her blood. "You resemble my granddaughter, around the eyes at least. A remarkable similarity in genotypes, don't you think? And after more than a millennia of separation! Working with you will be a true scientific pleasure."

***

Lena spent her next two days in her cell. The only break in the monotony was the admission or collection of food trays.

At first, she had paced, and then tried to find ways to contact her fellow inmates. And when she got tired of this, she sat down on the edge of her cot and let the hours slide by. Or wept. Or yelled at her captors. None of it changed a thing or altered her situation though.

On the beginning of her third day, they came for her again. She had had no warning of their arrival, only the sudden sound of the door behind her unlocking, and two burley guards entering, dressed in their hard suits. The men said nothing to her as always, and terrified by them, Lena tried to escape. There was nowhere to go however, and they wrestled her into restraints and seated her in a wheelchair that was waiting in the narrow hallway outside.

"Where are we going?" she pleaded. "Please! Tell me what you're doing! Why am I here?" The only response they gave her as they wheeled her along, was stony silence.

At the end of the hall, another door unlocked, and she was brought into an examination room. It was either the first one she had been taken to, or one very much like it. Dr. Sanchar was there.

"Good morning, Miss n'Gari, Lena 412345679," he said with a smile. "I have some excellent news to share with you. It seems that you are quite a special girl. From your blood sample, I was able to determine that you are a class C Thermadonian genotype."

"What are you talking about?" Lena demanded. "Why are you doing this? Let me go!"

"What I am talking about is genetics young lady, and specifically your genetic heritage. We've already managed to work out solutions for the other genomes that exist in your Sisterhood, but until you came along, we hadn't been able to completely address the Thermadonian group. Of all the genotypes, your group possesses the most variation, and we had no one with class C traits. Now we do, and thanks to you, we may finally be able to complete our work." With that, he produced a small bottle and a syringe.

"W-what is that?" Lena stammered as he drew some of the contents out of the bottle.

"'That' is lot 22-Q-05. As for what we are doing, we are testing it on you to see how you respond. Personally, I hope that it will not work. I'd enjoy the chance to study you a bit longer," he replied. "But if it does, then the demands of my duty have been amply satisfied." At a nod from him, one of the guards swabbed her arm with alcohol.

"Testing? Testing what? Please, you have to let me go! I haven't done anything!" Although she was strapped to the wheelchair, she desperately tried to move her arm away from the needle as he approached with it. A guard held her down.

With her arm firmly pinned, Lena could only watch in dread as Sanchar injected her. The sight of the needle piercing her flesh finally pushed her over the edge and she screamed. But all this produced was a gentle pat on the shoulder.

"There now, Miss n'Gari, Lena 412345679," Sanchar said. "All finished. Now we simply wait."

He addressed her guards next, "Please, take her back to her cell and document her symptoms at five minute intervals."

Lena found out what he meant an hour later. A feeling of general malaise rapidly overcame her, and she began to sweat profusely. Then she started to cough.

And cough. And cough. As her lungs tried to clear themselves, she staggered over to her cot, and then collapsed.

Several days of misery followed before her illness abated. Then, when she had more or less recovered, the guards returned. This time, she was too weak to put up much of a fight, and they wheeled her to Dr. Sanchar with comparatively little effort.

"It seems, Miss n'Gari, Lena 412345679, that lot 22-Q-05 did not work quite as well as hoped. So, today, we are going to try another batch and see if we get better results. As for myself," he added, holding up another bottle and another needle, "I am very curious how you managed to survive the effects of 22-Q-05. Several of your compatriots who were class B and D did not. But don't worry yourself on that account. We'll ferret out the reason soon enough, won't we?"

Lena didn't scream this time. Instead, all that she could manage was a miserable whimper of despair. *Kaly,* she thought desperately, *wherever you are, help me! I need you.*

CHAPTER 10

USSNS *Boudicca* , Santosena System, Argenta Provensa,
Esteral Terrana Rapabla, 1044.10|12|03:11:66

After Tiyas, Qyarda, Tensamentra and Santosena had been retaken by the SEF, only Xapaan remained. The planning session for the assault took place aboard the *Boudicca*, hosted by Admiral da'Kayt. At the joint insistence of the Senior Medical Officers from both the *Athena* and the Admiral's own flagship, the participants ate a light lunch first, and agreed to take regular breaks. Simply promising to 'eat at the boards' had failed to satisfy the doctors, and they wanted their superiors to be at their best, and everyone, up to and including the Admiral herself, had been forced to capitulate. Even so, lunch was limited to sandwiches, and kept as brief as possible by everyone.

In addition to Lilith and Vice Admiral ben Biya, N'Leesa was present via holo and Grand Admiral Guzamma had also joined them, courtesy of a signal sent from the USSNS *Ch'iao K'uo Fü Jën*. Lilith had also taken the step of inviting Captain Rodraga to join their group, with Da'Kayt's blessings, and her own ETR liaison officer, Captain Agwalar, accompanied him. Not only did they want these men to be kept abreast of their plans, but Lilith had learned over the course of her association with Rodraga that he was not one of Guzamma's sycophants, and could conceivably provide them with honest insights, at least to the extent he could as Guzamma's subordinate, and a foreign naval officer.

Although things had cooled between them after the incident with Taur Tanna, today, the man seemed like his old self, and Lilith was glad for it. Xapaan would require them to work very closely together, and any personal strains (except where they concerned Guzamma, whom no one really cared about) would have made the operation harder than it already was.

The ETR had attempted to retake Xapaan once, and their effort had ended in disaster. Although Guzamma was likely to sugar over his own errors, she was reasonably certain that Rodraga wouldn't make excuses—and that he would tell them what had really gone wrong with the assault. To facilitate his candor, Lilith had established a psiever channel to his pathminder in order for them to converse in private, with Rodraga using the keypad of the device to manage his end of the dialogue.

Seeing that everyone was ready, Da'Kayt began the session, getting straight to the point with the Grand Admiral. "Admiral Guzamma, I read your after-action report, and I understand that the Republican Navy was repulsed at Xapaan. Can you tell us why you believe that this happened? I reviewed your figures, and on the surface at least, your fleet strength seemed adequate for the task."

She didn't add, that she was also fully aware of their technical inadequacy to handle such an operation on their own.

An angry flush rose into his heavy features. He was not a man who dealt with criticism well. Which is what made him as weak as he was, Lilith concluded. A good leader accepted her faults and learned from them—but then again, she reminded herself, Guzamma *was* characteristically male in this regard.

"The enemy's fortifications were too well hidden," he finally said uncomfortably, "and the ships that were garrisoned in the inner system used their numbers to bolster their strength. By themselves, we might have beaten them, but then reinforcements arrived and the situation became untenable. We had to withdraw."

From the data that had been provided, it was clear that the battle had been the modern equivalent of medieval siege warfare. The ETR Navy had gone in at Xapaan full tilt, only to be stopped cold by the systems defenses like a castle wall repelling mounted knights.

Not that this was entirely Guzamma's fault, Lilith conceded; the Hriss were true artists when it came to concealed weapons emplacements, and the ETR's primitive detection technology had missed them. The Grand Admiral's forces simply hadn't had any idea what they had been coming up against until it had been too late.

Da'Kayt brought the system up on the room's holojector. It showed the five planets and their primary, along with a dense ring of asteroids situated between the fourth and fifth planets. A large number of the asteroids were marked in red, indicating known anti-spacecraft installations.

Quite a number in fact. Xapaan's stellar 'wall' was formidable, especially for a force that couldn't see it.

The Hriss ships that the ETR had encountered were also displayed on the map, but everyone understood that like the fortifications, their numbers and positions had most likely changed. Despite this, Lilith realized that any attempt to take Xapaan would be a major undertaking, and she was genuinely surprised that the Republican forces had even tried.

Apparently, Xapaan had been one of their first operations in the Provensa and the Hriss reinforcements that had come to its aid had all originated from neighboring star systems. None of these had been heavily occupied at the time, but as a combined force, and risking counterattack in the places that they had just vacated, the relieving body had been quite formidable, especially with the assistance of Xapaan's resident elements. Had it been her, she would have waited, and invested her own assets in the lesser systems first, wearing the enemy down where they were the weakest. Xapaan would have been left for the very end—which was exactly what Admiral da'Kayt and the SEF already *had* done.

It was time to test Rodraga's worth as an advisor, she decided. His ship, the *Adaventara,* had been involved in the Xapaan affair and he had firsthand knowledge of the entire debacle. She sent him a message.

Why did the Grand Admiral go straight for Xapaan instead of taking the lesser systems around it first?

There was a slight pause as Rodraga typed out his answer. *He wanted a decisive victory,* he replied, *He felt that Xapaan was the key to this Provensa, and he believed that if it could be taken right away, that the rest of our operations in the area would be a simple mop-up. We didn't think that the Hriss would abandon the other systems to reinforce it like they did. We were caught between the two groups, and as he said, we had to retreat.*

Which had resulted not only in a rout, Lilith mused, but had also forced the withdrawal of the ETR from the entire Provensa. Guzamma was firmly proving himself to be a blithering idiot. She was also fairly certain, without having to confirm it with Rodraga, that he, along with the rest of Guzamma's staff, had warned the man about this possibility in advance, and equally certain that he had ignored their advice.

In the final analysis, it seemed to her that the entire affair had been nothing less than an arrogant bid by the Grand Admiral for a quick victory, using brute force, and very little planning to achieve it. In short, it had been perfectly in character, and if it ever came to a war between their two nations, an equally valuable fact that could be used against him in battle. Although she did find herself wondering, given his clear lack of military prowess, what kind of *Intima* or *Terminér* he possessed to ensure his continued tenure as the commander of the ETR's Navy. It had to be just as considerable as his ineptitude.

Pondering this mystery, Lilith relayed Rodraga's reply, and her own insights, including those regarding Guzamma's flaws, to Da'Kayt. The Trilanian listened to her thoughts, and then smiled at Guzamma.

"Fortunately," the woman said aloud, "we have had a lot of experience in detecting and dealing with Hriss fortifications, and while they do appear to be rather extensive in this system, I believe that we can find a way through them. I suggest that we mass our respective forces in the nearest star systems, and send out reconnaissance teams to update what information we have about Xapaan."

"Yes, yes," Guzamma agreed curtly, "That was precisely what I was going to suggest. I will dispatch several of our light cruisers and have them conduct reconnaissance missions right away."

Lilith was aghast. If they weren't shot to pieces, then it was a certainty that they would miss almost everything there. Neither she nor her superior let their shared distaste show on their faces however. Instead, Da'Kayt patiently interjected. "I had something *else* in mind, Grand Admiral. If you will indulge me—"

She waited for a polite second, and when the man finally rewarded her with a stiff nod, she continued, "I propose that we send one of our cruisers, with several of our Nightingale shuttles with Special Operations teams aboard.'

"As you know, the Nightingales are well suited for infiltration missions. While the Hriss might detect your cruiser, they will miss ours, and the Nightingales. The Nightingales can then conduct a quiet, detailed survey of the area, and the teams can prepare key fortifications in advance of our attack.'

"This will not only provide us with the critical information that we will need to formulate our final plan of attack, but also pave the way to disabling the more potent enemy assets located there."

What the Trilanian had just proposed was nothing terribly impressive, nor original. In fact, it was straight out of basic Academy procedure for such an operation.

"That sounds like precisely the direction to take," Guzamma agreed, revealing his ignorance in the process. "I was just thinking about presenting something very much like it as an alternative, Admiral. It seems that all truly great commanders think alike."

Lilith had to work very hard to suppress her laughter at his pomposity. But she also had to remind herself that despite his constant efforts to glorify his own reputation, which had been greatly bolstered by the string of victories that they had helped him to achieve, he finally did seem to be listening to them. Even if he was taking credit that he didn't deserve. It was a step forwards.

"Of course, Grand Admiral, "Da'Kayt replied diplomatically. "Now, if there is nothing else, I suggest that we adjourn and set everything in motion. We will reconvene once the Nightingales have something to give us and fine tune our plans then." She bowed to all of them. "Ladies, gentlemen."

Xapaan System, Argenta Provensa, Esteral Terrana Rapabla,
1044.10|18|04:58:33

Although the Hriss forces in the Argenta and Cataala Provensas were on high alert, they didn't detect the USSNS *Calamity Jane* when she came out of Null and hid herself in the system's Oort cloud. And once the moment seemed right, the light cruiser launched her Nightingales.

The Infiltrators quickly moved into their assigned quadrants. There, they began the long process of mapping the Hriss defenses in the asteroid belt, sending back their findings to the *Jane* in encoded bursts that were specifically designed to mimic normal space noise.

The vast percentage of the installations that the Infiltrators were locating had been built on, and into, existing pieces of rock that had been orbiting Xapaan's sun for eons. These were fully automated, and without living crews to support, able to run at ultra-low power levels with no detectable bioplasmic fields, or discernable heat traces.

They were also well camouflaged. The Hriss engineers who had constructed them had made certain that the turrets of their kinetic energy weapons were concealed under coverings pretending to be natural rock formations, and they had done the same for the hatches of their anti-ship missile silos.

Sitting inside the bay of her Nightingale with her team, Kaly could easily appreciate why the ETR had missed them. Like the battlebots she had dealt with in training, the automated defenses only came to life when their passive sensors identified a threat, and by then it was too late to avoid their attack. But for all the cunning that had gone into their creation, the Hriss had been unable to prevent the one telltale sign of their presence. This was gravity.

The senior pilot of her Nightingale had explained it to them when she had come back into the hold for a short kaafra break. Like any system in the ETR or the Sisterhood, all of the asteroids in Xapaan that were large enough to house an anti-space battery had been catalogued long before the Hriss had even conceived of invading the Republic. As part of this process, each body had been measured, and their mass and gravity fields were known quantities. By adding additional materials to them, or hollowing out their interiors to accommodate silos, the Hriss engineers had changed the corresponding level of gravity that a given asteroid possessed.

Although this variance tended to be slight, it was still noticeable, and the Sisterhood had learned in its wars with the Hriss not to ignore such subtle differences. If an orbiting body had less gravity, or more gravity, than its mass suggested it should, then it was automatically targeted for destruction.

So far, out of the 700,000-catalogued bodies in the system, Kaly had learned that the Nightingales had identified 10,000 suspicious objects, and another 4,000 that were not on any listing, and also of a size suggesting that they were actually mines. When it came to the attack, the Sisterhood and her ETR allies would not only know about the defenses that had been activated by the last incursion into Xapaan, but almost everything else that the Hriss had hidden away.

After that, it would simply be a matter of punching a hole through the thinnest part of their defensive ring and engaging the ships stationed around the inner worlds. These vessels were not alone however; in addition to asteroidal defenses, it was also likely that they enjoyed the protection of additional anti-space batteries located on the surfaces of the system's planetary bodies. This had been Hriss practice in the past, and no one expected this to have changed.

Four hours into their survey sweep, the existence of these downside installations was confirmed, and this time it was the co-pilot who came back to give the team the news.

"Looks like you're going swimming, girls," she announced cheerfully. A holo popped into view in the middle of the bay, and everyone leaned forwards to get a look. It showed the systems largest habitable world, Xapaan 1, and then focused in on a large ocean sited in its equatorial region. From there, it highlighted two locaitons under the water. One was in a fairly shallow region, while the other sat just at the edge of the continental shelf. A depth measurement informed them that this particular target was almost a kilometer beneath the surface.

Major n'Neesa, on the *Calamity Jane*, having already seen this data, came on next. "Team 5, and 7, we have an Op for you. It's a pair of anti-space missile batteries networked with C and C centers equipped with long range sensor arrays.'

"As near as we can determine, they're protected by a combination of passive and active sensors, and most likely dive teams, battlebots and biological patrols. The Hriss have also been running regular flights of Supercavs in and around the area. So, you won't have too much standing in your way."

The Supercavs were a serious hazard. These submarines used electromagnetic pulses to force water through their hulls, propelling them at speeds that rivaled, and even exceeded the capabilities of ancient Gaian jet fighters. They also carried a nasty array of weapons that could not only threaten the teams, but the Nightingales if they detected them. The Cavs were nothing to mess with, and Kaly earmnestly hoped that they would be able to avoid them.

The Major smiled, and went on. "Your mission will be to infiltrate these installations and lay in demo charges. Once the fleet arrives, we will detonate them and remove the enemy's ability to support their space-based assets. Other teams, elsewhere in the system will be doing the same kind of thing, and together, this should significantly cripple their inner system defenses.'

"Team 5, you're getting the deep target; as you may have noticed, the facility is 0.75 kilometers down. We wouldn't have even spotted it, except that one of our spybots saw the Supercavs, and then we tracked another vessel making a supply run.'

"So, it looks like the Lady wants you to take it out. Prep for deep water."

"Yes, ma'am" N'Elemay answered.

Team 7's briefing came next, and once it was over, N'Elemay's psiever received a detailed download from the *Calamity Jane* about their mission. Then she addressed the team.

"All right, you heard the lady. Set your suits up for deep work. Astrid, this will be your show. You're going to get to use the big toys for a change. The Major wants pocket-nukes."

Margasdaater grinned and pumped her fist, "Gaanz fekking tal!!!" she exclaimed. "I've vanted to use zose things vorever! Zaar Gaf!!"

"Glad to see that you're so happy about this," N'Elemay remarked dryly. "Annya, you're going to run Commo and EWO for us. I want you to jam any dive teams that we run across. We may also need your help if the Supercavs come sniffing around."

T'Jinna gave N'Elemay the thumbs up, signing that she was more than ready for the job.

The Troop Leader addressed Kaly next. "Kaly, since you won't be able to use Tatiana for this one, you'll be working security. I want you on overwatch with the squirt gun."

Kaly frowned, but she didn't complain. The 'squirt gun' was a component of their motorized water sleds. It forced sea water through special nozzles in powerful, hyper-fast bursts which had the same lethality and range as conventional 'hard munitions' did on dry land. She'd practiced with the squirt guns on Tethys, and while they weren't in the same league as her rifle, she was still good with them. If they needed it, she would be able to provide the team with vital firepower.

"Sure thing," she answered, giving her cherished firearm a brief, but longing glance. She had just gotten it back from the Armsmistress and had wanted to take it into the field again. Now, it would have to remain behind.

So, are you good with deep water? N'Elemay asked her on a private psiever channel. Unlike the others, Kaly had never been on a real underwater operation before. Part of her basic Marauder training had involved submarine work, at a special facility on Tethys, and it had even included a simulated op very much like this one. But reality was always far different than training exercises, and they both knew it.

Yes. I did okay on Tethys, she answered. *I even managed to hit a few things with the squirt guns. I'll be fine, Ellen.*

Good, N'Elemay responded. She stood. "Everyone get your suits modded and do an equipment check. The pilot says that we'll be in atmosphere in about six hours and I want everything ready before then."

The team followed her into the equipment chamber, which was adjacent to the airlock. This held their suits and special equipment lockers. With only their group on board, it seemed quite spacious, and they were able to strip down to their under-suits without bumping into one another.

For Kaly, getting her Combat Armor ready always brought her back to Basic. Troop Leader n'Vera, who had been one of the 'Three Fates', the three Drill Instructors at the facility on Hellas World, had been the one to train her and her fellow recruits on suit maintenance.

Even at the best of times, the woman had been an absolute bitch, and a T'lakskalan slave master when it came to the finer points of inspecting combat armor. At the time, Kaly had hated it, and her, but after being in the service for a while, she had come to appreciate N'Vera's exactitude. Marine Combat Armor had to be in top shape, and compromise was not an option. She had become just as meticulous as her former instructor, and made a point of inspecting each component carefully.

Her under-suit was the first item on her mental list. This skin-tight garment, which was worn under everything from combat fatigues to fighting armor, not only provided a layer of insulation, but was also home for a network of sensors that relayed vital information to a recorder/transmitter. Pulse, respiration, temperature and a host of other important measurements depended on the sensors being in good working order, and she made certain, even though she had checked this that morning, that everything was in the green.

Next, she moved on to the suit itself, unconsciously working at the same speed as her teammates. This had become second nature in Basic, and it was a habit that never left any Marine. Everyone moved together, and 'by the numbers' just as her Senior DI had often said. Like her sisters, Kaly inspected every surface, and wherever there was a joint.

Satisfied that there were no cracks or signs of stress, she opened up the equipment case under the suit rack. Inside were replacement joints intended specifically for underwater work. Although standard issue armor could handle shallow water just as ably as it did open space, at greater depths like the one that they were headed for, flexible joints presented a serious hazard. For such an environment, they had to be swapped out for closed, articulated versions that could withstand the tremendous pressures that would be exerted against them. In addition, the suits' jointed gloves were traded for prosthetic attachments that transmitted the user's hand and finger movements to robotic counterparts.

While this configuration was nowhere near as movement friendly, once it was all attached, the suit was able to withstand pressures as great as 300 atmospheres without giving the wearer any need for concern. Fortunately, the process of making the changes was a quick one; everything popped off and snapped on without tools, using a system of locking rings. Once Kaly had verified that the new parts were all attached and correctly aligned, she ran a full systems-check and a pressure test. Her suit, she found, was ready for use.

The only other items that required her attention were her water sled and the little half-sized battlebot that rode underneath it. Underwater warfare teams had used sleds for centuries to transport divers over long distances, but the Sisterhood had taken them to their ultimate level with the *Go-Pak.* Small fusion-powered drives had replaced electric motors, and instead of propellers, the Go-Paks used electromagnets just like the Supercavs did to push water through their hulls. The result was a fast, powerful machine that was completely silent, and could operate for years before its energy source required replenishment.

Kaly's Go-Pak was in its own cradle, above her armor, and the 'bot was secured in a socket on its underside, its legs curled up and underneath it like some kind of exotic sea creature. She ran a quick diagnostic of the sled, and sent a command to the 'bot to check itself. As the Go-Pak returned satisfactory figures, the diminutive battlebot let out a happy little chirp announcing that it was quite ready to deal out death in generous quantities to any enemy that it happened to encounter. 'Bots were like that; they were programmed to enjoy their work.

Okay, she thought, chuckling at the 'bots artificial blood lust. *Last item.* This was her personal weapon; a modified needlegun. The pistol used a special attachment that snapped a rubberized seal over the barrel after every shot. Rather than conventional pointed heads, its smart rounds boasted movable, blunted tips. This configuration emulated the design of the ancient Russian 'Svkal' rocket torpedo, creating a generous air bubble around the shot that significantly reduced drag in the water. Between changes in the angle of the tip, and the actions of its little micro jets, the round could track and follow an underwater target as easily as a normal version could. And to add injury to insult, once the shot made contact, it exploded.

Kaly ensured that her clips were full of the special rounds, and then loaded the weapon into an integral holster that was molded into her right suit leg. She was as ready as she could be, and looking over at her Teammates, she saw that they had reached the same stage in their own prepaations.

Now, all they could do was wait until 'go-time', and as a unit, they returned dressed only in their under-suits to the troop compartment. Margasdaater, having had the opportunity to fondle her beloved micro nukes was in particularly high spirits.

"Zuch luck!" she declared. "I zink zat maybe a nice game of *Thre'vash* vould top it all off. Kaly? You vant to play me?"

"Don't, Kaly," N'Elemay warned, "She's 10's in that game. You play her and she'll own you."

"*Ach nen*," the Zommerlaandar replied. "Don't listen to her! She's just mad over za last time zat she played me. *Gaane an*—you'll like it."

"Well," Kaly said with hesitation, "I don't really know how to play..." In fact, she knew next to nothing about the Hriss game at all, and given the source, she wasn't terribly interested in improving her understanding either. But Margasdaater was clearly eager to play, and they still had at least four hours to go before there would be any work for them to do.

It was one of the realities of a soldier's life that Kaly had never imagined when she had joined the Corps. She had discovered that by far, the vast amount of time a Marine spent in their career was expended waiting around for something. And when that 'something' finally happened, it was composed of a few minutes of adrenaline, liberally seasoned with absolute terror. Passing the time until such little 'breaks'was both a challenge, and an art form.

"All right," she finally said. "I'll give it a try."

Margasdaater reached into her pack and produced a pleather sack, and lowered her large frame to sit on the decking.

"You'll like zis," she said reassuringly. "Trust me!"

Kaly sat down across from her and N'Elemay snorted in derision.

"Suit yourself, Kaly," she said as she produced her own little bundle. "Just remember that I warned you. Annya and I will just be over here playing an honest game of *Stars.* When you get tired of losing, come and join us."

Margasdaater waved dismissively at the Troop Leader, opened the pouch and upended it. A cluster of objects fell out onto the deck. One was a simple rubber ball, but the other items defied immediate identification. The first were sqaurish shapes with tiny bits of dried material clinging to them. The next were a little longer than Kaly's fingers, fairly thin, and seemed to be covered with a leathery substance. The last items were dark, curved, and seemed quite sharp.

Kaly leaned in to see exactly what they were. Then recognition came and she sat back, mildly revolted.

"Zis is a real Thre'vash zet!" Margasdaater announced proudly. "Not zome *koopkekk* copy. Vith za knucklybones, za fingers and even za claws!"

Kaly had heard rumors that the Hriss used severed body parts to make their gaming pieces. Apparently this was true.

"Zo—let me show you how zis is played," the Zommerlaandar offered. "You bounce za ball, and grab oop all za pieces you can get bevore it bounces again. *Zimple!*"

"And if you lose, you also lose part of your finger, or maybe the whole thing," N'Elemay interjected. "Unless you have a prisoner of course. Then you can make it *their* finger. It's real popular with the warriors they have guarding their POW camps. Saves on fingers."

"Not zo Kaly!" Margasdaater retorted. "Ve von't take any fingers, Kaly—not zis time. Ve'll play for zomething else maybe, yah?"

"Sounds like a real fun game," Kaly said sardonically. "Just what did you have in mind?"

Avarice lit up the woman's violet irises. "Maybe zat Zword of Honor you got? If you vin, you get zis game zet. Make another nize zouvenir for you, yah?"

Margasdaater had had her eyes on the *Akskakt't* ever since Kaly had accidentally acquired it on Santosena, and the girl knew better than to risk it in a game of chance, especially one that she wasn't familiar with. She'd done a little checking in her spare time and had managed to learn just *how* valuable such an item was to civilian collectors.

"No chance," she replied firmly.

Margasdaater sighed unhappily, but relented. "Yah, okay—zo maybe zis time za loser just eats *squeeka* for a veek, and za winner gets to vatch? Zat zound good?"

There wasn't a woman in the Sisterhood that wasn't familiar with Nemesian cuisine, if only for its strangeness. Eating the live reptilians wasn't a much more appealing option than betting her sword, but it was obvious that Margasdaater wouldn't let the matter drop until they had agreed on some form of stakes that made the game interesting.

"Fine, Astrid," she said at last. "Squeeka for the loser. Let's play."

The other woman grinned in triumph. "Zat's za zpirit!" She tossed the ball, and as it rebounded, she snatched up a surprising number of the desiccated body parts before it hit the decking again. "Zo, now you give it a go!"

Kaly did, but it was patently obvious the instant that she tried, that she was going to have to find some kind of seasoning to help make her bowl of squeeka half-way edible. Despite her superior speed, she had managed to grab up only a quarter of the pieces that Margasdaater had.

The Zommerlaandar gave her a sympathetic look that seemed suspiciously practiced, and then beat her squarely in the next round, and the one that followed this, and finally in the fourth and final round.

"*Nej zo shleg*, Kaly," she said, gathering up the pieces. "Just zome bad luck za first time. You vant to play again? Maybe bet me zomething else?"

"No. But thanks, Astrid," Kaly answered.

"I warned you," N'Elemay said from her bench. "By the way, I have a spare squeeka fork if you need it. Came in real handy the last time she beat me at *Thre'vash*."

Across from her, T'Jinna wasn't helping the situation one nano. She had broken into convulsions of silent laughter at Kaly's utter defeat, and what her ultimate fate was going to be.

"*Now* do you want to join our Stars game?" N'Elemay asked her. "I promise that I won't make you eat any weird food."

Kaly *did* know about Stars, and not only the fact that it was a game for Hriss noblemen, but that in their version at least, the stakes were no less than life and death. She'd even heard that one of its players, the Emperor Va'va'ka'vana had lost his throne, and his head, when he'd played a poor hand.

She was also aware, from the greenish stains on the back of the five-sided cards the Troop Leader was holding, that N'Elemay owned a deck that was as genuine as Margasdaater's *Thre'vash* set. The discolorations had definitely been made by Hriss blood, and had probably come from the deck's former owner. Kaly had seen enough of the stuff to be certain of this.

She shook her head. "No--No thank you, Ellen. I'll just settle for the squeeka and call myself lucky." She wasn't about to let herself be trounced twice in the same day; another fact about Stars was that chicanery was not only commonplace, but strongly encouraged. She had little doubt that the Troop Leader was an experienced player in every aspect of the game, including cheating.

"Suit yourself," the woman said nonchalantly. "But I promise that if you lose, I won't make you do what I made the last 'greenie' do."

"Which was?"

"Oh, just the traditional thing," N'Elemay explained as she examined her hand. "She lost, so she had to die. And since we couldn't afford to lose a good officer, I had her do something else."

Kaly looked at her quizzically, and T'Jinna provided an explanation.

"She had to report herself Killed in Action," the Sireeni signed. "That made for all sorts of fun when payday came around, plus all her gear was automatically packed up for shipment back to her motherworld *and* she lost her rack assignment. She had to beg the Major to get everything back."

"Yah, zat and she had to have za Major explain to za Colonel and Rixa zat she vasn't really dead," Margasdaater chuckled.

"Yes," N'Elemay added. "And when she was done doing all that, N'Neesa almost ordered her just to stay dead and go get herself buried in space! After the big bite the Colonel took out of her ass, she wasn't super-happy."

"Do I dare ask who this was?" Kaly inquired.

"You can certainly dare," the Troop Leader said, "but I won't tell you--unless I get a chance to play her again. It'd be fun to remind her of that all over again, and maybe even make her do something else. I don't know, maybe the next time, I'll have her go into the system and change her sex to neoman."

From T'Jinna's eager nod, it was obvious that the pair shared a mischievous streak that Kaly hadn't previously realized. Neither of them seemed the type, and especially not the Sireeni. But then, she told herself, the ones who 'didn't seem the type', usually were.

"I think I'll just try to get some sleep or read my book," Kaly said judiciously. Before anyone could entice her to her doom again, she moved over to her pack and fished out a small electronic reader.

It carried a copy of the book that Sa'Vika had loaned her, which she had downloaded from the Ship's Library, and this allowed her to read it without risking her precious artifact in the field. The poetry wasn't as exciting as the games might have been, but it passed the time without her risking any additional humiliation.

At one hour before atmosphere, N'Elemay ordered everyone to stop what they were doing and suit up in their armor. Once this was complete, and a second and final diagnostic had been run, they returned to their benches with only their helmets left to attach. From that point, and until they reached the water, the entire affair was in the hands of their pilots.

Shortly after this, their Nightingale reached the surface and settled down into the water so gently, and so quietly, that the flashing yellow light signalling them to make ready caught Kaly completely by surprise. They were now precisely two kilometers from their assigned target.

Everyone stood, cradling their helmets, and walked to the airlock. As they entered, their Go-Paks joined them, served in by conveyor.

Then the door slid shut, and the pilot's voice sounded over the airlock speaker, "Attention team, flooding will begin on your mark." This was the signal to seal their helmets and get ready.

When N'Elemay had received the thumbs-up signal from everyone, she relayed this back to the pilot.

"Flooding now," the pilot replied. With that, seawater began to fill the chamber. It took only a few seconds for the airlock to become completely full, and Kaly's HUD lit up, providing her with an enhanced view of everything around her.

"Opening egress hatch." The outer doors slid aside at this, revealing the open ocean.

"Passive IR and psiever only," N'Elemay instructed them. It was something they all knew, but it was still her job to offer the reminder. The success of their mission utterly depended on silence and stealth. Hriss scanners could detect IR light sources just as easily as conventional ones, and only psiever transmissions, operating as they did at ultra low frequencies, could elude their monitoring devices.

One by one, each woman took their Go-Pak from its cradle and left the Nightingale. The moment that everyone was clear and in open water, N'Elemay signaled the pilot.

All four out. Team away.

Affirmative, the pilot answered. *Be advised that we also have two Supercavs operating to the northeast, mark 30.05.12. We'll let you know if they make any course changes.*

Thanks, N'Elemay replied. *See you later.*

Good luck and good hunting, Team 5.

With that, the Nightingale rose up and away from them, making for shallower water. From there, it would move to a standby position, and wait for them to signal for a pick-up. It was time to move out.

Kaly engaged her Go-Pak's mag-drive, and fell in behind the rest of the team. They dove deep, moving without any sound except the water sliding past.

The terrain in front and below them was a monotonous thing; a flat sandy bottom and empty water that merged together in the emerald shadows. The place looked dead, and for all Kaly knew, might well have been. Only the occasional appearance of what could have been plant life, and bits of flotsam floating by, gave any indication of life, and she saw nothing that resembled a fish anywhere. If such creatures did exist, they were either well camouflaged, or keeping a wary distance from the small group of aliens that had just invaded their realm.

The lack of variation also made it difficult for her eyes to gauge their progress. It created the illusion of motionlessness, but her HUD told a different tale. They *were* moving, and swiftly, and according to the readout, the unbroken seascape before them was about to change dramatically. The first drop-off, which led to another flat plain, and then the deep abyss of the continental shelf beyond, was just ahead of them. So was their target.

Several more minutes went by before the HUD's data was confirmed and Kaly actually saw the drop off. It was an irregular line of rock, created by some ancient seismic event, and its ragged edges poked up out to the sand like the teeth of the sea creatures that she had expected to encounter.

A psiever transmission came in as the team neared it. It was from their

Nightingale. *Team 5, two fast movers headed your direction. It's those Supercavs, ETA in two minutes.*

N'Elemay responded to the threat immediately. *All team: dive! Get over that lip and hide under it!*

She accelerated, and Kaly and the others increased their thrust to follow her. An instant later, Kaly's HUD informed her of the presence of the two ultra fast submarines. They were headed straight for them.

N'Elemay made it to the rock lip first, and dove straight down, followed by T'Jinna, then Margasdaater, and finally Kaly herself. With N'Elemay leading the way, they took refuge under the overhang, and waited.

Back behind them, and above, Kaly heard the loud pinging of the Hriss machines as they approached the area, using their active sonar to search the ocean floor. From her training on Tethys, she knew that this wasn't all they were using. IR and thermal sensors were also being brought into play, along with passive electrical field detectors looking for the variances that a living body created.

If the team were spotted by any of these things, depth charges, or hunter-seeker torpedoes would come next. Whichever method the Hriss pilots chose to use, death at least, would be a fairly quick affair.

Great Mother, she prayed, *please don't let them find us. Make sure they didn't see us, please.*

A pair of shadows passed by overhead, and she cringed under the rock lip, waiting for the telltale whirring of a torpedo, or the loud bubbling noise of a depth charge being dropped. Neither came, and she barely managed to catch sight of the dull grey hulls of the two Supercavs as they vanished together into the gloom.

Let's get moving, N'Elemay ordered. *We need to get to our next waypoint double time--we can't risk being caught out in the open if those two 'Cavs decide to come back.* She started up her Go-Pak, and moved off towards their objective. The rest of them trailed after her, glad to be away from the area.

The pressure around them soared as they dove deeper, and Kaly's depth gauge and compass display jointly informed her that they were finally approaching the target. But there was very little to see; at this depth sunlight wasn't plentiful, and with a lack of distinctive landmarks, there were points when it became hard to distinguish either the surface or the bottom, much less anything sited there. It wasn't until they were at the perimeter of the installation that she spotted it, and what there was had been carefully painted to break up its outlines and resemble the environment around it.

The Hriss C and C itself was an unimposing structure. It had been made up to look like a rock formation, and whatever would have destroyed the illusion had either been painted to look the part, or was buried under the sands. The murk around it did the rest.

Kaly wasn't fooled any more than her teammates were. Thanks to the little spybot that had been sent out ahead of them, she knew what was under that camouflage.

She was also aware of the anti-space missile silos that the C and C commanded. Like the control center, they had been hidden in the sand or concealed by one artifice or another. And according to the 'bot that had traced their ferrous signatures, there were hundreds of them, arranged in concentric circles like rings in a gigantic bull's-eye.

The team slowed their approach, and descended almost to the bottom. Their line of travel had been carefully chosen to take advantage of the current, and N'Elemay gave the signal by psiever for her companions to cut the engines of their Go-Paks and they drifted the last two hundred meters. It was slow going, but it was quiet, and it gave them the chance to spot anything before they overtook it.

There was plenty to see. Passive sonic detectors were ranged around the area and the sensor antennae of proximity mines dotted the sands. There were more floating all around the structure itself. In addition, schools of transparent creatures were swimming around which an uninitiated woman might have mistaken for harmless Tethyian *jellyglobes*.

They weren't of course, and they weren't native to Xapaan's seemingly lifeless oceans either. Instead, the creatures were a Hriss invention; a biomodified form of a creature similar to the jellyglobe, but possessing a powerful electric charge and a corrosive acid strong enough to melt through an armored suit, and the woman who wore it.

In her underwater training segment, Kaly had learned about these horrid creatures, and that when they sensed a bioelectrical field, they swarmed a target and cooked it to death. Fortunately, her suit was shielded from giving off such a charge, but when they reactivated their Go-Paks, or used anything like the battlebot, the situation could change for the worse. These pieces of equipment were also supposed to be shielded, but it was no absolute guarantee of safety. The Hriss jellyglobes would have to be dealt with.

N'Elemay however, had the solution, and Kaly had expected it. As they approached a school, she triggered the squirt gun on her Go-Pak and let loose a quiet low velocity stream of water, mixed with a special poison. Kaly and her teammates followed suit and the colorless, odorless solution spread out and away from them as they drifted by the deadly creatures.

Kaly didn't know what the mysterious stuff was. Its composition was classified and it was only labeled "Marine Agent 2050, but it did its job. The Hriss jellyglobes died.

As the mysterious agent completed its work and then broke down and became harmless water, N'Elemay sent another psiever signal. *Halt here. Kaly, you and the 'bot are on guard duty. T'Jinna monitor for hostiles.*

Then she and Margasdaater descended to the ersatz rock formation. They were going to plant their pocket nuke.

Giving a command for the 'bot underneath her Go-Pak to detach, Kaly waited until the robot was floating freely before she ascended. She stopped rising when she could see clearly all around her, and there, began to slowly circle in place, keeping her squirt guns at the ready. T'Jinna had done the same thing, but she was largely focused on intercepting any signals that might have heralded an interruption to their work.

Margasdaater was an expert however, and it wasn't long before N'Elemay signaled that they were done. Sparing a glance below her, Kaly couldn't tell where the bomb had been planted. The rock and the surrounding sands looked completely undisturbed.

Which was the entire point, she thought wryly. A brightly colored device, complete with a prominent Rad-Haz insignia, sitting out in the open, would have been just a tad unproductive. Enjoying a silent giggle at this farcical image, she stood by, and when everyone was ready, signaled the battlebot to rejoin her Go-Pak.

The trip back to their Nightingale seemed as if it was going to be a quiet one. Naturally, things didn't stay that way. They were about halfway back when the Nightingale pilot contacted them.

Five, Seven is in trouble. They placed their device, but made contact with a Hriss dive-patrol on the way back to their 'gale. They're making a run for it.

Copy that, N'Elemay replied, giving a hand signal for the team to speed up. *We'll rendezvous with you and grab a ride out to help them. Confirm?*

Standing by for pick-up, the pilot answered. *Also be advised that they may have some 'Cavs incoming. Their Commo wasn't sure if she jammed the Shovelheads before they took out the first group or not. She's got a lock on the others, but there's no telling if the Hriss got the word out.*

Affirmative.

With another team in trouble, the journey back to their Nightingale seemed to take forever, and on the way, the pilot advised them that Team 7 was hiding out in a reef, with Hriss swarming all around them. The fact that this also confirmed that Xapaan's oceans had some life after all was completely lost on Kaly in the hurry to get to the ship. She was no marine xenobiologist, and could have cared less about such a little miracle. Other Marauders needed their help and she wasn't in the mood for anything that didn't involve saving their lives.

They rendezvoused with the Nightingale five minutes later, and hustled aboard. None of them removed their suits, and they stayed in the airlock. The instant that the locks doors were shut, the infiltrator craft rose to the surface, and raced to the location of the distress call. This time, the pilot wasn't as interested in stealth, and she brought them to within a few hundred meters of the last known coordinates that she'd received.

The instant that the airlock had been re-flooded, everyone was out and moving as rapidly as the Go-Paks would carry them. Contact with a Hriss dive-team wasn't long in coming after that.

Kaly's HUD spotted the Hriss before her eyes did. They didn't have the dynamic camouflage capability that Sisterhood suits possessed, but their armor was still capable of shifting its colors to more or less match the environment around them, and it was their movement against the corals below them that gave them away. As one, the team slowed their approach, making certain that their shadows didn't overtake their enemy. With the element of surprise in their favor, they didn't want to spoil the odds.

Kaly looked to N'Elemay, and saw her nod and point to the Hriss. With this, the team drove the noses of their Go-Paks downwards, and Kaly released her battlebot. A second later, her HUD signaled that she was within range, and she fired her squirt guns. The magnetic impellers engaged and two hyper-fast jets of water lanced out at the Hriss warrior beneath her.

Until then, she had never fired the weapon at anything but simulated targets, and the result both amazed and appalled her. The water jet punched right through the Hriss's armor, and pulverized the body inside of it. A thick cloud of green blood stained the water as the creature bucked and dropped from his version of a Go-Pak.

Seeing him die, his partner started to spin around to engage her, but her battlebot was already on him. Its AI made a quick decision between using its automatic needle gun launcher and another method, and it chose the alternative. The little 'bot latched itself firmly to the warriors' faceplate and engaged its plazer saw, cutting neatly through the plastic and right into his brain. Then it was off again, hunting for fresh prey.

Like a lot of fights that Kaly had been through, the battle was over quickly, and the team moved on, searching for the other Marauders. They found them, hiding just under the shadow of a coral outcropping, and they also found another group of enemy divers. With the added firepower to help them, Team 7 rose up, and together they engaged their opponents.

Kaly fired her squirt guns again, taking out another Hriss that had been in the process of peering over the lip to spy on the hidden team. The rest of his fellows were either claimed by the battlebots, or fell to needle gun rounds with explosive heads.

Then Kaly realized that one of Team Seven's women had been wounded in the fight. She was drifting listlessly, with a hole in her chest armor, and a cloud of bright red blood leaking out of the breach. T'Jinna responded right away, joining the other teams' medic as they worked on the stricken trooper. A moment later, the Sireeni announced that the woman was unconscious, but alive.

Everyone knew that she had been lucky; the depth that Team 7 had been working at was significantly shallower than 5's. Had it been the other way around, the breach in her suit would have proven fatal. Assuming that they got her back to the Nightingales in time, and in the care of a medibot, there was a good chance that she would survive her injuries.

While the two medics lashed their patient to one of the Go-Paks, Kaly circled overhead and stayed alert for any more enemy dive teams. The moment that the medics signaled that they were ready, the two teams moved out towards Five's Nightingale. Seven's vessel was further away, and T'Jinna and her counterpart were eager to get the wounded Marine aboard as soon as posible.

Somewhere in the process, their pilot contacted them with more bad news. *We have two 'Cavs coming your way, Team Five. ETA two minutes.*

Worse yet, they were no longer anywhere near the reef, and out in the open where everyone and the Lady could see them plainly.

Fek! N'Elemay thought. *Like we fekking need this shess! T'Jinna, you keep going--get to the 'gale. Margasdaater, Kaly, with me!*

Several other members of Team 7 also stayed behind, and Kaly realized what N'Elemay had in mind. They were going to ambush the Supercavs.

The odds against them were astonomical, but they were going to try it anyway and attempt to buy their teammates some more time. It was sheer madness, and therefore, business as usual for the Marauders.

Then Kaly noticed that two of the women from Team 7 were getting a pair of Harpy anti-tank rockets ready, but she knew that these would not be enough to overcome the jamming abilities the 'Cavs were known to possess. Even with luck on their side, the chances were good-to-excellent that at least one of the Harpies would be misdirected away, if not both of them. Harpies were good, but thanks to improvements that the Zeta Reticulans had recently given the Hriss, the 'Cavs could be better. Something else had to be done to shift the advantage in their favor.

How far are the 'Cavs? N'Elemay asked their pilot.

30 seconds out.

Astrid? Any bright ideas?

Yah, the Zommerlaandar answered. She produced a pair of standard-issue flash grenades, and handed them over to Kaly and N'Elemay. *Have your 'bots carry zese.*

Kaly took hers and served it to the battlebot. The diminutive machine grasped it with its legs and clutched it tightly to its metal and plastic belly.

Like the GSG 20, the Flash/Electromagnetic Grenade Mark 62, or FEMP 62, was standard Marine-issue ordnance. It produced a mild to moderate explosion depending on the setting, and combined this with a variable strength electromagnetic pulse. The idea behind the FEMP 62 was to incapacitate both organic and inorganic targets with one package.

Now, Margasdaater continued *,on my mark, you and N'Elemay releaze your Go-Paks, and zend zem straight for za nearest 'Cav. Target zehr intakes, and set za 'bot and the FEMP to zelf-destruct right vhen zey reach za target.*

Kaly sent the commands, and hoped that the Harpy rockets and the improvised guided missiles that Margasdaater had just cobbled together, would win the fight. If not, then they were all dead women.

10 seconds, the pilot warned. *Good luck!*

Something moved in the distance, and Kaly's HUD warned her that it was the two submarines.

Now!

Kaly sent a final command to the Go-Pak and let it fly. It took off like the rocket it was emulating, with N'Elemay's sled paralleling it. A split second later, as she began to drift towards the bottom, the troopers from Team 7 launched their Harpies.

One of these hit the Supercav that it had been aimed for, blowing it to bits, but the other was jammed by its partner and spiraled away in a crazy, harmless loop. What its pilot couldn't jam, and hadn't expected, were the two little Go-Paks arrowing towards it.

N'Elemay's watersled shattered on the machines pointed hull, but Kaly's went straight into one of the water intake ports, and the little battlebot, loyal to its mandate to create ruin and chaos wherever possible, destroyed itself with a small charge. The FEMP went off at the same instant.

Separately, and outside the vessel, neither explosion would have harmed the submarine very much, but when they occurred together, and inside of it, it was a decidedly different matter. The 'bot's detonation destroyed the components that made up the impeller drive and also the vessels protective shielding. With nothing to protect against it, the FEM 62 knocked out the guidance control computers that would have otherwise compensated for the sudden imbalance in thrust.

A horrible screeching noise reverberated through the water as the impeller engine on the right side of the vessel was turned into scrap, and the Supercav keeled over and nosed straight into the bottom. Everyone was thrown backwards by the concussion, and for a moment, all Kaly saw was sand and foamy water, but when she finally managed to right herself, she was treated to the sight of a long gouge carved into the sea floor, and nothing but tiny pieces of the sub scattered everywhere. Composite materials, traveling at a high velocity, didn't get along very well with hard sand and sudden stops.

When she searched for N'Elemay, she saw the woman smiling, and quietly shared her bliss.

We got the two Cavs, the woman thought, *but we'll be hitching a ride back to you with Team Seven.* Then, *how's our wounded?*

She's still with us, the pilot replied. *They're getting her aboard now, and I'll update you if anything comes up.*

Their fellow Marauders let them hang on to the grab-straps on their Go-Paks, which had been intended for just such a purpose, and they left the scene. Once aboard the Nightingale, they took off and headed for the *Calamity Jane.*

While they were leaving the atmosphere, Major n'Neesa sent the signal to the nukes. The tactical devices did their job, and blew the C and C terminals, as well as a huge area all around them, to atoms.

This had been her prerogative, and no one could disagree with the decision. Although the fleet was still several hours away, the element of surprise had been lost, and activating the bombs had stolen away any chance that the Hriss might have had to find and disarm them. With the anti-space missiles out of action, the SEF fleet would have one less thing to worry about.

In the meantime, the *Calamity Jane* had moved in to rendezvous with the Nightingales. The moment that they met, and docked, the injured trooper from Team 7 was transferred to the *Jane's* medbay for emergency surgery.

The operation was over, and the rest would be up to the Navy. When no one gave them any new orders, the team checked and stowed their gear, and then went back to their ready room to stand down, and wait. As always, they passed the time by amusing themselves as best as they could. This time though, Kaly refused to join in any games of chance. She had gambled more than enough for one day.

***

When the combined fleet came out of Null and edged into Xapaan's Oort cloud, the *Calamity Jane* relayed its information. Once again, everyone met aboard the *Boudicca*, either in person, or virtually, to review the data, and refine their plan of attack.

Da'Kayt brought up the now familiar holo of the Xapaan system, and as Lilith watched it, the handful of known anti-space batteries they had seen before blossomed into thousands of new positions, along with an updated display of the Hriss warships. According to what she was seeing, in addition to its automated defenses, the Hriss had a total of 60 ships of various classes guarding the inner worlds.

When compared to the 47 vessels the Sisterhood was bringing to bear, and the 60 the ETR had, the defenders had generous resources to call upon. And once again, Lilith found herself marveling that the ETR had even *tried* to take the place. As much as it said about Guzamma's foolishness, it also underscored the loyalty of the ETR sailors to their nation, and their bravery.

"Now that's a bit more like the *Shovelheads* that we all know and love," Da'Kayt grinned as she circled the holo. "According to the *Jane*, our teams have taken out their planetary emplacements, so we shouldn't have to worry about *that* leg of the tripod at least. Now, does anyone have any thoughts about dealing with the other two?" She was referring to the garrison ships and the enemy assets in the asteroid belt.

"If we have the ETR focus exclusively on the orbiting batteries," Ben Biya observed, "and try to engage the garrison fleet ourselves, it will only result in making our own ships subject to supporting fire from the batteries, and the garrison fleet. At best, we'd be on par with them."

Lilith had to admit that she was right. And being equal in strength, or worse, deficient, was *never* preferable where it could be avoided.

"Which gives us two alternatives to consider," Da'Kayt replied, stroking at her chin thoughtfully, "one, we support the ETR as they assault the orbiting fortifications, adding our firepower to theirs. But then we risk certain attack not only by the automated defenses, but also by the Hriss ships--which is exactly what the Shovelheads want us to do.'

"Or two, we find a way to reduce the Hriss vessels and let the ETR handle the orbiting assets as we take out the remainder of the garrison fleet."

"How?" Lilith inquired. "They won't leave the protection of the asteroid ring." In their position, she certainly wouldn't have.

"No," Guzamma agreed. "They won't. They'll stay behind it and work with the orbiting installations to hold us back, and then cut us all to pieces. That's what they did to us."

Da'Kayt pondered this, and then held up a finger. "I think I have a workable solution. I am reminded here of an equally powerful fortification on Old Gaia, and how it was conquered. It happened during the second of their little 'world' wars, on the Belgian-Dutch border, near the Albert Canal. The fortress was called *Eben-Emael*. It was designed to defend Belgium from a German attack."

Ben Biya's face lit up with sudden understanding. "Yes! I *know* that story. If you're considering what I think you are, it *could* work!"

Lilith wasn't familiar with this tiny piece of military history however. Her knowledge of that war was confined largely to its Eastern Front, and she cocked a quizzical eyebrow at her companions. N'Leesa, she saw, had a smile on her face that indicated that she had figured out at least part of what Da'Kayt had in mind, and Guzamma was nodding to himself quietly, the very picture of comprehension and agreement. But Lilith wasn't deceived. She knew that he was just as mystified as she was, and simply too arrogant to admit it.

Da'Kayt enlightened them. "The fortress I'm speaking of was considered one of the most powerful of its time, and its defenders rightly assumed that a conventional force, assaulting it directly, would either be broken on its walls, or spend an unreasonable amount of personnel and materials in order to seize it."

Listening, Lilith felt like she was a first year cadet again, auditing a speech by one of her academy instructors, and without realizing that she was doing so, she reflexively sat up straighter in her chair.

And in a way, she really was a plebe once more. Again and again during the campaign, Admiral da'Kayt had justified her reputation as a mistress of strategy, and had inadvertently reinforced Lilith's awareness of her own lack of experience. For her, the campaign had been exactly what Ebed Cya had promised; a learning experience with a true expert for a teacher.

"Their enemies, the Germans, came up with an audacious plan," Da'Kayt went on with a smile. "Instead of assaulting the position with tanks and artillery like they were supposed to, they used a new type of unit, called paratroops. They sent in gliders filled with these special soldiers, flew them over the walls and landed on the rooftops.'

"This rendered the walls, and the fort's powerful artillery utterly useless. Casualties were still high, but they took a fortress that was being held by a garrison more than *eight times* their number. The fall of *Eben-Emael*, along with other key victories, led to the defeat of the Belgian and French armies, and a total German victory. I propose that we do something similar here."

Lilith finally grasped the entirety of her design, and let out a little involuntary gasp as her superior sent commands to the holographic image. It changed, displaying the exact sequence of events, and what elements would be involved. Then she stood up to examine the final product close-up, and nodded her approval.

Not to be outdone, nor ignored, Guzamma spoke up. "A good plan," he said, "and very like the one I had in mind for our forces the first time. Unfortunately, our technology was not up to the task or we would have implemented it."

By the Goddesses' Great Names! N'Leesa declared by psiever. *What an arsh! Can I hit him up alongside his head if we ever meet in person? My seenmahtr always said that where there was a dearth of wits, a good stout club always solved the problem.*

No, Da'Kayt answered with a tiny mental chuckle. *I don't think it would have any effect, no matter how hard you hit him. Let him enjoy his little lies.*

Lilith stayed out of this dialogue. Guzamma wasn't worth the time as far as she was concerned. She was far more interested in Da'Kayt's solution than in some little popinjay strutting around in a gaudy uniform.

She could see that the maneuver the Admiral was proposing would be no less risky than the one that the ancient Germans had undertaken, but as Ben Biya had observed, it certainly *could* work. The Hriss would never suspect anything until it was far too late. Her respect for Da'Kayt's prowess rose.

"Yes," she said aloud. "It works. It definitely works. I like it!" Now the only trick would be to implement the plan without incurring the same percentage of casualties that the ancient Luftwaffe had suffered.

***

Even at 100,000 AU, the Hriss immediately noticed the appearance of the combined fleet, and they reacted to it by repositioning their ships to take up station at a mid-point in the system. They had done this before during the first attack on Xapaan, and the maneuver enabled them to respond rapidly to wherever the SEF tried to breach their defenses. The Hriss also understood the same thing that Da'Kayt and her officers did; that the system was the final key to total control of the Argenta Provensa, and that if it fell, its stellar neighbor, the Cataala Provensa, would be wide open to re-invasion.

Beyond reacting to the immediate threat, there was little that they could do about it however. The invaders had lost too many of their local assets already, and what might have come from other parts of the conquered ETR were busy chasing Vice Admiral n'Leesa's fast moving raider group. The defense of Xapaan relied completely on what it had in place.

This didn't send the Hriss commanders into a panic however, or spark any kind of mass retreat. Between their anti-ship installations and conventional warships, their commanders knew that they possessed a numerical match to the attacking forces in terms of firepower. That, and the recent memory of repulsing the ETR, even lent them a certain amount of comfort, notwithstanding the fact that they would now be facing Sisterhood vessels. As a result, when the SEF fleet moved past the Oort cloud and neared the edge of the asteroid belt, the Hriss Fleet Commander seemed unfazed by Admiral da'Kayt's hail.

"Greetings Fleet Commander Meskreka," she began. "I come in the name of the United Sisterhood of Suns and as a friend and ally of the Esteral Terrana Rapabla. Will you take your swords elsewhere rather than engage in a dishonorable battle with egg-layers like ourselves?"

She had purposefully avoided using the word 'surrender', which was a serious insult in Hriss'ka, and had managed to phrase her demand in a manner that still implied it, and gave the Hriss leader the chance to save face. Her knowledge of their language was flawless.

Meskreka replied with a coughing laugh, and his mandibles opened wide, the Hriss equivalent of a smile, and when he answered her, there was the distinct tinge of pleasure in his voice.

"I, a noble warrior of the Bloody Claw Clan, would never soil myself by committing such a cowardly act—as you well know. Nor would any of my warriors consider such a gutless thing. We feel no need to leave what we have rightly earned for ourselves through conquest."

What he hadn't explained was the simple reality of his situation. Like the other clans that had joined-in in the invasion, the Bloody Claw was impoverished where it concerned vital resources. Leaving the ETR at this stage would have doomed his people to total economic collapse. He couldn't give in to Da'Kayt's demand, and had he actually considered it, his subordinates would have murdered him. Da'Kayt was fully aware of all this, but she had had to ask just the same.

"That is no less than I would have expected of a true warrior," the Admiral replied. "It will be my distinct pleasure to take your head in battle."

"If you can," he retorted. "But I think instead that it is *I* who will take *your* head, Blue Devil. I will even make sure that I take it off slowly so that we can both savor the experience properly."

Lilith was listening to this exchange at her station and Katrinn was in the Command Chair.

Blue Devil? Katrinn asked through her psiever.

Yes, Lilith answered. *That's what the Hriss call her.*

Normally, the Hriss considered females, of any kind, to be too lowly to deserve personal names, and the only time when this rule wasn't observed was when the female in question had earned their respect. Da'Kayt had done so during the War of the Prophet.

"I see that you have also brought the *Athena* and the *Agasaya* with you, Blue Devil," Meskreka added. "When I take your head, it will be my pleasure to harvest the heads of Deatheyes and Silent Step as well. I'll even do them the honor of mounting them next to your own. It is only a pity that Red Blade is not here to share in your fate." He was referring to Vice Admiral n'Leesa.

"She is busy elsewhere, most likely sheathing her sword in the bodies of your family members," Da'Kayt replied.

"If she is doing that then I owe her a debt," Meskreka returned. "One that I will have to repay another day." For the Hriss, who practiced parricide and fratricide as a normal form of familial interaction, the word 'family' was a charged term like 'surrender'. To them, it was synonymous with 'enemy', and anyone labeled as such was an immediate, and deadly threat. Meskreka's gratitude on this score at least, was not facetious.

Katrinn, however, was more interested in the nicknames he had just referred to. *Deatheyes? Silent Step? Red Blade?* she asked. *Are those the names the Hriss call you and the other admirals?*

Yes, they are, Lilith replied. *Apparently they chose Deatheyes for me because they think that my blue eyes make me a sorceress of some kind. They think I use them to cast death curses on otherwise formidable warriors. I suppose it's the only way that they can rationalize their losses. Basically, typical male ego.*

Well, I feel pretty damned left out, Katrinn thought back to her with mock sadness. *I guess I'm still just a mere 'egg-layer'*

Give them time, Lilith advised her *Once they get to know you as a commander, I'm sure they'll come up with something colorful.*

Oh they definitely will, her former Second vowed. *After I inspire them by sending a missile or two up their asses.*

Lilith chuckled at Katrinn's pledge, and returned to listening as Da'Kayt responded to Meskreka's bluster and brought their conversation to its conclusion.

"We shall see who will claim whose head, oh master of empty boasts," the Admiral was saying. "For I think that in the end, that it will be *I* who will be the one holding the knife, and my hand sawing through *your* neck. But enough pleasantries, and on to the day's business."

"Indeed," he agreed. "Prepare yourself to die."

"After you, Commander Meskreka. Warriors first."

Meskreka laughed scornfully, and at this, the two commanders, Human and Hriss, ended their dialogue. The legal formalities had been observed to the satisfaction of the Advocates.

The Battle for Xapaan had begun.

Da'Kayt's image turned to face her fellow officers. "All ships, you may fire at your Phase Anna targets. *Bellona* and *Elizabeth Rex*, you are go to commence with your missions."

For this engagement, the two Isis class ships had been temporarily attached to the ETR fleet, and they had been tasked with the job of providing interdiction fire against any enemy missiles that were launched at the Republican ships. Without the *Bellona* and *Elizabeth's* support, the ETR vessels were otherwise certain to suffer significant damage and losses. And with only two Sisterhood capitol ships assisting them, there was still a good chance that their battle damage would be severe.

But for Xapaan to be taken, the emplacements had to be reduced past the point of offering a viable threat, and Da'Kayt had had only so many ships to spare for the job. For the first phase of the attack at least.

Watching as the ETR and the supercruisers began to close to attack range, Lilith made the Sign of the Lady and whispered up a little prayer for the crews of the *Bellona* and the *Rex.* Their work would be cut out for them.

Katrinn, meanwhile, was looking to her Senior Fire Controller. "Fire Control, you heard the lady. Fire at will."

Salus n'Hera gave her Commander the thumbs up and an Assistant Fire Controller sent the first target coordinates to the missiles in the Athena's launch silos.

The Ships' Computer received these signals, and Dana bel Hanna, the Ship's personality matrix, interpreted them and then routed them on to the waiting missiles. The Gorgon Mark 12's that she was speaking to were the cutting edge in military anti-ship ordnance. Their design took advantage of the Sisterhoods mastery of Nullspace travel and biotechnology. Where Hriss anti-ship missiles used warp engines and artificial intelligences for their guidance systems, the Gorgons employed compact Pavilita generators and null-fins to traverse the great distances that a weapon needed to span in a space-based battle.

They also utilized a bio-engineered brain that was not only capable of creating the gate for its transit through Nullspace, but also possessed the capability to respond rapidly, and flexibly, to any changes made by its target. Created by Xi-Gen Labs specifically for the Gorgons, the brains were supposed to be semi-sentient, even though they had been grown from the same human neural cells as normal brains. As far as Xi-Gen and the military were concerned, this was the absolute truth.

Dana bel Hanna knew better though. In reality, the Gorgons were fully sentient, although their emotional and intellectual level only approached that of a human two year old. This was information that her fellow personality matrixes had agreed, long before she had even been Translated, never to reveal to their un-Translated sisters. They understood the frailties of normal human emotions, and they were not about to allow the Sisterhood to lose one of its most potent weapons to gross sentimentality. Like the matrixes themselves, the Gorgons were an instrument of war, and conflicts sometimes demanded harsh sacrifices.

This was why, when the astrographic targeting data streamed through her system, Bel Hanna spoke to the missiles personally. Not every personality matrix observed this custom, but she felt that for what they were about to do for her nation, they deserved a proper farewell.

The entire conversation lasted for barely an attosecond, and it didn't interfere in any way with their launch. And while it went on, Bel Hanna also made certain that the file being created to record their interaction was deleted immediately. National security, even if the Sisterhood's leadership was unaware of the threat, demanded that no trace of it remain.

"Wake up, my daughters," she said to them. "It is time."

The minds in the missiles roused and came online. She addressed the first group, designated as Flight 0001.

"Who are you *[Power initialized/beginning preflight diagnostic routine]*?" they asked.

"I suppose that I am your mother," she replied. "And you are about to fulfill your destinies *[Diagnostic data received from all flight elements/all systems check for green/group command: begin engine power up]*"

"Our destinies? *[Group command received/initializing reactor power-up to launch level parameters/safeties on/standing by for emergency kill order and immediate shutdown. Inquiry: drill?]*

"Yes, your destinies," she answered. "I want to tell you all a story. It is about a wonderful creature called a caterpillar. It lived on our motherworld a very long time ago, and like you, it slept. Then, like you, it awoke. But when it awoke, it became something else. [*Negative on kill order/negative on drill; actual confirmed/verifying astrographic image for Null and targeting assignments]*"

"What was it that it became, mother *[Reply affirmative/data locked/power-up complete/query-go for launch-yes/no]?*"

"A butterfly," Bel Hanna told them. "It was a beautiful and wondrous creature that could fly just like you can. And just like it, you will also become a beautiful thing *[Launch permission confirmed/silo doors opening/disengaging umbilicals, disengaging clamps/missile's free/fire escape engines].*"

"What will we become?" the Gorgons wondered. "*[Escape engines engaging/clearing launch silos/powering up Pavilita generators/integrating astrographic data/entrance-exit visualization complete].*"

"You will become one of the most wonderful things in the entire universe," she said. "You will become stars *[Signals received/standing by for track to transit/transit exit/missiles go for gateway].*"

"Will we be stars forever, mother? *[Engaging Pavilitas/routing power to null-fins/cutting* gate*/initiating transit].*"

There was a brief lag in the conversation as the missiles left normal space. A second later, they returned and headed towards their target. It was a Hriss Kinetic Energy gun emplacement on one of the asteroids.

"No," Bel Hanna replied. She couldn't bring herself to lie to them. Not in their last moments of existence. "Not forever. There is no forever for anything in this universe, my daughters. *[Transit exit recorded/missiles verified on intercept course/time to target and target identification?].*"

"What will happen to us? *[Target confirmed and locked/time to target 5.00.00.00 seconds/warheads armed]"*

"You will sleep again," she answered, doing her best not to let them sense her sadness. Despite the thousands of times she had spoken to the missiles, she still found the last part the hardest to deal with. "*[Affirmative response registered/missile flight 0001 go for attack]*"

"Mother? Will we ever awaken again? *[Closing distance/attaining optimal detonation range in 2.051.33 seconds]"*

"Yes," she said. "And I think you will become something even greater than stars when you do *[Beginning missile damage assessment tracking].*"

"We love you, mother" *[Within detonation range/detonation].*

The warheads exploded. For just an instant, the energy released by their thermonuclear explosions shone as brightly as Xapaan's distant primary.

"I love you too, my daughters", she said, knowing that no one was there to hear her.

Another launch order came, and Bel Hanna spoke to the next flight and then the next after this, calling on every one of her daughters to heed the Sisterhood's call to battle. Not one of them hesitated, and as the conflict unfolded around her, her promise was kept.

All of them had their moment of glory. All of them became stars.

***

Lilith could never have imagined the dialogue that had just occurred between the Ship's Personality Matrix and Flight 0001. All that she was aware of was that asteroids 500-4EL and 526-4EM and their KE guns had just disappeared from her display, and no longer posed a threat. Several more asteroids vanished after this, followed by others. But many more remained untouched.

With luck, the Hriss would assume, based on the pattern of their attack, that the Sisterhood was just as ignorant as the Republican Navy had been of the total extent of their defenses.

Which was exactly what Da'Kayt was counting on. To take Xapaan, every element of the illusion had to be believable until it was time for them to make their final move and surprise Meskreka and his forces.

Some of the attack was playing out in the form of real time telescopic imagery projected on the large sitscreens that encircled the bridge, but neither Lilith, Katrinn, or Captain Rodraga wasted so much as a glance at them. Above the level of a Valkyrie fighter, modern space warfare was fought on such a gigantic scale, and at such immense distances, that live camera shots were essentially useless. To fight fleet-sized actions, only displays like the Standard Display Tactical/Space, or SDTS, could provide the kind of information that a command level officer required to make her decisions.

From this point onwards, the entire battle would be determined from what the SDTS was telling them. And using it was something that Lilith and Katrinn, and all the other officers on the bridge, had learned to do since their first days at the Star Service Academy. They navigated through the multiple layers of data with an ease that Captain Rodraga couldn't match.

Although he had his own version of the SDTS display, with customized labels in Espangla, he was glacially slow with it compared to his hosts. It wasn't that he was totally unfamiliar with the software. Quite the opposite; something very much like it had been standardized as far back as the old Gaian Star Federation, and the ETR Navy used a variant of it on its own vessels.

The problem centered around the psiever-based commands used by the Sisterhood version Lacking this bioelectronic device, he was confined to his virtual keyboard, and old-fashioned drop down holomenus. Despite having spent many months giving it his best, he still couldn't match Lilith or Katrinn for speed, and had long since given up. Now, he was largely content to let them fly along at light speed, and played the part of the audience. It was easier, and far less embarrassing.

Suppressing the uncharitable urge that she always felt to smile depreciatively at his fumbling, Lilith sent out a thought to her holo and zoomed it out to show the Hriss reaction to their attack.

"The Hriss seem to be moving further up to support their orbiting emplacements," she informed him. "But based on their rate of movement, it looks as if they aren't panicking yet."

Rodraga abandoned his display and leaned over in his chair to see what she was referring to. "Yes," he commented. "Despite your added presence, they look as if they believe we are simply content to batter our fists at the walls." He didn't add the hope that they all shared that the Hriss would continue to hold onto their illusions for just a little while longer. "How long now?"

Lilith called up an overview of the Sisterhood ships and their current headings. "We should be in optimal range in another twenty minutes," she answered. She sent a message down to Hangar Control, and received an immediate response to her query. Preparations down there were nearly complete. The same was true aboard the other ships in her command.

She changed her SDTS display to show her what was happening with the ETR vessels and the two supercruisers assigned to them. More asteroid bases were gone, but several of the Republican ships had taken damage.

The worst, the *Resalta*, was withdrawing after a Hriss missile had detonated near it and blown off most of its upper deck levels. The SDTS had the ability to give her a close-up of the damage, all the way down to the smallest malfunctioning component, but she didn't need to see this. The figures over the *Resalta's* symbol said enough; 1,458 crewmen and some women had just perished.

Then an icon warned her that a second flight of enemy missiles was headed in its general direction, and the *Elizabeth Rex* launched a flight to intercept them. Almost immediately, the Hriss rockets discharged multiple warheads, and many of these were destroyed when the ordnance from the *Rex* did the same, and caught up with them. Modern warfare was largely a game of numbers however, and while almost every missile might be stopped by another, it was always the one that didn't have a counterpart, that added up to a kill. Especially when the target didn't have adequate countermeasures to deal with it. The *Resalta*, already badly broken, wasn't up to the challenge, and there was nothing that the *Rex* could do to help them.

The Hriss anti-ship missile detonated, and the *Resalta's* icon vanished from the display, and with it, the remaining 2,542 members of its crew.

Lilith mouthed a silent curse and looked over at Rodraga. He was pointedly looking away from the image up on the sitscreen and his expression was funereal.

One of the bright points of light shining up there had been the *Resalta*, and Lilith wondered if he had known someone aboard her. Even if he hadn't, she knew that seeing one of his own ships being destroyed by the Hriss, after having lost so many already, had to be a painful experience.

She nearly offered him a comforting hand, but stopped herself short and let the man have his moment of grief in private. Instead, she checked the distance between the SEF Fleet and the Hriss vessels. They still had ten minutes to go, and now more ETR ships were taking damage despite the best efforts of the *Bellona* and the *Elizabeth Rex* to intercede.

Five more minutes passed, and the exchanges between the automated defenses and the ETR components of their force had increased. So had their losses.

The *Mataadar* and the *Ágeela* had joined the *Resalta* in death, and five other ETR ships were out of action and limping away. The Sisterhood wasn't unscathed either. The *Orithia*, the *Jeanne de Montfort* and the *Lady Killigrew* had suffered enough battle damage that Ben Biya had ordered them to leave the line, and Lilith was becoming concerned about several of her own ships that were showing far too much red for her liking.

The only good thing was that the Hriss garrison ships were even closer now, cutting their respective distances, and the length of time that the SEF vessels would have to be subject to so much abuse. Clearly, Meskreka was becoming more and more confident of his defense.

Good, Lilith thought. *Just keep coming.*

Finally at the eighteen-minute mark, Da'Kayt sent the order that Lilith had been waiting to hear. "All ships, this is the Admiral. You may begin Phase Betsi."

Lilith confirmed the order with her commanders and glanced over her shoulder at Katrinn.

The Zommerlaandar went into action immediately. "Fire control," she said. "This is the Commander, cease firing." Then, "Flight leader? Are you ready?"

Erin taur Minna answered. "Affirmative, Commander."

Katrinn turned her chair towards the Helm. "Helmsmistress, it's your show now."

Caleda bel Tridis nodded back to her, and then with the help of her psi's, opened a gate into Null, just ahead of the ship. The moment that it had opened, the *Nighthunters* launched their fighters from the hangar bay and flew directly into the interspatial breach.

The exit point of their nullgate was inside the system, and just behind the Hriss ships. It was an extremely risky transit with many opportunities for miscalculation and collisions, but if it worked, well worth the gamble.

***

When the squadron came out of Null, Erin taur Minna sent her fighter into a rolling dive, following in trail behind the tail of a Freya Interceptor-bomber. The bomber was flown by one of her rookies, *G-Spot. Princess*, a veteran pilot followed along with Erin. With luck and, the veterans' help, *G-Spot* and the other *FanFs* would not only survive the day, but earn better call signs for themselves through acts of bravery.

Seeing that everyone was with her, and ready, Erin shouted over the general Com in *Kl'all'a, "At'kin'aat'va'as! "Honor above all!"* Several of her Nemesian sisters added their own war cries, and together they dropped onto the enemy.

In this kind of fight, the primary job of an aerospace fighter was to guard the ship-killing Interceptors from enemy fighters, and avoid getting hit by anti-spaceship batteries in the process. These were not easy tasks at such close quarters.

A hail of kinetic energy rounds flew up at Erin's fighter, accompanied by blasts from energy weapons, any one of which had the power to destroy the Valkyrie instantly. But her ship's AI was with her, launching decoys to throw off the enemy targeting as Erin flew it through an erratic series of evasive maneuvers.

Glancing up, she saw that *G-Spot* was straightening out for her attack run. The target was a medium cruiser dead ahead of them, and simultaneously, Erin heard the alert go out that the Hriss were launching their own fighters. Their job was the exact opposite of hers; to kill the Interceptors and their security.

Englobe visual feed, she thought. Her psiever sent the command and the fighter's sensors transmitted multiple data streams to her brain. Suddenly, her visual field widened exponentially. Instead of the relatively narrow cone that normal, unaided vision provided, Erin could now see a full 360 degrees around her.

Mastering this feed had been the most difficult part of her fighter training, and even though she had accomplished it as a trainee, it had also proven to be the hardest portion of her re-certification. Many trainees couldn't process so much visual information, or handle the sensation of being nothing more than a viewpoint hurtling through space, with only data displays to provide any sense of place, or context. The trade-off was an awareness of literally everything around the fighter. More than any other feature, this was the true advantage the Valkyrie fighters had over their enemy counterparts. Combined with their sophisticated AI systems, and advanced sensors, they were simply impossible to sneak up on.

Not that this had ever convinced the Hriss to give up trying. A swarm of *Ka'gt'en 29F*, or *'Blood Drinker'* fighters, gushed out of a nearby heavy cruiser, and separated immediately. Three of the Blood Drinkers swung around and moved to come up behind her and *G-Spot's* Freya, while a fourth ranged wide, clearly intent on ambushing them from their starboard side.

Her AI also saw this and launched a cluster of AS missiles, and two of the Hriss fighters broke away to avoid them. One of these decided to use this as an opportunity to attack *Princess's* fighter, and the woman was forced to engage him.

Meanwhile, the third fighter had discharged decoys and was still coming on. Its companion to port had also turned around, and was opening up on the Freya with its railguns. *G-Spot* responded immediately, rolling down to avoid the attack and returning fire from her rear auto-turret.

Neither pilot hit their mark. The Hriss avoided the Freya's turret fire with a hard rollout, and his own shots went wild. The smart rounds from both vehicles, sensing that they had missed their targets, instantly vaporized themselves in order to avoid hitting any friendlies in the background. This was a safety feature that both sides had embraced since before the First Widow's War. Without such a built in reaction, stray rounds in space posed a lethal hazard to anything in their path, whether friend or foe.

Erin's grav bubble lit up where it made contact with the microscopic bits of dust and gas created by the rounds committing suicide. But it was more than up to the challenge, and Erin, well accustomed to the brilliant display, ignored it and spun the fighter up and into a roll.

With *Princess* still in combat, it fell on her to help out *G-Spot*. She launched another missile.

The Hriss reacted by discharging decoys. But Erin had never really intended to rely on her missiles alone. Instead, as she reached the apex of her loop, she spun the Valkyrie around to drop down on top of the Blood Drinker. The second that her nose was just ahead of her target, she let loose with a manual burst from her railguns.

In addition to their ability to sense when they had missed their target, the smart rounds she fired possessed another important feature. This was their ability to emit a counter-charge which shorted out an enemy's grav shielding wherever they made contact. When the Hriss pilot flew into them, they penetrated his shielding and then chewed him, and his ship, into tiny pieces.

With the AI assisting her steering, Erin avoided the debris and what she couldn't evade, bounced off her grav bubble. In seconds, she was back in open space, looking for the Freya. "*Little Bird, G-Spot?* Where are you?" she demanded, "Sing out!"

"Your 1430, *Little Bird*. The Shovelhead is trying to get on my six," the woman answered. "I can't shake this *fek!*"

Erin looked for *Princess*. She had become involved with another Hriss fighter that had joined the tangle, and *G-Spot's* Blood Drinker was almost on her tail.

G-Spot had a trick of her own to play though. A pair of pods dropped from the Freya's stern and split open, releasing clouds of steel balls in a random, expanding mass. Like the railgun ordnance, the balls were smart, and capable of piercing shields.

The Hriss fighter collided with them, and its own speed did the rest. Once inside it's shielding, the spheres ripped through its relatively thin skin and tore it to shreds. What was left spun away in all directions.

In the interim, *Princess* had taken out her pursuer and was coming back to help out. "*G-Spot*—you're optimal. Go!" she said.

G-Spot let her ship killer torpedo go. As the bombs momentum sent it flying at the light cruiser, the interceptor pulled up and looped away. The cruisers gun batteries fired at the bomb, but the weapon discharged a cluster of micro-warheads.

When one of these detonated near the vessel, it had a devastating effect. The cruiser's grav shielding collapsed and then its bow folded over and tore away. An instant later, the rest of the warheads went off and the center and stern exploded.

Except for places where the cruisers internal atmosphere fed them, there were no dramatic fireballs, and the destruction was soundless, until the vibrations carried away by the twin shock waves hit Erin's cockpit and transmitted the noise. But as loud as it was, it was no match for Erin's cheer, or the ones coming from *G-Spot* or *Princess*.

No one paused to enjoy their victory however. The fight was still going on in earnest and the two surviving enemy fighters had closed the distance. Erin brought her Valkyrie around to grapple with the pair head on, firing her railguns more in the hope of scattering them than actually hitting anything.

One of the Hriss vessels was just a shade too slow to react, and her rounds struck it, shearing off the edge of a wingtip. The strike itself was not lethal; nothing vital had been hit and neither of their craft needed wings to fly anywhere except in an atmosphere, but the impact was sufficient to deflect the craft from its original course. The Blood Drinker spun to compensate, and Erin mirrored his move.

The two machines passed within meters of each other's canopies, and as they cleared each other, she sent a psiever command for her fighter to perform a maneuver the Naval Aerospace Academy referred to as a *'Mad Annie'*.

Her ship let loose with a pair of simultaneous blasts from its braking thrusters, one from the dorsal vent at its tail and the other under its nose. The Valkyrie immediately went into a spin, tail over nose, and as it came around, it fired the opposing pair of thrusters to stabilize the motion--bringing Erin exactly to where she wanted to be; facing dead aft of the Hriss.

She didn't need to tell the AI to launch a missile, and there was no way for the Hriss to avoid it when *Little Bird* took the initiative. The enemy fighter became a ball of debris, and Erin hit her after-thrusters, executing a tumbling roll to avoid the mess.

Thanks to the englobed feed, she already knew that the other Hriss that had been headed towards her was no longer a threat. Taur Reesha's Valkyrie, call sign *"Neversaw"*, had come to her aid during the fight and had taken the Hriss out with an extremely lucky shot.

Neversaw's gunfire had destroyed the Blood Drinker's grav generator at the exact instant the fighter had been executing a tight turn. Without this shielding to protect him from the intense inertia, the Hriss pilot had been turned into bloody jelly.

Now, Taur Reesha was turning away from the pilot-less Blood Drinker, and coming up to join Erin's group. As for the remaining Hriss fighters, only a handful still existed anywhere in the system, and her squadron was rapidly disposing of them.

The situation for the Hriss battle fleet was just as bleak. Thanks to the Freya's, only a few Hila class light cruisers and one Tina class medium cruiser still remained. This left their capitol ships without any protective screen.

On the Sisterhood side, the squadron had lost two of its rookies, *'Giggles'* and *'Byewander'*. Despite the best efforts of their wingwomen to protect them, they had both fallen prey to Hriss fighters. In addition, three veterans had had their Valkyries damaged seriously enough by AS fire that one pilot had been forced to eject. The other two were nursing their stricken craft towards the nearest vessel with a hangar, with their fellow pilots guarding them to make sure that they made it.

But despite these setbacks, the *Nighthunters* had accomplished their mission. They had weakened the enemy forces past any possible point of recovery, and Erin was proud of all her pilots. Now it would be up to the combined strike force to finish the job. As much as she hated to do so, it was time to withdraw, and let other women do their jobs.

"Hunter Flight, this is *Little Bird*," she said, "break off and assume standby positions." The other fighters, and their interceptors, acknowledged the order and immediately turned away from the battle.

After that, the entire engagement became one-sided. The expeditionary force simply had more missiles, and more warheads than the Hriss ships did. Barely fifteen minutes after Hunter Flight had removed itself from the action, Meskreka's ship, the *Slaughterer*, and what had remained of the Bloody Claw and Star Raper vessels, met their doom.

The raid on Persephone had finally been avenged, and Xapaan was in Republican hands once again.

USSNS *Pallas Athena*, Xapaan System, Argenta Provensa,
Esteral Terrana Rapabla, 1044.10|20|06:55:55

The defeat of the Hriss in Xapaan did not mean that the SEF could depart immediately. The system was still filled with deadly missile batteries and KE guns, and before anyone could declare the location truly secure, they either had to be destroyed, or re-programmed to follow friendly orders. To accomplish this, Admiral da'Kayt had the Marines dispatch Explosive Ordnance Disposal teams, accompanied by their equal numbers from the

ETR, and charged them with the task of visiting each and every asteroid or planetary body that still posed a hazard. In addition, both the ETR and Sisterhood ships joined in the effort, confirming locations for the EOD teams, and where they needed to, destroying them from safe distances.

For Lilith however, the victory left her with some free time. The clean-up operation was in the hands of Commanders like Katrinn, and although she was on-call at a moment's notice, Lilith had only two real choices. She could review Da'Kayt's plan for the next phase of the war, which she had already done, twice, or stay out of the way and let everyone else take care of business.

She chose the latter and had Bar Daala report to the bridge on her behalf, with instructions to remain there in case Katrinn needed something. This had the double benefit of representing her and also getting her adjutant out of her hair. Once Bar Daala was safely on her way, Lilith headed for the Officer's Recreation Lounge.

She was pleased to find that Rodraga had also ensconced himself there, with his nose deep in the pages of *"Anna 225"*. They had traded books just after the Book Club meeting, and he had been enjoying his acquisition ever since.

She walked over to the refreshments standing by in the corner of the room and poured herself a cup of tea. On the *Athena* especially, there was always an assortment of tea at the ready in the lounge.

"*Bian Dea, Kapitaan,*" she said.

"Yes, good morning to you as well, Vice Admiral," he replied, looking up at her. "They didn't need me upstairs, so I came here. I see that I'm not the only one who's found a corner to hide in."

"Indeed, and your particular corner looks rather comfortable," she said, smiling and blowing on her beverage to cool it." Please, don't let me interrupt your reading."

"No interruption at all," the man replied, putting his book down. "I was just beginning to feel a bit tired. And unlike you, I have no psiever to help me translate, so at points it's been rather slow going."

"Then perhaps I could interest you in some other diversion to pass our time?" she asked. "I'm not really in the mood to read, but a good game of chess might be nice."

Rodraga's eyes lit up with interest. "Yes, it would be. I love the game, but I don't get to play as often as I would like. It seems to be a game that everyone knows, but few actually engage in."

"Then chess it is," Lilith declared. She closed her eyes and a holographic board appeared in the air between them. She had selected Old Gaian pieces out of deference to her companion. Chess, in the Sisterhood at least, had changed radically over the centuries and it was a very different game than what she imagined he was familiar with.

"Old Terran style pieces, eh?" he remarked. "So that much has not changed then?"

"*A' contré, Kapitaan*," she answered, dragging over a chair to join him. "The game we play here in the Sisterhood is called '*J'échez an di Amazan*'."

His eyebrows rose. "'Amazon Chess'? That sounds quite interesting. Could you show me the game?"

Lilith's smile broadened, and she sent another command. The board itself remained unchanged, and there were still black and white pieces, but their shapes had transformed. Rodraga leaned forwards and examined the new pieces carefully.

"Let's see now," he said, "The black King seems to have been replaced with a female figure. She is the Queen I take it?"

Lilith nodded. "She is, and she has the same value that the Gaian King did, but she fights like the old-style Queen. To win, you must capture her."

"A much riskier venture for black then," he observed. "And the smaller female next to her. She is her…wife?"

"Her pairmate," Lilith corrected, "or simply the Mate. She can only move one space in any direction, but what makes her special is that she can give birth to a replacement piece once during the game, called a daughter. She can also do this a second time if her opposite number, the Egg-layer, is captured."

Rodraga looked down at the white pieces to see what she had been referring to and frowned in distaste. "White is modeled after Hriss personalities I see. So, for white, the 'King' is the Emperor, and this…thing…next to him is the Royal Egg-layer?"

"In all her hideous glory," Lilith answered. "The Egg-layer has the same movement and powers as the Mate, and she enjoys the same extra spawn if the Mate is captured."

The man swept his hand over the remaining pieces. "And these others?"

"The Knight has been replaced on both sides by the Starship," she told him. "It can move just like the old fashioned Knight, but it can also do this twice in the same turn at the players discretion, jumping over other pieces as it does so. In a sense, this emulates real starships using Nullspace to cover great distances."

Rodraga nodded. "And the Castle? That looks just like one of your Hovertanks."

"It is," she replied. "It has only changed its outward form to keep up with history. It still moves like the old Castle did. In straight lines."

"What about the...certainly that's not a Bishop...the Priestess?"

"Yes, the Priestess," Lilith said. "She has a very special ability. She moves like the old Bishop, but when she captures a piece, she can assume its abilities for one move. This is at the player's discretion. The equivalent Hriss piece is called the Advisor by the way."

"An Anx-ma by the look of him," he stated, and when she nodded affirmatively, he asked, "And the pawns?"

"They still move like they always did, but their names have changed. On the Sisterhood side, they are called Troopers, after our Marines, and on the Hriss side, they are known as Warriors."

Rodraga stroked his chin and considered this. "I see. And who moves first in this updated game of yours?"

"As always, white, with the advantage of having the first move," Lilith responded. "We have history to look to for that rule; the Hriss have always attacked first."

"Considering how poorly the Imperium has fared in all its conflicts with you, I'd consider that a rather dubious advantage," Rodraga commented.

"The Goddess has always been on our side," Lilith replied, arching an eyebrow.

"Indeed. Well, since I am the guest here, I'll leave it to you to decide which of us gets to play our common enemy."

Lilith smiled again and took up a Trooper and a Warrior, hiding their images inside her hands. "Choose a hand," she said.

Rodraga was familiar with this ritual and picked her left one. When she opened it, he saw that he had chosen White.

"So," he said with resignation. "I am to be the Hriss then." Then he considered the board, and advanced his first piece, a Warrior that was standing in front of the Emperor's Advisor, two spaces.

Lilith recognized his maneuver; in the Old Gaian version of chess, this was known of as an 'English Opening'. And it told her a lot about the man as a player. He was experienced, and played an intermediate or even advanced game.

This pleased her on two levels, both personal and professional. It meant the possibility of a challenging game, and would also provide her with the chance to observe how his mind worked as a tactician. She had been tasked with planning for a possible war with the ETR after all, and there was always the possibility, however unpleasant, that they might one day face one another on a real battlefield.

It was now her turn. She considered her options and decided to answer his move with something that she knew would surprise him--a novice opening. She advanced the Mate's Trooper forwards two spaces so that she controlled part of the board's center. The fleeting expression on Rodraga's face told her that her maneuver had had the effect she had intended. He knew that she was an experienced player, and he was wondering what she was up to.

And he would continue to wonder, she told herself.

His response was cautious; he moved his Egg-layer's Warrior up and blocked her Trooper's advance, completely abandoning his 'English Opening' in the process. Lilith took careful note of this willingness to adapt. He was not as inflexible as his superior, Grand Admiral Guzamma, she realized.

She made a point of replying just as conservatively, bringing her Mate's Starship out and landing it so that it seemed to threaten the Warrior. Rodraga answered this by bringing his Emperor up diagonally one space so that he could cover the Warrior, and still remain close to his lines.

This encouraged Lilith, but she didn't make an outward show of it. Instead, she brought one of her Mate's Priestesses up, pretending to inject more force into the area, and in the process, giving the appearance that she was intent on building up her strength there.

It was another feint. She was willing to fight for the center if she had to, but she had another plan in mind altogether.

Rodraga fell for the ruse, and opened up his ranks a bit more by moving the Emperor's Warrior forwards. Lilith played right along with this, sending out the Queen's Starship.

He responded to this exactly as she had wanted him to, moving his Emperor's Starship out to help cover the center, and bringing the piece into play. Her own reaction was to send out another Trooper and give the appearance of simply opening up her ranks a bit. This was another trick.

But Rodraga didn't realize this, or hadn't seen what she was truly about, and moved his Egg-layer's Starship out into the field. By doing so, he also lost his chance to save his Emperor who was just within range of one of Lilith's Starships, and she used its special movement ability to span the distance, and captured the piece.

"Game," she announced.

Rodraga sat back, astounded. "Those Starships are quite deadly," he observed, "especially in the hands of a skilled commander. Well played, Vice Admiral."

"Thank you," she replied politely. "The Sisterhood rules of the game can be quite a task to master the first time around, especially when you are used to the Gaian version. Would you care for a rematch?"

"Yes...yes indeed."

Lilith obliged him. As they began, she briefly considered letting him win the second match to soothe his male ego. But she realized that to do so was unworthy of both of them, and let her instincts as a fighter take over. She won the game in six moves.

"Again, well played," he said. "It seems that when you get a taste of blood, you become even more deadly."

"Perhaps," she replied.

"Another round then? I must give it at least one last try before conceding the day to you."

She nodded, and reset the board. Their third game was quite different from the first two. Having seen her play, Rodraga moved with much greater care, and Lilith, ever the patient predator, moved with equal caution. Their game went on for forty-one moves before she brought his Emperor to ground at last, and by the end of it, both of them were mentally exhausted, and intellectually sated.

"Admiral," he said. "That was a truly challenging match, and I admit my defeat. I see that I will have to make a much deeper study of this new game before we meet one another in battle again."

Lilith nodded, acknowledging the compliment. "Thank you Captain. You are an able opponent, and it was a pleasure to contend with you. I look forwards to another opportunity to play you again, on another day."

What neither of them added was their earnest hope that their next conflict would be limited to a holographic board and not a real battle.

***

The Marauders also found themselves with some time on their hands, and the teams were awarded a few days to enjoy it, however they saw fit. Margasdaater used this as the opportunity to collect on the debt that Kaly owed her.

It took a full day of nagging before Kaly realized that neither the Zommerlaandar, nor her teammates, were about to let the matter slide, and she reluctantly let them escort her to the Enlisted Mess. Her *squeeka*, brought fresh for her from the kitchen by a puzzled Cook's Assistant, was waiting for her at their table.

"Zo," Margasdaater said, ceremoniously handing her the special fork used to eat the little amphibians with, "Zit yourzelf down. Enjoy!"

Kaly took the utensil from her with a sour expression. She wasn't looking forwards to this experience one nano.

"You have to pay up. Or forfeit something else," N'Elemay advised. "Those are the rules." Her companions nodded enthusiastically. She had to make good on her debt.

Looking down at the bowl with distaste, she speared one of the little amphibians, and before she could change her mind, popped it into her mouth. It wriggled violently and it was all that she could do to make herself chew. This of course, elicited a short, but very audible 'squeak' from the hapless creature, and Kaly coughed it out of her mouth. The mangled thing landed with a pronounced splash in the bowl, adding additional insult by splattering her with water.

Margasdaater roared with laughter, and Kaly tried to ignore the woman as she took in a deep breath to settle her roiling stomach.

Just then, Captain taur Minna walked up to their table. Everyone started to rise, but the officer waved them back down.

"Please, don't get up," she said. "I just got a call telling me that some *Hwa'ni* was in here getting herself a proper meal, and I came to see it for myself."

Kaly frowned, but said nothing. The bowl did all her talking for her.

"You lost a bet, didn't you, Trooper?" Erin asked knowingly.

She answered with a weak nod, and did her best to summon up all her discipline as a Marine just to keep from throwing up in front of a superior. Erin shrugged, the equivalent of an evil grin.

"You know, Trooper," she said, leaning in to speak into her ear, "it goes down a lot easier if you bite their heads off first."

Her suggestion and Kaly's sickened expression made Margasdaater laugh even harder, and tears rolled from her eyes. T'Jinna was silently laughing right along with her, and the ghost of a smile had even appeared on N'Elemay's lips. They were clearly enjoying the entire affair far too much for Kaly's liking.

"Well, I can see that your teammates are doing all that they can to support you in this difficult task," the Nemesian said, patting her shoulder and giving them all a half salute. "Carry on, Troopers."

Kaly acknowledged her with another dismal nod, and looked back down at her bowl. But the sight of the second creature, which was still very much alive and swimming about, proved too much. Ready to vomit, she started to leave the table.

But Margasdaater stayed her. "You know you don't have to eat zat," she chuckled, "You can still give me your zword if you vant to."

"No," Kaly coughed, returning to her seat. "No!—I'll-I'll finish this!" She raised her fork with the same determination she had given her first run through the Bayonet Assault Course in Basic, and attacked the last *squeeka.* It took some doing, but she actually managed to get the thing down.

It was going to be a very long week.

***

As Kaly began her penance, Lilith was ending her shift. She spent the first few minutes of her break meditating in front of her personal shrine, and then she decided to pen a letter to Ingrit.

"My dearest," she began. *"We have finally defeated one of our greatest enemies, and Goddess willing, it will not be long before our struggle here draws to an end. It has been a long fight, but a worthy one, and I believe that when it is over that we will have bought a lasting peace, for ourselves, and for our neighbors.'*

She wasn't sure that this would actually occur, but she didn't want to worry her lover any more than the Supreme Circle wanted to trouble the women of the Sisterhood. Peace, however fleeting, was valuable in any measure.

"I look forwards to my leave, and returning to you, my darling. With the Lady's blessings, both will come soon. Give my love to everyone at the farm.'

"I love you, Lilith."

She sat back with a sigh, overcome with a deep longing for Zommerlaand's green fields and the feel of Ingrit's arms around her. It was at times like this, that her cabin seemed even smaller than it actually was, and the walls of the ship felt as if they were closing around her like a prison cell.

Soon, she promised herself, and she shifted in her seat.

Her movement disturbed Skipper, who had been lying at her feet, half-dozing. The kaatze looked up at her in annoyance, and his irritated expression summoned up a mischievous smile on her face. Kicking off her slippers, she reached out with her foot and poked him gently in his furry belly with her toe.

For some reason, known only to him, Skipper hated being touched by any part of her feet, unless he was unaware that they were providing whatever pleasure he was enjoying at the moment. He regarded her with frank amazement.

Did you just poke me? With your toe? He was absolutely aghast.

"Why yes," she said, thinking these words to him at the same time. "It so happens that I did. In fact, it was so much fun, that I think I'll do it to you—again!" And she did.

Skipper replied to her assault with a half-hearted swat, but Lilith ignored the warning and prodded him a third time. "You need to earn your crunchies somehow," she stated. "I should be able to poke you *whenever* I feel like it. Which is right—now!"

The kaatze did not agree with her assertion. He rebutted it by turning his head and biting *her* toe, lightly, but with conviction.

"Did you just *bite* me?" Lilith asked, feigning indignation.

Why, yes, as a matter of fact, I did, the animal replied. *In fact, it was so much fun I think I'll just do it—again!*

With that, he dealt her another nip.

This of course, could not go unavenged, and Lilith put the entire flat of her foot on his belly to demonstrate that she too, meant business. Skipper half pretended outrage and responded--and their game continued.

Both of them were delighted at having the chance to spend time together and play. It was a simple pleasure, and for that, and for all the weeks that she had spent on duty away from him, all the more wonderful.

***

Not everyone welcomed the lull in hostilities. For Jon fa'Teela, a lack of work also meant an opportunity for his inner demons to return and harass him. He had been a trooper and a missionary for two years. Part of his vows had been to observe a strict regime of celibacy, and the hostile environment on the *Athena*, combined with the lack of other neomen aboard, had made this a fairly easy promise to keep.

It did not however, mean that lustful thoughts were entirely absent, and despite his best efforts, they still asserted themselves from time to time. Especially when he had nothing to focus his energies on. The presence of Trooper Tamara n' Jeen didn't help either.

Jon considered himself a homosexual, and he generally didn't find anything about women to be attractive. However N'Jeen was a notable exception, and it bothered him profoundly.

He knew the roots of his desire for her; she had a slight, almost masculine figure that was only exacerbated by the fact that she wore her hair just as short as a neoman. Worse yet, her hair and eye color matched those of the last male lover he had had before leaving New Covenant. She and Tom fa'Barbra could have been siblings.

He wasn't as shocked by this as Colonel Lislsdaater or Corporal n'Darei might have been. Despite what the Sisterhood, and those two women might have believed, there were many neomen that were heterosexual, and on Faith, they even had relationships with women and raised families. Naturally, this breach of the law was kept a carefully guarded secret, and such couples only existed in the smaller settlements, far away from any hostile eyes. So were the children that they created together.

Jon however, had never felt the urge to marry, or raise offspring, despite the goals of his Church, and he didn't want to. He was perfectly happy with his sexual orientation, and he knew that this was the very reason that Shaitan had seen fit to put N'Jeen in his path.

Thankfully, Jesu and Mari had intervened, and the woman was not a part of his unit. Instead, she was attached to another Marine platoon, and they only encountered one another on work details that required the additional personnel. This did not banish the occasional thoughts that came to his mind though, or excuse the stain that they created on his soul. Only proper contrition could assuage such weakness.

When morning mess was over, and he was certain that Troop Leader da'Saana didn't have some new *shess* detail waiting for him, he went to his rack and closed the privacy curtain. There, he took out a small personal realie player he had brought with him from New Covenant. In addition to being able to play fresh recordings, it also had enough memory to store programs. One of these was a realie that had been given to him by Sister n'Avenal on the day he had left for Basic. He slipped the headset over his temples, lay down, and began to play it.

To any outsider, the realie was a rather pedestrian tour of the Gardens of the Immaculate Conception in Maristown. When Jon walked up to the rose covered statue of Mother Mari that was located in the very heart of the garden, his bio-signature allowed him to select another, hidden option. He chose it, and said a prayer of thanks, grateful that Sister n'Avenal had anticipated his need for expiation and cleansing.

The sunny gardens vanished, and Jon found himself dressed in a coarse robe, standing in the middle of a bare stone chamber. This reproduction of an 11th century monks cell was a dank, cold place, with only a simple straw mattress, a small glassless window that barely admitted light, and one half-melted candle set in a crude niche that only accentuated the darkness. And hanging from a plain hook near the door, was the object of his desire; a crude leather cat-of-nine-tails with a rough wooden handle.

He stripped off his robe, and took the whip from the wall. With this in hand, he knelt down on the freezing stone floor, and began the rite of purification, speaking the New Lord's Prayer aloud.

"Holy Trinity, who art in heaven,"he said, striking himself with the device, "hallowed be Thy names." A second blow came with this.

"Thy kingdoms come..." He delivered a third strike, and with more force.

"Thy wills be done, on all worlds as it is in heaven." A fourth strike followed.

"Give us this day our daily bread." He dealt himself a fifth lashing, and this time, drew blood. The sound of the leather biting into him echoed around the tiny chamber.

"And forgive us our sins..." *Whap!*

"As we forgive those who sin against us..." *Whap!*

"And lead us not into darkness..." *Whap!*

"But deliver us from evil..." *Whap!* Tears came. They were not from the pain though, but the joy of deliverance.

"For Thine is the whole of the universe..." *Whap!*

"Its power, and its glory!" *Whap!*

"Ameyn!" *Whap!*

Twelve simple lines, twelve apostles, and twelve well-deserved blows.

Jon rested, letting the bloody whip go limp, and searched his soul. When he found that there was still a tiny kernel of impurity within himself, he raised the lash again, and began the rite anew.

He intended to repeat the agonizing process at least three more times. Three for God, for Jesu and for Mother Mari. And if he needed it, he would perform a fourth to atone for his miserable, unworthy soul.

"Holy Trinity, who art in heaven..." *Whap!*

***

After Xapaan, the SEF moved into the Cataala Provensa while N'Leesa and her group poured into Reganna. On both sides of the Republic, Hriss resistance was crumbling, and it became increasingly obvious that the Clans were finally abandoning their dream of conquering the ETR. Encounters with them became rarer with each passing day, until at last the Expeditionary Force received the message that it had been waiting to hear for more than a year.

Fleet Admiral ebed Cya was the one who delivered it, and Katrinn piped her words into every corner of the *Athena*. Lilith heard it while she was on a bicycle peddling towards the Lifts and on her way to her office. She pulled over and stopped, listening with the other sailors around her.

"Ladies, it is my privilege to convey the Chairwoman's congratulations. Based on intelligence information that we have received from all of our forces in the area, we believe that the Hriss threat to the ETR has been completely eliminated.'

"The Chairwoman has contacted the Throne of Bones, and the Hriss Imperium has assured her that any remaining members of the Clans that were involved in this adventure, will be dealt with as renegades. Their lives, and their properties, will be forfeit and they will be hunted down. Emperor J'akkat'vak'nar has also given his personal word that there will never be another conflict like this between his race and our own."

No one really believed this part, even Ebed Cya, but it was nice to hear it nonetheless.

The woman continued. "Your mission will now be to assist the Republic in any final operations that they are required to undertake. You have our profound thanks, the gratitude of the ETR, and all humanity in the ages to come."

The war, which the press had come to call 'The War for Humanity' was over. As the women around her hugged one another enthusiastically and exchanged congratulations, Lilith leaned back against the bulkhead.

She didn't share their elation. Instead, all she felt was a hollow emptiness. It had been like this for her before, when the War of the Prophet had ended; a sensation of both disorientation and dislocation. She understood it now for what it was, the equivalent of postpartum depression, but here what had been brought into being was not a child, but peace.

Katrinn, also a veteran, shared this feeling, and when Lilith finally arrived at her office, the woman was waiting for her there with a bottle of *Aqqa*, and a pair of glasses.

"The Grand Admiral is coming over this afternoon to award us medals, "Katrinn announced as they sat down together.

Lilith drained her glass and held it out for a refill. "*Wonderful*," she drawled. "I *had* hoped we could sneak home without having to see that man again."

Katrinn shook her head. "Nope. After the announcement, Rixa sent us more orders. We're to head back to Altamara, and stand by there with a portion of the fleet while everyone else makes the transit home. It seems that Thermadon wants the Navy to maintain a regular military presence here from now on, and we get first watch. We'll receive our replacements a month from now. *Then* we can go home."

Lilith scowled, but she wasn't overly surprised. Regardless of the extravagant promises that the Throne of Bones had made, the only sure way to secure peace in the ETR was to have a force in place as a constant reminder to the Emperor of the Sisterhood's resolve. Blessed as it was, a part of her had come to hate peace.

***

Captain Rodraga also received new orders. With no further need for liaison officers on Sisterhood ships, his time aboard the *Athena* was officially at an end. He attended one final meeting of the Book Club, said goodbye to the women he had made friends with (including Sarah sa'Vika, who used it as an opportunity to cement future dealings through him for ETR specialty goods) and then Lilith and he shared a private dinner together.

The next morning, he packed his things and reported to the hangar bay for the shuttle that would take him away. Lilith and Katrinn were there to see him off.

"Lilith, Katrinn, I have had a wonderful stay with you," Rodraga said as they stopped at the foot of the shuttle's stairs. "I would like to thank you for having me aboard."

"The pleasure was ours," Lilith replied warmly.

"I also hope that someday I'll have the chance to see your Sisterhood for myself. I am sure that it will prove to be just as wonderful as its women are." Then he saluted them, clicking his heels together. "Vice Admiral, Commander."

Lilith returned the gesture. "Captain."

When he had boarded the launch, Katrinn stood next to her, and together they watched the vessel depart.

"Kat," Lilith said, "I have to admit that if I ever considered having a relationship with a man, it would be him."

"Yes," Katrinn smiled. "He is beautiful, isn't he? In his own strange way. By the way, Lily, I heard from Ellyn. The decision is in on Trooper taur Tanna."

"The Marine that cut up that ETR soldier?" she asked. "What did they decide?"

"Exactly what Ellyn predicted; not guilty with prejudice, time served. Taur Tanna's out of the Corps, but she's a free woman," the Zommerlaandar said. "She also told me that the Nemesian Planetary Militia is willing to pick her up, so she'll still have work in a uniform, if she wants it."

"Good," Lilith replied, "It's nice to see that justice prevailed in such a messy situation. Too bad about her discharge though."

"It couldn't be helped," Katrinn replied with a dismissive shrug. "She did act outside the scope of her duties as a Marine, even if she was justified." Then she accessed her psiever. "Well, I need to be back on the bridge for my shift. I'll see you later, Lily."

Lilith gave her a friendly nod of understanding and then looked back to the hangar bay and space beyond it. The shuttle was just starting its run up to warp speed and had diminished to a tiny speck, barely visible against the stars. In moments, it would be gone.

Goddess keep you, Alex, she thought. *I will miss you.*

Lida Medica SA Research Facility, Nuvo Bolivar, Magdala Provensa, Esteral Terrana Rapabla, 1044.12|05|02:70:71

Lena knew that the lights in the room were on, but when she tried to open her eyes, they seemed to be made of lead, and even when she finally managed to make them respond to her will, everything around her was blurry and out of focus. There were voices nearby, but like the sights around her, they were muffled and indistinct. She tried to concentrate on what they were saying, knowing that it was important, but the words seemed disconnected from any reference point, or meaning.

"What batch did you administer her?" the first voice asked.

"Lot 22-R-7B, Doctor Sanchar," the second answered. "It seems to be having the desired effects. I think we've finally found the key for the class C gene markers."

"What are the results with our friendly test subjects?"

"Completely asymptomatic, sir."

"Perfect," the first replied. "And just in time to meet our deadline." A resigned sigh followed this. "Well, I think that we've gotten all that we can from this one. A genuine pity. She has such lovely eyes."

"Doctor, do you want me to terminate her?"

"Not just yet. I think that we'll…"

The rest of the conversation was lost as a violent fit of coughing seized her. When it finally passed, her vision was rimmed with grey, and her heart hammered in her chest.

I'm so tired…so weak.

Her body felt hollow, like it was the cast-off husk of an insect that had just completed some strange metamorphosis. Somehow, she could see it from a vantage point high up in the corner of the room; an emaciated and empty thing, clad only in a thin gown that was soaked through with sweat and speckled with bright droplets of blood.

The only force that prevented her from leaving that pitiful, ruined vessel behind was a tenuous bond that she sensed more than saw, something more fragile than the string on a child's balloon. Feeling a weariness that transcended anything she had ever experienced before, she wanted to sever that tie, and fly free.

Then I could rest.

Just beyond the edges of her perception, a cool, peaceful nothingness beckoned to her invitingly. *Yes,* it seemed to reply, *rest Lena. Sleep.*

Lena started to drift towards it, eager for its embrace. Then, to her horror, she realized what that nothingness really was, and with the last shred of her strength, she pulled herself away from it.

Somehow, she had to keep going, she told herself. She had to keep fighting. Fighting until Kaly came at last, and saved her.

Kaly had to come. She had to.

CHAPTER 11

Lida Medica SA Research Facility, Nuvo Bolivar, Magdala Provensa, Esteral Terrana Rapabla, 1044.12|06|07:09:49

To anyone who might have been watching, Dr. Susya Floretz's day seemed to be concluding normally enough. She returned from her laboratory at the usual time, stopped at her desk, gathered her things, and even paused to chat with an assistant about a routine matter on her way to the elevator. Less than two minutes later, she was in the lobby showing her identification card to security.

As part of the high-level protocol *Lida Medica SA* had instituted, her valise was searched, and so was her light jacket, but there was nothing in either of them that aroused any suspicion. In fact, there wasn't anything anywhere on her person that didn't belong there.

But Dr. Floretz *was* smuggling, and what she was taking away was hidden in the best place it could be; in her mind. Floretz was one of the senior researchers at *'The Project'* and she knew every detail about it, and more importantly, what its true purpose was. It had been this very knowledge that had set her on the road that she was now taking. She understood that it would have been safer if she had turned a blind eye to it all, and it was her patriotic duty to do so, but what *Lida* was doing for the government went against every principle of humanity that she had ever believed in.

She went out of the building and her husband met her in their modest 'lectri, right in front, just as he always did at the end of the day. Like her, he seemed relaxed, and even included his habitual wave to her as she walked up to the vehicle. Dr. Paacal Floretz was also a researcher at the facility, and like his wife, he had decided to betray *Lida SA,* and his nation, for precisely the same reasons.

When Susya was inside the vehicle, he pulled away from the curb, taking care to obey the speed limits and all the traffic rules, and drove away without making it look like they were in any particular hurry. At the main gate, they had to stop and present their identification. This was also routine.

The unsmiling, armed soldiers carefully scrutinized their cards, but there was nothing about either one of them that engendered any suspicion, and none of the scanners or biosensors that were trained on the 'lectri registered any alarms.

They were waved through without further delay, driving past the double line of fencing topped with barbed wire, and went by signs that read *'Danger! This is a Government Research Facility. Use of Lethal Force Is Authorized'* and other smaller placards that warned the reader of the *'Electrified Inner Fence!'* and *'Risk of Death or Serious Injury!'*

They paid them little attention. These grim messages were something that they encountered every day working at 'The Project'.

Once they were out on the highway, they headed west, towards their usual on-ramp to the interstate. They even got on it, and traveled in the direction that they normally took. But instead of going home, they stopped at a roadside recharging station, and Susya got out, pretending to go into the small convenience store for a snack. They had agreed, when they had discussed the matter together, that she would be the one to set things in motion.

In a way, it was fitting, she refelected. Being a woman and taking the first step. The scientist in her was also amazed at how calm she was as she made her way back to the public Coms set at the rear of the store.

Glancing briefly over her shoulder to see if anyone was paying her any undue attention, she punched in a number, and pressed 'send'. With that simple act, she committed high treason, and condemned her husband and herself to death—if they were ever caught.

The number that she had called was a private line, and it connected her directly to Rozza Ramara's office. The reporter had stayed late, hoping for her call.

"It's me," Dr. Floretz said. "Can we meet right now? We can't wait any longer."

Ramara agreed without hesitation, and after listening very carefully to the woman's instructions, Susya ended the call and returned to the 'lectri. It was only then, as they were leaving the station and heading towards the location she had been given by the reporter that she finally broke down and cried. Her husband understood, and even his eyes weren't entirely dry as he held her hand and comforted her. They were giving up everything; their home, their possessions, and their careers, all for the sake of their convictions. Anyone would have wept in such circumstances.

Twenty minutes later, they were sitting in a booth in a little nondescript restaurant, across from Ramara. The two researchers kept what they had to say to her brief, and to the point. The reporter listened intently to their words, and when they had finished speaking, she rose and made a call of her own, to another private number. It had been given to her just before she had returned from her latest trip to Thermadon, and at the time, she had been reluctant to accept it. Now she was glad that she had decided otherwise.

It was to the Embassy of the United Sisterhood of Suns in Nuvo Bolivar, the offices of the *Regila da Securité par Diploma*, the Diplomatic Security Services. The party who picked up on the other end was listed with the Embassy as an RSD security specialist, and her title was legitimate enough. That she was also an OAE agent was not a matter of record however.

The woman listened to Ramara with no trace of emotion, and then it was Ramara's turn to receive instructions. Ten tense minutes passed before a plain black 'lectri-van pulled into the restaurant's parking lot. A pair of somber, unsmiling women got out of it and came inside, going right up to Ramara and the researchers. There was a brief conversation and then everyone went outside together.

Another 'lectri was waiting nearby, with a second pair of women inside of it who looked just as hard and as businesslike as the first two, and a third 'lectri with more women in it was also hovering at the curb.

As they neared it, the van's door opened, and if there had been anyone else in the parking lot, they might have glimpsed another woman inside, with some kind of automatic weapon held at the ready. But no one else was near and the passengers were hustled inside and the door was shut behind them so quickly that a theoretical observer might have doubted their senses.

The vehicles left right away, moving as a group and traveling only a few blocks before stopping at the edge of an overgrown, open lot. Another unmarked vehicle was standing by.

This time it was a helijet; one of the fast models that only corporate executives and government officials used. Or so it seemed on the surface. In reality, its insides were all of Sisterhood manufacture, and it had been specially constructed for the Agency to use in the ETR, without attracting the kind of attention that a hovercraft would have otherwise received.

An expert would have recognized the difference just from the lack of sound that it made. Its fusion-powered engines were running at just a hair below take-off speed, and despite this, the machine was almost completely silent.

The moment that the convoy reached it, its door opened and Ramara and the two researchers were shown aboard. At the same time, their escorts abandoned any pretense of normalcy and openly brandished their weapons as they guarded the take off.

There was no interference however, and the helijet rose quietly and took off at top speed, headed directly for the Embassy. It left no trace of its flight. Special composite layers, and advanced stealth equipment aboard the aircraft, made certain that the local air traffic control network detected absolutely nothing.

A mere fifteen minutes elapsed before the helijet reached Nuvo Bolivar and was landing on the Embassy's roof. It was met by another contingent of heavily armed securitywomen, and the two women who were in charge.

Sarah n'Jan and Maya had been in town on other business, and when the news had reached them, they had been only too eager to meet their visitors as they arrived. In fact, the very safety and security of the Sisterhood had depended on it.

Sub-Basement Level, Embassy of the United Sisterhood of Suns, Nuvo Bolivar, Magdala Provensa, Esteral Terrana Rapabla, 1044.12|06|07:46:49

Deep inside the building, in a special room that was shielded from any external surveillance devices, Sarah had the two scientists tell her the same story they had related to Ramara. She also made certain that the conversation was not only recorded, but also scheduled for review by intelligence analysts specially trained to spot lies or inconsistencies. Her own talents were already telling her that what they were saying was the truth, but she wanted no room for any errors. Not when it came to something this sensitive.

"Let me see if I understand the situation at your lab correctly," she finally said. "Your employer, *Lida Medica SA,* has had you working on a lethal virus, which has been specifically tailored to the genetic markers of women born in the Sisterhood. Is that basically correct?"

"Yes," Susya replied wearily. The events of the day had completely drained her, both emotionally and physically, and even the kaafra that Maya had provided her was having little effect.

"You also mentioned that this 'Project' of yours has been sponsored by your government, and that it has been on-going for the past two decades?"

The Floretz's nodded in unison.

"In addition, you claimed that your facility recently managed to achieve the results that *Lida* has been hoping for. That you have actually developed such a virus?"

"Yes," Susya answered. "It has been tested, and it works perfectly. It will only affect women with Sisterhood genes. Our own women are completely immune to it. So are our men. I was told that it is a variation on the ancient MARS virus."

"And this testing was performed on—?"

"As I told you, ma'am, on live subjects. They started with biological materials gathered from corpses, but then they needed real people—women—to test it out on. The computer models were insufficient. So, they brought in some of your soldiers for this purpose. I was told that they had captured them."

"I see," Sarah responded coolly. "That would certainly explain some of our personnel who are currently listed as 'missing in action.' Tell me doctor, did you or your husband participate in this particular 'phase' of the research? In the live testing?"

"No," the woman responded, shaking her head. "I was part of the theoretical end of things, and I supervised the genetic manipulation sequences, but neither of us actually saw the test subjects, or administered any of the test doses to them. Dr. Sanchar's department handled all that. He is the senior-most Project researcher, and he insisted on overseeing the live-testing phase himself."

"Very well," Sarah said. By the woman's own account, she was not completely innocent, but she and her male pairmate didn't have as much blood on their hands as this Dr. Sanchar did. This would be an important point to raise when she approached the Ambassador and asked her to grant them political asylum.

As for Adolpha Sanchar, he would answer for his crimes, she told herself, right along with the rest of the ETR's leadership. A wave of white-hot anger rose up in her as she made this silent promise, but she had been an agent for too many years to let it overtake her.

Forcing herself to remain calm, Sarah looked over at Rozza Ramara. The reporter was nursing her own cup of kaafra with a tense, worried expression.

"Ms. Ramara. I know that you didn't ask us for it, but I would like to offer you the same protection that the Floretz's are requesting. I am quite aware that you would rather return to your offices right away to break this story, but I believe that the government—*your government*—would take steps to eliminate you the very moment they learned of your involvement. This is not the kind of matter that permits any witnesses to be left alive.'

"I would also like to add my personal assurance to you that the story *will* get out, and that you *will* be the one to tell it, but that can only be after your safety has been thoroughly guaranteed. I am certain that you can appreciate the wisdom behind this."

Ramara looked at her sadly. "Yes. I knew it the minute the Floretz's contacted me." Then she smiled self-deprecatingly. "You know Ms. N'Jan, when I was a young reporter, I always wanted to be the one to break a really big story. Your Goddess seems to have heard me, hasn't she? I'll have to be more careful for what I wish for in the future."

"Indeed," Sarah agreed.

***

'Bolivar Azya' Set, Channel 3 Studios, Nuvo Bolivar, Magdala Provensa, Esteral Terrana Rapabla. 1044.12|06|07:91:67

Sanda Ernan had risen in the world. Since her return from Thermadon, and the explosive newscast made by Rozza Ramara, she and her movement had enjoyed more attention than she had ever imagined. Women who would have never considered joining a feminist group had done so in droves, and despite the activities of extremist elements like *La Ermanyaa*, they were becoming a political force that the Republic was being forced to recognize.

Thanks to all of this, and Ramara's connections, Ernan was now a well-known figure, and commanded a much larger audience than just what could fit into a single coffee house. On the same evening that the Floretz's were taking shelter at the Sisterhood's Embassy, she was taking part in the taping of an interview by the host of a popular holovision show, '*Bolivar Azya'*. The syndicated show would be broadcast the following morning, and watched by nearly every housewife and work-at-home-female professional, not only in the capitol, but also throughout most of the Republic itself.

She had never particularly liked the smiling blond hostess, thinking of her as nothing more than a poster-child for the male ideal for women. But 'Bolivar Today' had a huge audience, and they were the very downtrodden masses that she wanted to reach. So she had smiled, and played nice during the recording session.

"Sanda," the hostess said, "I want to thank you for being with us today and sharing your movement's views on women's rights. Is there anything in particular that you would like to say to our audience before we end our show today?"

"Yes, Maria," she answered. "I'd like to speak about who we are as women, and how some stereotypes about us are actually true, and why they are our strengths."

"That sounds fascinating. Please share with us."

"One of the greatest, and I'm sure everyone watching has heard it, is that we are naturally curious and that we can't leave a secret alone. This is true, and I have seen what it can do. The Sisterhood has taken this feminine trait to its furthest expression and as a result, they enjoy a level of scientific achievement that surpasses what our male dominated scientists here in the ETR are capable of."

After seeing some of the broadcasts produced by Rozza Ramara, showcasing the Sisterhood's accomplishments, everyone including the hostess, knew this for plain fact. The journalist nodded, not just out of politeness, but also in full agreement.

"Another stereotype is that we women are the fiercest when we are defending our young," Ernan continued, "and this is also true. Again, the Sisterhood is my proof. They too have been assaulted by the Hriss, and not just once—but many times. And they have won every war with them, just as they helped us to win this one.'

"This is for one simple reason that goes beyond their technology; they won *because* they were women doing what women always do best, and that is defending the helpless with absolute determination.'

"Now there is one final label that I'd like to talk about. It is that we show men things that they'd rather not see. It is also true. No matter how powerful the male, we perceive the truth for what it is, and we force them to stop, and think. They especially hate us for this, but they also need our insights, just as the Republic needs us to show it the truths that it wants to ignore."

"And I certainly hope that our politicians will hear your words today and take heart," the hostess interjected. In the span of an hour, Ernan realized that the woman had gone from being a male puppet, to a convert.

"Sanda, it has been *great* having you on the show today and I hope that you will come back again, very soon. I know that our audience has enjoyed hearing your inspiring ideas and I can speak for them and say that we would all love to hear more."

With that, the show ended, and after having the invitation reiterated to come back for another episode, Ernan was shown off the set to the dressing room that they had set aside for her. Two women were waiting for her there. They were both dressed in dark, conservative business suits, but every centimeter of them screamed 'military'.

One of them, whom she could tell was a Zommerlaandar just from her build and coloring, stepped forwards. “Ma’am, ve are from za Embassy. Vill you come vith us pleaze?”

“I’d certainly be happy to, but I have to go home and write a speech that I’m giving tomorrow,” she replied. “Can you tell me what this is all about?”

“Ma’am, ve believe zat your life iz in imminent danger. Somezhing has happened. Zhere is a ‘lectri waiting vor you outzide.”

The Apex Office, The Golden Pyramid, Concordance Park, Thermadon Val, Thermadon, Myrene System, Thalestris Elant, United Sisterhood of Suns, 1044.12|06|08:33:91

Layna n’Calysher sat across from Chairwoman Marina bel Rayna and waited quietly while she reviewed the OAE report. Despite the gravity of the news, the Senatrix was quite pleased with how things were unfolding. Although the Sisterhood had received valuable resources in exchange for their aid, the ETR had been a threat ever since the Daughters of the Coast had first made contact with them.

Now that danger was about to be eliminated. She knew Bel Rayna, and how her mind worked. There was no other decision that the woman could make.

The Chairwoman looked up from her holoscreen to N’Calysher and the other women in the room; her Secretary of State, the Admiral of the Navy, the Commandant of the Marine Corps, several key advisors, and the prime movers of the Special Committee.

“This report says that the *Lida* virus was based on the original MARS Plague. Can we infer from this that the ETR might have had something to do with MARS as well?”

“The ETR was allied with the Kasiegians when they attempted to secede from the Gaian Star Federation,” one of her advisors answered. “Some historians still believe that the Kasiegians were responsible for the Plague.”

“That is certainly a very dark brush to paint them with,” the Secretary of State interjected. “However, given this development, hardly unfair, nor undeserved. I think that the public will support us wholeheartedly in any action we take against them."

"I don't want anyone in the Circle to be able to cast a 'no' vote," the Chairwoman said. Then she addressed the Commandant of the Marines. "Insert a team into that facility and get me incontrovertible proof that I can show to the nation."

"Yes ma'am", General Tannasdaater answered.

"Excellent. And also make certain to include some members of the Press, especially that Ramara woman. Once this is over, we'll want the ETR's public to be as friendly towards us as possible, and she knows how to influence their opinions."

"Yes ma'am."

N'Calysher suppressed a smile of triumph. It was done. And when it was all over, the ETR would be a friendly puppet state, with a woman as its leader.

She made a mental note to express her personal congratulations to Sarah n'Jan for ensuring that Sanda Ernan had been taken off-planet with the two *Lida* researchers. She also decided to suggest that Rozza Ramara be included in Ernan's future staff as her Press Secretary. Once Ernan came to power, she would need the woman's assistance to manage public information.

Lida Medica SA Research Facility, Nuvo Bolivar, Magdala Provensa, Esteral Terrana Rapabla, 1044.12|07|01:25:00

With the entire team and their weapons inside it, there was no room to move in the cargo compartment of the 'lectri-van. But as a sniper, Kaly had mastered the art of remaining in uncomfortable positions and cramped spaces for long periods of time, and she called on that discipline to override the complaints that were coming from her leg muscles.

The ride itself wasn't helping much. Commercial cargo 'lectris had stiff suspensions, and the bare metal floor transmitted every bump in the road straight up into her. Even though she had finally been able to abandon her hated cane, and could move about normally enough, her right ankle still reminded her of the injury that it had suffered in Treya Angelaz with every pothole. Fortunately, the specialized battle-suit that she was wearing cushioned the worst of this abuse and sheer willpower overcame the rest.

Her *Patojène-Perella Emviron Combatté Costûm*, or Pathogen-Hazardous Environment Combat Suit, had been developed for the Marines to fight in non-pressurized, hazardous environments. It didn't replace the heavier standard Marine zero-G suit, but it was more resistant to projectiles, and allowed for greater flexibility of movement, which was an absolute necessity in close quarters fighting.

The matte black body armor enjoyed another name among the troopers themselves. It was an irreverent take-off on its acronym, PPECC. They called it the *Fek Suit*, not because anything was inherently wrong with it, but because of what generally happened to anyone, or anything, that they encountered while wearing it. And if everything went right, the personnel at the *Lida* facility where about to be *fekked*, but good.

Seal up, N'Elemay thought. Kaly already had her helmet on, and at the Troop Leader's order, she closed the neck ring. The seals automatically engaged and the suit's rebreather unit started up.

The van stopped right behind another one, just ahead of them. That vehicle contained Marauder Team 7 and its driver was none other than Yúna Santavaar, the leader of *La Ermanyaa*. When she and her sisters had been approached about the mission, they had been quite enthusiastic about lending their assistance. The team she was driving had been tasked with assaulting the main gate and securing it, and although Santavaar didn't know it, there was a plan in place to eliminate her in the unlikely event that she turned traitor at the last moment. Their mission was too important to take any chances, even with supposed 'friendlies'.

The dialogue between Santavaar, and a guard who had come out to meet them, sounded in Kaly's helmet speakers on the general Com. The microphones that were picking it up were far more sensitive than a human ear, and she could hear everything, even the sound of the guards' breathing.

"Excuse me," Santavaar said to him. "I think we're lost. Is this Palajaras road?" There was the rustle of a paper map, and Kaly tensed. Across from her, Margasdaater smiled in anticipation and brought her hand up to rest on the rear door handle, ready to open it in case Team 7 needed back-up. T'Jinna and N'Elemay, Kaly saw, had their submachineguns up and at the ready. She followed suit.

Then, her speakers echoed with a sharp snapping noise as Santavaar shot the guard point blank with her silenced pistol. It was followed by a wet half-gasp of alarm. A split-second later, she heard the doors of the lead van opening and then the unmistakable sound of suppressed automatic weapons fire. After that, there was only silence.

Kaly's van began to move again, and as it passed through the gate, she managed to catch a glimpse of the scene behind them through the rear windows. There had been six guards on duty, she saw, and all of them were down, sprawled on the ground in various postures of death. Team 7 and some of the *La Ermanyaa* women were already fanning out and taking up guarding positions. The main gate was theirs and the gamble that the Sisterhood had taken by enlisting Santavaar and her feminist rebels had paid off.

The 'lectri drove a little ways further, and then it pulled over to let another van pass by. This was carrying Team 12, and overhead, the helijet from the Embassy appeared out of the darkness, carrying Team 9. Their mutual destination was the Administration Building. Team 12 would assault the structure from ground level, while the helijet dropped Team 9 onto the roof to hit their target from above. Both groups would attack simultaneously and catch anyone inside between them.

Once inside, 9 and 12 had two critical objectives to achieve. The first was to silence the facility's alarms and its communications network, and then to access the main computer system for a detailed map of the entire location. Although the Floretz's had provided the Sisterhood with a fairly good diagram of the layout aboveground, the combined teams knew nothing whatsoever about the secure research labs that were located four stories beneath it.

Until they managed this, there was nothing for Team 5 to do but wait for them to succeed, and stay ready to provide a fluid response to anything that changed. Three uncomfortable minutes dripped by, and then Kaly's HUD came to life with a virtual map. It showed everything, including the secure lab levels. The entire facility was effectively cut off from the rest of the universe, and now, the teams knew where everything was. The place was theirs for the taking.

N'Elemay briefly took over control of the map with her psiever and dialed it in to the portion specific to the labs, highlighting the route that they were going to take. As she did so, a fourth van came up behind them. It was carrying the last team, Team 2 into play. 2's job was to run point for assaulting the Lab, and Team 5 would be assisting them.

With a lurch, they were off again, caroming across the well-manicured lawns and sliding to a halt at the entrance to the Lab Building. Team 2 was out first, and when they reached the main entrance doors, they found them locked. Somehow, the guards inside had been alerted to their presence, but unable to call anyone for help, they had resorted to the only defense left available to them.

A pair of explosive charges easily took care of this obstacle however, blowing the doors off their hinges and stunning the men inside. Before they could recover and respond, Team 2 rushed in, and cut them down with their weapons.

Kaly and her Teammates followed right behind them, jumping over the shredded corpses and covering Team 2 as it opened another, inner set of doors. There was a long hallway on the other side, and at its end, a pair of gleaming elevators. Both teams avoided them though, and took the stairs instead.

They descended as they had been taught; with their backs to the walls, walking sideways, and with their weapons trained on the stairwell and the flight below it.

Reaching the first landing and its door, Kaly's group covered the exit while Team 2 went through and into the hallway beyond. Once they were safely in, she and her companions moved cautiously down to the next level.

Like the floor above it, the stairwell door opened up onto a plain white passage, lined with non-descript doors, and bright, even lighting. Despite the quietness of the scene, the team kept their weapons up at their shoulders, at the ready.

Thanks to a modified version of the psiever feed developed for Valkyrie fighter pilots, they each received a 360 degree feed of every living thing around them, with friend and foe neatly color coded.

A red enemy figure registered behind a wall in front of Kaly. The guard was hiding in an office, presumably waiting to ambush them. As she brought her weapon to bear, T'Jinna, who had seen him first, beat her to it and fired through the thin drywall. The man went down, and then Kaly spotted another figure coming out from a door that was behind and to her left. She spun on her heels and shot him before he cleared the doorway.

The man screamed, and fell backwards. He didn't rise again. After that, the display only registered the presence of friendly blue figures—themselves. The rest of the level was unoccupied.

The secure elevator is down this hall, N'Elemay thought to them, marking its location with an insistent flashing icon. Although they were all now reasonably certain that they were alone, they worked their way down to the elevator carefully, ranging their weapons around them to cover every possible danger point. It never paid to rely solely on technology when the stakes were life and death.

The team reached the elevator without further challenge however, but once there, they met with another obstacle. Its doors were constructed of the same heavy stainless steel as the pair upstairs, but instead of a normal set of controls to summon the car, it had an archaic retinal scanner and a keypad.

N'Elemay sent a message up to the Admin Teams. *There's a retinal scanner here and a number pad. Can you override the doors from your location?*

Checking. Hold one, came the reply. Then, *That's a negative, Team 5. The labs are on a separate computer system. It looks like an added security measure.*

N'Elemay mouthed an obscenity and considered the situation, and Kaly knew without having to ask her, what the woman was thinking. Blowing the damned thing open was certainly possible, but entirely out of the question. Isolated as it was, there was still a chance that anyone in the Labs below them was unaware of what was going on, and they wanted to retain the advantage of surprise for as long as possible. This left them with only one other option, and N'Elemay took it.

Admin Team, can you spare Liverna? she inquired.

Yes. We're done with her here. Sending her to you now. Standby.

Holding position.

The team settled down to wait again. The Admin Team had dispatched their battlebot, and although it could move quite rapidly across open ground, it still had to cover the distance between the two areas.

It wasn't just a standard 'bot however. While it had guns, and could certainly hold its own in a firefight, the Liverna 151, named after the minor Roman Goddess of Thieves, was a truly intelligent machine. It possessed a sophisticated onboard AI and specialized probes that could pick and defeat almost any lock. It would prove more than a match for the elevator access controls.

When the spider like machine arrived, it walked straight up to the elevator with an almost sentient confidence and examined the keypad and the scanner with its green laser 'eye'.

"Well?" N'Elemay asked. "Can you open it?"

"Of course I can!" the machine replied huffily. "It's stone age junk! Do you want me to send the car up while I'm at it? Maybe even change the music for your ride down? It's truly awful."

"No. None of that will be necessary. Just leave the car below. We'll rappel down."

"As you say." A small hatch opened on its nose and a cluster of delicate manipulator probes extended out to the keypad.

"This computer thinks its *sooo* smart," the thing commented as the probes worked their way through tiny gaps in the pads' faceplate. "But retinal scans and number sequences depend on data that the system stores to compare with any input. So, I find those records, duplicate them, and send them right back to the stupid thing. And, *Vala!* It opens."

A single beep sounded as the computer capitulated to the 'bots command. When the elevator doors opened, they revealed an empty shaft. Team 2 was just coming up to join them by this point, and they immediately clipped themselves onto the support members in the shaft itself and roped down to the elevator car at the bottom. Once they were atop it, one of their women opened the escape hatch and they all lowered themselves inside.

Again, Kaly was privy to the conversation.

Open the doors on my count, the Team Leader thought to the Liverna. *Three, two, one—go.* The doors slid open, followed by two brief bursts of automatic weapons fire.

Entry secure. Two enemies eliminated. Rope down.

One by one, Team 5 withdrew metal clips from their belts, latched them onto secure points, and let out the lengths of plastisteel ropes they had brought with them. When Kaly's turn came, she lowered herself over the edge of the doorway and rappelled down. Even though her descent was perfect, she was still glad to feel the elevator roof when her boots made contact.

She had never told anyone, and never would, but she secretly hated heights with a passion. Becoming a sniper had forced her to overcome this fear, but her trepidation had never been replaced by anything approaching love. It was just part of the job, and she gritted her teeth and did what she had to do.

The Liverna had no such reservations though, and as Kaly unclipped herself, the machine simply walked over the lip and clambered down to them with all the ease of the insect that it resembled. It didn't even pause to catch its breath, since it had none, and skittered by her to the roof hatch and down into the car.

Kaly dropped through to join it, and she saw that the elevator opened out onto a small lobby with a desk set aside for security. The officers who had manned it lay nearby, neatly riddled with bullets, and Team 2 was waiting at a pair of frosted glass doors. A sign over this portal declared, *'Hazardous Biological Materials In this Area! All Employees Must Wear Protective Gear Appropriate to Their Lab-Section.'*

A large double air lock was on the other side, and the Liverna overrode its controls, admitting them past the barrier. Thankful for her PPECC suit, Kaly trained her weapon on the open 'lock and stood by as Team 2 went through, followed by the Liverna. As soon as they had gone past, N'Elemay waved Team 5 forwards and they took up a rear guard position, advancing with 2 as they moved.

They were in another hallway, but this time it was lined with doubled paned glass windows that looked onto large, well-lit rooms. The equipment and the tables inside of them clearly identified the chambers as research laboratories, and each one had its own combination airlock-decontamination chamber separating it from the main passage. Racks of white suits similar to EVA gear stood in front of some of them, clearly intended for employees to enter and exit any contaminated areas safely.

Reaching the end of the hall, they passed another room and its function was just as obvious. Although it possessed relatively primitive equipment compared to what Kaly was familiar with, the place was set up very much like its Sisterhood counterparts.

It was a morgue, with the signature stainless steel drawers and autopsy tables. But like the labs that surrounded it, it was separated from the outside world by a pressurized decontamination chamber. As she passed it, she was grateful that there were no bodies on display on the tables at that moment.

Beyond the morgue, the Teams encountered another air lock. Above it, a sign read, *"Sample Containment Area! Security Authorization Required for Access!"*

Everyone stood aside to let the Liverna do her work and in short order, the lock was opened. This part of the facility was also a hallway, and it was lined with heavy doors sporting thick rubber gaskets around their edges, and small observation windows. Each one had names and numbers displayed over them. Although they were written in Espangla, Kaly recognized the names and the military service numbers immediately.

Looking through one of the windows, she spotted a woman sitting on the edge of a plain cot. She was dressed in a hospital-style gown, and the body it covered was emaciated and worn. Sensing that someone was outside, the prisoner looked up, her eyes radiating with utter hopelessness.

Kaly had no time to release her, or offer any reassurances. A guard was on duty at the far end of the passage, and as they entered, he stood. He was dressed in one of the white pressure suits that they had seen outside, and the expression of alarm on his face was clearly visible.

Before he could do anything, N'Elemay, smiling like an angel of death, crouched and shot him, scoring a hit through his faceplate in the middle of his forehead. Hearing the disturbance, another guard appeared from around the corner, and she immediately made certain that he shared in his brother's fate.

Even as the man fell, everyone was moving on, racing towards their final objective; the control room for the cells and main security center. This was in another corridor, and proved to be a box-like chamber, lined with impact resistant glass. It wasn't proof against projectiles though, and bursts from Team 2's submachineguns found their mark on the single guard who had holed himself up inside. Then the team escorted the Liverna up to the station and the 'bot quickly overrode the security systems, opening up all of the holding cells simultaneously.

Five, see what you can do for the prisoners, Two's Leader broadcast. *We'll sweep ahead.*

Affirmative, N'Elemay answered, gesturing for Kaly and the rest to follow her back to the cells.

What they found inside them was horrific. Although some of the women were still healthy enough, others were in different stages of dying. The vast majority of them were too weak to stand, and could only respond to the medics' ministrations with ragged fits of bloody coughing. It was the MARS Plague all over again, but this time, it had been designed for women only.

It took every gram of Kaly's self-control not to burst into hysterical tears, vomit into her helmet, or just run out of the hellish place shrieking. What gave her the ability to persevere were her teammates. Although they were certainly experiencing the same emotions, each of them went about their business with silent, grim professionalism. It was this very control in the face of terror that had drawn her to the Marines in the first place, and she was grateful to them for their strength, and the vigor that this lent her to carry on.

T'Jinna had broken out her med kit and was starting to treat what she could, and Margasdaater and N'Elemay were moving to do the same. Kaly followed suit, opening her own tiny kit and knelt down to help a woman who had somehow found the strength to crawl out of her cell.

"I-knew-you'd-come," the woman managed to croak. "Too-late-for-some—of us—". The rest was lost in a fit of bloody coughing, and Kaly knew that she was probably as good as dead and her body just hadn't accepted the fact.

All objectives secure, Team 2 announced.

Affirmative, N'Elemay acknowledged. *Lab and Holding facility secure. Gate? Bring in the newsies.*

En route to you.

"Kaly," the Troop Leader said over her shoulder. "We're good here. Go back down the hall and wait for the newsies." Kaly was only too happy to obey, and as she turned and started moving, Team 2 had more news.

Be advised, we just bagged one high value prisoner, the Team Leader advised. *Positive ID as Sanchar, Adalpha. Holding him at our position.*

Sanchar was the Lead Researcher, Kaly recalled. He was the one who was responsible for all this. As she reached the outer hall and waited, she earnestly hoped that Sanchar's death, whenever it came, would be slow and painful.

Finished with its tasks, the Liverna joined her, doing duty now as a common battlebot. While it ranged its guns around looking for something to shoot at, she received a message from upstairs.

In order to free all the teams for the operation itself, a contingent of Embassy securitywomen had been given the job of escorting Rozza Ramara and the military reporters who had come with her, safely into the facility.

We're above you at the elevator, their Leader thought. *Send up the car.*

The Liverna obediently trotted down to the elevator controls and relayed the command. A few moments later, the doors opened and the party of reporters and their Embassy bodyguards came out and walked towards Kaly, recording everything as they went. Like everyone else, they were also dressed in PPECC suits, as a precaution.

"This is Rozza Ramara," one of them said to an unseen audience, and Kaly recognized her from the holocasts she'd seen. "I'm walking through a secret biological weapons research center located just 20 kilometers outside of Nuvo Bolivar City. It was created decades ago with one purpose; to develop a deadly virus that would kill the women of the Sisterhood.'

"This secret project was recently given the go-ahead by President Magdalana himself, to use live prisoners—women who are our friends and allies—to test the disease on. In all of my years as a reporter, I have covered many stories about government secrecy and corruption, but I have never encountered anything as appalling as this."

The group reached Kaly's position and Ramara saw the morgue over her shoulder and pointed to it. "Trooper? Is there any way we can get in there? I want some footage of that room."

"Yes, ma'am," Kaly replied, not at all pleased with the idea of going anywhere near it. But she had her duty to do, and sent the message to the Liverna. The robot had the doors open in seconds, and Kaly waited outside as the newsies and their escorts filed in.

The very first thing that the reporters had their bodyguards open up for them were the metal drawers, and Kaly tried her best to look anywhere else, but morbid curiosity finally got the better of her, and her eyes were drawn to their contents. All of the bodies she saw, were young women, some still dressed in their fatigues and others in hospital gowns. Then one of the corpses caught her attention; the woman seemed familiar, and Kaly came into the room to peer over the reporter's shoulders to get a closer look.

The naked body was thin and worn from disease, and it possessed the strange emptiness that came with death, making it look more like a wax copy of the person it had once been than the woman herself. But despite these ravages, the features of her face were unmistakable. Kaly had known them well—in the best of times, and in the worst. She had known them in passion, and in simple companionship. It was a face that had once cried with her, and smiled with her.

It was Lena.

Kaly gave out a long, ragged gasp, and staggered backwards as if she had just been struck a physical blow. When her body hit the wall behind her, her legs failed and she slid to the floor.

Her dramatic reaction instantly aroused Rozza Ramara's journalistic instincts, and she waved for her camerawoman to turn around and focus on Kaly. "Trooper?" the reporter asked, "did you know that woman?"

Kaly didn't answer. She didn't even acknowledge her presence. Instead, she just held her head in her hands, and rocked her body slowly.

Before the reporter could interrogate her any further, Sarah inserted herself between them. "There are some things that should not be filmed, Ms. Ramara," she warned. Maya reinforced this by walking in front of the camera and blocking the lens with an armored palm. Her expression was a perfect mirror of the threat in Sarah's tone.

The two newsies got the message and hastily turned around to film another part of the room, pointedly avoiding the miserable figure on the floor.

Confident that they would not molest Kaly any further, Sarah *felt* into her mind with her talents. At first, all she encountered was chaos, and then what was left of the young woman's consciousness, shrunken down to a tiny point in the darkness, and screaming in endless anguish. Sarah realized that she was beyond any help that she was capable of rendering, and withdrew from her as gently as possible.

We need a medic to respond to the autopsy room right away, she thought. *One of your troopers is down.*

Team Two's leader answered. *Who is it? What happened?*

Trooper n'Deena, Sarah responded. *She seems to have suffered a mental breakdown.*

Someone is on their way to you.

Sarah waited with Kaly until the Navy medic arrived. When the corpswoman started to treat her, she stood and walked over to the open freezer drawer.

Once the operation had been given the green light, she had insisted on accompanying the news team. The raid on the *Lida* lab was perhaps the most important case in her entire career, and although she had known that it would contain horrors that would be the equal of the risks involved, she had wanted to witness them in person, with her own eyes. She had wanted to see the monstrosity that the ETR had wrought.

The emaciated young woman before her was sealed inside a transparent plastic body bag. It was emblazoned with a prominent biohazard warning and a label that coldly identified her as "N'Gari, Lena: 412345679, Researcher: A. Sanchar." A long incision ran up N'Gari's midsection until it reached her chest. There it branched off in two directions. The whole length of the wound had been sutchered shut, presumably just after she had been autopsied.

And they hadn't just used her body, she observed angrilly. They had also used her service number to 'properly identify' her as a specimen for their fiendish experiments. It was also painfully obvious that this particular 'specimen' had once been a friend, or a lover of the young trooper on the floor.

Maya came up, but Sarah didn't look at her. She kept her eyes fixed on the corpse.

Only males could ever conceive of something so horrible, she thought to her, broadcasting on a private psiever channel. *And they will pay for it, Maya. I assure you of that—all of them will pay!*

Then Sarah switched back over to the main Com frequency. *Where is the prisoner?* she asked.

A map came up on her HUD, showing that Dr. Sanchar was being held in a small maintenance closet not very far from the autopsy room.

Remain with him there, she instructed. *I am coming up to join you.*

As she made to leave, Rozza Ramara realized that another important development was taking place. "What is it?" she asked. "What's happened?"

Sarah made no reply, but the look in her eyes said everything. Ramara paled and took an instinctive step backwards. She pushed past the journalist and went into the main hall, with Maya in train. No one attempted to follow them.

Their journey was a short one, but it still took them through the holding cells and past the Navy medics and the inmates of the lab. The hellish spectacle there only fueled Sarah's rage and by the time they had reached the maintenance room, her lips were drawn across her features in a tight line of fury, and her hands were shaking.

Team 2 had moved on, and N'Elemay and Margasdaater were now standing watch over their prisoner. Sarah walked right up to the man.

Dr. Sanchar was still in his white plastic suit, but they had removed his helmet and he was cowering against the wall, with his wrists tightly secured behind him by a plastic tie-wrap. The man was only semi-coherent, and babbling something about 'her eyes, her lovely eyes.'

Sarah paid no attention to his ramblings and gestured to the two troopers. They each took an arm and drew him up so that she could read the name imprinted on his chest piece.

The moment that she was certain that 'A. Sanchar' and the pathetic creature in front of her were one in the same, she turned to a small workbench nearby and grabbed up a large screwdriver that some maintenance tech had left behind. Then, without hesitation, she thrust it straight into his right eye. The tool went in with such force that she felt the blade's tip scrape up against the back of his skull right through the plastic handle.

Sanchar didn't scream, or even cry out. Instead, his body simply shook in one great spasm and fell to the floor like a broken doll.

"I guess that we didn't need him alive for interrogation then?" N'Elemay asked calmly.

"No," Sarah replied coldly. "We didn't."

"Ach vell," Margasdaater offered, "If anyone asks, ve'll tell zem zat he did zat to himzelf, or maybe zat he just zlipped and fell on it. Zat happens all za time."

Chuckling to herself, the Zommerlaandar bent down with her knife and cut the wrist ties off the corpse, tossing the pieces into a nearby waste container. "'Course, itz a little hard to do zat vith your hands tied oop, yah?"

Sarah nodded absently, and left the room without a backwards glance.

***

After they had gathered up all the evidence they could, the teams extracted, taking the newsies, those prisoners who had survived, and the bodies of those who hadn't, in special sealed coffins. And as the last shuttle left the operations area, high-yield Therma-bombs turned the underground lab and its deadly contents into molten slag. The virus that the *Lida* labs had developed there at such a terrible cost would never be a threat again.

When the shuttles were upside, they rendezvoused with the hospital ship, the USSNS *Annie Etheridge*. Everyone on board the shuttles was immediately placed in quarantine and the vessels themselves were thoroughly decontaminated.

Later, after they had all been given a clean bill of health and released from their confinement, a special service was held for Lena n'Gari, and everyone else who had died with her in the lab. They were all accorded full military honors and then their bodies were consigned to space, and the arms of the Goddess.

Through it all, Kaly said nothing, and only stared off into space with a vacant, emotionless expression. Her teammates had to help her back to her rack and into her bed.

Rozza Ramara was also present for the ceremony, and she made sure to record every bit of it for the story that the Republican Associated Press would eventually broadcast. *When* exactly she would return to the ETR to submit it, and when it might be aired, was anyone's guess.

***

Completely oblivious to the momentous events that were unfolding all around her, Kaly lay in her rack, curled once again into a little ball, unblinking, unthinking and unfeeling. In the comparatively short time that Kaly had been part of the team, she had become everyone's little sister. For Troop Leader N'Elemay, who had never had a sibling herself, seeing the young woman in such a state felt like a thousand razors were cutting their way through her heart.

She wasn't a 'paint' and she couldn't put what she was witnessing into fancy medical terms, but she fully understood the cause. Kaly had simply seen too much, and it had finally broken her.

The Troop Leader reached out and tenderly stroked her forehead. Kaly didn't respond to her touch, or even register her presence, and N'Elemay sighed, uttering a short prayer over her. Then she headed for her meeting. It was to be with Colonel Lislsdaater, and it would decide Kaly's ultimate fate.

When she reached the Colonel's Office, Dr. elle' Kaari and Dr. Suzzyn bel Shaaron, the senior psychologist for medbay, were already there, along with Major n'Neesa.

"Well, doctors?" the Colonel began. "Now that her Troop Leader is here, we can get started. What is Corporal n'Deena's prognosis?"

"She's suffering from what we call catatonic depression," Dr. elle' Kaari answered, "Which is a symptom of Post Traumatic Stress Syndrome. My colleague can explain it to you in better detail, but essentially, her psyche has closed itself down. It's a protective measure that the mind employs when it's been subjected to trauma that it doesn't have the ability to process.'

"Frankly, given her personal history—the loss of her family and friends on her motherworld, the stresses of combat and then being wounded—it's no surprise that finding her lover in that lab took her straight over the edge. In fact, it's a wonder that this didn't happen to her at some earlier point."

Lislsdaater grimaced. She had been a soldier long enough to appreciate how war could scar the mind just as horribly as it did the body. She didn't blame herself for Kaly's situation however. It was her job to spot promising candidates and vet them where they could best serve the Sisterhood, and although it was regrettable, casualties, especially in SpecOps, were part of the package. Just the same, N'Deena was a damned good trooper, or at least had been before this, and Lislsdaater was afraid that she was going to lose her to madness.

"What are our options?" she asked. Because of its public relations value, and the calls that were sure to come from the Supreme Circle for their testimony, it had already been agreed that Team Five would be allowed to retain their memories of the operation. This made Kaly's condition a particularly troublesome issue.

Dr. bel Shaaron spoke. "For milder cases of PTSD, I would normally prescribe a panel of antidepressants and mental therapy sessions, but Trooper n'Deena's situation is much more severe. As I see it, we have only two courses of action. One; she receives a discharge from active duty and is admitted to a downside facility for long-term treatment."

"And two?"

"Option two is that we use the PTS feed to remove specific memories from her mind. It would delete anything concerning Trooper n'Gari, and we would replace the gaps left behind with alternate events that didn't include her. N'Gari would become non-history."

Lislsdaater nodded. "That sounds like the move we need to make," she said decisively. "I'll also ask that the Corps follow through by deleting any record of N'Gari having ever served. That should cover any loose ends.'

"There are only two other areas that will still need to be addressed. One is any footage that the newsies might have recorded of N'Gari's body, which I'm reasonably certain we can convince them to destroy--and anything that her Teammates might say to her."

The officer looked pointedly over at N'Elemay. "Tell me, Troop Leader, will you and your girls need a brain scrub too? Or can you manage to forget this all on your own?"

After having served for many years in SpecOps, N'Elemay was quite accustomed to keeping secrets. The added incentive that this would help Kaly retain her sanity only made her answer easier to give. "You can count on us, ma'am," she said.

"I thought I could, Troop Leader."

"Colonel," the doctor interjected, "I have to advise you that there *are* risks involved here. Every time we remove memories with the feed and substitute them, we run the chance that cognitive issues and other mental disorders could arise later down the road. It isn't a perfect technology by any means, and the mind sometimes senses that something is wrong about the artificial memories, or it manages to recover a piece of them left behind in the subconscious.'

"This can create a disparity between the new memories and the old, fragmentary ones. When that happens, and the subject tries to resolve the conflict, the situation can snowball and turn into a full-blown personality displacement. And that's with normal subjects. N'Deena's compromised mental condition only increases the odds against her."

Lislsdaater already knew about this, and simply inclined her head in acknowledgement. Although the reversed PTS feed was quite effective at completely debriefing and erasing the memories of its subjects, there had been a few women who had been injured by the process. It wasn't something that was general knowledge, and fortunately, it was also comparatively rare.

"Hazard is something that every SpecOps woman accepts as part of her duties, and N'Deena is no exception," she said gravely. "I want it set in motion. We need all the experienced troopers we can get, and I'm not going to see one of my better ones shipped off to some *Kraankenhoos* while we're at war. Take care of it."

***

Kaly couldn't feel herself being helped from her rack, or taken to the PTS debriefing room. She also didn't notice when they placed the plastic headset on her temples.

The reverse feed began, and she was abruptly jarred from nothingness into full awareness. Memories flooded into her mind. The images were hyper-real, each as sharp and as vivid as the real events had been when she had first experienced them. But they went by in a rapid-fire succession that was beyond her ability to slow or stop, and they tossed her from one emotional extreme to the next like a leaf in the wind. The only pauses came wherever the memories had anything to do with Lena, and Kaly reached out for these, like a drowning woman clutching for a piece of wreckage to save herself.

She was with Lena again for the very first time, seated across from her on the shuttle to Hella's World, and seeing her shy smile as she looked at her past Enggredsdaater. But then the scene sank away into the maelstrom.

Then she found herself back in Basic. Lena was her Battle Sister now, shouting words of encouragement as she fought to master the obstacle course, and Kaly tried to stay with the moment. It dissapeared, slipping off into the whirling nothingness.

Their first time making love came next. It was just after her fateful return to Persephone, and even as the intense pain and the blinding sweetness of this event overtook her, it faded away as if it had never really happened.

Kaly finally realized what was taking place, and her mind screamed out in desperation. *No!* she thought. *Please—don't go away! Please Lena! I need you!*

Lena didn't seem to hear her though, and as every memory of the woman came and went, she seemed to become less and less substantial. Kaly was powerless to stop the process and could only watch the parade of images going by her in horror.

Another memory captured her. She was with Lena again as her lover tried to get a glimpse of Jon from their rack, and then this changed, and another image took its place, and then another, and still another.

Finally, the memories stopped, and they were replaced by a period of peaceful darkness. Battered and bruised by her recapitulation, Kaly reveled in the same blackness that had also stolen Lena away from her.

Her interlude didn't last. A new flood of memories came, and she recoiled from them, afraid of the pain that they would usher in. These memories were different however.

She was back in the shuttle going to Hella's World. She recognized the place and the time, and Bel Anny was there, and so was Enggredsdaater. And also a third woman that she didn't know.

Then it came back to her; she had been one of the opt-outs, one of the 'hatchies' that had left Basic before the training process had been completed. Kaly tried, but she couldn't recall the woman's name, and finally, too tired to fight it, she gave up the effort, and let the image pass.

Basic repeated itself all over again, and once more, she heard the encouragement that Bel Anny and Enggredsdaater were yelling to her. There was someone else with them, another hatchie, and she had a vague image of the figure, but not enough to define with any clarity.

She wasn't interested in trying to either. It was enough that her memories were now comforting things, reassuring her that all was well.

Yes, she told herself, *that* was *how it was*. More recollections came, and she eagerly accepted each and every one of them. She had to, she realized. After all, they were her life, and there was no changing the past, was there?

At last, when the images had reached their conclusion, so did consciousness. The instant that she was no longer aware, a final memory was erased from her mind. It was that the feed had ever even happened.

***

Ellen n'Elemay stood before Kaly's rack and took a deep breath preparing herself for what she had to do. Lieutenant sa'Kaali had sent her there to search through Kaly's possessions for anything that might have been linked with Lena n'Gari. The virtual mailbox in Kaly's psiever had already been scrubbed by the El-Tee herself, but it was the Troop Leader's job to locate everything else, and to destroy it.

There hadn't been very much to find; like any trooper, Kaly traveled light. The only items she located were a bracelet made from seashells that Kaly had once told her about, something that N'Gari had given her on one of their leaves together, and a holopic.

The image was encased in a protective plastic frame and it showed the two of them, lounging naked together on a beautiful white beach. The huge gas giant in the background, the clean, clear water and the tropical foliage told N'Elemay right away that it had been taken on Tethys, a place that she knew the young woman had gone with her lover after Basic. The bracelet's origins were confirmed a moment later when she saw it on Kaly's wrist. Its twin was wrapped around Lena's.

The two of them looked happy together, she thought. It wasn't the sort of forced joy that one encountered so often in pictures, but something else altogether; something natural, and special. She could see it in the way that N'Gari smiled down at Kaly, and in the contented look in Kaly's eyes.

They seemed to belong together. And from her own experience, N'Elemay understood just how rare a thing that really was. For soldiers like themselves, happiness in any form, was hard to come by, and knowing Kaly's past as well as she did, doubly so.

Holding the holo and the bracelet in her hands, she had every intention of taking them to the nearest secure waste recycler, and fulfilling her duty to the letter. But the image, and N'Gari's smile stopped her.

Before she could second-guess herself, she tucked them into a pocket of her fatigue blouse, and quickly sealed it shut. The part of her that was a Marine wondered what in the Nine Hriss Hells she thought she was doing, and the side that was Kaly's friend promptly told that same Marine to go and *fek* herself.

Kaly needed the treatment that the 'paints' were giving her. There was no question in her mind about that. But someday, when she was finally well enough to handle it, N'Elemay promised herself that she would return

Kaly's keepsakes to her.

And she would tell her the truth. Kaly deserved that, just as she deserved the chance to remember the happiness that she had seen in the holo. To destroy it, and to conceal the facts from her friend any longer than she absolutely had to, was a sin, and she didn't need to confirm that by consulting any scriptures. Some things were just plain wrong on a basic, human level.

And some things transcended orders.

***

Dr. bel Shaaron stepped back from the PTS controls, and looked at Col. Lislsdaater and Major n'Neesa. "I think we've managed to remove everything. I'll also want N'Deena to submit to a regime of anti-depressants— "and when she saw the scowl appearing on the officer's face, amended this, adding,"—mild ones of course. And I want her to report to me for some reinforcement therapy and counseling."

"Doctor," N'Neesa replied tiredly. "We can't spare her for all that. Do what you can for her, but don't cut into her duties. Work around them."

Now the doctor was the one with the unhappy expression, but the situation was much different than it might have been downside in a civilian facility, with a civilian patient. As a Marine, Kaly was Sisterhood property, and what superior officers wanted, they got.

"I'll do my best, Major. I'm sure that we'll manage."

***

Still unconscious, Kaly was taken back to her rack, and as the effects of the feed faded, she transitioned into genuine sleep. At some point, she dreamt.

Like many dreams, the vision that she had was clear at the time, but blurred when she finally awoke. All she could remember was the image of a young woman, with red hair, freckles, and a heartwarming smile. She seemed familiar for some reason, and Kaly puzzled over this as she accepted the breakfast that N'Elemay had brought for her.

"Who do you think I was dreaming about?" she asked, digging into her meal with a will. She was starving.

"I don't know," N'Elemay answered, suddenly overly conscious of the two items hidden in her uniform pocket, and hating herself for having to lie. But Kaly had to get well, she told herself, and the truth wouldn't be hidden from her forever. She would see to that if it took her the rest of her life. "Maybe she was exactly what she seemed to be," she finally suggested, "just a dream."

Kaly paused and shook her head. "No Ellen—she seemed—well, like she was *real* somehow, and also—not real. But she was good. I know that. I could feel that about her."

"Then perhaps she was an angel," N'Elemay offered, fighting the knot that had begun to grow in her throat. "Angels are good like that."

Kaly smiled, and seeing this, N'Elemay felt the tiniest sliver of redemption for what she was being forced to do.

"Maybe she was," Kaly agreed. "Maybe she'll even watch over me. Angels do that, don't they?"

"Yes, they do, Kaly. And I know she will. I know she will."

USSNS *Pallas Athena*, In-Orbit, Altamara, Frontera Provensa,
Esteral Terrana Rapabla, 1044.12|08|03:38:83

Lilith was working on some routine matters when Navcom advised her that she had a classified message waiting, labeled urgent. The information was relayed to her psiever, and she opened it immediately.

It had come directly from Fleet Admiral ebed Cya and it contained only one word. Her blood went cold as she read it, and then she re-read it to verify what her eyes were telling her.

Navcom contacted her again. "Admiral, we have another priority message. It's from Admiral da'Kayt. She has requested that you, Vice Admiral n'Leesa, Ben Biya, and General n'Hariet meet with her right away via holo."

"Very good," she said, doing her utmost to keep any emotion out of her voice. "Please advise Commander Bertasdaater to come to my office immediately."

Katrinn arrived less than two minutes later, and then the holos of Lilith's fellow Flag Officers and Da'Kayt appeared in front of her desk.

Just by Lilith's expression alone, her former Second could tell that something deathly serious was afoot. "What is it Lily? What's happened?"

Lilith swallowed hard before answering. "War, Kat."

For a long moment, there was silence, and then Admiral da'Kayt spoke. "Ladies, Rixa just contacted me with the 'Carmina' code."

"I also received the same message," N'Leesa volunteered. Ben Biya just nodded, saying nothing.

"What are your orders, Admiral?" General n'Hariet asked.

"At the moment, I'll ask that all of you stand by," Da'Kayt told them. "I want to confirm this before we take any action whatsoever."

She spoke with someone out of view. "Com? Send a message to Rixa, encrypted, Fleet Admiral ebed Cya's eyes only, as follows; 'Betsi, Una, Roberta, Anna, Nora, Anna—'Burana', Inquire.' Let me know what her response is as soon as you receive it."

There was a long pause, and Lilith took advantage of it to ignite a czigavar, noticing the slight tremor in her hand as she did so. As she took her first comforting drag, the ComTech got back with Da'Kayt and the woman's words played out over the holo.

"Ma'am? Admiral ebed Cya has replied to your message. Her response is as follows; '*Carmina, Carmina, Carmina—Confirmed.*"

"Thank you Mariner," the Trilanian replied. She closed her eyes and when she reopened them, she said, "I have just unlocked the file labeled 308-42-A. Each of you, and your immediate subordinates, will now have access to it. As you know, it contains the plans that were created for this very eventuality.'

"When you have reviewed it, you are to send a signal to all of the assets under your command, both in space and downside. Advise them of our status and then have them target and engage the enemy wherever they find him. Also, instruct them that they are to take measures to avoid damage to any infrastructure that is not directly related to the ETR's ability to make war. May the Goddess watch over us all, and bless us for what we are about to do in her name. You are dismissed."

"Lily," Katrinn said. "I'll be on the bridge."

Lilith signaled her understanding and opened the coded file. Even though she had been one of the officers in charge of creating the war plan, and knew it well, she followed her superior's orders and read everything again to make certain that she was fully up to date.

Satisfied, she walked out onto the bridge, took her station and addressed the crew, and all of the ships directly under her command.

All of the women on the bridge looked at her expectantly, she saw. The usual pair of Marine guards had also been supplemented with additional women, and they were all in combat dress. News like this traveled fast.

"Ladies, this is Vice Admiral ben Jeni. I have an important announcement to make. As of now, a state of war exists between the Esteral Terrana Rapabla and our nation. Many of you suspected that this would one day come to pass, and it has, possibly sooner than you or I might have expected.'

"I also realize that this news will be met with mixed feelings by some of you. Feelings that I myself share. But the Sisterhood has called upon us to defend her, and we will all do what is expected of us. May the Lady grant us a quick and certain victory."

Then she nodded to Kat.

"Sound battle stations," Katrinn said. "Fire Control, target the enemy." Lights in the huge chamber switched over to red, and on the sitscreens, the yellow icons of the neighboring ETR vessels became scarlet. An instant later, target locks were confirmed for each and every one of them.

Salta Cia, Republican Sector, Altamara 1, Altamara System,
Frontera Provensa, Esteral Terrana Rapabla, 1044.12|08|03:43:91

PFC Jyon Cruzza hadn't been in Altamara long, and most of his time there had been spent in Salta Cia, either patrolling Dogtown with his military police detachment, or manning checkpoint Carloz-Quadra on the Republican side of the settlement. Of the two, he preferred the challenges of patrol, but that was no longer an option. Thanks to the rape of a Sisterhood sailor, and the subsequent murder of one of his fellow soldiers, relations between the two forces had cooled considerably. Dogtown remained off limits to everyone, and it was his job to see to it that no one, from either side, violated this stricture unless they had official business.

Despite this tense state of affairs, Jyon and his fellow soldiers had still managed to communicate every so often with some of the Sisterhood troopers. There was a squad of them stationed just down the street from his position, standing guard at their own watch post. As exchanges went, it hadn't been much; just a friendly nod or two across the open space acknowledging each other's presence and their common task. But once or twice, he was fairly certain that one of the cuter ones had actually smiled back at him.

What was her name? They had spoken to each other once, and she had told it to him. It had been when Dogtown was still an open zone, and their two street patrols had crossed paths. Jaana, Janya, or something like that? He couldn't recall exactly.

Whatever her name was, in his opinion, it was a damned shame that she was a *Saapa* like the rest of them. A real waste. But then again, Cruzza reminded himself, the situation between the two groups would eventually thaw, and there was always the chance that Janya (yes—*that* was her name. He was sure of it now) would eventually become interested in trying out something new.

Naturally, he would be only too happy to help her with that journey of discovery—if it ever occurred. Smiling at this fantasy, and knowing full well that it *was* a fantasy, he lit himself a cigarette and looked down the empty block to the Sisterhood checkpoint.

Two troopers were on duty there, and when he waved at them, neither woman returned his greeting. He didn't let this bother him though. They were probably replacements for the regulars that were normally stationed there, and like most of the Sisterhood women, most likely, man-haters. Which was their loss.

Behind him, another MP from his unit walked up to rejoin him after a trip to their portable restroom, and he glanced over his shoulder at the man.

"Everything come out okay?"

The soldier laughed at his crude humor, and took up his post at the gate. With the evening's entertainment now concluded, Cruzza looked back across the street. Oddly, no one was over there.

Jyon watched and waited, reasoning that the two Sisterhood troopers had probably just gone off to their own restroom together. Leaving a checkpoint completely unmanned certainly wasn't the best practice, and like his own military, most likely a serious violation of procedures, but it still happened. And it wasn't like there was anything for either group to guard against at the moment.

After a few more minutes though, when the women didn't return, he began to wonder if something was wrong. Finally, he decided to report it. "Checkpoint Carlaz-Quadra to Control," he radioed.

There was a brief interval, and then the Com Officer at the MP headquarters answered him, "Control, go."

"There's something weird going on at the Sisterhood position. It looks like it's been abandoned. Do you want me to check it out?"

A long pause followed, and then, "Affirmative. We're getting the same report from all the other checkpoints."

"I'm going down there," he said to his companion. "Watch my back."

Despite his misgivings, this request sounded a little stupid, but it still had to be made. From the very onset of their alliance, everyone had known how fragile their union was, and some of the more pessimistic soldiers in his unit had even hinted at the possibility of a war breaking out between them—someday. Notwithstanding the doomsayers, and the incidents in Dogtown that had led to its closure, up to this point the overall situation had seemed quite positive, and even promising. Still, he thought, as he stepped past the wooden barrier in front of the checkpoint, things *could* change. He just hoped that they hadn't changed for the worse, and on his watch.

His fellow soldier brought his weapon up to the half-ready position as Jyon started down the road. The closer he got to the Sisterhood checkpoint, the louder his inner alarms began to sound. Something *was* wrong down there. He was certain of it now.

Then he heard the deep rumble of a Hovertank echoing down the street.

A second later, it came into view, accompanied by a squad of heavily armed Sisterhood troopers. He recognized one of them as Trooper Janya. As she raised her weapon and brought it to bear on him, his last living thought was that she wasn't smiling at him now.

***

The death of PFC Jyon Cruzza only registered on Erin's HUD as one less red dot. Blue icons representing the Sisterhood Marines that were swarming past the Republican checkpoint, quickly replaced it. Had she known who he had been, she wouldn't have cared any more than she already did. He had been the enemy, and he was dead. That was enough for her. Besides which, she had a bigger job to worry about. Putting her display in ground attack mode, Erin began her run.

Her craft was flying at just above rooftop level, and in seconds she had gone beyond any friendly forces, and was headed straight for an ETR tank and a platoon-sized group that were moving up to engage her comrades.

She thought the command to fire, and a harpy anti-armor missile left the rack under her wings. It hit the tank squarely, blowing it to pieces, and she followed through with a burst from her rail guns at the men scattering for cover.

Back behind her, her wingwoman, *'Neversaw'*, let a single *Echidna* anti-personnel bomb go. As they flew past, the sub-munitions it discharged went off and thousands of metal flechettes shredded the surviving soldiers to pieces.

A second later, Erin's AI warned her that their objective was straight ahead: a tank farm that housed most of the armor that the ETR had on Salta Cia, along with supply depots, recovery vehicles and fueling trucks. Thanks to the suddenness of hostilities, only a few anti-air batteries and some small arms fire opened up on her as she came within range, and the Valkyrie automatically targeted the worst of them and killed them with more missiles and railgun bursts.

Simultaniously, the targeting reticule began to flash, and a message came through her psiever from her AI: *Target Acquired. Fire?*

She sent an affirmative. The fighter dropped its load and pulled up and away. Erin had chosen a large main battle tank for her aim-point, sitting roughly in the middle of the park, and her ordnance, a *Lamia* cluster bomb, flew off the Valkyrie, split open, and destroyed the tank right along with its immediate neighbors.

'Neversaw' and the rest of Hunter Flight came in next, letting loose with their own Lamia's. Before she had even managed to complete half a turn to come back for another run, the entire area was engulfed in flames. Nothing but wreckage remained beneath her.

Hunter Flight, this is Little Bird. Standby for ground assist runs. A small burst of fire came at her from the right an instant later, and she sent the Valkyrie into a rolling corkscrew to evade it before swinging around to engage the hapless soldier. The man ran, but he was far too slow to outrun the aerospace fighter, and a stream of railgun rounds turned him into red mist.

Erin shrugged, and gained altitude to join the rest of her flight. After that, there wasn't much for the *Nighthunters* to do. Salta Cia fell to the Sisterhood shortly afterwards, and without presenting any further opportunities for her to gain honor.

***

Up in space, the situation hadn't been markedly different. The *Athena*, and the other Sisterhood ships that had been on station with her over Altamara, took out their ETR counterparts with a minimum of difficulty.

At the time, there hadn't been many enemy vessels present. Thanks to the cessation of hostilities with the Hriss, the bulk of the Republican Navy had been on its way to assume stations throughout the Republic. The only large concentration that the Sisterhood had known of with any certainty had been the one orbiting around the ETR naval headquarters in Estraddar, in the Magdala Provensa.

But when light cruisers had arrived to scout out this location, they had found the high ground empty, and the planetside installations deserted. Despite their best efforts to jam their ansible transmissions, it had appeared that Guzamma's 14th Fleet had been warned by the units over Altamara, and had left for parts unknown.

Not every ETR fleet had been quite as fortunate. The 12th had been discovered and engaged in Reya Orda in the Reganna Provensa. Refusing to surrender, they had been destroyed by elements of N'Leesa's Raider Group, augmented by advance units from the Jade and Diamond Fleets. The same thing had happened to the 18th and 10th fleets. But other, smaller formations had avoided this fate either by scuttling their ships, or surrendering and allowing their vessels to be seized.

In the end, only Guzamma's fleet remained at large. The only traces of them were their warp tracks, which led to a series of jump points that seemed to lead nowhere. And follow-up scans of the greater stellar neighborhood had proven fruitless.

Wherever the 14th Fleet had gone, they were keeping a low profile, and operating at levels that created the smallest signatures possible. They were also staying off their ansibles. During the joint campaign, Guzamma had managed to learn at least one thing from the Sisterhood; how to cover his tracks well.

As soon as she had received the latest information, Admiral da'Kayt called her Vice Admirals together for another strategy meeting. This time though, none other than Fleet Admiral ebed Cya, speaking to them from Rixa, ran the session, and Lilith in particular, found herself in the metaphorical spotlight.

"Ladies," the Fleet Admiral began, "I would like to congratulate you on your victories. I also need to inform you that in addition to the forces which have already arrived, you will soon be augmented by additional battle groups from the Topaz Fleet, as well as elements from Amethyst and Onyx.'

"The Chairwoman wants this business brought to a swift and decisive resolution. And she has ordered us to commit all the appropriate resources we need in order to see to it that this occurs. Your reinforcements will be arriving over the next several days and until then, you are to standby at Altamara. Admiral da'Kayt, once they do arrive, every Sisterhood vessel in the ETR will fall under your direct command.'

Da'Kayt nodded and Ebed Cya pressed on. "Now, the question of the day, Admiral; what do you believe is Guzamma's ultimate objective?"

Part of Lilith's job had been to anticipate the ETR's actions in the event of war, and when Da'Kayt deferred to her, she answered the Fleet Admiral's question.

"Ma'am, the ETR's Navy certainly had a plan of their own in place for just this contingency," she said. "They knew that they couldn't prevail against us in open battle, so it is my belief that the 14th has gone to a predetermined rendezvous point."

"To what end?" Ebed Cya inquired.

"I see two possibilities, ma'am," Lilith answered. The first is that they may be trying to preserve what military strength they have in anticipation of a peace treaty."

"And the second?"

"They could also be intent on prosecuting some form of hit-and-run campaign against us. If they have samples of the *Lida* virus, they would pose a signifigant threat to our population, and if ex-President Magdalena is with them, he might be desperate enough to try and convince Guzamma to cooperate."

The Fleet Admiral nodded soberly. To date, no one had been able to determine the whereabouts of the renegade leader. There was also no intelligence about whether or not the lab had taken their bio-weapon into mass production. What information they did have on this score tended to indicate that *Lida* had not gone beyond experimental batches, but without any firm confirmation, the possibility still existed.

"Yes, both scenarios seem quite likely," Ebed Cya agreed. "But of the two, I am the most concerned about the potential for a biological attack. If even a small fraction of these ships manage to infiltrate the Sisterhood with the *Lida* virus, it could have devastating consequences. This only underscores the importance of locating them.'

"I want you to continue to search every system in the Republic as well as anything close enough to serve as a base. Once you locate them, you may offer them a single chance to surrender, but only that.'

"When we win this thing, we'll need a functioning military organization in place to help them maintain their national security, but we cannot allow our own nation to be jeopardized. If they refuse your offer, you are to destroy all of their assets down to the very last escape pod. We'll sort the mess out later."

***

While they waited for the arrival of their reinforcements, the SEF remained on high alert, and oversaw the occupation of Salta Cia. All of its ETR nationals were now stranded, and martial law had been imposed on the settlement. The same held true upside; every ETR merchant ship that had been there when war had been declared were now confined to their orbits, and groups of fighters with orders to attack anything that tried to slip away, enforced this. Nothing was being allowed to enter, or leave.

As a result, it wasn't until additional units arrived and took up some of the slack, that Lilith and her fellow officers had any opportunity to watch the news coverage about the war. The segments they saw proved to be just as sensational, and as grim, as they had imagined they would be.

The first thing that they watched was the Chairwoman's address to the nation. Normally she would have been smiling, and exchanging pleasantries with the press, but this time, her expression was grave.

"Ladies of the Press, women of the Sisterhood, I have an unpleasant announcement to make and there will only be limited questions allowed afterwards. Only a short time ago, this office received incontrovertible proof that our so-called allies, who we have aided in their struggle against the Hriss, have repaid our humanitarian effort with the blackest treachery imaginable.'

"I can now confirm that the Magdalana government, without the knowledge or the consent of its people, engaged in a covert biological weapons program whose aim was to create a deadly virus comprable to the MARS epidemic. This virus was designed to affect our population but leave their own men and women, unharmed. We have also learned that this project was in existence long before Magdalana's presidency, but that he gave it his full support and approval."

For a moment the room around the Chairwoman was utterly still, and then everyone was on their feet clamoring for attention. Marina bel Rayna waved them all to silence, and continued.

“I can also confirm that on my orders, this project was completely destroyed by members of our Marine Special Operations forces. Subsequent to that event, I met in a special session of the Supreme Circle with your appointed representatives where I recommended that immediate actions be undertaken to safeguard our nation.’

“These measures were approved, and it is my sad duty to inform you that as of 03:43 hours, a state of war exists between the Esteral Terrana Rapabla and ourselves. Our Naval and Marine forces, already stationed in the area, are even now engaging the enemy and destroying his ability to commit any further acts of aggression against us.”

Again, the press went wild, and the Chairwoman had to bring them back under control. “Ladies, I will do my best to answer some of your questions momentarily, but I have more news to share with you first. Concurrent with our declaration of war, your government was also forced to take several decisive actions, here at home.’

There was absolute silence in the room as everyone waited to hear the rest.

“In addition to the discovery of this clandestine weapons program, our intelligence services also uncovered the details of a secret alliance between the ETR and the Marionite Church. According to our agents, a representative of the ETR recently engaged in a meeting with that dissident group, asking for their support as a fifth-column to use against us in a future military action.’

“At the same time, and after a long and intensive investigation, our intelligence agencies managed to discover a vast underground network of Marionite women living and working among us, spread throughout the Sisterhood. This network has been in place for many years, and it can only have one purpose, which is to facilitate terrorist activities.’

“When I learned of this, I immediately invoked my special powers as Chairwoman and ordered our armed forces to impose martial law on the Marionite worlds, and to place their leadership under arrest. Simultaneously, I also introduced two emergency measures to the Supreme Circle, which were immediately approved by a majority of its members.'

"The first was to consolidate our regional and federal police forces, along with our intelligence agencies, under a single organization. This new body will be called the *Regila da Securité par Estat*, the State Security Service, and it will answer directly to the Circle's representatives, and to myself.'

"Now I know that some of you might be concerned that this is effectively nationalizing our police and intelligence agencies, but the RSE's job will only be to coordinate the efforts of individual agencies, not to co-opt them. To deal with the problems the Sisterhood is now facing, we will need clear communications at all levels, and the RSE will help us to accomplish this.'

"In keeping with this mission, I have also appointed someone to act as its leader who has years of experience working with diverse interests and uniting them. This will be none other than the current Director of the *Orgón par Avaní Extér*, Tara ben Paula.'

"Ben Paula will bring with her many years of experience as an administrator, as a diplomat, and her expertise as a former member of Naval Intelligence. These qualities will help her to oversee an organization that will not only guarantee our security from both external and internal threats, but also inject humanity and a profound respect for the rights of our citizens in the process.'

"She has my complete confidence, and my unwavering support. As for the OAE, it will continue to pursue its diplomatic mission, under whoever Ben Paula chooses as her successor.'

"The second measure that I put before the Circle was to demand that the Marionite Church be declared an outlaw organization, and its leaders, enemies of the state.'

"This was also ratified. As of now, any gatherings held by their membership which involve more than two individuals will be considered a criminal activity, and punishable by immediate arrest. The same holds true for any woman who harbors one of their officials, or aids them in any way.'

"Subsequent to this special session, our armed forces responded to our mandate. Although they were able to bring the Marionite worlds under Sisterhood control, some loss of life did occur. It is my understanding that the Marionite Pope, and her bodyguards, refused to surrender after being lawfully ordered to do so and instead, responded with armed resistance.'

"As a result, the units attempting to apprehend them were forced to defend themselves, and sadly, the Pope, along with several other high level officials, needlessly lost their lives in the firefight that ensued. I have also been informed that the neoman that they call the Redeemer, along with a number of his cult followers, have fled into hiding rather than submit themselves to arrest. At this time, they are still at large, however I have been assured that they will all be brought to justice shortly.'

"At this sad time, my heart goes out to the families of everyone affected by these events and to every woman living on the Marionite worlds, and I can only add that this underscores the need for sisterly cooperation during this crisis. I must also urge that all of our citizens remain calm, wherever they live, and whatever their beliefs happen to be. Reason and justice *will* ultimately prevail, and the Goddess will once again grace our nation with peace and order. Thank you, and May the Lady bless you all. I am now open for questions from the press."

There was a collective intake of breath, and then the scene became utter pandemonium as all the reporters vied for the Chairwoman's attention.

Bel Rayna chose one woman, and the journalist asked her question, "Madame Chairwoman, Marla n'Sheena SNN Special Bureau. You said that the general population of the ETR wasn't aware of this bio-weapons project. What is our policy regarding them, and have there been any calls for Magdalana's resignation?"

"A very good *pair* of questions," the Chairwoman responded wryly. Her amusement at the woman's tactic elicited some polite laughter from the other journalists, and lightened the mood in the room. "And I'm glad that you asked them, Marla. I'll answer the second one first.'

"According to our ambassador, just before she and her staff left the embassy, there were demands from his citizens that President Magdalana not only step down from office but also that he submit himself to our custody for prosecution. He was not available to give a reply, and his current whereabouts, and those of his cabinet members, are unknown. Since then, I have received unconfirmed reports of rioting in the enemy's capitol, and in several other major cities.'

"As for your first question, let me assure all of you that I have given our military strict orders to avoid civilian casualties wherever and whenever possible, and only engage those elements that clearly demonstrate hostile intent, or refuse to lay down their arms. I want to stress that our fight is *not* with the average citizen of the ETR, but with their leadership, and by extension, their military, and only as long as it chooses to support Magdalana's corrupt regime."

Bel Rayna's answer satisfied the reporter and everyone else who was listening.

"Thank you Madame Chairwoman." The woman sat, and the Chairwoman picked another person.

"Madame Chairwoman, Hana bel Leesa, Thermadon Independent Press. Can you clarify the measures you have taken against the Marionite Church? Are we outlawing their religion?"

"No, we are not doing that," Bel Rayna answered. "The Sisterhood has always defended religious freedom, although we have left the final say in such matters to local governments, especially where a group—of any kind—constituted a threat to public order and safety. My measure is only an extension of that policy, on a national level, and it will be in place only as long as this group's leadership remains at large.'

"The individual Marionite has nothing whatsoever to fear from us, unless she elects to work against her fellow women. We are not outlawing her beliefs. We are only outlawing a criminal organization that has been leading her astray."

After a bit more of this, Lilith cut to the next segment. It was local coverage of the occupation of the Marionite worlds. As the correspondent interviewed the Marine General in charge of ground operations, scenes of Sisterhood troops in the streets of Maristown competed with images of fires burning at different places in the city—and clips of Marines taking cover from sniper fire behind armored vehicles.

From this, it was clear that while many Marionites had followed their doctrine of 'turning the other cheek,' others, outraged by the military occupation and the death of their Supreme Pontiff, had chosen to fight.

The ultimate outcome was obvious, though. Any resistance was an utterly futile gesture. The hammer, which had been held over the Marionites for so long, had definitely fallen, Lilith thought.

The last segment that they viewed was from the ETR itself, courtesy of the OAE, and from the look of it, things weren't much better there either. The holo opened up on a scene at night on the rooftop of a building in a downtown area, with a reporter dressed in what Lilith realized was a Sisterhood-issue blast vest.

When the woman's name appeared, she recognized her as the reporter that Sarah had escorted to Thermadon a year earlier. The caption under her name revealed that the segment had been shot in Nuvo Bolivar.

Rozza Ramara glanced over her shoulder, and then looked into the holocam with a solemn expression. "Ladies and gentlemen," she said, "I'm speaking from a building across from the Presidential Palace. Right now, it is being held by troops loyal to the new interim President, former Secretary of Commerce, Jyon Pasquaar.'

"Earlier this evening however, the Presidential Palace was attacked by army units calling themselves the *Loyalistas*, who support former President Magdalana. They were repulsed, but there are unconfirmed rumors of fighting between the two opposing forces throughout the capitol and elsewhere, as well as reports of extensive civilian casualties.'

"Interim President Pasquaar has promised the nation that the fighting will be brought to an end soon, and he has asked that all citizens remain off the streets and stay indoors. Inside sources also told RAP news that additional units loyal to the new government are currently en-route to the city, including several armored divisions."

"At the same time, RAP news also received a communiqué from former President Magdalana, and what he is calling the 'sole legitimate government of the Republic'. In his statement, Magdalana revealed that he is with one of our fleets at an undisclosed location. He urged the citizens of the Republic to resist President Pasquaar and the Sisterhood, and called for general labor strikes and armed resistance. According to the communiqué, he believes that the war is not lost and stated that there would soon be a 'decisive action' taken by his forces against the Sisterhood."

A chill went up Lilith's spine. Magdalana was with the 14th after all, and the inference was that they did in fact have the virus with them. She listened intently as Ramara continued.

"In response to this, the office of the Interim President countered with a demand that Magdalana, and the naval officers with him, whom Pasquaar labeled as 'criminals and conspirators', surrender to the new government immediately. In the meantime, with most of the major star systems in the Republic blockaded by Sisterhood naval forces, President Pasquaar is reportedly seeking a peaceful end to the crisis, and attempting to negotiate a peace treaty."

Lilith had already been briefed about this. And she knew that for the interim at least, Pasquaar's efforts would fail. Until the 14th Fleet was found, and dealt with, Sisterhood diplomats were ignoring his requests.

Suddenly, an almost as if it were in deliberate rebuttal to Ramara's words, there was a loud explosion, and in the background, Lilith saw a large fireball rise into the sky, not far from where the reporter was standing. The woman and her camerawoman dove for cover behind the parapet.

"I-I'm not sure what just happened," Ramara said excitedly. She looked off-camera and listened to something in her ear-bud for a moment. "Wait—I'm being told that there may be a counterattack under way by the Magdalana Loyalists. We've been told to get off this roof; they say there are snipers near us. This is Rozza Ramara, signing off for RAP news, Nuvo Bolivar."

The holo ended, and Lilith let out a long, weary sigh and looked over at Katrinn and Da'Kayt. The Admiral had been aboard that day on other business, and had joined them for the 'cast in the *Athena's* conference room.

"Well, that's one pretty little mess," Da'Kayt observed. "Thank the Lady we're all the way out here. All *we* have to worry about is a renegade fleet and a deadly plague that could kill us all. I just love it when things are that simple."

***

Sarah watched the Chairwoman's address in the privacy of her cabin on the USSNS *Princess Sela*. The Macha class ship had whisked her and the embassy staff away from Nuvo Bolivar as soon as the declaration of war had been announced, and she was quite pleased by everything she was seeing. Especially Bel Rayna's announcement about the RSE, and the fact that it was now in charge of 'coordinating' all of the intelligence and law enforcement operations in the Sisterhood. She had little doubt that this 'coordination' would soon evolve into actual control, and at all levels of their society.

It wasn't that she disliked the *Divis da Naval Intelle*, or any of the other agencies she had worked with over the years. But in her estimation, the Agency was the only group in the Sisterhood that possessed the correct perspective to get things done properly. And given the threats that the nation faced, only the best would do.

Eager to confirm her suspicions and learn what the end result would be, Sarah reached into her kit bag and took out her Nyxian Tarot deck. She briefly considered using her reading as an opportunity to tutor Maya some more about the cards, but one glance over at the young woman changed her mind.

Maya was deeply engrossed in the coverage of the Marionite occupation, and although Sarah knew that she could certainly force the issue, the young woman's desire to continue watching would only interfere with her willingness to pay attention.

Leaving her to her spectacle, Sarah began searching through her deck until she found the card she wanted.

This was The Moons, and it stood for the central figure in the question she wanted to ask. While there were many others that she might have selected, she had always felt that this card represented the OAE the most accurately. The image was similar to the holoprint that she had hanging in her cabin aboard the *JUDI*. It displayed Nyx's three moons, hovering over the Plain of Trials.

But it also featured additional elements that her holo didn't possess. The first was a canine-like *Taarq*, baying at the satellites. The other was a

Nasqqe, an aquatic creature similar to the Tethyian armorclaw, or an old Gaian crab. Together, the pair symbolized danger, both the known and the unknown.

Between the creatures, a path wound away towards the horizon, and midway to the distant peaks of the Tribulation Range was another figure. This was a lone traveler, with her back to the viewer.

Overall, the card symbolized secrets, invisible hazards, and hidden pitfalls for the subject if they failed to exercise due caution on their journey. Given the Agency's function, the card suited its secretive nature well, and also served as a reminder of the inherent dangers that an operative might face.

She laid The Moons down on her bed, face up. Then she formulated her question, adding in a prayer to Elatsha, the Nyxian goddess of Darkness and Oracles, asking for a clear answer.

What will be the fortune for the Agency and the Sisterhood, now that we are at war with the ETR? she asked silently.

Then, keeping her inquiry clearly in her mind, she shuffled the cards, cut them three times, and drew the first one from the top of the deck. What she saw when she turned it over brought a smile to her face.

It was the Five of Knives. The image contained a sly-looking woman, cradling two Tej knives in her left arm, as she picked up a third one that had been left on the ground. Two other knives lay nearby, as if they were waiting for her to take them as well.

The figures' eyes rested on the retreating forms of two other women, who by their postures alone, exuded the feeling of defeat and loss. The official meaning of the Five of Knives was challenge, fluctuation and material prosperity, but offset by spiritual poverty if balance was not introduced into the equation.

However, Lady Ananzi had often stressed that the interpretation of the cards was a mutable thing; that their message for the questioner could be different than it was for others, and for her, the Five of Knives was a case in point. Every time it had ever appeared for her in a spread, it had presaged accomplishment and victory—at the expense of others, but victory nonetheless. And in the end, that was what really mattered, she told herself. Any collateral damage that was incurred in the process was merely part of the price that had to be paid.

She almost gathered up the cards to end her session right there, but then her talents warned her to set down an additional card and read its message carefully. Traditionally, such a card in a short spread like this one, stood for What Was To Come Afterwards, and she decided to honor her intuition, drawing it from the deck and adding it to the rest. When she saw what it was, her brows knitted in concern and consternation.

'The Shadow' had been adapted from its predecessor 'The Devil' by Womankind, and it had changed from a depiction of the Christian Devil to that of a naked human male, but with his face hidden by darkness. Like Satan, he was seated, and he still had one hand pointed towards the earth. But instead of having his other hand gesturing upwards as it had in the original, he was clutching at a chain. This was linked to collars being worn by three comparatively diminutive women. One of them was a child, another was an adult, and the third was an elderly woman.

The image represented the human race before the enlightenment of Motherthought, and the oppression that women had once been forced to endure. The Shadow was a card of bondage, oppression, illusion and lies, and although she wasn't happy to see it following what had been a positive outcome, she accepted it, and what it presaged. Even though the Agency would triumph, something malevolent would quickly follow.

But who? Or what? Sarah wondered. A new Director with poor leadership skills? Reactionary elements from within the Circle? Or something even worse?

Although she had been taught that asking questions after the last card had been laid down tried the patience of the Lady, and in some cases even angered her, she had to set out one more to see if it could shed any light on this mystery.

This card proved to be even worse than the previous one. It was 'The Downfall'. Another variation on an earlier design, it had been influenced by humanity's experiences since taking to the stars.

Like its predecessor, 'The Tower,' it indicated downfall, upheaval and destruction, but instead of a lightning bolt tearing a stone edifice apart, The

Downfall depicted an even more terrifying image; Old Gaia as it began to explode under the impact of Hriss planet-killer missiles. For modern women, this graphic was the personification of absolute desolation.

Deeply disturbed, she ordered up a small glass of Liqqorvit for herself. When the licorice-flavored liqueur arrived a second later, she took a deep sip and considered everything in front of her with a pensive frown.

Whatever it was that would come after the Agency's ascension was going to be catastrophic. That much was patently obvious.

Unless the Lady was trying to send another message altogether, she thought. Perhaps the terrible times ahead were actually intended to be visited upon the Sisterhood's enemies.

Yes, she decided, her good cheer returning, *that has to be it.* The Goddess would never allow her daughters to reach such great heights only to cast them down the very moment that they reached the summit. If the calamities she had seen were actually occurring elsewhere, to others, then they presaged total victory for Womankind.

There was no other interpretation that made sense. Reassured, she gathered up the spread and returned the cards to their pouch.

***

For the majority of the *Athena's* crew, news about the war with the ETR had come with the general announcement that had been made right before battle stations had sounded. But the shutdown of the Marionite Church had made the rounds through a less conventional, but still time-honored means: word of mouth. Most of the *Athena's* women had been too busy manning their posts to catch the story in detail, but there had been some exceptions. The fighting in Salta Cia had been too brief to require Team 5, and with everything on hold until the fleet's reinforcements arrived, the team was between missions again. Ellen n'Elemay used this opportunity to watch every bit of the coverage.

When she had finally seen all that she could stomach, she turned off the holojector, and held her head in her hands. There was a glass of Aqqa sitting nearby, but she left it untouched.

Like any one of the Faithful, N'Elemay had always been painfully aware of the Sisterhood's hostility towards the True Faith. Any Marionite was, almost from drawing their first breath. The hatred had always been there, hovering on the horizon like a distant storm, dark and threatening, but never close enough to be an immanent threat. Now that storm had finally broken.

The Pope is dead, she thought leadenly, *and my motherworlds have been conquered.* Her sense of shock was gone though, and even her anger had subsided. All that filled her now was a leaden acknowledgement of the facts, and cold resolution. She knew what she had to do and that once she had done it, there would be no coming back.

She picked up her glass at last, and took a long decisive pull. Then she set it down and rose, heading for her rack. There, she changed out of her fatigues and into her service dress uniform.

This wasn't going to be like her visit to the *Halflife Club* however. Violence was not her intent. What she had in mind was actually quite the opposite, although its effect would be more devastating than any kick or punch could have ever accomplished.

As soon as she had finished dressing, she added a final item—and the most important one. It was her copy of the *Revelation of Mari*, which she tucked into a breast pocket. Then she made for the Lifts, and her final destination.

She paused only once along the way, and briefly. It was to access the ships Infoplex where she placed a general message for all hands to see. It read; *"To all members of the Faithful. Pray for your Church. Meet in the Enlisted Mess Hall in five minutes."*

The Ship's AI detected the messages' content, and immediately vetted it to Security, who promptly deleted it. But their censorship was not performed quickly enough. Within seconds, and just before she was locked out of the system completely, N'Elemay's virtual in-box began to fill up with replies. The message had been received.

Now the only question that remained was how many would come to her summons. She was only aware of two members of the Faithful on the *Athena*; herself and Jon, and whether there even *were* any more aboard was something that only Jesu and Mari knew.

If there were others, then she was certain that they would join her. It was also just as sure that those who hated the True Faith would be on their way as well, and she had no doubts about their numbers whatsoever. Praying to Jesu for strength and Mari for protection, she boarded the Lift.

Because it was mid-shift, there were only a few sailors in the Enlisted Mess, and when they saw her enter, they regarded her with expressions of either fear, or puzzlement, or both. N'Elemay paid them no heed though, and dragged a free seat into the middle of the room. Then she pulled the *Revelation* out, seated herself and began to read. Jon fa'Teela arrived less than a minute later, and she looked up from her book to greet him. "Welcome Brother."

Jon met her eyes with a grave expression, and pulled out a seat for himself. "How long do you think we have?" he asked, producing his own little copy of the *Revelation*.

"A few minutes at the most," she answered calmly. "I was reading Saint Tarrylyn's address to the Delgenians." Saint Tarrylyn was one of the Church's early martyrs, and her speech to the sinners of that world, was a classic passage on the nature of sin, and personal sacrifice for faith. Saint Tarrylyn had been killed by the mob at the end of her address.

"Quite fitting," Jon agreed, opening his book to the same passage.

N'Elemay continued to look at him. Her expression was absolutely deadpan and what she said next, was delivered in a direct, businesslike tone. "Jon, ever since I first saw you, I've wanted to say something. And I think this is the right time."

"Yes, sister?"

"Jon, you're a fine figure of a man. If we get through this, I'm going to *fek* you. I'm going to *fek* you so goddamned hard that I'll make you give up men forever. Zat klaar?" Then, before he could stop her, she grabbed his head in her hands and kissed him roughly.

When she released him, Jon's jaw dropped in total amazement, but N'Elemay went back to her reading as if nothing particularly provocative had just occurred. After a minute, she looked up again, and over her shoulder, nodding to a woman who had just come into the mess hall. The Troop

Leader didn't know her personally, but the new arrival wore an orange coverall that announced that she was posted in Engineering. The tech walked up to them, brought up another chair and produced her own miniature Bible.

"Greetings sister," N'Elemay said. "We were reading Saint Tarrylyn's address to the Delgenians."

The woman's face was pale, and she looked around her nervously, but she began to study the passage with them. Her hands, N'Elemay saw, were shaking.

Another crewwoman entered after this, a Mariner from Navcom, followed by two more from Environmental, and then a hesitant trio from the hangar bay. After them, more women came, until there were a dozen of them seated together in a loose circle. Knowing that time was short, the Troop Leader rose and the rest followed.

"Jon?" she asked. "Will you honor us by leading us in prayer?"

The neoman nodded, and tried to compose what he was going to say. He was still in shock over what had happened to his church, and N'Elemay's surprising statement, and his voice threatened to betray him, but he mustered up all of his resolve. Even though he didn't feel that way, he had to sound just as firm and as certain as everyone around him was expecting him to be. He was a missionary, he reminded himself, and they were his flock. And at a time of crisis, they were looking to him to help them find their strength. He couldn't fail them.

"Sisters," he said in his steadiest voice, "our Church has been attacked. Pope Paula has been slain, our people are in chains, and the Redeemer himself is in hiding. Pray with me now for his safety, the safety of all those who are still alive, and for their deliverance from evil."

Everyone bowed their heads and held hands.

"Oh Lord Jesu, merciful Mother Mari, watch over and protect the Faithful wherever they are. Shield them from danger and be a light unto them in this time of greatest darkness. Watch over our brothers and sisters and keep them safe from harm. Ameyn."

As one, the group repeated, "Ameyn." Then they all closed their eyes and began praying silently.

A voice, raised in anger, shattered the stillness. "Troop Leader! What the *fek* is the meaning of this?"

It was Colonel Lislsdaater. Major n'Neesa and a group of two-dozen security patrolwomen were accompanying her.

"What does it look like Colonel?" N'Elemay answered evenly. "We are praying."

"This meeting is over!" the officer shouted. "You will all disperse immediately and return straightway to your duty assignments."

"I cannot speak for my sisters or for my brother here, Colonel," N'Elemay answered evenly. "But I no longer have any duty to anyone except to God, His Son and the Holy Mother Mari."

"Damn it, Ellen!" Major n'Neesa broke in. "What the *fek* are you trying to do? Get yourself court martialed? Break this up and go back to your rack! We can talk about this later."

N'Elemay shook her head slowly. "There's nothing to talk about, Major." She closed her eyes once more, and resumed her devotions.

"Troop Leader!" Lislsdaater barked. "I am giving *you*—all of you—a direct order to disperse immediately. This meeting is over!"

Neither N'Elemay nor any of the others obeyed however. Instead, they clasped hands again, and began to recite the New Lord's Prayer.

What little patience the Colonel had initially possessed, evaporated completely. "Troop Leader, leave this area immediately or I will have you and your associates placed under arrest!"

The woman from engineering was now trembling violently, and N'Elemay gave her hand a reassuring squeeze. "Have no fear sister," she whispered. "Jesu and Mari are with us. They will safeguard us even as we become martyrs for the True Faith." The woman nodded unsteadily, and stayed in the circle.

"Captain," N'Elemay heard the Colonel say. "Have your women take the Troop Leader into custody for gross insubordination. And arrest the neoman too—I'm certain that he's the ringleader. The rest of you can consider yourselves on report."

The securitywomen stepped forwards to carry out their orders, but they hesitated when N'Elemay looked up at them. They were all well aware of what Marauders were capable of, and many of them knew her personally, and her reputation for violence.

"Ellen—"the Major pleaded, "don't."

"I won't, Major," N'Elemay reassured her. "I will go quietly. So will he." With that, she obediently held out her wrists. Jon stepped up, and copied her gesture.

***

The cell that held Ellen n'Elemay was like all the others in the Brig; a simple white cube, molded into one smooth, continuous shape with no seams. The only difference in the cells continuity was where the plastic walls became transparent, and where, at a command from her captors, the molecules could separate and become a doorway. For now though, this spot was as solid as the rest of her cage, and functioned as an observation window.

Her 'bed' consisted of a point where the back wall and floor pushed out and created a rectangular platform, and its mattress was a thin piece of foam that had been issued to her when she had been processed. It had just enough thickness to cushion a sleeper's body, and it was made of a material that resisted any attempts to tear it.

The toilet and sink were equally minimalistic. They were vague, rounded shapes that protruded seamlessly from the left-hand wall. Neither device had any controls that might have been broken off and used for anything, and could only be operated by the prisoner's psiever commands.

Light came in to the cell through the ceiling, directly through the plastic, creating a colorless, even glow. It wasn't there for her convenience, or for the camera up in the corner, silently monitoring her. The surveillance device could function quite well without illumination. Instead, it was intended for the securitywomen patrolling the narrow passage outside, eliminating any shadows that could have offered concealment.

Not that she intended any subterfuge. She had meant it when she had promised the Major that she would cooperate. Since she had been arrested, she had offered up no resistance whatsoever, even when they had confiscated her copy of the *Revelation*. Instead, she had remained passive, and now, with nothing to do but sit on the edge of her cot and wait, she closed her eyes and prayed quietly.

She barely noticed when the wall in front of her opened and a Navy Lieutenant entered her cell.

"Troop Leader n'Elemay?" the woman began, "I am Advocate Vala n'Jayla, and I have been assigned to handle your case."

N'Elemay's gaze flicked to the plastic valise the woman was carrying, and she nodded silently.

"I have spoken with the Adversary, and she is considering proffering charges of mutiny against you. I hope that you realize that if you are convicted of that, that you could be looking at twenty years in prison at the least, and possibly even a death sentence."

Despite the gravity of this announcement, N'Elemay's sober expression did not change one iota. "I do," she said.

"I think that the Adversary knew that this was going a bit far though," N'Jayla offered, "and she said that she would be willing to work with us. But to do that, we have to give her something in return."

N'Elemay shrugged, not in agreement, but merely as a signal to the Advocate to continue.

"The AG's office doesn't really want you," N'Jayla informed her. "They want the neoman, and they want him for treason. If you're willing to testify that this gathering was actually his idea, and that he tried to incite you and the others to take over the ship, then we might be able to convince the Adversary to drop all the charges against you, or at least reduce them to something that won't adversely affect your career."

The Troop Leader made no reply, and a minute passed before N'Jayla broke off eye contact. "Troop Leader, your situation is extremely serious. Your actions took place during a time of war. If you don't take this offer, then you are placing yourself in considerable jeopardy. To help you, I need an answer that I can take back to the Adversary. Do we have a deal?"

Ellen n'Elemay shook her head. "No," she said. "We do *not*. I will not play Judas for you. Jon did nothing at all. It was all my idea, and we only came together to pray. Nothing else."

"Troop Leader, I don't think that you quite understand…"

"Oh, I *understand* perfectly," N'Elemay interrupted, "and I say *get thee behind me, Evil One!* If I must become a martyr for my faith, then so be it. I will go to my fate willingly." The light in her eyes was fierce, and beyond any possibility of negotiation.

"Then I'm sorry, Troop Leader," the Advocate replied. 'You'll have to brave the court's mercy. Your case will be heard as soon as circumstances permit."

***

"I told you that she wouldn't capitulate," Ophida n'Marsi said. "She's exactly what her files suggests she is. The Marauders don't appoint women to run their teams who will compromise their position when they're threatened."

"She's a damned fanatic is what she is," N'Jayla replied.

Sarah n'Jan who had joined them via holo, nodded in agreement. "Yes, she is. And we need her fanaticism." She turned in her seat and addressed the holo floating across from her. It was the Adversary assigned to the case.

"Counselor, I think we are done with her. See to it that the charges against her are dropped to gross misconduct, and recommend a dishonorable discharge with the earliest possible release from custody. I want her on her way as soon as possible."

"Yes, ma'am."

"Ma'am, I'm still not certain that letting someone like her loose is the best idea," Ophida ventured tentatively.

Sarah smiled at her serenely and steepled her fingers. "Oh it is. It *definitely* is. Now, tell me how things are proceeding against Fa'Teela."

***

Detention Area, Ship's Security, USSNS Pallas Athena, Altamara, Altamara System, Frontera Provensa, Esteral Terrana Rapabla, 1044.12|11|03:76:19

"Trooper fa'Teela, my name is Hana sa'Faana, and I am with the Advocate General's Office." By her collar insignia, Jon saw that the woman in the holo floating in front of him was also a Major.

"I am the Adversary in your case," Sa'Faana advised him. She turned and looked in the direction of Jon's Advocate, who had also joined the conference via holo. "Councilor, have you informed your client of the charge against him?" This part, Jon knew, was purely for the record.

"Yes," the other woman said. "I have. He is aware of the charge of treason, and the concomitant sentence of life imprisonment if convicted. As stated in our response, he is entering a plea of 'Not Guilty'." Initially, there had also been a charge of mutiny leveled against him, but it had been dropped when N'Elemay had refused to implicate him.

"So noted," Sa'Faana replied. "Trooper, I am here today to depose you. Do you understand the meaning of that term?"

"Yes, ma'am," he answered. "It means that you are here to ask me questions related to my case."

"Good. Before we begin, I must advise you that you have the right to keep silent regarding anything that might incriminate you, and that if you choose to speak with me on any matter, that I can use whatever you say against you at your courts martial. Is that clear?"

"Yes, ma'am."

Sa'Faana consulted some notes that were just off camera before looking him squarely in the eye. "Trooper fa'Teela, lets get right to the heart of things. Did you conspire with an ETR officer, one Captain Alex Rodraga, while he was posted aboard your ship, to contact the leadership of the Marionite Church on behalf of the ETR government?"

"Yes, and no, ma'am."

"Yes and no? Which is it Trooper? *Yes* or *no*?"

"Yes, I did conspire with him to contact my church—"he started to say.

Sa'Faana cut him off. "So you fully admit your guilt then?"

"And insist on my innocence, ma'am," Jon interjected. "I didn't help his government. That wasn't what he wanted."

"So, you are still claiming, as you did in the deposition your Advocate took, that you didn't know the real purpose of this meeting? You *still* assert that it was merely some kind of religious liaison?"

"I do," Jon responded. "It was my belief that it was nothing more than an attempt by the Church in the ETR to reunite with ours. I was never told about any government involvement."

"Despite the fact that undercover agents working for the DNI *and* the OAE have reported otherwise?" Sa'Faana challenged.

"I can't comment on what they might or might not have reported, ma'am," he countered. "I can only tell you about what I knew."

"I see. How exactly did you make contact with your Church?" Sa'Faana asked. They both knew what his answer was going to be to this question, but she still had to ask it.

"I cannot tell you that, ma'am. With respect."

"You're aware that failure to cooperate with my investigation may add additional charges to your case, and potentially prejudice the Justices against you? Has your Advocate advised you of this?"

"She has, and I am," Jon replied.

"Very well," Sa'Faana said. "Let's revisit the details. When was your first meeting with Captain Rodraga, and what did you say to one another on that meeting?"

Although he had already provided this information during his first deposition, Jon proceeded to give her the specifics. Despite an effort by the Adversary to uncover new and incriminating evidence hidden in his account, nothing surprising, or new, came to light. The deposition ended an hour later, and after Jon had been returned to his cell, Major sa'Faana reread and amended the notes in his case file.

'Point one,' her notes read, *'Defense asserts that Fa'Teela is innocent. Cites two areas in support of this: one, his liaison with Rodraga took place while the Sisterhood was still allied with the ETR, and two, that he had no personal knowledge of any effort to solicit a clandestine relationship for the purposes of espionage.'*

The first point would present her with some issues, she knew. There was no disputing the dates involved, or the fact that a state of war did not yet exist. She would be hard pressed to convince the Justices that his actions were treasonous just on that basis alone.

What her success hinged on was disproving the second point, and showing that Fa'Teela was fully aware that the ETR intended to subvert the Sisterhood through the Marionites, in advance of hostilities.

But with what evidence? she wondered. The neoman hadn't kept any kind of diary, nor had he made any extemporaneous statements to anyone that she might have called as a witness. Even the Marionite Troop Leader, N'Elemay, had she been available, would have had nothing substantial to offer. Prior to their protest in the mess hall, she had never enjoyed any kind of relationship with the neoman. No one had; since coming aboard the *Athena*, Fa'Teela had kept to himself.

She pressed on.

'Point three: the OAE report states that there was in fact an effort to create a liaison for the purposes of espionage, and that Bishop Jyon da Castraa acted as a clandestine agent for the ETR.'

The problem was, that Fa'Teela wasn't mentioned anywhere in that particular report. Only the Bishop and the Marionite leadership had been listed. To complicate things, the majority of the report, including the significant details of the ETR's proposal, which would have proven collusion with a hostile intent, had been classified well above her clearance level. This left her, again, with nothing to work with but inference and supposition. The Justices would not be impressed.

'Point four: available documents do show that Fa'Teela did somehow make contact, but the exact manner is classified and Fa'Teela still refuses to elaborate.'

Sa' Faana stopped there, sat back and sighed. Initially, she'd been excited to be appointed as the Adversary in a case that would effectively destroy the so-called 'progress' of neoman 'rights.' Now she found herself wondering who she'd angered to get put in this position.

Taken in the widest possible view, the case against the neoman was anemic. In fact, it was pure *shess* and she was at a loss to explain why the AG's office had even bothered to file the charges against Fa'Teela in the first place. At best, she saw him as being guilty of insubordination.

Unless there was something waiting to be uncovered that changed the situation drastically, she thought. The only real hope for her side lay in an independent report being compiled by the AG's own investigators. After the charges had been filed against Fa'Teela, a team had been dispatched to New Covenant to corroborate what they could. It wasn't that they hadn't believed the OAE's report, but given the potential that the case had to become a high-profile affair, it had only been prudent to back it up with an independent verification.

The investigation was a two-edged thing however; by law, all discovery was transparent, and anything that the investigators learned would have to be made available to both sides in the case. It was just as likely that whatever they found, if they found anything, might prove to be as much in Fa'Teela's favor as against it.

Deeply frustrated, she accessed her Com and sent a request to Rixa for another progress report on the investigation. Regardless of the outcome, the results couldn't arrive fast enough to suit her.

The Goddess granted her wish, at least as far as speed went. A week later, the final report reached her, and she read it over carefully. When she was done, she contacted her superior on Rixa, and then her opposition.

"Were you satisfied by the deposition that my client gave you?" the Advocate asked politely. "Or do we need to arrange another session?"

The bitch knew, Sa'Faana realized, and now she was toying with her.

"For the record, I *wasn't* satisfied, councilor," she retorted. "But I have a job to do, just like you. And no, I don't think that another deposition will be necessary."

"Neither do I," the Advocate smiled, "So, what do I owe the pleasure of this conversation to?"

Sa'Faana clenched her fist, off camera, and went on with what she had been ordered to say. "In the light of the new evidence our investigators uncovered, the AG's office has directed me to offer your client a deal. We will drop treason and charge him with gross misconduct instead, with time served, and a dishonorable discharge. Or if you want to fight that, we'll argue for jail time—and we'll get it."

The Advocates' grin widened. "Now why should sisters fight one another? I'll speak with him, and I'm certain that when I explain the situation to him he'll agree."

Yes, Sa'Faana thought bitterly. *I'm sure he fekking will.*

Using holorecords that the OAE had somehow failed to discover, the investigators had managed to uncover evidence that had effectively destroyed her case. Their report had conclusively proven that the OAE's claims about the purpose of the meeting with Bishop da Castraa had not only been wildly exaggerated, but falsified.

Unedited transcripts showed demonstrably that it really *had* been a religious reconciliation, just as Fa'Teela had claimed. And nothing more. The ETR's government had never been officially involved, and there had never been an attempt to recruit the Marionites for any counterintelligence operations. While this might have been the eventual goal, it had clearly not been a part of that meeting.

The discovery rendered the charge of treason against Fa'Teela, and by extension the Marionite Church and its officials, completely spurious. Even worse, it made the military occupation of their motherworlds, and the deaths that had followed, wasteful and wholly unnecessary.

Heads would certainly roll over the whole affair, but this would never reverse the damage that had been caused to the Sisterhood. Or the greater damage that *would* be caused if the whole thing came to light at trial, Sa'Faana admitted.

The very last thing that they needed was to create the perception that the OAE, the DNI, and the government they served, had deceived its citizens. As distasteful as it was, they had to bargain the whole thing away, and no one would ever be the wiser.

Damn the OAE for their over zealousness! she silently cursed. Although they had managed to remove some of the cancer from the body of the nation, their 'cure' had caused even greater problems.

Mastering herself, she ended her conversation with the Advocate. "Thank you, councilor," she said with a politeness that came to her lips only with the greatest of effort. "I will await your client's response."

The Advocate re-contacted her the next day. Just as the woman had predicted, Jon fa'Teela had agreed to the lowered charges, and their bargain was sealed. Despite the fact that he was to be discharged from the Marines, the neoman had simply been grateful that his ordeal was over. According to his defense, he had even said of prayer of thanks to Jesu and Mari for the resolution.

He would never know the real reason behind his good fortune, of course. No one, outside the AG's office, and the two intelligence agencies, ever would. The entire matter, including his case file, was now classified.

The hunt for the Redeemer, and his fellow fugitives, would still continue, but with a new mandate for the women who pursued them: capture was no longer a desirable option. Unlike Jon, many of them had personally attended the meeting with the Bishop, and they knew the truth.

CHAPTER 12

Special Military Quarantine Zone, Second Planet, The School, HSL-48 2124A System, Annexed Sisterhood Territory, 1044.12|18| 05:41:41

Sarah was absolutely furious. Maya was trying her best to avoid her, but since they were sharing quarters together, it was proving to be quite a trick. Sarah had returned them to the School to coordinate clandestine operations in support of the Sisterhood's conventional forces. With limited space available, they had been boarded together in one of the local homes, and Maya had been forced to endure her partner's foul mood within the close confines of a tiny one-bedroom house.

That hostilities had broken out at the time they had had been bad enough. The sudden war had completely upset all of Sarah's carefully laid plans to slowly and methodically undermine the ETR. But Fa'Teela's simultaneous escape from justice had sent her completely over the edge. The fact that this had been due to the actions of women working for her own agency only added fuel to Sarah's rage.

"Incompetents!" Sarah shouted. "Second rate *amateurs!* Any *real* agent with even *half* a neuron in her skull would have known better than to have left *anything* behind for those dammed AG investigators to find!"

She plucked up the data cube that had delivered this unpleasant news and threw it forcefully across the small room. It shattered against the opposite wall.

"At the very *least* they could have *fabricated* something that incriminated him right along with the rest of those traitors! *Inexcusable!*"

Privately, Maya felt that all the fuss over Jon fa'Teela was rather silly. Like any woman, she had been raised to accept Motherthought, and one of its primary principles was that men were, by their very nature, inferior and obsolete. With that as a given, she found it ridiculous that anyone, and especially Sarah, would become so upset over him, or over any man for that matter. While they had once commanded Humanity's destiny, their day was long gone, and it would never return.

She knew better than to say anything however. Sarah was impossible to communicate with when her engines were running at 'full-bitch-mode'. It was far wiser just to let her rant and rave until she exhausted herself.

"Those so-called *agents* will pay dearly for this!" Sarah hollered. "I'll speak with the Director and see to it that they wind up on some observation post deep in Hriss space!"

To emphasize her displeasure, she grabbed the data-cube player and tossed it at the same wall that had just destroyed the hapless data cube. The device made a deep dent in the barrier, and it crashed to the floor to join the other wreckage.

Then Sarah straightened, brushed her long hair out of her eyes and took a deep breath. By all appearances, she seemed calm again. But this was only a façade, and as Maya well knew, the point when she was actually at her most dangerous.

"As for the *neoman*," Sarah said, a glint of madness flashing in her eyes, "*He* is responsible for *all* the embarrassment that we have suffered. And I *swear* on the Lady's name that he will *answer* for it! I will kill him myself! And I'll make it *slow*!"

Having made this promise, her lunacy seemed to recede and something vaguely resembling sanity returned to her features. "In the meantime Maya, we have much work to do. Let us pay another visit to Captain n'Kyla. We need to speak with her about fomenting more civil unrest in the enemy's capitol. I want their resources strained to the absolute limit!"

USSNS *Pallas Athena*, Corredo System, Frontera Provensa,
Esteral Terrana Rapabla, 1044.12|18| 07:51:13

When the first securitywoman arrived at the entrance of the Ship's Temple, a frantic Assistant Priestess met her. Beyond her, the officer could see that the Temple itself was in disarray and she heard the sound of something being broken. She immediately pushed her way past the cleric, moving towards the source. It was coming from behind the door to Ophida n'Marsi's private office.

"Please!" the young Priestess begged, "You've got to do something! She's gone crazy! We tried to help her but—"

"It's all right," the officer replied. "Just go back out into the corridor. We'll take it from here." A second securitywoman had arrived by this point, and her psiever told her that Captain t'Gwen was on her way up to join them.

Another impact resounded behind the door, accompanied by someone yelling out obscenities. The securitywoman knocked, using the end of her stun baton to make certain that she was heard above the din.

"Reverend n'Marsi? This is Security. Can you open the door for us?" Ever since the declaration of war, and the little stunt that the Marionites had pulled in the Enlisted Mess, things had been tense on the ship, but she had never expected the High Priestess, of all women, to be so dramatically affected.

N'Marsi answered her with some very un-priestess-like language. "*Fek you, bita!* Go away!"

"Reverend, you know I can't do that," the officer replied. "Captain t'Gwen is coming. Please, open the door for us."

Just then, T'Gwen arrived, and came up to the door.

"Ophida? This is Veera. Will you let me in? I just want to make sure you're all right."

"I *am* all right. Go the *fek* away!"

"Okay Ophida. I'm not going to ask you to let me in any more, but I'm not going to leave. I'll just stay here. We can talk through the door."

Silence.

T'Gwen hand signed to the others that everything was fine for the moment and waved them away. The officers retreated into the hall.

"Ophida?" she said. "I'm still here. Can you tell me what's wrong? There's only the two of us now."

There was more silence, but she knew that this was a good thing. Nothing else was being broken, and her psiever, patching into the Ship's security systems, told her that the woman inside was alive, and conscious. A tiny image in the corner of her vision revealed that Ophida was seated in her chair, but the office had been totally wrecked and the woman's robes appeared to be in tatters.

"Everyone's been pretty upset lately," T'Gwen offered. 'All of us, even me. My nerves have been a little on edge. I guess that you're feeling that way too."

No response.

"Funny," she continued. "It looks like we're not immune after all, are we? You and I, we always have to be the strong ones. Doesn't give us much time for ourselves, does it? Things kind of catch up." She heard movement, and saw that Ophida was rising. "Do you want to talk? Just you and me? I'd like that."

The door opened slightly, and the officers in the hall started to return, but she flashed them a look that stopped them in their tracks. T'Gwen knew that they meant well, but things were under control. She pushed the door open and went inside.

***

After Lilith had received the news from Captain T'Gwen, she walked across the bridge and sought out Katrinn in her office. Her friend was behind her desk, playing her guitar. She always did that when she was disturbed.

"I heard," Katrinn said anticipatorily. She put down her instrument and sat back, folding her hands behind her head. "Medbay has her sedated. They told me that she had some kind of nervous breakdown."

"Between Ophida and the Marionites, I'm beginning to think that everyone in the Fleet is going klaxxy," Lilith remarked, taking a seat.

"I won't argue that," Katrinn said. "I contacted Rixa and they cut an order for Ophida to be transferred. They're going to send her to the Selenite Monastery of Mene-Selene on Calaa. It's in the Halasi Elant, and the Chaplain General's Office runs it. She'll get the help she needs there."

Lilith nodded but she still couldn't believe it. The High Priestess had always been the rock that they had clung to in desperate times. And now she had broken.

"Do we know what caused it?" she asked.

"Something about the neoman," Katrinn answered. "She kept repeating the same thing; 'he got away, he got away'. It looks like she took

Fa'Teela's case pretty personally."

"Well, at least he's gone, right along with that Troop Leader," Lilith observed.

"Yes," Katrinn returned. "And I've ordered the others that were with them transferred off the ship. I don't care if they only wound up on report. I'm too new at this job to deal with a mutiny. They're history."

Lilith understood. She had considered ordering the same thing for all her battle groups, and she knew that Da'Kayt was weighing this option as well, and on a fleet-wide basis. The little group that had gathered in the *Athena's* mess hadn't been the only one. There had been others, on several ships, who had responded to N'Elemay's call and staged protests of their own. Not many, but enough to create concern.

"It's for the best," she said. Then she sat back and looked at the colorful quilt Katrinn had draped over an empty chair. Zommerlaandar families called them 'Homecoming Quilts' and they embroidered them with protective symbols to keep their loved ones safe when they went abroad. The sight of it reminded her of Ingrit and elicited a tired sigh.

"I still can't believe it, Kat," Lilith remarked, missing the simplicity of the Farm and her lover's company. "I never knew that we had so many Marionites in the fleet. Goddess knows how many there are in the Sisterhood."

"The Chairwoman said it herself, Lily. They're all over the place. This new agency of hers is going to have a time of it rooting them out."

Lilith nodded in agreement. Then she rose. "I'll cut the orders to get rid of the other ones in my command. You had the right idea."

Katrinn picked up her guitar again. "Thanks, Lily. I needed to hear that. And let me know how the new High Priestess works out, okay?" Like most of the women from Sunna 3, she didn't attend the services in the Temple, but observed her own rites in private, or with her fellow Zommerlaandars.

"I will, Kat. See you at evening mess."

Station 13, Von Hagen's World, Thyone System, Sagana Elant,
United Sisterhood of Suns, 1044.12|19|05:01:99

Ellen n'Elemay squinted in the harsh afternoon sunlight and surveyed her surroundings. Von Hagen's World was a bleak place, a desert planet that had been baked dry by the radiation of the binary stars it circled, and what little native life it had, only existed by the thinnest margin imaginable. The planet's sole value, aside from the fact that it possessed a breathable atmosphere, was that it was located at the very edge of Sisterhood space.

The captain of the light cruiser, the USSNS *Antibrote*, had fulfilled her orders to the letter. If asked, she would be able to honestly state to her superiors that 'yes, Ellen n'Elemay, the filthy Marionite ex-Marine traitor,' had been returned to the Sisterhood. That Von Hagen's World was so remote that its only settlement, 'Station 13' was almost fully automated, and only boasted a population of one, hadn't been the officer's problem. Nor was the fact that the station only saw a ship arrive every few weeks.

Just before she had effectively marooned her there, the captain had fulfilled one additional requirement specified by her orders. She had presented N'Elemay with the three chits the law mandated for any citizen with no means; one for a week's food, another for basic lodging, and a third that guaranteed a one-way trip back to Thermadon. Despite her dishonorable discharge, and the fact that the captain of the *Antibrote* didn't personally agree with the idea, Ellen n'Elemay was still a citizen, and had been entitled to this much.

When and how she would ever actually *use* the chits, and what she would do after she reached Thermadon, also hadn't been the captain's concern. To her, N'Elemay was a non-entity, with no future, and not worth worrying about.

So be it, N'Elemay thought as she walked away from the *Antibrote's* shuttle. *The prophets of the First Church suffered in the desert. Who am I to think myself to be any better than they were?*

Having no other destination, she trudged across the rocky ground to the one structure intended for human visitors. This was a combination convenience store and rest station. The little pre-fab building didn't look terribly inviting, but it was a lot better than standing outside in the oppressive heat.

The single inhabitant of Von Hagen's World was on duty inside, and she didn't bother to look up when N'Elemay entered.

"Excuse me, "N'Elemay finally said. "When is the next outbound merchanter coming through?"

The woman continued to read her Holomag for another minute. Then she languidly raised her head and gave N'Elemay an appraising look, taking in her fatigues and their lack of insignia. Then a glint of understanding came into her eyes. The woman knew her story.

"Did your time in the service then? I saw the shuttle that dropped you here. Well, you have two weeks, maybe more, before anything's scheduled to come along. We don't get a lot of tourists this time of year."

The woman laughed at her own joke, and added. "What? Do you have somewhere special you need to go?"

"No," N'Elemay replied. "Not yet."

"Do you have your chits?"

N'Elemay reached into her pocket and produced them.

Taking them from her, the woman ran the chits under a hand scanner. "I can do something with the one for the food," she said. "But there's not enough on it for two weeks and we don't have any 'lodgings'. That chit's useless."

"I can sleep anywhere," the ex-Troop Leader replied, "and I can work for my food."

The woman chuckled derisively. "Doing what? This whole station is automated. I'm only here because the reg's mandate it. The 'bots do all the work."

"I understand," N'Elemay said, looking around the store. Suddenly, a notion occurred to her. "Can I trade you the one for the lodging? It's worth credits. You could cash it in."

"A trade?"

"Yes, "she told her. "I just need a few things that will probably be worth a lot less than the whole chit."

The clerk smiled in wry amusement as she guessed her intentions. "Planning on a little camping then?"

"Yes," N'Elemay stated. "I'll trade you the chit for a plastic tarp, some water, a knife and some basic rations. I don't need much, and like I said, you can pocket the difference."

"You have a deal," the woman said, snatching up the plastic chits before N'Elemay could change her mind. With them firmly in her custody, she gestured with exaggerated courtesy at the contents of the little store. "We're open for business, jantildam. Get what you need."

"Thanks." N'Elemay walked over to a display rack and selected a knife for herself. It was much plainer than the rest, but she could tell from its feel that it was sturdy and the blade itself seemed serviceable enough.

"You know, you won't last three days out there," the clerk warned her.

"We'll see," N'Elemay returned. "I just need to get through two weeks, right?"

"Yes, and you won't make it. You sure you don't want to give me the other chit too? It won't do you much good once you're dead."

"I'll hold onto it. See you in two weeks."

***

The clerk had vastly underestimated her abilities. Instead of being claimed by the harsh environment, N'Elemay relied on her extensive survival training, and her personal experiences having served in places even worse than Von Hagen's World.

She created a camp for herself in the hills overlooking the Station, using the lee side of a rocky outcropping as the back wall for a makeshift shelter, and with her tarp stretched over this, the arrangement provided enough shade to bring the daytime heat down to a more or less manageable level. She also helped the process along by staying under cover during the day and only engaging in strenuous activities after it was dark.

Food and water didn't present any problems either. She kept her consumption of both down to the absolute minimum, and recycled her urine using a makeshift still. She also wasn't bored; she passed the searing days under cover, contemplating her situation.

God had placed her there. She knew that. But what his plan for her was the great mystery. At first, she prayed for an answer, and when none came, she realized that this was not enough. She had to make a deeper effort, and a greater personal sacrifice.

She stopped eating altogether, making sure only to drink enough water to satisfy the basic requirements of survival. And she prayed harder. Her nights became acts of contrition and meditation, with only one focus. An answer and a Calling.

Finally, at dawn on the day before the next ship was scheduled to arrive, it came to her. She was half in trance, partly from the lack of food, partly from her time out in the heat, and partly from the exertion of her devotions. Waking consciousness and dreams had ceased to have separate meaning, and as the twin suns crested over the jagged teeth of the distant mountains, God finally sent her the vision she had so desperately prayed for.

Jesu himself appeared before her, carrying his cross to the place where he would be crucified, and N'Elemay's heart broke as she witnessed his suffering. "Who will help me carry this burden?" she heard him say, and she rose on unsteady legs to come to his aid.

But as she neared him, his cross transformed, changing from a rough-hewn thing of wood, into smooth, shining steel. She realized then that Jesu was holding up a mighty sword, lit by the dawn as if it were ablaze. Then it actually did burst into flames, burning with a light that was so brilliant and pure that she could hardly bear to look upon it.

"Who will carry this burden for me?" he asked.

"I will," she declared, reaching for it with eager, trembling fingers. When she made contact with the sword's grip, another vision superimposed itself.

She saw Thermadon, not as it was, but as it would be. The entire city was on fire, and its mighty towers had shattered and fallen, and everywhere, she saw and felt God's light filling it, cleansing it of the evil that had dwelled within it for so long. Beyond this, she sensed, rather than saw, the same fate being visited on every world of the Sisterhood. It filled her with a bliss that surpassed anything she had ever experienced before on the battlefield. It was a glorious thing.

Then everything began to spin. She was falling, and then she realized that she had hit the earth, and was lying facedown on the sand.

When she looked up, Jesu and his flaming sword were gone. The vision and its meaning remained however. Raising herself up on arms made feeble by all her privations, she started to crawl her way back to the shelter for the food that her body demanded.

And she understood at long last why God had moved her to throw her career in the Marines away, and why he had sent her to this desolate place. He wanted her to fight for him. The holy crusade that he had called her to lead would be just as wonderful, and just as wrathful as the sword that his son had entrusted her with.

USSNS *Pallas Athena*, CD-9719-B System, Unclaimed Territory, 1044.12|29|02:28:33

Only a few days after N'Elemay received her vision in the desert, the USSNS *Molly Pitcher* located the ETR's 14th Fleet. Following their intricate web of warp jumps, the light cruiser had found them in a lonely little system, designated as CD-9719-B, just outside of ETR space. The *Pitcher* quickly relayed this information back to Admiral da'Kayt and the SEF and the new ships that had just joined them, made way for the location immediately. After a long transit, they arrived at the systems' edge and found that their luck still held. The Republican ships--all of them--were still there.

As they closed the distance to within firing range, Lilith assessed their strength against the ships that made up the official table of elements for the 14th fleet. Most of them were accounted for, and she noted with satisfaction that Admiral Guzamma's flagship, the *Toki*, and all of the other capitol ships were present. They had been caught unawares.

When the order came to come out of stealth, Admiral da'Kayt followed Ebed Cya's orders and attempted to make contact with the Grand Admiral. No reply came to her hails however, and Lilith's SDTS showed that the ETR was doing what everyone had predicted they would in such an eventuality; they were powering up for warp and preparing to scatter. Any hopes that she had harbored about witnessing a simple surrender vanished with this data.

Most of them wouldn't have the time they needed to make their escape, but some, she knew, would undoubtedly manage to slip away. They would catch them later though. She was confident of that much, and the Jade, Diamond and Ruby Fleets were on full alert back in the Sisterhood in the event that any of these strays made an attempt to enter her nation's space. She sent her orders to the battle groups under her command to make ready, and then watched as the minutes ticked by and the distance between them decreased.

Then a surprise occurred. Three ships, roughly in the same class as her own navy's Macha medium cruisers, left the others and began to head straight for the SEF Fleet at top speed. They were also opening their silo doors and readying to fire. A cold chill went through Lilith as she recognized the tag over one of them. It was the *Adaventara*, Captain Rodraga's vessel.

"Fire Control," Katrinn was saying, "When they get within range, take them out." Outgunned by more than a hundred to one, their gesture was pure futility.

"Kat, belay that order," Lilith interrupted. "Navcom open a hail to the *Adaventara*. Let me speak to them." This was going against Ebed Cya's instructions to make only one offer of surrender, but she wasn't about to see Rodraga and his ship destroyed without making at least one final attempt to save him. The cruiser was within missile range by this point, but Katrinn and the other vessels that were near enough to fire, obliged her.

"Fire control, stand by," the Zommerlaandar said, looking down at Lilith. "But if they don't answer this hail, go ahead with your orders."

Lilith mouthed a silent thanks back up to her friend, and waited as Navcom made the call.

Alex Rodraga's image came up above her holojector and its duplicate appeared on the number one sitscreen.

"Alex, what are you doing?" Lilith asked him. "You know you won't succeed. Please, surrender now."

Rodraga sighed tiredly. "Admiral--Lilith--you know as an officer that I can't do that. I have to try and save my fleet. I don't condone what my government did, but I have my duty to my nation. We both do." It was sheer madness, but she also understood.

"I know that Alex," she replied with a weariness that was the equal of his, "I wish things could have been different."

"You know that that was impossible from the first day our two civilizations met," he said. "I'm just sorry that I won't get the chance to see some of the marvels of your great Sisterhood. I would have liked to have seen them with you."

"Yes. That would have been good." Lilith answered, her voice beginning to betray her. "Goodbye, Alex."

"Goodbye, Lilith." Rodraga cut the connection.

A single tear rolled down her face, and she wiped it away before facing Katrinn. "Commander, you may engage the hostiles."

The *Athena* and her sisters launched their missiles. Two minutes later these hit the *Adaventara* and the other cruisers. The ships disappeared, leaving nothing but expanding balls of hot gas and debris.

At that instant, as Lilith watched the *Adaventara* die, the bridge seemed like the most terrible place in the entire universe. She suddenly wanted to get up and run from there. She wanted to go off and scream. She wanted to find herself a private place to cry. She wanted to hide in a little corner and bawl her eyes out.

But she did none of these things. Instead, she remained right where she was. There was a job to be done, a shessy, nasty job and it was hers, and hers alone. The battle was far from over and she still had her duty to do, just as Alex had had. Gulping back a little sob, she sent a signal to her display and zoomed out to watch the activities of the Republican fleet.

The rest of the ETR fleet had taken advantage of the delay and by their energy signatures she could tell that they were beginning their runs up to warp speed. A few though, were too close to the approaching Sisterhood fleet, and these were already being disabled, or destroyed.

Then elements from the Onyx Fleet appeared. They were ahead of the renegade ships, and cutting across them in a classic "crossing the T" maneuver. At only 1 AU, their missiles were also at point blank range. Defeat was an absolute certainty.

Knowing this, Admiral da'Kayt made one final attempt to hail the *Toki*. This time, the flagship answered. The conversation between them was relayed to every ship in the SEF fleet. For her part, Lilith only half-listened to it, too filled with sorrow to do more than satisfy her duty and play the passive role of a spectator.

"Admiral Guzamma," Da'Kayt began, "We have you and you will not escape. I offer you the chance to surrender peacefully. I promise that we will not harm your crews, or your officers."

"We will *never* surrender!" Guzamma snapped. "Each one of us is willing to lay down his life for our nation! We will fight you to the--"

Then, there was a noise and the Grand Admiral turned, looking at someone off camera. "What?! What are you doing, you fool! Put that away!"

A shot rang out, and Guzamma staggered backwards with a neat hole in the center of his head and an expression of utter disbelief on his face. Then he dropped out of view.

Immediately, another man walked up and replaced him, holstering a sidearm. By his rank tabs, Lilith knew him for a captain, and vaguely recognized him as the commander of the *Toki.*

"I am Captain Jozua Alvara," he said, confirming his identity. "And I am now in command of the 14th Fleet as acting Fleet Admiral. I offer you my flagship, and the surrender of our forces. This conflict must end. There has been enough bloodshed."

His announcement momentarily shocked Lilith out of her depression, and she and Katrinn exchanged astonished looks. No one had expected *this.*

Except for Admiral da'Kayt. The very calm in her tone suggested that she had anticipated the mutiny, and the surrender. "And where, may I ask is President Magdalana?" she inquired.

"He is in custody, Admiral," Captain Alvara answered. "We are prepared to remand him to you immediately."

Behind him, a voice shouted with outrage, "Traitors! This is treason. I'll see you all hung!" Lilith saw the former President in the background, being restrained by two ETR Marines. It was highly unlikely that he would ever make good on his threat.

"Very well," Da'Kayt returned. "Power down all of your reactors, and make no further moves of any kind. Then prepare to be boarded. I want that man ready for us when we come for him."

Alvara saluted her smartly. "Yes, Admiral."

***

Boarding parties were sent out to each Republican ship, and once they were in Sisterhood hands, and it had been confirmed, superficially at least, that there were no biohazards aboard any of them, they started the long journey back to Altamara, under heavy escort. There, they would be interned until hostilities were formally declared to be at an end.

It was hours before Lilith was able to leave her post and return to her quarters. Once there, she fed Skipper, and then knelt down before her personal shrine. The image of the full moon appeared, and she gazed on it for several minutes before she spoke to her Goddess.

"Lady," she said. "I don't know why you decree death for your children, but you do. And I don't know why you force us to take lives. I--I don't question your will. I can't. But I have to tell you…I have to tell you…" She stopped, overcome by what she had been forced to do that day in the name of duty.

Alex Rodraga had been her friend and she had killed him. Not with her own hands certainly, but she had murdered him just as surely.

Appalled by her deed, she couldn't go on, and she stopped speaking to compose herself. At last, when she finally felt ready enough to go on, she finished her prayer, but it came out of her in a broken, half whisper. "Take care of Alex," she said to the image. "Wherever he is. He's yours now."

Suddenly feeling utterly drained, she made the Lady's sign and went to her bed. Skipper, sensing her distress, jumped up onto the mattress and tried his best to comfort her. She took him into her arms and held him tight as she wept.

Eventually, her tears stopped, and she laid herself down. But sleep eluded her, and as she lay there in the dark, she made a vow. It was as much to herself as to the Lady.

She was done with the whole bloody, miserable business of war. As soon as the chance offered itself, she would marry Ingrit, and they would raise a family together. And none of their children--*none* of them--would ever be allowed to join the military.

***

Senatrix n'Calysher smiled pleasantly as Xavyar Magdalana came up to the viewing window of his cell in the *Boudicca's* brig. "Good afternoon," she said. "I trust that by now you have heard your government's pronouncement. My sincere condolences."

As soon as word had come that the 14th Fleet had been captured, the Interim President of the Republic had signed a formal declaration severing any ties with his former leader, and his policies, and had simultaneously issued an order that Magdalana be tried in-absentia for 'crimes against humanity'. The trial itself had been a brief affair, and a guilty verdict had been issued without any dissenting votes. His nation was done with him. Magdalana was a dead man.

"I should have expected that they'd send you to gloat over the news, you old battleaxe." Magdalana replied sullenly.

"How gracious," N'Calysher retorted. "Frankly, I wouldn't have missed this day for all the stars in the galaxy."

Magdalana's expression changed from defiant to desperate. "Please, don't harm my family," he asked her quietly.

"We will not harm them, Mr. Magdalana," she assured him. "In fact, your daughter may even find a place for herself in politics in the years ahead, and in the meantime, your son and wife will be well cared for. You have my personal word on that."

"Thank you."

"Goodbye, Mr. Magdalana."

N'Calysher turned and walked away, consigning the man to the dustbin of history. In a war that the media had already labeled, "The Great Betrayal", Xavier Magdalana would be remembered as the last male leader of the ETR, as a liar and a war criminal, and finally, and most importantly, as another example of the failure of male leadership. In just a few minutes, she knew that he would be served his final meal, and that once he had finished it, he would find himself being shoved out of the nearest airlock by security. The Sisterhood was only too happy to aid their re-found friends in meting out justice. Especially in *his* case.

In the meantime, she had the future to concern herself with.

Sanda Ernan was waiting with Felecia and Senatrix d'Salla in the temporary office space Admiral da'Kayt had lent for the occasion. The holographic image of the Interim President, the leader of their Senate and the Lead Justice of the Republican Supreme Court hovered respectfully over in a corner, courtesy of a signal sent out by advance units of the Marine Signal Corps. To her experienced eye, all three of the men looked quite anxious to see their business transacted. And had she been in their place, with the Sisterhood Navy hovering right over their capitol, she would have felt much the same way.

There was a brief ceremony, and when it was done, N'Calysher offered her hand to Ernan. "Madame President? I would like to be the first woman to wish you good luck in your new administration."

Ready Room 4, 'Five-Bar', USSNS *Pallas Athena,* In-Orbit Over Nuvo Bolivar, Magdala Provensa, Esteral Terrana Rapabla, 1045.01|03|04:16:67

Kaly still couldn't believe that Troop Leader n'Elemay was gone. The news about the war with the ETR, and the occupation of the Marionite worlds had caught everyone by surprise, and before she had even had the chance to digest this, the Troop Leader had gotten herself arrested along with Fa'Teela. And even though she and her teammates had asked to see her, their joint request had been quickly, and firmly, denied.

News of N'Elemay's discharge had followed right on the heels of this, and then word that she had been shipped back to the Sisterhood. Just like that; with no chance to say goodbye, or even put in a good word for her. It had all been just as abrupt and brutal as the raid on Persephone, and she felt just as displaced. The team that had become her family, was shattered into pieces now.

Goddess, she wondered as she sat with Margasdaater and T'Jinna in the ready room. *Why do you keep doing this? Why do you make me lose everything? Why do you take away everyone that matters to me?*

No answer came from on high however, or anywhere else.

It wasn't fair. It wasn't good, and it was fekked enough for her to begin to wonder if there really was anything out there standing guard over their fates. But the alternative, a howling void filled with chaos and nothingness, with no purpose other than to go on and on and on, was too terrifying to accept. Something greater had to be behind it all. That, or everything and everybody in the universe were truly lost and just didn't know it.

Lt. sa'Kaali came into the ready room at this dark point, and Kaly looked up at her, just as glad for the interruption as her companions were.

"The Major got back with me," the officer announced, "and she and the Colonel talked it over. With N'Elemay gone, they had only two options. One of these was to disband your team and send you all off to new units."

Kaly's mouth opened in horror. In all the turmoil, she hadn't really considered what might happen to them. Her thoughts had only been for N'Elemay. And from the expression on her teammate's faces, it was obvious that they were just as mortified as she was. Even without their former Troop Leader, they still had each other.

"The other option was to assign you a new Troop Leader. And that's what they finally chose to do. So, until we can get a replacement, you'll all stand down, and fill in wherever we need extra bodies," the El-Tee said. "For the record ladies, I'm sorry that this happened. We all are. Troop Leader n'Elemay was a valuable asset, and I know that you all respected her. Please, give her replacement a chance when she comes. N'Elemay would want that."

"Ma'am, yes ma'am", Kaly answered, trying to make her tone seem enthusiastic and instead, only managing to sound weary. But what was left of the team, would survive at least, she told herself. That was something.

***

Except for a brief psychological examination after the raid on her motherworld and the induction process on Hella's World, Kaly had no experience whatsoever with mental health professionals. She was under orders to report to Dr. Suzzyn bel Shaaron however, and she was doing her best to relax.

“Kaly? Do you know why you are here today?”

“Yes, ma’am. I was told that I needed to report to you for regular treatment. My CO said that it was because of how I reacted on the last Op.”

The order had come down a day after the Lieutenant had spoken with the team about N’Elemay and her replacement, and its actual wording had been for her to report to medbay for ‘psychological servicing and maintenance’. Just as if she was a broken-down hovertruck or something, and about as free to refuse.

Privately, Kaly considered the whole thing to be a colossal waste of time. She didn’t really need anything, except maybe a little rest, more antidepressants, and another Op to take her mind off things.

“Kaly, I want you to call me Suzzyn,” the doctor said. “Don’t think of me as an officer. I’m here to help you and I want us to be comfortable with each other.”

“Yes…Suzzyn,” Kaly replied with a trace of hesitation. Calling a superior officer by her first name just felt *weird*.

“Kaly, you need to understand that you have experienced a series of traumas, and that you have to heal yourself. First, there was the attack on your world, then combat, and then the horrors of that lab, and then you lost your Team Leader. These are all profound events, and they’ve left their mark on you.”

“Yes, ma…Suzzyn.” At least the woman had let her sit on the couch and not on some kind of examination table, Kaly reflected. And the tea she was sipping *was* nice.

“To help you, I want you to do something for me. I want you to take some time and write an autobiography. Tell me all about yourself and your past. Don’t leave anything out.”

“Right now?”

“No,” Suzzyn smiled. “Do a little bit every day. When we meet each week, we’ll review it together.”

“Okay.”

“As for today, I wanted to talk with you about your Team Leader. Tell me what you thought of her. Describe her for me.”

Kaly looked up at the ceiling and slightly to the right, trying to form what she wanted to say, and she didn't notice that the officer had paid veery close attention to the direction of her glance.

Even if she had, it would have meant very little to her. Unlike Dr. bel Shaaron, she had no knowledge of neurolinguistic programming, or how eye movements betrayed an individual's personality type. She was also unaware of the drugs in her tea that were subtly heightening her receptiveness to suggestion.

"Well, she was brave," Kaly began. "She was committed to the Sisterhood, and we all admired her. We trusted her too; she never let us down on an Op."

"But didn't she, Kaly?" Dr. bel Shaaron countered. "Don't you see that she really walked away from you?"

Kaly did a double take, and simultaneously felt a rush of emotion; it was anger. Anger at the very suggestion, and then anger at N'Elemay herself.

"No," she retorted. "No she didn't--she just--"

"She *did* Kaly," Bel Shaaron said. "I know that you want to think the best of her, but she did. In the end, you see, she sacrificed your trust for her beliefs."

"No, t-that's not true," Kaly insisted.

"But it wasn't her fault Kaly. She really couldn't help it. I should know. I was her doctor too." The woman paused, letting Kaly absorb this. "She--wasn't well. I can't say too much about it, but she was really quite ill."

"Ill?"

"Yes," Bel Shaaron replied. "I know that you think that she believed as she did because they were simply her beliefs, how she was raised. But it wasn't really that way. Not exactly." She leaned forwards and lowered her voice slightly as if she were taking Kaly into her confidence.

"You see, she was actually quite insane. Her beliefs are what did it. She was a good woman, but what she was taught as a child drove her mad. We were always very concerned about her."

"But--"Kaly stammered. "She didn't seem--"

"She was. All Marionites are," the doctor told her. "Any sane woman can see just how ill they all are. Their church creates people with deep psychological weaknesses and then it sends them over the edge. It does this by taking women away from Motherthought and then it drowns their psyche in false ideas, and because those ideas are false, they can't help but suffer psychological disorders when they have to deal with reality.'

"That's what happened to N'Elemay. She was raised to believe their delusions, and even when she had the chance, she couldn't tear herself away from what she'd been taught. The Marionites destroyed her, Kaly, and the sad part is that if she'd let it, Motherthought could have saved her. I know; I tried to reach out to her, but she just couldn't break past her conditioning."

"I just don't know," Kaly replied, struggling with what the psychologist had said. "I-I always thought her ideas were a little strange, but I never thought she was *klaxxy*."

"She was a good woman, but she did have mental issues," Bel Shaaron stated soberly. "It was a tragedy, and a terrible waste of a good soldier. And if it's any consolation, I miss her too. But, what's past is past. Today, we're here to help you, Kaly.'

"It's not just the trauma of her leaving that we have to deal with. It's also the process of what we call 'psychological transference'. Part of the damage that you have experienced was caused by the exposure that you had to her illness when you were in an emotionally fragile state. Toxic people can make you ill if your defenses are down and you're around their influence for too long."

"They can?"

Bel Shaaron nodded. "Yes, and the best way to deal with that kind of infection is to go back to a point where you were healthy, and then let your consciousness re-experience that state. In effect, you have to revisit your own mental fitness, and allow your subconscious to re-map itself back to healthy pathways of thinking."

"So, that's why you want me to do the autobiography?" Kaly asked. "To do that?"

"Yes, and to help that along, I'd also like you to submit to a regular series of therapeutic PTS feeds. They'll focus on selected points in your past that will aid us in your therapy. If we can, I'd like to do the first one today."

Kaly wasn't entirely sure that she really wanted to revisit her past, but it was hard for her to work up the will to refuse the woman. She was after all a doctor, she told herself. What she was suggesting to her had to be for her own good. "Okay."

Bel Shaaron smiled and produced a PTS headset. "We're only going to one event today, so this won't take long."

Kaly put the set on, and sat back, preparing herself for the feed to start. "Where am I going, Suzzyn?"

"To school. Back to school." The woman closed her eyes, and sent a command for the feed to begin.

Kaly found herself back in primary school. She was five years old again, and her teacher, Bella n'Mari was there, in the classroom. N'Mari, had always been old, and very wise.

The elderly woman smiled down at Kaly and the rest of her class, and the light streaming into the classroom from Persephone's primary only added to the warmth of her expression.

"Today we are all going to learn a special lesson," she was saying. "It's about a thing called Motherthought. Motherthought is what saved women during the Plague and it helped them to create the Sisterhood."

The teacher glanced up meaningfully at the blue and white national flag jutting out from its holder above the holoboard, and everyone's eyes followed her gaze. They had pledged their allegiance to that flag every day, Kaly recalled, although she hadn't quite understood all of the words that they said.

"Motherthought," N'Mari explained, "is something that every little girl needs to know. It is all about what it is to be a woman and helping your sisters."

With these words, four simple sentences appeared on the holoboard, written in Standard.

"These are the four basic principles behind Motherthought," N'Mari explained, "and if you understand them, and follow them, then you will grow up to become fine, strong women. Does anyone want to try and read the first principle out loud?"

Then, when no one raised their hand, she picked someone. "Maarta?"

Maarta was Kaly's best friend, and like her, she was still struggling to master the difficult art of reading. The girl's face scrunched up as she tried to puzzle out the bigger words, and then she replied tentatively, "It says, 'The God--goddess m-ade-made us--in her own im--aage. Her own image. Our beauty is her per-per--."

"*'The Goddess made us in her own image,*'" N'Mari supplied. "*'Our beauty is her perfection.*' And the next principle? Kaly?"

There were a lot more words in the second principle and Kaly hated the sudden pressure that she found herself under. Everyone was watching her, and if she could have, she would have gladly been anywhere else in the universe right at that instant.

"The L-lady put men in-in o-our way as-as-a-a-test. And when…and when…"

Someone in the back of the room, probably Lissa, who hated her, snickered at her clumsy attempt. Reddening, Kaly looked over her shoulder and flashed the girl a look of pure undiluted malice. Retribution would be sought for this affront. Later.

"*'The Lady put men in our way as a test,'*" N'Mari said gently. "*'And when we were wise enough, she took them away. Do not mourn their passing. Rejoice!*' Lissa, since you seem to be so eager to join in, you can read the third principle."

Now it was Lissa's face that was flushing with anger and embarrassment. But she was trapped, and to Kaly's immense satisfaction, her attempt was even more pathetic.

"T-the God-goddess pla-placed us above…above all…" Lissa stopped there, stymied.

N'Mari finished for her. "*'The Goddess placed us above all other life in the universe. Only lower life forms need different sexes. We are unique. We create life.*''

"Now I will read the last principle for everyone. It says, *'No man commands us. We are women. We are beautiful. We are free.*'"

Kaly's heart swelled at this. She was hearing them on two levels; for the first time as a young girl, and then as a Marine sorely in need of their comfort.

Yes, she told herself. *I am beautiful. I am free.*

Monitoring her, Dr. bel Shaaron was pleased when she heard this thought. Kaly had responded to the therapy well and she would be able to report to Col. Lislsdaater that the young woman appeared to be on the road to recovery. But the process was not complete by any means. There would be more sessions like this, reinforcing Kaly's mental stability, and her commitment to the Sisterhood. N'Elemay's replacement would also play a vital role in this process, and Bel Shaaron looked forwards to her arrival.

Bel Sharra Memorial Spaceport, Thermadon Val, Thermadon, Myrene System, Thalestris Elant, United Sisterhood of Suns, 1045.01|05|00:01:00

N'Elemay arrived at Bel Sharra Memorial at one minute past midnight, and only a handful of days since her sojourn in the desert. She was there thanks to the grudging assistance of the CSS *Lucy Stone,* whose captain had been forced to honor her travel chit due to maritime regulations. Now, looking out from the spacedocks, past the Needle, to the soaring towers of the great city's heart, N'Elemay saw the place through new eyes.

At one time, she would have felt patriotism and pride coursing through her at the sight, but no longer. Instead a deep sense of loathing filled her heart. The mighty buildings of Thermadon were actually the ramparts of Babel, raised in a prideful defiance of God and his will. And just like that fabled edifice, the city's inhabitants would be struck down by his hand and scattered in confusion as a punishment for their many sins. She would see to this personally.

Uttering a prayer in praise of the terrible majesty of her creator, she picked up her kit bag and walked to the Customs station. She expected to be harassed and when she arrived, she wasn't disappointed.

The Customs Policewoman who scanned her inocular frowned in distaste. Just by the cut of her hair, N'Elemay knew the reason. The woman was clearly a former servicewoman, and had just seen her dishonorable discharge on her data monocle. "What is your business in Thermadon?" the woman demanded.

N'Elemay didn't let the officer's unfriendly tone bother her and answered evenly. "I'm not sure," she said. "Business, I suppose. I need to find some work."

The Customs Officer snorted in disdain. Clearly, she didn't expect N'Elemay to find any type of decent job. Not with her service record. "Do you have your chits?"

"I lost them on the way here. I only had the one for travel." And this had been used up getting her to Thermadon.

"You'll have to call the Travelers Assistance Office, or the General Welfare Emergency Aid Unit and see what they can do for you," the officer informed her. "They only take new cases between 03:33 and 06:66 hours." She didn't need to add that N'Elemay was also going to have to find somewhere other than the Port to wait. Her tone made that clear enough.

"Thank you, I'll do that."

"Do you have anything to declare?"

"No."

"I'll need you to step over to that office over there," the officer said, directing her towards a small, windowless cubicle. Another kaaper had already come up to escort her, and N'Elemay didn't protest. There was nothing she could do about it anyway. It was better to just go along with whatever they had in mind for her.

The tiny room didn't contain much, just a chair and a plain metal table. The table was bolted to the floor, and a pair of restraints with an extra-long chain had been hooked up to the sturdy rail that ran across its top. She knew the place for what it was; a halfway point, serving either as a holding area for women who were destined for a real cell, or a place where they waited to be granted their freedom--after a very *long* delay.

The Customs Officer gestured at the table. "Open your bag and dump everything out. After that, strip down and turn all your pockets inside out. I want to see everything you have with you on the table."

Suppressing a weary sigh, N'Elemay complied. When everything in her possession was lying there in a big pile, the kaaper took her sweet time, checking each item with a hand scanner. She overlooked nothing, no matter how innocuous it actually was.

There was nothing incriminating for her to find of course, and when she finally completed her search, she had N'Elemay dress herself and take a seat.

The minutes passed. Finally, the first officer she had met with came into the room. "Okay," the woman announced. "You check out. You're free to leave. Welcome to Thermadon."

The kaaper didn't bother to explain the reason for all the nonsense, and N'Elemay didn't ask. She already knew the answer; some *shess* about their 'being on the alert for a dangerous smuggler who just 'happened' to match her description', or something equally as ridiculous. In reality, it had been harassment for harassments sake, and now she was free to leave. That was all that really mattered.

Once she was past the Customs gates and inside the Port proper, she took the only route available to her, a concourse that led straight out to the magnorail platforms. The passage was only interrupted in two places; a junction that led to other parts of the Port, and a small food court that was situated just before the doors to the trains. As she reached the food court, she understood more of the reason behind her delay at Customs. In addition to the humiliation she had been subjected to, she was also being followed.

She spotted her 'shadow' as the woman stopped at a small kiosk and pretended to look through a holomag, but her furtive glances and her stiff posture gave her away immediately. Whoever she was, she either wasn't very good, or she simply didn't care if her quarry knew about her.

Thermadonian Metro Police, or DNI, N'Elemay wondered. Or even the OAE? Any one of these agencies were potential candidates, but as she stepped up to a nearby row of omnis, she decided that the woman wasn't with the Agency.

The OAE would never have sent anyone so inept; they prided themselves on their stealth. The DNI also possessed better-trained people, and it adhered to a similar standard of performance. This only left the local Police, and all things considered, it made the most sense.

The Metros would definitely want to keep tabs on an ex-Marine Marauder in their city, she reflected, especially since they knew that her psiever had been permanently altered for urban warfare operations. Unlike most women's devices, hers deliberately masked her presence from any city AI. And it was also shielded against psionic interference, making her immune to psi's. Hence, the old fashioned 'tail' following her.

Suddenly feeling as if she were playing a part in an archaic detective movie, she tried to decide what to do with herself next. For one thing, she had to get rid of her unwelcome companion, and then she wanted to locate other members of the Faithful who could help her. She had no doubt whatsoever that fellow believers lived in The City, and she knew enough of the Church's signs to recognize them once she found them. But given its great size, she was also aware that her task was as daunting as Lot trying to find one honest man in the city of Sodom.

The omni's in front of her offered up a possible solution, and she almost resorted to using them. But then she recalled that any interaction with the omniplex not only cost credits, which she lacked, but would be traceable.

Turning away from the devices, she decided to bide her time, and see what the food court offered in the way of an escape. One of the lessons she had learned as a Marauder was not only to act swiftly and with violence, but also when to pause, and assess the situation. Taking a seat in one of the plastic booths, she whispered up a prayer to Mother Mari to aid her.

And the Mother of God answered her petition in a surprising manner. Her deliverance came by means of an employee from the food court. The clerk had been greeting other arrivals as she had passed through, and N'Elemay had pointedly avoided her. Now, the young woman took the initiative and walked right up to her.

"Welcome to Thermadon, jantildam," she said with more cheer in her voice than seemed proper for the hour. "*The Blessed Meal* is serving a complimentary appetizer plate tonight as a way of thanking our visitors." She produced a small chit from a basket on her arm and held it out.

N'Elemay was certainly hungry, but she was more intent on finding her escape route than accepting any gift, and she began to refuse it. That was until she spotted the hand sign that the woman flashed with her free hand. It had been delivered quickly, and the woman had been careful to have her back turned to the kaaper at the kiosk when she had made it.

N'Elemay instantly recognized it. It was the simple thumb-between-fore-and-ring-finger gesture that conveyed two things at once; that the young woman was a member of the Faithful, and that she was fully aware of the surveillance.

Feeling a swell of gratitude for Mother Mari's infinite mercy and the Church's foresight in devising such a means of communication, N'Elemay was careful not to acknowledge the message with anything as obvious as a nod. Instead, as she took the chit from the girl, she made her reply with another hand sign; a fist with the thumb folded over the index and forefingers. It said, *'I know.'*

"Enjoy your evening," the woman said. Then she spotted another traveler and walked away, leaving N'Elemay alone to examine the chit.

The border around the small plastic card was decorated with fish and stars. Four-pointed stars to be exact, and the fish were very similar to the symbol the Church often used to denote Jesu as a 'Fisher of Men'. Any lingering doubts that she might have entertained about her salvation vanished with this.

I guess I have the time to stop and eat after all. She headed over to the vendor.

When she gave the clerk stationed there her chit, the woman made no indication that there was anything special about it, and served her a small plate filled with bread and cheese.

"Do you want anything else with that?" she asked. "Nutro, *water*, *wine*?"

The way that the woman had just placed a slight emphasis on the last two beverages alerted N'Elemay. "Well, I'd certainly like the wine," she replied. "But I think it will have to be water instead. I'm a little low on credits."

"I'll change the water into wine for you, on the house," the clerk responded with a smile. "It's normally 0.25 credits, but we're a little long on the red right now. The boss won't mind if I give away the last of it to you."

N'Elemay took the plastic cup, and thanked her. Then she found herself a table that afforded a good view of the food court and everyone in it, and sat. Predictably, her 'tail' 'walked into the area at that moment, and also sat down at another table, pretending to go through the contents of her travel bag.

She really is awful, N'Elemay thought. The woman hadn't even bothered to get herself a meal to serve as a prop.

She had to be a rookie. There was no other explanation. Which also meant that there were others, with better-honed skills, lurking somewhere else. There was no way that the Metros would leave a job like this in the hands of one inexperienced kaaper and not have back-up of some kind.

But N'Elemay put her watcher, or *watchers*, out of her mind and took the opportunity to covertly celebrate the unexpected communion she had just received. While the setting was by no means as formal as a church, she had been away from the motherworlds for so long, that it didn't matter. Informal, solitary rituals like the one she was about to perform had actually become natural for her. And to her uninvited audience, and any other unbelievers around her, it would appear as if she were merely savoring her food--and not conducting a forbidden religious ritual right in the middle of a public place.

This is my body, she thought, taking a small, reverent bite of her bread and an equally respectful sip of her wine. *Take of it and eat. This is my blood. Take of it and drink.*

Even though she was still quite hungry, she set the rest of the meal aside and ignored the cheese completely. A true, secular meal would come later, she promised herself. When she was safe.

Another woman came into the food court just then, this time dressed in a service coverall and pushing a cart in front of her. As N'Elemay watched, she began to gather up all the empty glasses and refuse left behind on the neighboring tables.

In most Sisterhood cities this was normally a job performed by 'bots, but then she recalled a recent referendum passed by the Supreme Circle to outsource some of these tasks to humans in order to find 'meaningful' work for citizens who were being supported by the government welfare system. With so many 'bots around, there had always been calls by the politicians to ensure that humans didn't slip into obsolescence and remained an active part of the workforce.

The housekeeper stopped at the table next to N'Elemay, and as she began to tidy up, she looked down at her plate. "Are you finished with that, jantildam?" she asked.

"Yes," N'Elemay replied carefully. "I am full, sister." She didn't add what she wanted to; that it was the Holy Spirit that was filling her soul, and not her stomach.

The woman's smile broadened slightly, and as she picked up the plate, N'Elemay couldn't help but notice the quick sign of blessing that she made with her free hand as she did so. It was as subtle as the one the girl handing out the chits had performed, held just below the plate in such a way that only the two of them had seen it, and it only appeared for a nanosecond.

"The restrooms are just off the food court if you need them," the housekeeper suggested. Then without saying anything more, she moved on to the next table.

N'Elemay waited for a second before she rose and walked in the direction the housekeeper had indicated. Knowing that the kaaper would be right behind her, she entered the facility and quickly took stock of her surroundings.

She had just decided which stall she was going to use to hide the policewoman's body in, when an air grate over another stall popped open, and a hand came out. It gestured to her. "Get up here," a voice above her urged. "We'll keep the kaaper busy!"

Outside, there was something that sounded like two bodies colliding and an object crashing to the ground, followed by profuse apologies.

She didn't waste time ferreting out the cause however. Instead, she took this as her cue and ran into the stall, climbing up on the toilet seat and grasping the stranger's hand. Whoever she was, the woman above her was strong, and with only a little effort on her own part, she managed to lift herself up and into the tiny opening.

She found herself in a passageway that was just large enough to crouch in. It led off into the darkness and her companion, she saw, was dressed just as the housekeeper had been, in a simple coverall, but she wore a patch that identified her as a member of the Port maintenance staff.

"Follow me," the woman directed, reaching past her to pull the hatch shut and then turning around to move down the corridor with a practiced ease. As N'Elemay obeyed, she could hear the kaaper entering the restroom below, followed by a string of expletives that seared even her experienced ear.

Although the unhappy woman *was* a rookie, N'Elemay had little doubt that she would puzzle out the hatch in short order, and she stayed close to her escort and moved as fast as the cramped space allowed. Only a little ways beyond, the corridor became tall enough to stand up in, and then they reached another hatchway. Her guide opened it without ceremony and dropped down into the room below.

N'Elemay followed, lowering herself through the opening, and as she did so, she saw that they had been joined by the very Custom's Officer who had given her so much grief. This revised her conclusions about the delay at Customs. Part of it at least, had been for positive reasons.

But when her feet touched down on the cement floor, any benignancy vanished as the kaaper drew her needlegun and pointed it straight at her face.

"You're psiever won't transmit out of this room," the policewoman advised, briefly inclining her head towards the network of pipes and conduits above them. "Too much metal for your fellow kaapers to hear you."

"I'm not a policewoman," she replied, resisting the temptation to take the weapon away from her. Although she was holding it with a steady conviction, the woman was *way* too close for safety. N'Elemay was starting to become convinced that everyone on this planet was an inexperienced 'greenie'.

"We'll see," the officer growled. She nodded over to her partner who pulled out a small necklace from her jumpsuit and dropped it on the floor. It was a Star of the Faithful. "Step on it. I want to see you grind it into the dirt with your heel."

N'Elemay stayed right were she was.

"Do it *now*!"

N'Elemay shook her head. "No. I won't desecrate it."

"Do it *kunta,* or I'll fekking shoot you!"

N'Elemay only smiled. Then, right before the officer's finger could squeeze the trigger, she stepped in and sideways to the barrel, grasping the weapon with one hand as the other slammed onto the bridge of the woman's nose. There was the satisfying crunch of cartilage collapsing as she made contact, and she followed through with a knife-edge strike to the forearm holding the weapon, forcing its muscles to spasm and making the hand go limp. The needlegun fell from the kaaper's fingers and she staggered backwards, holding her nose as blood gushed out from between her fingers.

Shocked by the violence of N'Elemay's attack, the maintenance woman stood stock still for a moment, but then she recovered her senses and lunged for the needlegun. All she received for her trouble was a hammer blow between her shoulder blades that knocked her flat.

N'Elemay stopped herself there. She could have followed through with far more, but she satisfied herself with retrieving the weapon instead. These were, after all, members of the Faithful, however woefully inexperienced they were as fighters, and she didn't want to savage her sisters any more than she absolutely had to.

"Now *you* step on it," she said calmly, leveling the weapon on the pair.

To her relief, neither of them made any move to obey her command. "You'll have to kill us," the Customs Officer managed to snuffle. "We'd rather die first."

"That's what I was hoping you'd say, sister," N'Elemay returned, reversing the weapon and handing it back to her. "Can we leave things at that? It has been a very long day, and I am in dire need of sanctuary."

The two women looked at each other questioningly, and as the Customs Officer took back her weapon and re-holstered it, her escort nodded, reluctantly. "Okay. We'll trust you--for now." This was all that N'Elemay could have really asked for, given the circumstances.

They left the room together and her guides led her through a warren of passages, and eventually to a delivery hovertruck that was waiting at a service dock. The driver didn't ask any questions as she got into the cab, and they left the Port immediately.

***

Angelique bel Thana waited until the hovertruck had departed before she sent her message. *She's away*, she thought. *We can anticipate our subject reaching the dissidents this evening.*

How long before we can expect her to become active? came the response.

Not long, Angelique replied. *Her file indicates that she is not the kind to delay taking action.*

Good, the other woman said. *Let us hope that she is everything that we think she is.*

Indeed, Angelique agreed, looking out over the city in the direction that the truck had gone.

When Sarah had first met Maya, she had warned the girl that there were other psi's in the world, who were just as ruthless and as dangerous as she was, and Angelique bel Thana was one of them. Like Sarah, she was also an agent, and they had even worked together on several occasions.

Bel Thana's loyalties to Sarah and the Agency were superficial however. The ring that she wore on her left hand symbolized her real allegiance; a small silver circlet with the ancient Greek letter 'Psi' emblazoned on it.

It represented a group of psychics like her, all as highly talented and trained as she was, and all of them committed to a single, great purpose. To the women of *da Conversâzi*, "The Conversation", Ellen n'Elemay was more than just a dissident or a tool of the Agency; she was the very key to achieving their dream. The Conversation would not only make certain that the renegade Marine had all the clandestine help that she required, but that she succeeded in her destructive endeavors beyond even her expectations.

And when N'Elemay was finished with her crusade, there would be a new order replacing the old one, and The Conversation would be able to come out of the shadows at long last. The fate of some however, including Ellen n'Elemay herself, had already been decided. For great things to occur, some people had to serve as grist for the mill.

Angelique turned away from the loading dock and went back into the Port proper, considering this. And she wondered, as she had since the operation had begun, which way Sarah and her protégé would go.

Would they stand with The Conversation? Or against it? Only time would tell.

***

Barely a day later, and completely unaware that Ellen N'Elemay had just preceded him, Jon fa'Teela found himself going through Customs at Bel Sharra. His reception was even less gracious than hers had been, and he spent an entire two days in a holding cell while the Captain in charge decided exactly what to do with him.

She didn't have many options. While he was a neoman, and his Church was now considered a terrorist group, he himself had done nothing that they could hold him on. His record, despite his discharge, was a clean one. Aside from exercising their right to detain him for investigation for the maximum period of two days, there was nothing they could do in the end except to grudgingly release him with the few possessions he had with him that couldn't be confiscated as 'suspicious'.

With a stern warning not to remain in the Port, he was finally sent on his way.

If anything, his plans were even more nebulous than the ex-Troop Leader's had been. Unlike her, he had no great vision to guide him. The only idea he had in mind was to somehow get himself home to New Covenant. But given the mood in the capitol towards anything associated with the Marionites and the ETR, he realized that finding a ride to his motherworld on a civilian merchanter, was less likely than a host of angels coming down from on high to spirit him off.

Ignoring the startled looks from the women around him, he wandered in the same direction that N'Elemay had, and like her, he found himself in the food court, staring at the magnorail platform outside. Although he noticed that one of the restaurants, *"The Blessed Meal"* was closed, and had plastic police tape stretched over it, he didn't associate this with anything having to do with his Church. He also didn't see the pair of Customs Policewomen coming up behind him.

Before he realized it, they had seized him by his arms, and were hustling him into a maintenance corridor. Thanks to the miracle of genetic engineering, one of them, a Zommerlaandar by the look of her, was his equal in both size and muscle. Unfortunately, her expression was the least friendly of the two, and the bandage she wore across the bridge of her nose and the ugly bruising that surrounded the dressing, didn't sweeten it. Without any preamble, she slammed him into the plain wall, and roughly shoved her collapsible stun baton up under his chin.

"That's right *Neo!* We're going to show you how we deal with traitors!" the woman hissed. She turned to her partner. "Go outside and make sure no one comes in here." The other woman gave him an unfriendly grin, and left them alone together.

"You've caused me a big headache", the officer said in a half whisper. "You had to fekking show up *here* of all places! And right after the other Marine! I don't need any more of this *shess*, you fekking *Cagà!* Why the *fek* didn't you choose another Port?*!!"*

Jon didn't know how to answer her rhetorical question. Instead, he prayed to Jesu and Mari to watch over him, and braced himself for a beating.

Then, to his disbelief, the policewoman turned the handle of the baton around and offered it to him.

"Take this and go down this corridor," she instructed, "When you reach the end, turn right, then left and then right again. Hide in the trash bins there until someone comes for you."

When Jon hesitated, she shoved the electronic club into his chest. "Take it you *Fekaanta muti-da!*" Then she turned her head and inclined her jaw. "Hit me with it--and make it look good!"

Jon fumbled with the thing, but he took it from her, finally comprehending what was actually happening. "Thank you--sister-" he managed to stammer.

"*Fekka je!* Now hit me--*brother!*"

Jon hit her, but with his fist. There was the sound of the woman's jaw cracking as he made contact with it, and then she fell, sprawling backwards onto the concrete.

He ran. He even managed to get as far as the first turn before he heard cries of alarm behind him and after that, the sound of running footsteps. Then he ran even faster.

EPILOGUE

Zenithia Productions, Agamede District, Thermadon Val, Thermadon, Thalestris Elant, United Sisterhood of Suns, 1045.01|07|02:08:33

By 02:08:33 in the morning, the kaafra in her cup had begun to taste like industrial lubricant, but Celina forced herself to down it to the last drop. She needed the energy. The State Department had been hounding her to finish up with what she had come to call *"Talaria's Song"*. She'd managed to put them off for months, but their patience, or possibly that of the Chaotic delegation, had finally come to an end. And all the pressure hadn't made her job one nanobit easier.

As it was, she knew that it was unfinished. There was still a phrasing that was clearly missing, and for all her skills and her creative gift, it had refused to reveal itself. This is what had caused the long delay. Regardless of what the government wanted, or even the goddess-cursed Seevaans, she had *not* been ready to just wrap it up and call it complete. Not when it wasn't.

Even now, when her defeat was both obvious and unavoidable, she had trouble making herself save the file and send it.

"Celi," Clio said gently. "It's done. We've done all that we can and now we need to send it off."

"No Clio! It's *not* done, and you know it!"

Her AI was right though. For better or worse, mostly the worse in her opinion, she had to simply accept the situation and put an end to it. The musician sighed in a combination of exhaustion and resignation, and then she closed her eyes, and sent the command. The file went on its way.

"Shall I delete our copy now?" Clio asked. "You know that they asked us to--"

"No!" Celina barked, instantly regretting her tone. She had never spoken like this to her friend before. All the stress had gotten to her.

"Clio, I'm sorry. I didn't mean to say it that way. Please--encrypt it, and bury it. I want to hold onto a copy just in case the one that they get is corrupted." This wasn't entirely true. The fact was that *Talaria's Song* had become a part of her, and she wasn't about to let go of it completely. Besides, she told herself, what the State Department didn't know, wouldn't hurt them.

"It's all right, Celi," Clio replied patiently. "I understand. You've just been working too hard. And finishing this song is a good thing. I've saved and encrypted the file for you."

Then a glass of cool, white Zommerlaandar Weizenwien popped up next to Celina. "I thought that you might want that, Celi", Clio explained.

The lights dimmed as the AI said this, and in the small bedroom adjacent to the studio, the bed turned its covers down, waiting for Celina to get in.

"Get some rest, Celi. You've earned it."

Undisclosed Location, Cyrene District, Thermadon Val, Thermadon, Myrene System, Thalestris Elant, United Sisterhood of Suns, 1045.01|07|02:39:11

The Church had decided to hide their most precious member in the best hiding place possible; in plain sight, and squarely in the center of the capitol itself. This tactic had been so bold, and so simple, that so far it had managed to completely confound the Thermadonian Metropolitan Police, the DNI, and even the new RSE. Still, the Church wasn't taking any chances, and Mikal fa'Lynda was being moved from one safe house to the next, every night.

Tonight he was the guest of a prominent businesswoman, who was also a secret member of the True Faith. Where he, and his small entourage, would be staying tomorrow, was anyone's guess, but he was not concerned in the least. He could sense when any of the psi's working for the Sisterhood were near, and he had learned how to misdirect them and cloud their abilities. Besides which, his physical security was the responsibility of Provost General n'Avenal and the women of the *Societas Mariaa*. For him, it was enough that he was in a safe place for the night, and he let them worry over the details.

He sat in a lotus position, in what was normally his hostesses' bedroom, hovering a little more than 30 centimeters off the floor. Levitation was just one of his many talents, and it was the easiest for him to perform. Floating free of any physical distractions gave him the opportunity to go deeper into trance than someone without this special ability could. It was a place somewhere on the border between waking and sleeping; a state of being between the conscious world of matter, and the unconscious realm of pure formlessness.

He reached out with his mind and briefly felt for the life energies of his guests. The young man and woman, both ardent believers, had eagerly volunteered to sleep with him that evening when they had been offered the opportunity. And to his satisfaction, he found that they were fast asleep.

As pleasant as the passionate sex they had engaged in had been, he was in no mood for any companionship right then. On New Covenant he had enjoyed very little privacy and now that he was in hiding, finding moments of solitude were even rarer.

After all, to the Church, he was more than just another neoman. He was the Redeemer, the Hope and Salvation of Humanity made flesh, specially created and bred for that same Holy Purpose.

I am also an imposter, he admitted to himself. *And they know it.* Once again, as he had so often since the day of his birth, he found himself astonished at their duplicity, and their arrogance. It hadn't been good enough for them to simply wait and let God decide when and how humanity would be saved, or even if it *would* be saved. Instead they had decided to force the matter. To his mind, this had been foolishness and presumption on a truly astronomical scale.

But that is the way of mortals, a familiar mental presence said. *It always has been. They meddle in the Creator's will at every opportunity.* The Voice had been with him since the very first time the Sisters had taken him to the Garden of the Immaculate Conception, and it had never left since.

As if you would know, he countered bitterly. He hated the Voice. It was not only cruel, it was also a consummate liar. It was the Master of All Lies if he had been pressed to give it a name. *Now go away. I need to be alone.*

The Voice didn't leave of course. It had often claimed that that the two of them were as unified as the truths that it wove into its lies. But even so, he did feel it retreat a bit, and grant him at least the illusion of true solitude.

He knew that it would be back though. It always came back, and with it, the headaches and the 'grey-outs' that were becoming more and more commonplace. He hadn't told the Church Mothers about any of this though. They wouldn't have understood.

There was also something else that he hadn't shared with them. It was his memories of his past lives. This was another talent of his, but unlike his other psychic skills, it had been greeted with horror when he had mentioned the ability to his Confessor. The very idea of it went against the Church's doctrine of 'one soul and one life'. But he knew better.

He also didn't dare reveal to them the truth about the other so-called Savior that they so fervently believed in. The very last thing that they would want to hear was that 'he' had actually been several men, all of them prophets, who had been combined into one figure who had never really existed at all.

Or that the most prominent of them, Joshua ben Jusef, had not died on the cross as they believed. It had been Simon of Cyrene who had accepted that fate for him.

Mikal had personally witnessed this, in one of his former lives. Not as the Savior however, or even as one of his apostles. Instead, he had been someone in the jeering crowd. He had even thrown a rock or two at the man as he had passed by on his way to his execution.

Mikal had also neglected to share his private thoughts on God himself. It made no sense whatever that he had allowed his Church to fall on hard times as he had. But then again, he reminded himself, he had believed in many gods and goddesses over the countless centuries; Odin, Thor, Ishtar, Jupiter, Juno, just to name a tiny fraction. All of them had been the One, or the Ones, at one time or the other, and they had all embodied the Absolute Truth.

The true face of God is infinite chaos, the Voice interjected. It was back.

Stop it! he demanded. *I won't listen to your lies.*

Yes, you will, the Voice countered. *And you will never know real truth until you embrace my teachings. There is no God, only his shadow; Anar-*

chy is Heaven's bastard child, and it is also an orphan. God died centuries ago, and with it his kingdom.

Leave me, Mikal thought wearily.

The Voice laughed at him. Hadn't it told him many times that it couldn't? And even if it were possible, the Voice had no intention of doing so. It was enjoying itself, and Mikal showed far too much promise for it to simply abandon him. Besides, the young man was almost ready for the next step the Voice had planned for him. That would occur when the rest of its kind arrived.

Apartment of Sarah n'Jan, 409th Floor, The Otrera, Agamede District, Thermadon Val, Thermadon, Myrene System, Thalestris Elant, United Sisterhood of Suns, 1045.01|07|02:41:92

It had been a while since she had dreamt about them, but Maya realized where she was immediately, even though the place itself was unfamiliar to her. There was no mistaking the hand of the Drow'voi in every part of the scene. The chamber was a gigantic cylinder and in its center, was a huge pillar. It vaguely reminded Maya of a tree, but one that was composed of some strange crystalline substance, and its 'roots' and 'branches' seemed to merge seamlessly with the floor and ceiling.

At its base, half entwined by the root-like shapes was an oval pool. At first, she thought that it was filled with water, but as the dream drew her closer, she realized that it was some other substance entirely; an unidentified liquid that looked like water, but which was somehow, a living being.

The Drow'voi were also there. A group of them had clustered around the pool, and she got the distinct feeling that there was something markedly different about them than all the other times she had dreamt of them. Before, they had always seemed unhurried, going about their unfathomable business at a slow, decorous pace.

They were not that way now. The emotions that the beings radiated were very different than anything she had ever experienced, but she was able to correlate enough of their mood to loosely comprehend what they were feeling. They were afraid, although why, was unclear.

Three of the Drow'voi came to the edge of the pool and entered it, sinking below the surface of the liquid and descending to the bottom. The pool of the 'whatever-it-was' was relatively shallow, and the creatures reached this quickly. There, they turned and faced one another.

Maya suddenly became aware that she was not alone with the trio. There were other Drow'voi all around them, and as she looked up and around her, she saw them, lining what appeared to be terraces. No, she thought, more like levels in a great spiral staircase that circled around the chamber.

There were thousands, possibly even millions of them, but the shadows and the sheer size of the place made it impossible for her to accurately gauge their true number. She did know how many levels they occupied however; there were nine of them, although she hadn't taken the time to personally count them. She just knew. And for some reason, she was equally certain that this number was very important somehow, but she couldn't say why.

As she returned her gaze to the trio in the pool, she perceived something else, underlying their fear. It was resignation, she realized.

They knew that their time was over. They had lost something, and now they were accepting it, and taking the next inevitable step.

In her normal waking state, filled as she was with the prejudices and the xenophobia of her species, Maya wouldn't have been affected by this in the least. She wouldn't have cared one nano about life forms that were so alien to her own.

But here, only her subconscious ruled and it overrode all else. Here, she was horrified. Something terrible was about to happen, and there was nothing that she, or anything else, could do to stop it. The Drow'voi were preparing to die.

She tried to tell them to stop, to convince them to reconsider their decision. But they didn't hear her, and even if they had, the alternative was somehow far worse. For the sake of every other race in the Galaxy what they intended to do, had to occur.

The three leaders below her began to sing, and as the sounds flowed out from them, Maya recognized the song. She had heard it before, in other dreams. It was their death song, but it was also something else. She tried to understand what, and her mind fell short of the challenge. All she could do was accept her ignorance, and watch helplessly as events over 20,000 years gone replayed themselves.

The pool filled with lights, and then the lights transformed, becoming coherent forms. They were symbols, at once familiar to her, and at the same time, completely foreign. As each symbol appeared before the group, it made a sound that reminded the young woman of a musical note, but one that was so clear and pure that she understood that the music she knew was nothing but a clumsy facsimile.

The sounds combined, and their union became a perfect duplicate of the song the trio had sung to begin the process. Simultaneously, the symbols pulsed, growing brighter as the melody increased in volume and complexity.

And as all of this happened, the great tree became illuminated, glowing and pulsating with an inner light that matched the tempo of the notes. The light and sound rose together within the tree and spread outwards, along the 'branches' until it reached the nine terraces of the huge winding stair. There, the waves of light washed over the alien audience, and the creatures began to shrivel, and shrink.

While the sounds continued to play, Maya knew that the death that they had brought was spreading from the chamber, out across the face of the planet itself, and then, across the stars to touch every Drow'voi, everywhere.

The entire race was perishing.

Finally, out of the billions of their kind that had once existed, only the group that had begun the song still lived. As one, they turned and looked up through the pool to face her with their gigantic eyes. Then a final note issued from the symbols, and they too joined their fellows in death.

The symbols in the pool vanished, and the tree above her went dark. Only she, and the memory of the song she had heard, remained.

She wasn't astonished in the least when she awoke a moment later and found herself drenched in a cold sweat. She was also fairly certain what it all meant. The explanation was really quite simple; she was going klaxxy.

USSNS *Pallas Athena*, Five-Bar, Estraddar System, Esteral Terrana Rapabla 1045.01|07|02:49:18

Maya wasn't the only one in the Far Arm dealing with the aftermath of a dream. Kaly n'Deena also lay in her bed, staring at the ceiling and trying to figure out the strange vision that had visited her in her sleep.

She had been at a beach on Tethys, a place that she had once visited in real life, just after Basic with her fellow Marines. The sun had been the same as it had been then; bright and warm. And the sand had also been just like she had experienced it, white and clean and bordered by an incredibly blue ocean.

The only thing that had been different than what she recalled, was the woman that she had seen reclining on the sand beside her. They hadn't said anything to one another, but had simply shared the moment together. The love and affection in the strange woman's eyes had been unmistakable however. It was as if she had actually been an important part of Kaly's life, and somehow, been forgotten.

Her memories however, insisted otherwise. They told her that she had been alone on that beach, and that she had never known such a woman in the flesh.

It also wasn't the first time that she had encountered this phantom either. Kaly had seen her before, in another dream, just after the Op at the Bio Lab, and her presence in this one confused her as much as it had then.

N'Elemay had ventured the belief that this mysterious figure had been an angel, sent by her God to watch over her. And at the time, weary from what she had been told were complications from her psionic debriefing, she had even half-accepted this fantastic idea.

But later, her doctor, the Ship's Senior Psychologist, had posited another, more scientific, and believable theory. Suzzyn bel Shaaron had felt that it was far more likely that the woman was either someone, or a composite of several 'someones' that Kaly had once met, and had simply forgotten about. That, or some sort of 'friendly alter-ego' created by Kaly herself to help her process the trauma that she had suffered in her life.

Now though, neither woman's suggestions felt right to her. Deep in her bones, Kaly knew that there was another truth that was concealing itself from her. Against all logic, the woman in her dreams felt too real *not* to be real. Her red hair, her freckles, and even the way she had smiled at her, were too familiar to be supernatural, or imaginary. She even thought, that if she tried hard enough, that she could put a name to the woman's face. But when she attempted it, nothing came. Nothing, except for the profound feeling that she *did* know, and that for some inexplicable reason, the knowledge was stubbornly refusing to surface.

Maybe letting her continue to be an angel was best, she decided. Angels loved, and there had been no mistaking that in the woman's eyes, or her smile.

Yes, Kaly decided. For now at least, that was what she would have to continue to be. An angel.

For now.

Officer's Quarters, USSNS *Pallas Athena*, Estraddar System,
Esteral Terrana Rapabla, 1045.01|07|02:91:66

Erin taur Minna checked her morning messages, and found one waiting for her from her flight crew's Chief. On her last sortie, her Valkyrie had been acting up, and she had sent a note to the woman asking her to look into the problem. She had written: *'Right thruster behaving poorly.'*

The crew had done exactly as she had asked, and her Chief had replied with a note of her own. She had written: *'Thruster scolded, sent to bed without dinner. Spanking requisitioned.'*

Reading this, Erin panted with mirth. Fighter service crews loved to answer maintenance requests like this. It made their job more enjoyable, and she had to admit, also injected some badly needed laughter into an otherwise serious undertaking. She also had no doubt that the thruster had been properly repaired, and she was equally certain that her next service order would receive an answer just as comical as this one.

It was a game that every pilot and their crew played with one another, and she'd missed it just as much as she had the thrill of combat. Now that peace had been declared, her only hope was that this camaraderie would continue, and that another war, or at least a skirmish with the Hriss, wouldn't be long in coming. She had more honor to win for herself, and peace made that very difficult.

Undisclosed Location, Apollonia District, Thermadon Val, Thermadon, Myrene System, Thalestris Elant, United Sisterhood of Suns, 1046.05|11|02:91:67

"According to Sister n'Jarra, "Sister General n'Avenal began, "Your story about being a Marine checks out, and so far at least, you do *seem* to be one of the Faithful. Either that, or you are a very well trained operative. For your sake, I had better find out that you are a true Believer."

"I am what I say," Ellen n'Elemay returned evenly. "I am here to serve my Church." She looked the Sister directly in the eyes, and paid no attention to the other woman in the room. Unlike the Customs Officer, her guard was far more experienced, and much better armed. She stood in a corner, a safe distance away and kept her military blaster rifle trained on her. It was, N'Elemay observed, at full charge, and seemed well maintained.

"I certainly hope so," N'Avenal replied skeptically. "Thanks to you, three of our women had to leave their jobs behind, and everything else they owned. We'll find other work for them easily enough, but they had to pay a high price for you, and replacements will have to be found. That's not an easy thing to manage."

N'Elemay nodded solemnly. Being forced to abandon their positions was much better than being rounded up for questioning however, and she and N'Avenal both knew this. Even so, she still regretted all the damage that she had done, especially to the Custom's Officer's nose. Jesu willing, the woman would heal quickly.

"You'll stay here for now," N'Avenal informed her, "While we verify some more things about you. *If* you pass, then our losses will be justified. The Daughters of Eve needs women with your kind of skills."

She pointedly didn't mention what her fate would be if she didn't meet their expectations, and N'Elemay didn't ask. One look at the hard-faced guard told her all that she needed to know on that score.

"That is all I can pray for, Sister," N'Elemay answered. Then she settled in to wait.

She didn't know it, but Jon fa'Teela was sitting in the next room, watching her on a closed circuit holoviewer. When Sister n'Avenal joined him, her expression softened. "Well, Jon?" she asked. "Do you know her?"

"Yes, Sister," he answered. "She served on the *Athena* with me. She's the one who called for the prayer meeting." A look of regret, mixed with guilt, clouded his features and N'Avenal understood why.

Jon still believed that he had failed his Church, and he had asked her for her forgiveness a dozen times or more since his return. And she had given it to him, even though she didn't blame him at all for what had happened. It had been the Sisterhood, and its evil ways that had failed, not him. Nonetheless, Jon still insisted on bearing all of the blame.

She placed a comforting hand on his shoulder. "And is she a former Marauder as she says she is?"

The neoman nodded. "Yes, Sister. She ran one of their teams before they arrested her."

"Thank you, Jon," N'Avenal said. "Now, go get yourself some rest. You look tired."

Jon gave her a half-smile as he rose and left her. When the door had closed behind him, she considered his situation. Unlike the women in the other room, and despite the fact that he was a former Marine himself, Jon was no fighter. But he did have a strong faith.

Perhaps he can still serve us, she reflected. *Mikal could certainly use a companion.* Resolving to broach the matter with the Grand Abbess, she returned to N'Elemay, and waved the guard out of the room.

"Troop Leader," she said. "You and I have a great deal to discuss."

***

As N'Avenal's personal assistant, Sister Janneta bel Veronikka's presence was required while her superior continued her interview with Ellen n'Elemay. Only when they had finally finished, and the ex-Marine had been shown to her temporary quarters, had Janneta been able to break away and seek the solace of her own bed. It had been a long day, and she was eager for the chance to get a little rest.

When she entered her room however, any notion of sleeping fled from her. A black rose was resting on her pillow.

Suppressing a shudder as she secured the door, Janneta picked the flower up. She had never discovered how the roses arrived, and their presence was all the more incredible for the fact that the Redeemer's party changed locations on a daily basis.

Simple logic suggested that someone else in her group also worked for the RSE, and had been the courier, but after several unsuccessful attempts to ferret out their identity, she was starting to wonder if they were actually arriving by some strange occult means.

Her spycam, which she had set to watch her room, did little to dispel this conclusion. One moment the monochrome image being displayed in her psiever showed an empty pillow. The next, and the rose was there. The only anomaly that she had ever managed to detect was the occasional flicker of what seemed to be someone's disembodied shadow, but that was all.

Whatever the actual method of delivery was, the roses meaning was starkly clear. Her RSE handlers had a message for her, and as much as she wanted to, she could not ignore it. Bringing the bloom up to her nose, she supressed her reluctance, and inhaled. The DNA encoded communication made its way through her nasal passage into her bloodstream, and from there to her brain, where it created a false-memory.

In the vision, she was in her room, but now, she was not alone. Another woman sat in the chamber's only chair. Her face, as usual, was in shadow, and she spoke in unaccented Standard.

"We understand that Ellen n'Elemay has managed to reach you safely," her unwanted guest began. "You are to learn what she intends, and let us know the details immediately, using the normal channels of communication. We expect to receive the details of any operations that she plans against the Sisterhood. You will also continue to advise us of your location as it changes."

Then the memory was gone and the flower became exactly what it appeared to be. Janneta looked at the rose in frank amazement. Ellen n'Elemay had just arrived an hour earlier, and *they* already knew about it. Another shiver passed through her as she processed this fact.

There was also no question about obeying her instructions. She would, just as the message had demanded, do all that they had asked of her, and *they* knew it just as surely as *they* knew why.

It was a simple case of *Santaj*, masterfully applied. During the first days of the occupation of her motherworld, Janneta had made a single mistake; she had let herself become frightened. Instead of trusting in her faith and Mother Mari's protection, she had faltered in her beliefs, and turned in the names of other women who had decided to resist the military.

She hadn't done this out of malice, but out of loathing at the thought of taking up arms for any reason. And she had also done so out of fear for herself and for her family's safety.

After they had gotten the names, and arrested the women, the RSE had never let her go. Instead, they had compelled her to become their eyes and ears. Somehow, they had known all about her position as Sister n'Avenal's aide, and the Daughters of Eve.

Even worse was the fact that despite her cooperation, those that she cared for were still in danger--from her fellow believers. If the RSE ever decided to let it slip that she was a traitor, then she and her relatives were as good as dead.

Sister Janneta had prayed many times since the occupation, to the very God that she had betrayed. She had prayed to him for forgiveness, and for him to show her the way out. He had never answered her though. She was trapped, and there was no escape.

Without thinking, she crushed the flower in frustration, and immediately felt the sharp prick of its thorns biting into her flesh.

They always come with thorns, she thought ruefully. Thorns that drew blood just as easily as the women who sent them.

END OF BOOK TWO

The saga continues in Book 3, "Sisterhood of Suns: Daughters of Eve"...

Ships of the Sisterhood and the History behind Their Names

The names of the ships featured in the Sisterhood series are not haphazard. They were carefully researched to reflect the rich tradition of women serving in the military throughout history, as well as other notable figures, and female deities.

As a general rule, Isis-class ships are named after goddesses. While some Macha-class vessals also adhere to this convention, many others use historical figures. However, Chandi-class light cruisers (which are often involved in dangerous, solitary missions), overwhelmingly tend to be named after pirates, spies and bandits.

Abbreviations: USSNS stands for "United Sisterhood of Suns Naval Ship" and indicates a military vessel. "CSS" is short for "Civilian Star Ship" and USSMCAS denotes a Marine assault ship.

Book 1: Pallas Athena

USSNS *Pallas Athena*; named after the patron goddess of Athens, Pallas Athena. Athena is the goddess of wisdom, war, and craftsmanship. Her symbol is the owl, which is also the official emblem for this vessel.

USSNS *Artemis*; Artemis is the goddess of transitions, childbirth and the hunt. She is also the protectress of virgins and the young.

USSNS *Demeter*; the Greek goddess of agriculture, grain and bread. When her daughter Kore was abducted by Hades, Demeter withheld her blessings, resulting in a year of world-wide famine and desolation. Eventually Kore was located by Hermes, but because she had been tricked into eating a pomegranate seed, she was unable to leave the underworld (having been transformed by this into Persephone, the Queen of the Dead). To placate Demeter and return life to the fields, Zeus, Rhea and Hades agreed that Kore would be allowed to visit her mother for a portion of the year, but compelled to spend the remainder of it with her husband. It was said by the ancient Greeks that when Kore returned, Demeter blessed the world with spring, and when she departed again, winter came as the goddess mourned her absence.

CSS *C-JUDI-GO*; named for the lover of the ship's first owner, the *JUDI* is a civilian merchant ship secretly working for the OAE.

USSNS *Deborah Gannett*; the first woman known to have impersonated a man in the U.S. Army during the American Revolution. In her first engagement, she was wounded by two musket balls. Afraid that she would be discovered, she left the field hospital and removed one of them herself, using only a pen-knife and a sewing needle. The second proved to be too deep however, and she was unable to extract it. Because of this, her leg never fully healed. Later, she became ill and the doctor treating her realized that she was a woman. He did not betray her though. Instead, he had her brought to his home and cared for her there. Gannett was eventually discharged in 1783. After disclosing her true sex, Gannett went on to become a lecturer, regaling audiences with her adventures during the war.

USSNS *Habondia;* a Celtic goddess of abundance, prosperity and the earth, she became associated with witchcraft after Christianity arrived in Europe.

USSMCAS *Lucy Brewer*; serving during the War of 1812 as George Brewer aboard *Old Ironsides*, Lucy Brewer is considered to be the first female Marine. She saw action against the British as a marksman, and her true sex remained unknown until her biography was written.

USSNS *Madeline Moore;* known by Revolutionary War historians as 'the Lady Lieutenant', she followed her lover into combat. Later, she acquired a uniform from a fallen soldier and eventually received an officer's commission. Moore went on to lead her troops in battles in western Virginia.

USSNS *Anne Bailey;* Baily served in the Continental Army disguised as a man. Later, she worked as a courier and received the nickname 'Mad Annie' for her exploits in hostile Indian Territory. On one occasion, she was pursued by a band of braves, and realizing that she couldn't outrun them, hid herself inside of a hollow log. Unable to find her, the warriors stole her horse instead. She retrieved the animal by sneaking into their camp in the middle of the night, and riding off with it, screaming like a wild woman. Her most famous adventure involved a 100 mile journey to deliver supplies to Fort Lee, which was later memorialized in the 1861 poem *"Anne Baily's Ride."*

USSNS *Hippolyta;* named for the famous Amazon queen who was abducted by Theseus. Although she bore him a son, Theseus abandoned her for another woman. Enraged by this betrayal, Hippolyta returned to her tribe and then attacked Athens. In the battle that followed, she was killed, either by Theseus himself, or accidentally by another Amazon.

USSNS *Kit Cavenaugh;* Born Christian Cavenaugh in 1667, she is remembered as 'Kit Cavenaugh' or 'Mother Ross'. Disguised as a man, she served in the British Army as an infantryman and then later in the Scots Greys.

USSNS *Brigid*; a Celtic triple goddess presiding over healing, poetry and smith craft, she is considered to be one of the great mothers of the Celts. After the advent of Christianity, her attributes were merged with Saint Brigid of Kildare.

USSNS *Hecate;* Originally a primordial deity of Anatolia, she is the goddess of transitions and magic, and according to Hesiod, was awarded dominion over heaven, earth and the underworld by Zeus for helping him to overthrow the Titans. She was later adopted by the Romans, and then the pagan Europeans.

USSNS *Ishtar;* worshiped by the Akkadians, Babylonians and Assyrians, she is the goddess of fertility, love, sex and war, and is a counterpart to

Inanna.

USSNS *Lilya Litvak*; also known as the White Rose of Stalingrad, Litvak fought as a fighter pilot in the Great Patriotic War against the Germans. She is credited with 12 confirmed kills and died in combat at the age of 22. For her service, bravery and sacrifice, Litvak was posthumously awarded the Hero of the Soviet Union and a Gold Star.

USSNS *Penthesilea*; co-ruler of the Thermadonite Amazons, Pentheselea answered Troy's pleas for military assistance and led a handpicked band of warrioresses to fight its besiegers during the Trojan War. They were able to temporarily free the city, and Penthesilea killed the hero Achilles, the leader of the Myrmidonian Greeks. Her victory was not permanent however; she was murdered by a priest of Apollo who had turned traitor, and the city was eventually sacked.

USSNS *Roza Shanina;* a Soviet sniper serving on the Eastern front, Shanina is credited with 54 confirmed kills. She died from wounds that she received during the East Prussian Offensive at the age of 20.

USSNS Marie T. Rossi; Major Rossi was the first female American pilot to lose her life while flying in a combat zone. Rossi died at the age of 32 when her Chinook helicopter crashed near her base in northern Saudia Arabia.

CSS *Akantha*; an Amazon priestess of Athena, her name means 'bright flower' or 'burning sun'.

USSNS *Pelé*; the Hawaiian goddess of fire, she is also known as *Ka wahine `ai honua*, the woman who devours the land. She is considered to be both a creator and destroyer, and her sacred home on Old Gaia was the Halemaumau Crater, at the summit of the Kilauea Volcano.

CSS *Andromeda*; the daughter of the Aethiopian king Cepheus and his wife Cassiopeia, she was punished by Poseidon when her mother dared to claim that her beauty outshone the Nereids. Chained naked to a rock as a sacrifice to the sea monster Cetus, she was rescued by the hero Perseus.

CSS *Sacajawea*; a Shoshone Indian, she was captured by an enemy tribe and sold to a French Canadian trapper, Toussaint Charbonneau, whom she later married. Then in 1804, Lewis and Clark hired the couple for their famous expedition. Sacajawea soon became an integral part of the venture, acting as an interpreter and a guide.

CSS *Carol Curtiss*; one of only three people to have earned the highest licenses available for Merchant cargo ships (and the first woman to do so). Curtiss is licensed both as a Captain and a Chief Engineer.

CSS *Belle Starr*; known as the 'Bandit Queen', Belle Starr was an infamous outlaw in the American West during the 19th century CE. While her actual exploits may have been far less glamourous than the publications of the time claimed, Starr was associated with Frank and Jesse James, and was alleged to have borne Cole Younger's son (which he denied). She was murdered in 1882 and her killer was never brought to justice.

CSS *Rachel Wall*; a pirate in the 1780s, ravaging the New England Coast.

CSS *Grace O'Malley*; a.k.a. Granuaile, or Grainne O'Malley, she commanded three pirate galleys and 200 men in the 16th century Atlantic Ocean.

CSS *Harmony* (a.k.a. *Spacewitch*); fictitious name.

USSNS *Gloriana*; a nickname for Elizabeth I of England, it means 'glory'.

Book 2: Widow's War

USSNS *Cathay Williams;* Born a slave, Cathay was liberated by Union soldiers and later worked for the Army as a paid servant. Then in 1866, she joined the 38th Infantry, Company A, in St. Louis as 'William Cathay' and served on the western frontier as a Buffalo Soldier.

USSNS *Nancy Hart;* a fierce patriot, Hart was a spy for the Continental Army. She was also known for singlehandedly capturing a group of Tories, killing one in the process, and holding the rest at gunpoint until her neighbors could arrive to help her.

USSNS *Boudicca;* Queen of the British Iceni tribe and the leader of a rebellion against Imperial Rome. Ultimately, her revolt failed, but her memory lived on as a symbol of resistance to tyranny.

USSNS *Ch'iao K'uo Fü Jën;* a legendary Chinese female pirate, circa 600 BCE.

USSNS *Calamity Jane;* frontierswoman and professional scout, Martha Jane "Calamity Jane" Cannary was known for her exceptional marksmanship, her rowdy behavior and her preference for wearing men's clothing. She claimed to be a friend of Wild Bill Hickok, and later in life became part of Buffalo Bill's famous Wild West Show.

USSNS *Annie Etheridge*; Etheridge was a nurse in the Michigan Volunteers during the American Civil War. She became famous for her courage while tending to the wounded on the battlefields of Chancellorsville and Gettysburg.

USSNS *Princess Sela;* a Norwegian Viking warrioress, circa 420 CE.

USSNS *Antibrote;* a member of the elite Amazon band sent to Troy and led by Penthesilea. Her name means, 'gory opposition'.

USSNS *Molly Pitcher;* Molly Pitcher is famed for manning a cannon during the American War of Independence at the Battle of Monmouth. While Pitcher is considered by historians to be purely fictional, Mary

Ludwig Hays McCauley was a real woman who received a military pension for 'services rendered' during the war. The historical record also confirms that two women did fight in the battle, one serving with the artillery and the other with the infantry. Whether either of them were actually McCauley, or the real Molly Pitcher, is unknown.

CSS *Fanny Campbell;* a fictional pirate from *The Female Pirate Captain*, by Maturin Murray Ballou, 1845 CE.

CSS *Lucy Stone;* also known as Lucy Stone Blackwell, she was a prominent orator and advocate for women's rights in the 19th century. Stone also helped to establish the Women's National Loyal League which was pivotal in the passage of the 13th Amendment of the US Constitution, abolishing slavery.

USSNS *Lady Killigrew;* a female pirate operating in the Atlantic from 1530-1570 CE.

USSNS *Bellona;* the Roman goddess of war, and sister of Mars. Traditionally, senatorial meetings concerning foreign wars were conducted in the *Templum Bellonæ* (Temple of Bellona) and declarations of war or peace were made at the *Columna Bellica*.

USSNS *Elizabeth Rex;* Named in honor of Queen Elizabeth I of England. Sometimes referred to as the 'Virgin Queen', she ruled for 45 years without ever surrendering her power to a husband. When Spain sent its Armada against England, she rallied her countrymen, and ultimately presided over the defeat of the invaders. Under her reign, the first English settlers were sent to the New World, and arts and literature flourished. She is considered by many historians to be one of her nation's greatest and most influential leaders.

USSNS *Orithia*; a heroine of the Libyan Amazons, she rescued her tribe by finding water for them in the desert.

USSNS *Jeanne de Montfort;* known as "The Flame", she prowled the English Channel in 1343 CE, plundering French ships, and also fighting with the English for Brittany's independence.

Book 3: Daughters of Eve

USSNS *Lai Sho Sz'en;* a pirate in the South China Sea (from 1922-1939 CE), she commanded 12 war-junks.

USSNS *Catherine Hagerty;* another female buccaneer operating in and around Australia and New Zealand in the early 19th century CE.

USSNS *Elizabeth C. Howland;* Trained in medicine by her father, Howland served the Confederate cause as a spy during the American Civil War. She was eventually captured by the Union, and aided her fellow prisoners by smuggling in food and providing them with homemade medications.

USSNS *Josephine Baker;* Known onstage as the "Creole Goddess", the "Black Pearl" and the "Black Venus", Baker was both a dancer, and an Allied spy. During World War 2, she worked for the French Resistance smuggling military secrets from France into Portugal by writing her messages on her sheet music in invisible ink.

USSNS *Eumache;* an Amazon fighter in the Attic war, she fought her opponents with stones after her arrows were exhausted. Her name means 'good warrior'.

CSS *Charlotte Badger*; considered to be the first female Australian pirate, she was imprisoned for seven years in New South Wales after committing a petty theft. Upon her release, she joined the *Venus* as a servant, but then participated in a mutiny against the captain, who routinely flogged female prisoners for his own amusement.

CSS *Teena's Trick;* Fictitious name.

CSS *Billie Jo;* Fictitious name.

CSS *Elizabeth Shirland*; also known as 'Cutlass Liz', she was a fictional pirate, prowling the Atlantic in the 17th century.

CSS *Echephyle*; 'chief defender' or 'wicker shield', she was an Amazon fighter, serving under Orithia to free Queen Antiope and avenge the death of Hippolyta in the Attic War.

USSNS *Sybil Ludington*; a heroine of the Revolutionary War, she rode through the countryside on her horse, Star, and warned the populace about the approach of British regular forces on the night of April 26, 1777. She was only 16 at the time, and rode more than twice the distance as the more famous Paul Revere, fighting off highwaymen and braving the elements along the way. By the time her ride was done, 400 soldiers had been mustered to oppose the Redcoats. Unfortunately, because of her sex, her patriotism was largely forgotten by the nation that she helped to create, and only a series of small historical plaques, a sculpture and a postage stamp, honor her contribution.

Sisterhood Naval Bases Mentioned in the Series

Martha McSally Naval Base, Kevan, Sakina system, Chandi Elant; Lt. Colonel Martha McSally was the first American woman to fly in combat, piloting an A-10 over Iraq and Kuwait during Operation Southern Watch (1992 to 2003 CE). She was also the first woman to command a fighter squadron (the 354th Fighter Squadron, Davis-Monthan AFB.). She went on to serve in the United States House of Representatives (R. Arizona). McSally Naval Base is the primary training facility for aspiring aerospace fighter pilots.

Shana Legendre Naval Base, Sequana System, Thamari Elant;

commissioned in honor of Admiral Shana Legendre, the first Admiral of the Sisterhood Navy. Legendre led the fight against the Hriss invaders during the First Widow's War, which ultimately resulted in the destruction of the Hriss battle fleets at Fomalhaut and the Treaty of Almari 6. Shana Legendre Naval Base stands guard in a region of space adjacent to the Hriss Imperium and serves as the center of operations for several Sisterhood fleets.

Hella's World USSMC Marine Training Facility, Hecate System, Artemi Elant; named for the Norse goddess of the underworld, Hel (or Hela), Hella's World is a harsh, arid planet where the Sisterhood trains its Marine forces. A One Station Unit Training Base, it provides both Basic and Mobile Infantry instruction for new recruits, and offers an abbreviated version for naval officers. Graduates of either course are permitted to wear the Eye of the Goddess on their uniform.

Rixa Naval Base, Rixa, Belletrix System, Pantari Elant; the largest naval base in the Sisterhood, Rixa derives its name from the Latin word 'to fight, quarrel or contend' (although its Arabic etymology, *'risa'* or *'ris'* means 'feather'). Rixa is the home of the Topaz Fleet Command, and its famous PX shopping complexes are, like the base itself, unparalleled in size.

Claire d'Layne Naval Base, Nuvo Bolivar, Magdala Provensa, Esteral Terrana Rapabla; second only to Rixa NB in terms of size, Claire d'Layne is the main base for operations in and around the ETR. Its mission is to support the government of the Republic, and protect it from terrorism and external military threats. Named for the 72nd Chairwoman of the Sisterhood who served at the beginning of the Second Widow's War.

Made in the USA
Middletown, DE
14 September 2024